RIDERS IN THE CHARIOT

Patrick White was born in England in 1912, when his parents were in Europe for two years; at six months he was taken back to Australia, where his father owned a sheep station. At the age of thirteen he was sent to school in England, to Cheltenham, 'where, it was understood, the climate would be temperate and a colonial acceptable'. Neither proved true, and after four rather miserable years there he went to King's College, Cambridge, where he specialized in languages. After leaving the university he settled in London, determined to become a writer. His first novel, *Happy Valley*, was published in 1939 and his second, *The Living and the Dead*, in 1941. During the war he was an RAF Intelligence Officer in the Middle East and Greece. After the war he returned to Australia.

His other novels are *The Aunt's Story* (1946), *The Tree of Man* (1956), *Voss* (1957), *The Solid Mandala* (1966), *The Vivisector* (1970), *The Eye of the Storm* (1973), *A Fringe of Leaves* (1976) and *The Twyborn Affair* (1979). In addition he published two collections of short stories, *The Burnt Ones* (1964), *The Cockatoos* (1974), which incorporates several short novels, the collection of novellas *Three Uneasy Pieces* (1987), and his autobiography *Flaws in the Glass* (1981). He also edited *Memoirs of Many in One* (1986). Penguin have recently published *Patrick White Speaks*, a collection of his essays, articles and speeches. In 1973 he was awarded the Nobel Prize for Literature.

Patrick White died in September 1990. In a tribute to him *The Times* wrote, 'Patrick White did more than any other writer to put Australian literature on the international map ... his tormented *oeuvre* is that of a great and essentially modern writer.'

Patrick White

Riders in the Chariot

Penguin Books

PENGUIN BOOKS

Published by the Penguin Group
Penguin Books Ltd, 27 Wrights Lane, London W8 5TZ, England
Penguin Books USA Inc., 375 Hudson Street, New York, New York 10014, USA
Penguin Books Australia Ltd, Ringwood, Victoria, Australia
Penguin Books Canada Ltd, 10 Alcorn Avenue, Toronto, Ontario, Canada M4V 3B2
Penguin Books (NZ) Ltd, 182–190 Wairau Road, Auckland 10, New Zealand

Penguin Books Ltd, Registered Offices: Harmondsworth, Middlesex, England

First published in Great Britain by Eyre & Spottiswoode 1961
First published in the United States of America by
The Viking Press 1961
First published in Canada by
The Macmillan Company of Canada Limited 1961
Published in Penguin Books 1964
20 19 18 17 16 15 14 13 12

Printed in England by Clays Ltd, St Ives plc
Set in Linotype Times

For Klari Daniel and Ben Huebsch

The Prophets Isaiah and Ezekiel dined with
me, and I asked them how they dared so
roundly to assert that God spoke to them;
and whether they did not think at the time
that they would be misunderstood, & so
be the cause of imposition.
Isaiah answer'd: 'I saw no God, nor heard
any, in a finite organical perception, but my
senses discover'd the infinite in everything,
and as I was then perswaded, & remain
confirmèd, that the voice of honest
indignation is the voice of God, I cared not
for consequences, but wrote. . . .'
I then asked Ezekiel why he eat dung, & lay
so long on his right & left side? he answer'd,
'the desire of raising other men into a
perception of the infinite: this the North
American tribes practise, & is he honest who
resists his genius or conscience only for the
sake of present ease or gratification?'

WILLIAM BLAKE

Part One

1

'Who was that woman?' asked Mrs Colquhoun, a rich lady who had come recently to live at Sarsaparilla.

'Ah,' Mrs Sugden said, and laughed, 'that was Miss Hare.'

'She appears an unusual sort of person,' Mrs Colquhoun ventured to hope.

'Well,' replied Mrs Sugden, 'I cannot deny that Miss Hare is *different*.'

But the postmistress would not add to that. She started poking at a dry sponge. Even at her most communicative, talking with authority of the weather, which was her subject, she favoured the objective approach.

Mrs Colquhoun was able to see for herself that Miss Hare was a small, freckled thing, whose stockings, at that moment, could have been coming down. To tell the truth, Mrs Colquhoun was somewhat put out by the postmistress's discretion, but could not remain so indefinitely, for the War was over, and the peace had not yet set hard.

Miss Hare continued to walk away from the post office, through a smell of moist nettles, under the pale disc of the sun. An early pearliness of light, a lamb's-wool of morning promised the millennium, yet, between the road and the shed in which the Godbolds lived, the burnt-out blackberry bushes, lolling and waiting in rusty coils, suggested that the enemy might not have withdrawn. As Miss Hare passed, several barbs of several strands attached themselves to the folds of her skirt, pulling on it, tight, tight, tighter, until she was all spread out behind, part woman, part umbrella.

'You could get torn,' Mrs Godbold warned, who had come up to the edge of the road, in search of something, whether child, goat, or perhaps just the daily paper.

'Oh, I could get torn,' Miss Hare answered. 'But what is a little tear?'

It did not matter.

Mrs Godbold was rather large. She smiled at the ground, incredulous, but glad.

'I saw a wombat,' Miss Hare called.

'Not a wombat! In these parts? I do not believe you!' Mrs Godbold answered back.

Miss Hare laughed.

'What did it look like?' Mrs Godbold called, and laughed. Still looking in the grass.

'I will tell you,' Miss Hare declared, laughing, but always walking away.

It did not matter to either that much would remain unexplained. It did not matter that neither had looked at the other's face, for each was aware that the moment could yield no more than they already knew. Somewhere in the past, that particular relationship had been fully ratified.

Miss Hare went on, together with her emancipated skirt. With the back of her hand she hit a fence-post, to hear her father's blood-stone ring. She would knock thus on objects, to punctuate periods which, otherwise, might never have had an end. Now she heard the redeeming knock. She heard the wings of a bird suddenly break free from silence. She sang a little, or made sounds. All along the road – or track, the older people still called it – which rambled down from Sarsaparilla to Xanadu, the earth was black and oozy in the early morning of early spring. In all that dreamy landscape it seemed that each particle, not least Miss Hare herself, contributed towards some perfection. Nothing could be added to improve the whole.

Yet, was she not about to attempt?

Miss Hare stood still in the middle of the road. So she had stood in the post office, only, then, she had worn the kind of expression people expected.

'This is something of an occasion, Mrs Sugden,' she had said.

There were those who could never understand Miss Hare's manner of speech, but the postmistress had grown used to it.

'Well, now,' Mrs Sugden said, arranging some papers nicely, and the little glue bottle which use had almost glued up.

Then she waited.

'Yes,' said Miss Hare.

She could not find the horrid pen. She could not find the telegraph forms, sandy like her own skin.

'I have been in touch with a person. A widow. In Melbourne. In an advertisement,' she said, and found the forms. 'I am engaging a housekeeper for Xanadu.'

'Well, now, I am real pleased!' said Mrs Sugden, and was truly.

'You will not tell?' asked Miss Hare.

How she hated the vicious pen.

'Oh dear, no!' protested Mrs Sugden. 'What is an official position if not a position of trust?'

Miss Hare considered. The post office pen pricked the paper.

'I will tell you all about it,' she decided. 'But must write the telegram. To Melbourne.'

Mrs Sugden knew how to wait.

Miss Hare began to write.

'She describes herself as a lady – capable and refined.'

'Oh, dear, I should hope so!' exclaimed Mrs Sugden, blushing for other possibilities. 'In these days, and under the same roof!'

Miss Hare ploughed her way through the ugly desert of the telegraph form.

'I am not afraid,' she said, 'of anything. Or not of the things people are afraid of.'

'There are other things, of course,' agreed Mrs Sugden, who, in her official position, must have experienced an awful lot.

The postmistress waited. Miss Hare had on that old hat, wicker rather than straw – it was so very coarse – which she wore summer and winter regardless, and which gave her at times the look of a sunflower, at others, just an old basket coming to pieces. From where they were standing at the counter Mrs Sugden was able to look down at the kind of navel right at the centre of the crown. Miss Hare was that short. All was hat, and a hand extended from it, having trouble with a pen. The pen appeared to be resisting. Mrs Sugden stood and wondered where the hat could have come from. Nobody remembered seeing any other.

'It is all due to my Cousin Eustace Cleugh,' began Miss Hare, who had just managed the signature. 'He came here very many years ago. You will not remember. The way people sometimes used to send their sons on a visit to relatives in Australia. It seemed astonishing then. To *Australia*! Two wars have made a difference, of course, and the food parcels. But my Cousin Eustace came – he was somehow on my mother's side, through Aunt Fanny of Banjo Downs. Oh, it was splendid! The bachelors' quarters full. And they lit the chandelier almost every night. And balls, with music from Sydney. My mother said I should mingle with the guests – I was then a young girl; my hair had just been put up – but how could I mingle when I

9

must watch all the people who had come to Xanadu? There was one girl – I must tell you – called Helen Antill, in a dress embroidered with tiny mirrors. I overheard my mother remark that perhaps she should not have invited that Miss Antill. "Nor any other girl," my father replied; "nor young men either." My father had to have his joke. "And let us enjoy our pudding in peace," he said, "and bread sauce." My father was fond of bread sauce with a roast fowl, and one of the cooks used to make him a special kind.'

'Ah?'

'With *crushed onion*!' cried Miss Hare.

Mrs Sugden shifted foot. Much of her life had been spent in waiting.

'But let me see – my Cousin Eustace, who came and went, was in some way disappointing to my parents, though in after years he made amends. Oh dear, yes, he made me a little allowance, because his circumstances permitted, from the island of Jersey where he lives. That began already during my mother's lifetime. Fortunately. Because something – I never understood what – happened to my father's business.'

Miss Hare's voice trailed off. She took up the second, and equally horrid post office pen. But her gesture remained an irrelevant one.

'What do you know!' said Mrs Sugden.

'Oh, yes,' sighed Miss Hare. 'I thought *you* knew. I had been receiving the allowance so many years. Till suddenly the island of Jersey was overrun. Like that.'

Miss Hare did, in fact, spill the remaining post office ink, but Miss Sugden appeared not to care.

'By Germans?'

'Who else?' replied Miss Hare, not without contempt. 'Like darkness. For years there was no communication from our relative, until on a Friday morning, exactly seven weeks ago, a few lines arrived to say my Cousin Eustace was safe. Although in only moderate health and reduced circumstances, he considered it his duty to continue rendering me some small assistance.'

Mrs Sugden was suitably rejoiced at such a lifting of the clouds.

'And so you were able to engage this lady.'

'This woman has almost agreed.'

Miss Hare could be at moments both realistic and stern.

'Her name is Mrs Jolley,' she added, and, as the extent of the morning struck her through the window: 'I do hope she is capable of being happy at Xanadu. Sydney is not Melbourne, and here on the outskirts, there is such a lot of grass.'

'Anybody can be happy if they have a mind to be,' offered the postmistress, regardless of whether her maxim was cut to fit the situation.

Some flies had died on the counter which separated the two women, who found themselves examining the bodies.

'What,' asked Mrs Sugden, taking a deep breath, 'what became of the girl called Helen Antill, who wore that lovely dress?'

'Oh, she went away,' said Miss Hare. 'Everybody goes away.'

She began to swing her right leg. Her face, which narrative had turned moist and crumbly, was become dry and stale again. Ordinarily when she spoke, her mouth stayed stiff, almost as if she had had a stroke.

'She went away, and married, but somebody we had never heard of, and lived in a house, and had children, and buried her husband. Once I saw her looking out of the window at something.'

Mrs Sugden looked away, as if she, too, had seen.

Just then there was a crunching, and a person approached – it was, in fact, the newcomer to Sarsaparilla, Mrs Colquhoun – with the result that Miss Hare let the present fall like a shutter.

'Thank you,' she said to Mrs Sugden, whom she could have met only the moment before, and left.

So there was Miss Hare, on the track which the Council had begun to call a road, sometimes even avenue, which led down from Sarsaparilla to Xanadu. At one point doubts had invested her, and turned her stony still, but uncertain prospects could not long resist the surge of her surroundings, and she soon went on. Where the road sloped down she ran, disturbing stones, her body quite agitated as it accompanied her, but her inner self by now joyfully serene. The anomaly of that relationship never failed to mystify, and she stopped again, to consider. For a variety of reasons, very little of her secret, actual nature had been disclosed to other human beings. She stood still. Thinking very intently. Or allowing her instincts to play around her. Although no other human being was actually present, she did resent what must eventually recur. She stroked leaves sulkily. She broke a shaggy stick. Other people would drive along a bush road looking out of the windows of a car, but their minds embraced almost nothing of what their flickering eyes saw. Whole towers of green remained unclimbed, rocks unopened. Or else the intruders might stop their cars, and go in search of water. She had seen them, letting themselves down into the cold, black, secret rock pools, while remaining enclosed in their own resentful goose-flesh. Whereas she, Miss Hare, whose eyes were always probing, fingers trying, would achieve the ecstasy of complete, annihilating liberation without any such immersion.

Now, for a moment, she looked angry.

But drifted on dreamily.

All that land, stick and stone, belonged to her, over and above actual rights. Nobody else had ever known how to penetrate it quite to the same exent. She went on through her peculiar territory, lolloping, stopping. Often stopping. The sky had quickened, and was now a lively blue. The rather scrubby, indigenous trees, not so much of interest to the eye as an accompaniment to states of mind, were at the moment behaving with docility, a certain languid melancholy. Until she arrived at the bottom, where the road turned, and curled, and rose. The slope, gentle at first, climbed to abrupter terraces, with dispensations of fern and moss, and soft, rotting carpets, and there the trees, it seemed, grew straighter, taller and invariably she would turn dizzy if she stared too long upward at their scintillating crowns.

The owner never approached her legal property by following the official road to the gates – those, with their attempt at heraldry, were chained and padlocked, anyway – but took a short cut that she and the Godbold children always used, or an even shorter one, as now, known only to herself, and along which she had to push and struggle, actually to tunnel. But the way developed over good, soft loam, and velvet patches of leaf mould, lovely if the knees were allowed to sink for a moment into a surface from which would rise the scent of fungus and future growth.

So Miss Hare was pushing and struggling now, because it was what she liked, and chose. Scratched a little, but that was to be expected once the feet were set upon the paths of existence. Slapped by a staggy elder-bush, of which the buds had almost reached the edible stage. Whipped by the little sarsaparilla vine, of which she could have drunk the purple up. Stroked by ferns, and ferns.

At one stage she fell upon the knees of her earth-coloured, practical stockings, not because she was discouraged, or ill – she had reached the time of life where acquaintances and neighbours were always on the lookout for strokes – but because it

12

was natural to adopt a kneeling position in the act of worship, and because intense conviction will sometimes best express itself through the ungainliness of spontaneity.

So she rested a little upon her knees, under the great targe of her protective hat, and dug her blunt, freckled fingers into the receptive earth. She knelt for a while in the tunnel that led to Xanadu, and anybody would have found her more grotesquely ugly, less acceptable than they had thought. If family had remained to her, other than her Cousin Eustace, who was at a distance, and a handful of Urquhart Smiths, who had decided to forget, they would have turned away on recognizing such a travesty of their otherwise irreproachable strain.

In the past the Hares had always blamed the Urquhart Smiths, and the Urquhart Smiths, with equal determination, had blamed the Hares. But now there were not many of either to argue and discuss. If it had not been for Norbert Hare himself one might have expected normality from such an untainted, bourgeois stock, for Norbert was the son of old Mr Hare, the wine merchant at Wynyard, as everybody knew. The Urquhart Smiths, understandably, knew it better than anybody else, and, forgetting the Smiths in favour of the Urquharts, were always ready to remind their Eleanor who had married Norbert.

Eleanor was of that branch of the family at Mumblejug, of whom Sir Dudley, it will be remembered, arrived in New South Wales during the last century to represent the Queen. Renowned for his silk hats and horsemanship, Sir Dudley was an exemplary man, as his descendants had continued to tell long after everybody else had forgotten. If his daughter Eleanor was less remindful than some of the collaterals, it was perhaps because of her discreet temper, her indifferent health, and, certainly, her unorthodox marriage. Of four sisters, she was the only one to survive. All lovely, gracious girls, three were buried before they had been matched, under the gum trees, outside the little Gothic church which Sir Dudley had built at Mumblejug, not so much to exalt the spirit, as to perpetuate a materialist tradition.

So solid, so lovely-old, so *English*, Sir Dudley's church seemed to proclaim the situation at Mumblejug as indestructible. And then Eleanor went and did that terrible thing, of marrying Norbert, the son of old Hare the wine merchant at Wynyard. People of account, quite unacquainted with the Urquhart Smiths, were shocked into sympathy with them.

13

Eleanor, however, departed with her portion, and many lesser individuals laughed.

It was not that anybody failed to respect old Mr Hare. Nobody suspected his fortune of being anything less than considerable; nor were the matrimonial expectations of nice people particularly sanguine in such a recent society, unless the arrival of some Honourable roused intemperate hopes. All considered, a girl might have done worse than catch a Hare, and if practical minds did not quickly and quietly accept Eleanor Urquhart Smith's choice, the fault lay with her husband, who was original.

Norbert Hare had never been given to half measures. He did, or contemplated doing things which nobody else would have thought of. He once rode a grey horse up the marble stairs at Xanadu, as far as the landing, it was said, where his mount took fright, and deposited a mound of glaring yellow on the runner. Although they were not always executed, Norbert was for ever conceiving plans: for building a study at the top of a Chinese pagoda, or stable in the shape of a mosque, for breeding *escargots de Bourgogne*, or planting medlars, or printing poems – his own – on sheets of coloured silk, woven for that purpose on the property. The wine merchant's son had received an education, which his own peculiar temperament ensured was of a spasmodic and eclectic kind. At one period he had considered writing a treatise on Catullus, until discovering he was out of patience with that poet. Norbert had, in fact, written quantities himself: epigrams and metaphysical fragments, which he would read aloud to anybody he succeeded in cornering. The fragment, it appeared, possessed for him a greater distinction than the whole. There were all those pieces of marble he brought from Italy. He brought the mosaics for a bath, all nymphs, and vines, and a big, black, baleful goat. Two Italian artisans were imported purposely to fit the pieces together, after it had been promised they would receive a regular supply of *vino*. The Italians came and practised their art, and drank their wine, and one of them, it was never decided which, got an Irish girl with child. Norbert and Eleanor were absent a good deal, of course, in foreign parts, because it was the period when Australians of That Class – and Norbert was soon of That Class – were returning home to show they were as good as anyone else. So the Hares had to go, nor could the discreet Eleanor prevent rumours trickling back: that Norbert had been involved in a duel while passing through Perugia, and that in London he had fallen down in public while under the influence of strong drink. It was all in character. But Norbert's grandest gesture, the one that caused people to suck their teeth, to gnash them, or to set them in a kind, sad smile, was the building of his folly at Sarsaparilla outside Sydney. His Pleasure Dome, he called it, his Xanadu, and recited the appropriate verses to lady guests as they strolled in their veils and the afternoon, inspecting the freshly-laid foundations of porous yellow stone.

Nothing exquisite can be created in a hurry, and Xanadu was no exception. It cost time and patience; everybody grew exhausted. But there it stood finally: golden, golden, in a frill or two of iron lace, beneath the dove-grey thatching of imported slates, its stables and bachelor quarters trailing out behind. So Norbert, son of old Mr Hare, the wine merchant at Wynyard, was vindicated at last, if only in his own sight. He liked to climb up through his house, and on reaching the top, with its little, actual dome of faintly amethyst glass, spend a private hour devouring the flesh of a cold fowl, skimming opening lines from obscure poets, or just staring out over his own property. Or beyond, it could have been – beyond the still manageable park which he had ordered to be planted, beyond even the grey, raggedy, native scrub, for his eyes appeared momentarily appeased, and that end might not have been achieved, if anchorage in time and space had forced him to recognize the native cynicism of that same, grey, raggedy scrub.

The scrub, which had been pushed back, immediately began to tangle with Norbert Hare's wilfully created park, until, years later, there was his daughter, kneeling in a tunnel of twigs which led to Xanadu. Speckled and dappled, like any wild thing native to the place, she was examining her surroundings for details of interest. Almost all were, because alive, changing, growing, personal, like her own thoughts, which intermingled, flapping and flashing, with the leaves, or lay straight and stiff as sticks, or emerged with the painful stench of any crushed ant. Her hands, almost always dirty and scratched, from the constant need to plunge into operations of importance – encouraging a choked plant to shoot, freeing a fledgling from its shell, breaking an afterbirth – were now hung with dying ants, she observed with some distress. One slithered from her father's bloodstone ring, which she wore not as a memento of her father, but because its device officially confirmed her ownership of Xanadu.

Once or twice in the far past she had attempted to play with the ring on her father's hand.

'It is not a toy,' he had warned. 'You must learn to respect property.'

So she had begun to.

The mother, also, had worn rings, amethysts for preference. She favoured the twilight colours. Her clothes were in no way memorable, except perhaps her collection of woolly wraps, of such lightness they could not possibly have weighed upon her. The little girl was allowed to touch the clothes and rings her mother wore, even to grow rough with them. Too delicate to protest much, unless an issue exceeded the bounds of taste, Eleanor Hare wished most earnestly to do what was right, as wife and mother.

'I am so afraid, Norbert, we shall not love our child enough. With my health and your interests.'

'Oh, *love*!' the father replied, and laughed fit to shatter it for ever.

'I had no intention of causing you pain,' his wife complained, before withdrawing into herself, under a big woolly shawl, a sage green, and a hot water bottle which she would hold to her neuralgia.

'If only you would prevent her knocking over coffee cups,' he requested, 'especially into the laps of guests, and snapping off dahlias, and stamping up and down the landing while I am reading. I need a certain amount of silence while I am thinking something out.'

'It is only reasonable,' she agreed, 'that a child should learn to respect other people's needs.'

Anybody's reasonableness, and particularly his wife's, was what infuriated him most.

So the child learned, as far as her natural clumsiness would allow, to move softly, like a leaf, and certain words she avoided, because they were breakable. The word LOVE, for instance, brittle as glass, and far more precious. Oh, she could go carefully enough in the end, in little, starched movements. And had learnt to love, even, but after her secret fashion, the labyrinths of corridors, the big, cool, greenish rooms, the golden walls of stone, the tunnels through the shrubberies.

And now Miss Hare got up, as far as her tunnel would allow, to continue struggling, bundling, pushing with the shield of her great wicker hat, to burst forth, not without shaking, and panting, and ridiculousness, into the presence of her noble love.

16

On extricating herself from the embrace of twigs, there remained perhaps another two hundred yards of less grudgingly gracious green: a pomegranate almost gone to wood, a crab or two, spidery with first blossom, several sad, but soothing pines. The ground continued to rise, increasing her breathlessness, tearing her calves open as she climbed. All, whether within or without, was leading upward now.

So Miss Hare came home, as always, for the first time. She stepped out beyond the trees where lawn began. Certainly the grass appeared a bit neglected, but the eyes, and not necessarily the eyes of a lover, were invariably transfixed by their first glimpse of Xanadu. Miss Hare herself had almost crumbled as she stood to watch her vision form.

2

She liked to come downstairs early. She would even get up in the dark, bumping things before she found her balance. She liked to come down, and sit, and listen to the house, after her own footsteps had died away, and the sound of the primus on which she had brewed a pot of tea. Then, she would sit and wrinkle her nose at the smell of kerosene, while she thawed out, if it were winter, or relaxed in summer after the weight of the heavy nights. Later she would start to walk about, touching things. Sometimes she would move them: a goblet, or a footstool, and once a heavy buhl table, from which the brass had risen to set traps for clothes and flesh. But mostly she let things lie, out of respect. Or she would draw a curtain, cunningly, to look out at the spectacle of morning, when all that is most dense becomes most transparent, and the world is dependent on the eyes of the beholder. Then Miss Hare's mouth would grow slack and loving as she formed the solid trunks of gums out of the grey embryos of trees.

She was at her best early in the morning. Except on this one. She jerked the curtain. And it tore uglily. A long tongue of gold brocade. But she did not stay to consider. It was several mornings since she had taken the postmistress into her confidence. It was the morning before the arrival of the housekeeper at Xanadu.

'A housekeeper!' she said, feeling her knuckles to test their infirmity, and finding they were, indeed, infirm.

A housekeeper though was less formidable than a person, and this was what Miss Hare dreaded most: an individual called Mrs Jolley, whose hips would assert themselves in navy blue, whose breathing would be heard, whose letters would lie upon the furniture addressed in the handwriting of daughters and nieces, telling of lives lived, unbelievably, in other places. It was frightening, frightening.

Miss Hare often cried in private, not from grief, but because she found it soothing, and she did now. It was frightening though. Naturally she found it impossible to like human beings, if only on account of their faces, to say nothing of their habit of relating things that had never happened and then believing that they had. Children were perhaps the worst, because they had not yet grown insincere, and insincerity does blunt the weapons of attack. Possible exceptions were those children who grew up in one's vicinity, almost without one's noticing, just being around; that was delicious, like air. Best of all Miss Hare liked those who never expected what they would not receive. She liked animals, birds, and plants. On these she would expend her great but pitiable love, and because that was not expected it ceased to be pitiable.

Once, it was related, a naked nestling had fallen into her lap, and she had reared it by some mysterious method of her own, warming it down her front, it was suspected, and ejecting juices into its beak from her mouth. The nestling had grown into a dove. Some of the Godbold children had been shown it. Then it flew away, of course, but would return sometimes, Miss Hare told. She would talk to it. Everybody except the Godbold kids thought it a lot of rot, Miss Hare talking to birds. But you could learn, she insisted. Miss Hare said you could learn to do anything provided you wanted to, but there were an awful lot of things you did not want enough.

Like learning to love a human being. Like the housekeeper, whom the telegram and her own increasing infirmity were bringing to Xanadu.

'Ah, no, no, no!' she protested and whimpered in the cold early morning air.

And the house repeated it after her.

Most of those landowners who wished to show how rich they were had already gone on to build in brick at the time when Norbert Hare decided to cut his dash in stone. To Mr Hare, brick was plain ugly; it did not please him a little bit, and what was Xanadu to suggest, if not the materialization of beauty, and climax of his pleasure? *Pleasure* is a shocking word in societies where the most luxurious aspirations are disguised as humble, moral ones. It is doubtful whether any rich, landowning gentleman of the period would have admitted to his house's being more than *necessary* or *practical*. Material objects were valued for their *usefulness*; if they were also intended to *please*, not to say *glorify*, it was commonly kept a secret. Only Norbert Hare, notoriously rash, had been heard to confess that the word *useful* sounded to him less modest than humiliating. It was so intolerably grey and Australian. *Brilliant* and *elegant* were the epithets applicable to Norbert's aspirations, certainly to his most ambitious, his Pleasure Dome at Xanadu. Although by no means a sincere man, there was one point in his life at which sincerity conferred with taste and individualism. Xanadu was Norbert's contribution to the sum of truth, *brilliant* and *elegant* though the house was, created in the first place for its owner's *pleasure*. More would have admired it openly, if they could have felt the principles of their admiration to be sound. As it was, other monied gentlemen voiced more loudly than ever their enthusiasm for the *practical* qualities of brick, and were persuaded that if the turrets of their purple mansions conformed to the pattern then condoned, nobody was going to accuse simple, down-to-earth sheep-keepers of acting in any way *flash*.

Norbert, of course, did not keep sheep; his family might have laughed a little longer if he had. What he possessed was the fortune of his wine-merchant father, who died conveniently soon after his son's marriage, followed by several commercial brothers, trustful to the point of overlooking brilliance in a nephew. Norbert Hare inherited all, and thus comfortably endowed set about leading the life of a country gentleman, such as he understood it from his reading and his travels, with none of the colonial encumbrances of sheep and acres which made the undertaking virtually impossible. What he required, and did in fact acquire, was an exquisite setting for his humours: the park of exotic, deciduous trees, the rose garden which his senses craved, pasture for the pedigree Jersey cows which would fill his silver jugs with cream, and stables for the horses which he drove himself with virtuosity – always greys, always four-in-hand. Thus surrounded and provided for, he was soon engrossed in living up to it all: advising on the drenching of a cow, or blistering of a horse (Mr Hare always knew), marshalling the cinerarias in extra brilliant ranks, interfering in his daughter's education, tearing down a wall, throwing out a wing, or running upstairs to jot down some thought which had occurred invariably to someone else before him.

Despite the inevitable frustrations and migraines, life at Xanadu was never squalid. Out of its bower of rather unhappy exotic trees, out of its necklaces of rosebeds (the complexions of the blooms themselves protected by little parasols, which occupied practically the whole of the second gardener's time) aspired the lovely languid house. Round it they had trained wistaria, which at the height of the Hares' glory had not attained to vulgar opulence, and which never failed to please the eye in the same way as a feather boa on the right neck. In the spring its heavy, clovy scent invaded the great, greenish rooms; the marble staircase and the malachite urns dissolved beneath the onslaught, and the gilded mirrors led by subtle, receding stages far beyond the bounds of vision.

The beauty of it antagonized some of those whom the Hares were in the habit of regarding as friends, to say nothing of the practical relatives, Ted Urquhart Smith, for instance, one of the cousins from Banjo Downs.

'What becomes of all this flummery when Bert has blown the cash?' asked Ted on one occasion, indicating with calloused hand the drawing-room at Xanadu, in which it was almost impossible to tell where glass ended and light began.

Addie, his sister, permitted herself a titter.

His Cousin Eleanor hesitated. Grave even as a girl, life with her husband had made her graver still.

'But I think Norbert's fortune is very prudently invested,' she replied at last. 'And then, a house is said to be an investment in itself.'

The wife of Norbert Hare seldom committed herself to positive opinions. Two positives in that relationship would have been intolerable.

Once, in a fit of rage, the husband accused his wife of having become the mouthpiece of social cliché.

'But it is what people prefer, Norbert,' the poor woman protested, with vehemence for her. 'Too much of what is unexpected is too upsetting.'

Before there was any call for it she began to wear, together with her apologetic amethysts, colours which suggested mourning. She would cough thinly, from behind an expression that invited inquiry into the state of her health, and visitors would take the hint, not that they really cared to discover how Mrs Hare's health was poor, but it provided a useful topic with which to hack a way into the tangles of conversation.

She was not a snob, though there were many who accused her of it. She suffered, rather, from seeing the weak exposed to those whom she considered strong, and so she would attempt to keep her friends separate, in compartments that she hoped might protect them from one another. She was completely unreal, and would impart temporarily to those of her equals with whom she came in contact something of her unreality. Yet she was not ineffective against the peacock colours of the stage at Xanadu, and provided the perfect flat foil to her husband's fustian. The one cataclysmic reality to challenge her playing of the part was the presence of her daughter, but that was a fact she had failed from the beginning to embrace, an event the significance of which she had recoiled from relating to the play of life.

After several years of tedious and frustrated childbirth, Mrs Hare had succeeded in having this little girl. They named her Mary, because the mother, fortunately, was too exhausted to think, and the father, who would have plunged with voluptuous excitement into the classics, or the works of Tennyson, to dredge up some shining name for a son, turned his back on the prospect of a daughter. So Mary the latter became, but an innocent Protestant one.

Mrs Hare had soon taken refuge from Mary in a rational kindness, with which she continued to deal her a series of savage blows during what passed for childhood.

'My darling must decide how best she can repay her parents for all she owes them,' was amongst the mother's favourite tactics. 'See all these beautiful things they have put here to be enjoyed, not smashed in thoughtless games.'

And, in answer to a frequent question:

'Only our Father in Heaven will be able to tell my pet why He made her as He did.'

Paddling in her own delicious shallows, it never occurred to Mrs Hare to raise her eyes to God, except to call Him as a formal witness. She accepted Him – who would have been so audacious not to? – but as the creator of a moral and a social system. At that level, she could always be relied on to put her hand in her purse, to help repair vestments, or support fallen girls, and her name was published for everyone to read, on a visiting card, inserted in a brass frame, on the end of her regular pew.

The little girl appeared gravely to accept the attitudes adopted by her mother, but was not genuinely influenced. Unattached, she drifted through the pale waters of her mother's kindness like a little, wondering, transparent fish, in search of those depths which her instinct told her could exist.

Her father's attitudes were less acceptable than her mother's.

Once in her presence – or she had been standing, rather, in the drawing-room alcove, apart, touching the waves of an emerald silk with which the day-bed would fascinate the fingers – her father had thrown down his cap with more than his usual violence and shouted:

'Who would ever have thought I should get a *red* girl! By George, Eleanor, she is ugly, ugly!'

Which – it sounded – was the worst that might be said.

With more than her usual kindness, Eleanor Hare motioned to their child, and when the latter had come forward – because, what else could anyone do? – the mother smoothed a sash, and sighed and suggested:

'Plain is the word, Norbert. And who knows – Mary's plainness may have been given to her for a special purpose.'

Because she was inexperienced, or because she was born hopeful, Mary did not immediately begin to hate her father. She decided on a watery smile, which only made her uglier, and her parent more enraged.

She remained altogether without companions, because it never occurred to anybody that she was in need of them, and she did fairly well without: with sticks, pebbles, skeleton leaves, birds, insects, the hollows of trees, and the cellars and attics of Xanadu. She did have a pony, but preferred to be with it rather than to ride upon it – which would have entailed the company of her father – and soon learned to oblige most of its wishes by studying the quiver of a nostril, the flicker of a muscle, and the varying assertions of silence.

Once when, unavoidably, in the company of her father, and they had gone down to inspect a rested paddock, she had thrown herself on the ground and begun to hollow out a nest in the grass with little feverish jerks of her body and foolish grunts, curling round in the shape of a bean or position of a foetus. So it appeared to him. But, in answer to his quick-drawn demand for an explanation, the child had replied simply:

'Now I know what it feels like to be a dog.'

He had been so shocked and disgusted by the expression on her freckled face, that he told her to get up at once, and decided not to think about the incident again.

On very few occasions Mary Hare and her father, approaching from their opposite sides, arrived simultaneously at a common frontier of understanding, and then only when alcohol, despair, or approaching death loosened the slight restraints of reason – when, indeed, he came closest to resembling in her eyes a distressed or desperate animal.

Throughout her life the daughter would remember an incident which occurred about that time, and on which she would employ her intuition in attempting to interpret what her mind failed to understand. She had been standing on the terrace. It was the hour of sunset. Earlier in the afternoon they had gone driving along the roads and lanes round Sarsaparilla, even as far as Barranugli, so that her father might show himself. How relieved she felt to be alone at last, able to look at and touch and smell whatever she saw, without danger of being asked by her parents for explanations. The urns on the terrace were running over, she remembered, with cascades of a little milky flower, which would shimmer through darkness like falls of moonlight. But at that hour the light was gold. Or red. So splendid that even she, a red girl, had no need to feel ashamed of the correspondence.

Then her father came outside. He had been tasting a new brandy which they had sent out for his personal opinion, and his mouth was still wet and shining from his recent occupation. His eyes, in the dazzle from the sun, appeared almost vulnerable. There they stood, the father and daughter, facing each other, alarmingly exposed. He came forward, and seemed at once both puzzled and assured. Fondling her. Which was not his habit. And it was not altogether pleasant: his hands playing amongst her hair. She was reminded of a pair of black-and-white spaniels she had seen lolloping and playing together, too silly to help themselves. But just because her father's temporary silliness and loss of control had reduced him to the level of herself and dogs, she did submit to his fondling her.

She did not remember what he said, not all of it, for that, too, was silly and confused, only that at one point he had shaken his head, as if to dash the sunlight out of his eyes, both drowning and smiling, and spoke in a harsh voice, which, although addressing her, did not seem designed for her attention.

Her father said:

'Who are the riders in the Chariot, eh, Mary? Who is ever going to know?'

Who, indeed? Certainly *she* would not be expected to understand. Nor did she think she wanted to, just then. But they continued there, the sunset backed up against the sky, as they stood beneath the great swingeing trace-chains of its light.

Perhaps she should have been made afraid by some awfulness of the situation, but she was not. She had been translated: she was herself a fearful beam of the ruddy, champing light, reflected back at her own silly, uncertain father.

Then he had started frowning, and it became obvious they were again driving along the road from Barranugli to Sarsaparilla, returning through the comparatively humdrum light of the afternoon already past.

'I do not like the offside front mare,' he complained. 'Must replace the offside front. She moves lame, without her being lame at all.'

For he required perfection in horses, as in everything, and usually got it, except in human beings.

He looked at her, and was again irritated, she saw, because she was such an ugly little girl, and she, for her part, could do nothing for him but smile back in the way of those from whom nothing much is expected.

Yet, the father's rather oblique remark, made when he was drunk, and uttered with the detachment and harshness of male egotism, encouraged the daughter to expect of life some ultimate revelation. Years after, when his stature was even further diminished in her memory, her mind would venture in foxy fashion, or more blunderingly worm-like, in search of a concealed truth. If fellowship with Himmelfarb and Mrs Godbold, and perhaps her brief communion with a certain blackfellow, would confirm rather than expound a mystery, the reason could be that, in the last light, illumination is synonymous with blinding.

In the meantime, life at Xanadu was disturbed less by transcendental problems than the economic and social ones which come to those who enjoy nerves and invested income. The Hares never talked about money. To Mrs Hare that would have been an act in the poorest taste. To her husband, on the other hand, money was something he did not care to think about, but which he hoped fervently would still be there. He was not unlike a traveller walking into a landscape which may prove mirage. Fortunate in his inheritance from the wine-merchant father and commercial uncles, and in the devotion of an individual just stupid enough to be honest, just intelligent enough to be practical, who managed his late father's business, Norbert was pretty certain that his landscape was an actual one. But it unnerved him to discuss it, and if drink or insomnia forced him to consider his financial future, he would buy reality off by writing to his London agent to order a fireplace in Parian marble, or a Bonington, which, he was assured, would soon be coming up for sale. In that way he was fortified.

In that way they continued to live at Xanadu, and soon it became clear the daughter of the house was a young girl. They put up her hair, and the nape of her neck was greenish and unfreckled where the red hair had lain. She was no prettier, however, and unnaturally small.

The mother began to sigh a good deal, and remarked:

'It is time we thought about doing something for our poor Mary.'

But immediately wondered whether her suggestion might not have sounded vulgar.

The father could not feel the situation deserved his interest.

'If anything is to happen, it will happen.' He yawned, and showed his rather handsome, pointed teeth. 'How does it happen to at least ninety per cent of the unlikely human race? How did it happen to us?'

'We grew fond of each other,' his wife ventured, and blushed.

The husband laughed out loud.

And the wife preferred not to hear.

Not long after, Mrs Hare displayed excitement and her husband cynical interest when it was announced that Eustace Cleugh intended to undertake a tour of the world, in the course of which he would visit his relations in New South Wales. Except that he was a member of an English branch of Urquhart Smiths, not a lot was known about Mr Cleugh, but blank sheets are always whitest. Mrs Hare *had* heard that her Cousin Eustace was *awfully nice*, neither young, nor yet middle-aged, comfortably off, and that his mother's brother had married the Honourable Lavinia Lethbridge, a daughter of Lord Trumpington.

'What does Mr Cleugh do for a living?' Mary asked her mother.

'I don't exactly know,' replied the latter. 'I expect he just lives.'

So it all sounded most desirable.

Eustace Cleugh, when he arrived, was not surprised at a lot of what he heard and saw, for, as an Englishman and an Urquhart Smith, he had preconceived notions of what he must expect from colonial life in general and the Norbert Hares in particular.

'Breeding is ninety per cent luck, whatever the experts and Urquhart Smiths may tell you,' Mr Hare announced the first

25

night at dinner. 'And when I say luck, I mean bad luck, of course.'

'There are so many *rewarding* topics!' his wife complained, looking at her cherry stones.

Mary Hare stared at her cousin. An absence of interested upbringing had at least left her with a thorough training in observation, and although she looked deeper than was commonly considered decent, she often made discoveries. Now she confirmed that this man was, in fact, as her mother had forewarned, neither young, nor yet middle-aged. To Mary Hare it seemed probable that Mr Cleugh had always been about thirty-five. As she herself was of indeterminate age, she hoped they might become friends. But how was she to go about it? In the first place, he was of her father's sex. In the second, his beautifully kept, slightly droopy moustache, and the long bones of his folded fan-like hands, appeared unaware of anything beyond the person of Eustace Cleugh. Perhaps if he had been a dog – say, an elegant Italian greyhound – she might have won him over by many infallible means.

But as that was not the case, she could only offer him an almond.

Which he accepted with an unfolding of hands. Now also he began to unfold his mind, and to offer to the audience in general – everything that Eustace spoke was offered to a general, rather than to a particular, audience – an account of a journey he had made with a friend through Central and Northern Italy.

'After a short interlude at Ravenna,' Mr Cleugh picked his way, 'not in itself of interest, but there are the mosaics, and the *zuppa di pesce* – and they are essential, aren't they? – we went on to Padua, where the Botanic Gardens are said to be the oldest in Europe. They are not, I must admit, particularly large, or *fine*, as gardens go, but we found them to be of peculiarly subtle horticultural interest.'

Mrs Hare made the little social noises that one made. But her husband had begun to blink, repeatedly, and hard.

'In Padua, poor Aubrey Puckeridge was struck down by some ailment we were never able to diagnose, part tummy, part fever, in what turned out to be – our guidebook had sadly misinformed us – a most primitive *albergo*.'

Mrs Hare made the same, only slightly more appreciative noises.

'And did he die?' asked Norbert.

'Well, no,' replied Eustace Cleugh. 'I hope I did not imply.

I intended only to suggest that poor Aubrey was awfully indisposed.'

'Oh,' said Mr Hare. 'I thought perhaps the fellow died.'

Eustace Cleugh noticed that his cousin's husband had been drinking a good deal of his own poisonous wine.

Mary Hare was fascinated by Mr Cleugh's story, not so much by the narrative as how it issued out of his face. She put it together in piles of dead leaves, but neatly, and matched, like bank-notes. It made her sad, too. So many of the things she told died on coming to the surface, when their life, to say nothing of their after life in her mind, could be such a shining one. She wondered whether Mr Cleugh realized how dead his own words were, and if he was suffering for it. There were, after all, many things he and she had in common, if they could first overcome the strangeness of their separate existences, and crack the codes of human intercourse.

'When he got better, and left that primitive *albergo*?' she asked, for a start, offering him her assistance.

But Eustace Cleugh no longer felt inclined.

He had only glanced at his cousin's ugly child, and promised himself that, during his visit, he would look as little as possible in that direction. Her short, stumpy hands were particularly repulsive, and the flare of hair that had not yet submitted to the tyranny of pins. He shuddered inside himself. Even while concentrating on the pattern of his dessert plate, he was conscious of how shockingly the girl was put together. It was almost as though the presence of any kind of physical monstrosity was a personal insult to Mr Cleugh.

'I expect Cousin Eustace is tired.' Mrs Hare was making his excuses. 'My own arrival in a strange house exhausts me beyond anything.'

Eustace, of course, turned a smile on the company, because his manners were perfect, and became murmurous in protest.

But he did retire early, and not to the bachelors' quarters because, said Mrs Hare, he was a member of the family.

Mary soon realized that her life would remain unchanged by their cousin's being with them, because she did not see so very much of him; he was always either reading or writing – his tastes appeared studious – smoking or thinking, or walking in the bush to study the flora of Australia.

Once she suggested:

'If you like, I shall come with you. I shall take you to places that probably no one else has seen. Only you mustn't mind crawling and scrambling. And sometimes there are snakes.'

He could smile very obligingly. He said:

'That is a good idea. Yes. Why have we not thought of it before? Yes, some day. When there is more time.'

Because there were also social engagements: gentlemen were brought, who told him about their sheep, and ladies, who wished to be told about Home, some mythical land that existed largely in their imaginations. A lot of this did at last surprise the visitor, for it had never occurred to him that sheep could be taken seriously, and together with his English acquaintances, he had always considered that, of all civilizations, real and imagined, only the Italian was worthy of consideration.

All the time Mrs Hare remained aware that something must be done for Mary, and so it was decided to give the ball. This was such an undertaking in itself that it did not occur to her how her daughter might be affected by it.

The latter did venture:

'Do you think Cousin Eustace cares about dancing? He is far too polite to say whether he does or not.'

But already, mentally, the mother was at the dressmaker's. She was calculating how many oyster patties, and wondering whether in the final hour the maids would obey her orders.

Even on the night, everyone was inclined to ignore Mary Hare. Those who were kind enough thought to respect her feelings by not noticing her appearance, but those who were cruel hoped to spare their own by refusing to see what could only upset them.

She appeared dressed in a silvery white, because she was a young girl, and this was to be the moment of her triumph, or sacrifice. She stood about, touching the papery stuff of her skirt with disbelieving hands, wearing jewels which her mother had brought from her own box: a little brooch in knots of pearls, and pearl dog-collar which the mother herself no longer wore, and which had lost much of its lustre from lying on velvet instead of on living flesh.

So there she was, dressed to kill, as one young fellow remarked, only it was Mary who was killed, by her own pearl dog-collar.

Certainly it was rather tight. She was always inclined to be red, however, in patches, according to weather and emotion, to say nothing of rough. Her hands caught in the splendid stuff of her silvery dress, and she was reminded of the many awkwardnesses of behaviour of which she had been guilty. Perhaps the most grotesque detail of her whole appearance, those who discussed it remembered afterwards, was a little bunch of ridiculous flowers that she had pinned half-wilting at her waist: frail fuchsia, and rank geranium, and pinks, and camomile – all stuffed together, and trembling, and falling. It did certainly look peculiar, and most unsuccessful, but she had not been able to resist one touch of what she knew by heart.

The evening developed, in gusts of music and tinkling of glass. The ugly, forgotten girl should have felt miserable, but was preserved finally from unhappiness by the wonder of it, by the long shadows and the pools of light, by the extraordinary, revealing faces of men and women, by receiving a glass of lemonade, off a silver salver, from a servant who pretended not to recognize, in their own house.

There were a great many important guests: landowners, professional men and their wives – only those who were rich, hence socially acceptable. And house guests. The bachelors' quarters were full of young men down from the country, with high spirits, good teeth, and brick-red skins.

And the dancing. And the dancing.

Mary Hare, without aspiring, loved to watch from some familiar corner, protected by mahogany or gilt, in cave of chalcedony or malachite, peering out. From there the dancers could be seen riding the swell of music (the best that Sydney could provide) in the full arrogance of their intentions. Or, suddenly, they would lose control, whirled around by the un-suspected eddies. But willingly. As they leaned back inside the slippery funnels of the music, they would have allowed them-selves to be sucked down, the laughter and the conversation trembling on their transparent teeth.

There was, in particular, the girl Helen Antill, whom some considered, in spite of her beauty and assurance – *extravagant*. Miss Antill wore a dress embroidered with little mirrors, oriental it could have been, which reflected the lights, and even, occasionally, a human feature. She carried, moreover, a fan, curiously set in a piece of irregular coral resembling a hand. The fan was of peacocks' feathers. Most unlucky.

But Miss Antill could not have been perturbed.

Mary Hare, watching, thought she might have loved some-thing like this, just as she fell spontaneously in love with the smooth limbs of certain trees, the texture of marble, and long, immaculate legs of thoroughbred horses spanking at their exercise. Even Mrs Hare became carried away by Miss Antill's performance, and although she had at first suffered qualms on seeing the effect her guest would have upon those others present, admiration overcame her protective instincts as a mother, and she began to move quickly through her house, searching and frowning, her grey mist of chiffon trailing like an obsession after her.

'Where is Cousin Eustace?' she asked cursorily of Mary.

'It is some time since I noticed him,' replied her daughter, and as she diverted her attention, realized how strange it was that she should be addressing her own mother.

Mrs Hare frowned again. At the point of sacrificing a daughter, she continued to expect that the latter should do her duty.

'You should see to it that he is not alone. When there is nobody else, you should keep him company. In fact, any young girl of serious intentions makes sure that hers is the company he wants.' Then Mrs Hare sighed, realizing the difficulty of most situations. 'Men do not know what they want without a little guiding.'

'But I should hate to *guide* someone,' replied Mary.

'The way you say it you make it sound like *drag*!' despaired the mother. 'I meant to imply that a slight touch on the elbow works wonders.'

'Cousin Eustace hates to be touched.'

Mrs Hare preferred to interrupt a conversation that had become so physical. She would bear her cross, and in becoming thus a martyr, she was convinced that only she herself was aware of the source of her martyrdom.

So she continued the search for her relative, strengthened by her disappointments, and the vision of Miss Antill in her successful dress.

Eustace Cleugh had, in fact, performed most nobly almost all that had been expected of him that night. He had appeared to listen attentively to all those statistics with which the graziers had provided him. He had lent a sympathetic ear to graziers' wives, condemned to use up their lives on Australian soil, removed from all those material advantages which their sensibility, not to say spirituality, required. He had danced, how he had danced with the daughters. At least, his body had accepted the dictatorship of music, and his face had not let him down. But now he had gone upstairs, into the study of his cousin Norbert Hare, to nurse his numbness, and to look through an album of engravings of German churches in the Gothic style.

Here his Cousin Eleanor found him.

'Eustace,' she exclaimed, 'I cannot imagine how you have

allowed yourself to overlook Miss Antill. Such an exquisite dancer, and a lovely girl. I cannot rest until I see you lead her out.'

And she took him by the wrist, *guiding,* as she was convinced.

Eustace Cleugh was far too well brought up to wrench himself free of gentle compulsion. All he said was:

'Yes, Miss Antill is very lovely.'

So Mary Hare watched their cousin brought downstairs. She watched him move out across the treacherous floor. That he was *brought*, and that he no more than *moved*, was something which perhaps only Mary noticed, but she, of course, spent so much of her time observing timid behaviour: of birds, for instance. Now here was her cousin, Eustace Cleugh, netted by the music and Miss Antill. How the mirrors in the dress flashed and reflected. Eustace did not struggle, but revolved most correctly, holding his partner; Mary alone saw how he was held. Almost the colour of nougat, his face asked the expected questions: about theatrical entertainments, the races, and the weather. In the short space of his visit, he had grown surprisingly well informed on matters of local importance.

But Miss Antill seemed to remain unconvinced. As they revolved and revolved, the phrases into which she bit could have tasted peculiar. She could not quite believe in some *thing*, some failure – was it her own? Or could the bird have died before the kill? They continued, however, to revolve. As Miss Antill clutched her partner's expensive cloth and the travesty of experience, she could have been flickering, although it was attributed by almost her entire audience to the clash between light and mirrors. Such splendour as hers did not encounter uncertainties.

Then there was a pause in the music, and Mr Cleugh did behave very oddly, everybody agreed. He simply excused himself, wiped his face with a horribly white handkerchief, and walked away. It was in the end far less humiliating for Miss Antill, in spite of the slight she had suffered, for practically the whole population of the bachelors' quarters rushed upon her, to say nothing of several susceptible solicitors and elderly, unsuspected graziers.

Eustace Cleugh disappeared in the direction of the terrace. One or two ladies just noticed in the confusion of movement that dotty Mary went, or rushed rather, after him, dropping wilted flowers as she ran, but everybody was too distracted by the scene they had just witnessed to envisage further developments of an incomprehensible nature. Besides, they had been taught firmly to suppress, like wind in company, the rise of unreason in their minds.

Eustace was on the terrace, Mary found, not quite in darkness, for the lights of the house cast a certain glow, tarnished but comforting.

'Oh,' she began, 'I shall go away if you would rather.'

Though she would have hated to be sent.

'No,' he said. 'There is no reason to go away. In this glass house. One is fully exposed everywhere.'

'Is it different, then, in other houses?'

He laughed. He sounded almost natural.

'No,' he replied. 'I suppose not.'

'How you hated it,' she said. 'The dance with Miss Antill. I am sorry.'

He began to tremble. If she had not pitied, she might have been shocked. But there had been moments when she had absolved even her father from being a man.

Cousin Eustace did not speak. He stood and trembled.

She touched some ivy. Painfully.

'And you will not forget it,' she said.

'There comes a point where one can't remember everything,' Eustace replied, with reason as well as feeling.

Then she touched the back of his hand, and he did not withdraw. Of course her skin told her immediately that she could have been a dog, but she was grateful to be accepted if only in that form. In fact, she would not have thought of expecting more, and mercifully it had never yet occurred to her to think of herself as a woman.

After a bit, he began to cough and move about without direction or elegance, like an ordinary person when nobody is there. Rather clumsily. But he did not repudiate his companion.

'Oh, dear!' He sighed, and laughed, but again roughly, and unlike him. 'Do you ever crumble? Suddenly? Without warning?'

'Yes,' she cried. 'Oh, yes! Often. Truly.'

It was most important that he should know.

But he was yawning. It could have been that he had not heard her reply, or that he had heard, and did not believe in the existence of anything outside the closed circle of himself.

She saw, however, that he was tamed, and that in future she might walk calmly, though quietly, in his vicinity, and watch him, and he would not mind. Only soon after the ball at Xanadu, Cousin Eustace resumed his tour of the world, as had always been intended, and took refuge finally on the island of

Jersey, with a housekeeper, and what eventually became a famous collection of porcelain.

Even if her husband had allowed it, Mrs Hare would never have been able to forget how her cousin had insulted her guest. What she did forget, conveniently, was that she had expected of him something impossible, not to say indelicate. It was only in after life, in the regurgitation of memories, that she sometimes came across her true motive for giving the ball at Xanadu. It would drift up to the surface of her mind, almost complete, almost explicit, but always it had a horrid, quickly-to-be-rejected taste.

If Mary was less upset by Eustace Cleugh's behaviour, it was because she already expected less of the human animal, and in consequence was not surprised when he diverged from the course which other people intended he should take. The ugliness and weakness which his nature revealed at such moments were, she sensed, far closer to the truth. So she could understand and pity her cousin, even understand and pity her father, even when the latter looked at her with hate for what she saw and understood. In her time she had seen dogs receive a beating for having glimpsed their masters' souls. She was no dog, certainly, and her father had not beaten her, but there had been one occasion when he did start shooting at the chandelier.

It was a summer evening, on which the weather had not broken. The expected storm still hung heavy on the leaden mountains to the west, and the air was full of flying-ants, dashing themselves against glass and flesh, and fretting off their wings in the last stages of a life over which they seemed to have no control.

As the servants, with the exception of an old coachman who was somewhere in the region of the stables, had not yet returned from a picnic, the family had just finished helping themselves to a supper of cold fowl. This fowl had been coated, all with the best intentions, with an egg sauce, to which in the heat and the dusk the flying-ants were fatally attracted, their reddish bodies squirming, with wings, without, as they died upon the baroque carcase of the anointed fowl.

'Loathsome creatures!' protested Mrs Hare, to whom any insect was a pest.

Mary did not contribute an opinion, as the remarks of parents seldom seemed to ask for confirmation, but continued to eat, or munch, rather loudly, a crisp stick of celery, and to scratch herself, because the heat had made her prickly. In intolerable circumstances, she alone was tolerably comfortable.

To the others, it was insufferable. The light in the dining-room had turned a dark brown.

Then Norbert Hare took the fowl by its surviving drumstick, and flung it through the open window, where it fell into a display of perennial phlox. It was one of his misfortunes to be led repeatedly to ruin his effects.

He was still eating. His mouth was, in fact, too full. His cheeks were swollen, and his eyes appeared almost white.

'Norbert!' cried his wife. 'Whatever are the maids going to say?'

Knowing that she herself, with a lantern, would rummage amongst the phlox.

Then Norbert Hare took a loaf of bread, and flung it after the boiled fowl. He took a carving knife, and decanter of port wine, and threw.

He felt freer.

His wife began to cry.

'There,' he said, for himself. 'But it is never possible to free oneself. Not entirely.'

His wife cried and cried.

'I am to blame,' offered the daughter, in case that was what they wanted.

'If we are to decide on the objects of blame,' her father shouted, 'it could well be the boiled fowl.'

And seemed to madden entirely.

He was running and pouncing on some intention not yet matured.

Then he seemed to remember, and went to a desk, and got out the pistols.

In the drawing-room at Xanadu, separated from the dining-room by folding doors, there was a chandelier of exceptional loveliness, which money had brought from some dismembered European house, and of which the crystal fruit now hung above antipodean soil. The great thing loomed and brooded, at times fiery, at times dreamily opalescent, but always enticing away from the endless expanse of flat thought. Mary Hare loved it, though she had always believed her passion to be secret.

Now her father went, after loading, and shot into the chandelier.

He looked very small and ridiculous standing beneath the transparent branches.

'Munching! Munch-ing!' he shouted.

And shot.

'O God, save us all!' he shouted.

And shot.

There fell at intervals an excruciating crystal rain. How much actual damage was done it was not yet possible to estimate, although Mrs Hare did attempt spasmodically.

'There!' shouted Norbert Hare. And: 'There!'

'Come! I cannot endure your father any longer!' announced the mother, and drew her daughter into a little room which was only used when the doctor came, or someone asking for money.

Then, when the door was locked, she cried:

'I do not know what I have done to deserve so much!'

The daughter remained silent, for she knew she was the greater part of what her mother had to endure. Besides, it was of more interest to listen to what her father might be doing.

The sound of shots was less frequent, but boards cracked, rooms shook, the whole house seemed under the influence of his passion. He must have been running about a good deal. Until, suddenly, silence took over, its passive structure rising in tiers of indifference and layers of suffocating feathers.

'What do you think can have happened?' asked his wife, perhaps as she was expected to.

'It is probably less fun when nobody is looking,' suggested the daughter, but without bearing a grudge.

'That is true,' agreed the mother, startled to realize the truth had been spoken by her daughter.

For Mary was stupid, and the truth something that one generally avoided, out of respect for good taste, and to preserve peace of mind.

'I shall go out now,' said Mary at last, 'and look.'

'How brave you are!' the mother cried, with genuine admiration.

'I am not brave,' said her daughter.

But she was unable to explain that, burning as she was, there could be no question of her dying; life itself would have been extinguished.

She found the house big and empty. The weather had changed at last, with the result that a cold wind was blowing through the rooms, scattering dead ants from the sills. The curtains tugged, swollen, at their rings.

Then her father came downstairs, very quietly, as if he had been reading in his room, and come to get a glass of water. The situation might have continued innocent enough, if it had not been for the appearance of the outraged house, and the eyes of the man who had just arrived at the bottom of the stairs.

He was looking at her, trying to engulf her in a tragedy he

was preparing. Looking, and looking. It might have been horrible if less protracted.

As it was, and perhaps realizing his error of judgement, he took the pistol she had failed to notice he was still carrying, and shot it off at his own head. And missed. A piece of plaster thumped down from a moulding on the ceiling.

The sound could have completed his exhaustion, for he tumbled immediately into a big, strait, wing chair, which stood at hand. All of it he did rather clumsily and ridiculously, because it had not been thought out, or else he had lost interest in the sequence of events.

But it seemed for a moment as though she would not allow him to break the thread. She could not prevent herself from continuing to look, right into him, as he sat in the uncomfortable chair, and although he had forgiven her for the crime of being, it was doubtful whether he would ever forgive her for that of seeing.

She did not expect it, of course.

She went and picked up a pistol lying on the floor, and put it back where it had been in the first place, whether innocently, or through an inherited instinct for malice, he was too exhausted to inquire of his own mind.

He continued to sit, looking at his own waistcoat.

'All human beings are decadent,' he said. 'The moment we are born, we start to degenerate. Only the unborn soul is whole, pure.'

As she had turned away from him, and stood picking at some flaw in the lid of the little desk, he had to torment her. He said:

'Tell me, Mary, do you consider yourself one of the unborn?'

'I don't understand such things,' she replied. 'Not yet.'

And looked round at him.

'Liar!'

He would never forgive her her eyes, and for refusing to be hurt enough.

'Oh yes, you can twist my arm if you like!' she blundered, through thickening lips, for his accusation was causing her actual physical pain. 'But the truth is what I understand. Not in words. I have not the gift for words. But know.'

The abstractions made her shiver. If she could have touched something – moss, for instance – or smelled the smell of burning wood.

He continued sitting in the chair, and might even have started to relent.

So, she saved him that further humiliation by going outside, and there were the stars, swimming and drowsing towards her as she put out her hands. She was walking and crying, and gulping down the effusions of light, and crying, and smearing her cheeks with the sticky backs of her rough hands.

Long after her father was dead, and disposed of under the paspalum of Sarsaparilla, and the stone split by sun and fire, with lizards running in and out of the cracks, Miss Hare acquired something of the wisdom she had denied possessing the night of the false suicide. Sometimes she would stump off into the bush in one of the terrible jumpers she wore of brown ravelled wool, and an old stiff skirt, and would walk, and finally sit, always listening and expecting until receiving. Then her monstrous limbs would turn to stone, although her thoughts would sprout in tender growth of young shoots, or long loops of insinuating vines, and she would glance down at her feet, and frequently discover fur lying there from the throes of some sacrifice. If tears ever fell then from her saurian eyes, and ran down over the armature of her skin, she was no longer ludicrous. She was quite mad, quite contemptible, of course, by standards of human reason, but what have those proved to be? Reason finally holds a gun at its head – and does not always miss.

Often in the evening as she watched from the terrace of her deserted house for the chariot of fire, the woman wondered how her father would have received her metamorphoses: probably with increased disgust, although a suspect visionary himself, and on one occasion at least, standing together at the same spot, she had actually seen him twitch the veil. Now, if she had outstripped him in experience, time and silence, and the hints of nature had given her the advantages.

So she would wait, with the breath fluctuating in her lungs, and the blood thrilling through her distended veins. She waited on the last evening before the person called Mrs Jolley was expected to arrive. And sure enough, the wheels began to plough the tranquil fields of white sky. She could feel the breath of horses on her battered cheeks. She was lifted up, the wind blowing between the open sticks of fingers that she held extended on stumps of arms, the gold of her father's bloodstone ring echoing the gold of trumpets. If on the evening before the arrival of a certain person an aura of terror had contracted round her, she could not have said, at that precise moment, whether it was for the first time. She could not remember. She was aware only of her present anguish. Of her mind leaving her.

The filthy waves that floated off the fragments of disintegrating flesh.

Later, when she got up from the ground, she did not attempt to inquire what might have bludgeoned her numb mind and aching body, for night had come, cold and black. She bruised knuckle on knuckle, to try to stop her shivering, and began to feel her way through the house, by stages of brocade, and vicious gilt, by slippery tortoiseshell, and coldest, unresponsive marble.

3

The following day, which was that of Mrs Jolley's arrival, Miss Hare did not dare look out of the house before the morning was advanced, for fear she might suffer a repetition of her experience the night before. She did not feel strong enough for that. Still, she rose as usual, in the dark, bumping and charging as she pulled her jumper on. This morning she lit the kitchen range with twigs she had gathered, and small logs sawn slowly in advance. She also swept a little in the room which she had decided the housekeeper should use. But she did not draw curtains until she saw a well-established sunlight lying on the floor. Then she waited for nothing further, but went outside, and became at once involved in many little rites, both humdrum and worshipful.

The morning glittered still with pendants of swinging light and stomachers of dew. The formidable blades of taller grasses were not yet wiped free of wet. In some cases she performed for them what later the sun would do better. But she soon gave up. It was too much for her at her age. She scattered crumbs instead, and birds came down, hobbling and bobbing at her feet, clawing at her shoulders, and in one case, holding on to the ribs of her hat. With a big pair of rusty scissors, she cut crusts of bread into the sizes she knew to be acceptable. Bending so that her skirt stuck out straight behind, she became magnificently formal, like certain big pigeons, of which one or two had descended, blue, out of the gums. All throats were moving, wobbling, and hers most of all. In agreement. In the rite of birds.

Other dedicated acts were performed in order. She drew water, and set bowls. Several days earlier a snake had issued out from between the stones of the house, very black and persuasive, with tan bands along the sides. Her eyes had glistened for the splendid snake. But although she had stood still, at once, it had failed to sense the degree of sacerdotal authority vested in the unknown woman, and returned by way of the crack in the stone, into the foundations of the house. Every morning since, she had put a saucer of milk, but the snake remained to be converted. She would wait, and eventually, of course, perfect understanding would be reached.

Morning wore away. A wind had risen, and was slashing at things, and funnelling down her front. Then she did give a slight gulp of panic, not as the result of direct physical discomfort, but because of the remoter mental pain she must suffer in the afternoon.

To say to the woman.

Miss Hare went inside.

At least she had her house. She could show her house. Its splendours would speak for her, in voices of marble and gold, to say nothing of the lesser insinuations of watered silk. So she wandered here and there, letting in always more light, and the blades of light slashed the carpets, smoking, and pillars of gold rose up in the shadows of some rooms, where they had never been before.

In a little room which had never been much used – it was, in fact, that in which she and her mother had locked themselves the night of the false suicide – she picked up a fan, of some elegance and beauty, of tortoiseshell, tufted with flamingo, which an Armenian merchant had given to her mother one winter at Assouan.

Miss Hare held the fan, but she did not dare open it on seeing her own face in the glass.

The gust of cold panic recurred.

It was time. The light told her, not her stomach, for she was seldom hungry all day long, living, it would have seemed, almost on experience; nor did clocks signal the hour at Xanadu, for clocks had stopped, and she no longer bothered to wind them up. But light told all that was ever necessary. And now the windows were gaping long and cold, with a cold, whitish light, of later afternoon.

Miss Hare began running about, doing things, and not. She did the things to her clothes that she had seen other people do. Only, she was inclined to hit, where others might have given a pat. There was nothing she could do about hair, and besides, she would be wearing the inevitable hat.

Mrs Jolley got off the bus at the post office corner at Sarsaparilla. It could only have been Mrs Jolley, her black coat composed of innumerable panels – it appeared to be almost all seams – over what would reveal itself as the navy costume anticipated by Miss Hare. The hat was brighter, even daring, a blue blue, in spite of the mourning of which her future employer had been forewarned. From the brim was suspended, more daring, if not actually reckless, a brief, mauve eye-veil. She remained, however, the very picture of a lady, waiting for identification at the bus stop, but discreetly, but brightly, and grasping her brown port.

Oh dear, then it must be done, Miss Hare admitted, and sighed.

Mrs Jolley was all the time looking and smiling, at some person in the abstract, in the rather stony street. At one corner of her mouth she had a dimple, and her teeth were modelled perfectly.

'Excuse me,' began Miss Hare at last, 'are you the person? Excuse me,' – and cleared her throat – 'are you expected at Xanadu?'

Mrs Jolley suppressed what could have been a slight upsurge of wind.

'Yes,' she said, very slowly, feeling her way with her teeth. 'It was some such name, I think. A lady called Miss Hare.'

The latter felt tremendously presumptuous under Mrs Jolley's glance, and would have chosen to postpone her revelation.

But Mrs Jolley's white teeth – certainly no whiter had ever been seen – were growing visibly impatient. Her dimple came and went in flickers. Her expression, which might have been described as motherly by some, became suspect under the weight of its suspicion.

'I am Miss Hare,' said Miss Hare.

'Oh, yes?' replied the disbelieving Mrs Jolley.

And tried to fetch her teeth to the rescue.

But the brutal wind of a cold afternoon was not prepared to allow any nonsense. It flung the mauve eye-veil into Mrs Jolley's eyes and even bashed her black coat.

'Yes,' confirmed Miss Hare. 'I am she.'

Mrs Jolley scarcely believed what she was hearing.

'I hope you will be happy,' continued the object, 'at Xanadu. It is a large house. But we need only live in bits of it. Move around as we choose, for variety's sake.'

Mrs Jolley began to accompany her mentor over the stones, in shoes which she had purchased for the journey. Black. With a sensible strap. But, even so, she thought her ankles might not stand the walk, and the fangs of the road metal were eating through her soles.

'You haven't a car, then?' she asked.

'No,' said Miss Hare. 'No cars.'

Level with the Godbolds' shed, the blackberry canes snatched at Mrs Jolley's coat.

'We never owned a car,' Miss Hare was saying. 'Even in the days of my father. Naturally cars were only beginning. But horses. My father fancied horses; he was quite splendid when he drove his greys four-in-hand.'

Mrs Jolley could not believe any of this. Remembering the trams, she could have cried.

'In our family,' she said, 'everybody has their own car.'

'Oh,' said Miss Hare. 'No. No cars.'

The sound of the two women's breathing would intermingle distressingly at times. Each wished she could have repudiated the connexion.

'It is a satisfaction to a mother,' said Mrs Jolley, on twisting ankles, 'to know that each one of them – three girls – is each settled comfortable.'

'Of course,' agreed Miss Hare.

She could not believe, though. Not a bit.

Then they walked down the track which the Council had begun to call an avenue, and which led to Xanadu. Arriving at the end, the employer guided her companion through the fence, and they began the less tortuous, the longer of the short cuts.

As her responsibilities loomed, Miss Hare drew ahead. Mrs Jolley followed, occasionally hearing something tear. The silence was shocking in the undergrowth.

In the circumstances, the nascent green of oaks and elms, massed to overwhelm the scrub, issued too shrill, the grace-notes of crab and plum blossom, sprinkled at intervals on black nets of twigs, too sickeningly poignant.

Mrs Jolley remarked:

'A good thing I put me lisle stockings on.'

Her mauve eye-veil was less gay.

'The burs do prick a little, but they pick off quite easily,' Miss Hare thought to offer over her shoulder.

She had grown nervous, as if, at the back of her mind, there was something dreadful she could not remember.

They went on.

'We shall arrive soon now,' she encouraged.

They went on.

'There!' her voice revealed.

Mrs Jolley did not answer, almost failed to look up.

They climbed the approach. Under the stranger's feet the tessellated floor of the veranda sounded hollow as never before.

But the house was hollowest.

Miss Hare had opened the front door. They had gone in. They had stood for ages.

'Well,' Mrs Jolley said at last, 'it is easy to see it's a long time since you had a lady here.'

Nor did the voices of Xanadu protest. They agreed in all coldness of stone.

'A house is not the less for what you make it,' said Miss Hare.

'Nor any more,' added the darker voice of Mrs Jolley.

Neither could have offered adequate explanation of what she had just said. Each saw what she saw, or rather, Miss Hare was beginning to remember what she had forgotten. The veins in her temples were writhing. It was as if some stranger with sly eyelids had touched the real door, with a finger, and there stood the interior.

'That was the drawing-room,' she said, the tense forced upon her. 'And the dining-room through the folding doors.'

But forced most brutally.

They were standing in the present, in the late hours of an afternoon in spring, when the light can be merciless. The white light fell amongst the furniture, where a bandaged memory awaited diagnosis.

'I have never seen anything like it,' confessed Mrs Jolley, withdrawing as far as possible into her clothes.

Where time had not slashed, the light was finishing the job. Cabinets and little frivolous tables seemed to splinter at a blow. Even solid pieces in marquetry, and the buhl octopus, were stunned.

Catching on to the thread of their original intention, the two women strayed here and there, but always retreating. Now a shutter had begun to bang. Old birds' nests, lying on the Aubusson, or what had become, rather, a carpet of twigs, dust, mildew, and the chrysalides of insects, trapped guilty feet with soft reminders. On one side of the dining-room, where weather had torn the slates from an embrasure in the course of some historic storm, an elm had entered in. The black branches of the elm sawed. The early leaves pierced the more passive colours of human refinement like a knife. The little rags of blue sky flickered and flapped drunkenly. In places the rain had gushed, in others trickled, down the walls, and over marble, now the colour of rotten teeth.

'Or places where dogs have pissed,' Miss Hare noticed and sighed.

'I beg yours?' asked Mrs Jolley, wondering.

But her employer did not answer – her thoughts were her own, whether she cared to utter them or not – so the house-keeper saved up what she believed she had heard, to let it ripen on the shelves of her mind before she took it down for use.

At last Miss Hare cleared her throat, and that, too, sounded dusty – she was really quite exhausted. She said:

'I think I shall take you up to your room now.'

As the stair wound upward, by slow convolutions, through the well of light, its loveliness tortured the throat of the owner.

'I would sit here sometimes,' she said, 'and listen to the music, and watch the dancers. Oh, it was splendid down there.'

As the stair wound upward, past the closed doors, passages tunnelled off, into distance and a squeaking of mice.

'Of course, a great many of these rooms,' she said, and waved, practical again, 'have not been opened for years. There was no reason why they should have been. Not after the death of my mother. She died at the beginning of the War. The Second, yes, it was the Second War. It was Father who went during the First. And Mother, I found her sitting in her chair. But this is not the time to tell family history. And on the stairs.'

'I am a mother,' said Mrs Jolley, 'and am always glad to hear of anybody in like circumstances.'

Her ring chinked on the wrought iron. Despite shortness of breath, she did, and would act firmly. Her corset could not assure enough as she followed up the stairs. She would act as befitted a mother and a lady; it was only to be hoped the two duties would not clash.

'Here,' said Miss Hare, 'is the room I have prepared. I have made the bed. Although people have different ideas on the making of a bed. There,' she said.

Would the door open?

Mrs Jolley wished it would not, and that they might be left, instead, looking at each other on the landing, however unsatis-factory that solution might be.

But the door did open, easily, even, one would have said: eagerly.

'Well,' said Mrs Jolley, 'we shall see.'

And smiled.

She had a blue eye that would see just so far and no farther, which was perhaps why she could recover while still professing shock. Miss Hare hoped that her housekeeper's face was kind, but suspected that the dimple had not bewitched more than the one man.

Mrs Jolley did not know where to begin, and would stand kneading her bare arms, as if they might not have got their final shape. In that spring weather her milky arms were dapple-blue against the silk jumper – she had knitted it herself – oyster-toned but sagging now.

Mrs Jolley was a lady, as she never tired of pointing out. She would repeat the articles of her faith for anybody her instinct caught doubting. She would not touch an onion, she insisted; not for love. But was partial to a fluffy sponge, or butter sandwich, with non-parelles. A lady could never go wrong with pastel shades. Or Iceland poppies. Or chenille. She liked a good yarn, though, with another lady, at the bus stop, or over the fence. She liked a drive in a family car, to nowhere in particular, but looking out, in a nice hat, at faces on a lower level. Then the mechanism with which her superior station had fitted her would cause her head to move ever so slightly, to convey her disbelief.

She preferred to believe, however, and so Mrs Jolley would go to the pictures. To sit at the pictures sucking a lolly – not a hard one – after dropping the paper, along with memories and intentions, under the seat, was to indulge in sheerest velvet. It was a pity, though, about the hard lollies; the smell of a hot, moist caramel almost drove her nuts. But she would sit, and the strangest situations would pass muster as life. That lean young fellow, in crow's-feet and leather pants, might just have reached down, and put his hand – it made her lolly stick; and Ava and Lana, despite proportions and circumstances, could have been a couple of her own girls. Best of all was a picture about a mother. She knew by heart the injustices to expect, not to mention the retribution, so that, at the end, the wurlitzer rising from its well only completed her apotheosis. When she smelled the *vox humana's* rose and violet breath, and felt the little hammers striking on her womb, then she was, indeed, fulfilled, and could forget her hubby, who had died in the lounge at 10 p.m., as she was handing him his second cup of tea. Grave as that injustice was, she had survived, and, it appeared, might have experienced enough of life and dreams to parry any further blows.

Miss Hare was afraid she might be afraid of her house-keeper. She said:

'I hope you will get used to things.'

'I miss the trams,' Mrs Jolley replied.

The clang of them was in her voice, and in her eye, the melancholy plume of violet sparks.

'Oh dear,' said Miss Hare, 'I cannot say I was ever attached to a tram.'

'I miss Saturday evening,' Mrs Jolley said. 'Dropping in at Merle's or Dot's or Elma's. Elma is the youngest – married a stoker, not that he is not a gentleman, because none of my girls would never ever have entertained the idea of anything else but a gentleman.'

'I am surprised you could bear to leave them,' said Miss Hare, almost not loud enough.

'Ah,' said Mrs Jolley, and took the mop, 'that is life, if you know what I mean.'

Then she screwed the mop in the bucket, and took it out, and looked at the head.

'Or death,' she said.

Miss Hare was terrified.

'As if it was my fault,' said Mrs Jolley. 'Sitting in his own chair.'

'A chair makes it seem more natural,' Miss Hare ventured to suggest.

Remembering her mother, who had died in similar circumstances, thus she comforted herself.

'I can just imagine you and your mum,' Mrs Jolley said, and laughed. 'Living here amongst the furniture. Like a couple of mice.'

'Oh, there was Peg, too, and William Hadkin.'

'Peg who?'

'I can't remember her name. If we ever knew it. She always seemed old. And had always been here. When the maids left – after the troubles overtook us – Peg stayed, and became a friend. And died, too. But after Mother. I was quite alone then.'

'And who was the gentleman you was speaking of?'

'William was a coachman. He was very deaf.'

Miss Hare paused.

'He was what they call *rather simple*. Which means that what one knows is of a different kind. Actually, William knew an awful lot. And was not so deaf. I did not like him.'

'And this Mr Hadkin, did he die too?'

'No. He simply went away.'

'Strike a light!' said Mrs Jolley. 'No wonder! What did all you people live on?'

'Things,' said Miss Hare, and yawned. 'Bread, for instance. Bread is lovely. I love to tear the ends off, and eat it just like that. Going along. And give it to the birds. It is so convenient. But, of course, we had the little allowance from my cousin, Eustace Cleugh, of which I wrote you. Certainly it was not very much, and that was discontinued in the War. Oh, I forgot. There was the goat. I had a goat, and would milk her. Yes, I missed her.'

'What happened to the goat?'

'Please don't ask me!' cried Miss Hare. 'I don't know!'

'All *right*!' said Mrs Jolley, whose turn it was to be afraid. In that house.

But Miss Hare was sad rather than afraid. She could not answer questions. Questions were screws that spiralled down into the brain. She looked at the bucket of grey water, from which the woman's mop was spreading ineffectual puddles. The woman whose three daughters' husbands had built with bricks, boxes in which to live. So childish. For the brick boxes of the daughters' husbands would tumble like the games of children. Only memories were indestructible.

So Miss Hare snorted – she was bored, besides, with Mrs Jolley – and went off into the passages of Xanadu.

But memories also tormented. They flapped like old rags of curtains, the priceless ones with gold thread, and moths flew out, always grey, or night-coloured, scattering their suffocating down.

'We must wrap up our furs, Mary,' Mrs Hare had said, 'very carefully, now that summer is here, in sheets of the *Herald*. And put them in strong canvas bags, with draw-necks. I shall feel uneasy otherwise.'

Mrs Hare had remained mostly happy, right to the end, in the ritual of a past life.

And Peg would run, on her sticks of legs, and say from between her naked gums, which her mistress permitted, because, well, of everything:

'Yes, m'mm. No one likes to have moths on their mind. But leave it to me. No, miss, I will see to it.'

And the servant would show the canvas bags, their necks well-and-truly drawn. Yes, those geese were dead, the daughter saw, and stuffed with the balls of paper Peg had put, to simulate. But the mother was pacified.

46

Mrs Hare, gentle in her youth, distinguished in maturity, had become a horse of polished ivory in her old age. She would sit quite still for half an hour, then suddenly toss her head, at a thought, or fly. It was her long, refined face that gave the impression, and long, ivory teeth, which she loved to exercise on the fingers of cinnamon toast brought to her by Peg. Afterwards she would continue to sit, while her elderly, refined stomach rumbled with tea and toast, and the waning light worked still further, with uncanny, Chinese skill, at the polished portrait of an ivory horse.

Sometimes she would walk through what remained of the gardens, leaning on her stumpy daughter's arm, but she did not notice very much. She preferred to remember social triumphs and the Borromean Isles.

Once she asked her daughter:

'Where is the grotto, Mary? The grotto that your father had them build out of shells. Or was it lumps of rock crystal?'

The daughter grunted, for, after all, nothing more was expected of her.

Once Mrs Hare started to complain:

'I used to hope my daughter would become an ambassador's wife. She would have long, beautiful legs, and carry a fan, and manage other people's conversation. In the end there is nothing one has managed. Not even of one's own.'

'Still,' she continued more cheerfully, 'you would not have been walking with me in the garden, in those circumstances, and I might have fallen over on my own, and broken something.'

Again the daughter grunted, because what else could she have done?

Then the mother began to hit the grass.

'Horrid, horrid tufts!' she cried, beating the tussocks of paspalum with her stick, so that the tassels of the grass trembled.

'Don't!' begged the daughter. 'Please!'

Such impotent caprice was, at least, quickly diverted.

'But do not think I am not devoted to you, Mary,' insisted the mother. 'I can truly, honestly say I do love everybody now. Even your father.'

For Mrs Hare, whose passions had always been watery, it was perhaps easier.

'Even one's disappointments seem, at the end, to have a kind of meaning,' she said towards sunset.

And would have squeezed her daughter's arm if she had had the strength.

Instead, they went inside, the disappointing daughter, and the mother who was, in the end, supported by her disappointments.

Months later, looking at the figure of the dead woman seated so naturally in her chair, the daughter cried because she could not mourn in an approved manner. With passion, perhaps, but that the mother would hardly have appreciated or understood. So she mourned life, instead, such as she herself suspected it of being, from sudden rages of the sky, and brown gentleness of young ferns.

It was fortunate that Peg had been there, because it was Peg who knew what to do. She sent William to Sarsaparilla, and the postmistress telephoned, and some men arrived to take the body. It was a day of rain, and the hall had smelt of wet rain-coat quite a while afterwards.

Those were the last dealings Mary Hare had with her mother. For Peg had said:

'Don't you bother to go to the funeral, Miss Mary, if you feel it will upset you. Who will hold you if you take a turn? We'll sit here together, you and me, and eat a piece of bread and dripping in front of the stove. And let the parson look after things; that's what he is there for.'

Peg, although an elderly woman, had preserved some link with childhood, which allowed her to recognize the forms of reality through the rough sheath of appearance. She remained an admirable companion. Mary loved Peg. She would sit and rub her own wrinkles, and watch the maid's tranquil face: that of an elder sister in steel-rimmed spectacles, a sister who knew approximately the plan of an outside world, but who had not forgotten all the games.

Because she was of that district, Peg used to go about a lot. She would ride her bicycle at the hills, and it was surprising how she got to the top. Such a frail thing. Not much more than the sawing sound of her own washed-out, starchy dress. Peg laundered and cleaned to perfection, but cooked badly. She liked to make jam, and render down beeswax, and usually smelled of one or the other. She would suddenly appear from under beds, holding a pad of waxy cloth, when a person least expected. In her steel-rimmed spectacles. In a dress that had once been pale blue, now almost white.

'Read to me, Peg,' her mistress Mary Hare would command.

'Read yourself!' Peg advised, and laughed. 'What shall I read, ever?'

'I can see it better if you read it out. Do, Peg!' begged Mary Hare. 'Let us read Anthony Hordern's catalogue.'

'Dear, you are a caution!' Peg had to laugh.

She was rather pale around the eyes.

Peg liked best to read the Bible, but not aloud, as her mistress did not care for it. The maid was always busy with the Gospels. She found the Epistles too dry, and did not go much on the Revelations – in fact, she showed no inclination to discuss that end of her battered book.

'You ought to be having a study of this,' Peg used to say, glancing up from her Bible.

She had always worn an exposed look on account of her pale eyelids, but her innocence had protected her.

'Oh dear, no!' protested her mistress, almost in fear. 'I know that that is nothing for me.'

'It is for everybody,' Peg would insist earnestly.

'Not quite. It is not for me.'

'But you won't try it. How have you ever found out?'

'I will find out what I am to find out, in my own way, and in my own time. I am different,' maintained Mary Hare.

'Yes,' sighed Peg. 'Different and the same.'

She could not marvel at it enough.

Although the two women were in many ways not unlike, Peg was without that arrogance which snared her mistress frequently. Mary Hare loved Peg, but she loved her own arrogance. It was her great pride, and if nobody else recognized her jewel, then, she would still deck herself. That way she achieved distinction, perhaps even beauty, she was vain enough to hope.

But Peg was not taken in. She would say in her slightly gritty voice:

'You are not flying into one of your tantrums, Miss Mary?'

And Peg was always right, the way glass is, and water – all that is blameless.

Which made it the more desperate when Mary Hare went into Peg's room, and saw that her friend had died. Just after dressing. On a dry morning. Peg had lain down again on the bed, in her dress that had once been a brighter colour. There she lay, very brittle, like a branch of one of the good-smelling herbs, rosemary, or thyme, or the lemon-scented verbena, that people used to break off and put away.

After a while the mistress dared to touch her maid. Then, she knew, at last, she was, indeed, alone. She stayed a long time in a corner of the room, looking, and it was only in the course of the morning that she remembered William Hadkin.

William was somebody Mary Hare had never taken to, perhaps because, on the night of her father's shooting match, when all the other servants were still away at the picnic, he had remained in the grooms' quarters, together with his deafness. That deafness of William's was something Mary had never been able to believe in, because of the thundering of her own emotions on the night in question. Yet, he had remained faithful, and in the days of her mother would take them for little drives in an old buggy that had survived. And on a pittance. Though, of course, he was old, nor ate, nor needed very much. By the time Mrs Hare died, he had practically given up shaving, because of a tender skin, yet was always seen in the same length of stubble, with the same rivulet of spittle in the same white ravine. He had the same smell, too, of most old men. Which again could have been a reason why Miss Hare had not taken to him. Old men, on the whole, are smellier than old women.

It was William, of course, that his mistress told of Peg's death.

'Well yes,' he said. 'I was reckoning she would die. There was nothing to her.'

He was greasing a strap of harness, for which there was no longer any use, but it helped to keep him in practice.

'I would not have let myself think,' began Mary Hare.

'That was what all you people was such artists at,' said William Hadkin, stroking his leather.

'What do you mean?' asked Miss Hare.

She began to tremble, but not with rage.

'As far as I can see, lookin' back and all,' William said, 'you was the race of pretenders.'

'Some of us had imagination, if that is what you mean.'

'To set the house on fire without the matches!'

'That is enough, William,' said Mary Hare, as she had heard her parents. 'You must go about Peg.'

'All right! All right!' he said. 'Don't agitate me!'

He stood looking at the holes in the strap.

'I wonder you stayed if you could not bear us,' his mistress said.

'I stayed,' he said, 'because I got used to it. There's a lot of that sort of thing going on, you know.'

Because his mistress was always the first to recognize the truth, there was really nothing for her to say.

The last and worst encounter with William Hadkin occurred a few weeks after her maid's death. She came across him just after he had killed a cock. There was the bird's head, shamefully detached and dead, while William watched and laughed as the body danced out the last steps of life in a shambles of its own blood.

Mary Hare stood very still. She could not find the strength to move even when her boots were sprinkled with the cock's blood.

William observed.

'Well,' he said, laughing, 'you've gotta eat, if it's only an old stringy rooster.'

And continued to laugh.

'See,' he said, 'what I meant the other day? The rooster got so used to it he can dance without his bally head.'

'The way I see it, you are a murderer,' accused Mary Hare.

'What! To kill a cock for you to eat?'

'There are ways and ways of killing.'

'That is something you should know.'

'How? I?'

'Ask your dad.'

Mary Hare turned so pale. She remained standing by the woodshed long after the groom had gone about other business. She was left looking at the wattles of the dead cock.

Soon after that, William Hadkin, without a word, sorted his thoughts apparently, and disappeared from Xanadu. Now, at last, I shall be free, and all to the good, murmured Mary Hare, afraid. But remembered the goat, and at once her spirits were restored.

The goat had appeared already before Peg's death. From where it had come was never discovered. A white doe heavy in kid, it would follow the women for company, choosing its leaves and grass with a certain finical air. After the doe had been delivered of a dead buck, Peg said they should milk their goat, which Mary proceeded to do. She lived for it. In time her mind grew equal to the tranquil wisdom of the goat-mind, and as she squatted in the evening to milk her doe, after they alone were left, their united shadow would seem positively substantial. So much so, the woman's love began to conflict with her reasoning, and she grew quite frantic that something might happen to the animal: some disaster to follow those which she had been permitted to outlive, or, simply, that it might decide to leave.

So, when night began to fall, the mistress would run to shut her creature in a little, tipsy shed, within sight of the kitchen, on the edge of the yard. Heaping boughs and pouring endearments, she would padlock her goat every night, and return, and return, to see whether her love might not have vanished in the course of some devilish conjuring act. But there the goat would be. As she shielded her lamp, the white mask glimmered at her through the dark. The amber eyes pacified her fears, and the long lip would move in what she knew was sympathy.

Even on the morning of the mistress's severest trial, the abstraction of a goat's mask continued to communicate. Even though the goat itself had become a skull and shred of hide in the ruins of the black and smoking shed.

How she herself survived the holocaust of her discovery, Mary Hare could never be sure. But the morning was kind. Leaves were laid upon her face. The earth was soft to her trembling knees. For she went off into the scrub almost immediately, and remained there how long nobody was able to tell her, because nobody knew that she had gone. She remained there probably two or three days, for she returned stiff and scratched, hungry, at least for one who was almost never visited by hunger, and anxious to recall even the painful reason for her absence.

As she sat chewing a crust of stale bread, for which she had immediately rummaged in the crock, she had to suppose:

Eventually I shall discover what is at the centre, if enough of me is peeled away.

Never in her life, she felt, had she reasoned so lucidly, with the result that she swallowed a whole lump of softened bread.

Mrs Jolley was in two minds.

It could have been the cobwebs. She would drag them down. They could have been ropes. They could have been chains. Then she would pick, and flick, not to say dash, and bash, all thumbs and fingers, elbows too, as she struggled to divest herself. But would never be free. The grey skeins clung, like a sense of guilt.

'Who isn't nuts!' she would cry at times. 'But, of course, a person can always give notice – tomorrow, or the day after, any day of the week.'

Nobody would have thought to accuse Mrs Jolley of not being rational at every pore, even at moments when, netted in cobweb, clamped with bobbypins, teeth upstairs in the tumbler, her answer might stumble. As she pursed her lips, and turned her head, to disengage the reluctant words, was she guarding a secret, or merely having trouble with her lolly?

At least she would remain a lady, whatever else might come in doubt.

For the mirrors had begun to follow her down the passages, and on one occasion, she had been compelled to finish a flight of stairs at the run. For no obvious reason. Her legs had simply taken over, and her calves, still strong, and firm, and glossy, had bulged rather frantically; her breasts were jumping under the corset by the time she reached the top.

'Everybody has their off days,' Mrs Jolley liked to say.

When, for instance, one of her eyes – blue for mothers – would water from the corner.

'I am so afraid you are not happy at Xanadu,' remarked Miss Hare – it was at breakfast, over the crispies, in the kitchen.

'It is not that I am not happy,' answered Mrs Jolley. 'I am always happy, of course, more or less. It is that a lady does expect something different.'

Miss Hare mashed her crispies.

'What?'

'Oh, you know,' said Mrs Jolley, 'a home, and a hoover, and kiddies' voices.'

'I do not know,' replied Miss Hare. 'This is my life. This is my home.'

And she munched the crispies.

'You are that hard at times,' Mrs Jolley protested, 'and unwilling to understand.'

Miss Hare munched her crispies.

'When a loved one passes on, it is as if you was lost for a bit. See?'

Miss Hare would not. She was familiar with the core of rock she must acquire to match Mrs Jolley.

'As if a bit of you went with him. And if you don't follow, too, it is because of a sense of duty to others. I once read in a horoscope' – here Mrs Jolley picked up the cloth – 'that my sense of duty is very, very highly developed.'

'I am not preventing you from following whoever you wish to follow,' Miss Hare replied, 'If that is what you mean.'

'You know that I was referring to my late hubby,' said Mrs Jolley, 'and you will not hurt my feelings, however hard you try.'

That face!

'Oh dear, it is breakfast,' sighed Miss Hare.

Mrs Jolley went off into laughter. She laughed, and laughed, and laughed.

'I will not ask what you find so amusing,' announced Miss Hare.

'People are funny!' Miss Jolley laughed.

Her throat had knots in it, almost a goitre, and farther down was the cleft upon which the eyes of her late husband, presumably, had rested, whether in approval or disgust.

Miss Hare, who had finished her crispies, turned the plate upside down as usual.

Mrs Jolley had stopped laughing. Very, very patiently she said:

'You are a dirty girl. That is what *you* are!'

And stood back to look.

'A habit is a habit,' said Miss Hare.

'Dirty is dirty,' replied her companion.

'Mrs Jolley, two people cannot live together unless they respect each other's habits. That is something I have learnt by painful degrees in my relationships with birds and animals.'

'I am not a bird, or an animal,' Mrs Jolley replied. 'I am a . . .'

'No. I know what you are. Please, do not tell me!' Miss Hare begged.

'You do not know me,' Mrs Jolley said, 'any more than you don't know nothing at all.'

'No,' Miss Hare agreed. 'You are often right.'

'I know what I am,' said Mrs Jolley, 'and more's the pity. My late husband thought he knew, but didn't. He thought he knew. Oh, yes, he knew everything. He had taken night courses, and collected stamps. He was paying off a cyclopaedia, for years, in the oak cabinet, beside the settee.'

Quite suddenly Mrs Jolley began to cry.

Miss Hare sat as still as she could, and watched.

'All I did,' Mrs Jolley cried, 'was to make him a clean and comfortable home, and yet, that night when I handed him his cup of tea, you would have said I had committed a crime.'

Miss Hare watched. The kitchen at Xanadu was one of those big, old, black kitchens which swallow up, but Miss Hare was never swallowed. She was feeling very bright now.

'Do you mean that your husband blamed you for his death?' Mrs Jolley almost choked.

'You are that hard!' she protested. 'And this house! You can hear your own thoughts ticking, along with the mouldy furniture. I will leave, of course. But, in the circumstances, not yet.'

Then she stopped. She seemed to have immediate control over her emotions, or almost anything, if she wished. Mrs Jolley was what Miss Hare supposed they called a practical woman.

'There!' said Mrs Jolley. 'Finished now!'

And pursed her mouth up.

But Miss Hare was not finished. Her train of thought, she feared, had only started. If she had not been so fascinated, she would have retreated from the presence of Mrs Jolley, who was responsible.

'What you have just told, has made me remember something,' she said. 'Only one person ever blamed me for his death.'

'Who?'

Mrs Jolley took possession of Miss Hare's disgusting, fascinating, down-turned plate.

'My own father.'

'You have not spoken much about your dad,' Mrs Jolley slowly realized.

'There is so much to tell, and almost all of it painful,' said Miss Hare.

'But your own father.'

'A long time ago. He died most horribly. By drowning in a cistern.'

'Where?'

'Out there. Across the yard. It collects the rain-water from the roof, and in those days was allowed to remain open. It was only closed later, on account of the mosquitoes.'

'And your father fell in?'

'Oh, there are some people – I might as well say from the beginning – will tell you other things. My father was said to be unstable.'

'And you saw it?'

'I sometimes wonder exactly what.'

Norbert Hare had experienced his moments of illumination. Doors had opened once or twice in music, or he had turned a corner on an Italian street, or descended dizzily, breathlessly, his vision grown milky and unreliable, from a too reckless encounter in the stone branches of some Gothic forest. On occasions release had even come simply by watching the line of hills beyond his property of Xanadu, although he was inclined to suspect deliverance by inexpensive means. Whatever the source of his experience, he was, however, aware of a splendour that he himself would never achieve except by instants, and rightly or wrongly, came to interpret this as a failure. He would sometimes laugh, unpleasantly, and what seemed irrelevantly, to those who heard, with the result that many of his acquaintances and neighbours became convinced that Norbert was mad. Only his daughter, Mary, obviously more than a little dotty herself, sensed his dilemmas. She might even have understood them if she had been allowed.

But the mere idea was preposterous.

One steamy morning in summer, at the time of year when the whole world was living palpably under grass, in a crushing scent of crushed grass, in a mercilessly gentle murmuring of doves, Mary Hare rose up, actually, visibly, out of her father's thoughts. At one of those moments when two people would give their souls to escape each other, neither could begin. There she was, rooted in his path, where it led beneath the camphor laurels, and meandered on into the yard.

'You, Mary!' exclaimed Norbert Hare, the sharp corners of his mouth outlined in dry, white salt.

There was no need for him to give further expression to his feelings.

Of course, she could not answer. She stood and twisted a stalk of grass.

A trick of light had endowed her with what could have been a shadow of beauty under the old goffered bonnet she was wearing: a country beauty, botched and brown, and quickly gone. But her father would not allow. He might have been denying the possibility for years, for now he said, from a long way off, but very distinctly, as some sounds will convey themselves in a stillness and from a distance.

'Ugly as a foetus. Ripped out too soon.'

Then their emotions were whirling, the spokes of whitest light smashing, the hooks grappling together, hatefully.

The sweat was running down her body, she could feel, in molten streams. She caught sight of his tightening mouth, and his throat strung with gristle.

'If you think we cannot put an end to it! But I am the one to choose!'

Whether she had heard this as she was walking away, she had never been quite certain; perhaps she would have liked to hear it.

But a stench was rising from the flesh of bruised grass. She was being surely suffocated under a pall of leaves.

Till his great voice began to call through a megaphone of stone.

She went back then, and realizing that it came from the cistern, looked in to see him treading water. The hair hung above his eyes in a straight, black, wet fringe. His eyes were awful – very pale and far-seeing – as his voice, under the influence of cold and fear, continued to reproduce a desperate glug-glug of water. How cold the water was she could remember from once dipping her hand, in time of drought, into a bucketful a gardener had drawn up.

And now her father.

'Get some-thing, Mar-y!' her dream seemed to be giving tongue. 'Some-one!'

At the same time it sounded silly. He was like some spaniel thrown in against its will, and whose genuine dog-tragedy appeared to be drowning in comical acts.

She ran, though. She got a pole; it was an old, bleached clothes-prop. She stood above him, away up, in the light, on the rim of the cistern.

Then he appeared more afraid than before, as if she were looking truly monstrous from that height and angle, as she held the pole towards him.

He was crying now, like a little boy, out of pale, wet mouth. 'Some-one!' he was crying. 'Mary! Don't! Have some pity! For God's sake! Run!'

Although rigid, her pole was merciful, but he warded it off with his hands, which were blue, she observed, and he would bob under, and return, each time his deathly fringe falling into place again on his forehead.

So she gathered up her dress at last, holding it bundled over her stomach, and ran, by whatever made her. She was two beings.

She ran through the deserted morning. It laid clammy hands upon her. She fell once, bumping along gravel. The house could have been a shell from which even the echo of distance had withdrawn. The little frail parasols, which protected the complexions of the roses, were on that morning untended by the second gardener.

By the time Mary Hare fetched William Hadkin and a boy, it was plain her father's folly had caught up with him; regret was of no assistance. He was gone by then. A frog plopped. A leaf fluttered, floated. When they finally dredged him up from under the black water, his pale eyes looked fearfully at those who had failed to rescue him, and for the first time the daughter realized how very similar his expression was to one of her own.

After that, Sarsaparilla learned how Norbert Hare had fallen into the tank at Xanadu. Although those who pulled him out said they would have taken a bet he had jumped, and others had even begun to consider whether – but that would have been uncharitable, not to say unthinkable. So there the matter rested, or was hushed up, rather, for the sake of a proper funeral.

At first the widow was not expected to recover from her grief. Or was it shock?

'How I feel for your poor mother!' said Mrs Jolley. 'Even now. Even after she has passed on. Only one who has been a wife and mother can ever fully sympathize.'

'There are those who believe that they, and only they, can understand a dog.'

'I beg yours?' asked Mrs Jolley.

'Nothing,' replied Miss Hare, and laughed into her cup. 'We were talking about my mother. She felt for herself, I think. More than enough.'

'You are a hard one!'

'I was hardened.'

'But not all hard,' added the blotchy woman, after a second's thought, and softer. 'Or I would be dead of it.'

'Well, I never!'

'Oh, there is a great deal that I truly, truly love.'

'Are you a Christian?'

'Ah,' sighed Miss Hare. 'It would not be for me to say, even if I understood exactly what that means.'

'I am,' said Mrs Jolley. 'I attended the C. of E. ever since I was a kiddy.'

And would batter somebody to prove it.

'I mean,' persisted the housekeeper, 'didn't anybody bother with your religious education?'

Miss Hare was too embarrassed to answer.

'So as you can believe. You do believe in *something*, don't you?'

Miss Hare hesitated. Then she said, very slowly:

'I believe. I cannot tell you what I believe in, any more than what I am. It is too much. I have no proper gift. Of words, I mean. Oh yes, I believe! I believe in what I see, and what I cannot see. I believe in a thunderstorm, and wet grass, and patches of light, and stillness. There is such a variety of good. On earth. And everywhere.'

'But what is over it?' Mrs Jolley had to burst out.

'That!' Miss Hare cried. 'That! I would rather you did not ask me about such things.'

She had got up, and was swaying and trembling, so that Mrs Jolley became afraid. How she hated that blotchy face. Just supposing it had a fit!

'I am sorry I started all this if it is too much for you,' the housekeeper said, very firmly, not looking any more, and controlling her voice.

'Oh no,' breathed Miss Hare.

And went away.

Mrs Jolley listened, hoping she might hear a body fall. She hoped Miss Hare might die, even. Then all that was bright and solid, all that was known and vouched for must prevail.

So Mrs Jolley rushed at the oven, to bake a cake, although it was not a day of celebration, but she liked to bake, a pink cake for choice, with non-parelles, and something written on it. With the Mothers' Union and the Ladies' Guild, with the Fellowships, Senior and Junior, pink was always popular, and what is popular is safe.

Mrs Jolley sang and baked. She loved to sing the pinker hymns. She would even sing those of which she did not know the words. She sang and baked. And saw pink. She loved the Jesus Christ of long pink face and languid curls, in words and windows. All was right then. All the homes and kiddies saved. All was sanctified by cake.

At Xanadu the great kitchen almost cracked black open.

Mrs Jolley sang and baked. Brick by brick her edifice rose, but a nice sandwich, of course. Round. Whereas it was the square brick homes which she celebrated. And populated. With her mind she placed the ladies and the kiddies – not so many gentlemen – as if they had been sandwich flags: the little girls, with their fresh frocks, and tiny rings and vanity bags; the lovely little boys, with freckles and quiffs and teeth that too much cake had destroyed. Mrs Jolley sang and praised. To destroy or to save was the same when you had paid the premium.

As the time approached to ice her cake, the smell of delicious baking and support of family morality had made this woman strong. So she must remain; it was only nerves that had caused her to falter a moment, and the company of that poor dill.

Ah, dear, you had to laugh, though!

When Miss Hare returned, Mrs Jolley had burst open. Her white teeth were gashing the kitchen.

'Will you share the joke?' asked the mistress.

'Would I share!' Mrs Jolley rocked.

Until Miss Hare had to smile in self-defence.

'Ah, dear, I am bad!' Mrs Jolley cried, and laughed. 'That is what I am!'

She looked at Miss Hare. If she had not been breathless, she would have blown down the whole dusty house of cards on the owner's head, and walked away into the perspective of certainty.

4

At what stage she had begun to fear Mrs Jolley, Miss Hare was not sure, though she thought it probably dated from the morning when the housekeeper had presented her with a pink cake, and on it written, really most beautifully, in fancy script: *For a Bad Girl.*

'What a beautiful cake!' Miss Hare had exclaimed, with something like horror.

'I would not claim to be artistic if my son-in-law, the stoker — he is the husband of Elma, the youngest — had not told me that I was,' Mrs Jolley replied.

But she coughed for decency's sake.

'You must not mind the joke,' she added. 'Two ladies living together should cultivate a sense of humour.'

As she watched her employer, the milky dimple was in its place.

'Oh, how I agree!'

Miss Hare laughed, and her right leg stiffened as she kicked the kitchen flags with her heel.

Then Mrs Jolley lowered her eyelids.

Yes, it was from the moment Mrs Jolley lowered her eyelids that Miss Hare had begun to feel afraid. Of course, she did not fear for her person. She could come to no physical harm; she was too old, too ugly, too poor, too unimportant in anybody's life. But she did sense some danger to the incorporeal, the more significant part of her. Time and isolation had rendered this, she had felt until now, practically indestructible. Even history, wars had not coerced her inner being. Except for her relationship with her father, the brief unpleasantness with William Hadkin, and the death of her poor goat, she had had little experience of evil. Newspapers she never read; living, not reading about it, had been her life. So the world had revolved on the axis with which she had provided it, until Mrs Jolley brought the virtues to Xanadu.

Days after the lettering had been consumed, Miss Hare was

haunted by the pink cake. She must, she *would* understand it, though there were pockets of thought which her mind refused to enter, like those evil thickets in which might be found little agonizing tufts of fur, broken swallows' eggs or a goat's rational skull.

How much Mrs Jolley knew it was difficult to tell. She would lower her eyelids and go disguised. There was always the veil of conversation – Miss Hare dreaded it most of all: the piles of brick that Mrs Jolley built to house her family in, the red brick boxes increasing and encroaching, the sons-in-law, all substantial men it appeared, straining at their clothing, mopping up their gravy before they retired to the pleasures of chenille and silky oak. And the children: too good, too clean, too nice – too bad in fact.

Nothing but faith could have resisted such very material opposition, and Miss Hare did have hers, to revive which she would run off into the bush, and after picking up the crystal thread, follow it over pebbles. Each pool would reveal its relevant mystery, of which she herself was never the least. Finally she would be renewed. Returning by a different way, she would recognize the Hand in every veined leaf, and would bundle with the bee into the divine Mouth. If she no longer raised her eyes to the evening sky it was because she had not yet recovered all her strength. Morning is for the weaker souls; in that she walked gratefully, and not without considerable deep knowledge.

On such a morning of confusion and solution, she found herself closer to the dark man than she had ever been before. Already she had come across this person once or twice on the roads round Sarsaparilla, although she gathered from the Godbold children that he lived somewhere at Barranugli.

He was an abo, or something, Else the eldest Godbold *thought*.

He could be a Syrian, or Indian, or a sort of gipsy, Gracie shouted.

Maudie yelled that Gracie did not know a thing.

Anyway, Saturday the black got drunk and was lying in the nettles, Kate knew for certain.

Else shushed her sister.

It was Maudie who added the only sober, factual information. He worked at the place that made the bicycle lamps, where their dad had gone for a bit, until he got fed up – Rosetree's factory, just outside of Barranugli. Maudie had seen the black knocking off along with the other men. He was carrying his tucker bag, and a big square piece of board, she had wondered for what.

There were six Godbolds, all girls, some of whom could usually be seen in the scrub round Xanadu, lugging a puppy, or nursing a bird, and intent on business of their own. In one way and another the Godbold girls knew a lot. Their bodies and the soles of their feet were hard, and their minds, on the whole, sensible.

That they were not better informed on the subject of Miss Hare's black was rather surprising, though Miss Hare herself was not surprised, nor would she have wished it otherwise, for she respected privacy. Seldom did she meet human beings, and those she did, she would not know how to address. She preferred to peer at them through leaves, when she herself was practically reduced to light and shadow. Then, at last, she was truly in her element.

So she would peer out at her dark man on those occasions when he walked through the lanes which ran past Xanadu. Once she had entered through his eyes, and at first glance recognized familiar furniture, and once again she had entered in, and their souls had stroked each other with reassuring feathers, but very briefly, for each had suddenly taken fright. From then on, they had been inclined to avoid each other, until on that specific morning, not long after Miss Hare's trial by Mrs Jolley had begun, the dark person actually spoke.

It was like this.

Miss Hare had come out from behind a clump of eggs-and-bacon, on the edge of the scrub, at the bend in the road below Xanadu. She had come out and was herself standing on the edge where, she realized at once, she had been caught. For she heard feet approaching over stones. And there he was, the dark man, almost level with her.

On this occasion the stranger appeared to take their situation for granted. He was all bones, and might have seemed to shamble if it had not been for a certain convinced bearing. His full lips were slightly, lazily open on obviously excellent teeth, and his voice sounded agreeable, direct, and unexpected. For he addressed her immediately, as though it had always been intended that he should.

'The water,' he said, and pointed, 'is creeping up on you. Don't you know it? Eh? You are standing in a bog.'

Miss Hare did, then, look at her feet.

'The water,' she repeated, or choked.

'In a minute you will know all about it,' warned the voice. 'It will come in over the tops of your shoes.'

Then he passed, and she was left standing at the roadside where she could recently have witnessed a procession.

Her shoes did not matter, of course. It was a mild morning, ruled by a still air. The leaves were resting together.

As the man continued along the road the stones were crunched steadily but easily beneath his feet. He was excessively thin and slack-bodied, but his shoulders she saw were at peace. At least for the moment. It was doubtful whether a human being, any more than the weather, could remain permanently at rest.

She watched his back, gratefully rewarded. Both the illuminates remained peacefully folded inside the envelopes of their flesh. Each knew it was improbable they would ever communicate in words. Yet they had exchanged a token of goodness which would remain for ever in each other's keeping. From behind closed eyelids each would have recognized the other as an apostle of truth. And that was enough.

Then the water did come in over the tops of Miss Hare's shoes as the stranger had predicted, but she did not altogether mind nor did she withdraw immediately.

When she got in, Mrs Jolley had returned from church.

'Oh, the lovely hymns!' the latter exclaimed. 'And the sermon! The clergyman was lovely.'

'I am glad you were satisfied,' said Miss Hare.

'Religion is not a meal,' protested the housekeeper.

'It is everything anyone wishes it to be.'

'There are the heathens, of course. And what have you been up to, I would like to know?'

'I have been in the bush,' Miss Hare confessed.

Mrs Jolley sucked her perfect teeth.

'And on a Sunday!'

'Every day is the same,' replied Miss Hare.

'But Sunday is not a day for scarecrows,' Mrs Jolley could not resist.

'No,' Miss Hare began, rather more timidly. 'It is a day for Christians.'

Mrs Jolley did not hear.

'Did you see nobody you knew?' she asked her employer, but very cold. Employer, indeed! On that wage, she was doing a favour.

'No,' said Miss Hare, in a sense truthfully.

But feared for what, in truth, had also been a lie.

'That is,' she corrected herself, 'I saw the dark man.'

'Pooh! Some dirty abo bloke! I would not have an abo come

near me. And in the bush. They are all undesirable persons. And in the bush! You will run into trouble, my lady. Mark my words if I am not right.'

Though she had to smile, and not to herself.

'I am told the aboriginals *are* a very dirty lot. And drunk and disorderly,' Miss Hare had to admit.

But it was she herself who felt dirty. Mrs Jolley had dirtied her.

Mrs Jolley had hung her fur on the back of the kitchen chair. It was a silver fox, she would declare, and a present from the family. Mrs Jolley's fur was, incontestably, a reminder.

Miss Hare felt miserable.

Mrs Jolley began to know it. She yanked a pan out of a cupboard and clanked it extra hard.

'And what was the name of this abo?'

'I do not know,' said Miss Hare, 'but will inquire of the Godbolds, if it is of interest.'

'Who are the Godbolds?'

'They are some children. Their mother is my friend.'

'You don't say! You have a friend then?'

'Yes.'

'Is she a nice lady?'

'She lives in a shed below the post office and takes in washing.'

Mrs Jolley breathed hard.

'I would not of thought that a lady like you, of Topnotch Hall, and all, would associate beneath them. Mind you, I do not criticize. It is not my business, is it? Only I cannot truly say I have ever been on any sort of terms with a lady living in a shed.'

But by now Miss Hare was too rapt to have been acquainted with any other.

'Ah, but she,' she told very humbly, 'she is the best of women.'

Miss Hare would remember how she used to listen for the footsteps on the stairs. Very firm, rather heavy, relentless, they had seemed, until time and familiarity drew attention to the constancy of those sounds. Soon the woman lying in the room above could barely endure the tumult of her own emotions as she waited for the door to open.

It was during a winter of the Second World War that people – at least one or two of them – began to wonder what had become of that old Miss Hare. It was a harmless thought, and so quickly dropped until one morning, running through the frost across what had been the lawn at Xanadu, young Gracie who, of all the Godbolds, had made that place her especial hunting ground, saw something at a window and went and told her mum.

Although she had not seen *much* because of the dressing-table mirror jammed against the window, she thought she had recognized a piece of old Miss Hare. And Miss Hare had looked queer. Now Gracie Godbold had never seen a ghost, but if she had she knew it would have looked sort of misty-dirty like.

So it was natural for the mother, a conscientious woman, to put on her hat and sober coat and go down to investigate.

Nobody ever heard what emotions Mrs Godbold had experienced in the rooms and on the stairs at Xanadu. Discreet by nature, she was also uncommunicative. But she did at last, by peering and calling, arrive at the cell which contained the survivor, somewhere in the centre of that vast and crumbling comb.

Miss Hare was lying on a bed of pomp and tatters.

She said: 'Mrs Godbold is it? I have been feeling rather unwell for several days. But hope it will pass with patience. I do not believe in fussing and doctors, because look at the animals. Oh dear, but I become breathless, and it is terribly cold when the frost sets in.'

'I see,' said Mrs Godbold, and thought.

She began very soon to do things. Simple, but soothing, as accorded with her own nature. She made Miss Hare comfortable. She washed her at evening, using a crystal basin the Hares had brought from Vienna – was it? – but long ago. She heated bricks and wrapped them in a blanket. And from the shed in which she lived she brought, on that and many evenings after, milk in a little white-enamelled can, a brown egg and a slice or two from an enormous loaf.

So Mrs Godbold nursed Miss Hare the winter the latter had pneumonia. Many people remained unaware because Mrs Godbold did not talk, and Godbolds were no-hopers of the worst kind, and who, anyway, ever saw or spoke with that old, dirty, mad Miss Hare.

Yet she reappeared. She had begun, very tentative, supporting herself on the furniture and, like a dog, listening for familiar sounds on the empty stairs.

'You see, Miss,' said Mrs Godbold. 'Soon you will be outside again.'

'Ah,' said Miss Hare, 'then I shall breathe.'

But quickly looked at her companion's somewhat flat and pallid face.

'I shall be sorry, too,' she added, 'because you will come to me no more.'

Mrs Godbold made a little noise that was difficult to interpret.

Then they glanced together out of the window at Xanadu, on which the mists had begun to hang, so that if it had not been for their own group of solid statuary, the world might have seemed at that hour ephemeral and melancholy.

For Miss Hare, Mrs Godbold had become and indeed remained the most positive evidence of good. Physically she was too massive, and to some no doubt displeasing: too coarse, too flat of face, thick-armed, big of breast, waxy-skinned, the large pores opened by the steam from her copper. But nobody could deny Mrs Godbold her breadth of brow. She wore her hair in thick and glistening coils, and her eyes were a steady grey.

As for her existence, that was endless. She knew by heart the grey hours when the world evolves, and would only rest a while to enjoy the evening star. Strangled by the arms of a weaned child, she was seldom it seemed without a second baby greedy at her breast, and a third impatient in her body. She would scrub, wash, bake, mend, and drag her husband from floor to bed when, of an evening, he had fallen down.

'You will exhaust yourself,' Miss Hare warned.

'I am used to it,' Mrs Godbold replied. 'And am strong besides. When I was a girl we would work in the fields and walk for miles. That was in the fens. Before I came out. Flat country certainly, but it does not let you eat it up all that easy.' She laughed. 'We would skate, too, all of us girls and boys; we was nine in the family. We would skate across the flooded country during a hard winter, miles and miles, everything so brittle. The twigs on the hedges looked as if you could have broken them off like glass.'

Her eyes were suddenly brightened by what she was telling. Solidity in herself seemed to give to the glass twigs some mysterious, desirable, unattainable property of their own.

Once while Miss Hare was feverish and really very ill she confided in her nurse:

'I am afraid I may fall and hurt myself on so much glass. Will you let me hold your hand?'

'Yes,' agreed the other, and gave it.

She might have severed it if necessary with its wedding ring and all.

66

'Gold,' Miss Hare mumbled. 'Champing at the bit. Did you ever see the horses? I haven't yet. But at times the wheels crush me unbearably.'

Mrs Godbold remained a seated statue. The massive rumps of her horses waited, swishing their tails through eternity. The wheels of her chariot were solid gold, well-axled, as might have been expected. Or so it seemed to the sick woman whose own vision never formed, remaining a confusion of light, at most an outline of vague and fiery pain.

'Never,' complained Miss Hare. 'Never. Never. As if I were not intended to discover.'

Whereupon she succeeded in twisting herself upright.

'Go to sleep. Too much talk will not do you any good,' advised the nurse.

And looked put out, at least for her, as if the patient had destroyed something they had been sharing.

'Oh, but I am ill,' Miss Hare whimpered.

Mrs Godbold let the silence slip by. Then, ever so gradually, she had ventured on a suggestion.

'I will pray for you,' she said.

'If it will do you any good,' Miss Hare sighed. 'I hope you will take the opportunity. But leaves are best, I find, plastered moist on the forehead.'

Then she drifted off, and Mrs Godbold continued to sit beside her for a while. Evening was a perfect silence. The tranquil light interceding with the darkness held for a moment a thread of cobweb in its balance.

When she was recovered, Miss Hare decided on one occasion to sound her friend.

'I believe we exchanged some confidences while I was so ill.'

Mrs Godbold did not wish to answer but felt compelled to.

'What confidences?' she asked, turning away.

'About the Chariot.'

Mrs Godbold blushed.

'Some people,' she said, 'get funny ideas when they are sick.'

Miss Hare was not deceived, however, and remained convinced they would continue to share a secret, after her friend had returned to carry out her life sentence of love and labour in the shed below the post office.

That some secret did exist Mrs Jolley also was certain, with her instinct for doors through which she might never be admitted. Not that she wanted to be. Oh dear no, not for a moment.

'Sounds a peculiar person to me,' she had to comment when her employer had concluded the story of her illness, or such parts of it as were communicable.

Miss Hare laughed. Her face was quite transformed.

Mrs Jolley swelled, only just perceptibly.

'And what will become of her?' she asked, 'in that shed, with all those children, and the husband – what about the husband?'

Had she put her finger on a sore?

'Oh, the husband comes and goes. On several occasions he has hit her, and once he loosened several of her teeth. He has been in prison, you know, for drunkenness.'

'Oh, yes, the husband!' she was forced to add.

And she began to sway her head from side to side, in a manner both troubled and grotesque, which gave her companion considerable satisfaction.

'There is so much evil,' finally cried the distraught Miss Hare. 'One forgets.'

'I can never forget,' Mrs Jolley claimed. 'It is always with us, in the daily papers, not to mention the back yard.'

'I had forgotten,' Miss Hare realized, 'until *you* reminded me of it.'

'But,' said Mrs Jolley, doing something dainty with a white of egg, 'why doesn't she leave this husband?'

'She considers it her duty to stay with him. Besides, she loves him.'

Miss Hare pronounced with difficulty that amazing word.

'One day, on my way past, I shall give her a piece of advice.'

'You would not dare!' cried Miss Hare, protecting something breakable. 'She is a very sensitive woman,' she said.

'Squeezing the water out of sheets!' retorted Mrs Jolley.

Then Miss Hare suspected that her housekeeper might ultimately have everybody at her mercy.

'Nobody who is a believer could fail to derive consolation from her faith,' Mrs Jolley decided.

'Few could fail to believe in Mrs Godbold,' Miss Hare followed up.

But feebler. Mrs Jolley had experience of words. Mrs Jolley had her family in a phalanx, her three daughters, and her sons-in-law, to say nothing of the incalculable kiddies.

'None of all this,' said Mrs Jolley at last, 'is what I am used to. I have always moved in different circles.'

Miss Hare believed it, but also feared.

'Mrs Flack agrees,' said Mrs Jolley, 'that I have been faced with things recently which I cannot be expected to understand or accept.'

'Mrs Flack?'

'Mrs Flack is a friend,' said Mrs Jolley, and let fall a veil of sugar from her sifter. 'A lady,' she said, 'that I met on the bus. And again outside the church. The widow,' she added, 'of a tiler who fell off the roof while contracted at Barranugli years ago.'

'I have never heard of Mrs Flack.'

'Different circumstances,' continued Mrs Jolley with dignity if not scorn. 'Mrs Flack resides in Mildred Street, in a home of her own, with every amenity. Seeing as her husband, the tiler, had the trade connexions that he had, they were able to fix things real nice. Oh, and I almost forgot to tell: Mrs Flack's father was a wealthy store proprietor who saw to it, naturally, that his daughter was left comfortable.'

'Naturally,' Miss Hare agreed.

Expected to evoke for herself the apparition of Mrs Flack, her mind would not venture so far. And there the name rested, unspoken and mysterious.

Indeed, Mrs Jolley, too, became a mystery now. She would appear in doorways or from behind dividing curtains and cough, but very carefully, at certain times. She carried her eyes downcast. Or she would raise them. And look. And Mrs Jolley's eyes were blue.

'I was looking for the ashtrays,' Mrs Jolley would explain. 'All my girls are smokers, of course. And the trays need emptying.'

Then she would retire. She was most discreet now and silent.

Again she would appear.

'Do you need anything?' Mrs Jolley would ask, or breathe.

What can one possibly need? Miss Hare used to wonder.

'No,' she would have to confess.

She would go on sitting in her favourite chair, which was old but real.

'Some people are given to one thing and some another,' Mrs Jolley would say, and finger. 'Now, *we* have the Genoa velvets in all our lounges. But Mrs Flack – the lady I was telling you of – she goes for *petty point*.'

But Mrs Flack would at once withdraw.

'Do you need anything?' Mrs Jolley would repeat.

Miss Hare's face fumbled after some acceptable desire.

'No,' she would have to admit, ashamed.

Then, on one occasion, Mrs Jolley announced:

'I had a letter.'

She had followed her employer out to the terrace. It was almost evening. Great cloudy tumbrils were lumbering across the bumpy sky towards a crimson doom.

'I did not see your letter,' Miss Hare replied.

'Oh,' she said, 'it was at the P.O. All my correspondence is always directed to the P.O. A matter of policy you might say.'

Miss Hare was observing the progress of a beetle across the mouth of a silted urn. She would have much preferred not to be disturbed.

'It was a letter from Mrs Apps,' Mrs Jolley pursued. 'That is Merle, the eldest. Merle has a particular weakness for her mum, perhaps because she was delicate as a kiddy. But struck lucky later on. With a hubby who denies her nothing – within reason, of course, and the demands of his career. Mr Apps – his long service will soon be due – is an executive official at the Customs. I will not say well-thought-of. Indispensable is nearer the mark. So it is not uncommon for Merle to hobnob with the high-ups of the Service, and entertain them to a buffy at her home. *Croaky de poison*. Chipperlarters. All that. With perhaps a substantial dish of, say, *Chicken à la King*. I never believe in blowing my own horn, but Merle does things that lovely. Yes. Her buffy has been written up, not once, but several times.'

Miss Hare observed her beetle.

'Now Merle writes,' the housekeeper continued, 'and does not, well, exactly *say*, because Merle is never one to *say*, but lets it be understood she is not at all satisfied with the steps her mum has taken to lead an independent life since their father passed on, like that, so tragically.'

Mrs Jolley watched Miss Hare.

'Of course I did not tell her half. Because Merle would have created. But you will realize the position it has put me in. Seeing as I am a person that always sympathizes with the misfortunes of others.'

Mrs Jolley watched Miss Hare. The wind had started up and the housekeeper did not like it in the open. She was one who would walk very quickly along a road and hope to reach the shops.

'Everybody is unfortunate if you can recognize it,' said Miss Hare, helping her beetle. 'But there are usually compensations for misfortune.'

Mrs Jolley drew in her breath. She hated it on the horrid

terrace, the wind tweaking her hair-net, and the smell of night threatening her.

'At a nominal wage,' she protested, 'it is hard lines if a lady should have to look for compensations.'

'How people can talk!' Miss Hare exclaimed, not without admiration. 'My parents would be at it by the hour. But one could sit quite comfortably inside their words. In a kind of tent. Do you know? When it rains.'

'Your parents, poor souls!' Mrs Jolley could not resist.

So that Miss Hare was cut. She removed her finger from the beetle, which ultimately she could not assist.

'Why must you keep harping on my parents?'

The marbled sky was heartrending, if also adamant, its layers of mauve and rose veined by now with black and indigo. The moon was the pale fossil of a moth.

'Who brought them up?' Mrs Jolley laughed against the rather nasty wind. 'I have always had consideration for Somebody's feelings, particularly since Somebody witnessed such a very peculiar death.'

Miss Hare was almost turned to stone amongst the neglected urns, and the Diana – *Scuola Canova* – whose hand had been broken off at the wrist.

'Will you please leave me?' she asked.

'That is what I have been trying to convey,' insisted Mrs Jolley. 'No person can be put upon indefinitely. And I have been invited,' she said, 'or it has been suggested by a friend, who suffers from indifferent health, that I should keep her company.'

Miss Hare was gulping like a brown frog. It was not the eventuality that appalled, so much as the method of disclosure, and the shock.

'Then, if you really intend,' she mumbled.

Mrs Jolley could have devoured one whom she suspected of a weakness.

'It is not as if you wasn't independent before,' she reminded, and smiled. 'We could hardly call ourselves Australians – could we? – if we was not independent. There is none of my girls as is not able, at a pinch, to mend a fuse, paint the home, or tackle jobs of carpentry.'

Mrs Jolley had assumed that monumental stance of somebody with whom it is impossible to argue.

'Perhaps,' Miss Hare answered.

When all was said she would remain a sandy little girl. Her smiles would weave like shallow water over pebbles.

'So,' sighed Mrs Jolley, 'there it is. I cannot say any more. Nothing stands still, and we must go along too.'

Then she drew in her breath as if she were restraining wind.

Or else she could suddenly have been afraid.

'Do let go of me, please!' she said, rather loud but still controlled.

'Miss Hare!' she said louder. 'You are hurting my wrists!'

But Miss Hare for her part could not resist the black gusts of darkness that were bearing down on her, and if she did not know the satisfaction of recognizing Mrs Jolley's fear, it was because she became engulfed in her own; she was removed from herself, at least temporarily, at that point.

As for Mrs Jolley, night had closed on her like a vice, leaving her just freedom enough to wrestle with the serpents of her conscience. So the two women were thrashing it out on the gritty terrace. The wind, or something, had torn the house-keeper's hair-net, and she hissed, or cried, from between her phosphorescent teeth.

Several afternoons a week, after putting on her gloves and hat with eye-veil, Mrs Jolley would not exactly go, she would *proceed*, rather, to her friend's residence at Sarsaparilla. Up the hill and into the street, it was not far, but far enough to turn a walk into a mission. How much solider a pavement sounded. Mrs Jolley would stamp and kick until she felt satisfied. The mere sight of a bus passing through a built-up area restored a person's circulation, as rounds of beef and honey-combs of tripe fed the spirit, and ironmongery touched the heart. So Mrs Jolley would continue on her way, under the lophostemons, as far as Mildred Street. Five minutes from the Cash-and-Carry, with doctor handy on the corner, it was a most desirable address. So Mrs Jolley would proceed, smiling at the ladies in the windows of their brick homes. She might correct the position of a seam or two. Then she would be ready to arrive.

If Mrs Flack's brick looked best of all, her tiles better, brighter-glazed, it was perhaps because of her late husband's connexions with the trade. There KARMA stood, the name done in baked enamel. Considering the delicate state of her health, the owner risked too much for neatness, though certainly she paid an elderly man a few shillings to mow the grass and had almost succeeded in encouraging an older one to do the same for less. On Thursdays, besides, a strong woman coped with any stooping or lifting, but that arrangement might possibly be discontinued. Depending on developments.

Mrs Jolley loved the latch at Mrs Flack's. She loved the rustic picket gate. She loved the hedge of Orange Triumph. To run her glove along the surface of Mrs. Flack's brick home gave her shivers. The sound of its convenience swept her head over heels into the caverns of envy.

As for Mrs Flack herself, she would seldom greet her friend with more than:

'Hmmmm!'

Or:

'Well I never!'

Or at most:

'I did not look at the calendar, but might have known.'

Yet Mrs Jolley understood the significance of it all. She might have been a cat, except that she was rubbing on the air.

Mrs Flack was sometimes described as having rather a yellow look, although more accurately speaking she was a medium shade of buff. For many years, she told, she had suffered from derangement of the bile. She was the victim of gallstones, too, and varicose veins, to say nothing of her Heart. She was wedded to her Heart, it might have seemed, if it had not been known she was a widow. Yet, in spite of such complications and allegiances, she would get about in a slow, definite way, and even when she had not been there, was remarkably well informed on everything that had happened. Indeed, it had been suggested by those few who were lacking in respect, that Mrs Flack was omnipresent – under the beds, even, along with the fluff and the chamber-pots. But most people had too much respect for her presence to question her authority. Her hats were too sober, her reports too factual. Where flippancy is absent, truth can only be inferred, and her teeth were broad and real enough to lend additional weight and awfulness to words.

Remarks collapsed on Mrs Jolley's lips in the presence of her friend. *Her friend*. The word was quite alarming, if also magical. Mrs Flack would look up from lashing the Orange Triumphs with the jet from her plastic hose, or, seated in her own lounge behind a prophetic steam of tea, would simply look, before pronouncing.

'That poor soul,' she might begin, 'who we both know – there is no need to mention names – how she has survived all these years on a slice of bread and dripping, and her relatives well-to-do, not to say downright wealthy. They did, for their

73

own convenience, after the death of the mother, deliver her to an institution, but the person screamed and screamed, and clung to the railings with her two hands, so that they were forced to take her back. It only goes to show. I am always thankful that, in my case, there are no ties, no encumbrances, not even a mortgage on the home.'

'Ah,' Mrs Jolley had to protest, 'I am a mother.'

Mrs Flack would pause, pick a burnt currant from a scone and appear to accuse it terribly.

'I cannot claim any such experience,' she would declare.

Then, after frowning, she would fall to laughing, but feebly – she was an invalid, it had to be remembered – through strips of pale lips.

Like cheese-straws at a buffy, Mrs Jolley would be reminded, and immediately regret her disrespect.

'I did not mean,' she would hasten, dashing at a few crumbs. 'That is to say, I did not intend to suggest.' And then: 'Are you truly quite alone?'

'Yes, dear.' Mrs Flack would sigh.

At that moment something would happen, of such peculiar subtlety that it must have eluded the perception of all but those involved in the experience. The catalyst of sympathy seemed to destroy the envelopes of personality, leaving the two essential beings free to merge and float. Thought must have played little part in any state so passive, so directionless, yet it was difficult not to associate a mental process with silence of such a ruthless and pervasive kind. As they continued sitting, the two women would drench the room with the moth-colours of their one mind. Little sighs would break, scintillating, on the Wilton wall-to-wall. The sound of stomachs, rumbling liquidly, would sluice the already impeccable veneer. Glances rejected one another as obsolete aids to communication. This could have been the perfect communion of souls, if, at the same time, it had not suggested perfect collusion.

Mrs Jolley was usually the first to return. Certain images would refurnish the swept chamber of her mind. There was, for instance – she loved it best of all – the pastel-blue plastic dressing-table set in Mrs Flack's second bedroom.

Mrs Jolley's face would grow quite hard and lined then, as if a pink-and-blue eiderdown had suffered petrifaction.

'Alone perhaps, but in a lovely home,' she would be heard to murmur.

'Alone is not the same,' Mrs Flack would usually reply.

And smile.

It was not all that sad. They both knew it was not sad. They understood that a dénouement might be reached in the drama of their wishes – if they so wished.

As tea and contentment increased understanding of each other, as well as confidence in their own powers, it was only to be expected that two ladies of discretion and taste should produce their knives and try them for sharpness on weaker mortals. Seated above the world on springs and *petty point*, they could lift the lids and look right into the boxes in which moiled other men, crack open craniums as if they had been boiled eggs, read letters before they had been written, scent secrets that would become a source of fear to those concerned. Eventually the ladies would begin. Their methods would be steel, though their antiphon was always bronze.

'Take doctors, for instance,' Mrs Flack might say. 'Doctors are only human beings.'

'You are telling me!' it was Mrs Jolley's duty to interpose.

'But must be expected to act different.'

'And do not always.'

'Very often do not. Mrs Jolley, I am telling you that this doctor at the corner, in giving me a needle – which I have to get regular for certain reasons – pulled me quite close. "Is it necessary?" I asked – myself, of course – "and according to medical etiquette, to press against a lady's form in giving her a simple needle?" His breath was that hot, Mrs Jolley, and the odour, well, I am not one to insinuate, but if it had been *my* breath, I would of been ashamed to advertise the fact.'

'Ttst, ttst! The doctors! And to think that a lady, on some occasions, must submit to an examination by such hands!'

'Ho, an examination! I have never had one, and do not intend to. No, never!'

'There are the lady doctors, of course.'

'Ah, the lady doctors!'

'Do you suppose the lady doctors ever attend to gentlemen?'

'I do not know. But they would not attend to me, never. I have my own ideas about the lady doctors.'

Mrs Jolley would have liked to hear, but etiquette did not permit.

'Ah, yes.' Mrs Flack would sigh, and lapse.

Though each knew she must soon revive. It was but the pause between movements, when initiates clear their throats, and frown at some innocent who gives expression to his pleasure. Mrs Jolley had quickly learnt.

'Thursday night,' Mrs Flack had indeed revived, 'Mrs

Khalil's Lurleen was seen three times outside the Methodist church.'

'In the open?'

'On the grass.'

'Accompanied?'

'Ho! Mrs Khalil's Lurleen!'

'But with a gentleman?'

'With three. And all of them different. Between the pictures going in and coming out.'

Then Mrs Jolley had to laugh.

'Girls will be girls, eh?'

'I should hope not,' said Mrs Flack, whose pale lips would become transformed at times into two strips of adhesive tape. 'Such girls should be run out. But when the Law – well, what can you expect at Sarsaparilla?'

'Did you say the Law?'

'I will not go into that,' Mrs Flack replied. 'Except that the constable's own braces was found in the paddy's lucerne on the block below the pictures. There is no denying ownership when the name is put in marking-ink.'

'He could have lost them.'

'He could have lost them.'

'Or thrown them away.'

'Or thrown them away. With the price still visible on the brand-new leather. No, Mrs Jolley, Constable McFaggott is far too close to lose or discard his belongings in the paddy's lucerne, unless the duty that took him there had turned him lighter-headed than usual.'

Then Mrs Jolley began to hiss like any goose. Her pink-and-blue was changed to purple.

'What do you know!' She sat and hissed, and would have known more.

But Mrs Flack had folded her arms. She was holding the blanched points of her yellow elbows.

'We have not kept to the subject,' she said, or accused.

For Mrs Flack could sense with only half her instinct that her friend had something which she wished to tell.

The occasion was, in fact, the day after Mrs Jolley had approached her mistress on the terrace, and been involved in something rather nasty. How nasty, the housekeeper scarcely dared remember. But would touch her wrists from time to time. Certainly on setting out, so brisk and bright, on the visit to her friend, she had fully intended to confide, perhaps even make the great decision. Yet could she, finally? Or would she?

'That poor soul at Xanadu,' Mrs Flack had begun to lead, 'I do feel sorry for the sick and simple.'

'But in her case has had her day.'

'There are all kinds I must admit.'

'But has had her day, Mrs Flack. All that lot has had their day.'

Mrs Jolley could not pass her tongue quick enough along her stripped lips, nor twist her nice openwork gloves into a tight enough knot.

Mrs Flack's eyes began to dart, so that her friend was unpleasantly reminded that somebody was behind the skin.

'We must think of ourselves as well, of course,' Mrs Flack agreed.

'We must think of ourselves.'

'Without killing *Her*!'

'Not likely!' Mrs Jolley laughed. 'She must run the risk though. Like any girl in a kennel beneath the roof. When the heat used to crack. Or shelling peas. Or pushing the pea-pods through the sieve. Or blacking the grates. Or blacking the grates.'

'Are you bitter, Mrs Jolley?'

'Bitter, no. I am just remembering.'

'One thing I never was, was bitter,' Mrs Flack announced.

Then they sat for a moment to experience once again that delicious process of disembodiment and union.

But time was passing. Mrs Jolley got up, brisk, good body that she was, and slapped her dainty gloves together.

'Well,' she said, 'it has been lovely, Mrs Flack. And now I must get back to that poor lady of mine.'

And sniffed and smiled and blinked at once.

At which her friend became her most dignified and formal. The classic gestures might have been detached from a frieze.

'If you was ever to decide, we would consider this as *your* chair,' said Mrs Flack, laying two fingers and a ruby ring on an excessive bulge in the upholstery.

Mrs Jolley could not bring herself to look, let alone comment. But the implications were understood.

'It was the one He used to sit in after an early tea,' on this occasion Mrs Flack went so far as to confide. 'He liked his comfort and an early tea. No one else will never ever have the use of that chair, without it is a certain trusted friend.'

Yet Mrs Jolley had become far too agitated to decide. Her mouth, her gestures were unlike themselves. Two masters could have been contending for the strings. She was forced to reply:

'I am expecting a letter that will help me give a straight answer on the future. You know how it is.'

'Only the person herself knows how it is,' Mrs Flack said, and smiled.

In the hands of Fate, and exhausted by conflict, Mrs Jolley held her head humbly and acceptant. She allowed herself to be led along the hall, past *The Two Little Princesses with their Dogs*, and a bloodhound that Mrs Jolley herself had worked in wool while waiting for her late husband to propose.

The two ladies seldom continued their conversation at parting, unless to consider briefly the prospects for rain or fine, and soon Mrs Jolley would be going down the street, still holding her head in a chastened way, like a communicant returning from the altar, conscious that all the ladies, in all the windows of all the homes, were aware of her shriven state. For there was no doubt friendship did purify.

Although there was no more mention of Mrs Flack she was always there at Xanadu. Miss Hare could feel her presence. In certain rather metallic light, behind clumps of ragged, droughty laurels, in corners of rooms where dry rot had encouraged the castors to burst through the boards, on landings where wallpaper hung in drunken brown festoons, or departed from the wall in one long limp sheet, Mrs Flack obtruded worst, until Miss Hare began to fear, not only for her companion and housekeeper, at the best of times a doubtful asset, but, what was far more serious, for the safety of her property. So far had Mrs Flack, through the medium of Mrs Jolley, insinuated herself into the cracks in the actual stone. Sometimes the owner of Xanadu would wake in her lumpy bed and listen for the crash. Or would there be a mere dull tremendous flump as quantities of passive dust subsided?

Either eventuality terrified Miss Hare.

One night she got the hiccups, and the marble halls of Xanadu reverberated with the same distress. Glass tinkled as she wandered here and there, grazing with an arm or elbow. Lustre crashed somewhere in the drawing-room.

'What are you up to, clumsy girl?' Mrs Jolley called. 'Can't I leave you for two minutes?'

Already she was coming. Mrs Jolley would appear at crucial moments, now from above, it seemed, her detached soles smacking marble. She was carrying a lamp which flew through the darkness like a small bouquet of flowers. Mrs Jolley stood at last in the drawing-room holding her bunch of yellow flowers.

'You are not to be trusted, you know,' said the reliable housekeeper, catching sight of the glittery fragments of the silver-lustre jug.

'Aren't they my own things?' the owner dared.

'Oh, yes!' the housekeeper laughed. 'They are your own things all right.'

'And no one will take them from me?'

'Not till you have smashed them all to smithereens. Home, too, it looks like. What will you do then? Camp out under the bunya bunya and count the raindrops?'

'I have the hiccups,' said Miss Hare. 'Or had, rather. I believe they have been cured.'

Mrs Jolley's little yellow bouquet shook.

'It was the fright you got. You could set up and make your fortune throwing junk at all the hiccupers in creation.'

The darkness was reeling under the attacks of Mrs Jolley's mirth. Miss Hare, although cured of her hiccups, felt quite sick.

'Mrs Jolley,' she began, 'your FRIEND ...'

The formidable word seemed to thunder.

But Mrs Jolley, wheezing inside her iron corset, had bent to retrieve the fragments of jug, and was making an icy music with them, as she swept them together over the floor. It was probable she had not heard the word. Nor did Miss Hare know how she would have continued if her housekeeper had.

For, although Mrs Flack pervaded, she was nothing tangible. Then Mrs Jolley straightened up.

'You will not leave me?' Miss Hare asked.

The woman stood. It was as if she had discovered a swelling on her lip. It was most embarrassing.

'In the dark I mean,' Miss Hare explained.

'You was here before, wasn't you?' Now Mrs Jolley's voice quite clattered. 'Having the hiccups. And before that. And before that.'

She appeared annoyed.

'Oh, yes,' said Miss Hare. 'And shall be. If I am allowed. I shall throw back the shutter. I had forgotten the moon. I shall sit for a little. Quietly.'

Soon there were a few planks of moonlight, in which she continued to rock long after Mrs Jolley had withdrawn. For much longer than she had anticipated the wanderer kept afloat, and by extraordinary management of the will always just avoided bumping against the shores of darkness. Other shapes threatened though, some of them dissolving at the last moment into good, some she was able to identify unhesitatingly as evil. In the misty silence, the two women, her tormentors-in-chief, let down their hair and covered their faces with veils of it. Their words were hidden from her. On the whole, she realized, she was unable to distinguish motives unless allowed to read faces.

Towards morning Mrs Jolley appeared in the flesh, and wrenched the little tiller from the cold hands. As she joggled the boat in anger, dewdrops fell distinctly from all its protuberances.

'You do hate me,' said Miss Hare, observing evil in person.

The rescuer's face was quivering with exasperation. The mouth had aged without its teeth, and should have proclaimed innocence, but words flickered almost lividly from between the gums.

'I am only thinking of your health,' Mrs Jolley hissed. 'I am responsible in a way, though do not know what possessed me to take it on.'

Then evil is also good, Miss Hare understood.

'But you have not yet enjoyed all the pleasure of tormenting me,' she was moved to remark.

'I will not waste my breath arguing with loopy Louie,' replied Mrs Jolley, leading her charge towards the stairs.

At breakfast each of them treated the incident as if it had not occurred. It was a brisk morning. It seemed to Miss Hare that the light illuminated. She herself was exuberant with knowledge. She radiated discoveries.

'I see,' she said over the crispies, 'I am wrong about Xanadu. To be afraid. I shall not fear if it is taken away, because my experience will remain.'

'Experience!' exploded Mrs Jolley. 'What have you experienced?'

'For many years, when there were people here, I sat under the table amongst the legs and saw an awful lot happen.'

'There's always plenty happens in a big house, but it's only the servants that sees that. You were sitting on the same cushions as your mum and dad.'

'I was the servant of the servants. I was a very ugly little girl. The maids would read me their letters because I hardly existed, and sometimes would allow me to fetch them things, especially before they were going out in their big pink hats to meet their friends.'

Mrs Jolley breathed on nonsense.

'Better eat up your crispies,' she advised.

'But that is not the experience of which I wish to speak. Take water, for instance. If you are alone with it enough you become like water. You enter into it.'

Mrs Jolley had got up and was throwing the crockery into the sink. The plates were falling dangerously hard but somehow failed to break.

'Whether this can count as my contribution,' Miss Hare continued, 'I still have to discover. Perhaps somebody will tell me. And show me at the same time how to distinguish with certainty between good and evil.'

Mrs Jolley's face, which was still eating, had become a series of lumps. Obviously she was not going to answer, and it was not only because her mouth was full.

'For all I know, Xanadu, which I still can't help loving, is evil itself.'

'It is that all right!' cried Mrs Jolley, gulping the rest of the crust that had been giving trouble.

'Like certain things made of plastic,' Miss Hare added. 'Plastic is bad, bad!'

Now she felt definitely stronger, and Mrs Jolley was resenting it.

Soon afterwards the seeker went outside, temporarily fortified by her knowledge. Of course, she realized too the sad extent of her shortcomings, which were tingling as always in her fingertips.

It was only natural, and soon became evident that Mrs Jolley was preparing something, or a whole series of torments, as she ticked off the days. The housekeeper would stand for whole minutes in front of a calendar she had got from a grocer to rectify a deficiency, for Miss Hare herself had never stopped to think about time let alone the days.

'Who would ever have thought I had been here all that long,' the housekeeper once remarked aloud.

'*I* should have thought!' Miss Hare laughed. 'But it is nonetheless surprising.'

'It is because I have a conscience,' Mrs Jolley hinted.

'I dare say it is,' replied Miss Hare.

'And am waiting for guidance.'

'I would guide you if I could,' said Miss Hare quite sincerely. 'But you cannot tell other people.'

Then Mrs Jolley stirred up the dust, as she did frequently – her conscience made her – while achieving nothing by the act.

'You know,' said Miss Hare, 'I think I am now strong enough if you decide to go to your friend.'

Mrs Jolley was all murmurs.

Friendship, she said, sometimes involved a plunge.

'Friendship is two knives,' said Miss Hare. 'They will sharpen each other when rubbed together, but often one of them will slip and slice off a thumb.'

At this point Mrs Jolley flew into such a rage she tore down a curtain in the dining-room, and Miss Hare no longer minded. She sensed that for the moment she had the upper hand. Or was it that she, too, contained something evil which could take control at times? Some human element. Now she recalled with nostalgia occasions when she had lost her identity in those of trees, bushes, inanimate objects, or entered into the minds of animals, of which the desires were unequivocal or honest.

Depressed, if also enlightened, she was not altogether surprised at the incident by which Mrs Jolley became reinstated in her own esteem.

One morning, rather fresh because still early, the housekeeper had gone out into the yard, and was stamping about too much and too long to satisfy the listener. The latter was standing in a little scullery, in one corner of which she was able normally to feel at peace, in a scent of apples, sometimes a squeaking of mice; and always the broken light from an old bulging cane blind. But on the present occasion her heart was dealing her blows as she listened to the dubious activities in the yard, and at last, clearly and unmistakably, the scrape of a spade over stone sent her rushing, tumbling, down short but sudden flights of steps, over interminable flags, past the smell of stale water, until she arrived ungainly and ashamed in the doorway which gave access to the yard.

'Ah,' she cried at once, 'you have killed it!'

What survived of her voice rasped her throat cruelly, and surprised the brash air of morning.

'I'll say!' Mrs Jolley blurted.

She was completely out of place in the yard, and knew it. Her hair had escaped into tails, her decent dress was disarranged, but the unusualness of the situation, together with her own inspired bravery, made her enjoy dislocation. Her smile, which should have appeared fiendish, was agreeable and innocent as she stood looking down at the spade.

Or snake. Of which the halves were still twitching.

'You killed it!' Miss Hare protested and mourned. 'I used to put out milk and it would drink and sometimes allow me to stand by, but I never quite succeeded in winning its confidence. There is something wrong with me,' she said.

Panting.

'And so you killed the snake.'

'That is not killing,' said Mrs Jolley, propping the spade. 'That is ridding the world of something bad.'

'Who is to decide what is bad?' asked Miss Hare.

At least she had been given the strength to bear what had happened, and in the yard – where so much else had taken place: the sacrifice of her poor goat, to say nothing of her father's unmentionable end.

She stooped to pick up the limp pieces of snake.

Mrs Jolley began to shriek and hold her hair.

'It will bite you!' she cried. 'They say their bite stays with them.'

Miss Hare's freckled, horrible hands looked so tender and ludicrous.

Mrs Jolley fell to snickering, then to giggling.

'Brave me!' she tittered. 'How did I do it?'

Nor did she watch to see how her employer disposed of the corpse. She was exhausted by her triumph.

But almost at once began sulking again.

Mrs Jolley would sulk for days, even forgetting she was a lady and a mother until Miss Hare was tempted to ask:

'Does Elma believe in plastic?'

Or she would beg:

'Tell me about the time, Mrs Jolley, that Merle gave the buffy for the high-up officials from the Customs, and the white sauce got burnt.'

She was truly interested, and would have loved also to see the officials sitting at their varnished desks during the hours of business drinking milky tea.

Or she would ask:

'You have never told me – does Mr Apps wear a moustache?'

Or:

'I wonder whether I should be afraid to meet a stoker?'

Mrs Jolley would not answer because she was sulking, and Miss Hare was half ashamed for her own powers of emulating the cruelty of human beings.

'It is I who am bad,' she sighed half aloud.

All the time the house was full of reverberations. The wind would tear through it when the women forgot to close the shutters, which was almost always now, with the result that leaves had begun to litter the brocade, and once the lunch-wrap of a picknicker or commercial traveller was found in an epergne. If it had not been for her stereoscopic memories, Miss Hare would have felt surprised and pained.

Mrs Jolley said:

'It is too much for me.'

As for the blowing paper it was possible to roll that into a ball, which Miss Hare did, and threw it where it would not be seen.

But all the time it was obvious something must happen. Mrs Jolley was waiting for inspiration, Miss Hare for explanation, and to those who wait it usually comes in some form or another.

In the housekeeper's case it could have been that continued absence of material symbols had shaken her religious faith, thus causing a delay. Was it possible that the piles of purple brick to which she had been used to cling were as liable to crumble as the stones of Xanadu? This was too large, too unbelievable a bomb to receive into the ordered mind, and she thrust the possibility away from her. But bombs *are* unbelievable until they actually fall. Whether Mrs Jolley suspected this or not behind the trembling veil of her beliefs, she would open her prayer-book and search in vain for some efficacious prayer she might have overlooked. She would even invoke the image of her late husband, until remembering certain aspects of their leave-taking: an eyebrow which had stuck, the mouth biting on a last word, for ever, as if it were a stone. Then she would stop. She developed heartburn, and sometimes her teeth would remain whole mornings in the tumbler.

But, of course, the real cause of Mrs Jolley's distress was her employer. Once this was realized, Miss Hare had to suffer.

The housekeeper walked about the house humming with intentions. Doors which she had never yet opened she now tried and, in the course of it all, climbed to the little dome in amethyst glass, under which she found airlessness and a quantity of old chicken bones. She was always ferreting into wardrobes, through forests of long embroidered garments, in which the cold rain of metal beads would drizzle on the backs of her hands, and tendrils of feather and drifts of down, overlooked by nesting mice, revolt her nostrils. She had forced locks when necessary to interpret the letters stuffed inside a drawer, but never found more than words.

In the absence of a real weapon loaded with infallible lead, or furnished with a knife which would finish cleanly yet cruelly, she was becoming truly desperate. It was not possible that such tunnels of decayed magnificence should lead to an innocent and

84

empty arena. Faced with this ultimate suspicion, Mrs Jolley was standing one morning beside the buhl table, upon which she suddenly noticed – it might always have been there, but her pre-occupation could have caused her to overlook it – the fan tipped with flamingo feather, a present from the Armenian merchant in the hotel at Assouan. Mrs Jolley had barely opened the fan, a poor thing of broken tortoiseshell and tattered parchment, the feathers themselves deadened by the years, no longer flaming. She was standing, the fan half open, like her mind.

When Miss Hare realized only too clearly.

The latter had appeared in the doorway in her eternal wicker hat. That Mrs Jolley had discovered Miss Hare's fan was in itself insignificant; the mother's relationship with her child had been one of duty rather than love. But now the daughter saw that the fan could be a hinge on which something might depend, opening out immeasurably.

'I wish you would put it down,' she suggested. 'It is old and very fragile.'

'It is a lovely fan,' Mrs Jolley simpered.

Through her half-opened mind she appeared half-devilish, half-girlish.

'To carry at a ball,' she added.

Memories of occasions when she had offered trayfuls of ices to dancers spun garishly.

'I do ask you to put it down,' Miss Hare begged, without hope.

'How they danced in their swansdown,' Mrs Jolley laughed, 'till the moths got into it. All night and into the morning.'

Then a terrible thing happened. Mrs Jolley began to dance, slowly at first, tentatively, sliding her practical work-shoes across the floor of the drawing-room at Xanadu. Her face was still only trying expressions, her arms and her body positions. But courage, or her daemon, prevailed. The muscles of her cheeks no longer twitched. Her mouth became fixed in the china smile of obsession, bluish-white. She was sliding and gliding, creaking, certainly – it could not have been otherwise in such a carapace – but borne along out of reach or control, her own or her employer's.

Her *employer*! It had always made her laugh. More than ever now.

Sliding and gliding, out of the drawing-room into the dining-room. Even whirling.

Mrs Jolley threw back her head. Her throat was taut. The laughter rose up through it to be expelled in solid lumps.

'At the ball! At the ball!' Mrs Jolley sang.

And cracked. Whirling and coughing. It was the dust.

'However much you intend to hurt me I shall not be hurt,' Miss Hare called. 'I shall not watch.'

But followed after – or could she have been leading? – in her wicker hat. She was trundling and stumbling on her short blunt legs.

'All the young men were for ever persisting,' Mrs Jolley chanted, 'to dance with the daughter of Xanadu.'

At the same time she made a play, with her fan, with her eyes, which had grown too young for mercy: the blue eyes of future mothers.

'All the young men with moustaches and the smooth ones too.' How she shrieked. 'And the limp cousins!'

'Oh, dear!' panted Mrs Jolley.

A tuft of flamingo flew out of the fan.

Miss Hare followed. Or was she leading? In either case she trundled. And whimpered.

The figures of the dance, though developed deviously, through room and ante-room, along passages, across landings and up the dangerous flights of stairs, led directly into the past, and this had never seemed more grotesque, draped with calico and dry with rouge. As Miss Hare followed – or led – and Mrs Jolley danced, sometimes obscenely moulded to a partner's chest, sometimes compelling a gilded chair to execute a teetering step, all the dancers of all the waltzes returned to Xanadu: the grave bosoms and the little pippins, the veins of coral and of watered ink, the chalk cheeks and the tortured mops, and the gentlemen, the gentlemen. Never had the ache of patent leather been admitted to such an extent as on the occasion of Mrs Jolley's lethal performance. Never had the music from Sydney broken more brilliantly under the chandelier. Never had the conversation opened deeper wounds.

Shuffling, trundling, blundering, the dancers frequently threatened to tumble over the balusters. Miss Hare held her heart and Mrs Jolley her breath. In spite of the fascination of the arabesques it was possible to spin out of air and music, at the risk of death, the mistress preferred to see the one-step. It was so much kinder to the long beauties, working so hard and sad, as they pushed against the tum-ti-tum.

It was terribly sad in the great tatty brilliant rooms, in mirror and memory.

Miss Hare really had to protest at last.

'Stop! Please, stop!' she called, and the strings which controlled her actions mercifully held up her hand.

Then the dancers stopped. Mrs Jolley stopped.

'Thank you,' gasped Miss Hare. 'I cannot be expected to experience too much in one day.'

She was almost extinguished beneath the snuffer of her heavy hat.

Mrs Jolley was surprised, and might have sounded more reproving if breathlessness had not prevented it.

'You have led me such a dance,' she said. 'You could have broken both our necks, but I hardly like to offer criticism, not in my position, and because we know there are times when you are not in full possession of yourself. Even so.'

'Full possession?' asked Miss Hare.

So softly.

The housekeeper wondered whether she had gone too far, then decided to go farther. It was her opportunity.

'You will not remember an evening on the terrace,' Mrs Jolley was in a hurry, 'or what you said, or what you did, or how you passed out cold.'

'Which evening on the terrace?' asked Miss Hare.

Softly.

'I cannot be expected to trot out dates.' Mrs Jolley's teeth snapped. 'Or quote exact words. But I had the marks on my wrists for several days.'

'I *hurt* you?'

'I'll say! And might have done real damage if you hadn't passed right out.'

'And I can remember *nothing*.'

'It was like a kind of fit.'

An undulating dread threatened to drown Miss Hare.

'I told you nothing?' she had to ask. 'Nothing of importance?'

'That depends on what is important.'

'Tell me,' Miss Hare ordered.

Mrs Jolley wondered whether she would.

'Tell me, Mrs Jolley,' the mistress was insisting.

Then Mrs Jolley changed her tactics, partly because she sensed an impending *coup de grâce*, partly since she was a little bit afraid.

'It was about the Chariot.'

She inserted the remark, nor would fear prevent her watching the result.

'I will not be told lies!' Miss Hare shouted.

'The truth is always truest when other people call it lies,' Mrs Jolley answered in her triumph.

'You are a wicked evil woman!' Miss Hare accused. 'I knew it! All along I knew it!'

'Who is not wicked and evil, waiting for chariots at sunset, as if they was taxis?'

'Oh, you are bad, bad!' Miss Hare confirmed.

'And you are sick. I was foolish not to have called a doctor, but did not, well, out of respect for feelings.'

'You must never call a doctor. Never, never!'

'I will not be here,' said Mrs Jolley, 'long.'

'You will be with your thoughts, and that will be worse.'

'What do you know about my thoughts?'

'Only what you have told me.'

Mrs Jolley had some difficulty in releasing the handfuls of her apron.

'If we are two of a kind,' she mumbled.

Miss Hare could not accept the possibility of that, and was rootling in remote recesses for some evidence of her own election.

'What did I really say?' she coaxed. 'That evening? On the terrace?'

But Mrs Jolley was sulking.

If Miss Hare had not felt so exhausted she might have known more alarm. There was a hornet crying as it built its nest in a doorway. The housekeeper had evaporated in her usual manner. A windy desert somewhere could not have been emptier than the hornet's cry suggested.

Yet it was one of the lusher mornings of spring, after the grass had taken over. The immediate world appeared to be living under grass. Light was no longer distributed by the sun in honest golden metal; it oozed, a greenish, steamy yellow from the flesh of grass. As Miss Hare went out into the green prevalence, the arrowheads of grass pricked her; she was the target of thousands. But had experienced worse, of course. So she went on.

She went down through the militant, sharp, clattering grass, and through the patches of shade where the soft, indolent swathes lolled and stank. She went to where the orchard had once been, and which she had not visited it seemed to her for years. Neglect, however, had not cancelled celebration. The tangle of staggy trees paraded a fresh varnish, stuck by intermittent grace with virgin heads of blossom. There was the plum tree, too, the largest anyone had seen.

The plum had obviously reached the height of its glory for that year. Its crowded white dared the grass, brought the colour back to the sky. The sun had returned, moreover, in its own right, and hung a spangled banner on the tree.

Miss Hare went on pushing through the musky grass. She could have swum for ever on her wave, towards the island of her tree, holding out her hands, no longer begging for rescue, but in recognition.

And he came out from under the branches, from where he had been sitting, apparently.

'Oh,' she said then, and stopped, knee-deep in the waves of grass.

He stood outside the tree waiting for her, though it was nobody she had ever seen.

'I came in here,' said the man. 'I saw the tree.'

'Yes,' she said. 'It is mine. Isn't it lovely? And I have not noticed it for years.'

She was making little grunting sounds of happiness and recognition.

The man appeared to recognize or at least not to reject.

Which was comforting.

He was a very ugly man, and strange, she saw.

'Would you care to sit down in the shade,' she asked, 'and enjoy the tree?'

She was filled with such a contentment of warmth and light she would not have cared if he had refused. She had been refused so regularly.

But the man did not reject her offer.

'I am Himmelfarb,' he said, correctly but oddly.

'Oh, yes?' she answered.

At the same time they stooped to negotiate the branches which were to provide their canopy.

Part Two

5

When they were seated, on two stones which could have been put there for them at the roots of the tree, the two people ignored each other for a moment, staring back at the material world as if to take a last look at those familiar forms which further experience might soon remove from their lives. From inside their flowered tent, they could now observe how the masses of the orchard were broken by a hatching in grey wood. Only precariously alive, the trees were the greener for their sickliness, moodily defiant of the strong light, with little wizened oranges radiating a feverish gold. All was most extraordinarily exposed to mind and view from beneath the plum, and could have appeared to challenge hope, if it had not been for the evidence of continuity: a bird cupped in the grey goblet of her nest, a litter of young rabbits moving by clockwork into grass, the eyelids of a lizard denying petrifaction by the sun. It was perfectly still, except that the branches of the plum tree hummed with life, increasing, and increasing, deafening, swallowing them up.

At that point Mary Hare turned to her companion, wondering whether he was the kind of person to whom apologies had to be made.

'This,' she said, 'is what I am really interested in.' She wished her hands could have helped her out, but they would not. 'All these things, I mean' – making an awkward motion with her head – 'are what I understand.'

She realized she was at her most hopelessly inadequate. Her tongue was small and round and hard.

The man nodded, however. She saw he would take her seriously. So she eased her knees, in their ugly, brown, woollen stockings.

'It is still difficult for us to appreciate, except in theory,' said the man. 'Until so very recently, we were confined within ghettoes. Trees and flowers grew the other side of walls, the other side of our experience, in fact.'

Miss Hare made rather a face for the difficulties she had begun already to encounter.

'I must tell you something,' she said. 'I did not receive much education. My father was impatient. And then,' she confided – it was terribly hard but necessary, 'I was supposed to be simple. Still, there were always a great many things I was able to understand.'

The man could not have been less surprised, or perhaps he was excessively grave.

'I mean,' he continued, 'I am a Jew, and centuries of history have accustomed one to look inward instead of outward.'

'Oh,' said Miss Hare, 'there are others who do that!'

And paused.

'Sometimes it is quite horrible,' she murmured.

A prickly stillness had fallen round them.

Then she reached forward and jerked off, clumsily but successfully, a twig from her tree.

'There,' she said, showing him.

She was holding the blossom in her blunt grubs of fingers. Would he be disgusted by her as many people were?

He bent forward to look at the flower. She had never been so close to a man – even her father's moments of intimacy had been necessarily distant; he had always avoided any gesture that might have developed into an embrace – so, now it was natural that she should observe intently. She was looking into the little whorls of hair on his neck, just above the collar. The confusion and profusion of rather wiry, once-black hair excited her love for all living matter, while she felt as guilty as though she had discovered the secret a respected friend had not attempted to conceal.

The man was taking a somewhat exaggerated interest in the plum blossom.

'It is almost finished,' he was saying.

'It is only beginning,' she corrected. 'After this there will be a period that a lot of people consider dull. Little pin-heads of green fruit. Before the fat, purple, powdered ones.'

'But the worms come, too,' she remembered. 'The plums will be full of worms.'

All the time she was examining the pores of his skin. His ugly face had not yet opened to her, although she could feel there was nothing such a person would willingly hide. His face was stone, but must have possessed the warmth of statues in summer, which retain the heat of the sun after it has withdrawn. She was particularly fascinated by his great nose. It should have been cruel, but, on the contrary, it appeared so gentle, she would have liked to touch it.

'You investigate nature very thoroughly,' the man said, and laughed.

'I do not have to investigate,' she answered. 'By now I know!'

Then she blushed for what Peg might have called a boast.

He continued looking at the twig, although each knew the necessity had passed. Her hands took the blossom for granted, while continuing gently to hold, and he was reminded of some animals: dogs that have accepted the good faith of a master, cats resuming their suckling of a litter while a stranger looks on. In their freckled clumsiness, her hands appeared supremely trustful.

'I am afraid I did not catch your name,' her voice had begun to say, in the accents of another, a mother, perhaps, or governess.

'Himmelfarb,' he said.

'Oh, dear!' she protested. 'That is something I shall never learn. Haven't you something easier?'

'Mordecai.'

'Worse!' she cried. 'Much worse!'

And looked helpless, but pleased.

'I have been called by a great variety of names. Many of them in the heat of the moment. But in the end, no name is necessary,' he said. 'Not even the rightful ones.'

She looked down into her lap to avoid something she did not fully understand.

'Mine are very simple,' she ventured, and was almost too ashamed to disclose them.

But when finally she did, he appeared delighted and asked with some enthusiasm:

'Did you realize it is possible to distinguish the figure of a hare if one looks carefully at the moon?'

'No, I did not. But I am not at all surprised,' she replied earnestly.

'The sacrificial animal.'

'What is that?' she asked, or panted.

'In some parts of the world, they believe the hare offers itself for sacrifice.'

'Oh, no!' she cried. 'I do not like to believe that. One meets with too many knives by the way, without going deliberately in search of one.'

'The concept of the willing hare is surely less painful than that of the scapegoat, dragged out, bleating, by its horns.'

'Goats? Please don't tell me! I really do not understand any of these things.'

His natural and immediate silence calmed her, however, and she said:

'I don't think I ever met a Jew. Perhaps one. An old man who was useful to my father. A piano tuner. Are Jews so very different?'

'There is all the difference in the world.'

'Do you like it?'

'We have no alternative.'

'I understand,' she said. 'I, too, am different.'

He laughed, and picked up the twig of wilting plum blossom which she had let fall.

'That would appear, mathematically and morally, to make us equal,' he said. 'I am glad.'

Without irony, though. So that she was glad in turn. This Jew would not be one to go laughing at her.

'In the factory where I work,' the Jew told her, and he had returned inward, behind walls higher than those he had mentioned, 'I am considered the most different of all human beings.'

'Of course!' she cried. '*They* always behave like that. What do you make in your factory? Is it close? I cannot imagine it. Tell me,' she said.

'It is at Barranugli. We do make other things, but our particular item is bicycle lamps.'

'I should hate that!' she replied with great vehemence. 'But do you live close? I do hope.'

'At Sarsaparilla,' he said.

'Yes?'

'Below the post office.'

'In your own house?'

'So to speak.'

'Yes, yes, I do know a little brown house. Oh, a house is better! One can hide in a house.'

Until seeming to remember. Then she added:

'Up to a point.'

This mad, botched creature might subject him to the thumb-screws and touch him with feathers at one and the same time, the Jew suspected.

'I have a house,' she continued warily. 'Down there. Beyond the orchard. Perhaps I shall show you some day. We shall see.'

Because the Jew must understand the essential mystery and

glory which Mrs Jolley and her like could never recognize. Yes, glory, because decay, even the putrid human kind, did not necessarily mean an end.

'I am not very often free.'

The man seemed uneasy. He was not refusing. Rather, he was attempting to resist something which he might have desired.

'I know,' said Miss Hare. 'The factory. But you must breathe sometimes. Even a plant must breathe.'

Her own breath had begun to sound spasmodic, though triumphant. She had never spoken like this before to any human being. Unexpected seeds of thought were germinating in her mind, and she had the impression she might shortly grasp things which had remained, hitherto, the secrets of others.

'Several times I have trespassed in your orchard,' the Jew confessed, 'and sat beneath your tree.'

'That is a beginning,' the woman suggested gently.

As a child she had learnt to help fledglings on to twigs, and maimed or frightened animals to walk.

'So you will come here again, won't you?' Now she was pleading, only this time it could have been in her own interests. 'I want you to tell me things. About your life. Won't you?'

She was quite greedy. Her hands were helping to trap those words which eluded her.

'There are a great many details, incidents, which you could not hope to understand,' the Jew replied, colder, it sounded. 'Naturally.'

'Oh, yes,' she agreed. 'There is always so much one does not understand. But it does not matter. Because some little thing, something quite unimportant, will show. So clearly. One is almost blinded by it,' she gasped.

Suddenly she was choking with ideas and words. She did hope he would not consider her an imbecile.

With the result that the Jew was ashamed of the momentary feeling of revulsion she had roused in him. Nor was his remorse unrelated to a sensation experienced on somewhat similar occasions, when, for usually superficial reasons, his own feelings caused him to reject inwardly a member of his race.

'It is a long and involved story,' he confessed, sinking down against the trunk of the tree, so that the bark scored the back of his neck, without his being aware. 'Perhaps I shall tell you some of it,' he said. 'Another time.'

But the strange part of it was: he began, there and then, whether he realized or not, and perhaps he did not, until fully launched in giving the woman the most intimate, sometimes the most horrible details of all that had ever happened to him. But, of course, in that sultry, motionless air, it was like addressing some animal or not even that. He remembered seeing fungi which suggested existence of the most passive order. And she could become perfectly still. It was only later that he recoiled from such an attitude, as if he had been guilty of treading on life.

But now, beneath the tree, booming with bees and silence, he had gone right back, drowsily, painfully, exquisitely, into memory. He had hardly ever allowed himself before.

And the woman listened.

'Yes?' she would murmur, but only in the beginning; or, 'Oh, dear, no! No, no, no!'

With her hands she would try to ease the air of some difficulty they were experiencing together, or wrestle with impending terrors.

Mordecai Himmelfarb was born in the North German town of Holunderthal, to a family of well-to-do merchants, some time during the eighteen-eighties. Moshe, the father, was a dealer in furs, through connexions in Russia, many of whom crossed Germany while Mordecai was still a child. The reason for their move had been discussed, mostly behind closed doors, by uncles and aunts, accompanied by the little moans of distress with which his mother received any report of injustice to their race. If Moshe the father remained the wrong side of the door, preferring to stroke his son's head, or even to take a beer at the *Stübchen*, it was not from lack of sympathy, but because he was a sensitive man. Any such crisis disturbed him so severely, he preferred to believe it had not occurred.

Mordecai the child observed the stream of relatives which poured in suddenly and away: the cousins from Moscow and Petersburg, no longer quite so rich or so glossy; their headachy, emotional wives, clinging to the remnants of panache, and still able to produce surprises, little objects in cloisonné and brilliants, out of the secret pocket in a muff. The whole of this colourful rout was sailing, they told him, for America, to liberty, justice, and the future. He watched them go, through the wrought-iron grille, from his own, safe, German hall.

There were the humbler Russians, too: people in darker, dustier clothes, who had suffered the same indignities, whom his mother received with reverent affection, his father with an increase in his usual joviality. There was, in particular, the Galician rabbi, whose face Mordecai could never after visualize, but remembered, rather, as a presence and a touch of hands.

Pogroms had reduced this distant cousin of his mother's to the clothes he wore and the faith he lived. Whatever his destination, he had paused for a moment at the house on the Holzgraben in Holunderthal, where his cousin had taken him into the small, rather dark room which she used for calls of a private nature, and the visits of embarrassed relatives. The mother sat, dressed as always by then, in black, smoothing her child's hair. But without looking at him, the little boy saw. In the obscure room, talking to the foreign rabbi, for the greater part in a language the boy himself had still to get, his mother had grown quite luminous. He would have liked to continue watching the lamp that had been lit in her, but from some impulse of delicacy, decided instead to lower his eyes. And then he had become, he realized, the object of attention. His mother was drawing him forward, towards the centre of the geometric carpet. And the rabbi was touching him. The rabbi, of almost womanly hands, was searching his forehead for some sign. He was laying his hands on the diffident child's damp hair. Talking all the time with his cousin in the foreign tongue. While the boy, inwardly resisting less, was bathed in the stream of words, suspended in a cloud of awe.

Finally, his father had come in, more than ever jovial, shooting his shiny cuffs and arranging his already immaculate moustache, with its distinct hairs, and lovely, lingering scent of pomade. Laughing, of course – because Moshe did laugh a lot, sometimes spontaneously, sometimes also when at a loss – he joined his wife and her cousin in their conversation, though he altered the complexion of it.

And said at last, in German, not exactly his own:

'Well, Mordecai, quite the little *zaddik*!'

And continued laughing, not out of malice – he was too agreeable for that. If his wife forgave him his lapse in taste, it was because he had often been proved a good man at heart.

Moshe Himmelfarb was a worldly Jew of liberal tastes. Success led him by a manicured hand, and continued to dress him with discretion. Nothing excessive about Moshe, unless it was his phiz, which would suddenly jar on those tolerant souls who collected Jews and make them wonder at their own eccentricity. Not that relations were thereby impaired. Moshe, in deep appreciation of the liberation, and truly genuine affection for the *goyim*, would not allow that. And he was right, of course. All those emancipated Jews of his acquaintance were ready to support him in his claim that the age of enlightenment and universal brotherhood had dawned at last in Western Europe. Jews and *goyim* were taking one another – intermittently, at least – moist-eyed to their breasts. The old, dark days were gone. Certainly there remained the problem of Eastern Europe, and deplorable incidents often occurred. Everybody knew that, and had been personally affected, but the whole house could not be swept clean at once. In the meantime, money was raised by Western Jewry to assist the victims, and to all such funds Moshe was always the first to subscribe. He loved to give, whether noticeably generous sums to numerous religious missions, the works of the German poets to his son, or presents of wine and cigars to those Gentiles who allowed themselves to be cultivated, and with whom he was so deeply, so gratefully in love.

Happy are the men who are able to tread transitional paths, scarcely looking to left or right and without distinguishing an end. Moshe Himmelfarb was one of them. If he had seldom been the object of direct criticism, except in trivial, family matters, it was because he had always taken care not to offer himself as a target. Unlike certain fanatics, he recognized his obligations to the community in which he lived, while observing the ceremony of his own. Mordecai remembered the silk hats in which his father presented himself, on civic and religious occasions alike. Ordered from an English hatter, Moshe's hats reflected that nice perfection which may be attained by the reasonable man. For Moshe Himmelfarb was nothing less. If he was also nothing more, that was after other, exacting, not to say reactionary standards, by which such lustrous hats could only be judged vain, hollow, and lamentably fragile.

Yet, along with his shortcomings, and his acquaintances, many of them men of similar mould, smelling of prosperity and cigars, and filled with every decent intention, Moshe continued to attend the synagogue of the Schillerstrasse. That they did not grow haggard, like some, from obeying the dictates of religion, was because they were reasonable, respectful, rather than religious men, and might have pointed out, if they had been openly accused, and if they had dared, that the Jewish soul was at last set free. The walls were down, the suffocating rooms were burst open, the chains of observance had been loosed.

They would still sway, however, all those worldly Jews of the synagogue in the Schillerstrasse, when the wind of prayer smote them. Standing beside his father, the little boy would watch and wait to be carried in the same direction. He would stroke the fringes of his father's *Tallith*, or bury his face in the soft folds. He would wait for his father to beat his breast for all the sins that were shut up inside. Then he himself would overflow with a melancholy joy that all was right in the forest of Jews in which he stood. All the necks were so softly swathed in wool, that, however fat and purple some of them looked, he was comforted, and would glance up, towards the gallery directly opposite, where he knew his mother to be. But behind the lattice. The boy would not see her, except in his mind's eye, where she sat very still and clear.

For Mordecai the man, his mother remained a sculptured figure. Whether, in fact, life and fashion had influenced her sufficiently to create a continuously evolving series of identities, his memory presented her as a single image: black dress; the high collar of net and whalebone, relieved by a little, seemly frill; the broad, yellowish forehead, marked with the scars of compassionate thought; eyes in which the deceits of this world were regretfully, but gently drowned; the mouth that overcame secret ailments, religious doubts, and all but one bitterness.

It was evident from the beginning that the boy was closer to the mother, although it was only much later established that she had given him her character. To casual acquaintances it was surprising that the father, so agreeable, so kind, so generous, did not have a greater influence. By contrast the mother made rather a sombre impression, stiff and given to surrounding herself with certain dark, uncouth, fanatically orthodox Jews, usually her relatives. Of course, the boy loved and honoured his good father, and would laugh and chatter with him as required, or listen gravely as the beauties of Goethe or the other poets were pointed out. So that Moshe was delighted with his son, and would bring expensive presents: a watch or a brass telescope, or collected works bound in leather. But it was out of the mother's silence and solitude of soul that the rather studious, though normal, laughing, sometimes too high-spirited little boy had been created.

Frau Himmelfarb had never become reconciled to the well-ordered, too specious life of the North German town. As she walked with her child against the painted drop of Renaissance houses, or formal magnificence of Biedermeier mansions, her incredulous eyes would reject the evidence that men had thus confined the infinite. Only in certain dark medieval streets, Mordecai remembered, did his mother seem to escape from the oppression of her material surroundings. She herself would blur, as strange, apparently inexpressible words came struggling softly out of her mouth, and her feet would almost dance as she hurried over the uneven cobbles, skipping the puddles of dirty water, very light. She would visit numbers of the rather smelly, frightening houses and bring presents and examine children, whether for ailments or their knowledge of God, and even hitch up her skirt over her petticoat, before going down on her knees to scrub a floor neglected by the sick. Along the airless alleys, in the dark houses of the Jewish poor, his mother's Galician spirit was released – which, in his memory, had seldom happened anywhere else, unless during the visit of her cousin, the destitute rabbi, in their own ante-room, or while writing letters to her many other relatives.

The mother was one of a scattered family. It was her sorrow and pride. She liked to bring her writing things as though she had been a visitor and sit at the round table, with its cloth of crimson plush, in preference to the ormolu desk on which Moshe had lovingly insisted. Then the little boy would play with the plush pompons and occasionally glance at the letters as they grew, and shuffle the used envelopes, from which she would allow him later to soak the stamps. He had known his mother, on a single rainy afternoon, seal envelopes for Poland, Rumania, the United States, even China and Ecuador. Until, finally, there was nothing of her left to give.

He realized only very much later the important part her dispersed family had played in his mother's secret life: how, in her mind, their omnipresence might have ensured and hastened redemption for the whole world. Such a conviction, implied, though certainly never expressed, gave her a kind of distinction amongst the numerous pious ladies who were always in transit through her house, eating *Streuselkuchen* and drinking coffee, organizing charitable projects, announcing births, marriages, and deaths, daring sometimes even to indulge, in the presence of their hostess, in bursts of frivolous, not to say unseemly chat. But always returning to one point. The women clung together like a ball of brown bees, driven by the instinct of their faith, intoxicated with the honey of their God.

The presence of that God amongst the walnut furniture of the sumptuous house – for Himmelfarbs had moved from above the shop before Mordecai was able to remember – was unquestioned by the worldly, but prudently respectful Moshe, taken for granted by the little boy, even by the confident young man whom the latter eventually became, and who turned sceptical, not of his religion, rather, of his own need for it. Religion, like a winter overcoat, grew oppressive and superfluous as spring developed into summer, and the natural sources of warmth were gradually revealed. But there was no mistaking the love and respect the young man kept for the enduring qualities of his old, discarded coat. In the solstice of his self-love, in the heat of physical ardour, he would melt with nostalgia at the thought of it.

In the meantime, however, the little boy remained wrapped in the warm reality of the garment they had given him to wear.

When he was only six, the mother remarked with the casualness she always adopted for important matters:

'Do you realize, Moshe, it is time the child began to receive instruction?'

'*Yoÿ!*' The father, who loved his own joke, winced to express horror. 'Do you want to load the boy already? And worst of all, with Hebrew?'

'Yes,' she answered seriously. 'It is our own tongue.'

Moshe was often inclined to wonder how he had come to marry his wife. Whom he loved, however. So it was agreed.

It was usual for the boys of their acquaintance to attend the classes of Herr Ephraim Glück, the *Melamed*, but because of some special confidence the mother had, the Cantor Katzmann was engaged to teach her son the alphabet. Which the latter mastered at astonishing speed. And began shortly to write phrases, and recite prayers. And grew vain. He would turn his head aside, and mumble what he already knew too well, or declaim too loudly, with a shameful spiritual arrogance.

On one occasion the Cantor was forced to mention:

'If a Jew is proud, Mordecai, it is all the harder when he bites the dust. As he certainly will.'

The Cantor himself was a humble man, with several squint-eyed children, and a wife who nagged. His voice was his only glory. When it had been poured out to the dregs, he would appear emptied indeed, falling back upon his chair with a smile of deathly content. Mordecai remembered him especially after the climax of *Rosh Hashanah* and *Yom Kippur*, when it could have been the Cantor had attempted the impossible. The white, closed eyelids would not so much as flutter, as he sat and smiled faintly from behind them. He was a small man and his pupil loved him in memory, more than he had respected him in life.

At the age of ten the boy entered the gymnasium. Already before *Bar Mitzvah*, he had embarked on Greek, Latin, French, with English for preference. He had begun to carry off the prizes. Sources, both informed and uninformed, insisted that Mordecai ben Moshe was exceptionally brilliant.

'You see, Malke,' the father remarked, preparing in his mind an additional, expensive prize, 'our Martin is surely intended to become a man of some importance.'

Because he had developed the ridiculous and distasteful habit of calling their son by a German name, his wife would pinch her eyebrows together as if suffering physical pain, although she would let it be known that, in spite of her expression of torture, she was grateful for the boy's success.

'*Ach*,' she exclaimed. 'Yes,' she said, and found she had a cough. 'We have known from the beginning he was no fool.'

How her cough continued to rack her.

'But,' she was able at last to resume, 'all that is by the way. I only ask that Mordecai shall be remembered as a man of faith.'

So that the father's pleasure was cut by his wife's stern consistency, and in time he ceased to love, while continuing to honour. In his casual, but always amiable way, he allowed her to bear many of the burdens, because he saw she was suited to it, and she succeeded manfully, for inside her rather delicate body she had considerable strength of mind.

Alone with her son, she would often unbend, even after he was grown. She would become quite skittish in her private joy, with the result that the boy was sometimes ashamed for what appeared unnecessary, not to say unnatural, in one of natural dignity.

'Mordecai ben Moshe!' she would refer to him half-aloud, half-laughing.

To establish, as it were, an unmistakable identity.

She had the habit of forming in his presence a suggestion of ideas, sometimes in German, more often in Yiddish, and as he learnt to follow her murmur, he forged a chain out of it. There were many tales, too, of relatives and saints. She could become inspired. Her *Seder* table was the materialization of simple dogma. For the rites of the Sabbath she had a particular genius, and, watching the candles increase in light and stature as her hands coaxed, her husband was again convinced of his own genuine desire to worship.

By far the most agreeable of all the feast days observed by the family on the Holzgraben was that of *Succoth*, for it made the least spiritual demands on the father, or so the son began to sense. Ignoring, for some atavistic reason, the considerable

102

triangular garden, with its smell of toadstools and damp leaves, they improvised their tabernacle beneath the lattice on the balcony. The meals could not appear too often or too soon, which they ate beneath the stars at *Succoth*, above the *Stadtwald* at Holunderthal. The symbols of citron and palm flourished happily in the father's somewhat shallow mind. Because, by now it had been made clear, the bleak heights of Atonement were not for Moshe, only the foothills of Thanksgiving. In the circumstances, the additional duty laid upon the mother was a source of embarrassment to the parents; also in time, the father suspected, to the son. On returning home from the synagogue, after the travail and exhaustion of *Yom Kippur*, he might pinch the boy's cheek and look into his eyes and wonder to which side Mordecai was going to be drawn. As his hopes conflicted with his fears, Moshe would sigh, and again, more loudly, when the first mouthful of reviving coffee passed his lips.

The hopes of all converged upon *Bar Mitzvah*. The candidate approached the ceremony with a dangerous amount of confidence. He received the phylacteries and the shawl, together with many desirable presents from parents, uncles, aunts and cousins. He delivered ringingly and with a sculptural logic his discourse on the chosen subject, with the result that aunts turned to congratulate one another long before he had finished. They could have devoured the feverish face – to some extent a replica of each of theirs –underneath the plastered hair and pretty *Käppchen*. Mordecai was entranced, and did not listen continuously to anybody's voice unless it was his own. Somewhere behind him on the platform wandered the father who was relinquishing, not without a hint of tears, spiritual responsibility. There were some amongst Frau Himmelfarb's relatives who could not contain their ironic smiles on noticing poor Malke's Moshe. But were immediately recalled to a state of adequate reverence by a flash of silver from the Scrolls. After the ceremony there was a delicious meal at which the formally dedicated boy was caressed and flattered. His triumph made him proud, shy, exalted, indifferent, explosively hilarious and uncommunicative of his true feelings – if he was conscious of what they were.

Who, indeed, could tell which way the *Bar Mitzvah* boy would go? Certainly not the self-congratulating father; perhaps the mother, through the tips of her fingers or subtler colloquy of souls.

In the comfortable but ugly house, in the closed circle of

relatives and friends, protected by the wings of angels, illuminated by the love of God, Mordecai accepted the pattern which his race, his religion, and his parents had ordained. But there was, in addition, an outside world, which his mother feared, for which his father yearned and of which Mordecai became increasingly aware. There the little waxen, silent boy grew into a bony, rasping youth, the dark down straggling like an indecision on his upper lip, the lips themselves blooming far too soon, the great nose assuming manifest importance. It was the age of mirrors, and in their surfaces Mordecai attempted regularly to solve the mystery of himself. He was growing muscular, sensual, yellow: hideous to some, provocative to others. What else, nobody was yet allowed to see.

'Tell me, you ugly Jew, what it feels like to be one?' his friend Jürgen Stauffer asked.

In fun, of course. Friendship and laughter still prevailed. The forest flecked the boys' skins, as they rubbed along, elbow to elbow, the soles of their boots made slippery by thicknesses of fallen leaves.

'Tell me!' Jürgen laughed and insisted.

He was of that distinctive tint of German gold, affection showing in the shallows of his mackerel eyes.

'Oh, like something that runs on a hundred legs,' Himmelfarb replied. 'Or no legs at all. A snake, for instance. Or scorpion. Anyway, specially created to be the death of Gentiles.'

Then they laughed louder and together. Sundays had become warmer than the Sabbath for the young Jew, when he walked with his friend, Jürgen Stauffer, on the wilder side of the *Stadtwald* at Holunderthal.

'Tell me,' Jürgen asked, 'about the Passover sacrifice.'

'When we kill the Christian child?'

'So it seems!'

How Jürgen laughed.

'And cut him up, and drink the blood, and put slices in a *Brötchen* to send the parents?' Mordecai had learnt how to play.

'*Ach, Gott!*' Jürgen Stauffer laughed.

How his teeth glistened.

'Old Himmelfurz!' he cried. '*Du liebes Rindvieh!*'

Then they were hitting each other and grunting. Their skins were melting together. They could not wrestle enough on the beds of leaves. Afterwards they lay panting and looked up through the exhausted green to discuss a future still incalculable, except for the sustaining thread of friendship. In the

104

silences they would sigh beneath the weight of their affection for each other.

'But when I become a cavalry officer – and there is no question of anything else, because of Uncle Max – and you are the professor of languages, it is not very likely we shall ever see each other again,' Jürgen Stauffer reasoned.

'Then you must arrange to ride your horses,' Mordecai suggested, 'round and round whichever university I honour with my presence.'

'It is a vice, Martin, never to be serious. A hopeless, hopeless, vicious vice!'

From where he lay, Jürgen Stauffer thumped his friend.

'You are the hopeless one, not to choose a more civilized career.'

'But I like horses,' Jürgen protested. 'And then I am also a bit stupid.'

Himmelfarb could have kissed his friend.

'Stupid? You are the original ass!'

If they had not tired themselves out, they might have wrestled some more, but instead they lay and listened to the blaze of summer and their own contentment.

Occasionally the young Jew was invited to his friend's house, for the parents' liberal attitude allowed them to receive regardless of race. Gerhard Stauffer, the father, was of course the publisher. He even loved books, and an undeserved failure would make him suffer more than an obvious success would cause him to rejoice. His wife, a minor actress in her youth, had retired into life and marriage equipped with a technique for theatre. Frau Stauffer was able to convince a guest that the scene they had just enacted together contributed immensely to the play's success.

'Martin shall sit beside *me*,' Frau Stauffer would emphasize, patting the place on the sofa with the touch the situation required. 'Now that we are *comfortable*,' she would decide, while inclining just that little in the direction of her guest, 'you must tell me what you have been *doing*. Provided it has been *disreputable*. I refuse to listen to anything else. On such a *damp* afternoon, you must *curdle* my blood with indiscretions.'

Then Frau Stauffer smiled that deliberate smile. She had remained of the opinion that any line may be 'improved', and that every scene needed 'lifting up.'

But the boy was conscious of his lack of talent. Seated beside his hostess on her cloud, he remained the victim of his awkward body.

Or, advancing from an opposite direction, the host would court their unimportant guest, inviting him to give his point of view, showering newspaper articles and books.

'Have you discovered Dehmel?' Herr Stauffer might inquire, or: 'What do you think, Martin, of Wedekind? I would be most interested to hear your honest opinion.'

As if it mattered to that grave man.

The embarrassed boy was gratified, but could not escape too soon, back to his friend. The attentions of the parents flattered more in retrospect.

'You see,' said Jürgen, without envy, 'you are the respected intellectual. I am the German stable boy.'

But it could have been for some such reason that the young Jew admired his friend.

There was the elder brother, too, who would emerge mysteriously from his room, suffering from acne and a slight astigmatism and eating a slice of buttered bread. Konrad has outgrown his strength and must fortify himself, Frau Stauffer explained. Konrad came and went, ignoring whatever existed outside the orbit of his own ego. He seemed to despise in particular all younger boys – or was it only the Jewish ones? – that was not yet made clear.

'What does he do all the time in his room?' Mordecai asked the younger brother.

'He is studying,' replied the latter, with the air of one who could not be expected to take further interest. 'He is all right,' he said. 'Only a bit stuck-up.'

On that occasion Konrad Stauffer came out of his room chewing at a *Brötchen* with caraway seeds on top.

'What,' he said to Mordecai, 'you here again! Are you perhaps *en pension?*'

As everybody else was embarrassed, he laughed a little for his own joke.

There was the sister, Mausi, still a little girl. Her plaits glistened like the tails of certain animals. Once she threw her arms round the Jew's waist and pressed against him with all her strength and tried to throw him.

'I am stronger than you!' she claimed.

But neither proved nor provoked.

She stood laughing into the bosom of his shirt. Her breath burned where the V opened on his bare skin.

Best and most alarming of all were evenings in the big salon, when girls came in bows and sashes, their necks smelling of *kölnisches Wasser*. There were girls already corseted stiff and a few real young men, often the sons of cavalry officers. These absolute phenomena, themselves cadets, always knew what to do, with the result that younger boys would listen humiliated to their own, crude, breaking voices, and mirrors reminded them that the pimples were still lurking in their tufts of down.

One evening, after their elders had withdrawn to the library to amuse themselves at cards, somebody of real daring devised the most scandalous game.

'Which person in the room do you like best?' it was asked of each in turn. 'Why?' The next impossible question followed, and others, all headed in the inevitable and most personal direction.

Giggles and the braying of the adolescent jackass, widened the circles of embarrassment.

'Whom do you like, Mausi Stauffer?' finally it had to be asked.

Mausi Stauffer did not hesitate.

'Martin Himmelfarb,' she said.

Some of the young ladies might have burst, if their whalebone had not contained them. In the circumstances, they rocked and wheezed.

'Why, Mausi?' asked Cousin Fritz, the son of Uncle Max. The scar across his left cheek appeared unnaturally distinct.

'Because,' said Mausi. 'Because he is interesting, I suppose.'

'Come, now!' complained an upright young woman in steel spectacles, with a pale, flat rosette of a mouth. 'That is a weak answer. You may have to pay a forfeit. Fifty strokes on the palm of your hand from the edge of a ruler.'

Mausi screamed. She could not have borne it.

'We want to give you another chance,' said Cousin Fritz, so beautiful and hateful in his cadet's uniform. '*Why* does this Himmelfarber appeal to you?'

He made the name sound particularly exotic and ridiculous.

Mausi screamed. She tossed her plaits into the air.

'Because,' she cried and snickered and wound her thin legs together, and perspired in her crushed muslin. 'Because,' she screeched, in a voice they were dragging out of her, 'he is like,' she still hesitated, 'a kind of black *buck*!'

The bronzes might have tumbled from their pedestals, if, at that moment, a spinster lady devoted to the family had not returned in search of her scarf, and decided instinctively to remain.

In that same moment, Mordecai made down the passage for the lavatory.

As he came out again, Konrad Stauffer was trying the door.

'Oh!' exclaimed Konrad, mostly with his stomach, and recoiled.

He looked quite pale and blank, but could have been rehearsing a speech.

'Just a lot of stupid Germans,' he managed to utter breathily. 'Germans are all animals.'

'Aren't we also Germans?' Mordecai suggested.

'Those who pass judgement always exclude themselves,' the spotty young man replied and laughed. 'Haven't you found that out? Oh, dear!' He sighed. 'I don't propose to get involved in anything else tonight. I am going up to my room.'

Mordecai did not know what to make of Konrad.

Nor did he see him again for years. One result of the evening was that Frau Stauffer apparently decided to bring down the curtain on the comedy they had been enacting in their relationship with the young Jew. Jürgen grew increasingly elusive. Attempts at even indirect inquiry would start him kicking holes in the ground, or else he would mumble and fix his eyes on some point, which, he let it be understood, lay outside his friend's field of vision.

Often in this suffocating situation, Mordecai would struggle for breath. Then his mother, noticing his dark eyelids and the colour of his skin, prescribed a tonic and, after only half a bottle, he slept with a whore called Marianne, who lived beneath a gable in one of the older streets of the town. His body was flooded with a new, though at first dreadful, relief.

'You Jews!' Marianne remarked, looking him over during a pause, for which she was sufficiently generous not to charge. 'The little bit they snip off only seems to make you hotter.'

As for her client, he stared exhausted at her enormous beige nipples, and wondered whether his instincts would know how to navigate the frail craft in which he had embarked alone.

Thus committed to the flesh, the ceremonies of his parents' house soon became intolerable. The Sabbath, for instance, all through his boyhood a trance of innocent perfection, in which he would not have been surprised to see the Bride herself cross the threshold, was now transformed into a wilderness of hours, where good aunts and all those ugly girl cousins were continually setting traps of questions to catch his guilt. Prayers and food choked him equally as he waited for sunset and the scent of spices to wake him from his nightmare. Lovingly. And he, in turn, loved all that he was rejecting, not so much

108

by choice, it seemed to him at first in moments of self-exoneration, but by arrangement between unknown persons who controlled his future.

The severest torture remained the trial by charity. There were the humble, sometimes even ragged, unwashed individuals, whom his father, from sense of duty, or the need for self-congratulation, collected at the synagogue and brought home to the Sabbath table, where Martin-Mordecai would exert himself to offer friendly words, and recommend the most delicious dishes, to atone for the disgust the visitors roused in him. There was one creature in particular: a little dyer, whose skin was bathed in indigo; the palms of his hands were mapped indelibly in purple. This man's material affliction impressed itself on his conscience the evening the dyer slipped while crossing one of Moshe's handsome rugs. The boy felt himself to be in a way responsible. As his hands slithered on the old Jew's greasy coat, he grabbed hold of what seemed a handful of rag, and just prevented the guest from falling. But his own fright and nausea were in his mouth; he might have been the one who had all but suffered a serious fall, whereas the old man grew servile with gratitude for what he called a gentlemanly act, was moved to caress every inch of his saviour's back, and to bestow pretentious titles such as Crutch of the Infirm, and Protector of the Poor.

After Mordecai had escaped from the room and was washing himself, his mother came and stood in the doorway, to say in her driest voice, which tender feelings would force her to adopt:

'You are upset, my dear boy, and have not yet experienced the hundredth part.'

She watched her son thoughtfully.

'Dry your hands quickly now,' she coaxed, gentler, 'and come on back to us. We must not allow that poor man to guess.'

She would have liked to use her compassion to comfort those nearest to her, but the loving woman was unable to. More often than not, she saw her words salt the wounds.

The house was full of twilight situations and shaken attitudes. The son became amused. He would raise one shoulder and compose his mouth as the *Kiddush* introduced the Sabbath. He would barb the words of prayers with mockery, to aim at innocent targets. Even though he failed to destroy what he had loved most, his perversity had developed to the point where the attempt remained his painful substitute for ritual.

Then, as soon as his duties had been at least outwardly discharged, he would rush out. He would roam the streets, looking into lit windows, brush against passers-by and apologize with an effusiveness which could only be interpreted as insolence. Now that he was filled with a rage to live, the scents of the streets maddened him. He would try the breasts of the whores, propped on cushions, on their window-sills. He had an insatiable appetite for white flesh, of pale complaisant German girls, pressed against stucco, or writhing in the undergrowth of parks, beside stagnant water in a smell of green decay.

If he had not hardened quickly, he might have been consumed by his own disgust.

But he grew steely. He plastered down his winged hair. He wore a moustache. And studied.

All through the period of his worst disintegration, Mordecai remained, to the innocent and unaware, dedicated solely to his books. He did, in fact, cling to them, like fingers to a raft. And what more solid and reasonable than words as such? It was only in the permutations and combinations that they dissolved into that same current which threatened to suck down the whole, boiling, grinning crew of desperate, drowning souls.

At the university the young man's intellectual activities were narrowed down to the study of his preferred language – English. Its bland and rather bread-like texture became his manna. But, in opposition to his will and intentions, he would find his mind hankering after the obdurate tongue he had got as a boy from the Cantor Katzmann. His proficiency in Hebrew had grown with intermittent attention, and he would often read, late at night, both for instruction, and for the bitter pleasure of it.

In the second decade of the century Mordecai Himmelfarb received his Doctorate in English, and shortly after was informed that he would be permitted to continue his studies at the University of Oxford.

Moshe was overjoyed, not only for the impression the event would make on his acquaintances, but because of his admiration for the English, for the excellent quality of their cloth, boots, and the silk hats he liked to wear on formal occasions. If he also sensed the distance which separated the English temperamentally from himself, that added, if anything, to their fascination. And now his own son was to be removed to the side of the elect. The gap in their relationship, already wide, would necessarily widen. Already the old man visualized himself, the self-sacrificing Jewish father, standing on railway platforms in the steam from trains. The joyous, painful tears spurted in anticipation. For, that which moved and charmed Moshe most, was that which receded irretrievably: departing trains, the faces of the *goyim*, the relationship with his own son and, if he had dared to think, let alone whisper – he who contributed so generously to the Zionist Movement – the redemption of Israel as a possible event.

It was Moshe who broke the news to the boy's mother, and in that way, perhaps, less pain was caused.

Frau Himmelfarb, who was darning a sock, did not at first answer. She continued looking at the sock with the rather myopic patience characteristic of her.

'I did expect, Malke, that you would grasp,' her husband had begun to emphasize, 'the immense advantage it will give the boy if he decides on an academic career.'

His wife was looking closely at the sock.

'Well?' he asked, and reasonably, but was immediately driven to support his argument, not exactly by ranting, but almost: 'It is time we Jews recognized the world has changed!' Here Moshe actually trembled. 'All the opportunities that are open to us now!'

'Ah, Moshe! Moshe!' sighed the woman, in the way that had always irritated him most.

'That is not an answer!' he protested.

'However you and others may transform him,' his wife replied, 'I pray that God will recognize a good Jew.'

'It is of more importance today,' said the father, 'that the world should recognize a good man.'

All of which was heard, as it happened, by their son, who had come in, and was listening with that cynical, yet affectionate amusement with which he now received any idea that originated in his parents.

'Ah, Moshe' – his mother sighed again – 'you forget that when both kinds are divided up into good, bad, and indifferent, the Jews will remain distinct from men.'

'There you are!' fumed the father, realizing at last that his son was present. 'I make the simple announcement that you will be going to Oxford, and your mother embarks on a philosophical, not to say racial argument. Of Jews and men! I hope I am a man! What are you?'

'I would like to think I am both,' the young fellow replied, 'but sometimes wonder whether I am anything at all.'

Because this was nothing like what he had intended to say, Mordecai smiled.

'Then it has come to that!' cried the mother. 'There, Moshe! Where can it all end?'

In her distress she kept on turning and stretching the meticulously darned sock.

'That does not mean you may expect me to cut my throat!' the son continued, laughing, jerking up his chin and baring his teeth in what had, this time, only the rudiments of a smile.

'It is terrible to see one's best intentions completely misinterpreted.' The father felt himself justified in moaning.

'Oh, but I do appreciate them!' the son answered with dutiful alacrity. 'All you have ever done. All the kindnesses. You have been a good father. And you need not doubt I shall try to repay you.'

Moshe Himmelfarb began to cry.

'And mother,' the son almost shouted, because of his father's emotion, and because the mere mention of his mother involved him more deeply than ever in the metaphysical thicket from which he was hoping to tear himself free. 'Whose guidance,' he babbled, his voice carrying him to a crescendo of melodrama of which he himself was most aware, 'whose example and deeds, might well redeem the whole race. Excepting one who is beyond redemption!'

'We must certainly pray for you,' Malke Himmelfarb remarked gently, hanging her head above the now crumpled and rejected sock. 'My poor son!'

Long after he had rushed from the room, Mordecai continued to visualize the situation: the black hairs on his father's elegant, but frail and ineffectual wrist; the pulse, actual or imagined, in his mother's yellow temple; and the ornate, heartrending furniture, of which he had explored every grain, every crack and blemish, under cover of conversation, day-dream, and prayer.

Now he would have prayed, but could not. He was suffering and indeed continued to suffer from a kind of spiritual amnesia. Remembering an incident in the examination room, in which, at the end of an agonizing hour, the Italian language had flooded back into his mind, he hoped that some such release would take place on the present occasion – or he could have waited, weeks, if necessary, or even months.

But it did not.

At most, an occasional onset of compassion would deflect the blade of his cynicism, as on the evening when he watched his own father leave a fairground on the outskirts of the town, accompanied by a brewer's clerk named Goltz, known to him by sight and repute, and two anonymous girls of unmistakable occupation. As the young man watched from the shelter of a clump of pollarded trees, the bluish-white glimmer from the flares sluiced the faces of the three unsteady Gentiles and their Jewish clown. The action of the flickering light made the unnatural abandon of the elderly, respectable Jew appear quite maniacal. He, too, was flickering and fluctuating as he led the way through the hubbub of shouting and jerky music. His companions seemed to have reached the stage where only the conventions of revelry are obeyed. The clerk stopped for a moment and stuck his head inside a bush to vomit. The mouths of the others opened from habit in the dreadful dough of their faces to emit song or wind. Or an arm attempted to return the imagined pressure of an arm. Or lips sucked the air in imitation of a kiss. So the revellers advanced and almost brushed against their judge in passing. Without moving, the latter continued to watch, and was able to distinguish the pores of their skins, the roots of their hair, the specks of gold flashing in their teeth. If he did not catch their words, it was because those were drowned in the tumult of his distress, which continued long after the ridiculous old satyr, who was also his father, had disappeared. That his own desires were similar, that he had breathed on similar smeary faces, of similar sweaty girls and fumbled at the scenty dresses, made the incident too familiar and more intolerable.

Yet the young man had lived long enough, if only by one day, to embrace his father on retiring the following night. For a moment he had stood behind the chair. There was the scraggy, reprehensible neck. Would he plunge his knife, which he had learnt to use with the skill of any *Schochet*? Then the thought began to tremble in him: that reason is far too imperfect a weapon. So he had bent forward instead and Moshe interpreted what he received as an expression of gratitude, not of pity. The old Jew was at once brimming over with pride for the grateful son who appreciated all that was being done for him.

Very soon after, Mordecai left for Oxford. Although in those days the talk was of war, the Kaiser's unpredictable temper, and the refusal of the French nation to respect German ideals, it seemed most unlikely to the young man that an international situation would ignore the crucial stage in his career. Dressed in a top-coat of excellent, sober cloth and cut, and a travelling cap in tartan tweed, the kind thought of one of his

aunts, he presented a fine figure as they stamped about the railway platform. They were all there. Moshe had fallen in love
with the new leather, monogrammed luggage, with which he
had provided his son. But the mother could have been dazed
by the appearances of a material world, of which she had only
been allowed glimpses hitherto, and her clothes, as always on
occasions of importance and splendour, looked as though they
had been brought down from an attic. As for the son, he was
only too relieved at the thought of relinquishing the identity
with which his parents were convinced they had endowed him.
And at last the train did pull out. And later in the day the
boat sailed in, into the fog.

At Oxford Himmelfarb continued to distinguish himself
scholastically. Determined at the beginning to restrict himself
to books, he soon discovered he was an influence on the lives of
human beings. He was very prepossessing in his Semitic way.
He developed an ease of manner. Men hoped for his respect,
women competed for his heart, and he would always allow them
to believe they had succeeded.

There was perhaps one young woman who roused and sustained his passionate interest. The young people went so far as
to discuss marriage during their attachment, though neither
thought to ask a parent's advice on the desirability of the
match. Catherine was the daughter of a reprobate earl. The
father's pursuit of pleasure and the mother's early death had
allowed the girl more freedom than was customary. Frail and
pale, simple in almost all her tastes, and of exquisitely pure expression, Catherine could have passed for an angel if she had
chosen discretion. But Catherine did not choose. And her behaviour was frequently discussed, in raffish circles with knowledge and appreciation, in polite ones with imagination and
distaste. Fortified by birth and fortune, Catherine herself was
able to ignore opinion up to a point, and seemed to rise from
each debauch purer and whiter than before.

Their refinements of sensuality persuaded the young Jew that
he loved the girl. Each was perhaps a little dazzled by the
incandescence they achieved together and the lover naturally
wounded when, at what might have been thought the height of
the affair, his mistress was discovered in a hotel bedroom with
an Indian prince. For the first time Catherine must have sensed
the narrowness of the plank she was treading, for it became
known almost at once that she had gone abroad, for an indefinite period, with an aunt.

Her lover did receive a letter from Florence:

114

My darling M.,

I wonder whether you will ever be able to forgive me the shattering mistake I caused you to make. I do not expect it. I expect very little of anyone, realizing how little may be expected of myself. But would like to act sentimental, on such a wet night, in this stuffy little town, full of English Ladies Living Abroad. I might feel desperate if I had not learnt you off by heart, and were not still able to bring you close, in spite of the revulsion I know the actuality would produce in you . . .

The letter continued in somewhat literary strain, about the 'little green hills of Tuscany, with their exciting undertones of sensuous brown', but he had no inclination to read any farther. He tossed the ball into the basket, and loosened his tie. He did not see Catherine again, although from time to time he read about her. She continued to lead a life in accordance with the conventions of her temperament: in her maturity she was almost strangled by a boxer in a mews in Pimlico, and died old, during a bombing raid of the Second War, in a home for inebriates at Putney.

As for Mordecai, he now returned to his studies, with a rage that belonged to youth and an austerity that he had inherited from his mother, until, shortly after destroying the distasteful letter from his mistress, he received another, of a far more disturbing nature, from his father:

My dear son,

I can no longer postpone informing you of the momentous decision I have been forced to make. To come at once to the point: I had been receiving instruction for some time past from a priest of the Roman Catholic Church, and was baptized, I am happy to be able to tell you, last Thursday afternoon. A weight is lifted off my mind. For the first time in my life, I feel myself truly to be free. *I am a Christian!*

After a lifetime spent studying the Jewish problem, it seems to me that this is the only solution of it. I hardly like to write *practical* solution, but that is the word which came into my mind. To give so little and receive so much! Because it must be obvious to all but fools that the advantages of every kind are enormous. However, as one who has the fate of our people sincerely at heart, I do not wish to stress those advantages, only to pray that many more of us repent of our stubborn, fruitless ways.

You, Martin, I have felt for some time, are undergoing a crisis in faith. All the more likely, then, that reason may lead you into the right and safe path, when you are ready to decide. It is your dear mother for whom I fear there is little hope. She will choose to remain caught for ever in the thicket of Jewish self-righteousness, and the reasonable step I have taken will only continue to cause her pain. Still, I shall pray that some miracle will unite our two souls at last.

I will not trouble you with details of our business house – it is, besides, the summer season – nor shall I introduce comments on the international situation into a communication which is probably in itself a source of surprise and, possibly, dear boy, distress.

I shall remain always

Your affectionate father...

Mordecai had never felt emptier than on finishing reading his father's letter. If he himself had dried up, there had always been the host of others, and particularly parents, who remained filled with the oil and spices of tradition. And now his father's phial was broken; all the goodness was run out. One corner of memory might never be revisited.

All through this phase of private desolation, the young Jew forced himself to go about his business, although his associates frequently suspected him of watching somebody else, who stood unseen behind their backs. Of the letters he composed to his apostate father, he sent the one that least conveyed his feelings and must have caused a pang of disappointment in the recipient. For the letter was indifferent, not to say feeble, in the reactions it expressed.

Of his mother, Mordecai did not dare think, nor did he mention his father's act in the letter he immediately wrote to her.

It did seem for the first time that his own brilliantly inviolable destiny was threatened, by an increased shrivelling of the spirit in himself, as well as by the actions of those whom he had considered almost as statues in a familiar park. Now the statues had begun to move. Great fissures were beginning to appear, besides, in what he had assumed to be the solid mass of history. Time was no longer congealed, but flowing. Some of the young man's acquaintances had already packed their bags. They reminded him that war must come and that, as a German, it was his duty to return with them before it was too late, to serve the Fatherland.

Scarcely Jew and scarcely German, Himmelfarb was still debating when he received the letter from his mother:

My dearest Mordecai,

Your father will have written you some account of what I cannot bring myself to mention. You will see that I am at present with my sisters, where I shall remain until I have recovered from my loss. They are very kind, considerate, more than I deserve.

Oh, Mordecai, I can only think I have failed him in some way and dread that I may also fail my son.

Mordecai averted his face. He could not bear to see his mother. It was as though she had not survived the rending of the garment.

The letter did, at least, release her son from the doldrums of indecision. Very soon Mordecai found himself adrift on the North Sea. Ostensibly he was returning home. So far his will had supported him, but only so far. That which his pride had begun to represent as a steel cable was, in fact, a thread which other people cruelly jerked, tangled with their clumsy fingers, and even threatened to break. So the sea air wandered in and out of that insubstantial cabin formed by the young man's bones. His once handsome skin had lost its tones of ivory to a dirty yellow-grey. Those of his fellow passengers who addressed him soon moved away across the deck, sensing a situation with which their own mediocrity could not deal, of hallucination, or perhaps even madness. A few, however, plumped for a simpler explanation: the damned Jew was drunk.

Drunk or sober he arrived at Holunderthal with admirable punctuality. Inside the skeleton of the station, the faces of strangers appeared convinced of their timelessness. Only his father, in his dark, correct coat, admitted age. His moustache was fumbling with a welcome. Or some undue perplexity. The young man's Aunt Zipporah, his mother's sister, a woman he had always disliked, for a certain smell of poverty and association with disaster, spoke to him out of a strained throat.

The aunt and the father were making way for each other.

'Yes,' said Mordecai. 'We had the kind of crossing one expects.'

And waited.

'Tell me,' he said, finally. 'It is my mother.'

And listened.

The aunt began to cry like a rat that has been caught at last. Trapped inside the girders of Holunderthal *Hauptbahnhof*, it sounded awful. Inquisitive passers-by slowed down and waited for a revelation to dictate their proper attitude.

'Yes!' cried his Aunt Zipporah. 'Your mother. On Saturday night. But over quickly, Mordecai.'

His father had begun to nail him with his voice.

'It appears there was some internal malady she had been hiding from us, Mordecai.'

The aunt's grief gushed afresh.

'*Oÿ-yoÿ-yoÿ!* Moshe! There was no malignancy. I have it from Dr Ehrenzweig. Not the least trace of a malignancy.'

117

Such luxuriant grief made that of her brother-in-law sound mercilessly arid. But his desperation was of a different kind.

'Dr Ehrenzweig assures me,' he insisted, 'that she did not suffer. No pain, Mordecai. Up to the end.'

'Did not suffer! Did not suffer!' The aunt's voice blew and flapped. 'There are different ways of suffering! Dr Ehrenzweig was responsible only for his patient's body.'

The father had seized his son by an elbow.

'This woman is vindictive, because, naturally, she is biased!' Moshe shouted.

The fact was, Mordecai knew, his mother had, simply, died.

So they walked on, and into a *Droschke*, over the heads of half a dozen carnations, which some other traveller had discarded on finding them, perhaps, unbearable.

For the few weeks before the outbreak of war, young Himmelfarb remained in his father's house. The father brought presents to lay at his son's feet, without, however, finding forgiveness. The son resumed relations with relations, with the community who had received him at *Bar Mitzvah*, for, officially, he was still a Jew. But the voices of the elders would threaten to dry up as he approached, and upon his entering a room, young, modest girls would lower their eyes and blush. He accepted that he was an outcast. He only failed to realize that neither his father's apostasy, nor his own spiritual withdrawal was the true cause of their suspicion, and that almost every soul must endure the same period of probation before receiving orders.

Of gentile friendships, none remained. Jürgen Stauffer was reined in somewhere, waiting to ride across Europe; nor did Martin-Mordecai care to visualize his friend's face, its adolescence pared away to the bones of manhood, the chivalry of minnesinger translated into *Wille zur Macht* in the expression of the mackerel eyes. Stauffer the publisher had died of a heart, Mordecai was told; his wife had become involved in a prolonged and unpredictable middle-age. Only the elder son appeared once, briefly, under a hat, in the doorway of a tram. It was obvious Konrad Stauffer did not remember, or else he had decided not to. The face had adopted an expression of deliberate boorishness, which did not altogether convince. Himmelfarb had heard that Stauffer was the author of a volume of poems, which nobody had read, and that he was now writing destructive reviews and articles for a radical newspaper in their home town.

But soon the image of Stauffer was swallowed up, together

with the past, and that part of his life which Himmelfarb had dared to call his own. War did not come as a surprise, to him or anyone; that is, it did not erupt in the manner of volcanoes, it seeped over and into them. Some were appalled at the prospect of their becoming involved, but many sang, as if welcoming a lover, one who might certainly crack their ribs and bruise their flesh, but whose saliva intoxicated as it poisoned and whose passion liberated their more inadmissible desires.

Because the sequence of events in his personal life had left him sceptical and cold, war, his first too, affected Himmelfarb less than might have been expected. At the height of its folly, he was ashamed to realize, it was taking place only on the edge of his consciousness. However, as a good German, he had volunteered and was accepted to serve in the infantry. He was wounded twice. He even won a medal.

Once, in the mud and rain of a ruined French village, he enjoyed the half-pleasure of encountering his former friend Jürgen Stauffer. The shining lieutenant embraced the rather scruffy Jewish private – the sun was setting, there was nobody about – and, with only a little encouragement, would have risked creating a duet for opera out of their innocent situation.

'*Ach, Gott!*' cried the *Herr Leutnant*. 'Martin! Of all men, my old, my dearest Martin! At sunset! In Treilles! At the end of our victorious advance!'

The Jew wondered how he might clamber after, if only just a little of the way.

'It is heart-warming,' – the *Herr Leutnant* could not sing enough – 'to renew valued friendships in unexpected places.'

Something, certainly, whether skill or conviction, had caused the *Heldentenor* to glow. Cut out of felt and cardboard, his golden skin streaming with last light, he maintained the correct position, as they stood together in the shambles of a street. He smelled, moreover, his tired inferior realized, of boot polish and toilet soap.

'But how are you, Martin? You don't tell me,' the officer complained in different key.

The approach of caution had caused him to moisten unnecessarily his glistening lips.

'I am well,' answered the Jew. 'That is, my arches have fallen.'

How Jürgen Stauffer roared. His teeth were perfect.

'Still a joker! My good Martin! But keep your health. We are almost there.'

'Where?' asked the Jew.

The officer waved his hand. His brilliance could make allowances for the impudence of simplicity. So he forgave, still laughingly, still glancing back, over his shoulder as well as into the past, at some extraordinary misjudgement on his own part, as he walked away through the mud to rejoin a general who depended on his company.

Peace is sometimes more explosive than war. So it seemed to many of those who lived through what followed: rootling after sausage-ends and the heads of sour herrings, expressing in their songs a joy they no longer possessed, forced by hunger and the need for warmth into erotic situations their parents would not have guessed at.

Swimming and sinking, trampling and trampled, the rout of men-animals was carried along, and with them the Jew Himmelfarb. If he ever experienced the will to resist, he never exercised it, and even derived comfort from the friction of similar bristles on his own. During the first weeks of release, strange embraces, a delirium of experience, prevented him from returning to the bed that was, of course, waiting for him in his father's house. Besides, in those surroundings he might have laughed too loud, or farted in the dining-room, or done something of an irrational nature. For Moshe had re-married. He had taken a young woman called Christel Schmidt, with hair as heavy and yellow in its snood as horses' dung, and the necklace of Venus on her neck. *Trotzdem, nett und tüchtig.* And of no further significance. The lovers had met after mass. The girl consented, partly out of curiosity, but more especially because she could not bear to feel hungry. As for the old man, any flicker of prudence was probably extinguished by visions of a last frenzy of consenting flesh.

Mordecai and his practically innocent stepmother were both relieved to put an end to an ironic situation when, after months, the former was appointed to a readership in English at the University of Bienenstadt. Dr Himmelfarb departed, with the tentative blessings of his old father and an inkling that he had been directed to this far from lucrative post at a minor university for reasons still obscure. Several homely Jews insisted on offering him introductions to others, probably of their own kind, which he accepted with amused gratitude, and on a street corner, the disgusting dyer of his youth clawed at his arm, and repeated, it seemed, endlessly:

'There is a good man at Bienenstadt, a printer, a cousin of my late wife's brother-in-law. This man will receive you with lovingkindness, such as you were accustomed to in childhood, I need not remind you, Herr Mordecai. I recommend him to you with all my heart. His name is Liebmann.'

Dr Himmelfarb could not escape quickly enough from the grip of the dyer, who continued to call after him:

'An excellent man! *Lieb-mann* is the name!'

He might have begun to spell it out, if somebody impatient had not pushed him into the gutter.

Soon after, Himmelfarb left for Bienenstadt.

The town itself was in many ways similar to the one in which he had been born, smaller certainly, but illuminated by the same brush. Its blue and grey, and flecks of weathered gilding, swam together in a midday sleep. Words trickled from the mouths of the inhabitants in an untainted stream. Faces dimpled with a professional friendliness and a conviction that only they could ever be right. Yet, at Bienenstadt, Himmelfarb was soothed by the drone of days, even by the tone of its hypocrisies. Of his students, most obeyed his commands with the respect of earnest youth, a few, even, seemed of the opinion that he had more than knowledge to offer and would loiter in hot silence, when lectures were done, as if hoping for some revelation of a personal kind.

It was not that he was loved, exactly, but he could have been, if he had not withdrawn for the moment too far into himself to be reached. He had torn up all those introductions forced on him by acquaintances before his departure from Holunderthal, for he felt that to use them might have proved laughable or boring. He kept to his room a good deal, and read Spengler late at night.

Months had passed before he began to be tormented by a name, for which he could not at first account. It became a source of irritation, like somebody tapping out the same phrase repeatedly on a buzzer. He would even find the name on his tongue. Then he remembered: it was that of the dreadful dyer's Bienenstadt relative. Which made the whole business more ridiculous and irritating than before. He had no intention of forming any such connexion. As soon as he was aware of its origin, he laughed the smoke out of his lungs whenever the name recurred. He would light a fresh cigarette. His fingers, he noticed, were growing stained. And trembled slightly.

Then quite suddenly, on a certain afternoon, he stood up knowing that he must go in search of Liebmann the printer. He could not have been more relieved, not to say elated, as he heard his feet clatter on the cobbles in the older part of the town. His wingèd hair, too luxuriant by standards of elegance and worldliness, floated in the light breeze.

So he arrived at the house. He had chosen an hour, towards evening, when the printer's business affairs would surely have released him. Certainly the ground floor was still, deserted, padlocked. In a lane at the side he discovered a door, which could have communicated with the actual dwelling. Yes, said the between-age girl who came; but her father was not yet back from the synagogue. After a pause for her instincts to debate, she told him he should come in, and led him by the stairs to where the family lived above the press. He was brought into a room, in which the shutters had been pushed back, and a young woman was examining what appeared to be a paper-knife, which she had just unwrapped from a parcel.

'Oh, yes! Israel!' she said, and laughed, after the visitor left by her sister had made some reference to the dyer. 'We have not seen him for years. I cannot remember when.'

She might have made a face, if kindness had not prevented her.

Instead, she showed him the paper-knife she had just received.

'From a cousin,' she explained, 'who has returned from Jannina. But I shall have no uses for it,' she regretted, and now she did make the face, and it looked most comical. 'Who but a stage duchess ever used a real paper-knife to cut books or open letters?'

Their combined laughter was unnaturally loud.

'Surely there are other uses?' suggested the visitor, still laughing.

'Oh yes. Undoubtedly,' agreed the girl. 'It is so *sharp*!'

With the point of the knife she pricked the ball of one of her thumbs, which grew quite white, and caused them to laugh more brilliantly than ever.

Then they were both ashamed, because they had never behaved like this before. It was unnatural to both of them.

But exhilarating. Each was breathless.

The girl began to talk again.

'Yes, my father will come soon,' she said, but incidentally. 'Then, we shall have some coffee. I am the eldest. I am Reha.' After which she reeled off the names of several brothers and sisters. 'Didn't Israel tell you about the family? Of course, he scarcely knows us. No, my mother is dead.'

It was a big, old-fashioned room in one of the gabled houses.

'You will think I am an awful chatterbox,' she said, pushing back some hair. 'The others always shout me down. Do you like it here? I mean, at Bienenstadt?'

'Yes,' he said. 'I suppose I like it.'

'Tell me what you do,' she invited.

So he did, altogether naturally now.

Reha was a plump and rather dowdy girl. It was already evident how comfortable she would eventually become, and happy, if it were to be permitted. In looking at her, Himmelfarb was compelled to hold his head on one side, in a manner quite new to him, an attempt at delicacy perhaps. She did not invite attentions, let alone courtship, and had that rather homely face, yet he found himself trying to please, without expecting rewards, continually anxious lest some too florid gesture, or elaboration of thought, might convey pretentiousness where sincerity had been intended.

'English,' she murmured, frowningly. 'My vocabulary was always weak. I did not force myself to read enough.'

'I shall lend you books,' he promised.

Each was conscious of the classic obviousness of their remarks, but it did not seem to matter.

The father came in. He was a thin, small old Jew, with a game leg and perhaps some secret ailment, or it could have been that he had never fully recovered from the death of his wife. When he heard how the visitor was sent, he came out of himself, however, and repeated several times:

'Poor Israel! Poor Israel!'

In a tone of voice which suggested that the hopelessness of his relative's case might have endowed him with a virtue.

'In spite of his name, I must tell you, Israel is childless. Some early misfortune,' the printer continued, without stopping to consider how well-informed his visitor might be. 'But has devoted himself to other matters. The seed can be sown, you know, in many ways.'

It was clear the printer would have preferred to withdraw again into himself, but he remarked quite spontaneously and with a dry courtesy:

'I hope you will always come to us on the Sabbath, sir. Make this your home. There are passages in the Books I would like to discuss with you. I would like to hear your opinion of the general situation.'

However formally the suggestion was presented, the printer's yellow skin remained tinged with the faint glow of lovingkindness. The eyes were too innocent to avoid entering those of his fellow men, with the result that Himmelfarb was forced to lower his own, while hoping that his host's goodness might prevent him from recognizing the disorder which prevailed within.

The printer was saying:

'There are many problems that you may illuminate for us, Dr Himmelfarb. We live inside a closed circle. That is our great weakness.'

If the visitor had not contracted the muscles of his throat with all his strength, he might have startled his grave host by shouting a denial. That, at least, was prevented.

After some further conversation, he saw that Reha had returned with coffee. She was standing looking in distress and surprise at what, he realized, was the knot of his hands. But he released them quickly. The white vanished from his knuckles. And at once she made it appear doubtful whether she had noticed. She was pouring the coffee, inclining and smiling in the slight steam. It certainly smelled of real, pre-War coffee. And there were wedges of *Käsekuchen* besides.

Himmelfarb went to Liebmanns' on the Sabbath, as had been suggested. He was diffident about it at first, but longing supported him, and soon it became a habit. As the whole family appeared to take his presence for granted, it seemed at last, to him too, perfectly natural. When they handed him the Sabbath dishes at table, or expected him to join in their songs, it was assumed that his life as a Jew had never been interrupted. Sometimes his happiness was an embarrassment to him. But nobody noticed, unless Ari.

Ari, the eldest boy, was probably a specialist in scenting out other people's secrets, certainly their weaknesses. Bullet-headed in his *Käppchen*, he had whorls of dark hair along his cheekbones. He would mumble a grace through his broad, goat's teeth, eyes half closed, almost smiling.

In the synagogue Ari once turned to Mordecai and did not even bother to whisper:

'See that fellow over there? The one with the locks. He is so simple – that is to say, he is such a *good Jew* that, if his grandfather stuck on a mask, and told Abram he was Elijah the Prophet, he would believe it.'

Ari did not expect Mordecai to laugh, but laughed for himself. He was perfectly detached. But he was not a bad lad. He would go off tramping and singing across the *Heide* with other young Jews, members of an organization to which he belonged. He loved his family too and would sit at table with his arms round his sisters' necks.

Mordecai believed that, in time, he might even love Ari. Of

the Sabbath table, he loved the crusts. The crumbs beneath his fingers humbled him.

'What is it?' Reha might ask. 'Don't you like the carp? Or is it, perhaps, the *Biersoss*?'

In the silence after his reassurance, she would fidget with her plate. And look for something. Like his mother, she was myopic. In the beginning Reha had not been able to resist joking with their guest about the blind leading the blind, for Himmelfarb, as it turned out, had inherited indifferent sight, and shortly before his arrival at Bienenstadt had been forced to take to spectacles. These sat somewhat oddly on his face and might have weakened its natural defences if they had not been reinforced by an expression of increasing certainty.

For the young man who was no longer a stranger, the Sabbath became a steadfast joy, whether sitting in the twilight of the printer's house, or at the synagogue, touching elbows with his friend Liebmann, as they stood wrapped in their trailing shawls. As the coverings of the Ark were changed, in accordance with the feasts of the year, so his soul would put on different colours. He was again furnished with his faith. To touch the fringes of his shawl with his lips, was to drink pure joy.

In autumn, when the heat had passed, he sometimes persuaded Reha Liebmann, who was secretly appalled by open spaces, to go walking with him through the barren heathland which stretched to the north of Bienenstadt and, on a Sunday in October, as they sat and rested in a sandy, slightly more protected hollow, he suggested she should become his wife.

She would not answer at first, by any word, but was separating the grains of sand and could have been sad or bitter.

To tell the truth, it surprised the vanity in him but only for a moment.

She did begin, very slowly, very softly.

'Yes,' she said. 'Yes, Mordecai. I had been hoping. From the beginning I had been hoping. But knew, too, of course.'

If her words had lacked simplicity, such candour might have sounded complacent, or even immodest.

'Oh, dear!' She began to cry, 'I must try very hard. Forgive me,' she cried. 'That I should behave like this. Just now. I am afraid I may fail you also in other ways.'

'Reha, darling!' he answered rather lightly. 'In the eyes of the world a provincial intellectual is a *comic* figure.'

'Ah, but you do not understand,' she managed with difficulty. 'Not yet. And I cannot express myself. But we – some of us –

although we have not spoken – know that you will bring us honour.'

She took his fingers, and was looking absently, again almost sadly, at their roots. She stroked the veins in the backs of his hands.

'You make me ashamed,' he protested.

Because he was astounded.

'You will see,' she said. 'I am convinced.'

And looked up, smiling confidently now.

So that he wanted to kiss her – she was so good and tangible – but at the same time he was determined to forget the strange, rather hysterical assertions his proposal had inspired.

'Reha! Reha! If you only knew!' he insisted. 'I am the lowest of human beings!'

But it did not deter her from taking his head in her arms. It was as though she would possess it for as long as one is allowed to possess anything in this world. Yet she did so with humility, conscious of the minor part she would be given to play.

When at last they got to their feet, after comforting each other by words and touch, they were amazed and shy. The bronze trumpets were calling their names, in that remote and rather sour hollow of the *Heide*, as evening fell.

Soon the days were tumbling over one another, babbling in the accents of old women, younger sisters, and girl cousins, until the bridegroom was standing beneath the *Chuppah*, waiting for his bride. She came very softly, as might have been expected, like a breath. Then the two were standing together, but no longer bound by their awkward bodies, under the canopy of stuffy velvet, in the particular smell of sanctity and scouring of the old synagogue at Bienenstadt, in an assembly of tradesmen and small shopkeepers who were the seed of Israel fallen on that corner of Germany. The miraculous, encrusted *Chuppah* did actually open for the chosen couple; they were sucked out of themselves into an infinity of blue, and their souls were flapping together, diffidently at first, as two handkerchiefs will flutter and dispute each other's form and direction in a wind, until, reconciled by nature to the truth of the situation, they reach out, wrapped together, straining always higher, in one strong white tongue.

So the souls of the united couple temporarily abandoned their surroundings, while the bodies of bridegroom and bride continued to stand beneath the canopy enacting the touching and simple ceremonies in which the congregation might participate. How the old men and women craned to distinguish the gold

126

circlet that the young man was slipping on the bride's finger. The old, dusty men and women were again encircled by love and history. Their own lips tasted joyful wine and trembled to forestall the breaking of the cup.

For the bridegroom had taken the glass, as no happiness can be repeated; all must be re-lived, re-sanctified. So the bridegroom stood with the glass poised. It was unbearably perfect, immaculate, but fragile. It was already breaking – breaking – broken. During a second of silence, its splinters glittered on the brick floor.

There were, of course, a few present who had broken into tears for the destruction of the glass, but even they joined with the congregation in shouting with joy, all, out of the depths of their hearts. They were truly overjoyed by that which they had just enacted together. Hope was renewed in everybody. '*Mazel Tov!*' cried the toothless mouths of the old people, and the red, shrilly voices of the young girls vibrated with hysteria and anticipation.

Only the bridegroom seemed to have entered on another phase. He appeared almost morose, as he stood fidgeting beneath the now grotesque and brooding *Chuppah*. Time had, in fact, carried him too far too fast, with the result that the beard had sprouted again on his shaven jaw, and as he dipped his chin, thoughtful and frowning, the neck of the white *Kittel* which protruded unevenly above his wedding jacket was chafing against the bristles of incipient beard. So he frowned and bit one end of his moustache and heard the first delicately-stated message of falling earth which precedes the final avalanche of mortality.

Afterwards, at the house of the father-in-law, Mordecai was whirled around and around so often, to receive embraces or advice, that the thinking man succumbed temporarily to the sensual one. Without listening to much of what he was told, he laughed back out of his parted, swelling lips, quite unlike himself. And rubbed his eyes occasionally to rid them of the blur of candles. Always laughing rather than replying. The air, besides, was unctuous with a smell of goose fat and the steam from golden soup.

In the mood of relaxed sensuality which the wedding feast had induced, it did not strike him as tragic that there were none of his own present. Tactfully, his father had developed a severe chill, which kept him confined to his bed. His aunts, self-engrossed and ailing women, had never really recovered from the circumstances of their sister's death. But one figure did emerge from the past, and when he had put his arms round the bridegroom, Mordecai recognized the dyer from Holunderthal.

'I did not doubt you would see what was indicated,' slobbered the awful man into the bridegroom's ear. 'And know you will justify our expectations. Because your heart has been touched and changed.'

The guests were swarming around, and jostling them, so that Mordecai only succeeded with difficulty in holding the dyer off by handfuls of the latter's scurfy coat.

'Touched and changed?' He laughed back and heard it sound faintly stupid. 'I am, as always, myself, I regret to tell you!'

'That is so and that is why!' the dyer replied.

Pressed together as they were, Mordecai realized that the man's hitherto sickly body had a warmth and strength he would never have suspected. Nor was he himself half as disgusted as he had been on previous occasions, though now, of course, he had taken several glasses of wine.

'But you are all riddles – secrets!' In spite of their proximity it was necessary to shout to be heard above the noise.

'There is no secret,' the dyer appeared to be saying, or shouting back. 'Equanimity is no secret. Solitariness is no secret. True solitariness is only possible where equanimity exists. An unquiet spirit can introduce distractions into the best-prepared mind.'

'But this is immoral!' Mordecai protested, shouting. 'And on such an occasion! It is a denial of community. Man is not a hermit.'

'Depending on the man, he is a light that will reflect out over the community – all the brighter from a bare room.'

As they were practically bellowing at each other, nobody else had heard, which was perhaps just as well, and at that moment they were separated by the printer, who wanted to display his son-in-law to some acquaintance or relative.

As his self-appointed guide was sucked back into the crowd and lost, Himmelfarb accepted that the crippled dyer, who had come even to the wedding with the lines of his hands marked clearly in purple, was one from whom he would never escape. He had learnt the shape of the unshapely body, the texture of the unchanging coat; mirrors had taught him, long before their meeting, the expression of the eyes. Now, in the moment of perception, all the inklings were married together: the dyer's image was with him for always, like his new wife, or his own fate Now he was committed. So he continued to answer distractedly the questions of the wedding guests, while trying to reconcile in his mind what his wife had taught him of love, with what had hitherto been the disgust he had felt for the dyer. In the light of the one, he must discover and gather up the sparks of love hidden in the other. Or deny his own purpose, as well as the existence of the race.

In the circumstances he was amazed nobody realized the answers they were receiving to their questions were no answers, or that his wife Reha should look up at him with an expression of implicit confidence.

In the beginning the young people lived with the wife's father, but soon found, and moved into, a small, rather old-fashioned house, with rooms high but too narrow and a very abrupt staircase. Because it was situated on the outskirts of the town, at least the rental was low, which enabled the tenants to engage an inexperienced girl to help the wife of the *Dozent*, while the *Dozent* himself gave up smoking, and practised other small economies such as walking to his lectures instead of taking the tram. They were completely happy, the female relatives claimed, and indeed, they were almost so. In their small, closed circle. On the outskirts of the town. Those who look for variety in change and motion, instead of in the variations on recurring events, would have found the life monotonous and restricted. But Himmelfarbs gave no outward sign of wishing to diverge from the path on which their feet had been set. If they left Bienenstadt at all, it was to spend the same month each year in the *Schwarzwald*, at the same reliable pension where it was possible to eat *kosher*. Although there were also occasions when Dr Himmelfarb had had to absent himself for several days, representing a disinclined Professor at conferences in other university towns. And once, after some years, he had returned to Holunderthal, on receiving a telegram announcing the death of his father.

Moshe died of his young wife, it was commonly and truthfully said. But repentant. That is easy at the end. And was buried by a priest with a stammer, and an acolyte with a cold. The few friends who attended were sufficiently recent to keep the ceremony superficial in tone. Most of the faces were kindly, curious, reverent, correct, but a few who were bored, or who suffered from bad circulation, took to stamping ostentatiously, or slapping their sides, and one more cynical than the rest reflected how quickly a mild joke can become a stale one. All of these were anxious to get finished. But each clod had to count.

As they summoned the Mother of God to the side of the old Jew, who had not known Her very long, and then, it was suspected. only as a convenience. So the earth was scattered, and water – though not of tears, not even from the son, whose grief was deeper than the gush of tears.

The son, who had gone round to the wrong side of the grave, amongst the earth and stones, and who had no idea what to do by way of respect, stood looking yellow in the silver afternoon. Some of the mourners grew quite fascinated, if repelled, by his pronounced Jewish cast.

As they watched, Mordecai swayed from time to time. Because the weight was upon him. Because faith is never faith unless it is to be wrestled with. *O perfect Rock, spare and have pity on the parents and the children....* So Mordecai wrestled with the Rock, and prayed for his parent, that shifting sand, or worldly man, whose moustache had smelt deliciously and who had never been happier than when presenting a Collected Works in leather.

Himmelfarb remained no longer than was necessary in his native town. Fortunately the business had been satisfactorily disposed of a couple of years before. The widow, who was already preparing to forget about that chapter of her life, proposed to look for consolation at a foreign spa. There remained the house on the Holzgraben, which the son inherited, and decided to close until a suitable tenant could be found. He was most anxious to return as quickly as possible to the life he had made and which his increase in fortune proceeded to alter only in superficial ways, for his wife could never accustom herself to worldly practices and he remained engrossed in her, his students, and his books.

It was not generally known in Bienenstadt that Dr Himmelfarb himself had written and published an admirable and scholarly little monograph on the *Novels of John Oliver Hobbes*. Although the *Frau Doktor* had made a point of mentioning the fact casually to the ladies of her circle, the information was not absorbed. Why should it have been? The book would remain a scholar's minor achievement or, at most, an object of interest to some research student exploring the by-ways of literature. However, his large-scale work *English Novelists of the Nineteenth Century in Relation to German Literature and Life*, also written during the quiet years at Bienenstadt, was rather a different matter. Himmelfarb's *English Novelists* attracted a wider academic, not to say public, attention, and it was taken for granted that the author would soon be generally accepted as a standard authority. So that, before very long, there was an outbreak of smiling discussion amongst the ladies of the *Frau Doktor's* circle, of the rumours they had heard: how Dr Himmelfarb was likely to be offered the Chair of English at a certain university – gossip was in disagreement over which; perhaps *Frau Doktor* Himmelfarb – here the ladies of the circle wreathed themselves in golden smiles – might be able to enlighten them. But, when questioned on that matter of advancement, the *Frau Doktor* would look rather nervous, as if she had been asked to tamper with the future. She personally preferred to await the logical unfolding of events, which her husband's brilliance must ensure.

So she would avoid giving a direct reply. Or she would murmur something of tried banality, such as:

'All in good time. Our lives have only just begun.'

And offer her callers a second slice of *Käsekuchen*.

In a sense, no more rational answer could have been found, for, although the *Dozent* was turning grey – not unnatural in a man of dark pigmentation – and his fine figure had begun to thicken, while his wife had grown undeniably fat, it could have been argued that they were only beginning to mature in the full goodness of their married lives. In the small house on the outskirts of the town. In the shade of an oak, and the lesser shadows of beans, which the industrious country maid had coaxed to climb up sticks in the back garden. Nobody, least of all Himmelfarbs themselves, could really have wished to destroy the impression of peaceful permanence, strongest always in the mornings, when the feather beds lolled in the sunlight on the upper window sills.

Yet, Frau Himmelfarb began to suffer from breathlessness, which gave her, when off her guard, a slightly strained look, as if her assertion of happiness might be proving too difficult to maintain. Some of her callers, in discussing it, decided it was the proximity of the oak – too many trees around a house used up all the oxygen, causing those spasms which, in the end, might turn to asthma; while other ladies, more daring, were of the opinion that the absence of a family had provoked a nervous condition.

One of the latter, a gross creature by intellectual standards, whose husband was a haberdasher in a mean street, and who was received on account of a relationship, knew no better than to say outright:

'But, Rehalein, it is time you had a child. Why, the duties of the *Rabbanim* do not begin and end in books. Give me a good,

131

comfortable, family Jew. He may not spell, but he will fill the house with babies.'

Two other ladies, one of whom was noted for her readings from the *West-Östlicher Divan*, decided it was time to break off even forced relations with the haberdasher's wife, who was smelling, besides, of perspiration and caraway seeds.

While Reha Himmelfarb simply maintained:

'Who are we, Rifke, to decide what a man's duties shall be?'

And Himmelfarb loved his wife the better for overhearing.

They were brought together closer, if anything, in an effort to express that love of which it seemed no lasting evidence might remain. None would know how Himmelfarbs had rejoiced in each other, unless by an echo from a library, from the dedication in a book: *To my wife, Reha, without whose encouragement and assistance....* But words do not convince the doubting soul like living tokens, as the wife of the haberdasher knew, for all her simplicity, or perhaps because of it.

Watching his wife one evening as she lit the Sabbath candles, Himmelfarb would have said: Of all people in this world, Reha is least in doubt. Yet, at that moment, the hands of Reha Himmelfarb, plump and practical by nature, seemed to grow transparent and flicker in the candle flames.

At the same time she gave a little startled cry of pain.

'It was the wax from the candles! The hot wax, that fell when I was not expecting.'

She whispered quickly, and only just distinct, as though she felt her need to explain and desecrate a sacred moment.

By then the flames of the candles were standing straight and still, but what should have been the lovely, limpid Sabbath light shone wan and almost sickly and the faces of the two people reflected by the mirrors could have been soft, sweating wax.

The obligations of other ceremonies prevented him from commenting there and then, but later he came to her, and said:

'Reha, darling, I can tell you are badly disappointed.'

And took her resisting hand, and put it inside his jacket, so that it was closest to him.

'Why?' she cried. 'When our life together is so happy? And soon there will be the Chair. Everybody is convinced of that.'

He was half-exasperated, half in love.

'But not the babies that your Cousin Rifke advises as the panacea.'

She would not look at him. She said:

'We must expect our lives to be different.'

'Referring in cold abstractions,' he answered, 'to matters we

132

do not understand. But for our actual lives – for yours, at least, I would ask all that is comforting and joyous.'

'Oh, mine!' she protested. 'I am nothing. I am your footstool. Or cushion!' She laughed. 'Am I not, rather, a cushion?'

She did appear her plumpest looking up at him, happy even, but, he suspected, by her own effort.

Then she put her arms round his waist, and laid her face against his vest, and said:

'I would not alter a single detail of our lives.'

But at once went on to deliver, in a different voice, what sounded almost a recitative, of the greatest significance and urgency:

'On Monday I must start to make the jelly from the apples Mariechen brought from her village. There is an old book my mother used to mention which gives an infallible method for clarifying jelly. I have the title, I believe, amongst some papers she left. Pass by Rutkowitz's on your way home and see whether you can find the book. Will you, Mordecai? He has such a mountain of old stuff, you might come across anything.'

She looked up, and was in such apparent earnest, he was both moved and pacified.

On the Monday, as he was preparing to leave, Reha came with the title of the book. As it happened, he had forgotten.

'Don't forget the book!' she kept insisting. 'I shall not start the jelly. I shall wait in case you happen to find, at Rutkowitz's, the book!'

It was so important, her face implied.

Then he left, relieved that his wife was such a simple, loving creature. If her words sometimes hinted at deeper matters, no doubt it was pure chance; she herself remained unaware.

Rutkowitz was a quiet, elderly Jew, whose overflowing shop stood in one of the streets which plunged off behind the university at Bienenstadt. Himmelfarb remembered to pass that way before returning home, and rummaged in the stacks and trays for the book his wife so particularly required. Needless to say, he did not succeed in finding it, but discovered other things which amused and interested.

'You deal in magic, Rutkowitz, I see!'

Deliberately he addressed the grave bookseller with inappropriate levity.

The latter shrugged, and answered, very dry:

'Some old Kabbalistic and Hasidic works. They came from a collection in Prague.'

'And are of value?'

'There are some who may value them.'

The bookseller was a wary man.

Himmelfarb warmed to the characters, and the language moved on his tongue, where the Cantor Katzmann had put it in the beginning. He began, inevitably, to read aloud, for the nostalgia of hearing the instrument of his voice do justice to its heritage.

And so, he heard:

'I set myself the task at night of combining letters with one another, and of meditating on them, and so continued for three nights. On the third occasion, after midnight, I nodded off for a little, quill in hand, paper on my knees. Then I noticed that the candle was about to go out. So I rose and extinguished it, as a person who has been dozing often will. But I soon realized that the light continued. I was greatly astonished, because, after close examination, I saw it was as though the light issued from myself. I said: "I do not believe it." I walked to and fro all through the house, and, behold, the light is with me; I lay on a couch and covered myself up, and behold, the light is with me all the while. . . .'

The cautious bookseller was standing a little to one side, the better to disclaim complicity in his customer's private pursuits.

'Do you appreciate the physical advantages of mystical ecstasy, Rutkowitz?' Himmelfarb inquired.

But although they stood scarcely any distance apart, the bookseller had apparently determined to keep his understanding carefully turned away. He did not answer.

Himmelfarb continued to browse amongst the old books and manuscripts. Now he was entranced. The bookseller had left him, or else had ceased to exist. In the stillness of the dusk and the light from one electric bulb, the reader heard himself:

'The soul is full of the love of God, and bound with ropes of love, in joy and lightness of heart. Unlike one who serves his master grudgingly, even when most hindered the love of service burns in his heart, and he is glad to fulfil the will of his Creator. . . . For, when the soul thinks deeply on the fear of God, then the flame of heartfelt love leaps within, and the exultation of subtlest joy fills the heart. . . . And the lover dreams not of the advantages of this world; he no longer takes undue pleasure in his wife, nor excessive pride in his sons and daughters, but cares only to obey the will of his Creator, to do good unto others, and to keep sanctified the Name of God. All his thoughts burn with the fire of love for Him. . . .'

Himmelfarb found the bookseller seated at his desk in the lower shop, as though nothing in particular had happened –

and what, indeed, had? After coming to an agreement, the *Dozent* went home, taking with him several of the more interesting old volumes of Hebrew, and one or two loose, damaged parchments.

'Did you find my book?'

Reha had appeared in the hall as she heard her husband mounting the stairs.

'No luck!' he answered.

She did not seem in any way put out, but immediately called back into the kitchen:

'Mariechen, we shall start the apple jelly tonight. By the old method. The *Herr Doktor* did not find the book.'

Almost as though she were relieved.

Her husband continued on his way upstairs. He had debated whether to tell his wife about his purchases, but as she had ignored the books in his arms, he no longer felt he was expected to.

Often now, after correcting an accumulation of essays, or on saying good night to students who had come for tuition, he would sit alone in his room with the old books. He would read, or sit, or draw, idly, automatically, or fidget with different objects, or listen to the sound of silence, and was sometimes, it seemed, transported in divers directions.

On one occasion his wife interrupted.

'I cannot sleep,' she explained.

She had released her hair, and brushed it out, with the result that she appeared to be standing against a dark and brittle thicket, but one in which a light shone.

'I am not disturbing you?' she asked. 'I thought I would like to read something.' She sighed. 'Something short. And musical.'

'Mörike,' he suggested.

'Yes,' she agreed, absently. 'Mörike will be just the thing.'

As the wind her nightdress made in passing stirred the papers uppermost on her husband's desk, she could not resist asking:

'What is that, Mordecai? I did not know you could draw.'

'I was scribbling,' he said. 'This, it appears, is the Chariot.'

'Ah,' she exclaimed softly, withdrawing her glance; she could have lost interest. 'Which chariot?' she did certainly ask, but now it might have been to humour him.

'That, I am not sure,' he replied. 'It is difficult to distinguish. Just when I think I have understood, I discover some fresh form – so many – streaming with implications. There is the Throne of God, for instance. That is obvious enough – all gold, and chrysoprase, and jasper. Then there is the Chariot of Redemption, much more shadowy, poignant, personal. And the faces of the riders. I cannot begin to see the expression of the faces.'

All the time Reha was searching the shelves.

'This is in the old books?' she asked.

'Some of it,' he admitted, 'is in some.'

Reha continued to explore the shelves.

She yawned. And laughed softly.

'I think I shall probably fall asleep,' she said, 'before I find Mörike.'

But took a volume.

He felt her kiss the back of his head as she left.

Or did she remain, to protect him more closely, with some secret part of her being, after the door had closed? He was never certain with Reha: to what extent perception was revealed in her words and her behaviour, or how far she had accompanied him along the inward path.

For, by now, Himmelfarb had taken the path of inwardness. He could not resist silence, and became morose on evenings when he was prevented from retreating early to his room. Reha would continue to sew, or mend. Her expression did not protest. She would smile a gentle approval — but of what, it was never made clear.

Some of the old books were full of directions which he did not dare follow, and to which he adopted a deliberately sceptical attitude, or, if it was ever necessary, one of crudest cynicism. But he did, at last, unknown, it was to be hoped, to his rational self, begin fitfully to combine and permute the Letters, even to contemplate the Names.

It was, however, the driest, the most cerebral approach — when spiritually he longed for the ascent into an ecstasy so cool and green that his own desert would drink the heavenly moisture. Still, his forehead of skin and bone continued to burn with what could have been a circlet of iron. Or sometimes he would become possessed by a rigid coldness of mind, his soul absorbed into the entity of his own upright, leather chair, his knuckles carved out of oak.

Mostly he remained at a level where, it seemed, he was inacceptable as a vessel of experience, and would fall asleep, and wake at cockcrow. But once he was roused from sleep, during the leaden hours, to identify a face. And got to his feet, to receive the messenger of light, or resist the dark dissembler. When he was transfixed by his own horror. Of his own image, but fluctuating, as though in fire or water. So that the long-awaited moment was reduced to a reflection of the self. In a distorting mirror. Who, then, could hope to be saved? Fortunately, he was prevented from shouting the blasphemies that occurred to him, because his voice had been temporarily removed. Nor could he inflict on the material forms which surrounded him, themselves the cloaks of spiritual deceit, the damage which he felt compelled to do, for his will had become entangled, and his nails were tearing on the shaggy knots. He could only struggle and sway inside the column of his body. Until he toppled forward, and was saved further anguish by hitting his head on the edge of the desk.

Reha Himmelfarb discovered her husband early that morning. He was still weak and confused, barely conscious, as if he had had a congestive attack of some kind. After recovering from her fright, during which she had tried to warm his hands with her own, and was repeatedly kissing, and crying, and breathing into his cold lips, she ran and telephoned to Dr Vogel, who decided, after an examination, that the *Herr Dozent* was suffering from exhaustion as the result of overwork. The doctor ordered his patient to bed, and for a couple of weeks Himmelfarb saw nobody but his devoted wife. It was very delightful. She read him the whole of *Effi Briest*, and he lay with his eyes closed, barely following, yet absorbing the episodes of that touching, though slightly insipid story. Or perhaps it was his wife's voice which he appreciated most, and which, as it joined the words together with a warm and gentle precision, seemed the voice of actuality.

A second fortnight's leave, granted for convalescence, was spent at a little resort on the Baltic. Grey light and a shiver in the air would only have intensified for Himmelfarb the idyll of impeccable dunes and white timber houses, if it had not been for an incident which occurred at the hotel. They had come down early the first evening into the empty dining-room, where a disenchanted apprentice-waiter sat them at any table. Soon the company began to gather, all individuals of a certain class, of discreetly interchangeable clothes and faces. The greetings were correct. The silence knew what to expect. When something most unexpected, not to say disturbing, happened. A retired colonel, at whose table the new arrivals had been seated, marched to his usual place, seized the paper envelope in which it was customary for a guest to keep his napkin, and after retreating to the hall, passionately yelled at the reception desk that it was not his habit to sit at table with Jews.

Nothing like this had ever happened to Himmelfarbs. They

were shaken, trembling even. It was obvious that most of their fellow guests were embarrassed, though one or two had to titter. All necessary apologies were made by the management, but in the circumstances, the newcomers agreed they had no appetite, and left the room after a few spoonfuls of a grey soup. During the night each decided never again to mention the incident to the other, but each was aware that the memory of it would remain. However conciliatory the air of Oststrand became, and however punctiliously, in some cases ostentatiously, the more liberal-minded of their fellow guests bowed to them during the rest of their stay, the little, lapping waves continually revealed a glint of metal, and the cries of sea birds drove the mind into a corner of private melancholy.

Yet, the sea air and early hours restored Dr Himmelfarb's health, and he returned to Bienenstadt with all the necessary strength to attack the immediate future. For soon, those who had been whispering about the *Herr Dozent*'s peculiar break-down, were openly discussing his promotion and departure. He was, in fact, called to an interview at Holunderthal, and shortly after, it was announced that he had been offered, and had accepted, the Chair of English at the university of his home town.

So the couple had plenty to occupy them.

'The books alone are a major undertaking!' Frau Himmel-farb was proud to protest.

'I shall look through them,' her husband promised, 'and expect I shall find a number that I shan't miss if we leave them behind.'

'Oh, I am not complaining!' his wife insisted.

'Then,' he replied, with affection rather than in censure, 'your intonations do not always convey your feelings.'

In the end, all was somehow packed. At a last glance, only the wisps of straw and a few sentimental regrets appeared to linger in the house with narrow rooms on the edge of Bienen-stadt.

Professor Himmelfarb, the son of Moshe the furrier, was by now a man of private means, and might have led a life of pomp, if he had been so inclined. But was prevented by a sense of irony, as much as by lack of enthusiasm. They did, certainly, open up the family house on the Holzgraben. However forbid-ding the façade, in the Graeco-German style, with stucco pedi-ment and caryatids, at least the interior preserved a soft down of memories along with the furrier's opulence of taste. In the beginning the *Frau Professor* had been somewhat daunted by

138

the total impact of her establishment and surroundings. For, quite apart from the pressure of monumental furniture, the house faced the more formal, or Park side of the *Stadtwald*, with the result that the owners, standing at a first-floor window, looked out over shaven lawns and perfectly distributed gravel, across the beds of tuberous begonias and cockscombs, or down a narrowing *Lindenallee*, lined with discreet discus throwers and modest nymphs, to the deep, bulging, indeterminate masses of the *Wald* proper.

The public setting, however incidental, increased the value and importance of the solemn property, and in the years which followed the migration from Bienenstadt, while an illusion of solidity might still be entertained, it was only his sense of irony which saved Professor Himmelfarb from being impressed by his material condition, in particular when, returning from his walks in the *Wald*, he was confronted with the gradually expanding façade of what was apparently his own house, reared like a small caprice of a palace, at the end of the *Lindenallee*.

Thus exposed to the danger of complacency, a noise, half-ribald, half-dismayed, seemed to issue out of the Professor's nose, and he would be forced to glance back over his shoulder, embarrassed by the possibility that someone had heard, amused to think that someone might have.

In time, and his responsible position, he grew greyer, thicker, deeply-scored, until those who watched him on the podium were sometimes less conscious of his words, however subtle and illuminating, than of his rough-hewn, monolithic figure. On his regular walks he took to carrying a stick – it was thought to be an ashplant – for company rather than support, and was always followed by a little, moth-eaten dog called Teckel, whom he would address at intervals, after turning solemnly round. He dressed usually in a coarse, and if truth were told, rather inferior tweed, but was clothed also in an envelope of something more difficult to assess, protective and provocative at once. Those who passed him would stare, and wonder what it was about the large and ugly Jew. But, of course, there were also many to recognize and greet a person of his standing. Until the decade of discrimination, Germans as well as Jews were pleased to be seen shaking Professor Himmelfarb by the hand, and ladies would colour, and show their teeth, no doubt remembering some story of his disreputable youth.

As for his wife, the *Frau Professor* never on any account accompanied him on his walks through the *Wald*, and was only rarely seen strolling with her husband over the red, raked gravel

139

of the Park. Her upbringing had not accustomed her to walk, except to the approved shops, where in a light of bronze fish and transparent oils she would celebrate the mysteries of which she was an initiate. In her middle age, she had grown regrettably heavy of body, while preserving a noticeable gaiety of mind. And would lift up many who were cast down. On occasions, for instance, when the women sat and sewed garments for those of them who had been taken too soon, when young girls trembled and pricked their fingers over the *Tachriechim*, and older women grew inclined to abuse their memories, it was Reha Himmelfarb who restored their sense of continuity, by some remark, or simply by her presence. That which the women knew, all that was solid and good, might be expected to endure a little longer, in spite of the reminder of the white linen garments in their laps.

'Fat people have an advantage over thin; they float more easily,' was how the *Frau Professor* chose to explain her powers.

Although her own doubts and fears would sometimes rise, as perhaps her husband alone knew. Returning from a walk he would catch sight of her standing at a first-floor window. Looking. Then she would notice, and lean out, and wave, with her rather dark, plump hand, breathless, it seemed, with happiness and relief that she had not been called away before he had returned. Then, in the distance between the window and the street, their two souls were at their most intimate and loving.

'What did you see today?' Frau Himmelfarb would often ask.

'Nothing,' her husband would usually reply.

Though by this time he suspected that she, too, was not deceived by the masks of words. Indeed, all substances, of which words were the most opaque, grew more transparent with the years. As for faces – he was moved, touched, amazed, shamed by what he saw.

In all his dealings with his colleagues of the faculty, in the lectures to his students, in the articles he published and the books he wrote, Professor Himmelfarb appeared a man of straightforward character, of thorough, sometimes niggling intellect, and often epigrammatic wit. Nobody watching him tramp slowly, monotonously over the fallen leaves of the *Stadtwald*, or along the well-kept pavements of the town, would have suspected him of morbid tendencies and reprehensible ambitions. For he was racked by his persistent longing to exceed the bounds of reason: to gather up the sparks, visible intermittently inside the thick shells of human faces; to break through to the sparks of light imprisoned in the forms of wood and stone. Imperfection in himself had enabled him to recognize the fragmentary nature of things, but at the same time restrained him from undertaking the immense labour of reconstruction. So this imperfect man had remained necessarily tentative. He was for ever peering into bushes, or windows, or the holes of eyes, or, with his stick, testing the thickness of a stone, as if in search of further evidence, when he should have been gathering up the infinitesimal kernels of sparks, which he already knew to exist, and planting them again in the bosom of divine fire, from which they had been let fall in the beginning.

So he would return home, and, knowing himself to be inadequately equipped, would confess in reply to his wife's inquiries:

'Nothing. I have seen, I have done nothing.'

And she would hang her head, not from annoyance at his concealing something, or because there were matters that she did not understand, but because she sensed the distance between aspiration and the possibility of achievement, and she was unable to do anything to help him.

Yet, in their relationship, they shared a perfection probably as great as two human beings are allowed to enjoy together, and would spend whole evenings of contentment in the library of the house on the Holzgraben, while Professor Himmelfarb read, or corrected, inclined at his characteristic angle, and his wife occupied herself with sewing, or knitting, usually for the family of some Jew whose circumstances had been brought to her notice.

One evening when they had sat silently absorbed to the extent that the clock had withheld its chiming, Reha Himmelfarb suddenly scratched her head with a knitting needle – an act which many people might have considered coarse, but which her husband found natural – and broke their silence. It was unusual behaviour on her part.

'Mordecai,' she asked, 'what became of the old books?'

'Books?'

He could have been contemptuous, as he stared back at his wife through the thick glass of his spectacles.

'The Judaica.'

She sounded unnaturally jovial. Like some woman who, for secret reasons, was trying to insinuate herself into her husband's mind by matching his masculinity.

'You don't always express yourself, Rehalein.'

Because, by now, he was annoyed. He did not wish to answer questions.

'You know what I mean,' Reha Himmelfarb replied. 'The old Kabbalistic volumes and manuscripts in Hebrew, which you found at Rutkowitz's.'

Professor Himmelfarb put aside the book he had been reading. He was cruelly interrupted.

'I left them in Bienenstadt,' he answered. 'I had no further use for them.'

'Such valuable books!'

'They had no particular value. They were, at most, intellectual curiosities.'

Then Reha Himmelfarb surprised her husband. She went so far as to ask:

'You do not believe it possible to arrive at truth through revelation?'

Himmelfarb's throat had grown dry.

'On the contrary,' he said. 'But I no longer believe in tampering with what is above and what is below. It is a form of egotism.'

His hands were trembling.

'And can lead to disorders of the mind.'

But his wife, he realized, who had begun in a mood of gentleness and light, had suddenly grown dark and aggressive.

'You!' she cried, choking, it seemed, with desperate blood. 'Much will be made clear to you! But to us, the ordinary ones?'

'There is no distinction finally.'

He could not bring himself to look at the horrible erratic movements her hands, the needles, and the wool were making.

'When the time comes,' her dark lips began to blurt, 'you will be able to bear it. Because your eyes can see farther. But what can we others hold in our minds to make the end bearable?'

'This table,' he replied, touching it gently.

Then his wife put down her knitting.

'Oh, Mordecai,' she whispered, 'I am afraid. Tables and chairs will not stand up and save us.'

'God will,' he answered. 'God is in this table.'

She began to cry.

'Some have been able to endure the worst tortures by concentrating on the Name,' he heard his voice mumble.

And it sounded merely sententious. For he knew that he himself could do nothing for the wife he loved. At most, he could cover her with his body.

At that period Professor Himmelfarb was conducting his courses as usual, while working on his book *The Compatibility*

142

of Spirit: a Study in the Affinities between Late Nineteenth- and Early Twentieth-Century English and German Literatures, a work which some considered would establish the Professor's academic fame, but which others feared might not find favour with the existing régime.

For events had changed their course by then, and from imperceptible beginnings, had begun to flow deep and fast. Many Germans found themselves, after all, to be Jews. If parents, in the confidence of emancipation, had been able to construe the *Galuth* as a metaphysical idea, their children, it appeared, would have to accept exile as a hard fact. Some did, early enough. They left for the United States, and fell into a nylon dream, of which the transparent folds never quite concealed the evidence of circumcision. These were for ever turning uneasily in their sleep. Some returned to Palestine – oh yes, returned, because how else is exile ended? – but were not vouchsafed that personal glimpse of the *Shekhinah* which their sense of atavism demanded. These were perhaps the most deceived. How their soft, parti-coloured souls lamented! Oh, the evenings at Kempinsky's, oh, the afternoons at Heringsdorf! Others who were thrown upon the stones of Zion, took root eventually and painfully, by law of creation, as it were. Developing tough and bitter stems, they resisted the elements because, there, at last, it was natural to do so.

There were many, however, in the aching villas, in the thin dwellings of congested alleys, beside the *Gummibaum* in tasteful, beige apartments, who, for a variety of reasons, could not detach themselves from the ganglion of Europe: their bones protested, or they loved their furniture, or *they* must surely be overlooked, or they were drunk with kisses, or transfixed by presentiments of immolation, or too diffident to believe they might take their destiny in hand, or of such faith they waited for divine direction. These remained. And the air was tightening. All remarks, even the silent ones, were aimed at them. Their own thoughts suspected doors, flattened themselves against the walls, against the dying paper roses, and pissed down the sides of lavatory bowls, to avoid giving their presence away.

During the whole of this period of unreason, Mordecai Himmelfarb's mind no more than fumbled after a rational means of escape. As an officially guilty man he could not function normally, but attempted to, as far as he was allowed. He was not yet actually dismissed from his post, because, it was recorded, Himmelfarb had served in a German war. At this stage, he was merely relieved of some of his duties, eyelids were lowered, backs turned on an embarrassing and difficult situation. He went on foot more often than before, to avoid the unpleasantness of trams and buses, with the result that his clothes began to hang more loosely on the essential bones, and his face presented an archetype that would have shamed his apostate father. In his still regular walks through the *Stadtwald*, he now rested whenever necessary on the yellow bench. Coming and going, early and late, in thin or thickening light, in company with birds and cats, he felt he had got by heart each stone and sorrow of the town in which he had been born, and that he could interpret at last the most obscure meanings of a contorted world.

Of course he should have made every effort to reach a practical solution, if only for his wife's sake. Cousins had written from Ecuador. Their brother, Ari, he heard, had left for Palestine in charge of a contingent of youths, and was settled on the land. Only Mordecai had received no indication of what his personal role might be, of how long he must suspend the will that was not his to use. Determined not to fear whatever might be in store for his creature flesh, nor even that anguish of spirit which he would probably be called upon to bear, he might have resigned himself indefinitely, if it had not been for the perpetual torment of his wife's image.

At one point his colleague Oertel, the mathematician, an Aryan of stature who suffered and died for it finally, came to him and begged to be allowed help his friend leave the country before it was too late.

Himmelfarb hesitated. Human gestures were so moving in the reign of Sammael, that for one moment he felt weak enough to accept. If only for Reha. Who would not, he realized at once, have left without him.

'Oertel!' he began. 'Oertel!' When he was able to continue, he explained: 'The sins of Israel have given Sammael the legs on which he now stands. It is my duty, in some way, to expiate what are, you see, my own sins. But naturally you cannot, you cannot see! You cannot understand!'

He had become, of course, more than a little crazy, Oertel added in telling of Himmelfarb's refusal.

The latter returned to his wife, whom he loved too deeply to mention his colleague's proposition. They were still allowed to live in the house with the Graeco-German façade. Even after the Professor's dismissal, of which he soon received notice, they were allowed to continue living in their own house. But precariously. Now that the maids were gone, with regrets, or threats, an old Jewish body helped Frau Himmelfarb with her household duties. They were fortunate in having been people of private means, and could eke out their material substance, at least for a little. Sometimes, too, Frau Himmelfarb, discreetly dressed – she had always been that, if anything rather dowdy – would be seen selling an object of virtu. So they existed. In the still house the rooms were never empty. Thoughts filled them. From the upper windows, the Park never looked quite deserted. The flesh of tuberous begonias lolled on perfect beds, and waited, as if to take part in an exhibition of lust.

Once Himmelfarb had paid a visit to a former friend, the *Oberstleutnant* Stauffer who, he had been told, lived only two or three streets away in a state of eccentricity. Celluloid ducks in the bath, it was said.

The *Oberstleutnant* had appeared at his own front door in a little apron trimmed with lace.

'Jürgen!' the visitor began.

But saw at once that the forest in which they had become separated had grown impenetrable, and that, of the two, Jürgen was the deeper lost.

The *Oberstleutnant*'s face, or as much as remained stretched upon the bones, continued a moment to contemplate an abomination that had been conjured up on his doormat for his personal torment.

'The *Herr Oberst* is not at home,' he said at last.

Face, door, words – all flickering slightly.

'And is not allowed to receive Jews. On any account.'

So the door was closed on Jürgen Stauffer.

Again, this time in the street, the past disgorged. It was Konrad, the elder brother, who was by now generally recognized, for one of his novels in particular, which everybody had read, and which dealt, in bitter and audacious style, with the relations between officers and men in wartime. Konrad Stauffer had succeeded in pleasing a cautious public – it was said, even the *Regierung* – because he dared and shocked.

Konrad could afford to know absolutely anybody. Konrad said:

'Why, Himmelfarb! You have hardly changed! Except that everything is on a larger scale.'

As he took a valued acquaintance by the elbow.

His hands were sure. He was freshly, closely shaven, and finished off with a toilet lotion, which caught the morning sunlight, and made the skin look like new. Success had given

Konrad Stauffer the shine and smell of expensive, but very tasteful leather. Many people would probably have professed to loathe him if they had dared run the gauntlet of his arrogance.

'You will pay us a visit, I hope.'

Nor was he taking a risk.

'We are quite close.' He gave his address slowly and accurately, with almost deliberate ostentation. 'My wife will enjoy meeting you. But soon. We may be going away.'

There he smiled.

The phenomenon of Konrad Stauffer left Himmelfarb indifferent. Stauffer must have been aware of it, for he returned immediately after parting. To take the Jew by a waistcoat button. He could have been apologizing for himself.

'You will come, though?' he coaxed. 'You promise?'

In those times, who made promises? Now it was the Jew's turn to smile. But together they had generated some kind of warmth.

Even so, Himmelfarb doubted he would see Konrad Stauffer again. In so far as his will continued to function, it propelled him along the narrow path of existence, not up the side tracks of social intercourse, however attractive those promised to be. Besides, there was his book. Most of his time was taken up with annotations and corrections, for, although he no longer hoped to see it published, it would have pained him to leave it incomplete. In his leisure he walked less than before, not because glances wounded – he had grown impervious – but because he wanted to be parted as little as possible from his wife.

He could not bring himself to speculate on how dependent that soft and loving, yet secretive and unexpected creature might be. Instead he found himself depending on her. He would touch her sometimes for no immediately apparent reason. If he could not find her, he would go in search of her in the kitchen, where probably she would be doing the work of the almost senile crone who had replaced the cook. Then he would inquire about things with which he had been familiar for years.

'What is that?' he would ask.

'That is chopped chicken-liver,' she would reply, in a firm, even voice, to make it seem less odd that he should not recognize the obvious.

Indeed, she would join him in staring at the common kitchen bowl, as if its contents had been ritually of the greatest importance. Together they would stave off the agonies of mind, and the possibility of separation, by the practice of small, touching rites.

Then they heard that Dr Herz had disappeared, and Weills, and Neumanns, and Frau Dr Mendelssohn was no longer to be seen at the clinic. It was very quietly communicated, and as the people concerned were but distant acquaintances, and the rigours and monotony of life continued, one would not have noticed they had gone. Only the old woman who helped at Himmelfarb's became worse than useless. She could not sleep besides. Often in the night Frau Himmelfarb was forced to leave her own bed to comfort her maid.

But there will come a night when comfort is not to be found. Faith will spill out of the strong like sawdust.

On an evening in November, Himmelfarb was on his way home. He had just turned into the Friedrichstrasse. When he stopped. He could not go any farther.

A tram was galloping through the dusk. Along the pavement, the greenish, vegetable faces of pedestrians were trusting to instinct to lead them through a trance of evening. Already in the taverns the shaven heads were arranged at their regular tables. Pickled eggs were being cracked. Mouths were nuzzling the cushions of foam on top of the full stone mugs. There was no reason why one soul should suddenly sense itself caught in the web of darkness, why one man should lose control of his body at the corner of the Friedrichstrasse. Yet Himmelfarb experienced an ungovernable fear. He was actually running. He was running away. He was running and running, released from the moral dignity and physical heaviness of age. Some of the spirits of darkness swore at him as he passed, but he scarcely heard, nor did he suffer from the brutal thumps of collision, of which he was, surprisingly, the cause, in the hitherto normally regulated night.

Down the Friedrichstrasse he ran, across the Königin Luise Platz, into Bismarckstrasse, along the Krötengasse. His desperate breath had to sustain him as far as Süd Park. For by this time the condemned felt the need to be received with kindness. To be *accepted*, rather, by those who stood the right side of the grave.

The Konrad Stauffers lived in one of the iron-grey apartment houses, severe in form, but stuck at intervals with the garlands and festoons of concrete fruit and flowers which usually accompanied the highest rentals. The visitor appeared to be confirming the number of the house by touching the embossed figures

147

with quite distressing relief. Upstairs on the landing, he began to pull up his socks, as young men do automatically, on finding that, for better or worse, they have arrived. He was grinning most horribly, in his effort to resume the human mask, before ringing his friend's bell. His friends! His *friends*! That was the miraculous, solid brass point, the mask considered tremblingly. A friend was safer than one's own blood, so much better value than the arch-abstraction, God. So the man's hands trembled in anticipation. He rehearsed the business of social intercourse, of the inevitable cigars and *Kognak*.

A figure, possibly of future importance, still rather a blurry white, was opening the apartment door.

Inside, beneath the orange light from a lantern in the oriental style, Stauffer was replacing the telephone receiver.

He came at once towards the front door.

'I am so very, very glad you managed to get here,' Konrad Stauffer was saying.

'This is my wife, Himmelfarb,' he said, indicating the thin, upright blur of white.

'So very glad, dear Himmelfarb,' he kept repeating. 'We did wonder.'

'So interested in all that I have always heard,' his wife added appropriately.

Both the Stauffers were obviously shattered. But after he had fastened the front door with a little chain, Stauffer recovered enough of his balance to lead their guest farther into the interior, into what appeared to be a study, where some oriental rugs, at first entirely sombre, gradually came alive, and smouldered.

Frau Stauffer went immediately to an inlaid box, and lit herself a cigarette. The way she blew the smoke from her nostrils, she must have been dying for it.

Then she remembered. She could not offer their guest too much, all in abrupt, though conciliatory, movements.

'Are you, too, fascinated by these poisonous objects?' she asked, following it up with her exceptionally wide smile.

She had brought a dish of hastily assembled liqueur chocolates, of an expensive, imported brand, which had disappeared long ago from the lives of despised mortals. In the circumstances the tinsel forms, presented on their silver dish, glittered like baleful jewels.

And Frau Stauffer herself. In the feverish situation in which they were involved, and at the same time not, Mordecai realized she would probably have excited him in his sensual youth. A

148

raw silk sheath was supported to perfection by a body, of which the bones were just sufficiently visible under brown skin. But tonight, she had a cold, or something. She squeezed herself up against the central heating, in an old cardigan, and even this retained a kind of studied elegance, an accent of Berlin.

The Stauffers both had expectations of their guest, or so their faces suggested.

'I came here tonight,' Himmelfarb began, looking, smiling at the little, glowing *Kognak*, with which his host had provided him as a matter of course.

'Yes? Yes?'

Stauffer was too anxious to assist, his wife too nervous. In fact, she went twice to the door, to listen for the maid, although the latter, she explained, had gone in search of a pair of real live jackboots.

At the same time Himmelfarb realized he could never convey that sudden stampeding of the heart, sickening of the pulses, enmity of familiar streets, the sharp, glandular stench of unreasoning fear. For words are the tools of reason.

'I,' he was blurting shapelessly.

He who was nothing.

So they gave him another *Kognak*.

'Yes, yes, we understand,' murmured the sympathetic Stauffers.

Who remained obsessed with, and perhaps really only understood, an uneasiness of their own.

In their unhappiness, and to assist their once more becalmed guest, they began to talk about Schönberg, and Paul Klee, and Brecht. As liberal Germans, they offered up their minds for a sacrifice, together with liqueur chocolates, and *Kognak*, and a genuine Havana. But every gesture they might make, it was felt by all three, could only be dwarfed by those of circumstance.

Stauffer was slightly drunk. It made him look like a man of action, or at least an amateur of sabotage. Probably he was one of those intellectuals who had discovered the possibilities of action too late in life, perhaps too late in history. He was burning to do something, if not to destroy the whole tree of moral injustice, then, to root out a sucker or two. As he sprawled on the oriental rugs which covered his too opulent divan, the skin had become exposed between the cuffs of his trousers and tops of his socks, which gave him the appearance of being younger, more sincere, if also, ultimately, ineffectual.

Frau Stauffer was combing the hairless skin of her arm with long, pale nails. Under the film of oil which she affected as a make-up, her long, pointed face understood at least the theory of serenity.

Konrad was bandying the names about: Morocco, the Pacific, the Galapagos. But came closer to home, because that was what he knew better. He would know the Riviera best. All of it Himmelfarb heard without relating it to life.

'Bern,' Konrad was discoursing; at last he had come very close. 'A dull but decent city. Where we could meet for lunch. On Thursday. If you decide, Himmelfarb. I suggest, though, you carry nothing heavier than a toothbrush.'

A gentle snow could have been falling through the Jew's mind, without, unfortunately, obliterating.

Its soft promise was forcing him to stand up.

'I must go,' he announced.

Finally, fatally; all knew.

'I must go home to my wife. There is a dog, too. At this time of night, the dog expects to be taken out.'

'Your wife?' Frau Stauffer's breath was drawn so sharp, she could have been recoiling from a blow.

She was wearing a bracelet from which hung big chunks of unpolished, semi-precious stones, which tumbled and jumbled together, in a state of painful conflict.

'I did not realize that your wife,' Stauffer kept repeating.

The Jew was actually laughing.

He laughed through fascinating lips, the horrifying, magnified blubber that flesh will become. Because nobody could realize how his wife was present in him, at all times, until for one moment, that evening, when God Himself had contracted into first chaos.

'I am afraid,' the Jew said, 'I may have been guilty tonight of something for which I can never atone.'

'I am afraid,' he was saying, and saying.

The crumbled Jew.

'No, no!' begged the Stauffers. 'It is we! We are the guilty ones!'

They could not apologize enough, Konrad Stauffer, the unimportant success, and his over-simplified, over-complicated wife.

'We! We!' insisted the Stauffers.

How her bracelet cannoned off itself.

The Jew, who was seen to be quite elderly, made his own way to the door.

'I dare say there are reasons why *you* should not be included in a mass sentence,' he pronounced gently. '*We* can never escape a collective judgement. *We* are one. No particle may fall away without damaging the whole. That, I fear, is what I have done. In a moment of unreason. Tonight.'

They had reached the hall, and were standing in the orange light from the oriental lantern.

'But this is most, most horrible!' Stauffer was almost shouting.

He had become personally involved.

'We understood, in the beginning, you had come here to take refuge' – his voice was reverberating – 'because tonight' – always hesitating, choosing, however loudly, words – 'we were told, in fact, by telephone, just as you arrived' – here his voice blared – 'they are destroying the property of the Jews!'

'*Ach, Konrad!*' His wife moaned, and might have protested more vehemently against the truth.

But a fire-engine seemed to confirm what her husband had just told. It shot through the solid silence of the German suburb, leaving behind it a black tunnel of anxiety.

Only Himmelfarb did not seem surprised. He was even smiling. Now that everything was explained. Now that contingency had been removed.

'When all the time you did not know. Your wife!'

By now Stauffer was wrapped, rather, in his own horror. His man's expression had become that of a little boy, round whom the game of pirates had turned real.

Frau Stauffer's oiled face was streaming with tears as she held an ashtray for their guest to stub out his genuine Havana.

Then the little, unprotective door-chain grated as it withdrew from its groove.

And Himmelfarb was going.

He had already gone from that place, forgetful of his truly kind friends, whom he would have remembered with gratitude and love, if there had been room in his mind.

Süd Park was still, though attentive. A layer of exquisitely concentrated, excruciating orange was seen separating the darkness from the silhouette of the town. It is seldom possible to resume life where it has been left off, although that appeared to be the intention of the figure hurrying through the streets, top-coat flapping and streaming, flesh straining. In the Krötengasse groups of Jews stood in a glitter of glass. The voices of women lamenting quickened his pace. In the Bismarckstrasse a man was crying at the top of his lungs, until some of the crowd began to punch him, when the sound went blub blub blub blub, with intervals of bumping silences.

Himmelfarb was not quite running. He bent his knees, rather, to move faster, closer to the pavement. His own breathing had ceased to be part of him. He heard it panting alongside, like an unwelcome animal which refused to be shaken off. At the corner of the Königin Luise Platz the flames were leaping luxuriantly. In the Schillerstrasse the synagogue was burning. This more sober. An engine parked against the kerb. Several firemen were standing around. What could they do, actually? The rather ugly, squat, practical old building had assumed an incongruous, a Gothic grace in its skyward striving. All could have been atoned now that the voices were finally silenced.

As he entered the Holzgraben, the drops were falling from Himmelfarb, heavier than sweat, his neck was extended scraggily, in anticipation of the knife. This was his own street. Still quiet, respectable – German. A power failure, however, caused by the disturbances, had plunged the familiar into a dark dream, through which he approached the house where they had lived, and found what he knew already to expect.

Of course the door stood open. It was stirring very slightly, just as it had on those several other occasions when he had found it in his sleep.

The house was a hollow shell in which the pretending was over, although he could not yet feel it was empty for the darkness and silence that had silted it up.

He went in, feeling with his feet, which were long and wooden, like his sticks of fingers. In the darkness he stooped down and touched the body of the little dog, already fixed in time, like the sculpture on a tomb, except that the lips were drawn back from the teeth, denying that peace which is the prerogative of death. Most horrible to touch was what he realized to be the tongue.

Then the Jew began to cry out.

He called:

'Reha! Reha!'

And it returned from out of the house.

Always he had imagined how, in the worst crisis, she, his saviour, would come to him, and hold his head against her breast.

But she did not.

So he went blundering and crying.

He called to God, and it went out at the windows, through the bare branches of the trees, so that a party of people a street away burst out laughing, before they took fright.

152

He was mounting interminably through the house. The scent of spices was gone from it for ever, and the blessed light of candles, in which even the most stubborn flesh was made transparent. Moonlight shifted and fretted instead, on the carpets of the landings, and in the open jaws of glass. Cold.

When the searcher did at last arrive in the upper regions, he found the old servant. She began to cry worse than ever, principally for her own fright, while stifling it for fear of the consequences, since even the furniture had turned hostile.

Gradually she told what no longer needed confirming.

They had come, they had come for Himmelfarb.

But what could she add that he had not already experienced? So he left her to babble on.

He went, whimpering, directionless, somewhere down into the pit of creaking darkness. Calling the name that had already fulfilled its purpose, it seemed. So he descended, through the house, into darkness. And in darkness he sat down, as much of him as they had left. He sat in darkness.

6

'The Chariot,' Miss Hare dared to disturb the silence which had been lowered purposely, like the thickest curtain, on the performance of a life.

She did tremble though, and pause, sensing she had violated what she had been taught to respect as one of the first principles of conversation: that subjects of personal interest, however vital, are of secondary importance.

'You know about the Chariot then,' she could not resist.

But whispered. But very slow and low.

It was as eventful as when a prototype has at last identified its kind. Yet pity restrained her from forcibly distracting attention to her own urgent situation, for her mouth was at the same time almost gummed together by all she had suffered in the course of her companion's life. And so, the word she had dared utter hung trembling on the air, like the vision itself, until, on recognition of that vision by a second mind, the two should be made one.

'If we see each other again.' The stone man had begun to stir and speak.

The knot of her hands and the pulses in her throat rejected

any possibility that their meeting might be a casual one. But, of course, she could not explain, nor was her face of any more assistance than her tongue; in fact, as she herself knew, in moments of stress she could resemble a congested turkey.

'If we should continue to meet,' the Jew was saying, 'and I revert to the occasion when I betrayed my wife, and all of us, for that matter, you must forgive me. It is always at the back of my mind. Because a moment can become eternity, depending on what it contains. And so I still find myself running away, down the street, towards the asylum of my friends' house. I still reject what I do not always have the strength to suffer. When all of them had put their trust in me. It was I, you know, on whom they were depending to redeem their sins.'

'I do not altogether understand what people mean by sin,' Miss Hare had to confess. 'We had an old servant who often tried to explain, but I would fail as often to grasp. Peg would insist that she had sinned, but I knew that she had not. Just as I know this tree is good; it cannot be guilty of more than a little bit of wormy fruit. Everything else is imagination. Often I imagine things myself. Oh, yes, I do! And it is good for me; it keeps me within bounds. But is gone by morning. There,' she said, indicating the gentle movement of the grass, 'how can we look out from under this tree, and not know that all is good?'

For the moment she even believed it herself. She was quite idiotic in her desire to console.

'Then how do you account for evil?' asked the Jew.

Her lips grew drier.

'Oh, yes, there is evil!' She hesitated. 'People are possessed by it. Some more than others!' she added with force. 'But it burns itself out. Some are even destroyed as it does.'

'Consumed by their own sin!' The Jew laughed.

'Oh, you can catch me out!' she shouted. 'I am not clever. But do know a certain amount.'

'And who will save us?'

'I know that grass grows again after fire.'

'That is an earthly consolation.'

'But the earth is wonderful. It is all we have. It has brought me back when, otherwise, I should have died.'

The Jew could not hide a look of kindly cunning.

'And at the end? When the earth can no longer raise you up?'

'I shall sink into it,' she said, 'and the grass will grow out of me.'

154

But she sounded sadder than she should have.

'And the Chariot,' he asked, 'that you wished to discuss at one stage? Will you not admit the possibility of redemption?'

'Oh, words, words!' she cried, brushing them off with her freckled hands. 'I do not understand what they mean.'

'But the Chariot,' she conceded, 'does exist. I have seen it. Even if a certain person likes to hint that it was only because I happened to be sick. I have seen it. And Mrs Godbold has, whom I believe and trust. Even my poor father, whom I did not, and who was bad, *bad*, suspected some such secret was being kept hidden from him. And you, a very learned man, have found the Chariot in books, and understand more than you will tell.'

'But not the riders! I cannot visualize, I do not understand the riders!'

'Do you see everything at once? My own house is full of things waiting to be seen. Even quite common objects are shown to us only when it is time for them to be.'

The Jew was so pleased he wriggled slightly inside his clothes.

'It is you who are the hidden *zaddik*!'

'The what?' she asked.

'In each generation, we say, there are thirty-six hidden *zaddikhim* – holy men who go secretly about the world, healing, interpreting, doing their good deeds.'

She burned, a slow red, but did not speak, because his explanation, in spite of reaching her innermost being, did not altogether explain.

'It is even told,' continued the Jew, stroking grass, 'how the creative light of God poured into the *zaddikim*. That *they* are the Chariot of God.'

She looked down, and clenched her hands, for the tide was rising in her. She looked at her white knuckles, and hoped she would not have one of her attacks. Even though she had been lifted highest at such moments, she could not bear to think her physical distress might be witnessed by someone whose respect she wished so very much to keep.

'I shall remember this morning,' Himmelfarb said, 'not only because it was the morning of our meeting.'

Indeed, looking out from under the tree, it seemed as though light was at work on matter as never before. The molten blue had been poured thickly round the chafing-dish of the world. The languid stalks of grass were engaged in their dance of transparent joyfulness. A plain-song of bees fell in solid drops of gold. All souls might have stood forth to praise if, at the very moment, such a clattering had not broken out, and shoved them back.

'What is that?' Himmelfarb asked.

The two people peered out anxiously from beneath the branches.

A pillar of black and white had risen in the depths of the abandoned orchard, but moving and swaying. Silence creaked, and the weed towers were rendered into nothing. Plumes of dust and seed rose.

'Hal-loo? Oo-hoo! Coo-*ee*!' called the voice of conscience.

Miss Hare grew paler.

'That is a person I shall probably tell you about,' she informed her companion. 'But not now.'

Mrs Jolley continued to stamp and call. It seemed doubtful, however, that she would invade territory with which she was not already familiar.

'There is one of the evil ones!' Miss Hare decided to reveal just so much, and to point with a finger. 'How evil, I am not yet sure. But she has entered into a conspiracy with another devil, and will bring suffering to many before it destroys them both.'

Himmelfarb could have believed. It was obvious, from the way he was preparing his legs for use, that he had begun to feel he had stayed long enough, although the Arch-conspirator had gone.

'You will not leave me,' Miss Hare begged. 'I shall not go in. Not for anyone. Not until dark, perhaps.'

'There are things I am neglecting,' mumbled the Jew.

'It is I who shall be neglected if you go,' she protested, like a great beauty hung with pearls. 'And besides,' she added, 'you have not finished telling me your life.'

It made the Jew feel old and feeble. If she was willing him not to go, he wondered whether he had the strength to stay. At least, for that purpose.

'I know,' she said, gently for her, 'I know that, probably, the worst bits are to come. But I shall endure them with you. Two,' she said, 'are stronger than one.'

So the Jew subsided, and the tent of the tree contracted round them in the wilderness in which they sat. The lovely branches sent down sheets of iron, which imprisoned their bodies, although their minds were free to be carried into the most distant corners of hell.

7

How long Himmelfarb remained in the house on the Holz-graben after they took his wife, he had never been able to cal-culate. In his state of distress he was less than ever capable of conceiving what is known as a plan of action. So he lingered on in the deserted, wintry house, even after the old woman, his servant, had left him, to burrow deeper in her fright into the darker, more protected alleys of the town. He would walk from room to room, amongst the violated furniture, over carpets which failed to deaden footsteps. Whenever necessary, he would pick, like a rat, at the food he discovered still lying in saucers and bowls. Much of the time he spent sitting at his manuscript, and once found himself starting to prepare a lecture which, in other circumstances, he should have delivered on a Tuesday to his students at the University.

Sometimes he simply sat at his desk, holding in his hand the paper-knife a cousin had brought from Jannina. He was fasci-nated by the silver blade, the sharpness of which had suggested to the girl Reha Liebmann that it was intended for purposes other than those of opening letters and cutting the pages of books. In recollecting, her husband went so far as to explore the interstices of his ribs, and might have driven it into the heart inside, if he had been able to see any purpose in dying twice.

So this dead man, or distracted soul, put aside the useless knife. Unable to reason, he would drift for hours in a state be-tween spirit and substance, searching amongst the grey shapes, which just failed to correspond, and returning at last to his own skull and the actual world.

During several walks which he took at the time, because, for the moment at least, it did not seem as though they intended to molest the solitary Jew, he continued his search for a solution to the problem of atonement. Nobody, seeing him on the clean gravel of the *Lindenallee*, or the more congruous, because in-determinate paths of the *Stadtwald*, would have suspected him of a preoccupation practically obscene. Nor would they have guessed that the being, in grey top-coat, with stout stick, was not as solid as he appeared, that he had, in fact, reached a state of practical disembodiment, and would enter into the faces that he passed.

This became a habit with the obsessed Jew, and he derived considerable comfort from it, particularly after it had occurred to him that, as all rivers must finally mingle with the shapeless sea, so he might receive into his own formlessness the blind souls of men, which lunged and twisted in their efforts to arrive at some unspecified end. Once this insight had been given him, he could not resist smiling, regardless of blood and dogma, into the still unconscious faces, and would not recognize that he was not always acceptable to those he was trying to assist. For the unresponsive souls would rock, and shudder, and recoil from being drawn into the caverns of his eyes. And once somebody had screamed. And once somebody had gone so far as to threaten.

But their deliverer was not deterred. He was pervaded as never before by a lovingkindness. Only at dusk, when even human resentment had scuttled from the damp paths, the Jew would begin to suspect the extent of his own powers. Although that winter, of bewilderment and spiritual destruction, the concept of the Chariot drifted back, almost within his actual grasp. In fact, there were evenings when he thought he had succeeded in distinguishing its form on the black rooftops, barely clearing the skeletons of trees, occasions when he could feel its wind as it drenched him in departing light. Then, as he stood upon the rotting leaves and steadied himself against the stream of memory, he would drag his top-coat closer, by tighter, feverish handfuls, to protect his unworthy, shivering sides. One morning before it was light, Himmelfarb woke and got immediately out of bed. The cold and dark should have daunted, but his sleep had been so unusually peaceful, he had embraced an experience of such extraordinary tenderness and warmth, that he remained insulated, as it were. Now, as he blundered about in the dark, although he could remember nothing of any dream, he was convinced it had been decided in his sleep that he should prepare to join a cobbler, a humble Jew of his acquaintance, who, he happened to know, was still living in the Krötengasse. So he hurried to shave, cutting himself in several places in the excitement of anticipation, and when he had prayed, and dressed, went about putting into a suitcase the few possessions he felt unable to part with: an ivory thimble which had belonged to his wife, the vain bulk of his now unpublishable manuscript, as well as the ironic, but priceless gifts of his apostate father, the *Tallith* and *Tephillin*. Then he paused, but only for a little, in the thin light, before the door-bell sounded. Although he had not rung for a taxi, knowing that none would have accepted to come, he went down with his worldly goods, in answer to what seemed like perfect punctuality.

'Ah, you are ready then!' Konrad Stauffer said.

Himmelfarb was really not in the least surprised, in spite of the fact that it had already been decided in his mind, or sleep, that he should move to the house of Laser, a Jewish cobbler in the Krötengasse.

Now there was some wrangling for possession of the suitcase, a rather mechanical mingling of his cold fingers with the warmer ones over the disputed handle.

'Please let me!' Stauffer begged.

Himmelfarb suddenly gave way. Because it seemed natural to do so.

His friend was wearing a half-coat of soft leather, which smelled intoxicating besides. Everything invited to a sinking down. The fashionable car had begun to shine in the still hesitating light. Frau Stauffer was standing there, with an expression of having discovered things she had never seen before, holding an anachronistic muff, which only she could have translated into perfect contemporary terms.

All three behaved as though they had parted company yesterday.

'He was actually waiting for us!' Stauffer announced, and laughed for one of those amiable remarks which can be made to pass as wit.

'You must sit at the back, Himmelfarb,' he ordained.

'Get in, Ingeborg!' he commanded his wife more sternly.

She did so, slamming the door in a way which must always have irritated her husband as much as now. But in settling into her seat, she rubbed against him slightly, and there was established a peace which could, of course, have been that of an unclenching winter morning, if Himmelfarb had not remembered, from the previous meeting, occasional glances and certain lingering contacts of skin, which made it obvious that Stauffers still devoured each other in private.

They drove through the white streets.

'I expect you have not eaten. We also forgot,' Frau Stauffer called back to the passenger. 'I have a stomach like an acorn. But we shall put the coffee on as soon as we get there.'

Houses were thinning. Round faces would extend into long blurs.

'We are taking you to Herrenwaldau,' Stauffer explained.

His voice was very grave as he drove. His clipped neck was taut, but in spite of the wrinkles, had acquired a beauty of concentration above the leather collar.

'We have moved out there,' he continued, 'because nowadays it is more sympathetic, on the whole, to live amongst trees.'

159

Herrenwaldau was an estate which Stauffers owned, about seven or eight miles from the town. Himmelfarb remembered hearing several years before how they had bought what some people considered the State should have acquired as a national monument. The original structure, built towards the end of the seventeenth century by a duchess for the purpose of receiving her lovers more conveniently, was something between a miniature palace and a large manor. It had become most dilapidated with the years, although it was understood the actual owners had renovated part of it to live in.

Himmelfarb received everything, whether information on his own future, or glimpses of the rushing landscape, with a sensuous acceptance which he might have questioned, if the motion of the car had not precluded shame. As he was rocked, soft and safe, he noticed the upholstery was the colour of Frau Stauffer's skin. Outside, early light had transformed the normally austere landscape, where sky and earth, mist and water, rested together for the present in layers of innocent blue and grey. The soil would have appeared poor if the frost had not superimposed its glitter on the sand.

The Stauffers, who were obviously performing a familiar rite, seemed to have forgotten their passenger – they would mumble together occasionally about cheese or paraffin – although Frau Stauffer did at last grunt loud and uglily:

'*Na!*'

For they were driving between stone gate-posts, under great naked elms, crowned with old, blacker nests, and hung with the last rags of mist.

Nothing could disguise for Himmelfarb the coldness and greyness, the detached, dilapidated elegance of this foreign house, until, in a moment of complete loss, while his hosts were rootling in the car, he looked very close, and saw that the stone was infused with a life of lichen: all purples and greens and rusty orange-reds, merging and blurring together. Although it was something he had never noticed before, and it did not immediately mean to him all that it might in time, he was smiling when Frau Stauffer turned to him breathlessly, and said:

'There is nobody here! Nobody, nobody!'

Like a little girl who had achieved real freedom after the theory of it.

'Ingeborg means,' her husband explained, 'we have been without servants since the *Regierung* became obsessed by manpower.'

He looked the more grimly amused for having bumped his head in retrieving an oil stove from the car.

'But,' he added, 'there is a farmer who rents some of the land, and who repays in kind, and with a certain amount of grudging labour. They feed the fowls, for instance, when we are away, and steal the eggs while we are here. We must devise a routine for you,' he concluded, 'against the future. To avoid possibly dangerous encounters.'

Such possibilities were ignored, however, for the time being. The three conspirators were loaded high with parcels, and clowned their way into the house, which smelled in particular of fungus, as well as the general smell of age.

They showed Himmelfarb what was to be his room. They had only fairly recently discovered it, Konrad Stauffer told. Disguised from outside by a stone parapet, and from inside by panelling which masked its stairway, the small room could have been intended originally for the greatest convenience of the amorous duchess. The present hosts had furnished it in a hurry for their guest, with a truckle-bed, an old hip-bath in one corner, an austere chest, and the oil stove brought that day. Otherwise the small room was empty, which was how the visitor himself would have had it. As he arranged his insignificant possessions, he realized with sad conviction that the empty room was already his, and might remain so indefinitely.

In the house proper, he understood, as he caught sight of himself that evening in one of the long, gilt mirrors, he would never belong.

But a congenial meal was eaten off the blemished oak table, on which Ingeborg Stauffer laid her face, after the things had been cleared and the work finished.

'At Herrenwaldau,' she said, or foresaw, 'I shall never be completely happy. I am always anticipating some event which will destroy perfection. For instance, I am afraid of the house's being requisitioned for I don't know what squalid purpose. I can see some party leader, of the self-important, local variety, sitting with his feet up on the chairs. I can smell the face-powder, spilt on the dressing tables, by the mistresses.'

'My wife is neurotic,' interrupted Konrad, whose back was turned to them, as he did accounts, or looked through letters which had arrived in their absence.

'Certainly!' Ingeborg agreed, and laughed.

She jumped up and ran and brought little glasses from which to drink cheap, fiery *Korn*. At times she could shine with happiness. And play Bach rather badly on an indifferent harpsichord.

'Between Bach and Hitler,' Konrad said, 'something went wrong with Germany. We must go back to Bach, side-stepping the twin bogs of Wagner and Nietzsche, with an eye for Weimar, and the Hansa towns, listening to the poets.'

'You must allow me *Tristan* though,' his wife protested, and went and hung over his shoulder.

Her head, with the dankish, nondescript, yet elegant hair, grew dark inside the candlelight.

'All right. *Tristan*,' he agreed. 'Anyway, *Tristan* is everybody's property.'

Very gently she bit the gristle in the nape of his neck.

And he cried out, laughably.

Which seemed to remind them it was time to go to bed.

They played this game for several days, while Himmelfarb tentatively explored unopened rooms, and a wilderness of garden, in which unclipped box and yew would have disguised his movements, if a scent of thyme run wild had not risen from under his feet. Once or twice only a trembling of greenery separated him from some peasants, daughters of the tenant-farmer, it appeared, who had arrived on an errand, faces mottled and suspicious, knees dimpling milkily above worsted stockings. And once his back had only time to disappear as Frau Stauffer received someone of greater importance.

That evening his hosts were more silent and thoughtful. When, of his own accord, he took to descending less often from his room, he knew that he was interpreting their wishes. In fact, Ingeborg Stauffer began, as if by agreement, to bring him his meals. And there were the cans of water. Now there was seldom music at night. Silence had thickened in the house below him.

Ingeborg explained at last that Konrad had gone to Berlin. For there had been inquiries by local authorities about the uses to which their house was being put, the number of rooms, their visitors, etc. So Konrad had gone to arrange. There was almost nothing that could not be arranged, through the sister, who was a Minister's wife, the friend, it was even said, of a personage. Ingeborg gave her information with an embarrassment which she had decided it was necessary to overcome, and left her guest to contemplate the knife-edge of life on which they were all balanced.

Himmelfarb could just remember the thin, burning arms of Mausi Stauffer encircling his waist. Once she had almost destroyed him in the eyes of the world, and was now lifting him

162

up, unconsciously, no doubt, a *dea ex machina* created for the occasion by her brother.

The latter returned, satisfied enough, though ironic.

'Sometimes I have to tell myself that success, even of the acceptable, the almost honest kind, was never unaccompanied. Inevitably, it trailed a certain shadow of shame. The favoured one became always just that little bit contaminated,' said Konrad, who had climbed to the room beneath the roof, carrying an extra lamp, and a bottle of *Kognak*. 'I wonder whether the pure aren't those who have tried, but not succeeded. Do you think, Himmelfarb, atonement is possible perhaps only where there has been failure?'

'In that case many of us are saved who never suspected it!' the Jew replied.

Konrad was already breathing too heavily, and not from his ascent to the hidden attic.

'But you are the man of faith,' he mumbled.

'I am the eternal beetle, who finds daily that he has slipped back several stages behind where he thought himself to be the night before. And continues to claw. I would only like to think I am the beetle of faith, not of habit.'

'Better any kind of beetle than a nothing!'

Konrad Stauffer was, in fact, the slightest of men, who made his respect the more touching to the object of it. Himmelfarb felt the humbler for his friend's consideration, and would have liked in some way to convey his gratitude, but might never have occasion to.

Because Stauffer remained at Herrenwaldau for increasingly brief periods.

'Berlin again?' Himmelfarb once asked.

'Berlin is only one of many directions,' the other replied.

And continued to come and go.

In the intervals, his wife served their guest with a regularity that was unexpected. Her elegance persisted, though by then shabbier in its expression. She had grown thinner, bonier, from withdrawal into a world where she seemed not to wish to be followed.

Himmelfarb was even better able to respect such a wish since his own withdrawal into the empty room. There, in his obscure box, he was rarely unemployed, but had not yet arrived at that state of equanimity, of solitariness, of disinterest, from which, it had been suggested by the dyer, he might illuminate the vaster darkness.

Sometimes, competing with his struggle to reach out towards, to reflect upon an unconscious world, he would hear the voice of the radio, announcing, admonishing, clearing its gravelly throat. Or Ingeborg would arrive to complete the sense of what he had suspected. Because, as the chain of events was forged, it became possible to foresee the links. So, Ingeborg only confirmed.

One evening Stauffer returned, and Himmelfarb realized that his friend was also his contemporary, if anything older by a couple of years. For that youthful, sensual, forgivably superficial man had suddenly aged, just as his wife's body could no longer conceal its physical shabbiness, which a superficial shabbiness of clothes had hitherto only hinted at.

Stauffer announced that the British had declared war on Germany.

'Then we are, at last, thank God, wholly committed,' he remarked, more to relieve his own feelings.

After that, Himmelfarb did not see his friend again, and Ingeborg confirmed his impression that her husband was no longer at Herrenwaldau.

'Yes,' she repeated with noticeable intensity, 'it was best that he should go. And even if he is gone longer than usual, one grows accustomed to being alone; one can make it a habit like anything else.'

Like the removal of her guest's tray, for instance, an act she had learned to perform with an obliviousness, a simplicity which moved him every time he watched it happen.

'All this that you do for me!' He was forced to try to convey his feelings on one of the occasions when she had poured the steaming water from the waist-high can into the antiquated hip-bath.

'Oh,' she exclaimed, quickly, still panting from her struggle up the flights of stairs, 'don't you understand? We do it also on account of ourselves. It is most, most necessary. For more than ourselves. For all of us.'

And went away at once, biting her lip, and frowning at her shame.

Several times Himmelfarb was tempted to touch on the subject of her husband's employment, but she was gone before he was able to commit any such indelicacy, and afterwards he was glad.

Only once she did remark:

'You know Konrad will never do anything that *you* would condemn.'

She became increasingly, no doubt wilfully, detached. On the

164

night they heard, from their different parts of the house, the hysterical protests of the ground defences, and the cough and groan, the upheaval of prehistoric foundations when the British aeroplanes first dropped their bombs on a neighbouring target, Ingeborg did not appear. But, on the morning after, he noticed she had gathered back her hair so tight, her normally exposed face was even nakeder.

Yet it did not reveal.

As she held his empty cup at an angle, and contemplated the grey dregs of *Ersatz* coffee, she announced:

'My lovely drake is dead. My big Muscovy. How he would hiss at times, and behave as unpleasantly as any man. But such a strong, splendid bird.'

Himmelfarb felt he should ask how the drake had died.

'Who will ever know?' she answered softly.

It was not important, of course, beside the fact of death.

There was the night the bombs were dropped so close, the rooms changed shape for a second at Herrenwaldau. The Jew rocked in his attic, but knew himself at that moment to be closer than ever to his God, as his thoughts clung to that with which he was most familiar. As the moonlight filled with the black shadows of wings, and all the evil in the world was aimed at the fragile lichened roof, he was miraculously transported.

Afterwards when he had returned from this most ineffable experience, and the lower house no longer strained or tinkled, and only a recessive throbbing and whirring could be heard, the narrow stairway began to fill with the sound of footsteps, and he saw that Ingeborg Stauffer had come to his room, shielding a little lamp with her long trembling hand, against what had once been her assured and elegant breast.

'I was so terribly afraid,' she confessed.

'We were their target,' he realized, 'for some reason only they can know.'

'So very, very afraid,' Ingeborg Stauffer was repeating, and trembling.

Fear, he could see, had made her once more human, and for the first time old.

She was crying now.

So he comforted her, by putting his arms round her almost naked body – she had been preparing herself for bed; he soothed and caressed and strengthened. So that she was soon made warm and young again. And some of his own youth and physical strength returned. In the short distance from the spirit

to the flesh, he knew he would have been capable of the greatest
dishonesty while disguising it as need.

Then, by the light of the subdued lamp, he saw their faces in
the glass. He saw the expression of Ingeborg Stauffer. Who had
woken first. Whose disgust was not less obvious for being ex-
pertly concealed. As for his own face, it was that of an old,
inept man. Or Jew.

'We must try to sleep now,' she said.

She had never sounded kinder, gentler, than in leaving him.

Quite early, it seemed, the following morning, Himmelfarb
recognized sounds of approach in the outside world. By climbing on the table, and opening a little bull's-eye, he had found
that, after craning out, and peering through a balustrade, he
could distinguish below the empty sky a fragment of garden,
trees, and gravel drive. Now, on the morning after the mis-
guided raid, a truck drew up in his precious, because so limited,
field of vision, and several men – or one of them, perhaps, a
sergeant – began to get down.

Much later than usual, Frau Stauffer appeared briefly with
his coffee, and announced that the Army was in residence. To
examine damage and dispose of bombs. Naturally, she would
come to him now only when absolutely necessary. That morning the coffee had been almost cold he realized after drinking
it.

At the same time his room became particularly fragile, even,
he felt, superfluous. Was he preparing to break his shell? Indeed, the stillness could have been an egg, inside which he had
been allowed to grow in strength, until now reminded, by instinct, by men's voices, by the contact of steel with steel, of
some unspecified duty to be performed in an outside world.

Now, it seemed, the stillness could give him nothing more. So
he was walking up and down, restlessly, although from habit
very softly. And hardly noticed when, after days, his guardian's
footsteps again sounded normal on the stairs.

'They have gone,' she said, but with an imitation of relief.

For, in fact, they had not. They would never go now, so her
face told, although she had watched, and he had heard them
disappearing down the drive.

Himmelfarb sensed that the inmates of Herrenwaldau had
merely entered on a fresh phase of spiritual occupation.

And soon after, Ingeborg Stauffer came to him to say: .

'I know now that Konrad will never return.'

It appeared so obvious when spoken, only it was a conviction that until then they had not dared share.

'But have you received news?' Himmelfarb was foolish enough to ask.

'Not news.' She shrugged. 'I shall never, never receive news. I shall only ever know that I shall not see Konrad alive.'

Himmelfarb suspected she would not allow herself to say: *my husband* – it had come so glibly, so extravagantly from her in the past – but now she was not strong enough. In his pity he longed to touch her.

Her face had opened a little. She said,

'It is less dreadful when one had always known. He himself expected. Oh, I know that Konrad, in spite of his success, was an insubstantial man. We both accepted it. He had very few illusions. "My books will survive," he used to say, "just about as long as I." '

There was an organization of a secret, an illegal nature, of which she could not tell, of which in fact she knew very little. To this, Himmelfarb gathered, Stauffer had belonged. But his actual missions would remain undisclosed.

'You understand, in any case,' she said, repeating a remark she had made once before, 'he will have done nothing that *you* would ever condemn.'

Up to this she had been giving information, but now she gathered her elbows. She said:

'I loved him! I loved him!'

Her ordinarily marble face was mumbling and grunting, like that of some bereaved woman.

'*My dearest husband!*' she confided.

And went away.

Less than ever now Himmelfarb belonged to Herrenwaldau. The boards ticked during darkness. In the hours of darkness the dark-red heart swelled enormously beneath the rafters. His iron bed was straiter, crueller to his sides. Then his own wife came and took his hand, and together they stood looking down into the pit of darkness, at the bottom of which was the very faintest phosphorescence of faces. He longed – oh, most intolerably – to look once more at the face of Reha Himmelfarb, but it was as though she were directing his vision towards the other, unknown faces, and might even have become unrecognizable herself. The tears were flowing faster, from the unseen eyes. Of blood, he saw, on the back of his hand. The voices of darkness ever swelling. So that the quick-lime of compassion, mounting from the great pit, consumed him where he stood. Quite alone now. For Reha Himmelfarb had withdrawn; she already knew the meaning of what they had just experienced together.

Himmelfarb climbed up out of his dream into the morning. It was already quite light, though early. For some reason, he saw, he had lain down without undressing, no doubt to be prepared, and now, as if in answer to his foresight, the outside world had begun again to impinge on Herrenwaldau. From his table, through the bull's-eye, between the stone balusters of the parapet, he observed this time a car, followed by a truck, jerking to a stop on the weed-sown gravel.

This time an officer trod down. His splendour was unmistakable, and as if in answer to it, Ingeborg Stauffer had already come out to do the honours. She was wearing a simple costume of still fabulous cut, but on which Himmelfarb had more than once observed a crust of pollard along a lapel. Now she stood there waiting, in the old gum-boots she wore in winter when going out to feed her ducks.

It was very quickly revealed to the observer, even at that distance, that he was present on an occasion, certainly not of high history, of vindication, rather, of the individual spirit. The faces of several private soldiers were aware. An N.C.O. had forgotten to give orders. The officer, of course, obeyed all the etiquette of gallantry in carrying out his peculiar duty. Nor did Frau Stauffer forget what she had learnt. Her voice, always lighter when fulfilling its social functions, was carried upward on the frosty air. Naturally, the listener could not hear more than the upward scale of formal laughter. Frau Stauffer was even wearing the bracelet of large golden links, the lumps of unpolished, semi-precious stones, which always conflicted in motion, and would threaten to break up any serious conversation.

So she had known and was prepared. Certainly there was one moment of intense silence in which Himmelfarb could have sworn he heard a sound of most unearthly breaking, so high, so clear, so agonizing in its swift dwindling. Then Frau Stauffer bowed her head, in agreement it appeared. She got into the car, holding one hand to her breast, not to protect it from the inevitable, but to decorate that inevitable with its measure of grace.

When the car was turned round, so sharply, convulsively, that the wheels left their furrows in the drive, Himmelfarb did catch a brief glimpse of Ingeborg Stauffer's face as it looked out at the wilderness of her neglected garden. She, too, no longer in any way belonged, it seemed, to the framework of actuality. So there was no reason why she should protest at being forced so abruptly out of it. As she was driven away, her face was of that perfect emptiness which precedes fulfilment.

At the same time, the detachment of soldiers, under orders from its N.C.O., had begun to billet itself on Herrenwaldau. Voices were burring. Equipment clattered.

Himmelfarb, who had got down again inside his room, was resigned enough on finding that his own turn had come. He did not hurry. When he had prayed, and brushed his overcoat a little with his hand, and packed into the suitcase the meagre sum of his possessions, he descended into the body of the house. Although it was now filled with sounds of what might be considered as activity, boots bludgeoning frail boards, voices flouting the damp silence of antiquity, those of the rooms which he entered or passed remained gently aloof from their fate. Intending to surrender himself to the first person who questioned his presence there, Himmelfarb wound farther down. Several objects that he touched were sadly reminiscent. Yet it was a distant ceiling encrusted with faded blazonry which made him wonder whether it might be possible to take one more look at the town in which he had been born.

In the long saloon which the owners had used as a living-room, and which was not yet empty of their presence, a heap of cats snoozed on a patch of winter sunshine. A radio was shouting of war. Outside, on the terrace, a stocky youth, of country tints, stood holding a gun, and picking his nose. Himmelfarb wondered for a moment whether to address the soldier boy. But smiled instead. The soldier himself wondered whether to challenge the elderly gentleman, so evidently discreet, so obviously stepped out of the life of kindliness which he understood. In the circumstances, his own always dubious authority dwindled. The gun wobbled. He gave a kind of country nod.

Himmelfarb walked slowly on. He sensed how horribly the boy's heart must have been beating for the mildness in himself which he had not learnt to overcome.

But the strange morning was already unfolding, in which any individual might have become exposed to contingency. The evader walked with care, under the naked, cawing elms. It seemed as though he had abandoned the self he had grown to accept in his familiar room. It seemed, also, fitting that it should again be winter when he took the long, undeviating road along which friends had brought him – how long ago, months or years? – to experience silence and waiting. The winter air cleared his head wonderfully with the result that he found himself observing, and becoming engrossed by the least grain of roadside sand. There were occasions when he nodded at some peasant or child, too involved in the living of their daily lives to think of obstructing the stranger. From time to time, he rested, because his legs were proving humanly weak.

It took the Jew the best part of the day to cover the miles to Holunderthal. The winter evening was drawing in as he approached the darker masses of the town, which had begun already to receive its nightly visitation. The knots and loops, the little, exquisite puffs of white hung on the deepening distances of the sky, all the way to its orange rim. The riot of fireworks was on. Ordinarily solid, black buildings were shown to have other, more transcendental qualities, in that they would open up, disclosing fountains of hidden fire. Much was inverted, that hitherto had been accepted as sound and immutable. Two silver fish were flaming downward, out of their cobalt sea, into the land.

As Himmelfarb entered the town, he concluded the industrial suburb of Scheidnig was the target for the night. There the panache was gayest, the involvement deepest, although occasionally a bomb would fall wide and casual into the deathly streets through which he walked. There was a sighing of old bricks subsiding, the sound of stone coughing up its guts, and once he himself was flung to the ground, in what could have been a splitting open of the earth, if the pavement had not remained, and the hollow clatter of his suitcase spoilt the effects of doom.

As he walked deeper into the town, a wind got up, tossing the flaps of his coat, twitching at the brim of his hat. In the streets, the vagaries of human behaviour had been almost entirely replaced by an apparent organization of mechanical means, engines roared, bells rang, flak reacted, the hard confetti of shrapnel never ceased to fall, innocent and invisible.

Through which the Jew walked.

It did not occur to him to feel afraid. His mechanism could have been responding to control. Once, certainly, compassion flooded his metal limbs, and he stooped to close the eyes of a man who had been rejected by his grave of rubble.

Then wheels were arriving. Of ambulance? Or fire-engine? The Jew walked on, by supernatural contrivance. For now the wheels were grazing the black shell of the town. The horses were neighing and screaming, as they dared the acid of the green sky. The horses extended their webbing necks, and their nostrils glinted brass in the fiery light. While the amazed Jew walked unharmed beneath the chariot wheels.

Originally it had been his intention to revisit the house on the Holzgraben, but suddenly he foresaw the vision of desolation, the stucco skin stripped by bombs and human resentment. So he came instead to the police station which he knew so well, at the corner of the Dorotheenstrasse.

Now, when he went in, the hands of the man on duty were darting back and forth from official paper to official paper. To occupy himself. He was, it seemed, the only one left behind.

'They are belting hell out of the glove factory,' the man on duty informed the stranger. 'For God's sake! The glove factory!'

The man's rather fat hands continued to stray hopefully amongst the official documents. There was a wedding ring on which the flesh was closing. On the plump hand.

'Who would have thought,' said the man in charge, 'that Holunderthal was inflammable! For God's sake!'

'I have come,' Himmelfarb began, who was rootling in his wallet for the necessary proof of identification; tonight it was particularly important.

'To give myself up,' he explained.

'Now there is only disorder!' complained the policeman. 'We no longer have the time even to water our flowerpots.'

His large bursting hands were helpless. And the broad yellow wedding ring.

If he looked up at all, his mind's eye remained directed inward.

'Well?' he asked though. 'What do you want?'

'I am a Jew,' Himmelfarb announced.

Offering the paper.

'A Jew, eh?'

But the policeman was too distracted by his inability to lay his hand on some other document.

'Well,' he grumbled, 'you will have to wait. A Jew!' he complained. 'At this time of night! And on my own!'

So Himmelfarb sat down and waited on a bench against the wall. He saw that it was, in fact, night as the man had said, and heard that a miraculous silence had begun to flood the burning town.

Somewhere there was a voice, thick with conviction, yet at the same time wavery.

> 'War and peace come and go,
> Beer and kisses stay....'

sang the ageless German voice.

'Beer and kisses! Piss-pots!' The policeman snorted. 'Enough to make a man burst himself! Beer and kisses is for human beings.'

Then he looked up.

'A Jew, eh?' he said.

As the silence seeped in he was again able to recognize his duties.

Himmelfarb learned that he was being driven to the railway marshalling yards some miles to the south-east of Holunderthal. He had already heard, through Ingeborg Stauffer, that the place had suffered considerable damage as a target of importance in the war effort and national life. Now he gathered that, amongst its other uses, it served as an assembly point for Jews who were being moved to other parts of the country, even to other countries.

His particulars were taken on arrival, and immediately he was shoved inside one of a number of large sheds. As it was still night, and the shed was kept in total darkness due to the exigencies of war, it was not possible to estimate the number of his fellow occupants, only that the shed contained a solid mass, and that a mass soul suffered and recoiled. Inside the prevailing darkness, worse because it was imposed by man – or could it have been sent by God? – the lost soul mourned, and tried to deduce the reason for the unreasonable. At moments the voice of the mourner sounded like that of a child, but quickly thickened and intensified. Then the aged voice rose, it seemed, out of the depths of history. Crying and lamenting. Sometimes there were blows and kicks as more of the filthy Jews were settled in, and sometimes from the door a torch would reach out, and rend the veil of darkness, revealing patches of yellowish skin, or hands clutching at possessions, as if those were the most they had to lose. The guards might laugh at some indignity glimpsed, but on the whole, at the assembly point, they seemed to prefer a darkness in which to hate in the abstract the whole mass of Jews.

By morning light, which comes slowly and coldly into a bare shed in winter, Himmelfarb began to distinguish the features of individuals, though the way they huddled, bundled up against cold and misery, these members of his race were presented rather as the dregs. Certainly there were individuals still under the influence of decorum. Here and there a streak of white powder was visible in the grey shadows of an elderly lady's skin. An old Jew, wrapped in his shawl for warmth as much as worship, dusted its fringes before kissing them. So far the stench had not begun to rise. Except where a child had dirtied himself, and was wiped clean with difficulty. In that corner it was not possible to ignore the smell of shit. Nor the clamour of hopelessness. In the thin light a man's voice was reciting a prayer for the common good, but the voice of the mother which rose against it no longer believed she might be included in a rescue. The first slime of despair had begun to cling.

Once, as the Jews bestirred themselves at dusk, changing position, chafing limbs, snuffing at the heavy air after a breath of imagined freshness, tearing precious pieces from the stale loaves several had succeeded in husbanding, in a few cases even trying to improvise little meals on spirit stoves, Himmelfarb thought he saw the figure of the dyer he had known in his youth, and sat up from against the case which was numbing his ribs – to call, to greet, to seize the flying tails of all past experience, and hold them fast, lovingly. But the dyer, he realized, touching his own skin, must have died years ago, probably in peace, and could have bequeathed him, as he remembered, the peculiar duty of loving his children, in the limbo of awfulness to which they had been consigned, until he himself was in turn released.

So the legatary sat considering his obligations for the future. When an angry woman, the wife of a grocer, accused the gentleman, educated too, of stealing a rind of cheese she had snatched up on leaving, and with which she was preparing to comfort herself. She was quite abusive, until she noticed her property, fallen in the dirt between them.

The gentleman, a professor or something, smiled at the woman as he handed up the cheese. But she remained hostile to the one who was the cause of her shame.

There where they sat, amongst the cases and the bundles, the keepsakes and the books, the *Wurst* and the cooking utensils, Himmelfarb embraced the children of the dyer. Even when they would not have him. On the several occasions when he actually went amongst them, they were ready enough to speak, to exchange the material details of their woe, but grew shy and silent when his attempts at spiritual candour made them suspect an assault on their privacy of soul. Most of those present were still united with family or friends. To that extent, they were safe, they believed. In the circumstances, they were not prepared to give what the stranger merely wished them to accept.

So he and they continued to sit in the congested shed. At one stage a party of Jews from a near-by camp was herded in. Huddled together in their austere, striped robes, these peoples of shaven heads, receded eyes, and skeletal limbs, silently implied that it was no longer their function to speak, or even mix, with their own race, and it became generally accepted that these were the elect of suffering, who should remain apart. But at least the inmates of the shed had their fate in common, and sometimes the voices of all would unite in prayer·

'May it be Thy will, O Lord our God and God of our fathers, to conduct us in peace, to direct our steps in peace, to uphold us in peace, and to lead us in life, joy, and peace unto the haven of our desire. . . .'

The voices of the Jews rose together in prayer for the journey as, indeed, they were going on one, if not exactly an excursion to Hildesheim, or visit to relatives at Frankfurt.

The unintelligible rigmarole made the guards laugh.

For several days the Jews remained in the sheds at the marshalling yards the other side of Holunderthal. It was difficult to imagine any issue above their own, yet it was fleetingly remembered, a war was raging outside: at night the sky would be criss-crossed as they had once seen it, and the joyless confetti that the flak made would still be falling for the bride of darkness. On the third night, a bomb hit an ammunition train, and the whole of the solid world was rocked. After the sheds which contained the Jews had recovered their normal shape, even after the exploding target, and the sirens and the whistles had exhausted their frenzy, the prisoners lay and waited for something worse to be directed at them personally. They were unable really to believe there might be other objectives.

Finally, on a morning of iron frost, they were taken out. A little hammer tapping on the cold silence at a distance might have struck a note of desolation, if the hiss and drizzle of escaping steam had not created an illusion of warmth somewhere close. Men were coming and going on those mysterious errands of the anomalous hours before dawn. A party of shift workers, stamping and chafing themselves as they gathered, shouted at the guards to remind them of a few simple brutalities they might have forgotten. But those who were most intimately connected with the departure of the Jews, and who had only recently torn themselves out of warm bunks and a frowst of sleep, needed no spur to their resentment. As they prodded their charges along with the points of their bayonets, the guards worked some of it off in little, provocative stabs. One, surlier, and more sleep-swollen than the rest, inserted the blade between the great buttocks of a fat Jew, just so far, to hear the threatened victim bellow. There was a woman, too, crying for something she had left behind in the shed which had become her home. How she cried for the bare boards, which her mind had transformed, and the loss of one woollen glove.

Some of the travellers, however, mostly younger people, and an elderly person said to be a university professor, were determined not to be intimidated by the steely face of morning. Whatever might happen next, there was always the possibility that it might not be worse than they had expected. So their eyes would invest the most unpromising forms with hope: the long black centipedes of stationary trains, twisted girders, or just the vast spectacle of landscape as the light disentangled it from the mist. These more fortunate individuals enjoyed at least the protection of their vision, as they continued to stand, on the thin soles of their shoes, above the crunching frost, holding their cheap portmanteaux, briefcases, or corded chattels. And waited. Or shuffled. And waited. Or shuffled.

Until, from the slight intensification of pressure, the throb of emotion and remarks filtering through the mass, it became known that those in front were being induced to mount a train. And soon it appeared that this was, indeed, a train, none of the cattle-trucks of which everyone had heard, but carriages with orthodox compartments, certainly not of the newest – the stuffing was bursting out of many of the arm-rests – yet, a train, a train, of corridors, and windows which opened after a struggle, and white antimacassars – admittedly a little soiled where other heads had rested – but a train, a real train. So the Jews pushed, and some of them dared joke. At the ends of the corridors there were actually w.c.s, nor was there any thought of complaint amongst the passengers when it was discovered that the basins and lavatories were waterless. They were far too grateful.

What could have happened? they asked one another as they sat, still panting, still in heaps, still trickling with sweat inside their winter clothes. Nobody bothered yet to answer, only to ask. The pale light of morning was filled with a wonderful flashing of eyes, for the fire of all those people, so recently threatened with extinction, was suddenly rekindled.

As the train jolted slowly into motion, and the couplings wrestled to establish a grip, throwing the passengers together, a lady whose face had not yet formed behind its veil, offered the university professor a *Brötchen*, filled with the most delicate shavings of *Wurst*, and explained in the voice of one who knew, that the policy towards the Jews had definitely changed. So she had heard, the lady insisted, holding her head at a knowing angle, but whether the information had come to her by word of mouth, or intuition, she did not seem prepared to reveal. Nor was her news less joyous because necessity had made it believable. The compartment hummed with surmise, and the lady herself threw back her veil, to prepare for cultivated conversation in refined company.

The Professor, however, chewed greedily away.

'It could be so,' he breathed, and made it clear he did not wish to elaborate.

For he was so happy to munch, his eyes bulging like those of any abandoned dog bolting down its find of offal. He masticated, and ignored the fact that the exquisite wafers of *Wurst* stank, and that the elegant little varnished roll was by then practically petrified.

There were others in the compartment, of course. To tell the truth, it was rather tightly packed. There was a mother, whose sick child dirtied himself repeatedly, and could not be treated without the requisite drugs. There was a widower in a stiff black hat, the father of two little boys, who owned between them a wooden horse. There was a young man and young woman, who plaited their hands together from the beginning, and would not have been parted, least of all by death. And two individuals so insignificant, Himmelfarb never after succeeded in reconstructing their faces, however hard he tried.

So the train drew out, across Germany, it could have been across Europe.

And the numb landscape actually thawed. The naked branches of the beeches appeared to stream like soft hair, when their steely whips should have stung. The fields and copses were delivered temporarily from the grip of winter. Black water flowed between the dirtied cushions of the snow. Such a miraculous release. Some peasants in a yard stood and laughed round a heap of smoking dung. A little girl, as pale as sprouting cress, danced in a meadow, holding out her apron to catch what even she might not have been able to tell.

As the train lurched always deeper into Europe, the lady of the *Brötchen* wound round a black-kid finger the tendrils of her hair. Of quite a lively red. She was a native of Czernowitz, she was kind enough to inform, of inherited means, and her own talents. Circumstances, alas, had carried her from the scenes of her glory into Northern Germany.

The little boys looked up, jointly holding their painted horse.

Na, ja, sighed the father in the stiff black hat.

He had a long, drooping, doubting lip.

And the landscape flowed. The sky showed, not the full splendour of sky, but intimations of it, through rents in the cloud. For Himmelfarb, who had closed his eyes behind his spectacles – from accumulation rather than exhaustion – it was enough. After the days of darkness, too much had been revealed too soon. He was filled with it.

As he drowsed, and woke, and drowsed, the train rocked, smelling of other trains. The sick baby slept, whom the mother had managed to clean after a fashion.

It *was* the change in policy, insisted the Lady from Czernowitz, who had returned from the waterless w.c.

She had spoken to a rabbi, of Magdeburg, and been convinced. The train-load of Jews was the first to be carried into Eastern Europe. In future, all Central European Jews would be assisted to reach Bucharest, to make their connexions for Istanbul, where they would embark for Palestine. Neutral powers had interceded. Certainly, whenever it halted, laughter sounded from farther down the train, and songs of rejoicing in the corridor, so choked with bodies and baskets that joy alone could have leavened such a mass.

The Lady from Czernowitz shone with her own information, and the anonymous souls had to praise God. Only the wooden father of the two little boys no more than stared, and breathed.

Dusk had begun to powder the Lady from Czernowitz, laying the grey upon the white; a woman of less indefatigable mystery might have looked smudged. But she herself was quick to take advantage of the hour. She anointed herself from a little phial, and tried out a bar or two, in the middle register, on the evening star.

Her voice, she explained, had received its training from only the best teachers in Vienna. Her *Freischütz* had been praised at Constanza, and as for her *Fledermaus* at Graz! Recently, she had agreed to accept pupils, but only a few, and those exceptional. She had accompanied a young princess to Bled, and spent an agreeable season, of pleasure and instruction. Ah, the charm and distinction of the Princess Elena Ghika! Ah, the *Kastanientorten* beside the lake at Bled!

The younger of the little boys began to cry. He had never felt emptier.

Only the landscape filled. Darkness seeped along the valleys, and clotted in the clefts of the hills. Its black, treacly consistency arrived on the window-panes of the train.

Certainly it was sadder at night.

A man died on the train, in the night, and was dragged off, into a village to which he had never belonged. They watched his heels disappear with a jerk. Death irritated the guards, particularly since the frost had set in again, and the dead man's metal heels caught in transit in other metal. Later in the journey, but by daylight, several other people died, and remained in the compartments, in the very positions in which their souls had abandoned them.

Had the *Regierung* overlooked the dead in revising its Jewish policy? asked the mother whose sick baby was by then stinking terribly.

But the Lady from Czernowitz averted her face. It was her habit to ignore the insinuations of common persons. And how was *she* responsible for official omissions? Dedicated to music and conversation, all else bored her, frankly. Indeed, her skin looked quite fatigued.

One would, perhaps, be better dead, mused the mother of the sick child.

'Death!' The Lady from Czernowitz laughed, and announced, not to the rather common woman who had suggested it, nor yet to the compartment at large, but to some abstraction of a perfectly refined relationship: 'Oh, yes! Death! If I had not suspected it involved *des ennuis énormes*, I might have used my precious little cyanide. Oh, yes! Long ago! Which, I must admit, I never move one step without.'

And glanced down into her floury breasts. And patted herself. And laughed – or ejected an appearance of mirth out of her deathly face.

So she continued to crumble.

Oh, the aching, and the rocking, and the questions. For they had begun again to ask one another: Why the train? Why the train? Why not the cattle-trucks?

Until the father in the stiff hat could bear it no longer, and had to shout:

'The train – don't you see? – was all they had. The trucks were bombed. And so many Jews on their hands. There was no alternative.'

178

But solutions do not always console. Ah, if they could have opened something, and found the truth inside.

Like the two lovers, at least, whose faces were cupboards containing antidotes, but only efficacious on each other.

There was the professor, too, who had withdrawn farther than anyone else could follow. Himmelfarb, the guilty, would return at intervals, to observe that the faces of those he truly loved had grown resentful, and might in time begin to hate, in the manner of men.

So the train-load of Jews continued to lurch across Europe. The minutes gnawed at the bellies of the hungry, but the hours finally stuffed them with a solid emptiness. As they sat, the crumbs of dignity and stale bread littered the floor around their feet.

Once or twice air raids occurred. Then the train would lie up in darkness, alongside some placid field. In the darkened, reverberating boxes, many of the human beings no longer bothered to crouch, as if worse could not possibly happen to them. Their skins had become hides, rubbing on the napless plush, or against the greasy antimacassars, which was all that survived of *Mitteleuropa*.

And then, in a morning of deeper, dripping green, of blander blue, the train, which had drawn slower, silenter, far more purposeful, since a certain seemingly important junction, with its ganglion of silver, slithery lines, stopped ever so gradually at a little clean siding, paved with sparkling flints, and aggressive in its new paint, if it had not been so peaceful. On either hand, the forest rose, green to black. The siding was named FRIE-DENSDORF, the sign proclaimed.

Yet, they must be in Poland, insisted the Lady from Czernowitz, who had overheard at the junction a few phrases in the Polish tongue, of which she had acquired a smattering, for amusement's sake, let it be understood, or as an intellectual exercise.

The train continued to stand, in the dripping forests, at the siding of Friedensdorf. And German voices came. The doors were wrenched open. There was a crunching of boots on flints, and much official instruction.

'Welcome! Welcome!' announced the official voice, magnified, though muffled. 'Welcome to Friedensdorf!'

There was even music. Towers of music rose above the pointed firs. The giddier waltzes revolved glassily on discs, or alternately, invisible folk-dancers would tread their wooden round, with the result that the seed was in many cases sown, of credulity, in innocence.

See, some of the passengers were prepared to believe, and amongst them the Lady from Czernowitz, this was a kind of transit camp, for those who were taking part in the organized migration to the Land. Here they would be fed and rested, while awaiting trains from the other end.

Whatever the explanation, the passengers were soon brought tumbling out, and again there were those more timid souls who regretted their late home in the dilapidated train, just as they had protested earlier at eviction from a railway shed. But there they were, standing on the platform, in the damp, outside air, assaulted by a scent of pine needles, the waves of which, at the best of times, will float their victims back into the intolerable caverns of nostalgia. Already it was apparent that some of the older people, weakened enough by hunger and the privations of the journey, would not be able to endure much more, and those nearest to them were preparing to catch them if they fell. To say nothing of sick, or young children. To judge by the expressions on the hatched-bird faces, these had suddenly recalled the experience of former lives. Unlike most of the adults, who had had time to forget, they enjoyed the doubtful benefit of insight, with the result that many of them walked as though they suspected the crust of yellow excrement coating the earth had still to harden.

Nervous children of this kind were jollied by the adults. Or the guards. Some of the latter were so good. Himmelfarb could remember cracking peasant jokes with the honest German faces, in forest clearing and village street. Their voices expressed the good, rasping crudity of earth and apples. Now, as they marshalled the new arrivals, their teeth were as white as split apples, their mouths running with the juices of persuasion. Though, of course, the bestial moments occurred too. There is always the beast lurking, who will come up, booted, bristling, his genitals bursting from the cloth which barely contains them. Some of the guards, by their behaviour, made the passengers remember other incidents they would have preferred to forget.

But all were soon ready to advance, and did, though the ones behind were the more willing. Beneath the streamers of music, through the wet, cajoling pines, the party moved. It could have been a tattered, a lamentable sight. So amorphous, in spite of official attempts, and the baritone voice of an iron tower, which urged order and cleanliness on the guests of Friedensdorf. But here came the sick, the aged, the untouchables – the Jews: old women pick-a-back on their sons, stiff legs stuck out in spiralled stockings; grandfathers trailing *Tallithim* and the smell of years; desperate husbands protecting their wives' bellies from the crush; bourgeois with brief-cases and identical hats. So they arrived, and the precautionary gates were closed upon them. The mesh of tingling, spangled wire subsided.

'*Ach*, look now! I have torn my veil!'

The Lady from Czernowitz was inclined to whimper, but after a very brief contact between her black kid glove and her companion's arm was able to continue.

'I am assured,' she informed, 'that we shall be treated with the greatest consideration during our short stay. And shall reach Constanza unharmed. Or is it Istanbul? But to return, Professor, to our conversation, I must tell you the walks were magnificent in the forests of Bukhowina, where we would pick the little wild strawberries, and eat them with the finest sugar and faintly sour cream.'

More than a little disarranged, her flesh turned mauve beneath the last vestiges of powder, the Lady from Czernowitz was still able to glitter from behind the kohl. It was also perhaps the music. She appeared to react more feverishly to music, and now a hand had released something by Lehar, the frills of which fluttered from the iron tower.

'*Achtung! Achtung!*' interrupted the official voice, that rather warm baritone.

All new arrivals would proceed to the bath-houses. Men to the left, women to the right. All would take baths. Baths. Men to the left. To ensure absolute cleanliness, passengers would have to submit to a routine disinfection. Women to the right.

Through the palpitating air of the false thaw fell the cries of parting. It was most unreasonable, the official voice grumbled. But who had not been deceived by reason before? So the bodies of the unreasonable locked themselves together in a last, long attempt to merge. And, in many cases, were only prised apart by force, carrying with them into segregation convulsed handfuls of clothing and hair.

'Do you suppose, Professor,' cried the Lady from Czernowitz, 'do you suppose we shall be expected to undress in public?'

'Let us not be ashamed of our nakedness,' Himmelfarb advised.

But the Lady from Czernowitz suddenly screamed.

181

'I cannot bear it!' she shrieked. 'I cannot bear it! Oh, no! No! No! No!'

'I shall pray for us!' he called after her. 'For all of us!'

His hands dangling uselessly in the vacant air.

Nor did she hear his man's voice attempting to grapple with a situation which might have tested the prophets themselves, for she was borne away, in a wind, and stuffed inside the bath-house, in case her hysteria should inspire those who were obedient, duller, or of colder blood. The last Himmelfarb saw of his companion, at that stage, was the black and disordered bundle of her tearing clothes.

For the men were also pressed back, by ropes of arms, and in certain cases, by naked steel. It seemed as though the sexes would never again meet, at the prospect of which some of the women screamed, and one young man, remembering tender intimacies, rasped, and ranted, until almost choked by his own tongue.

'Achtung! Achtung!' the official voice prepared to inform, or admonish. 'After disrobing, guests are requested to hang their clothing on the numbered hooks, and to pile any other belongings tidily on the benches beneath. Everything will be returned aft ...'

But there the system failed.

'Achtung! Acht ... On numbered hooks ... Will be return ... Ftt ... Ftt ...'

Now Himmelfarb, who had been pressed inside the door of the men's bath-house, gave himself into the hands of God. His own were on his necktie. Most of his companions, on whom the virtue of discipline had been impressed by the country of their birth or election, were instinctively doing as they had been asked. One big fat fellow had entered so far into the spirit of the dream that his shirt was half-way over his head. Himmelfarb himself was still only watching the dreadful dream-motions.

'Into your hands, O Lord,' his lips were committing him afresh.

When something happened.

A guard came pushing through the mass of bodies, one of the big, healthy, biddable blond children, choosing here and there with a kind of lazy, lingering discrimination.

'You will remain dressed,' he ordered Himmelfarb, 'and report with me outside for camp duties.'

It seemed quite capricious that the guard should have picked on this elderly man, although there might have been an official reason for his doing so. Certainly Himmelfarb was still impressive. In height and breadth he was the guard's equal, but his eyes entered deeper than those of his superior, whose shallow blue did flicker for an instant. It could have been, then, that the physically luxuriant youth was deliberately wooing into his secret depths what he sensed to be a superior spirit. Or he could, simply, have been directed without knowing.

Several other Jews, of various ages and muscular build, were following the guard, stupefied.

Outside, the sanded yard appalled by its comparative emptiness, as well as by its chill, for mists were issuing out from the trees, to creep between the sweaty layers of clothes. The favoured stood around, fluctuating uneasily inside the cages of their ribs.

Then they began to notice that a number of other individuals, all obviously of slave status, dressed in miscellaneous garments, were assembled in a kind of informal formation.

One of them spoke to his neighbour, who happened to be Himmelfarb.

'The women will soon be going in,' the stranger informed, in faltering, faulty German. 'The women usually go in first.'

It was doubtful to what race the man belonged. He could have been a darker Slav, a Pole perhaps, or of Mediterranean stock, but there was no mistaking the evidence of inferior blood.

' "Going in"?' asked Himmelfarb. 'What do you mean by "going in"?'

'To the gas,' the fellow explained, in decent friendly tones.

But ghostly, Himmelfarb remembered, fleetingly, a colleague who had been dying of cancer of the throat.

'Yes,' whispered his new friend. 'The gas will be pouring soon. When it is over, we shall drag the bodies to the pits.'

It suggested a harvest ritual rather than the conventions of hell.

But just then the door of the women's bath-house burst open, by terrible misadventure, and there, for ever to haunt, staggered the Lady from Czernowitz.

How the hands of the old, helpless, and furthermore intellectual Jew, her friend, went out to her.

'God show us!' shrieked the Lady from Czernowitz: 'Just this once! At least!'

In that long, leathern voice.

She stood there for an instant in the doorway, and might

have fallen if allowed to remain longer. Her scalp was grey stubble where the reddish hair had been. Her one dug hung down beside the ancient scar which represented the second. Her belly sloped away from the hillock of her navel. Her thighs were particularly poor. But it was her voice which lingered. Stripped. Calling to him from out of the dark of history, ageless, ageless, and interminable.

Then the man her counterpart, brought to his knees by sudden weakness, tearing them furiously, willingly, on the pebbles, calling to her across the same gulf, shouted through the stiff slot of his mouth:

'The Name! Remember they cannot take the Name! When they have torn off our skins, that will clothe. Save. At last.'

Before she was snatched back.

And he felt himself falling, falling, the human part of him. As his cheek encountered the stones, the funnels of a thousand mouths were directed upon him, and poured out over his body a substance he failed to identify.

When Himmelfarb was able once more to raise his head, he realized that, for the second time in his life, he had fainted, or God had removed him, mercifully, from his body. Now it was evening, and a strange one. Those objects which had appeared most solid before: the recently-built bath-houses, for instance, and the iron towers, were partially dissolved in mist. The well-planned establishment which he had known as Friedensdorf was enclosed in a blood-red blur, or aura, at the centre of which he lay, like a chrysalis swathed in some mysterious, supernatural cocoon. Other forms, presumably, though not distinguishably human, moved on transcendental errands within the same shape, no longer that intense crimson, but expanding to a loose orange. Of blue edges. He was reminded suddenly and vividly of the long, blue-grey, tranquil ash of an expensive cigar he had smoked somewhere. Of stubbing out a cigar by the orange light from a little lantern of oriental design. Then, of course, he remembered his friend Konrad Stauffer.

When his tardier senses returned.

His surroundings exploded into the consciousness of the man who was lying on the ground. What had seemed soothingly immaterial became most searingly concrete. A wound opened in his left hand. The blue-black gusts of smoke rushed in at his eyes and up his nostrils. Men were shouting. He could feel the breath of orange fire. Explosives convulsed the earth beneath his body. Bullets pitted the air, but rarely. It was the fire that predominated. Friedensdorf was burning.

It was then that Himmelfarb realized he had lost his spectacles. The discovery was more terrible than fire. Engulfed in his affliction, he began to grope about him, touching stones, a strip of hot metal, a little lake of some liquid stickiness, a twig, a stone, a stone, in that fruitless journey across what must remain an empty desert.

As he crawled and searched.

Or looked up at the orange blur, which seemed by now to be invading the whole of existence. Somewhere on the left a machine-gun hawked fire. Even his own breath issued from his mouth in a tongue of fire. As he blubbered, and panted. Searching. To focus again the blessed shapes of things.

He had covered so much ground, it was unlikely now. Though his hands continued, for employment, to grope, and touch, long after he had strayed beyond reach of possibility. He touched wire. He tore his hands on the barbs of wire. He touched a cotton rag suspended from the same barbs. He was touching air. To the side of the rag, or flag of cotton, his hands suddenly encountered nothing but the soft air. There was, in fact, a small jagged gap, if not a vast triumphal arch in the peripheral fence. Someone had simply cut the wire.

Then the Jew had bowed his head, and went out, still upon his knees. He shuffled upon his knees anywhere, or where it seemed indicated that he should. Over the stones he hobbled, like some deformity. Upon his torn knees. He must get up, he knew, but apart from the stiffness of his limbs, which made of this unnatural position a temporarily natural one, he had not yet crossed, he suspected, the line dividing hell from life. When the barbs entered his forehead, and he was not surprised to put out his hands and grasp a fresh agony of wire. It was, of course, the outer fence.

He might have hung there, content just to be ignored by the tormentor's mind, if a moment of lethargy had not forced him to reach out for a fresh hold, to prevent himself from toppling. And for the second time, he found himself touching the mild, unobstructed air. And was goaded into wildest action by that very gentleness. All of him was tearing – flesh, breath, the stuff of his clothes – as he wrenched himself out of the grip of the wire. But got himself free, and manoeuvred through the narrow, the so very narrow rent, made by those who had cut their way out through the second barrier of wire.

The air was staggeringly cold that flung against his sweaty, bleeding forehead. Shapes welcomed, whether of men or trees, he had not the strength to wonder, but did at last touch bark. And dragged himself up, on to his feet. He wandered through a forest, from trunk to kindly trunk. The wet needles mingled with his skin, their scent spreading through that second maze, his skull, until he was almost drugged with freedom.

He walked on, and could have continued gratefully, if he had not come to what was by comparison a clearing, in which stood a band of virgin forms – young birches, they might have been – their skin so smooth and pure, he fell down against them, and lay crying, his mouth upon the wet earth.

Some time later men arrived. Whatever their complexion or beliefs, he could not have moved. They stood around him. Talking. Poles, he reasoned with what was left of his mind. And listened to their silence and their breathing as they carried him through an infinity of trees.

On arrival at a stench of pigs and straw, they laid him on the stove of a house to which they had brought him. He had no desire to leave the warmth and darkness. He lay with his head on a kind of hard block, when not actually at rest in the bosom of his Lord. Women came to dress his wounds. They would appear with soup. Thin and watery. A steam of cabbage. Sometimes there were dumplings in the soup, which made it rather more difficult.

On the third day, or so he calculated, they brought him somebody, a man of youthful voice, who spoke to him in German, and told him as much as the peasants knew of recent events at Friedensdorf.

Those of the prisoners kept alive by the Germans, to empty the gas chambers of corpses, and provide labour for the camp, had decided to mutiny, the Pole related. Weeks had been spent collecting and hiding arms and ammunition, and it was only after the arrival of the last train-load of Jews that the conspirators felt themselves strong enough to act. Then the slaves rose, killed the commandant and a number of the guards, exploded a fuel dump, set fire to part of the establishment, cut the wire, and were at that moment on their way to join the Resistance.

'And all those other Jews?' Himmelfarb ventured to ask.

The Pole believed most of them had died, some already of the gas fumes, the remainder by the fire which destroyed Friedensdorf.

He laughed.

'You are the lucky one!' he said.

And Himmelfarb, who had re-examined so often the sequence of his escape, could not bring himself to explain how it had been a miracle.

When he was rested and recovered, they dressed him and took him by the hand. That half-blind peasant could not have counted the number of hands he touched as he stumbled on his journey eastward. Moving always in the same obliterating, perhaps merciful mist, he learned the smell of wet grass, of warm hay, of bruised turnips, of cows' breath. He grew accustomed to hearing voices he could not understand, except when accompanied by touch, or expressing the emotions of songs. There were many common sounds he felt he had never heard before, and he found himself penetrating to unsuspected layers of silence. Above all, he learned to recognize that state of complete suspension in which men, like animals, wait for danger to pass.

It was not until Istanbul that Professor Himmelfarb recovered his sight, and something of his own identity. How the water shimmered, and the leaves of the trees were lifted. As he looked out from behind his brand-new spectacles, he had to lower his eyes, ashamed to accept the extravagant gifts that were offered him.

It was decided, then, that Himmelfarb, unlike many others, should be allowed to reach the Land, although, in the absence of some sure sign, or sanction, his own conscience continued to doubt his worthiness.

In the circumstances, he was reluctant to lift up his voice with those of his fellow passengers on the somewhat rusty freighter which carried them down the Turkish coast. The young Jews lounged on the fo'c'sle hatches, with their arms round one another, and sang. All those young people, the thickish, hairy youths and green-skinned girls, germinated in the night-soil of Europe, had come that much closer to fulfilling their destiny. For the Jews were at last returning home. They would recognize the stones they had never seen, and the least stone would be theirs.

But the rather remote figure of the elderly man, a professor, it was said, seemed to have no part in it. As he continued to walk the deck, he would hesitate, and turn, carefully, perhaps not yet altogether reconciled to the rather-too-fashionable, recently-gotten, second-hand shoes. Certainly there was an immense gap between the age of the preoccupied figure and those of the jubilant younger Jews. Some of the latter called to him, inviting him to participate in their relief and joy, and even made a few harmless, friendly-sounding jokes. They soon gave up, however, averted their eyes, and rummaged for peanuts in the little bags which had been handed to them, together with other comforts, by a charitable local Jewess on the quay at Istanbul. Voluptuously, they lulled themselves. They began again, mumbling at first, then stirringly, to sing.

A number of the older Jews attempted to claim their share of good things, and join in the singing, but found they had not the mind for it. The sea air had given their cheeks a new, a positively healthy tinge, and their eyes were glazed with formal contentment from watching the pattern of crisp little waves repeat itself over and over on the classic waters. But in some of the older faces, the smiles were seen to stick half-way, as if caught up on an obstructing tooth, one of those gold landmarks. And there were individuals who were forced to stop their mouths with handkerchiefs, for fear their joy might get out of hand and not be recognized as such. After all, nobody was used to it yet. They had acquired that new and rather unmanageable emotion along with their new clothes, in many cases ill-fitting, from the organization in Istanbul.

The chosen people stood or sat about the decks, or leaned over the rails and watched the quite incredible sea. But Professor Himmelfarb walked, or stalked, between those who finally took him for granted. The relief committee had given a surprising amount of thought to what they had interpreted as the feelings and tastes of the elderly, cultivated refugee, who would no doubt be absorbed into the academic life of the university at Jerusalem. They had fitted him out with clothes which approximated to the kind he must always have worn. The topcoat, for instance, of European cloth and cut, had belonged originally to a Doctor of Philosophy at Yale. Now, as the present owner walked in the sea breezes on the crowded deck, the dark, capacious, yet somehow oppressive overcoat held plastered awkwardly against his sides, nobody would have questioned the distinguished man's right to it. Unless himself.

At the reception centre he had stood too long with the coat in his hands, with the result that the Jewess who was supervising the distribution of clothing had been provoked to ask:

'Are you not pleased with your nice new overcoat, Professor Himmelfarb?'

The lady, who wore a moustache, and a wristwatch on a practical strap, had had some experience of kindergarten work.

'Yes,' he replied. '*Pleased*.'

But stood.

'Then, why don't you take your coat,' she suggested kindly, 'and go and sit with the others at the tables. Madame Saltiel is going to distribute a few comforts for the voyage. After that, there will be a cup of coffee.'

She touched him firmly on the elbow.

'But it is hardly right,' he said, 'that I should accept what is not yet my due.'

'Of course it is your due!' insisted the lady, who was very busy, and who, in spite of her training, could become exasperated. 'And it is *our* duty to make amends to those of our people who have suffered,' she tried to explain with gentleness.

'It is I who must make amends,' insisted her recalcitrant pupil. 'I am afraid it may soon be forgotten that our being a people does not relieve us of individual obligations.'

But the lady propelled him towards the tables where other Jews were awaiting further largess.

'I should take my coat, if I were you,' the lady advised, 'and worry no more about it.'

She was too exhausted to respect delicate scruples. The little points of perspiration were clearly visible on the hairs of her moustache.

So Himmelfarb took the excellent coat, carrying it unhappily by one of its arms, and had to be reminded that his overcoat was trailing in the dust.

It was in the same reluctant frame of mind that he entered, or returned, to Jerusalem – as if he alone must refuse the freedom of that golden city, of which each stone racked him, not to mention the faces in the streets. One evening on a bare hillside, which the wind had treated with silver, he lay down, and it seemed at first as though the earth might open, gently, gently, to receive his body, but his soul would not allow, and dragged him to his feet, and he ran, or stumbled, down the hill, his coat-tail flying, so that a couple of Arabs laughed, and a British sergeant grew suspicious. Yet, at the foot of the hill, he was again clothed in dignity, and chose a lane that led through the trapped and tarnished light of evening, back into the city which, it seemed, would never be his.

There were many familiar figures on the streets, with greetings which ranged from the expansive to the elaborately judicious. On King George Avenue he ran into Appenzeller, the physicist, of Jena, whom he had known from student days, rather a coarse-skinned, bristly individual, who battered the backs of those he met to gain the advantage over them.

Appenzeller did not believe in ghosts. He opened with:

'Well, Himmelfarb, I shall not say I am surprised. You were always so substantial. Do you remember how they used to say you would go far? Well, you have arrived, my dear!' How he laughed at his own joke, and the pores round his nostrils oozed. You have been up to Canopus, of course. Not yet? Well, we shall be expecting you. You will be useful to me,' he said. 'Everyone has his part to play.'

Himmelfarb remembered the infallible stupidity of Appenzeller outside the laboratory and lecture theatre.

'Later on,' was all he could reply, with a reticence which gave his colleague opportunity for contempt.

Appenzeller recalled how an almost girlish diffidence would overtake his massive friend at times. The physicist was one of those who automatically interpret reserve as an encouraging sign of moral weakness.

'It is fatal to brood, you know,' he advised, looking as far as he could into the other's eyes, though not far enough for his own satisfaction; he would have enjoyed dealing some kind of jovial blow. 'Besides, it is no longer a luxury when so many others have suffered too.'

Advice would swim from Appenzeller's skin, of which the pores had always been conspicuously large.

'I am about to go down to Haifa,' Himmelfarb replied.

The physicist was surprised, not to say disappointed, to see that his tentative remark appeared to have left no trace of a wound. Appenzeller's simplicity could perhaps have been explained by the fact that he himself had barely suffered.

'Family connexions,' that dry number Himmelfarb continued. 'I am told that I shall find my wife's eldest brother in some *kibbutz* out near Ramat David.'

'Ah, family!' Appenzeller smiled. 'I am happy to hear it.' He coughed and giggled.

'We shall expect you, then, on your return. Refreshed. You will like it here,' he added, 'if you don't find there are too many Jews.'

After making his joke, Appenzeller took a friendly leave, and Himmelfarb was glad.

The latter did go down to Haifa, by a series of wartime buses and military lorries. He was carried some of the way along the road to Ramat David, but preferred to walk the final stretch before the settlement at which he hoped to find Ari Liebmann, his brother-in-law. He walked along the road which ran between tough little hills, built as battlements, so it appeared, to protect the spreading plain of the *kibbutz*. Once or twice he kicked at the surface of the road. All this was consecrated, he could not quite realize. Once, at the side of the road, he got upon his knees, amongst the stones, in the smell of dust, unable to restrain his longing to touch the earth.

At the *kibbutz* they were all occupied with the business of living. A woman in the office rose from her papers, and pointed at a field. Ari Liebmann and his wife, she said, were down there, amongst the tomatoes.

Ari, whom he remembered as a youth of mobile face and somewhat mercurial mind, had set in one of the opaque moulds of manhood. He was rather hard, dusty, grizzled. When the two men had embraced, and cried, they went to sit down beneath an olive tree, as the farmer had to admit it was an occasion.

'Rahel!' he called out across the sprawling entanglement of tomato bushes.

'This is my wife,' he explained incidentally.

Reluctantly there came a woman, who, Mordecai realized, was something to do with him now. Ari's wife was built in the shape of a cone, and wearing a pair of very tight blue shorts. Her thighs and hips were immense, but her face was not displeasing; it had history in its bones.

When all three were seated, Ari decided:

'You must come to work with us. You can teach the young ones. You will be far better off out here. A Jew only begins to be a Jew in relation to his own soil.'

Both Ari and his wife had hard hands. They were stained with the juice from the young tomato shoots they had been engaged in pinching out.

'Rahel was born here. She will tell you. She's a *sabra*,' Ari explained, and he and his wife laughed.

These people are completely fulfilled, Mordecai sensed. They belonged to their surroundings, like the stones, or the olive tree beneath which they were sitting.

'There will be Jews enough to exercise their intellects on inessentials. This is what matters,' Ari boasted, indicating with his hand all that his community owned.

He was dangerously arrogant, Mordecai saw.

'Yes, come to us here,' Rahel invited. 'There will always be plenty for Jerusalem.'

Then Himmelfarb replied.

'If I could feel that God intended me to remain, either in Jerusalem, or in your valley, then you could be sure of my remaining. But He does not.'

'Ah!' exclaimed Ari. 'God!'

He began to score the ground with his stick.

'How we used to pray!' He sighed and marvelled. 'In Beinenstadt. Under the gables. Good for the soul!' He hunched and laughed; he could have been trying to rid himself of phlegm. 'You, I seem to remember, Reha had decided, were to play the part of a Messiah.'

If each of the two men had not experienced all that he had, this accusatory remark might have sounded more brutal. As it was, Mordecai made it refer to one of those other pasteboard selves silhouetted on the past.

And at that moment, besides, an olive dropped, green, hard, actual, on the stony soil of Palestine.

'What do you believe, Ari?' Mordecai was compelled to ask.

'I believe in the Jewish people,' his brother-in-law replied. 'In establishing the National Home. In defending the Jewish State. In work, as the panacea.'

'And the soul of the Jewish people.'

'Ah, souls!' He was very suspicious, jabbing the earth. 'History, if you like.'

Rahel looked out over the landscape of hills. She could have been bored or embarrassed.

'History,' Himmelfarb said, 'is the reflection of spirit.'

Ari was most uneasy in his state of unemployment. He fidgeted about on his broad behind.

'Should we continue to sit, then?' he asked, showing his short, strong teeth, 'and allow history to reflect us? That is what you seem to suggest.'

'By no means,' Mordecai replied. 'I would only point out that spiritual faith is also an active force. Which will populate the world after each attempt by the men of action to destroy it.'

'I did not tell you,' Ari interrupted, 'but Rahel and I have already made two splendid children.'

'Yes, Ari,' Mordecai sighed. 'I can tell that you are both fulfilled. But momentarily. Nothing, alas, is permanent. Not even this valley. Not even our Land. The earth is in revolt. It will throw up fresh stones – tonight – tomorrow – always. And you, the chosen, will continue to need your scapegoat, just as some of us do not wait to be dragged out, but continue to offer ourselves.'

'And where will you pursue this – idealism?' Ari Liebmann asked.

Now, it appeared, Himmelfarb was caught.

'Well,' he began. 'For example,' he hesitated. 'It could be,' he said, 'in Australia.'

No thought of that country had ever entered his head before, but now it presented itself, possibly because it was farthest, perhaps also bitterest.

'Australia!' his relatives exclaimed – nothing more, as if it were best to ignore the obsessions of the crazed Diaspora.

Rahel changed the subject.

'You will spend the night with us?' she asked, but at the same time it was obvious she hoped he would decide against it.

'No,' Himmelfarb said.

He had no wish to delay where there was no point in his doing so.

They began to walk towards the settlement.

'You must eat, at least,' they insisted.

It was only practical.

Although it was not yet mealtime, Rahel foraged in the kitchen, and produced bread, a cup of milk, and a little bowl of shredded carrot, which she put before the traveller, in the long, empty hall. Soon the cold milk was burning in his mouth, while the others sat on the opposite side of the table, tracing their own secret patterns on the surface of American cloth, when they were not watching him, it could have been hoping he would swallow down their guilt, quickly and easily, with the milk.

Then Rahel swept the crumbs from the cloth with the flat of her hand. She began to glance at her wrist-watch. The hour was approaching when she would go down to her children at the crèche. Her mouth was growing hungrier.

There was, besides, a bus which passed along the road at evening, and to catch that bus the relatives hurried Himmelfarb. His sister-in-law kept looking at her watch. It was natural, of course; she was obviously a practical woman.

Then, at last, as they stood in the meagre scrub of what would one day be a copse of pines, dust foreshadowed the approaching bus.

'Mazel Tov!' cried Ari Liebmann, squeezing his brother-in-law's hand too hard.

This time the two men shed no tears, for the waters of grief

193

ran deeper, more mysteriously than before. The dust of the Land lay around the two Jews. The light was winding them in saffron. Before the bus took Mordecai, and, after the initial travail, flung him upon the next stage of his journey.

From then on, how his dreams jolted him as he followed the rivers towards their source. In this journeying, it could not be said that he was ever alone, for his outer man was accompanied by his dedicated spirit, until, on a morning of antipodean summer, it was suggested the official destination had been reached.

'This is Sydney,' the passengers were told.

The party of immigrant Jews looked anxiously for those who must be waiting to receive them. Only the rather peculiar, not exactly difficult, but *different* passenger, Mr Himmelfarb, in his dark, sweaty, unsuitable clothes, stood, and continued standing, apart. He had, in fact, already been received. As the heat smote the tarmac, there appeared to rise up before him a very definite pillar of fire.

By the time the Jew had finished his story, the day was already relenting. The plum tree, which had, in the beginning, promised protection from the narrative, and finally intensified, if anything, a common agony of mind, began again to demonstrate its natural subtleties of form and sound. The shadows inside its brocaded tent lay curled like heavy animals, spotted and striped with tawny light. Although the blossom had become by now a rather frowsy embroidery against the depths of a whiter sky, an always increasing motion and music freshened the limp folds of branches. For an evening breeze was flowing down across Sarsaparilla to Xanadu, lifting and feathering in its course, trickling through the more suffocating scrub, laving the surfaces of leaves, and at last lapping on the skins of the two survivors seated at the roots of the tree.

Miss Hare might have shuddered if her body had not been so recently released from the rack. In the circumstances, the least movement was painful.

When she had got to her feet she mumbled:

'I must go home, or a certain person, whose name I shall not mention, will cause a disturbance.'

The Jew was also struggling awkwardly up, testing his legs to learn whether they were sound. Neither he nor his audience had any apparent intention of referring to what they had experienced together, nor was it suggested they should meet again, though both expected that they would.

'I must leave you at once,' said the Jew, glancing with some concern at the sun. 'It is very, very late.'

So they parted in the tender light. The smaller their figures grew, the more they appeared pressed. Bobbing and thrashing, they swam against the tide of evening, their movements cruelly hampered by anxiety and grass.

Part Three

8

The house at Sarsaparilla to which Himmelfarb now returned did offer advantages, but of its own, and not all of them obvious. Certainly its boards held together, and resisted the inquiring eye. There were the willows, too, which stood around, lovely when their wire cages first began to melt in spring, more beautiful perhaps in winter, their steel matching the more austere moods of thought. Otherwise there was little to enhance the small house, nothing that could have been called a garden. To plant one would not have occurred to the actual owner, who, in his state of complete disinterest, was unable to conceive of any hierarchy of natural growth. So, at evening, when he was not otherwise employed, he would sit on his veranda, at the very edge, as if it did not belong to him, gratefully breathing the rank scent of weeds. He would sit, and at a certain point in light, as the green leaped up against the dusk, the pallor of his face appeared to form the core of some darker, greener flame.

Now, on the evening of his parting from Miss Hare, the Jew was hurrying to reach his house. Dust floated, seed exploded. The backs of his hands met the thrust of thorn and nettle. Stones scuttled. Yet, his breathing had grown oppressed, and, in spite of his positive, not to say triumphant advance, began to rattle as he climbed the slope.

When he arrived.

When he touched the *Mezzuzah* on the doorpost.

Then, when the *Sh'ma* was moving on his lips, he was again admitted. He went in, not only through the worm-eaten doorway of his worldly house, but on through the inner, secret door.

Silence was never silence in the Jew's house. Speculation alternated with faintest scratching of boughs on timber. Nor were the rooms bare which he had furnished with the utmost simplicity of worship. Now he moved in a wind of purpose over the dry, yielding boards, as far as the cell where necessity had bullied him into putting several sadly material objects: a bed, a chair, the pegs for clothes, and a washstand such as those which clutter country auction-rooms with yellow deal and white, sculptural china. There was nothing else. Except that one wall included a window, opening on green tunnels, and the obscurer avenues of contemplation.

Arriving in this room, and centre of his being, the Jew appeared to hesitate, his hands and lips searching for some degree of humility which always had eluded him, and perhaps always would. There he stood on the faded flags of light, his knees still trembling from their recent haste, and in the absence of that desired, but unattainable, perfection, began at last to make his customary offering:

'Blessed art Thou, O Lord our God, King of the Universe . . .'

He flung his rope into the dusk.

'. . . who at Thy word bringest on the evening twilight, with wisdom openest the gates of the heavens, and with understanding changest times and variest the seasons, and arrangest the stars in their watches in the sky, according to Thy Will. . . .'

So he twined and plaited the words until his ladder held firm.

'With everlasting love Thou hast loved the house of Israel . . .'

So he added, breath by breath, to the rungs of faith.

'. . . and mayest Thou never take away Thy love from us. Blessed art Thou, O Lord, who lovest Thy people Israel.'

By the time night had fallen, dissolving chair and bed in the fragile box in which they had stood, the man himself was so dispersed by his devotions, only the Word remained as testimony of substance.

On arrival in the country of his choice, Himmelfarb had shocked those of his sponsors and advisers who took it for granted that a university professor would apply for a post equal to his intellectual gifts. Whether he would have received one was a doubtful matter, but refusal would at least have provided him, and them, with that wartime luxury, an opportunity to grouse.

Himmelfarb, however, had no intention of applying. His explanation was a simple one:

'The intellect has failed us.'

Those of his own race found his apostasy of mind and rank most eccentric, not to say contemptible. To anyone else, it was not of sufficient interest that an elderly, refined Jew should allow himself to be drafted without protest as a wartime body; he was, in any case, a blasted foreigner, and bloody reffo, and should have been glad he was allowed to exist at all. He was, exceedingly, and did not complain when told to report at a piggery. There, he became attached to those cheerful, extrovert beasts, enough to experience distress as it was slowly proved he no longer had the strength for all that was expected of him.

At the end of an illness, he was put to polishing floors in the same hospital where he had been a patient. He washed dishes for a time, in a military canteen. He cleaned public lavatories.

And was grateful for such mercies.

The reason the peace found him at Barranugli, employed in the factory for Brighta Bicycle Lamps, must be considered a shameful one. This man of ascetic and selfless aspirations had so far diverged from his ideals as to hanker after physical seclusion. He had taken to wandering at weekends round the fringes of the city, and on his wanderings had come across the small, brown house, standing empty in the grass, at Sarsaparilla. As soon as he discovered that white ant, borer, dry rot, inadequate plumbing, and a leaky roof had reduced the value of the wretched cottage, and brought it within reach of his means, then his carefully damped desires burst into full blaze, quite consuming his strength of mind. He could only think of *his* house, and was always returning there, afraid that its desirability might occur to someone else. He grew sallower, bonier, more cavernous than before. Until, finally, spirit was seduced by matter to the extent that he rushed and payed a deposit. He had to buy the derelict house.

Installed at Sarsaparilla, he promised himself treasures of peace, and when he had collected such sticks of furniture as he considered necessary, and his joy and excitement had subsided by several days, he went in search of employment in the neighbouring town of Barranugli.

It cannot be said he chose the job with Brighta Bicycle Lamps. Truthfully, it was chosen for him.

'This Brighta Bicycle Lamps,' said the official gentleman in the employment bureau, 'is a new, but expanding business, like. There's other metal lines besides: geometry boxes, and bobbypins. Several unskilled positions vacant. And let me *see*, I have an *idea*, I'm pretty sure the proprietor is a foreign gentleman of sorts. Mr Rosetree. Yes. Now, if you don't mind my *saying*, that is just the job for you. Kinda Continental.'

'Mr Rosetree,' Himmelfarb repeated.

Then, indeed, the Jew's eyes grew moist with longing. Then the *Kiddush* rose above the wall at sunset.

'Very well thought of,' continued the official voice. 'Have any trouble with your English, well, there is Mr Rosetree on the spot. You will not find another place anywhere around that's made for you personally.'

Himmelfarb agreed the position could be most suitable, and allowed himself to be directed. To abandon self is, after all, to accept the course that offers.

So he presented himself at Brighta Bicycle Lamps, which functioned in a shed, on the outskirts of the town, beside a green river.

Here, on arriving for his interview, he was told to sit, and was ignored for an appropriate length of time, because it was necessary that the expanding business should impress, and as the applicant was stationed right at the centre of Mr Rosetree's universe, impress it did. For, through one door, Himmelfarb could watch two ladies, so upright, so superior, so united in purpose, one plump and the other thin, dashing off the Rosetree correspondence with a minimum of touch, and through another door he could look down into the infernal pit in which the Brighta Lamps were cut out and put together with an excessive casualness and the maximum of noise. The machinery was going round and round, and in and out, and up and down, with such a battering and nattering, though in one corner it slugged and glugged with a kind of oily guile, and through a doorway which opened on to a small, wet, concrete yard, in which an almost naked youth in rubber boots officiated with contempt, it hissed and pissed at times with an intensity that conveyed hatred through the whole shuddering establishment. There was music, however, to sweeten the proceedings. There was the radio, in which for the moment a mossy contralto voice was singing fit to burst the box. *I'm looking for my speshul speshurrll*, sang the voice, nor did it spare the farthest corner. Ladies sat at their assembly trays, and repeated with dainty skill the single act they would be called upon to perform. Or eased their plastic teeth. Or shifted gum. Or patted the metal clips with which their heads were stuck for Friday night. There were girls, too, their studied eyebrows sulking over what they had to suffer. And gentlemen in singlets, who stood with their hands on their hips, or rolled limp-looking cigarettes, or consulted the sporting page, and even, when it was absolutely necessary, condescended to lean forward and take part in some mechanical ritual which still demanded their presence.

Bending down in the centre of the floor was a dark-skinned individual, Himmelfarb observed, whose temporary position made his vertebrae protrude in knobs, and who, when straightened up, appeared to be composed of bones, veins, and thin strips of elastic muscle, the whole dominated by the oblivious expression of the dark face. The blackfellow, or half-caste, he could have been, resumed possession of his broom, and pushed it ahead of him as he walked backwards and forwards between the benches. Some of the women lowered their eyes as he passed, others smiled knowingly, though not exactly at him. But the black man, involved in some incident of the inner life, ignored even the mechanical gestures of his own sweeping. But swept, and swept. As oil reveals secret lights, so did the skin stretched on the framework of his naked ribs. As he continued sweeping. It was an occupation to be endured, so his heavy head and the rather arrogant Adam's-apple seemed to imply.

Himmelfarb began to realize that the plumper of the two typists was trying to attract his attention. While remaining seated in the office, she was, it seemed, calling to him.

'Mr Rosetree,' she was saying, 'is free now, to see you.'

Both the typewriters were still. The thinner of the two ladies was smiling at the keys of hers, as she hitched up the ribbon of a private garment which had fallen in a loop over her white, pulled, permanently goosey biceps.

Fascinated by all he saw, the applicant had failed to move.

'Mr Rosetree,' repeated the plumper lady louder, the way one did for foreigners, 'is disengaged. Mr Himmelferp,' she added, and would have liked to laugh.

Her companion did snicker, but quickly began to rearrange her daintily-embroidered personal towel, which was hanging over the back of a chair.

'If you will pass this way,' almost shouted the plump goddess, perspiring on her foam rubber.

She feared the situation was making her conspicuous.

'Thank you,' Himmelfarb replied, and smiled at the hand which indicated doors.

She did not rise, of course, having reduced her obligations at the salary received. But let her hand fall.

Himmelfarb went into Mr Rosetree's sanctum.

'Good-day, Mr Himmelfarb,' Mr Rosetree said: 'Make yourself comfortable,' he invited, without troubling to consider whether that might be possible.

He himself was comfortable enough. Formally, he was a

201

series of spheres. His whole appearance suggested rubber, a relaxed springiness, though his texture was perhaps closer to that of *Delikatessen*, of the blander, shinier variety – *Bratwurst*, for instance. Now he might just have finished buffing his nails, and forgotten to put away his dimpled hands, while his lower lip reached out after some problem he would have to solve in the immediate future.

There was no indication Himmelfarb was that problem, but the applicant suspected he was the cause of a bad taste which Mr Rosetree, it became obvious, would have liked to spit out of his mouth.

'Any experience? No? No matter. Experience is not essential. Willingness is what counts.' Mr Rosetree asked and answered in the tone of voice he kept for minor emergencies.

'Only the remuneration,' he said, 'will be less. In the beginning. On account of you are lacking in skill.'

He dropped a rubber into a little bakelite tray, where it plunked rather unpleasantly.

'That is understandable,' Himmelfarb replied, and smiled.

For some reason he was feeling happy.

Is this one clever, or just stupid? Mr Rosetree debated. In the one case, he would have reacted in anger, in the other, merely with contempt. But now he was in doubt. And suddenly he would have liked to revolt passionately, against that, and all doubts. The air grew quite sultry with displeasure.

Himmelfarb was inwardly so glad, he remained unconscious of the change of climate.

'You are not from here?' he had to ask, but very, very cautiously, for he himself had worn disguises.

'I am an Australian,' Mr Rosetree said.

But saw fit to rearrange several objects on his desk.

'Ah,' sighed Himmelfarb. 'It only occurred. Excuse me, won't you?'

'But will not deny I came here for personal reasons. For personal reasons of my own.' Mr Rosetree tossed the rubber up, and attempted to catch it, but he didn't.

'I do not wish to appear inquisitive, but thought perhaps you were from Poland.'

Mr Rosetree frowned, and bent the nasty rubber double.

'Well,' he said. 'Shall we call it Vienna?'

'*Also, sprechen wir zusammen Deutsch?*'

'Not on the premises. Not on no account,' Mr Rosetree hastily replied. 'We are Australians now.'

He would have flung the situation off, only it stuck to him, like discarded chewing-gum. For Himmelfarb was plunging deeper into a conspiracy.

The latter lowered his voice, and leant forward. He was tired, but had arrived, as he very softly asked:

'Surely you are one of us?'

'Eh?'

Mr Rosetree was not only mentally distressed, he was also physically uncomfortable; he could not detach the pants from around his groin, where they had rucked up, it seemed, and were giving him hell.

'Yes,' Himmelfarb persisted. 'I took it for granted you were one of us.'

Then Mr Rosetree tore something free, whether material or not. He said:

'If it is religion you mean, after so much beating in the bush – and religion in these countries, Mr Himmelfarb, is not an issue of first importance – I can plainly tell you I attend the Catholic Church of St Aloysius.'

Nobody was going to threaten Mr Rosetree.

'The Catholic Church,' he emphasized, 'at Paradise East.'

'Ah!' Himmelfarb yielded. He sat back.

Just then there came into the room a gentleman in his singlet. He was of such proportions that the cardboard walls appeared to expand in order to accommodate him fully.

'There ain't no 22-gauge, Harry,' the gentleman announced. 'Not a bloody skerrick of it.'

'No 22-gauge?'

Here at last Mr Rosetree was given the opportunity to explode.

'That is correct,' said the gentleman of the singlet, who was mild enough once he had established himself; he stood there twiddling the hairs of his left armpit, and breathing through his mouth.

'No 22-gauge!' screamed Harry Rosetree. 'But this cheppie which I told you of, has promised already for yesterday!'

'This cheppie has dumped us in the shit,' the mild gentleman suggested.

For want of other employment, Himmelfarb sat and observed the belly inside the cotton singlet. There are times when the position of the human navel appears almost perfectly logical.

'What do I do to peoples? I would really like somebody to tell me!' Mr Rosetree begged.

His mouth had grown quite watery. He had taken the telephone book, and was picking up the pages by handfuls, in ugly lumps.

'Peoples are that way from the start. Take it from me, mate,' the foreman consoled.

At that point, the plumper of the two ladies in the outer office stuck her head in at the door. Her necklaces of flesh were turning mauve.

'Mr Rosetree – excuse me, please – Mrs Rosetree is on the phone.'

'For Chrisake! Mrs Rosetree?'

'Shall I switch her through, Mr Rosetree?'

'For Chrisake, Miss Whibley! Didn't Mrs Rosetree let you know?'

Mr Rosetree, it was obvious, would favour jokes about Men and Women.

Now he took the phone. He said:

'Yes, dear. Sure. And how! No, dear, I am never all that busy. Yup. Yup. Yup. What! You have decided for the epple pie? But I wish the *Torte*! Not for Arch, nor Marge, nor anybody else, will I never assimilate the epple pie. Arrange it for me, Shirl. Sure. I have business now.'

The pitching of his stick of gelignite into the domestic works made him look pleased, until he began to remember there was something else, there was, indeed, the treachery of all individuals connected with supply, but something, he suspected, more elusive. There was this fellow, Himmelfarb.

Then Harry Rosetree knew that a latent misery of his own, of which he had never been quite able to dispose, had begun to pile up in the fragile, but hitherto protected office, assuming vast proportions, like a heap of naked, suppurating corpses. He could have spewed up there and then, because the stench was so great, and his considerable business acumen would never rid him of the heap of bodies.

So he said thickly to the applicant:

'Come along Monday. You better start then. But it will be monotonous. I warn you. Bloody monotonous. It will kill you.'

'I have been killed several times already,' Himmelfarb replied. 'Probably more painfully.'

And got up.

These Jewish intellectuals, Harry Rosetree despised the bloody lot of them. Freud, and Mozart, and all that *Kaffee-quatsch*! If he did not hate as well, not only a class, but a whole race, it was because he was essentially a loving man, and still longed to be loved in a way that can happen only in the beginning. But there, his childhood was burnt down, not a trace of it left, except that the voices of the dark women continued to vibrate inside him.

'What's up, Harry?' asked the foreman, whose name was Ernie Theobalds. 'Done something to your leg? Never noticed it was crook before.'

'I done nothink.'

'You was limpin'.'

'It has these needles.'

And Harry Rosetree stamped to bear it out.

How the two ladies in the outer office were bashing into their typewriters now.

The bloke Himmelfarb had gone out, and was walking alongside the green river, where nobody had ever been seen to walk. The river glistened for him. The birds flew low, swallows probably, almost on the surface of the water, and he held out his hand to them. They did not come to him, of course, but he touched the glistening arcs of flight. It seemed as though the strings of flight were suspended from his fingers, and that he controlled the whirring birds.

Presently he remembered he had forgotten to ask his future employer about the money. But his omission did not disturb him, not in that green effulgence, which emanated from, as much as it enveloped, him. The water flowed, the light smote the ragged bushes. Nothing disturbed, except that for a choking moment he wondered whether he had dared assume powers to which he had no right, whether he might even accept, in his very humblest capacity, the benedictions of light and water.

Himmelfarb went on the Monday. He took his lunch with him in a brown, fibre case, together with one or two articles of value he would not have liked to leave at home; a fire could have broken out. He caught the bus to Barranugli, and was put down before reaching the town, at Rosetree's, on the river bank. They sat him at a drill, with which he was expected to bore a hole in a circular steel plate, over, and over, and over. Ernie Theobalds, the foreman, showed him how, and made one or two accommodating jokes. They gave him his union card, and that was that.

Each morning Himmelfarb took the bus to Barranugli, until the Sabbath, when the factory did not open – as on Sunday, of course. He became quite skilful at his unskilled job; there was a certain way of whipping off the steel plate. As he sat endlessly at his drill, it pained him to recall certain attitudes and

205

episodes of his former life, which hitherto he had accepted as natural. There was, for instance, the arrogance of opinion and style of the monograph on an obscure English novelist, indeed, of his critical works in general. Many phrases of many prayers that he had mumbled down in his presumptuous youth came to life at last upon his tongue. Most often he remembered those people he had failed: his wife Reha, the dreadful dyer, the Lady from Czernowitz, to name a few. Sometimes as he bored the hole, the drill grazed his flesh, and he accepted it.

A few of his workmates might have joked with him, offering some of the worn remarks that were currency on the floor, but refrained on perceiving something strange. Nothing like his face had ever been seen by many of them. To enter in search of what it might contain was an expedition nobody cared to undertake. If sometimes the foreigner found it necessary to speak, it was as though something preposterous had taken place: as though a fish had opened its mouth the other side of a glass wall, and brought forth faintly intelligible words instead of normally transparent bubbles.

So the plastic ladies and the pursy men bent their heads above their benches. Toothless lads hawked up a mirthless laughter, while the faces of the girls let it be understood that nobody would take advantage of them.

Once or twice the blackfellow paused in his rounds of sweeping, on coming level with the Jew's drill.

Then Himmelfarb decided. Eventually, perhaps, I shall speak, but it is not yet the appropriate occasion.

Not that there was reason to suspect affinity of any kind, except that the black would establish a certain warmth of presence before moving on.

After one such *rapprochement*, a blue-haired granny left off assembling Brighta Lamps. She threw up her hands, and had to shout to the foreigner:

'Dirty! Dirty!'

As the machinery belted away.

'No good blackfeller! Sick!' she shrieked.

Even if the object of her contempt had missed hearing, or had closed his ears permanently to censure, Himmelfarb was made uncomfortable, when he should have returned some suitable joke.

Mistaking embarrassment for failure to understand, a bloke approached, and whispered in the foreigner's ear:

'She means he has every disease a man can get. From the bollocks up.'

206

As Himmelfarb still did not answer, his workmate went away. Foreigners, in any case, filled the latter with disgust.

And the machinery belted on.

Sometimes Mr Rosetree's shoes trod along the gangway, and appeared to hesitate beside the drill, but only hesitate, before continuing. Himmelfarb did not take it amiss that his employer had not spoken since the morning of the interview. It was only to be expected in a business man of some importance, a husband, and a father, with a lovely home. For the ladies at the benches would often openly discuss their boss. Without having been there themselves, they seemed to know by heart the desirable contents of the rooms. Nor did they envy, except intermittently, perhaps when having a monthly, or payment on the washing-machine was overdue. On the whole, they admired the signs of material wealth in others.

So Mr Rosetree shone.

Sometimes he would come out of his office, and stand upon a ramp, and scrutinize the rows of workers, and rackety, spasmodic machines. Then the ladies would tilt their heads, looking personally involved, and even those of the men who were the worst grumblers would aim shafts of such harmlessly blunt brutality as to cause only superficial wounds if they had ever reached their target. Good money had made the most sardonic amongst them sentimentally possessive of that harmless poor coot, their boss.

As for Himmelfarb seated at his drill, he would at once grow conscious of his employer's presence on the ramp, though he had not raised his eyes to look in that direction.

Rosetrees lived at 15 Persimmon Street, Paradise East, in a texture-brick home – city water, no sewerage, but their own septic. Telephone, of course. Who could get through the morning without the telephone? It was already quite a good address, and would improve, but then Rosetrees would probably move on, to realize on the land. Because, what was land – such nasty, sandy, scrubby stuff – if not an investment? All around the texture-brick home, Mrs Rosetree listened mornings to the gumtrees thudding down. And all around, the homes were going up. The brick homes.

Harry Rosetree was very proud of his own setting. Sundays he would stand outside his apricot brick home, amongst all the advanced shrubs he had planted, the labels still round them so as you could read the fancy names if a neighbour should inquire. Who wouldn't feel satisfied? And with the Ford Customline, one of the first imported since the war? Then there were the kids. He was an indulgent father, but had every reason to be proud of Steve and Rosie, who learned so much so fast: they had learnt to speak worse Australian than any of the Australian kids, they had learnt to crave for ice-cream, and potato-chips, and could shoot tomato sauce out of the bottle even when the old black sauce was blocking the hole. So the admiration oozed out of Harry Rosetree, and for Mrs Rosetree, too, who had learnt more than anyone.

With greater authority, Mrs Rosetree could say: That is not Australian. She had a kind of gift for assimilation. Better than anyone she had learnt the language. She spoke it with a copper edge; the words fell out of her like old pennies. Of course it was really Shirl Rosetree who owned the texture-brick home, the streamlined, glass car, the advanced shrubs, the grandfather clock with the Westminster chimes, the walnut-veneer radiogram, the washing-machine, and the mix-master. Everybody knew that, because when she asked the neighbours in to morning tea and scones, she would refer to: *My* home, *my* children, *my* Ford Customline. There was a fur coat, too, still only one, but she was out to get a second while the going was good.

Who could blame her? Shirl Rosetree had been forced to move on more than once. Put it into gold, she would have said, normally; you can hide that. And had bought the little gold Cross, before leaving, in the Rotenturmstrasse, which she wore still. Whenever she got excited it bumped about and hit her breasts, but it was comforting to wear a Cross. Except. Marge Pendlebury had said early on: 'I would never ever of suspected you Rosetrees of being tykes. Only the civil servants are Roman Catholics here, and the politicians, if they are anything at all.' Shirl's ears stood up straight for what she had still to assimilate. Marge said: 'Arch and me are Methoes, except we don't go; life is too short.'

Then the little Cross from the Rotenturmstrasse bumped less gaily on Shirl's breasts.

She said:

'Do you know what, Harry? Arch and Marge are Methoes.'

'So what?' asked her husband.

'That is what people are, it seems.'

He patted her. She was a plumpy thing, but not always comfortable. Her frown would get black.

She could shout:

'*Um Gottes Willen, du Trottel, du Wasserkopf! Muss ich immer Sechel für zwei haben?*'

208

But would grow complaisant, while refusing to let him mess her perm.

'There is all the rest,' she insisted.

And at times the Rosetrees would cling together with almost fearful passion. There in the dark of their texture-brick shell, surrounded by the mechanical objects of value, Shirl and Harry Rosetree were changed mercilessly back into Shulamith and Haïm Rosenbaum. *Oÿ-yoÿ*, how brutally the Westminster chimes resounded then in the hall. A mouse could have severed the lifeline with one Lilliputian snap. While the seekers continued to lunge together along the dunes of darkness, arriving nowhere, except into the past, and would excuse themselves in favour of sleep, that other deceiver. For Haïm would again be peddling *Eisenwaren*, and as frequently compelled to take to his heels through the villages of sleep; and Shulamith, for all the dreamy validity of her little Cross, would suffer her grandmother, that gaunt, yellow woman, to call her home down the pot-holed street, announcing that the stars were out, and the Bride had already come.

If daylight had not licked quickly into shape, this kind of night-time persecution might have become unbearable. But morning arrived in Paradise East with a clatter of venetian blinds. And there stood the classy homes in their entirety of brick. There were the rotary clothes-lines, and the galvanized garbage-bins.

By daylight the Rosenbaums would sometimes even dare indulge a nostalgia for *Beinfleisch*, say, *mit Krensoss*. They would stuff it in, as though it might be taken from them. Their lips grew shiny from the fat meat, their cheeks tumid from an excess of *Nockerl*.

Then Haïm Rosenbaum might ask:

'Why you don't eat your meat, Steve?'

'Mum said it was gunna be chops.'

'Shoot some of this tomato sauce on to the *Beinfleisch*. Then you can pretend it is chops,' advised the father.

But Steve Rosetree hated deviation.

'Who wants bloody foreign food!'

'I will not have you swear, Steve!' said the mother, with pride.

She loved to sit after *Beinfleisch*, and pick out the last splinters, with a perfect, crimson finger-nail. And dwell on past pleasures.

Once Shirl Rosetree thought to inquire:

'What about that old Jew, Harry, you told us about, down at the factory?'

'What about this old Jew?'

'What is he up to?'

'For Chrissake! Who am I to know what is up to every no-hope Jew that comes to the country?'

'But this one seemed, well, sort of educated, from what you said.'

'He talks good. He talks so good nobody can understand.'

Harry Rosetree had to belch.

'You can smell the Orthodox,' he said, 'on some Jews.'

It made his wife laugh.

'Times change, eh? When you have to *smell* the Orthodox!'

But she would have loved still to watch the hands lighting the *Chanukah* candles. The Scrolls themselves were not more closely written than the faces of some old waxen Jews.

'Times change all right,' her husband agreed. 'But I do not understand why am I to keep a day-book of the doings of every Jew that comes!'

'Let it pass!' his wife said. She manipulated her jaws to release a noise, half-yawn, half-laughter, punctuated by a gold tooth. But came out with a remark she immediately regretted: 'You can't get away from it, Harry, the blood draws you.'

'The blood draws, the blood will run!' her husband said, through ugly mouth. 'Have we seen, and not learnt?'

'What blood?' asked the little girl.

There were often things in her parents' conversation that made her tingle with suspicion.

'Nothing, dear,' said the mother. 'Mum and Dad were having a discussion.'

'At the convent,' Rosie Rosetree said, 'there is a statue of Our Saviour, and the blood looks like it's still wet.' She made her mouth into the little funnel through which she would allow commendable sentiments to escape. 'It was that real, it made me cry at Easter, and the nuns had to comfort me. Gee, the nuns are lovely. I'm gunna be a nun, Mum. I'm gunna be a saint, and have visions of roses and things.'

'There, you see, Shirl, Rosie has the right ideas.' The father smiled. 'And as she is her old dad's sensible girl, her visions will become more realistic. No one ever got far on the smell of roses.'

Shirl Rosetree sighed. She frowned. It was true, of course. But the truth was always only half the truth. It was that that made her act sort of *nervös*. And all these family situations, as breakable as bakelite. Sometimes she was afraid she might be starting a heart, and would have liked to consult a good European doctor, only they all rooked you so. Or priest. Only you always came away knowing you had not quite told. And, in any case, what could a priest know to tell? Nothing. She never came away from the confessional without she had the heartburn. Some old smelly man in a box.

Now she had got the heartburn real bad. It was after all that *Beinfleisch*, with the good *Krensoss*. She knew it must be turning her yellow.

So Shirl Rosetree breathed rather hard, and fiddled with the little gold Cross in the shadow between her breasts, and said:

'I think we had enough of this silly conversation. It's the kind that don't lead anywhere. I'm gunna lay down, and have a read of some nice magazine.'

The voice of the Rosetrees proclaimed that a stranger was in their midst. If it hesitated to deride, it was for those peculiarly personal, not to say mystical reasons, and because derision was a luxury the Rosetrees were only so very recently qualified to enjoy. The voice of Sarsaparilla, developing the same theme, laboured under no such inhibitions, but took for granted its right to pass judgement on the human soul, and indulge in a fretfulness of condemnation.

'I would not of thought it would of come to this,' Mrs Flack repeated, 'a stream of foreign migrants pouring into the country, and our boys many of them not yet returned, to say nothing of those with permanent headstones still to be erected overseas. So much for promises and Prime Ministers. Who will feed us, I would like to know, when we are so many mouths over, and foreign mouths, how many of them I did read, but forget the figure.'

Then Mrs Flack's friend, Mrs Jolley, would clear her throat and add her voice:

'Yes, indeed, it makes you think, it makes you wonder. Who counts? It is not you. It is the one that greases the palm of a civil servant or a politician. It is never you, but the one that comes.'

'Not that many a civil servant is not a highly respectable person,' Mrs Flack had to grant.

'That is correct, and I should know, seeing as my own son-in-law is one. Mr Apps, who took Merle.'

'I would not doubt that even a politician has high principles in the home.'

'Ah, in the home! Oh, a politician is a family man besides. It is the kiddies that makes all the difference.'

211

Abstraction would elevate the two ladies to a state so rarefied they dared not look at each other, but each would stare dreamily into her own bottomless mind, watching the cotton-wool unfurl.

Once Mrs Flack's eyes seemed to focus on some point. It was in actual fact a plaster pixie, of which she had a pair, out on the front lawn, beside the golden cypresses, amongst the lachenalia.

'They say,' she said, 'there is a foreign Jew, living,' she said, and appeared to swallow something down, 'below the post office, in Montebello Avenue, in a weatherboard home' – here she drew back her strips of palest lips – 'a home so riddled with the white ant, you can hear them operatin' from where the kerb ought to be.'

'In Montebello Avenue,' Mrs Jolley confirmed. 'I did see. Yes, a funny-looking gentleman. Or man. They say, a foreign Jew. And for quite some time.'

'Mind you the home is rotten,' Mrs Flack pursued, 'but you cannot tell me, Mrs Jolley, that a home is not a home, with so many going roofless, and so many returned men.'

'Preferential treatment is to be desired,' said Mrs Jolley, 'for everyone entitled to it.'

'What do you mean?' asked Mrs Flack.

Which was terrible, because Mrs Jolley was not at all sure.

'Well,' she said, 'you know what I mean. Well, I mean to say,' she said, 'a returned man is a returned man.'

'That is so.'

Mrs Flack was mollified.

But Mrs Jolley had decided she must go. She was perspiring uncomfortably behind the knees.

Then Mrs Flack flung a bomb.

'What do you say, Mrs Jolley, if I walk a little of the way? There's nothing like the fresh air.'

This was revolutionary, considering that Mrs Flack never, never walked except when strictly necessary, on account of her heart, her blood pressure, her varicose veins, and generally delicate state of health. The fresh air, besides, was as foreign to her yellow skin as Jews to Sarsaparilla.

'Why, dear, if you think you ought.' Mrs Jolley had to speak at last. 'But I must hurry along,' she said. 'My lady,' and here she had to laugh, 'will be expecting me at Xanadu.'

'Only a little of the way,' Mrs Flack insisted. 'I was never a drag on anyone. But as far as Montebello Avenue.'

'Ah!' Mrs Jolley giggled.

It was certainly entrancing to walk together past homes which failed any longer to conceal, from Mrs Jolley in her mauve eye-veil, from Mrs Flack in her flat black hat with its cockade of dust.

'Here,' said Mrs Flack, adjusting herself so that she became as much edge as possible, 'are people who should not be allowed to live in any decent neighbourhood.'

Mrs Jolley almost dislocated her neck.

'I could not tell you in detail – it would make your flesh creep,' said the disappointing Mrs Flack, 'only that a father and a young girl, well, I will put it bluntly – his daughter. There is a little motor-car in which you could not squeeze a third. She in slippery blouses that might be wet for all they hide.'

'What do you know!' Mrs Jolley clucked.

She could not help but feel she had suddenly got possession of all knowledge, thanks to the generosity of Mrs Flack. Mrs Jolley walked, red, but brave.

'There is the post office,' Mrs Flack continued. 'There is that Mrs Sugden.'

'Oo-hoo! Mrs Sugden!' she had to call. 'How are we today?'

Mrs Sugden was good, thanks.

Mrs Flack hated Mrs Sugden, because the postmistress would never be persuaded to tell.

Then the two ladies began to tread more cautiously, for they had entered Montebello Avenue. Their ankles had begun to twist on stones. Where the pavement should have been, the grass, unpleasant in itself, oozing black juices when it did not cut the stockings, threatened to reveal the rarer forms of nastiness at some future step.

'If you are not loopy to go on living at Xanadu!' Mrs Flack called from her wading.

Mrs Jolley usually replied: A person must retain her principles; but today, it had to be admitted, Mrs Flack's grip on life was so much stronger, her friend had been reduced. So, instead, she answered:

'Beggars cannot be choosers.'

'Beggar *me*!' shrieked Mrs Flack, somewhat surprisingly.

Foreign parts and paspalum had made her reckless. Her waxen skin had begun to appear deliquescent.

'There!' she suddenly hissed, and restrained her friend's skirt.

It was as though an experienced huntsman had at last delivered a disbelieving novice into the presence of promised game. Not that the game itself was in evidence yet, only its habitat.

The two ladies stood in the shelter of a blackberry bush to observe the house in which the foreign Jew was living. The small brown house was suitably, obscenely poor. The other side of the fence, from which previous owners had pulled pickets at random to stoke winter fires, mops of weed were threatening to shake their cotton heads. Of course there were the willows. Nobody could have denied the existence of those, only their value was doubtful because they had cost nothing. The willows poured round the shabby little house, serene cascades of green, or lapped peacefully at its wooden edges. Many a passer-by might have chosen to plunge in, and drown, in those consoling depths, but the two observers were longing for something that would rend their souls — a foetus, or a mutilated corpse. Instead, they had to make do with the sight of guttering that promised to fall off soon, and windows which if glitteringly clean, ignored the common decencies of lace or net.

'Not even a geranium,' said Mrs Flack, with bitter satisfaction.

Then, if you please, the door opened, and out came, not the Jew, that would have been electric enough, but a woman, a woman. It was a thickish, middle-aged woman, in shapeless sort of faded dress. Some no-account woman.

It was Mrs Jolley who realized first. She was often quite quick, although it was Mrs Flack who excelled in psychic powers.

'Why,' Mrs Jolley said now, 'what do you know! It is that Mrs Godbold!'

Mrs Flack was stunned, but managed:

'I always thought how Mrs Godbold was deep, but how deep, I did not calculate.'

'It is wonderful,' said Mrs Jolley, 'to what lengths a woman will go.'

For the owner himself had just emerged. The Jew. The two ladies clutched each other by the gloves. They had never seen anything so yellow or so strange. Strange? Why, dreadful, dreadful! Now the whirlwinds were rising in honest breasts, that honest corsets were striving to contain. The phlegm had come in Mrs Flack's mouth, causing her to swallow quickly down.

Mrs Jolley, as she had already confessed, had noticed the man on one or two previous occasions as she came and went between Xanadu and Sarsaparilla, but had failed to observe such disgraceful dilapidation of appearance, such irregularities of stubble, such a top-heavy, bulbous head, such a truly fearful nose. In the circumstances, she felt she should apologize to her somewhat delicate companion.

But the latter was craning now.

'He is big,' she remarked, between her moist teeth.

'He is not small,' Mrs Jolley agreed, as they stood supporting each other on wish-bone legs.

'Who would ever of thought,' Mrs Flack just articulated, 'that Mrs Godbold.'

Mrs Godbold and the man were standing together on the steps of the veranda, she on the lower, he above, so that she was forced to look up, exposing her face to his and to the evening light.

It was obvious that the woman's flat, and ordinarily uncommunicative face had been opened by some experience of a private nature, or perhaps it was just the light, gilding surfaces, dissolving the film of discouragement and doubt which life leaves behind, loosening the formal braids of hair, furnishing an aureole, which, if not supernatural – reason would not submit to that – provided an agreeable background to motes and gnats. Indeed, the Jew himself began to acquire a certain mineral splendour as he stood talking, even laughing with his friend, in that envelope, or womb of light. Whether the two had been strengthened by some event of importance, or were weakened by their present total disregard for defences, their audience was made to know, but could not, could not tell. Mrs Jolley and Mrs Flack could only crane and swallow, beside the blackberry bush, beneath their hats, and hope that something disgraceful might occur.

'What is that, Mrs Jolley?' Mrs Flack asked at last.

But Mrs Jolley did not hear. Her breath was roaring through her mouth.

For the Jew had begun to show Mrs Godbold something. Whatever it was – it could have been a parcel, or a bird, only that was improbable, a white bird – their attention was all upon it.

'I believe he has cut his hand,' Mrs Jolley decided. 'She has bandaged up his hand. Well, that is one way!'

Mrs Flack sucked incredulous teeth. She was quite exhausted by now.

Then, as people will toss up the ball of friendship, into the last light, at the moment of departure, and it will hang there briefly, lovely and luminous to see, so did the Jew and Mrs Godbold. There hung the golden sphere. The laughter climbed up quickly, out of their exposed throats, and clashed together by consent; the light splintered against their teeth. How private, and mysterious, and beautiful it was, even the intruders suspected, and were deterred momentarily from hating.

When they were again fully clothed in their right minds, Mrs Jolley said to her companion:

'Do you suppose she comes to him often?'

'I would not know,' replied Mrs Flack, though it was obvious she did.

'Tsst!' she added, quick as snakes.

Mrs Godbold had begun to turn.

'See you at church!' hissed Mrs Jolley.

'See you at church!' repeated Mrs Flack.

Their eyes flickered for a moment over the Christ who would rise to the surface of Sunday morning.

Then they drew apart.

Mrs Jolley walked on her way, briskly but discreetly, down the hill. towards Xanadu. She would have liked to kill some animal, fierce enough to fan her pride, weak enough to make it possible, but as it was doubtful any such beast would offer itself, scrubby though the neighbourhood was, she drifted dreamily through the series of possible ways in which she might continue to harry the human soul.

The morning Himmelfarb's hand was gashed by the drill which bored those endless holes in the endless succession of metal plates, was itself an endless plain, of dirty yellow, metallic wherever sweating fanlight or louvre allowed the sword to strike. The light struck, and was fairly parried by defensive daggers, of steel, as well as indifference. Equally, wounds were received. Their past lives rose up in a rush in the throats of many of the singleted men, and gushed out in tongues of sour air, while a few went so far as to fart their resentment, not altogether in undertone. Some of the ladies, who had bared themselves as much as was decent, and who were in consequence looking terribly white, swore they must win the lottery, or leave their husbands. Over every surface, whether skin or metal. humidity had laid its film. Flesh united to mingle with it. Only metal appeared to have entered into an alliance with irony, as the machinery continued to belt, to stamp, and to stammer with an even more hilarious blatancy, to hiss and piss with an increased virulence.

Just after smoke-o, Himmelfarb's hand came in contact with the head of the little drill. Very briefly and casually. The whole incident was so unemotional, probably nobody noticed it. At the time, it caused Himmelfarb very little pain. As he had succeeded by now in withdrawing completely from his factory surroundings, he was usually unperturbed by such wounds as they might deal, even the mental ones. But here was his hand, running blood. There was a fairly deep gash along the side of the left palm.

After a little, he went quietly to the wash-room to clean the wound. There was nobody there – except, he then realized, the blackfellow, who could have been staring at himself in the glass, or else using the mirror as an opening through which to escape.

Himmelfarb rinsed his hand beneath the tap. The blood ran out of the wound in long, vanishing veils. At moments the effect was strangely, fascinatingly beautiful.

So it seemed to appear also to the blackfellow, who was now staring at the bleeding wound, whether in curiosity, recollection, sympathy, what, it was impossible to tell. Only that his active self seemed to have become completely submerged in what he was witnessing.

Then the pain began to course through Himmelfarb. For a moment he feared his workmate might address him for the first time, and that he would not be able to answer, except in the words of common exchange.

But was saved. Or cheated.

For the black was going, discarding some vision still only half crystallized, retreating from a step he did not know how to, or would not yet allow himself to take.

The blackfellow had, in fact, gone, and Himmelfarb, after wrapping an almost clean handkerchief round his left hand, returned to his drill for what remained of the working day.

That night his dreams were by turns bland and fiery. His wife Reha was offering, first the dish of most delicious cinnamon apple, then the dish of bitter herbs. Neither of which he could quite reach. Nor was her smile intended for him, in that state of veiled bliss which he remembered. Finally she turned and gave the apple to a third person, who, it was her apparent intention, should hand the dish.

But he awoke in a sweat of morning, less comforted by his dead wife's presence, than frustrated by his failure to receive the dish.

He rose groggily, but prepared as usual to say his prayers, arranging the shawl, not the blue-striped Bar Mitzvah *Tallith* – that had been destroyed at Friedensdorf – but the one he had received with fervour in Jerusalem, and worn henceforth, touching its black veins in remembrance of things experienced. But when it came to the laying on of the phylacteries, that which should have wound down along his left arm caused him such pain, he could hardly bear it. But did. He said the prayers, he said the Eighteen Benedictions, because how else would it have been possible to face the day? Then, after packing the *Tallith* and *Tefillin* – they were those few possessions he could not entrust to empty houses – into the fibre case, together with a crust of bread and slice of cheese, he caught the bus for Barranugli, and was soon rocked upon his way, amongst the *goyim*, on a sea of conversation dealing exclusively with the weather.

That morning the shed almost burst open, with sound, and heat, and activity.

Until Ernie Theobalds approached.

'What's up, Mick?' asked the foreman.

'Nothing,' the Jew replied.

Then he raised his hand.

'See,' he said. 'It is only this. But will pass.'

When Mr Theobalds had examined the wound – he was a decent bloke, as well as practical – he became rather thoughtful.

'You go home, Mick,' he advised at last. 'You got a bad hand. You see the doc up at Sarsaparilla. See what he says. You'll get compo, of course.'

'You never know,' said Ernie Theobalds afterwards to the boss, 'when one of these buggers will turn around and sue you.'

Himmelfarb took his fibre case, and went, as he had been told. He saw Dr Herborn, who treated him according to the book, and told him to lay off.

Every day he went to the surgery for his needle. For the rest, he sat surrounded by the green peace of willows, and that alone was exquisitely kind.

Gruelled by his throbbing hand, exalted by the waves of fever, he began again to doubt whether he was worthy of those favours of which he was the object, and in his uncertainty imposed upon himself greater tests of humility, in themselves negligible, even ludicrous, but it became most necessary that his mind should not accept as unconditional that which his weaker body urged him to. For instance, he set himself to scrub out his almost empty house, which he did accomplish, if awkwardly. With less success, he made himself wash dirty linen rather than allow it to accumulate. As he paddled the clothes with one hand and the tips of his excruciating fingers, he was almost overcome by his limitations, but somehow got his washing pegged out on the line.

There he was one day. The sky had been widened by afternoon. A cold wind from out of the south slapped his face with wet shirt; inseparable, cold folds of cotton clung to his shoulder.

When a person came through the grass, and stood behind him.

He looked round, and saw it was a woman.

Respect for his dignity seemed to prevent her breaking the silence immediately.

'I could have done that,' she said at last, after she had stretched the possibilities of discretion to their utmost. 'Any little bits that you have. If you would give them.'

She blushed red, all over her thick, creamy skin. It could have been blotting paper.

'Oh, no,' he replied. 'It is done.' And laughed, idiotically. 'It is nothing. Always I do a little. As it comes.'

He had grown quite frail on the windy hillside, like some miserable, scrubby tree unable to control its branches. He was clattering. Whereas the thick woman, with all her shortcomings of speech and behaviour, was a rock immovable in the grass. As they stood for that moment, the wind seemed to cut through the man, but was split open on the woman's form.

Then Himmelfarb was truly humbled. He began to walk towards the house. He was rather shambly. His head was bumpy on his shoulders.

'Why should you offer, I wonder, to me?'

Was this, perhaps, a luxury he was begging to enjoy? But he had to.

'It is only natural,' she said, following. 'I would offer to do it for anyone.'

'But I am different. I am a Jew,' he replied, from behind his back.

'So they say,' she said.

In the silence, as they walked, one behind the other, he could hear her breathing. He could hear the motion of the grass.

When she said:

'I do not know Jews, except what we are told, and of course the Bible; there is that.' She paused because it was difficult for her. 'But I know people,' she said, 'and there is no difference between them, excepting there is good and bad.'

'Then you, too, have faith?'

'Eh?'

Almost at once she corrected herself, and continued very quickly:

'Oh, yes, I believe. I believe in Jesus. I was brought up chapel, like. At Home. We all believe.' But added: 'That is, the children do.'

It was very awkward at times for the two people, who were by now standing in the bare house.

'So this is the Jew's house,' she could not help remarking.

Her eyes shone, as if with the emotions occasioned by a great adventure. She had to look about, at the few pieces of furniture, and through a doorway, at the small fibre suitcase under a bed.

'Sir,' she apologized at last, 'I am sticking my nose into your business. Excuse me,' she said. 'I will come again, just passing, and take any things you may have for the wash.'

Then she went, quickly and quietly, lowering her head, as if that might have been necessary to pass through the doorway.

'Oh,' she remembered, when she had already reached the step, 'I forgot to say. My name is Mrs Godbold, and I live with my husband and family in that shed.'

She pointed.

'And I am Himmelfarb,' replied the Jew, with dignity equal to the occasion.

'Yes,' she answered, softly.

She would not allow herself to appear frightened of a name, but smiled, and went away.

Two days later she returned, very early, when, through the window, the Jew was at his prayers. She saw with amazement the striped shawl, the phylactery on his forehead, and that which wound down along his arm as far as his bandaged hand. She was too stunned at first to move, but watched the prayers as they came out from between the Jew's lips. Through the window, and at that distance, the words appeared solid. When the intruder forced herself to leave, it did not occur to her to walk in any other way than with her head inclined, out of the presence of the worshipper.

Nor had it occurred to him to interrupt his worship. Never before, it seemed, as he stood exposed to the gentle morning, was he carried deeper into the bosom of his God.

Afterwards, when he went outside, he found a loaf of bread, recently risen, still warm and floury, that the woman must have baked, and wrapped in a cloth, and left lying on the edge of the veranda.

Mrs Godbold did not dare immediately to come again, but in the afternoon six girls appeared, of various sizes, some walking with a first appearance of grace, some struggling, one carried. There was a puppy, too, wearing a collar which could have been a piece of salvaged harness. As the children approached, they had been indulging in argument and giggles, Himmelfarb suspected, for some of the younger girls appeared mysteriously congested, and the eldest, who had reached the age where shame is easily roused, was rather primly disapproving.

It could have been the middle child who presented the Jew with a bunch of green.

'Silly thing!' hissed the eldest.

Then they all waited, silent, but explosive.

'For me?' asked the Jew. 'That is kind. What is it?'

'Cow-itch,' replied the child who had made the presentation.

Then, with the exception of the eldest, who began to blush and slap, all burst. The baby hid her face.

'T'is-urn't! It's cobblers'-pegs!' shrieked one.

'It's whatever you want it to be,' shouted the official donor. 'Lay off, Else! You kill me! Why do you always pick on *me*?'

'Silly old weeds!'

There were times when Else could hate her sisters.

'I am honoured and touched by your recognition,' Himmelfarb replied truthfully.

'Next time we'll bring flowers,' yelled a small and rather runny girl.

'Where from?' shouted another.

'We'll steal 'em over some fence.'

'Grac-*ie*!' moaned the unhappy Else.

'We ain't got a garden at home,' somebody explained.

'Mum's too busy.'

'And Dad's too drunk.'

'When he's there.'

Else had begun to cry a little, but said, very quick and determined:

'Me mother said if you have any things for the wash to give them to us she will do them early and return tomorrow afternoon if it don't rain and probably it won't.'

She was a slender girl, whose hair could not be relied on to stay where it had been so recently put.

In the circumstances, Himmelfarb could only go to fetch his dirty linen, and while he rummaged, the Godbold children began a kind of ritual dance, forging chains of girls round the rotten veranda-posts, shoving one another by force into fresh extravagancies of position, shouting, of course, always, and laughing. Only Else stood apart, opening seed-pods, examining leaves and secrets. Once she threw up her head, on its long and slender neck, and looked between the bushes at a face she could almost visualize. Once Maudie, of the cow-itch, paused in the frenzy of the dance, and stuck out her tongue at the eldest sister.

'Soppy cow!' Maudie shrieked.

> 'Luv-a luv-a luv-a,
> Who's a lovesick plover?'

chanted Kate.

Which was so unjust, because untrue. Else Godbold bit her lips. She was not in love, but would have liked to be.

When, at last, Himmelfarb produced the bundle of clothes, and his visitors had departed, the air remained turbulent. Physical forms, when they have existed with any intensity, leave their imprint for a little on the surroundings they have relinquished. So the golden chains continued to unwind, the golden circles to revolve, the dust of secrecy to settle. Himmelfarb was glad even for his wilting bunch of lush, yellow-green weeds.

It did seem as though goodness had been sown around the brown house below the post office, and might grow, provided the forces of evil did not stamp it flat. The Godbold children would come, in twos or threes, *en masse*, but never singly; whether by instinct, upbringing, or agreement, was never made clear. Yet, the mother would allow herself the luxury of an unaccompanied visit to her neighbour, as if, perhaps, nothing worse could befall one of her experience. Or, it could have been, she enjoyed protection.

She had come on such a visit the evening Mrs Flack and her familiar, Mrs Jolley, were passing judgement from the blackberry bush. She had helped dress her neighbour's improving hand, very competently, binding it up with a rag she had washed so clean it was positively stiff. She had conducted a consoling conversation on several small subjects, including that of laundry soap.

'During the war,' she said, with that dreaminess for past events, 'I would boil the soap up myself. In big tins. And cut it into bars.'

How Himmelfarb immediately became convinced of the importance and virtues of yellow soap really did not puzzle him.

'You know,' he could even joke, 'we Jews are suspicious of such crude soap since we were rendered down.'

But Mrs Godbold did not seem to hear, or the matter to which he referred was too distant and improbable to grasp. It could have been, within her scheme, that evil was only evil

222

when she bore the brunt of it herself; she alone must and would deflect, receiving the fist, if necessary, between the eyes. He rather sensed this, but could not accuse her innocence. Besides, he suspected it of being a vice common to Christians.

They had come out by then on to the front veranda, and were suddenly faced with assault by the setting sun. Digging in their heels, so to speak, to resist, they frowned and laughed.

'Tonight,' she mentioned, 'we are having corned breast of mutton. It is what my husband likes best. He will be home tonight,' she said.

And made a little noise as though to apologize for some untidiness of life.

'I cannot imagine your husband,' he had to confess. 'You do not speak about him.'

'Oh,' she laughed, after a pause. 'He is dark. Tom was good-looking. He is jack-of-all-trades, I suppose you might say. He was an ice-man when we met.'

The two people, standing on the front steps, were helpless in the solid amber of the evening light. The woman had perhaps reached the point where the obsessed are wholly their obsession.

'Tom,' she said, managing the thick words, 'I must tell you, although I do not like to, sir – our business is not yours – well, Tom, I must admit, has never been saved.'

So that the Jew remembered, in a cold gust, the several frontiers he had almost failed to cross.

'Of course,' she said, wetting her lips against difficulties to come, 'I will not let him down. I am myself only on sufferance.' Then she added, more for her own consolation: 'It could be that some are forgiven for something we ourselves have forgotten.'

But continued to search with her inward eye for that most elusive needle of salvation.

Until the Jew, whose own future was still obscure, deliberately brought her back.

'At least, Mrs Godbold,' he suggested, 'you have possibly saved my left hand by your great kindness and attention.'

She had to laugh. They both did. So complete was their momentary liberation, something of their simple joy shot up glistening out of them, to the complete bafflement of those who were watching from behind the blackberry bush.

Mrs Jolley saw her friend Mrs Flack, as they had expected, that Sunday after church, but such occasions are never for confidences, nor is it possible, desirable, after a service, to peel right down to the last and most revealing skin of that doubtful onion – truth. So the friends chose to wait.

It was not until several days later that Mrs Jolley had the opportunity for looking in. If to *look in* suggests a casualness that one does not associate with such a delicate operation as the tidying-up of truth, it must be remembered that ladies of refinement go scavenging rather in the manner of crabs – sideways. So Mrs Jolley was wearing her second-best. She was carrying, only carrying, her gloves, because there was something accidental about her being there at all. Nor was she made up – not that Mrs Jolley ever made up to the extent of acquiring the patent-leather look – but she had at least licked the end of a lipstick, ice-cream-wise, before setting out.

There she was then.

Mrs Flack professed to be surprised.

'I only looked in,' Mrs Jolley apologized, but smiled.

Mrs Flack closed the kitchen door, and stood across it, in the hall. Mrs Jolley realized there was some reason for doing so.

'Well, now,' said Mrs Flack, so dry.

Mrs Jolley smiled, some for friendship, but more for what she did not know was happening beyond the kitchen door.

'Did you have your tea, then?' she had to ask, in the name of conversation.

'You know I never take nothing substantial of an evening,' replied the offended Mrs Flack. 'My stomach would create on retiring. But I have, I must admit, just finished a weak cup.'

'I am sorry if I have come inconvenient,' Mrs Jolley smiled. 'You have a visit. A relative, perhaps.'

'That is nothing,' protested Mrs Flack, walking her friend towards the lounge. 'A young man has come, who sometimes looks in, and I will give him a bite of tea. Young people are casual about their insides.'

'I dare say you have known him since he was a kiddy,' Mrs Jolley assisted.

'That is correct. Since a kiddy,' Mrs Flack replied. 'As a matter of fact, he is my nephew.'

By this time they were in the lounge, seated on the *petty point*, beside the window. Today Mrs Jolley failed to notice the two plaster pixies, normally inescapable, and of which their owner was so very proud.

'Ah,' said Mrs Jolley, climbing stairs, as it were, scuttling down the corridors of memory at such a pace, her words could only issue breathless. 'A nephew,' she said. 'I understood, Mrs

224

Flack, seeing how you told, that you was quite without encumbrances.'

Then Mrs Flack sat and looked, calmly enough, out of her yellow face, only for rather a long time.

'It must have escaped my mind,' she said at last, with equanimity. 'It is liable to happen to anyone. Although a nephew,' she said, 'who is no closer than a nice piece of steak makes him, cannot strictly be called an encumbrance. As I see it, anyway.'

Mrs Jolley sympathized.

'It is only a kindness that I sometimes do,' Mrs Flack set the seal.

'Of course, you are very kind,' Mrs Jolley admitted.

Then they sat, and waited for the furniture to give the cue.

It was Mrs Jolley, finally, who had to ask:

'Did you hear any more about, well, You-Know-Who?'

Mrs Flack closed her eyes. Mrs Jolley shivered for fear she had broken an important rule. Mrs Flack began to move her head, from side to side, like a pendulum. Mrs Jolley was reassured. Inwardly, she crouched before the tripod.

'Nothink that you could call Somethink,' the pythoness replied. 'But the truth will always out.'

'People must always pay,' chanted Mrs Jolley.

She herself was, of course, an adept, though there were some who would not always recognize it.

'People must pay,' repeated Mrs Flack.

And knocked over a little ashtray, which probably no one had ever used, with a transfer of Windsor Castle on it. Windsor Castle broke in half. Mrs Flack would have liked to blame somebody, but was unable to.

Mrs Jolley sucked her teeth, and helped with the pieces.

'It always happens so quick,' she said, 'and yet, you know it's going to.'

'That reminds me,' said Mrs Flack. 'A dream. I had a dream, Mrs Jolley, and your late hubby featured in it.'

Mrs Jolley was stunned by the roses on the wall-to-wall.

'Fancy now! Why should you?' she said. 'Whatever put it into your head?'

'That is beside the point,' said Mrs Flack. 'They were carrying out your late hubby on the stretcher. See? I was, it seems – if you will excuse me, Mrs Jolley – you.'

Mrs Flack had turned pink, but Mrs Jolley grew quite pale.

'What do you know!' the latter said. 'What a lot of nonsense a person dreams!'

'I said: "Good-bye, Mr Jolley," I said,' said Mrs Flack.

Mrs Jolley pleated her lips.

'He said to me: "Kiss me, won't you" – then he mentions some name which I forget; "Tiddles", was it? – "kiss me before I set out on me last journey." I – or you – replied: "I will do it voluntary for the first and last time." He said: "Who killed with a kiss?" Then they carried him out.'

'He was dead before they put him on the stretcher! Died in his chair! Just as I handed him his cup of tea!'

'But in the dream. See?'

'What a lot of rot! Killing with a kiss!'

Mrs Flack, who might have been enjoying a view from a mountain, it was so exhilarating, said:

'Who will ever decide who has killed who? Men and women are hardly responsible for their actions. We had an example only last week in Montebello Avenue.'

Mrs Jolley had grown emotional.

'And did you kiss him?' she asked.

'I don't remember,' Mrs Flack replied, and smoothed her skirt.

Mrs Jolley's nose sounded soggily through the room.

'Fancy,' she said, 'us talking like this, and that nephew of yours only in the kitchen.'

Or not even.

For just then the door opened, and no bones about it, there stood a young fellow. It appeared to Mrs Jolley that his exceptionally fine proportions were not concealed by sweatshirt and jeans; he was obviously not used to clothes. Nor was Mrs Jolley to sculpture. She began to sniff, and look at other things.

'Oh,' exclaimed Mrs Flack, turning her head, supple now that she had strengthened her position. 'How was the steak?'

The young man opened his mouth. If his gums had run to teeth, he would have gone through the pantomime of sucking them to expel the shreds. Instead, he merely ejaculated: 'Tough!' – from between two remaining fangs.

Although classical of body, it had to be admitted the young man's head was a disappointment: skin – dry and scabby, wherever it was not drawn too tight and shiny, giving an impression of postage stamps; eyelashes – might have been singed right off; hair – a red stubble, but red. Nor did words come out of his mouth except with ugly difficulty.

'Ahlbeseeinyer!' the young fellow announced.

'Whereyergoin?' asked Mrs Flack, who had apparently succeeded in mastering his language.

'Muckinaround.'

Then Mrs Flack's brick residence shuddered as the nephew withdrew from it.

Mrs Jolley appeared thoughtful.

'A sister's, or a brother's child?' she asked.

Mrs Flack was thoughtful, too, and might have wished to remain so.

'Oh,' she murmured. 'A sister's child. A sister's.'

But only eventually.

'I did not catch his name.'

'Blue is what he answers to.'

Mrs Jolley decided she would not penetrate any farther, and was soon startled enough from the distance at which she had chosen to halt.

'I will tell you somethink of interest,' Mrs Flack suddenly said, and had drawn herself right together, into a needle-point.

'Blue,' she said, 'works – rather, I should say, he is *in charge of* the plating-shop – good money, too – at Rosetree's factory at Barranugli.'

'Rosetree's factory?'

'Don't be silly!' said Mrs Flack. 'Where the Jew works, that Mr Goldbold's wife is conducting herself so peculiar with.'

'You don't say!'

'I do.'

'What is more,' Mrs Flack added, 'Blue has eyes which will see what I want to know. I will make no claims for his brains. He was never ever a clever boy, but always most biddable. Blue will act upon an idea, if you know what I mean, Mrs Jolley, and no harm done, of course, if it is the right idea, and the right person in control.'

Mrs Jolley threw up her head, and laughed, but in such a way that Mrs Flack wondered whether her friend realized what a respectable hand her superior held.

'I will tell you something too,' Mrs Jolley began. 'My lady is in the habit of meeting the Jew. Under an old tree. In the orchard. There now!' she said.

And trembled, not from fear.

Principle prevented Mrs Flack receiving reports from others with anything but reserve. So, when she had wet her lips, she merely offered:

'What is it that gets into people?'

But, if her voice suggested old shammy, her mind was already trying out its steel.

Mrs Jolley had purpled over.

'Mrs Flack,' she gurgled in a thick stream, 'it is not right the way some people carry on. And what is to be done?'

'What is to be done?' Mrs Flack recoiled. 'I am not the one, Mrs Jolley, to ask. Am I the constable? Am I the Government, or the Shire Council? Clergymen are in a position to act, but seldom do. We are no more than two ladies of decent feeling. I would not dream of dirtying my hands. Besides, a person might get burnt. No, Mrs Jolley. It does not pay to hurry cooking. You must let it simmer, and give it a stir, like, to keep it nice. Then, when it is ready, you can be sure someone will be only too glad to step in and eat it up.'

But Mrs Jolley was sputtering.

'But her! Her! Under a tree! The squintiest thing I ever laid eyes on! And cracked, into the bargain!'

Mrs Flack could only respect the passion which inspired her friend's hate.

'I would of gone long ago, if I mightn't of been doing her a service. Mrs Flack, have you ever laid in bed, and listened for a house to crumble, and if you was to crumble with it, what odds, let it crash?'

'You would never catch me under any roof in such a poor state of repair.'

'If circumstances had ordered it?' Mrs Jolley snapped.

'Circumstances is not as cranky as some people like to think,' Mrs Flack replied. 'You could be as snug as Jackie, under the blue eiderdown, in my second room, if you was not so stubborn.'

Mrs Jolley was pricked. Her skin subsided.

'I still sort of hesitate,' she simpered between looser teeth.

'Xanadu will crumble without you ever give it a shove. Dust to dust, as they say.'

'Oh, will it though? Will it though? Will I see the neat brick homes, with sewerage, gutters, and own telephones?' Mrs Jolley was entranced. 'Will I see an end to all madness, and people talking as if it was stuff out of dreams? Nobody should ever be allowed to give way to madness, but of course they will never want to in the brick homes. It is in those big old houses that the thoughts of idle people still wander around loose. I remember when I would come downstairs to turn out the rooms. I can remember the loose thoughts and the fruit-peelings. And Them, laying upstairs, in Irish linen. Dreaming.'

Part Four

9

Mrs Godbold liked to sing as she ironed. She had a rich, but rather trembly, mezzo voice, which her daughter Else once said reminded her of melting chocolate. Certainly the girls would get that sad-and-dreamy look whenever their mother sang, and the kind of feeling that warm, soft chocolate will sometimes also give. Mrs Godbold would iron in long, sad, steamy sweeps, singing as she did. Sometimes her iron would thump the board to emphasize a phrase, just as it always nosed more gently, accompanied by tremolo, into the difficult corners of a shirt. Then the mouths of the older girls would grow loose with wonder for some ineluctable drama which was being prepared for them, and the younger ones stare hypnotized at the pores which had opened in their mother's creamy skin. But the singer sang, oblivious, transported by her own words.

Mrs Godbold preferred to treat of death, and judgement, and the future life. Her favourite was:

> I woke, the dungeon flamed with light,
> My chains fell off, my heart was free,
> I rose, went forth, and followed Thee.

Though she was also very partial to:

> See the Conqueror mounts in triumph,
> See the King in royal state
> Riding in the clouds His chariot
> To his heavenly palace gate.

At such moments faith or light did convince many eyes. It was certainly most extraordinary the way the light in Godbolds' shed almost always assisted the singer's words. Great blades of fiery light would slash the clouds of cotton-wool, negotiate a rather bleak window, and threaten targets so personal and vulnerable that more than one conscience trembled. Or else the prophetic voice might coincide with the cold white reckoning of a winter afternoon. That was perhaps the sheerest wonder of all. Then the woman in the apron would become the angel of solid light. The colder fell the air, the steamier, the more compassionate the angel's judgement. Outside, but visible through the doorway, which Mr Godbold had fixed crooked in the beginning, was the big copper, which the girls kept stoked with wattle sticks, and which always seemed to be glowing with half-concealed coals. The hint of fire and the great brooding copper cup could appear most awful in the light of Mrs Godbold's hymns.

There was only one person who remained sceptical, and that was Mr Godbold, if he happened to be present; if away from home, and that was often, he did not think about it much. Mr Godbold had no time for All That. What he had time for could be very quickly specified. It was beer, sex, and the trots, in that order. Not that he really enjoyed beer, except as a dissolver of the hard line. Not that sex was more than a mug's game, involving the hazards of kids and syph, though he did succeed in losing himself temporarily in the brief sexual act. Nor did a horse appeal to him as horse; it was simply that the material future – which, after all, was all that mattered of it – depended on those four bleeding legs.

Any cold mind would soon have concluded that this was an individual to avoid, but for some tart he had been trailing, and who had still to taste Tom Godbold's relentlessness, or his wife, who liked to remember the past, and what she had believed her husband to be before she actually found out, he possessed a kind of eroded beauty, a bitter charm. Time's acid had eaten into the bronze, coarsening the texture, blurring the features. He was scraggy by now, and veined. But his eyes could still destroy the defences of logic and prudence, by seeming to ask for indulgence, and sometimes even love. They were very fine, dark eyes. Those who allowed themselves to be undone were willing to overlook the beery, bilious warnings of the whites. He had, besides, a habit of laying a finger, or two, never more, on the bare skin of somebody's arm, almost tremblingly, or applying pressure to an elbow, with a gentleness in which a command was disguised as an entreaty. Then his wife would waver, and yield, and some woman, from whom he had been peeling the skins of discretion in an upper room, would tear off the last layer herself with reckless hands. It was only later that everybody sat up in bed and realized that Tom Godbold's tragic eyes had merely been looking deeper into himself. Then his most recent conquest would hurry into her protective clothes and ever after regret her impulsiveness. In his wife's case, her nature, of course, denied her the opportunity of flight. She had to suffer. Permanence enclosed her like stone, with the difference that thought burst through its veins in little, agonizing spurts, and she would lie there wondering whether she had conceived again in lust. For one so strong, it must be admitted she was regrettably weak. Or else kind. She would lie there until a thinning light released the pressure from her eyelids. Then she would creak out of bed and light the copper.

Faith is not less persuasive for its fluctuations. Rather, it becomes a living thing, like a child fluttering in the womb. So Mrs Godbold's faith would stir and increase inside the grey, gelatinous envelope of morning, until, at last, it was delivered, new-born, with all the glory and confidence of fire.

This almost biological aspect of his wife's faith was what the husband hated most. Nor was he the father of it. That, at least, he could honestly confess.

'But, Tom,' she would say, in her gentle, serious, infuriating voice, 'the Re-Birth, I think it is lovely.'

Then he would answer from between his teeth:

'You will not catch me getting re-born. Not on your bloody life!'

He would look at all those girls, of whom the very latest always seemed just to have spilled out of the cornucopia. There was always the smell of warm napkins, there was the unmistakable smell of recent and accusatory, wrinkled flesh.

'Jesus, no! I've had enough of births!' he would confirm, and go away, or reach for the sporting page.

There had been some exchange of words and opinions the evening Mrs. Godbold was observed visiting their neighbour. Tom Godbold had returned from work. He was at that time driving a truck for a firewood contractor, though he was thinking of giving it away and starting a line in poultry manure. The father was seated with his paper, the mother stood at her ironing. Children came and went. Although they raised their eyes to their mother, it was at their father's work-boots that they habitually stared, at the stiff, trowel-shaped tongues and blunt, brutal toes.

Mrs Godbold, careful to use her rather trembly mezzo *mezza voce* so as not to inflame feelings further, had just begun her favourite: 'I woke, the dungeon flamed with light ...' when little Gracie ran in.

'Mu-umm!' she shouted. 'Guess what!'

And pressed her face against her mother's side, which would smell, she knew, of scones and clean laundry.

'What?' Mrs Godbold asked, and braced herself against disaster.

'I am saved for Jesus!' Gracie cried.

But rather pale, as if, to please her mother, she was taking on something that might be too much for her.

Nobody was altogether glad.

'You are saved for *what*?' the father asked.

His paper rustled.

Gracie could not find the word. A robust child, she stood trying to look delicate.

'You are saved for Crap!' said the father.

Then he took his newspaper.

'Crap! Crap! Crap!' Tom Godbold shouted.

And beat his wife about the head with the sheets of newspaper, so that it could have appeared funny, only it wasn't.

Mrs Godbold bent her head. Her eyelids flickered. There was such a beating and fluttering of light, and white wings. She was, all in all, dazed.

'That is what I think,' bellowed the husband and father, 'though nobody in this place gives a bugger!'

The paper was scattered at this point, so that he was left with his hand, it suddenly occurred to him. After looking at it very briefly, he said:

'This is what I think of all caterwaulin' Christians!'

He caught his wife across the ear with the flat of his hand, with the result that the room and everyone in it rocked and shuddered for her, not least Tom Godbold himself.

'And Jesus,' he hurtled on, as much to deaden his own pain, 'Jesus sticks in my guts! He sticks that *hard*!'

In fact, he had to deal his wife a blow in the belly with his fist, and when she had subsided on the floor, against the table, a kick or two for value.

Where there had been a white silence, there was now an uproar, as if someone had taken a stick and stirred up a nestful of birds. There was a crying and clustering of children. All were pressed against the mother, that is, except the baby, and Else the eldest, who had not yet come in.

The father himself was ready to drown, but managed to swallow the waves of loathing, exhilaration, fright, and still rampant masterfulness that were threatening to overwhelm him.

'Well?' he gasped. 'Well?'

But nobody answered. The children were whimpering, away

from him. All was turned away, except his wife's face, which she still held exposed to whatever might come.

Such was her nature, or faith, he saw again with horror.

'I'm gunna get out of this!' he announced at last. 'I'm gunna get shickered stiff!'

When he had slammed the door, and gone stumbling up the hill, he heard her calling, but would neither stop, nor listen, for fear she might use some unfair advantage to weaken him. Once, for instance, she had called after him what they would be having for tea, and he had almost vomited up on the spot his whole bellyfull of hopelessness.

Mrs Godbold was, indeed, humourless and true enough to employ any and every means, but for the moment she was feeling queasy. Her children were stifling her, too, as they clutched and touched, trying to revive what they knew as certainty, but which they feared was slipping from them, fast and sure.

'It is all right,' she said. 'I must just get my breath. Leave go of me, though, all of yous. Oh, dear!' she exclaimed, holding her side.

But it had all happened before, of course. Everything has always happened before. Except to children. So the Godbold children continued to cry.

When their mother had got to her feet, it was better. She said:

'We mustn't forget that corned breast. Come on, Kate. It's your turn tonight.'

Only then did they see that they might expect to resume life.

And their mother dared sit a moment, though only close to the edge of the chair. She would have liked to talk to somebody about the past, even of those occasions which had racked her most, of emigration, and miscarriages, not to mention her own courtship; she longed to dawdle amongst what had by now become sculpture. For present and future are like a dreadful music, flowing and flowing without end, and even Mrs Godbold's courage would sometimes falter as she trudged along the bank of the one turbulent river towards its junction with the second, always somewhere in the mists. Then she would look back over her shoulder at the garden of statuary, to walk amongst which, it seemed at that enviable distance, faith was no longer needed.

In the flat, fen country from which she had come, she grew to expect what is called monotony by those who are deaf to the variations on it. A grey country. Even though a hollyhock in

233

her father's garden would sometimes flicker up in memory against a grey wall, or rose straggle over eaves, or bosomy elm heave in the heavy summer, it was winter that she remembered best, of many, many greys: boots clattering through grey streets; the mirror-grey of winter fens; naked elms tossing rooks into a mackerel sky; the cathedral – the greyest, the most permanent of all greys, rising into cloud, that sometimes would disperse, sometimes would unite with stone.

The cathedral was both a landmark and a mystery, to which the gentry owed allegiance, and were, in fact, loyal in their languid way, observing somewhat frightening rites before Sunday dinner. All of that the little girl knew, but understood none of it, because her folk were chapel, all, as far as her grandmother could remember. Of course her father did not; he did not even attempt to. It was not a man's job. The little girl quickly discovered that women remember; men act, and are.

The father was a cobbler. Very devout, in that he observed all the Sabbath demanded, and went to meetings besides, and saw that good was done, within his means, where good must be. In the same way he provided for his children, always enough, without ever contemplating their true needs, or entering into their minds. After his wife died, he seemed no longer to consider there was sufficient reason for coming inside; he would remain in the shop half the night cobbling. And sometimes the girl would go as far as the doorway, to where she could see the back of her father's neck underneath the naked light. He had hard hands, which felt of wax. He was perhaps a hard man, if just; anyway, he might have found it hard to love, although he was fond of his daughter, because she was his, and of all his children, because it was his duty before God.

The girl inherited his devotion to duty, in addition to which she was granted a rapture her father had never known. The thumping hymns would lift her up above the smoking paraffin stoves; it was not only good health that inspired her lungs, but also something of ecstasy. She never forgot herself, however. She never failed to look along the line, to threaten misbehaviour, or find the place for brothers and sisters. She regarded it as her duty; that was clear. She was the eldest, and had become virtually the mother.

There was some talk of the eldest girl studying to be a teacher when she reached a certain age, but that was silly. She would hang her head whenever the possibility was mentioned, as if it was a joke against her. She was not intended for any such dignity. Nor was she really bright enough, she herself was ready to admit, and felt relieved when the matter was dropped. Then she was to have gone into service with old Lady Aveling. It had been discussed at a garden fête to raise funds for the victims of an earthquake. The girl had stood watching the ferrule of a parasol, while her father continued to answer questions on her behalf. All the while the coolest imaginable young ladies in lacy blouses were shooting arrows at the targets which gardeners had set up for their pleasure, or calling back to beautiful young men whose politeness seemed a kind of insolence. How the arrows pierced the desperate, wooden girl. She was that perturbed for considering what might become of *her* children once she had entered the great lady's demesne. But, in the end, the plan fizzled, like the first, and she remained at home, helping in the house, holding it up in truth with the strength of her young arms. There was the grandmother, certainly, but an ailing body who did little beyond shell peas, seated in a wicker chair, on a brick path, amongst the gooseberry bushes, whenever there was a bit of sun. It was the eldest girl, already in a starched white apron at an early age, who received people when they came. Her broad face would consider the answer, and always find it in the end.

But work and duty did not overwhelm her youth. Far from it. There were many simple pleasures. There were the expeditions, alone with brothers and sisters, or in company with members of the congregation, in winter skating and nutting, in summer hay-making, or those long afternoons, dawdled away beside hedge or water, which are half-dreamed, half-lived.

Once Rob – he was the one who always dared most – had thought to suggest: 'Why don't we go up into the cathedral, and muck about? It is too cold outside, and there is nothing else to do. Eh? What about it, sis?' She was accustomed to hesitate because the responsibility would be hers, but on this occasion she did give in, not because the others were punching and pinching, but because she was already throbbing with expectation. She had never done more than look inside the cathedral in their own town, when now the string of children was suddenly being sucked right in by the gasping door, into the smell of hot-water pipes, and a world which, as it formed, did not so much reprove them for their audacity, as ignore them entirely in the beginning. The great, ringed forest rose around them, its stone branches arching above their heads against a firmament of blue and crimson, from which light filtered dimly down, or music. At first the children acted respectful. Their limbs had ceased to be their own. They had stuck holy expressions on their faces, like little grotesque masks. Thinking that they ought to, they admired uninteresting objects, such as plaques for the dead, and only exclaimed too loud on discovering the Italian greyhound of some recumbent duchess. Such authenticity in stone thawed their natural spirits. They grew confident. They were laughing, and patting unnecessarily hard, ruddy-faced even in that gloom, becoming redder for the smell that somebody made, and just loud enough to carry. Then they were swept away in one gust, though by different paths, clattering and dispersing, bursting, for all the hissing and snatching of their mentor, the eldest sister. She might as well have hoped to restrain with hands or threats a batch of freshly-hatched trout, as catch the children once they had been poured back into their own hilarious element. Soon she had lost them. Soon, that could have been Rob, leaning out from one of the stone branches above, in company with the purple saints.

She was glad, though, to feel exhausted by her powerlessness. She strolled a little, and let herself be influenced by the climate of mild solemnity. And was eventually composed enough to sit down on a rush-bottomed chair in an attitude for listening to sacred music. For the organ never stopped playing. She had been conscious of it, but only now began to hear. A music of a strength and solidity to strain the capacities of the harmonium at home. She had never heard anything like this, and was at first frightened to accept what she was experiencing. The organ lashed together the bars of music until there was a whole shining scaffolding of sound. And always the golden ladders rose, extended and extended, as if to reach the window of a fire. But there was no fire, only bliss, surging and rising, as she herself climbed upon the heavenly scaffolding and placed still other ladders, to reach higher. Her courage failed before the summit, at which she must either step right off into space, crash amongst the falling matchsticks, or be lifted out of sight for ever. For an instant she floated in the cloud of indecision, soothed by the infinitely kind fingers.

So, in the end, when the organ stopped, she was dazed and sweating. She felt foolish, for her tears, and her recovered awkwardness. And for a strange gentleman who was looking at her.

'Well?' laughed the man, with genuine pleasure and interest, but through a lot of phlegm.

She blushed.

He was a floury, funny-looking person. His wescoat was buttoned wrong. The scurf had fallen from his hair down on to his shoulders.

236

'I shall not ask you what you thought of that, because,' he said, 'it would only be a ridiculous question.'

She blushed even worse. There was no ground to walk on. She was feeling awful.

'Nobody else,' he said, 'ever conveys the essence of music in any of the bilge they pour out regularly, trying to.'

She began the business of extricating herself, but her chair shrieked like slate-pencils on the paving.

'That was the Great Composer,' the strange gentleman continued, in an agony of enthusiasm and bronchial obstruction.

But the reference made him look kinder.

'I can see you will remember this day,' he said, 'when you have forgotten a lot of other things. You have probably been taken closer than you are ever likely to come.'

Then he walked away, warding off something with his scurfy shoulder.

By this time the girl was again almost crying, but purely from mortification now. She escaped furiously to collect her lost children, and was only restored when everyone had been herded together. They went home soberly enough. They had bloaters for a treat, which the eldest sister ate more rapturously than any. As a young girl she had an appetite she would not have known how to disguise. It was only in later years that she learned to pick, in order to make things go round.

In youth and strength, she would devour, and sleep it off. Even after the disasters which swallow those concerned, she would drop down and sleep like a pig. Her capacity for physical exertion was, it must be admitted, enormous. At hay-making, for example, she would never falter, or on pitching up the hay to load, like a man. At the end of the day, when women and boys were leaning exhausted and fiery, her normally pallid, nondescript skin would seem at last to have come alive, like a moist, transparent brier rose, as she continued to pitch regularly to the drays. It was Rob who liked to stand on the load, to receive. He always had to climb to where it was highest and most awkward, as on the toppling, dead-coloured hay, on Salters' cart at Martensfield. When the girl had looked up, and for the first time, life, that ordinarily slack and harmless coil, became a fist, which was aiming at her personally. It hit her in the chest, it seemed. There was Rob, slipping, laughing, slithering, all wooden arms and legs, as the haymakers watched the slow scene. There was Rob lying in the field, his white eyelids. Herself watching. As the wheel of minutes ground. His mouth had hardly finished laughing, in time for the teeth to protest a little. They might have been grains of unripe corn. As the wheel of the cart trundled, lurched. Then the girl, whose strong back could formerly have held off the weight of the whole world, was tearing at iron, wood, stubble. She was holding in her hands the crushed melon that had been her brother's head. In the dying field.

Several people ran to help. And on the way. But it was she, of course, who had to carry her brother. It was not very far, her blurry mouth explained. From that field. To the outskirts of the town. She was strong, but her thoughts were tearing as she carried the body of her brother. It had been different when their mother died, in bed, at night, surrounded by relatives. Children were forgotten. Until, almost at once, the big girl had taken them on. She was lugging her brother around. So that he was hers to carry now. As her feet dragged along the first of the paving-stones, women clapped fingers to their mouths, and ran inside, trampling geranium and pinks, or burst from their cottages to gape at the girl who was carrying a dead boy, the sun setting in the grey streets, filling them for a moment with blood.

She brought the body to their father, who did not look at her straight, she saw, then, or ever again. He would sometimes look at her boots, that strong pair, which he himself had made, and on which blood had fallen.

The girl went upstairs, and slept. Some of the younger ones had cried, not for a dead brother, but for fear they might never shake their elder sister out of her terrifying sleep.

Time, however, tidies very quickly.

The girl found a new way, the woman remembered, of doing her hair, making it look neat and sleek, with a brown velvet ribbon. She refused to cut off her hair, as others were doing. She would have felt foolish. Or perhaps she was just dowdy.

She had been walking, she remembered, in the back garden, in her brown ribbon, and a scent of stocks. It was evening, and the tea was on the stove.

Her father had come out to her. He said, looking away, as always, somewhere over her shoulder, but smilingly, for him:

'I want you to come inside and meet Miss Jessie Newsom.'

He even touched her, so that she quailed.

'Miss Jessie *Who*?' she asked, although she had heard plainly.

He appeared to take it for granted that she had, for he went on with what he had prepared.

'She is a teacher. Over at Broughton.'

She noticed the adam's-apple, which had always seemed to make speech more difficult for their father.

She tore off a bud. Inside, it was a pale, peculiar green.

Then he told her, gently, but awfully.

'She is going to be your mother.'

But the girl saw to it, in her own case at least, Miss Jessie Newsom never became that.

She was a kind, cool teacher, with apparently confident hands. She was wearing a cameo brooch on the important night, and a cardigan which sagged rather, from the weighty decisions the teacher had been forced to make. In her belief that advantages were open to all those who cared to take the trouble, Miss Newsom had learnt to speak properly, but her origins continually reminded her of the secret cupboards, and sometimes she would blush for their contents.

She said:

'So this is Ruth. They tell me you have been the most wonderful girl. I hope you will not feel, Ruth, that I am in any way an intruder. I hope we shall be able to – shall we say – share the duties of family life?'

Jessie Newsom was so prudent.

But now she hesitated, because she found she was looking at the girl's forehead, which was all that had been offered of the face, and it was altogether expressionless.

Miss Jessie Newsom made an excellent wife and stepmother, the girl heard, both from those who had been shocked by Ruth Joyner's behaviour, and from her own brothers and sisters, whose letters dwindled as continued distance loosened their relationship.

Shortly after Miss Newsom's advent, the eldest girl had approached her father, and announced:

'I have decided to look for work now.'

To which the father replied:

'If that is how you feel, Ruth. We will try to find you something close by.'

'I have decided to emigrate,' she said. 'Chrissie Watkins's auntie hears Chris is doing well in Sydney. I have got all the information from Mrs Sinnett, and will write about the passage, if you will help me. And with money, too, in the beginning. I will pay the money back, of course, because of all these other children.'

The father made noises in his throat. What could he say, he wondered, to console? Instead, he brought out something typical of himself.

'You should learn to forgive, Ruth. That is what we have been taught.'

But she did not answer. In her misery, she was afraid she might have fetched up a stone. Nor did she dare touch, for she could have buried herself in her father's chapped lips, and been racked upon the white, unyielding teeth.

So she went. Her father bought her a tin box in which to pack her few things. Her brothers and sisters presented her with a mauve satin handkerchief sachet, on which was embroidered across a corner: *A clean nose is not a luxury*. She was wretchedly seasick, or unhappy. Other girls, who lit cigarettes, and crossed their legs with professional ease, and knew how to ask for something called a gimlet, did not care for her company. Her skirts were too long, nor did her conversation add anything to their experience of life. So she sat alone, and watched the ocean, the like of which she had never seen, so huge and glassy. And off the Cape an elderly gentleman, who had a business at some place – Gosford, was it? – proposed to her, but it would have been silly, not to say wrong, to let herself accept.

At night, while the other young women were fumbling with temptation on the steerage deck, she said her prayers, and was mysteriously, personally comforted. Released finally from the solid body, her soul was free to accept its mission, but hesitated to trust to its own strength. And hovered, and hovered in the vastness, until recognizing that the rollers were folded into one another, and the stars were fragments of the one light. So she would stir in her sleep, and smile for her conviction, and often one of her cabin mates, as she combed the knots out of her own salty hair in the merciless little flaky mirror, would question the expression of the sleeping girl's face.

On arriving in Sydney, Ruth Joyner discovered that her friend Chrissie Watkins had married, and gone to live in another state. So there was no one. But she found work easy enough, first in some refreshment room, where for a while she carried trays with the thick white cups and the fingers of fruit-cake or madeira. She would set the orders carefully down, and return to the urns, which smelled perpetually of dregs.

All was going well, it seemed – customers often smiled, sometimes even read her passages from letters, and once she was asked to examine a varicose vein – when the lady supervisor called Ruth, and said:

'Look, love, I will tell you something. You will never make

good as a waitress. You are too slow. I am only telling you, mind.'

Because, really, the lady supervisor was kind. She had only been standing a long time, and the heat had eaten the seams of her black satin.

Ruth Joyner then turned to domestic service. She took a situation as kitchen-maid in the house of a retired grazier. She would sit cutting the vegetables into shapes. Or, standing at the full sink, she would sing the hymns she remembered from Home. Until the cook objected, who was bringing out her own niece from Cork, and had never been accustomed to associate with any but Catholic girls.

Ruth had worked in several large houses before she came to that of Mrs Chalmers-Robinson, which was, in fact, her final situation, and which remained with her in memory as the most significant phase of her independent life. Though why, it was difficult to say. Certainly she met her husband. Certainly the house was large, and white, and solid, with a magnolia tree standing at the door. But Mrs Chalmers-Robinson herself was the flimsiest of women, and her servant Ruth Joyner received nothing of material advantage from her mistress, beyond her wages, and a few cast-off dresses she would have been too embarrassed to wear. But the house of the Chalmers-Robinsons (for there was a Mister, too) remained important in Ruth Joyner's mind.

She had been advised by an employment agency to apply for the situation, which was described as that of house-parlour-maid.

'But I have no experience,' the girl suggested.

'It does not matter,' said the woman.

Ruth had discovered a great deal did not matter, but at each fresh piece of evidence her brow would grow corrugated, and her eyes wear an expression of distress.

Even Mrs Chalmers-Robinson, who was on her way to a luncheon engagement, and who had just recovered a very pretty sapphire brooch on which she had recently claimed the insurance, did not seem to think it mattered greatly.

'We shall give you a trial,' she said, 'Ruth – isn't it? How amusing! I have never had a maid called Ruth. I think I shall like you. And I am quite easy. There is a cook, too, and my personal maid. The gardener and chauffeur need not concern you. Both the men live out.'

Ruth looked at Mrs Chalmers-Robinson. She had never met anyone quite so dazzling, or so fragmentary.

'Oh, and my husband, I forgot to say, he is in business,' the brilliant lady thought to add. 'He is away a good deal.'

Mrs Chalmers-Robinson looked at Ruth, and decided the face was about as flat as a marble tombstone. But one that was waiting to be inscribed. (She would make an effort to remember that, and work it up as a remark for luncheon.) But she did so hope she had discovered in this girl something truly dependable and solid. (If she contemplated Ruth Joyner literally as some *thing*, it was because she did long for marble, or some substance that would not give way beneath her weight and needs, like the elastic souls of human beings.)

Then Mrs Chalmers-Robinson got up, in mock haste, protesting mock hungrily:

'Now I must fly to this wretched lunch!'

And gashed her new maid with a smile.

Ruth said:

'Yes, madam. I hope you will enjoy yourself.'

To the mistress, it sounded quaint. But touching.

'Oh, we shall see!' She laughed. 'One never can tell!'

She allowed herself to feel sad for a little in the car, but turned it into an agreeable sensation.

Ruth had soon accustomed herself to life at the Chalmers-Robinsons'. She was quite perfect, Mrs Chalmers-Robinson remarked to her husband – not that perfection does not always have its faults – and it had to be admitted Ruth was slow, that she breathed too hard when handing the vegetables, and preferred not to hear the telephone. Then, sometimes, she would stand at the front door, particularly at evening, as if looking out on a village street. Her mistress intended to mention that, but failed to do so, perhaps even out of delicacy, or affection. So the massive girl continued to stand in the doorway, in the porch, beside the magnolia tree, and as the details of her dress and body, from the points of her starched cap to the toes of her blancoed shoes, dissolved in evening, she might have been some species of moth, or guardian spirit, poised on magnolia wings before huge, flapping flight.

For one so laborious, she moved very quietly, and succeeded in a way in permeating a house which, until then, had worn rather a deserted air. If the flour which dusts a big yellow cottage loaf had fallen on the marquetry table, where the visiting cards were left in a salver, it would have appeared less unnatural after the new maid's arrival.

Once Mr Chalmers-Robinson, on returning from a club at dusk, had brushed against her in the entrance.

'I beg your pardon, sir,' she said. 'I was listening to the locusts.'

'Oh!' he jerked back. 'The what? Yes! Damn pests are enough to burst anybody's ear-drums!'

What did one say, he wondered, to maids?

'I am glad you came, sir, tonight. There is something good,' she announced. 'There is crumb cutlets and diplomatic pudding.'

So that he began to feel guilty, and realized he was a stranger in his own house.

Mr Chalmers-Robinson preferred clubs, where he could come and go as he pleased, without becoming involved in intimate relationships, or irritated by insubstantial furniture. He liked men better than women, not as human beings, but in the context of their achievement and public lives. Women were too apt to reduce everything to a personal level, at which his self-importance began to appear dubious. He resented and avoided such a state of affairs, except when the sexual impulse caused him to run the risk. Then the personal did add somewhat to the pleasurable, and he could always write off his better judgement as the victim of feminine dishonesty. He was certainly attractive to women, in his well-cut English suits, smelling of brilliantine and cigars, and he accepted the favours of a few. If he ceased to find his wife attractive after he had bought her, he continued to admire her ability for getting out of tight corners, and eschewed divorce perhaps for that very reason.

E. K. Chalmers-Robinson (Bags to those who claimed to be his friends) was himself an expert at tight corners, though admittedly there had been one or two at which he had failed to make the turn. One such minor crash carried off a yacht, a promising colt, a Sèvres dinner service, and the personal maid, soon after Ruth Joyner appeared.

'My husband is a business genius, but no genius is infallible,' Mrs Chalmers-Robinson explained. 'And Sèvres, one has to face it, is just a little bit – well, blue.'

'I suppose so, madam,' Ruth agreed.

She liked genuinely to please, for which, all her life, she remained the friend of children.

Her mistress continued:

'Between ourselves, Washbourne has always been something of a trial. I used to hope it was only gallstones, but was forced gradually to the conclusion that she is a selfish old creature. You, Ruth, I am going to ask to take on a very few of her duties. No doubt it will be amusing for you to lay out my clothes, and hand me one or two things when I dress.'

'Of course, madam,' Ruth said.

And was soon initiated into mysteries she had never suspected.

Mrs Chalmers-Robinson had reached the stage of social evolution where appearance is not an end, but a martyrdom. Never for a moment must she cease tempering the instrument of her self-torture. She was for ever trying on and putting off, patting and smoothing, forcing and easing, peering into mirrors with hope, and retreating in disgust. She would hate herself bitterly, bitterly, at moments, but often at the eleventh hour, when she had worn herself to a frazzle, she would achieve an unexpected triumph by dint of a few slashes and a judicious diamond. Then she would look at herself in the glass, biting her still doubtful mouth – a Minerva in a beige cloche.

She would breathe:

'Quickly! Quickly! The side pieces.'

And Ruth would hand the little whisks of hair which the goddess used to wire beneath her helmet, for motoring, or luncheon.

But Mrs Chalmers-Robinson was not all on the surface. Not by any means.

Once she confided in her maid:

'I am going to let you into a secret, Ruth, because you at least have shown me loyalty and affection. I am thinking of taking up Christian Science. I feel it will be so good for me.'

'If it is what a person needs,' hesitated the slow maid.

Once her mistress had dispatched her to the bay with a toy bucket to fetch sea water for her pearls, because that was what the pearls needed.

'Oh, what I *need*!' Mrs Chalmers-Robinson sighed. 'I did at one time seriously consider going over to Rome. Because, as you realize, I have such an insatiable craving for beauty, splendour. But I had to give up all thought of it in the end. Quite frankly, I could not have faced my friends.'

'I believe,' Ruth began.

But Mrs Chalmers-Robinson had already left to keep an appointment, so she did not hear what her maid believed, and the latter was glad, because her struggling tongue could not have conveyed that infinite simplicity.

Alone in the house – for the cook would retire into livery indolence, and the gardener had a down on somebody, and the chauffeur was almost never there, for driving the mistress about the town – the maid would attempt to express her belief, not in words, nor in the attitudes of orthodox worship, but in the surrender of herself to a state of passive adoration, in which she would allow her substantial body to dissolve into a loveliness of air and light, magnolia scent, and dove psalmody. Or, in the performance of her duties, polishing plate, scrubbing floors, mending the abandoned stockings, gathering the slithery dresses from where they had fallen, searching carpets for silverfish, and furs for moth, she could have been offering up the active essence of her being in unstinted praise. And had some left over for a further expression of faith to which she had not been led. Whenever the door-bell rang, she would search the faces of strangers to discover whether she would be required to testify. Always it seemed that some of her strength would be left over to give, for, willing though she was to sacrifice herself in any way to her mistress, the latter would never emerge from her own distraction to receive.

So the intentions of the maid haunted the house. They lay rejected on the carpets of the empty rooms.

Not always empty, of course. There were the luncheons, and the dinners, but preferably the luncheons, for there the wives were without their husbands, and their minds could move more nimbly divested of the weight: wives who had stupid husbands were in a position to be as clever as they wished, whereas stupid wives might now put their stupidity to its fullest, its most profitable use.

It was the period wnen hostesses were discovering *cuisine*, and introducing to their tables *vol-au-vent, sole Véronique, beignets au fromage,* and *tournedos Lulu Wattier,* forcing their husbands into clubs, hotels, even railway stations, in their longing for the stench of corned beef. Mrs Chalmers-Robinson, in particular, was famous for her amusing luncheons, at which she would receive the wives of graziers – so safe – barristers, solicitors, bankers, doctors, the Navy – but never the Army – and, with discretion, the wives of storekeepers, some of whom, by that time, had become rich, useful, and, therefore, tolerable. Many of the ladies she entertained, the hostess hardly knew, and these she liked best of all. How she would glitter for the ones who had not yet dared venture on the Christian name.

Mrs Chalmers-Robinson had been christened Madge, but developed into Jinny in the course of things. Those who were really in the know, those whom she *simply adored*, or with whom she shared some of the secrets, would refer to her as 'Jinny Chalmers', while those whom she chose to hold at bay would see her in their mind's eye as 'that old Ginny Robinson'. And it was not true. Of course she would not deny that she took a drop of *some*thing if she happened to be feeling tired, but would drink it down quickly because she *so* loathed the taste, and later on, when her nerves demanded assistance, and Christian Science would not always work, she did cultivate the habit of standing a glass behind a vase.

But before a luncheon, Mrs Chalmers-Robinson would invariably dazzle. She would come into the dining-room, to move the cutlery about on the table, and add two or three little Murano bowls filled with different brands of cigarettes.

Even if she felt like frowning, she would not let herself. She might say:

'How I wish I could sit down on my own to a nice, quiet grill, with you to wait on me, and tell me something interesting. But I must congratulate you, Ruth. You have everything looking perfect.'

Although it was at her own reflection that she looked, and touched just once – she would not allow herself more – touched her inexorable skin. Then, quickly, she would moisten her mouth until it shone, and widen her eyes as if she had just woken. Her eyes had remained so lovely, they were terrifying in the face. Such a blaze of blue. They should have given pleasure.

Just then the bell would start ringing, and Ruth running, to admit the ladies who were arriving. The ladies would be exhausted from all the committees they had sat on, charity balls at which they had danced, race meetings to which they had worn their most controversial clothes. They had been working so hard at everything they had barely strength left to hold a brandy cruster.

The year Ruth Joyner started work at Chalmers-Robinsons', the ladies were wearing monkey fur. When the girl first encountered that insinuating stuff it made her go cold. The idea of monkeys! Then she heard it was amusing, and perhaps it was, the live fur of dead monkeys, that strayed down from hats, and into conversation, until forcibly ejected. In the drawing-room, the talk would be all of fur and people. Ladies sat stroking their dreamy wisps, while the smoke reached out and fingered, like the hands of monkeys.

Before one lunch, which Ruth Joyner had cause to remember, a lady told the company of some acquaintance common to them all who was dying of cancer. It seemed ill-timed. Several of the ladies withdrew inside their sad fur, others began knotting the fringes. One spilled her brandy cruster, and at least her immediate neighbours were able to assist in the mopping. Until the conversation could resume its trajectory of smoke, violet-scented, where for a moment there had been the stench of sick, drooping monkeys.

Everyone felt far better in the dining-room, where Ruth and an elderly woman called May, who came in when help was needed, were soon moving in their creaking white behind the chairs of monkey-ladies.

Mrs Chalmers-Robinson kept her eye on everyone, while giving the impression she was eating. She could knit any sort of party together. She heard everything, and rumbles too.

She whispered:

'Another of the little soles, Ruth, for Mrs du Plessy. Ah, yes, Marion, they are too innocent to refuse!'

Or, very, very soft:

'Surely you have not forgotten, May, which is the left side?'

But the wine had contented everyone. And already, again, there was a smoke, blurry and blue, of released violets, it could have been.

At the end, when a big swan in spun sugar was fetched in, the ladies clapped their rings together. It was so successful.

Ruth herself was delighted with the cook's triumphant swan. She could not resist remarking to a lady as she passed behind:

'It was the devil to make, you know. And has got a bomb inside of it.'

Which the visitor considered inexperienced, though comical.

Dressed in polka dots, and altogether devoid of fur, the lady was of some importance, if no fashion. She was the daughter of an English lord, a fact which roused the respect of elegant women who might otherwise have neglected. Beside her sat a barrister's wife. They called her Magda. Magda was amusing, it seemed, though there were nicer souls who considered her coarse. It was certainly daring of the hostess to seat the barrister's wife beside the Honourable, but daring Jinny Chalmers had always been.

After lunch Magda visibly eased some elastic part of her clothing, and began to light one of her cigars. A few of the ladies were thrilled to see.

'These weeds have on many occasions almost led to my divorce,' Magda confessed to her Honourable neighbour. 'I hope you will decide, like my husband, to stick it out.'

She spoke in a decidedly deep voice, which vibrated through

several of the ladies present, and thrilled almost as much as the cigar.

But the Honourable threw up her head, and laughed. Early in life, in the absence of other distinguishing qualities, she had decided on good nature.

The other ladies glanced at her skin, which was white and almost unprotected, whereas they themselves had shaded their faces with orange, with mauve, even with green, not so much to impress one another, as to give them the courage to confront themselves.

Now Magda, who had tossed off the dregs of her wine, and planted her elbows on the table, remarked, perhaps to the ash of her cigar:

'Who's for stinking out the rabbits?'

But very quickly turned to her Honourable neighbour, drawing her into a confidence, of which the latter humbly hoped she might be worthy.

'Or should we say: monkeys?' Magda asked.

But her strings so muted that the other ladies, however they strained, failed to hear.

'Did you ever see' – the barrister's wife was frowning now – 'a bottomful of monkeys? That is to say, a cageful of blooming monkey bottoms?'

Magda could not spit it out too hard.

'In fur pants?'

It was provoking that everyone but the distinguished visitor had missed it, especially when the latter threw back her head, in her most characteristic attitude of defence, and let out a noise so surprising that she herself was startled, by what, in fact, had issued out of memory, where as a little girl on a cold morning, she heard a gamekeeper deride his own performance over an easy bird.

On intercepting that animal sound, some of the ladies looked at their hands, kinder ones thought to gibber. But the parlourmaid offered the important guest a dish of chocolates, seeing that she had begun to enjoy herself at last amongst the monkey-ladies. The Honourable Polka Dots accepted a chocolate with trembling fingers, and after rejecting the noisy foil, plunged the chocolate into her mouth, from which there trickled a trace of unsuspected liqueur, at one corner, over the smear of lip-salve with which she had dared anoint herself.

The daughter of the lord remained with Ruth Joyner, not because the guest at table was in any way connected with what came after in the drawing-room, rather as some inconsequential, yet in some way fateful presence in a dream – Ruth did, indeed, dream about her once or twice – a stone figure, featureless, anonymous, stationed at a still unopened door.

Mrs Chalmers-Robinson could not have been altogether pleased with the incident which occurred right at the end of her otherwise successful monkey-luncheon. Or she could have sensed the approach of some more detrimental episode. For she suddenly pushed back her chair, obliquely, and her throat turned stringy to announce:

'Let us go into the drawing-room. I dare say some of you would like to make up a table for bridge after we have had our coffee.'

Magda was soon apologizing to her hostess, it sounded to the maid, as she managed that heavy silver tray, so could not give all her attention. But caught the drift afterwards, and it was something different.

'But I am most terribly sorry, darling. Would not have mentioned in the circumstances. Multiple Projects certainly down the drain. Such a noise, practically everyone else has heard. Then, bang on top, comes Interstate Incorporated.'

The maid bore her tray in the dance of service, surging steadily, sometimes reversing. Her starch no longer crackled, but the tinkling coffee crystals scattered on the chased silver as the ladies helped themselves from an overflowing spoon.

Under her complexion, Mrs Chalmers-Robinson had turned noticeably pale.

'Bags did not mention any of this,' she said, 'simply because he has not been here.'

Her confession was a doubtful weapon of defence.

'Abandoned as well? But darling, I shall bring my nightie. To say nothing of my toothbrush. I have made shift in so many similar situations, I am almost the professional proxy.'

Sincerity made Magda blink, or else it was the brandy weighting her eyelids. Her skin was livery as toads.

'Nothing is settled in a night!' Mrs Chalmers-Robinson bitterly laughed.

'Some things are!' Magda blinked.

The maid wove her dance. In her efforts to hear better, she forgot one or two of the steps, and bumped a lady in the small of her monkey fur. But was, in fact, hearing better.

'Then we are ruined!' laughed Mrs Chalmers-Robinson.

She made it sound like a picnic from which the thermos had been forgotten.

Magda swore she could kick herself.

249

'Darling,' she said, 'you know I adore you. I shall pawn the cabuchon rubies that Harry gave. They have always sat on me, anyway, like bloody boils.'

'Coffee, madam?' asked Ruth Joyner of her mistress.

But Mrs Chalmers-Robinson's attention was only half diverted. For the first time the maid realized the truth of what she had already known in theory: that a human being can hate a human being; and even though her mistress was looking through her, as if she had been a window, it began to break her.

'No, thank you,' Mrs Chalmers-Robinson answered whitely.

Before she wilted from the waist downward, and was lying, washed-out, on her own ordinarily colourless carpet.

In the natural confusion a Wedgwood coffee cup got broken. There was such a bashing and scratching of jewellery, tangling of sympathy and fur fringes, bumping and recoiling, bending and straightening, that even one or two of the guests felt faint and had to help themselves to something.

After much advice and a hard slap, Mrs Chalmers-Robinson began to stir. She was actually smiling, but from a distance, it could have been the bottom of the sea. She sat up, holding the ruins of her hair. She continued smiling – she could run to a dimple in one corner – as though she had forgotten the season of enjoyment was over. She was saying:

'I am so sorry. I have disgraced.' But stopped as she realized the presence of the undertow that must prevent her returning to the surface. 'Where,' she asked, 'where is Ruth?' Feeling the carpet, as if afraid her one hope of rescue was floating away from her. 'I shall have to ask you all to go. So maddening.' Her laughter was letting her down into a snigger. 'But Ruth, where is *Ruth*?'

After pushing a good deal, the maid reached her mistress, and began to pull her upright. It was not an elegant operation, but succeeded, finally, in a rush. The hostess was supported, and up the stairs, on the white pillar of her parlourmaid. At the top she would have liked to take something of a Napoleonic farewell of the dispersing guests, but the truth suddenly overcame her, and she was bending, and coughing against it, and stifling it with her handkerchief as the devoted servant bore her away.

It was a terrible evening that Ruth had to remember. Never before had she seen her mistress stark naked, and the latter's flesh was grey. Anyone less compassionate might have recoiled from the sac of a slack, sick spider, slithering out of its disguise of silk. But the girl proceeded to pick up what had fallen, and afterwards, when it was Mrs Chalmers-Robinson propped in bed, could look full at her again.

A good stiff brandy, and the prospect of a pity she considered her due, even if she paid it herself, had restored the mistress to the pink. She was dressed in pink, too. Pale. A very touching, classic gown, which stopped before it showed how much she had shrivelled. Nor had she forgotten to frizz out the sides of her hair beneath a bandeau embroidered with metal beads.

'Whatever happens, Ruth,' she said, 'and I cannot tell you, cannot even guess, myself, the details of the situation, I cannot, *cannot* give you up. That is, if you will stand by me in my trouble.'

The girl was very awkward, opening cupboards, and putting away.

'Oh, madam, I am not the one to let anybody down!'

She remembered the dead weight of her brother.

Mrs Chalmers-Robinson was agreeably racked. She would have given anything to be able to stuff a chocolate into her mouth. Instead, she looked at the open wardrobe. Such light as succeeded in disentangling itself from the bead fringes of the lampshade made the empty dresses look tragic.

'All my pretty things!' She began to blubber.

Ruth Joyner was breathing hard. But could bear worse blows, if it would help any.

'Freshen up my glass, will you?' the mistress begged. 'With just a dash of brandy. What will you think of me? Oh, dear, but I am not like this! It is the prospect of losing just the little personal things. Because, when it comes to breaking point, men are quite, quite merciless.'

This was the first time Ruth had experienced the breath of bankruptcy. She was not to know that Mrs Chalmers-Robinson would always discover some 'pretty thing' to help her make an appearance in those of the approved places where she would still be allowed to sign. There are always ways and means of circumventing a reality which has ceased to be real. Jinny Chalmers was something like the mistress of a dog who salts away biscuits for her pet against a rainy day, down loose covers; and in the least expected corners, except that in the case of Jinny Chalmers she was both the mistress and the dog.

Her maid was to come across something at a future date, in the toe of an old pink satin slipper. A dutiful girl, she would have to tell.

'Oh, yes,' Mrs Chalmers-Robinson would answer, but very

slowly, thoughtfully. 'That is a diamond. Rather a good one, too.'

And she would take it, and put it somewhere else, almost as if it did not exist.

But for the moment, Ruth Joyner remained unaware that tragedy can be stuffed with sawdust.

She said:

'Hold hard on the brandy, m'mm, and I will bring you a nice hot drink.'

She even said:

'Every cloud has a silver lining.'

She would have loved an old, burst-open sofa, because that happened to be her nature.

She was running upstairs, and down, with hot-water bottles and things.

Until she heard the key.

Mr Chalmers-Robinson let himself in round about ten o'clock.

Ruth said:

'She is taking it very badly, sir.'

He laughed. She noticed on this occasion the network of little veins on either cheek.

He said:

'I bet she is!'

But walked tired. He was still very well pressed, though. His cuff links glittered on the half-lit stairs.

'Something has given me a stomach-ache,' he said.

Forgetful of the fact that he was addressing a maid.

He could have been drunk, she thought. She wondered what they might have talked about if they had been walking together along the gritty paths of the Botanical Gardens, under banana leaves.

Coming and going as she had to be – it occurred to her, for instance, that he might decide to stay the night, and went to turn down the bed he used in the dressing-room – she could not help but overhear a certain amount on landings. She was also, to tell the truth, a little bit inquisitive. Though she did not listen, exactly. It simply came out from behind doors which made a half-hearted attempt at discretion.

Bags Chalmers-Robinson was telling his wife what had happened, or as much of it as was fit to share. Ruth Joyner imagined how her mistress's brows had darkened under the bead-embroidered, flesh bandeau. Could you wonder?

'It was after the merger,' he was saying.

252

Oh, she said, sarcastic, she had always thought one sat back and breathed after a merger, she who was no financial genius.

He replied that she was just about the sourest thing he knew.

'But the merger!' she insisted. 'Let us keep to the painful point!'

How he laughed. He said she was the most unholy bitch.

'I was always gentle as a girl,' she said, 'but simply made the mistake of marriage.'

'With all its perks!' he suggested.

He was helping himself, it sounded, from a bottle.

'Which disappear overnight,' she said.

The mattress was groaning on which she lay, or threw herself into another position.

The maid knew how her mistress could whip the sheets around her at a certain stage in a discussion.

'Look, Jinny,' he said, 'if only you give me your assistance, we can manage this situation, as we have the others.'

'I!' She laughed. 'Well! It positively staggers me to hear there are uses to which I can be put!'

'You are an intelligent woman.'

She was laughing very short laughs.

'If you hate your husband, no doubt it is because he is a stupid beggar who doesn't deserve much more.'

There was a pause then, in which there was no means of telling who was playing the next card.

The maid did not hear her mistress's husband go, because she began to yawn, and sag, and crept away finally. Somewhere in her sleep she heard, perhaps, the front-door knocker clap, and in the morning she found that Mr Chalmers-Robinson was no longer there; nor had he slept in the bed she had prepared for him.

Mrs Chalmers-Robinson was particularly funny and dreamy over a cup of early tea. She had frizzed out her hair in some different way, too.

She said:

'You will not understand, Ruth – you are too good – how other people are forced to behave contrary to their natures.'

'I don't know about that,' the maid agreed, but wondered.

Then the mistress suddenly stroked the girl's hand, almost imperceptibly, almost unconsciously, it seemed, until the latter pulled it away. Both were momentarily embarrassed, but forgot that it had happened.

On a later occasion, Mrs Chalmers-Robinson did remark:

'I think I am only happy, Ruth, with you.'

But the girl was busy with something.

Not long afterwards, a new man brought the ice. He clattered down the back steps, on a morning washed by early rain, though not so clean that it did not smell of lantana and midnight cats.

'Good-day there!' said the new man. 'Where's a bloke expected to put it?'

Ethel, who was always cranky early, and particularly on days when she was expected to dish up something hot for lunch, did not look up, but said:

'Show him, will you?'

'Yes,' said Ruth. 'The kitchen chest is just through here. In the larder. Then there's a second one, along the passage, beside the pantry. You'll have to mind the step, though.'

The man was crossing the girls' hall, where Ethel sat with a cup of tea, studying the social page. From the man's hands hung steel claws, weighted with double blocks of ice. It looked like rain was frozen in it.

Then he had to go and drop one of the big blocks. How it bumped on the brown lino, and lumps of ice shooting off, into corners. Ethel was ropeable, while Ruth tried to calm her down.

'It's all right, Ethel. I'll get the pan, and clean it up in two shakes.'

The man was already groping after the bigger of the broken bits. His hands were rather pinched and green from handling so much ice. But he did not seem to worry about his clumsiness.

'Good job we missed the cook's toe!' he joked.

But Ethel did not take it good at all.

'Oh, get on with it!' she said, hitting the paper she was reading, without looking up.

Ruth was glad to lead the man to the pantry ice-chest.

He had one of those long, tanned faces, too thin; it made her think of used pennies. He was rather tall and big, with hollow-looking eyes. He was wearing a greenish, old, digger coat, from which one of the buttons was hanging, and she would have liked to sew it on.

'That is it,' she said, closing the lid of the chest. 'And double on Saturdays.'

'If I stay the course till Saturday,' he said.

'But you've only begun, haven't you?'

'That don't mean I'm all that shook on the job,' he said. 'Ice!'

'Oh,' she said. 'No.'

They were crossing the girls' dining-room, where already there were pools of water from all those pieces of half-melted ice.

'No,' she repeated. 'But if it is you that comes.'

Then she thought she would have a look at his face, just once more, although it was a kind of face that made her shy. What it told her was so different from all she knew of herself; it was the difference between a knife and butter. But she would have gone on looking at the man's face, if he had not been in it. In her mind's eye, she saw him without his hat. She liked, she thought, black hair on men.

'Gunna rain,' said the ice-man.

'Yes,' she said, 'it looks like that.'

Looking at the sky as though she had just discovered it was there. Still, you had to show an interest.

'Yes,' he said. 'It's a funny old weather.'

She agreed that it was.

'You never know, do you?' she said.

Then he jerked his head at her.

She almost overbalanced from the step to watch the new ice-man go, the rotten stitches giving in the seams of his old overcoat.

'I thought you was going to do something about all this nasty mess,' the cook complained.

'Yes,' said the parlourmaid. 'I'll get the pan.'

'A cloth and a bucket,' said the cook, 'is what you'll need by now.'

That evening as she waited for the mistress to finish powdering herself, Ruth Joyner announced to the dressing-table mirror:

'There was a new ice-man called today.'

'But Ruth, when I expect to be *stimulated*!' Mrs Chalmers-Robinson protested.

Because she could not have felt flatter. She had a headache, too.

'I mean,' she said, and frowned. 'I should like to be taken out of myself.'

She would have liked to descend a flight of stairs, in some responsive model, of lamé, in the circumstances, and the faint play of ostrich feathers on her bare arms. Her legs were still exceptional; it was her arms that caused her anxiety.

'Tell me something beautiful. Or extraordinary. Even disastrous.' Mrs Chalmers-Robinson sighed.

She did also hope suddenly that she had not hurt the feelings of her dull maid, for whom she had about as much affection as she would ever be capable of giving.

Ruth thought she would not say any more. But smiled. She remembered as much as she had seen of the ice-man's rather strong neck above the collar of the greenish overcoat. If she did not dwell on that image, it was because her upbringing suggested it might not be permissible. Though it continued to flicker forth.

The following morning, as the mistress's spirits had not improved, the maid was sent to the chemist at the corner. When she returned, and had handed over the little packet, she could not resist looking in the pantry chest. The fresh ice was already in it, double for Saturday. So there she was, herself imprisoned in the mass of two solid days, from which no one would have heard her, even if she had been able to call.

Once she went and stood for company beside the cook, who had been very quiet all these days, and was now stirring mysteriously at a bowl.

'What is that?' the parlourmaid asked, though she did not particularly want to know.

'That is what they call a *liayzong*,' Ethel answered, with a cold pride that obviously would not explain further.

On Sunday evening Ruth went to service, and felt sad, and got soggy in the nose, and did not care to sing the hymns, and lost a glove, and came away.

On Monday she clattered early downstairs, in fresh starch, because she had heard, she thought.

'How are we?' the ice-man called.

'It's still you, then,' she said.

'How me?'

'Thought you was fed up.'

He laughed.

'I am always fed up.'

'Go on!' She was incredulous.

Then she noticed. She said:

'The button fell off that I saw was going to.'

'What odds!' he said. 'A bloody button!'

'I could of sewed it on, easy,' she said.

But he dumped the ice in the chest, and left.

Most days now, she coincided with the ice-man, and it was not all by trying; it seemed to happen naturally. Once he showed her a letter from a mate who was starting a carrying business between the city and the near country; and would he come in on it? The name, she discovered, was Mr T. Godbold, from the address on the envelope.

Once he asked:

'Got a free Sunday, eh? What about takin' a ride on the ferry?'

She wore her new hat, a big, rather bulbous velour, of which she had been proud, but which was unfashionable, she realized almost at once. They bought some oranges, and sucked them in the sun, down to the skins, on a little, stony promontory, above a green bay. Few houses had been built yet in that quarter, and it seemed that she had never been farther from all else in her closeness to one person. It was not wrong, though; only natural. So she half-closed her eyes to the sunlight, and allowed his presence to lap against her.

In the course of conversation, when they had thrown aside the orange skins, of which the smell was going to persist for days, she realized he was saying:

'I never had much to do with girls like you. You are not my type, you know.'

'What is your type?' she asked, looking in the mouth of her handbag, of which the plating had begun to reveal the true metal.

'Something flasher,' Tom Godbold admitted.

'Perhaps I could become that,' she said.

How he laughed. And his arched throat hurt her.

'I never had a girl like you!' he laughed.

'I am not your girl,' she corrected, looking heavy at the water.

He thought he had cottoned on to her game.

'You're a quiet one, Ruth,' he said.

Laying his hand, which she already knew intimately from looking at it, along her serge thigh.

But she suddenly sat up, overwhelmed by the distance she was compelled to keep between herself and some human beings.

'You are not religious?' he asked.

Now she wished she had been alone also in fact.

'I don't know what you would call religious,' she said. 'I don't know what other people are.'

Whereupon he was silent. Fortunately. She could not have borne his remarks touching that most secret part of her.

He began throwing stones at the sea, but looking sideways, or so it felt, at her hot and prickly serge costume.

Now, indeed, he did wonder why he had tagged along with this lump of a girl. Even had she been willing, it was never worth the risk of putting a loaf in some slow oven on a Sunday afternoon.

So that he got resentful in the end. He remarked:

'We're gunna miss that ferry.'

'Yes,' she agreed.

He continued to sit, and frown. He put his arms round his knees and was rocking himself on his behind, quite regardless of her, she saw. She waited, calmer.

While the girl watched, it was the man who became the victim of those unspecified threats which the seconds can conjure out of their gulf. Although he was screwing up his eyes, ostensibly to resist fragmentation along with the brittle sunlight and the coruscating water, what he feared more was to melt in the darkness of his own skull, to drift like a green flare across the no-man's-land of memory.

This suddenly shrivelled man gave the girl the courage to say:

'You are the funny one. You was talking about missing the boat.'

Nor could she resist dusting his back. It was her most natural gesture.

'Dirty old dust and needles!' she mumbled to herself.

He shook her off then, and jumped up, though her touch remained. He had always shivered at what was gentlest. Many of his own thoughts made him wince, and it was the simplest of them that fingered most unmercifully: touching a scab, dusting down, pointing, with the bread-dough still caked round arthritic joints.

But he became quite cheerful as they walked, and once or twice he took her by the arm, to show her something that attracted his attention, a yacht, or a bird, or the limbs of some tortured tree. Several times he looked into her face, or it could have been into his own more peaceful thoughts.

In any case, the lines of his face had eased out. And in her pleasure, she confessed:

'I could come out again, Tom. If you will ask me. Will you?'

He was caught there. She was too simple.

So he had to say yes. Even though he left her in no doubt how she must interpret it.

Curiously, though, she did not feel unhappy. She was smiling at the sun, the strength of which had grown bearable by now. She could still smell the smell of oranges.

It was the relentless procession of mornings that killed hope, and made for moodiness. And the slam of the lid on the ice-chest. For, sometimes the girl would not go out to receive the ice-man.

'That ice-man is a real beast,' the cook had to comment once. The parlourmaid did not answer.

'You are feeling off colour, Ruth,' said the mistress.

She was lying on a sofa, reading, and the maid had brought her her coffee as usual on the little Georgian salver.

'I hope there is nothing really wrong?'

The girl made a face.

'I am no different,' she said.

But had developed an ugly spot on her chin.

'I can see you ought to take up Science,' said the mistress. 'It is wonderful; you don't know how consoling.'

The opinions and enthusiasms of those around her would slide off the girl's downcast eyelids. She liked people to have their ideas, though. She would smile gently, as if to encourage those necessities of their complicated minds.

'I am not educated,' she replied on this occasion.

'Understanding is all that is necessary,' Mrs Chalmers-Robinson replied. 'And it does not always come with education. Quite the contrary, in fact.'

But Ruth continued listless.

Then the mistress had to say:

'I am going to give you something. You must not be offended.'

She took her into the bathroom, and gave her a little flask, in which, she explained, was a preparation of gin and camphor, excellent against pimples.

'One simply rubs it into the place. Rather hard,' she advised. 'I find it infallible.'

Because, really, Ruth's ugly spot was getting on her nerves.

'Of course, I know you will think, in my case, at least: Science should do it.' Here Mrs Chalmers-Robinson sighed. 'But when you have reached my age, you will have discovered that every little helps.'

Ruth took the bottle, but she did not think it helped. Although her mistress assured her it was having the desired result.

Certainly, one morning very soon after, the girl's skin was suddenly clear and alive. She began to sing in that rather trembly mezzo which Mrs Chalmers-Robinson so deplored. She sang a hymn about redemption.

'Do you feel happy when you sing those hymns?' her mistress was compelled to ask.

'Oh, yes, I am *happy*,' Ruth replied, and was extra careful with the brasso.

She said that that Sunday she was going to the beach at Bondi with her friend.

Mrs Chalmers-Robinson's bracelets rustled.

'I am glad you have a friend,' she said. 'Is she also in domestic service?'

The girl folded the rag with which she was polishing the door-knobs.

'No,' she said. 'That is, I got friendly, recently, with the man that brings the ice,' she said.

'Oh,' said Mrs Chalmers-Robinson.

She had composed her mouth into a line.

On Sunday when her maid was all arrayed, the mistress appeared somewhat feverish, her eyes more brilliant than ever before. She had done her mouth. There it was, blooming like a big crimson flower. With a little, careful, mauve line, apparently to keep it within bounds.

'Enjoy yourself, Ruth!' she called, brave and bright.

Before she settled down to Science.

'God is incorporeal,' she said, 'divine, supreme, infinite, Mind, Spirit, Soul, Principle, Life, Truth, Love.'

Mrs Chalmers-Robinson read and studied, to transform 'hard, unloving thoughts', and become a 'new creature'.

Ruth waited on the corner near the Park. She waited, and her sensible heels no longer gave her adequate support. On Sundays the few people in the street always belonged to someone. They were marching towards teas in homes similar to their own, or to join hands upon the sand. Whenever people passed her, the waiting girl would look at her watch, to show that she, too, was wanted.

When Tom came at last – he had been held up by meeting a couple of blokes – it was quite late, but she was that glad; her face was immediately repaired by happiness.

Oh, no, she had not had to wait all that long.

By the time they reached the beach at Bondi, the light was already in its decline. They ate some sausages and chips in a refreshment room. Tom was a bit beery, she thought.

'I near as anything didn't come this evening,' he confessed. 'I nearly stayed and got full. Those coves I met wanted me to. They'd stocked up with grog enough for a month of Sundays.'

'Then it was a pity you had asked me to come,' she said, but flat, with no trace of bitterness or censure.

'I sort of felt there was no way out.'

'It would have been better not to come.'

'Oh, I wanted to,' he said. And again, softer, after a pause: 'I wanted to.'

'I wish you would always tell me the truth,' she said.

It made him start jabbing the tablecloth with a fork.

'Like somebody's bleedin' mother!' He dug holes in the tablecloth, till the young lady began to look their way. 'Didn't your mother speak like that?'

'She died when I was young,' said Ruth. 'But there was my dad. He brought us up strict, I will admit. I loved him. That was why I came away.'

'Because you loved him?'

'It is wrong to love a person too much. Sinful in a way.'

'Sinful!'

Contempt made him blow down his nose, at which, at times, she could not bear to look, at the nostrils – they were beautiful – but she would again.

And his contempt was very quickly spent. He knew the cause of it was that which most attracted him to her: the unshakeable – which at the same time he was tempted to assault.

After their exchange, he paid the bill at the desk, and they went out. They began to walk along the beach, avoiding in the dark certain darker shapes, making through the heavy, stupefying sand, towards the firmer path beside the sea.

'We're going to get our shoes wet,' she warned, 'if we are not careful.'

Although the bubbly sea was casting its nets always farther afield, she did not intend to allow herself to be hypnotized by its action, however lovely. She could only see the imprudence of such behaviour. For a moment it was almost as though she were guiding those others, her brothers and sisters, or own unborn children.

He did not much care now, and even allowed her to take his arm. They walked sober for a time, in the indifferent grasp of friendship, along the unrecognizable sand. Until, finally, exhaustion made them lag. Their legs could have been trembling wires. Such frailty was satisfying, but dangerous, so that when he said they should sit down, she remained standing.

Then, suddenly, Tom was down upon his knees. He had put his arms around her thighs. For the first time, against her body, she experienced the desperate bobbing of a human being who had abandoned himself to the current. If she herself had not been pitching in the darkness, his usually masterful head might have appeared less a cork. But in the circumstances, she would not have presumed to look for rescue to what her weight might have dragged under, just as she resisted the desire to touch that wiry hair, in case it should wind about her fingers and assist in her destruction.

Instead, she began to cry out softly in protest. Her mouth had grown distorted and fleshy. She was bearing the weight of them both on her revived legs. But for how much longer, she did not like to think.

'Ah, no! Tom! Tom!' she breathed; her voice could have been coming from a shell.

As the mouths of darkness sucked her down, some other strangled throat in the distance laughed out from its game of lust. In the spirals of her ears, she heard the waves folding and unfolding on their bed.

Then the sand dealt her a blow in the back. It, too, was engaged apparently, beneath her, but with the passive indifference of thick sand. As the two people struggled and fought, the sand only just shifted its surface, grating coldly. The girl was holding the man's head away from her with all her strength, when she would have buried it, rather, in her breast. In the grip of her distress, she cried out with the vehemence of soft, flung sand.

'I would marry you, Tom!' she panted.

'That is news to me!' Tom Godbold grunted, rather angry.

He had known it, though; he had known many women.

But her announcement gave him an excuse to pause, without having to admit his lack of success.

'You don't know what you would be taking on,' he said as soon as he was able.

'I would be willing to take it on,' she insisted.

Again he began to feel oppressed by that honesty which was one of her prevailing qualities, and now, as in later life, he tried to ensure that it would not threaten him.

He reached out very gently, and tried by every dishonest strategy of skin to reach that core which he resented. Until at last she took his hand, and laid it against her burning cheek.

She said:

'But what is it, Tom? It is not as if I did not love you.'

By now, he realized, he was really very tired. He lay heavy on her. He rested his head against her neck. He was too exhausted, it seemed, for further bitterness.

It was only then that she allowed him to make love, which was at best tentative, at worst ashamed, beside her riper one. Her lover allowed her to hold him on her breast. She buoyed him up on that dark sea. He floated in it, a human body, soothed by a mystery which was more than he could attempt to solve.

Afterwards as he lay, pushing the wet hair back from her temples, he said to her:

'Perhaps, you won, Ruth. I dunno how.'

She did not move, as he continued to stroke her moist skin with the dry, rough skin of his hand.

'I hadn't thoughta gettin' married, but, for that matter, we could,' he said. 'It'll be tough, though, for both of us.'

She began to kiss the back of his hand, so that he had to pull it away.

'Make you a honest woman!' He laughed. 'Because, I suppose, by you, it is a sin, eh?'

'Both of us has sinned,' she said, with a dreamy tenderness which at the same time filled her with horror.

She sat up, and the little pearls of sweat ran down between her skin and her chemise towards the pit of her conscience. She sat up straight, and the darkness could have been a board at her back, of the hard pew. Hard words came up out of her memory, of condemnation, in the voices of old men assured of their own salvation.

'Both of us! Both of us!' she repeated with shapeless mouth.

But he could not have troubled less.

'Not me!' He laughed.

Again he touched her thigh, and the terrible and lovely part was that she now allowed him. She rested her head against him, and even her tears were a sensation of voluptuous fulfilment.

'But I would bear all your sins, Tom, if it was necessary. Oh, I would bear them,' she said, 'and more.'

That made him leave off. He was almost frightened by what he meant to her.

'I don't see,' he complained, 'why you gotta take on so, not when you got the conditions you wanted.'

But he, of course, was not to know what she had forfeited.

'No,' she said. 'I won't take on. We must go now, though. Give me your hand up.'

Very early she had sensed that her love was on two planes, one of which he might never reach.

They began to walk back. Once or twice she had to stifle something rising in her full throat, once or twice she dared to look up, half expecting sentence to be passed in letters of stars.

Soon after, the parlourmaid mentioned to the cook – it could not be avoided for ever – that she was going to get married.

'To Tom Godbold, the ice-man,' she had to admit.

'Well,' said Ethel, 'you *will* be finding out!'

Contrary to the cook's expectations, the ice-man himself referred frequently to the promise he was supposed to have made.

'And will he be keeping both of you out of the ice-delivery wages?' she asked of the prospective bride, hoping that she might receive an answer to colour her visions of a pitiful existence.

'Oh, no,' Ruth replied. 'He is giving that up. We are going to live at a place called Sarsaparilla. It is on the outskirts. Tom is going in with a mate of his who is a carrier.'

'These mates!' Ethel said.

But it all seemed to be settled, and it became necessary to tell the mistress. Who knew already, of course.

Recently Mrs Chalmers-Robinson had been enjoying every opportunity to exercise her intuition on what might be happening to her friends. Since her husband had got into financial difficulties, there were few who did not respect her feelings by avoiding her. It was as if it had been agreed amongst her acquaintance that she was far too ill to receive visits. Certainly some gift, if not sincerity, is required to transpose the witty tunes of light friendship into a key appropriate to crisis, and lacking that gift, or virtue, the ladies would glance into shop windows, or cross the street, on observing the object of their embarrassment approach. Jinny Chalmers painted on a redder mouth, and studied Science. Once or twice she was also seen dining with her husband at expensive restaurants, but everybody of experience knew how to interpret that. The Chalmers-Robinsons were convening a meeting, as it were, in a public place, where each would be protected to some extent from the accusations of the other, while considering what next.

For the most part, however, Mrs Chalmers-Robinson was to be found alone, in her depleted décor, in the house which had survived by legal sleight of hand. It had been very complicated, and exhausting. Now that it was more or less over, she lay on the sofa a good deal, and rested, and in time learned how to enter the lives of her friends from a distance. She found that she knew much more than she had ever suspected. If she had been capable of loving, compassion might have compensated her for that insight by which, as it happened, she was mostly disgusted or alarmed.

Except in the case of her maid, Ruth Joyner. Here the mistress was chastened by what intuition taught her. To a certain extent affection made her suffer with the girl, or it could have been she was appeased by a sensuality she had experienced at second hand.

When the maid told her mistress of her approaching marriage, the latter replied:

'I hope you will be terribly happy, Ruth.'

Because, what else would she have said? Even though her words were dead, the shape and colour of their sentiments were irreproachable, like those green hydrangeas of the last phase, less a flower than a semblance, which such ladies dote on, and arrange in bowls.

'I have been happy here,' Ruth replied, and honestly.

'I would like to think you have,' her mistress said. 'At least, nobody has been unkind to you.'

Yet she could not resist the thought that nobody is unkind to turnips, unless to skin them when the proper moment arrives.

So she had to venture on:

'Your husband, will he be unkind to you, I wonder?'

She positively tingled as the blade went in.

Ruth hesitated. When she spoke, it sounded rather hoarse.

'I know that he will,' she said slowly. 'I do not expect the easy way.'

Mrs Chalmers-Robinson was almost gratified. It related her to this great, white, porous-skinned girl as she could not have been related otherwise. Then her loneliness returned. Because she could not have been gathered into the bosom of anything so comic, or so common, as her starched maid.

She began to buy herself off then.

'I shall have to give you something,' she said. 'I must try to think what.'

'Oh, no, m'mm!' Ruth protested, and blushed. 'I was not expecting gifts.'

For, as she understood it, poverty was never a theory, only a fact.

The mistress smiled. The girl's goodness made her feel magnanimous.

'We shall see,' she said, taking up her book to put an end to a situation that was becoming tedious.

As she closed the door, Ruth Joyner suspected that what she had done in innocence was bringing out the worst in people. If she had seen her way to explain how she had surrendered up the woundable part of her by certain acts, everybody might have striven less. But to convey this, she was, she knew, incompetent.

So the house continued to bristle with daggers looking for a target.

The cook said:

'One day, Ruth, I will tell you all about the man I did not marry.'

And:

'It is the children that carry the load. It is the children.'

'My children will be lovely,' Ruth Joyner dared to claim. 'My children will not fear nothing in the world. I will see to that.'

Looking at the girl, the cook was afraid it might come to pass.

Then, a couple of evenings later, the bell rang from Mrs Chalmers-Robinson's room. She had gone to bed early, after a poached egg. So Ruth climbed towards the mistress from whom, she realized, she had become separated.

'Ruth,' Mrs Chalmers-Robinson began, 'quite frankly I am unhappy. I have something – no, that is underestimating – I have every, every-*thing* on my mind. Why do you suppose I was picked on? Upon? On! You know I am the last person who should be forced to carry weights.'

And she would have eased hers from off her hair, but encountered only the parting, which needed attending to.

It was obvious Mrs Chalmers-Robinson had had a couple.

'Sit down, won't you?' she invited, because that was what one said.

But Ruth remained standing. She had never faced the better-class people except on her two legs.

'Ruth,' said the mistress, 'Science, I find – though this is in *strictest* confidence, mind you – Science is, well, something of a disappointment. It does not speak to *me*, me *personally*, if you know what I mean.'

Here she beat her chest with her remaining rings. By that light the skin appeared as though it had been dusted with the finest grey dust.

'I must have something personal. All this religion! Something I can touch. But nothing they can take away. Not pearls, oh dear, no! Pearls get snapped up amongst the first. Or men. Men, Ruth, do not like to be touched. Men must touch. That is not even a secret. Give me your hand, dear.'

'You would do better with an aspro and a cup of strong black coffee,' advised the maid, almost stern.

266

'I should be sick. I am already sick enough.' Mrs Chalmers-Robinson shuddered.

Her mouth had wilted and faded to a pale, wrinkled thing.

'What do you believe, Ruth?' she asked.

Though she did not want to hear. Only to know.

'Oh dear, madam,' cried the girl, 'a person cannot tell what she believes!'

And much as she regretted, she was forced to wrench her hand away.

Then, it was realized by the woman on the bed, who would have given anything for a peep – she was all goggly for it – this white tower, too, was locked against her.

So she began to bare her teeth, and cry.

Although rooted firmly in the carpet, the white maid appeared to be swaying. The light was streaming from her shiny cuffs. But it no longer soothed; it slashed and blinded.

'If I was to tell,' the creature attempted, 'it doesn't follow that you would see. Everybody sees different. You must only see it for yourself,' she cried, tearing it out helplessly at last.

'Tell, Ruth, tell!' begged the mistress.

She was now quite soppy with necessity, and ready to mortify herself through somebody else.

'Tell!' she coaxed with her wet mouth.

One of her breasts had sidled out.

'Oh, dear!' cried the girl. 'We are tormenting ourselves!'

'I like that!' shouted the woman in sudden fury. 'What do you know of torments?'

The girl swallowed her surprise.

'Why, to see you suffer in this way, and nothing to be done about it!'

So obvious.

'My God! If even the patent saints fail us!'

There were times when her teeth could look very ugly.

'I am ignorant all right,' admitted the maid, 'and helpless when I cannot use my hands. Only when it comes to your other suggestion, then I feel ashamed. For both of us.'

Indeed, she streamed with a steady fire, which illuminated more clearly the contents of her face.

When the woman saw that she had failed both to rob and to humiliate, she fell back, and blubbered shapelessly. She was screwing up her eyes tight, tight, as if she had taken medicine, but her words issued with only a slack, spasmodic distaste, which could have been caused by anything, if not herself.

'Go on!' she said. 'Get out!' she said. 'I am not fit. Oh God, I am going round!'

And was hitting her head against the hot pillow. She could not quite succeed in running down.

'Take it easy, m'mm,' said Ruth Joyner, who was preparing to obey orders. 'I daresay you won't remember half. Then there will be no reason for us not to stay friends.'

'See?' her starch breathed. 'After you have had a sleep.'

She had to touch once, for pity's sake, before going.

In the short interval between this scene with her employer and her marriage to Tom Godbold, Ruth Joyner was engaged by Mrs Chalmers-Robinson in noticeably formal conversation. For the most part the mistress limited herself to orders such as:

'Fetch me the *grey* gloves, Ruth. Don't tell me you forgot to mend the grey! Sometimes I wonder what you girls spend your time thinking about.'

Or:

'Here I am, all in yellow. Looking the purest fright. Well, nothing can be done about it now. Call the taxi.'

On the latter occasion, Mrs Chalmers-Robinson was bound for a meeting of some new company formed round about the time her husband got into trouble, and of which she had been made managing director. But Ruth, of course, did not understand anything of that.

Only once since the débâcle had the maid encountered her employer's husband. Standing in a public place, he was engaged in eating from a bag of peanuts. His clothes were less impressive than before, though obviously attended to. He had developed a kind of funny twitch. He did not recognize the maid, in spite of the fact that she approached so close he could have seen the words she was preparing on her lips. He was comparatively relaxed. He spat out something that might have been a piece of peanut-shell, from out of the white mess on his tongue. And continued to look through and beyond strangers. So the girl had gone on her way, at first taking such precautions of compassion and respect as she might have adopted for sleepers or the dead.

And then, suddenly, there was Ruth in her ugly hat, standing before her mistress in the drawing-room. Her box had been carried off that morning. The ceremony would take place early in the afternoon.

It was evident that for the occasion of farewell Mrs Chalmers-Robinson had decided to appear exquisite, and to send her servant off, not, perhaps, with a handsome cheque, but at least with a charming memory. She was firm in her refusal to attend the service in the dreary little church. Weddings depressed her, even when done in satin. But she would lavish on the stolid bride a sentimental, though tasteful blessing, for which she had got herself up in rather a pretty informal dress. She had made herself smell lovely, Ruth would have to recall. As she received her maid from the Louis Quinze *fauteuil*, assurance, or was it indifference, seemed to have allowed her skin to fall back into place. Even by the frank light of noon, the parting in her hair was flawless – the whitest, the straightest, the most determined. And as for her eyes, people would try to describe that radiance of blue, long after they had forgotten the details of Jinny Chalmers' décor, her bankruptcy, divorce, and final illness.

Now she said, trailing a white hand:

'I expect you are the tiniest bit excited.'

And laughed with the lilt she had picked up early on from an English actress who had toured the country.

Ruth giggled. She was grateful for so much attention, but embarrassed by some new stays, which were stiff and tight.

'I won't be sorry when it is over,' she had to answer, truthfully.

'Oh, don't hurry it! Don't!' Mrs Chalmers-Robinson pleaded. 'It will be over soon enough.'

Then she moistened her lips, and remarked:

'You girls, the numbers of you who have been married from this house! Falling over one another! Still, it is supposed to be the natural thing to do.'

In certain circles, this would have been considered deliciously comic.

Yet Ruth could not help but remember sad things. She remembered stepping back on to a border of mignonette, along the brick path, in front of her father's house, while trying to disguise her misery, and how this had risen in her nose, sweeter, and more intolerable, as people said good-bye with handkerchiefs, to wave, and cry into.

'Oh, madam,' the words began to tumble clumsily. 'I hope it will be all right. I hope this Violet will look after things.'

'She has an astigmatism,' Mrs Chalmers-Robinson revealed with gloom.

'The milk is on the ice. And bread in the bin. If Ethel is not back. And you want to cut yourself a sandwich.'

If, indeed.

At last the nails were driven. Ruth realized she was biting on

269

a mouthful of hair. It became untidy, always, without her cap.

Mrs Chalmers-Robinson took the stiffly gloved hands in both her cajoling, softer ones.

'Good-bye, Ruth,' she said. 'Do not let us prolong last moments; they can become ridiculous.'

For that reason, and because emotion disarranges the face, she did not kiss her departing maid. But might have, she felt, if circumstances had been a little different.

'Yes,' said Ruth. 'They will be expecting me. Yes. I had better go now.'

Her smile was that stupid, she knew, but something at least to hang on to. So it stuck, at the cost of strain. She listened to her shoes squeak, one after the other, as she crossed the parquet. She had polished it the day before, till her thoughts, almost, were reflected in it. A fireworks of light, brocade, and crystal cascaded at the last moment on her head, just before she closed the door in the way she had been taught to close it, on leaving drawing-rooms.

So Ruth Joyner left, and was married that afternoon, and went to live in a shed, temporary like, at Sarsaparilla, and began to bear children, and take in washing. And praised God. For was not the simplest act explicit, unalterable, even glorious in the light of Him?

Mrs Godbold was sitting on the edge of the chair, in that same shed which had started temporary and ended up permanent. Several of the children continued to cling to their mother, soothed by her physical presence, lulled on the waves of her reflective mind. Kate, however, was going about sturdily. She had rinsed the teapot, saving the leaves for their various useful purposes. With an iron spoon, she had given the corned breast an authoritative slap or two. Soon the scents and sighs were stealing out of pan and mouths, as fresh sticks crackled on sulky coals, and coaxed them back to participation. Eyes could not disguise the truth that the smell of imminent food is an intoxicating experience.

Even Mrs Godbold, who had felt herself permanently rooted amongst the statuary of time, began to stir, to creak, to cough, all of it gently, for fear of disturbing those ribs which had copped most of her husband's wrath. She would have risen at any moment, to resume her wrestling, as a matter of course, with the many duties from which it was useless to believe one might ever really break free. When Else, her eldest, came in.

Else Godbold often got home later of an evening now. Since

it had been decided that her fate was secretarial, she had learnt to bash out a business letter, and would take on any other girl, for speed, if not for spelling. As for her shorthand, that was coming along, too: she accepted dictation, with disdain, and sometimes even succeeded in reading her results. In her business capacity, she caught the bus for Barranugli, every morning at 8.15, in pink, or blue, with accessories of plastic, and a cut lunch. Else had begun to do her lips, as other business young ladies did. Cleverly balanced on her heels, she could make her skirt and petticoats sway, in a time which might have provoked, if it had sounded less austere. Else Godbold was ever so impressive, provided her younger sisters were not around.

Now, when she had banged the shed door, because that was the only way to shut it, and kicked off her shoes, because she always felt happier without, she went up close to her mother, and said:

'Mum, I ought to tell you, I just seen Dad.'

Her breath was burning, not to say dramatic.

'Ah,' replied the mother, slowly, not altogether rousing herself.

For Mrs Godbold never tired of examining her eldest, and now that the lipstick was all but eaten off, and Else looking warm, yet dewy, the woman saw the hedges rise again in front of her, in which were all the small secret flowers, and bright berries, with over them the loads of blossom, or pretty fruit.

'Yes,' – she cleared her throat to continue – 'your dad went out not so very long ago.'

'And is drunk as sin,' hissed Else, 'already!'

Because in Godbolds' shed, it would have been silly, everybody knew, to mince matters at all.

Mrs Godbold compressed her nostrils in a certain way she had.

'He was coming from Fixer Jensen's.' The messenger refused to relent.

'He will likely be catching the bus,' suggested Mrs Godbold. 'Your father was not in the best of tempers. He will almost certain make for the city. Oh, dear! And in his work-things, too!'

'Not him!' said Else, and now she did hesitate, for one who had learnt that time is not to waste. She did go red, and incline a little, as if she would have touched their mother. 'Not him!' she repeated. 'Dad,' she said, 'was making for Khalils'!'

Then Else began quite suddenly to cry.

So natural a noise, it sounded worse, and that such a secretarial young lady should act like any little girl.

Mrs Godbold had to get up, no longer so careful of her ribs. 'To Khalils',' she said. 'From Fixer Jensen's.'

The youngest of the children understood their father had fallen from a low level to perhaps the very depths of the pit.

And Else heaving and sobbing like that, hot and red, in her business dress. Several others saw fit to join her.

But they did not know how to share her shame.

'Let me see now,' said the mother, really rather confused, when she could least afford to be. 'You will attend to the mutton, Kate. And don't forget there's cabbage to warm. Else! Else! This house is too small for having the hysterics in. Grace, keep an eye on Baby. Whatever is she doing with that nasty-looking nail?'

Although it was warm, even sultry, Mrs Godbold put on her coat, for decency's sake, and for moral support, her black, better hat.

To everybody, her preparations appeared most awful.

'I am going out now,' she announced, 'and may be a little while. I want you girls to behave, as you can, I know. Else! Else! You will see to it, won't you, when you have pulled yourself together?'

Else made some sort of sound out of her blurry face.

Before their mother was gone.

Mrs Godbold went up the hill towards the road, along the track which all of them had helped to wear deep. A blunderer by nature, she was fair game for blackberry bushes, but would tear free, to blunder on, because she was meant to get there, by pushing the darkness down if necessary. And dark it was by now. Once she slithered, and the long, green smell told her of cow-pats. Once she plunged her foot right up to the ankle in a rusty tin. Empty bottles cannoned off one another, while all the time that soft, yet prickly darkness was flicking in her face the names of Fixer Jensen and Mollie Khalil, with the result that the victim's knees were trembly as the stars.

If she had lived less retired, she might have been less alarmed, but here she had undertaken an expedition to the dark side of the moon. Fixer Jensen was a joke, of course, even amongst those inhabitants sure enough of their own virtue to enjoy a paddle in the shallows of vice. 'Better see Fixer,' they used to say, and laugh, anywhere around Sarsaparilla, if it was a matter of short-notice booze, or commodities that had disappeared, or some horse that had become a cert almost too late in the day. Fixer could fix anything, after picking his nose for a while, and denying his gifts. Who would not overlook a certain unloveliness of behaviour in one who served the community, and supported the crippled kiddies, besides, and bred canaries for love? Yet, there were a few humourless blobs and wowsers who failed to appreciate that obliging, and all in all, respectable cheat. Why, they asked, did the law not take steps to ensure that Jensen toed the line? Those persons could only have been ignorant or imbecile as well, for it was commonly known that two councillors, at least, accepted Fixer's services. Moreover, Mrs McFaggott, wife of the constable himself, was dependent on him for a ready bottle, and she, poor soul, without her grog, could not have turned a blind eye to the constable's activities. It was obvious, then, that Fixer Jensen's position was both necessary and legal, and that he would continue to oblige those who found themselves in a hole. Nuns had been seen arriving with ports, and little girls with dolls' prams, at Fixer Jensen's place, while almost any evening, after work, and before wives might claim their rights, the sound of manly voices, twined in jolly, extrovert song, could be heard blurting through the vines which helped to hold that bachelor establishment up.

Most of this Mrs Godbold knew, by hearsay, if not experience, and now visualized a mess of husband, songful and soulful, bitter and generous at once, as ready to lay his head on a bosom as bash it open on a stone. She would have endured all this, and more, if only she could have caught him by the shirt as he stumbled glassy from Fixer Jensen's, but after Else's recent report, Tom had gone frying further fish, of rather a different kind.

Mrs Godbold was almost tripped by her own thoughts at the corner of Alice Avenue, but kept her balance, and went on, turning her wedding-ring round and round, to achieve an assurance which hesitated to develop. She even whimpered a little to herself, something she would never have done by daylight, or in public. Only, in the streets of Sarsaparilla at night, she was less a wife and mother than a humour in a dark hat.

In which state she arrived at Khalils'.

And found, unexpectedly, discretion.

If a piece of the gate did fall off as she opened it, that is always liable to happen, and if the house itself had dissolved, the windows remained an inextinguishable yellow, only partially eclipsed by a variety of materials: crimson plush, check horse-

rug, brown holland, even, it seemed, a pair of old cotton
drawers, that the owners had stretched, for privacy like. All
was quiet, though, at Khalils'. So that when the visitor knocked,
the sound of her knuckles rang out, and she sank a little lower
in her shoes.

Slippers approached, however, rather annoyed.

'Waddaya want there?' called a voice through a tear in the
screen door.

'I am Mrs Godbold.' the darkness answered. 'And I have
come for my husband. Who must be here.'

'Oh,' said the voice – it was a woman's. 'Mrs Godbold.'

Then there was a long pause, in which breathing and mosquitoes were heard, and someone was waiting for someone else
to act.

'Mrs Godbold,' said the woman at last, through the tear.
'Waddaya wanta come 'ere for!'

'I came here for my husband,' the visitor persisted.

It was so simple.

But the door was whining and creating.

'No one,' said the woman, 'never came for their husband.
Never.'

She was distressed, it seemed, by some infringement of etiquette. She did not know what to do, so the door creaked, and
her slippers shifted grittily.

'You are Mrs Khalil?' Mrs Godbold asked.

'Yes,' said the woman, after a pause.

The sticky scent of jasmine hung low, touching strangers.
Loving cats pressed against the skirt.

'Aohh,' protested Mrs Khalil, 'whydya wanna go an' do
this?'

She could have been a decent sort. She was swinging the
door, and her cats were at least fed.

'You better come in,' she said, 'Mrs Godbold. I dunno watta
do with yer. But come in. It's no faulta mine. Nobody never
done this ter me before.'

Mrs Godbold coughed, because she did not know what to
answer, and followed the slippers of her new acquaintance,
slit slat slit slat, down a passage, into a yellow light and some
confusion.

'There we are, anyways,' Mrs Khalil said, and smiled, showing a gold tooth.

Mollie Khalil was not a bad sort at all. If she was Irish,
whose fault was that? And such a long way back. There were
those at Sarsaparilla who called her a loose woman, and those

could have been right. But an honest woman, too. Doing her job like anyone else. Lived *de facto* with a Syrian until the bugger shoved off, when she simply turned to, and set up whoring in a quiet way, in a small home behind the fire-station. She was no longer for the men herself, preferring comfort and a glass of gin. Besides, her girls Lurleen and Janis were both of an age, and there was a lady would come from Auburn, to help out when necessary.

'We might as well be comfortable,' Mrs Khalil now said. 'Us women!' She laughed. 'Take off your hat, dear, if you feel like it.'

But Mrs Godbold did not.

Mrs Khalil was wearing a loose, imaginative gown, in which her flesh swam free, as she moved about what was evidently her kitchen.

She said:

'This is my youngest kid, Janis, Mrs Godbold.'

She touched her child's rather frizzy hair as if it had been something else, growing on its own.

Janis was having a read of what her mother would have called a Book. She did not look up, but stuck out her jaw, and frowned. She was sitting in her shift. Her bare toes were still wriggly, like a little girl's.

'Siddown, dear,' said Mrs Khalil to her visitor, and moved something private from a chair.

In a far corner there was a gentleman still to be explained.

'This is Mr Hoggett,' she said. 'He is waiting.'

Mr Hoggett did not know what to say, but made a noise in the region of the singlet which contained his upper part.

Mrs Godbold sat down upon an upright chair. Her errand of love remained somehow imperative, though by now she knew it could not be explained.

Janis was turning the pages of her Book with a thumb which she licked scornfully. She was black, but not so black as not to know what she was worth.

'Ackcherly,' said Mrs Khalil, staring dreamy at the vision which represented her younger child, 'we was having a sorta discussion when you come around and knocked. I said death is like anythin' else. It is wotcha care to make it, like. It is howya go orff. But Mr Hoggett and Janis still had to voice an opinion.'

Mr Hoggett had not bargained for anything of this. He turned his head sideways. He scratched his navel through the singlet.

'Mr Hoggett's wife died,' Mrs Khalil said, and smiled a kind of dreamy smile.

' 'Ere! Cut it out!' Mr Hoggett had to protect his rights. 'I didn't come 'ere for this. A man can stay at 'ome and listen to the wireless.'

He looked around, accusing, and what was most unfair, at Mrs Godbold, who was innocent.

Then the bawd began to turn nasty. She struck several matches, but they broke.

'I toldya, didn't I? I couldn'ta made it plainer. Janis is bespoke. Some men make me wanta reach!'

But she got the cigarette alight at last. She began to breathe up smoke, and to move about inside her clothes. Mr Hoggett, who was pretty big, simply sat, in his singlet, expressing himself with his belly. He might have expanded further if Mrs Khalil's kitchen had not filled up already, with dishes, and baskets, and piles of women's underclothes, and cats, and an old gas stove with a glass face and mutton fat inside.

'Excuse us, dear, if business will raise its head,' Mrs Khalil apologized to Mrs Godbold.

The latter smiled, because she felt she ought. But the expression did not fit her face. It drifted there, out of someone else's situation. The chair on which she sat was so upright, the flesh itself could not upholster it. Or, at least, she must see to that.

At the same time, there was a great deal she did not understand. It left her looking rather sad.

'I could wait outside,' presently she said.

For her intentions, if they had ever formed, had finally grown paralysed.

'Oh dear no!' protested Mrs Khalil. 'The night air does no one any good.'

So Mrs Godbold's statue was not moved from off its chair, and just as she was puzzled by her own position, the sculptor's purpose remained obscure to the beholder.

In the kitchen's fearful fug, forms had swelled. For one thing, Mr Hoggett had expended a good deal of emotion. Now, when he suddenly laughed, right the way up his gums, it was perhaps entitlement. He slapped his opulent thigh, and looked across at Janis, and asked:

'Havin' a nice read, love?'

'Nao,' said Janis.

She had done her nails some time ago, and the stuff was flaking off. What she read, following it with a finger, was obviously of grave substance.

'There!' she cried. 'Mumma, I toldya! Thursday is no good. We are under the influence of Saturn. See?'

She slammed the Book together then.

'Oh, gee!' she said.

She went and threw the window up, so that she let in the moon and a scent of jasmine. A white, sticky stream of night came pouring in, together with a grey cat of great persistence.

'Gee,' said Janis, 'I wish I could make somethink happen!'

'That is somethink I would never dare wish for,' asserted her mother.

And blew a trumpet of smoke from her nostrils.

In the house behind, voices were laid together in the wooden boxes. They would rasp like sandpaper at times, or lie against one another like kid gloves.

Mrs Godbold listened to the minutes. She held up her chin. In spite of the aggressively electric light, the side of her face closest to the window had been very faintly moonwashed. It was only just visible, one paler splash.

Suddenly she bent down, for something to do, it could have been, and got possession of the smoky cat. She laid it along her cheek, and asked:

'What are you after, eh?'

So softly. But it was heard.

Mrs Khalil nearly bust herself. She answered:

'Love, I expect. Like anybody else.'

And Mrs Godbold had to see that this was true. That was perhaps the dreadful part. Now she really did understand, she thought, almost everything, and only prayed she would not be corrupted by her own knowledge.

The chair creaked on which Mr Hoggett sat. He was very heavy. And hair bursting out of his body.

'I would like to go away, somewhere on a train,' Janis said, and turned quick. 'Mumma,' she said, 'let me have me dress. Go on!' she coaxed. 'I gotta go out. Anywheres.'

'You know what was agreed,' the mother replied.

The girl began to protest and twist. She was very pretty underneath her shift.

In the dream in which she sat, and from which her marble must never be allowed to stir, Mrs Godbold could feel the drops of jasmine trickling down. She began, for protection, to think of her own home, or shed, and the white surface of the ironing-table, cleaner than moonlight, not to say more honest, with the bowl from which she sprinkled the clothes. She must

pin her mind on all such flat surfaces and safe objects, not on
her husband; he was the weakest side of her.

So she fixed her eyes on the floor of Mrs Khalil's kitchen, on
a harlequin lino, where much had been trodden in.

The moon has touched her up, Mrs Khalil saw, and for a
moment the bawd fell quite genuinely in love with that strong
but innocent throat, although, mind you, she was sick of men
and women, their hot breath, their double-talk, their slack
bodies, and worst of all, their urgent tones. She liked best
to lay around with the Sunday papers, a cat against her
kidneys.

Mrs Godbold paddled her hand in the grey cat's very nearly
contented fur. She no longer blamed her husband, altogether.
She blamed herself for understanding. She might have left,
indeed, if she had been able to withdraw her feet. But the
moonlight lay in sticky pools, even where invisible, smelling of
jasmine, and a man's stale body.

Then there was such a to-do, the wooden house was all but
knocked sideways.

'Don't tell me!' cried Mrs Khalil. 'It is that bloody abo
again!'

'Arrr, Mumma!' Janis had to draw the line at that.

'Wot abo?' Mr Hoggett was quick to ask.

As if they had not stalled on him enough.

'The only one. Our pet one,' moaned Mrs Khalil. 'Send it
orff, and it will turn up again like washin' day.'

'Arr, Mumma, no!'

Janis could have had the belly-ache.

'Is it 'im?' Mr Hoggett was fairly running sweat.

But nobody listened to that gentleman now.

For the screen door was screaming painfully. The boards of
the violated house were groaning and recoiling.

He came in. He had a purple bruise where he had fallen on
his yellow forehead, somewhere or other. He could not use his
body by now, but was directed by a superior will.

'You dirty, drunken bastard!' shouted Mrs Khalil. 'Didn't I
tellya we was not accepting any further visits?'

He stood, and a smile possessed him.

The bawd would have liked to deliver a piece on blacks,
but remembered dimly she had been married to one in all but
writing.

'This is no visit. This is a mission,' announced the abo.

So surprisingly that Mrs Godbold looked up. She had been
half determined to keep her eyes fixed firmly on the lino, in

case she might have to witness an indignity which she would not be strong enough to prevent.

'A mission?' shouted Mrs Khalil. 'Wot sorta mission, I would liketa know?'

'A mission of love,' replied the abo.

And began to laugh happily.

'Love!' cried Mrs Khalil. 'You got ideas in yer head. I'm tellin' you! This is a decent place. No love for blacks!'

Janis had grown giggly. She was biting the red stuff off of her nails, and scratching herself.

The black continued to laugh for a little, because he had not yet run down, and because laughter disposed him to resist the roomful of fluctuating furniture.

Then he became grave. He said:

'Okay, Mrs Khalil. I will sing and dance for you instead.'

'If you will allow me,' he added, very reasonable. 'And even if you cut up rough. Because I am compelled to.'

Many of the words were borrowed, but those could have been the cheaper ones. A certain gravely cultivated tone and assembly of educated phrases were what, it seemed, came natural to him. Even as he rocked, even as his thick tongue tripped over a word here and there, as his fiery breath threatened to burn him up, or he righted himself on the furniture, his eyes were fixed obsessively on some distant standard of honesty and precision. He would never quite lose sight of that – he made it clear – and it was what infuriated some of his audience most. Mr Hoggett, for instance, while affecting the greatest disgust, both for a moral situation, and for the obvious signs of vomit on the abo's pants, was most enraged by a tone of voice, and words that he himself would never have dared use.

'Where did 'e learn it, eh?' he asked. 'This one beats the band. So much play-actin', and dawg!'

The black man, who was conscientiously preparing the attitude and frame of mind necessary for his act, paused enough to answer, in a voice that was as long, and straight, and sober as a stick:

'I owe everything to the Reverend Timothy Calderon, and his sister, Mrs Pask.'

'Waddaya know!' exploded Mrs Khalil.

She could not help but laugh, although she had decided on no account to do so.

The blackfellow, who had at last succeeded in reconciling attitude with balance, now began to sing:

> 'Hi digger, hi digger,
> My uncle is bigger
> Than my father,
> But not as big as
> Friday night.
> Friday is the big shivoo,
> When the swells begin to swell,
> And poor Mother has her doubts.

> 'Hi digger, hi digger,
> The moon has a trigger,
> Which shoots the buggers down,
> Whether they want to be hit,
> Or to pro-cras-tin-ate. . . .'

'Go easy!' interrupted Mrs Khalil. 'I don't allow language in my place. Not from clients. If I'm forced ter use a word meself, it's because I got nowhere else ter go.'

'Why don't they lock 'im up?' Mr Hoggett complained.

'Why?' asked Mrs Khalil, and answered it easy. 'Cos the constable 'imself is in the front room, as always, with my Lurleen.'

By this time the black, who had started in a lazy, loving way, only lolling and lurching, as he sowed seed gently with his hands, or took out his heart to present to the different members of the audience, had begun to grow congested. He was darkening over, purpling even. His sandshoes began to beat a faster time. Short, stabbing gestures were aimed, not at another, but inward, rather, at his own breast.

He stamped, and sang faster:

> 'Hi digger, hi digger,
> Nail it! Nail it!
> Nail the difference till it bleeds!
> It's the difference, it's the difference
> That will bleed the best.
> Poppies are red, and Crimson Ramb-lers,
> But men are redd-est
> When they bleed.
> Let 'em! Let 'em!
> Le-ehtt . . . .'

So he sang, and stamped, and stamped on a cat or two, which yowled in their turn. Baskets fell, or lingerie, which the sun had hardened into slabs of salt fish. As the abo jumped and raised hell, Mollie Khalil appeared to have started jumping too, or at least her breasts were boiling inside the floral gown,

'Catch 'old of 'im, willya, please! Someone! Mr Hoggett, be
a gentleman!'

She had revived herself somewhat, with something, to cope
with a situation, and now was holding her side hair, so that
the sleeves had fallen back, from rather moister, black-and-
whitest armpits.

'Not me!' said her client, though. 'I came 'ere for a purpose.
Not for a bloody rough-'ouse.'

'But the constable!' she had to plead. 'He will disturb the
constable.'

> 'Okay for Daisy . . .'

sang the abo.

He was stamping mad. And cutting wood. Or breaking sticks.

> 'Okay for Mrs McWhirter . . .'

the abo sang, and stamped.

> '. . . and Constable O'Fickle,
> And Brighta Lamps,
> To see with,
> To see see see,
> And be with. . . .'

Just then Lurleen came in. At one moment, where the
shambles of sound fell back, leaving a gulf to be filled, her
bare feet were heard squelching over the lino. Lurleen was a
good bit riper than her sister. She suggested bananas turning
black. She was rather messed up. She had the bruised-eyelid
look, and some rather dirty pink ribbons just succeeded in
keeping the slip attached to her sonsy shoulders.

'I have had it!' she said. 'That man has one single thought.'

'Waddaya expect? Latin thrown in?'

'No, but conversation. There's some tell about their wives.
That's the best kind. You can put the screw on them.'

'Did he pay?' the bawd asked. 'Don't tell me! He said to
chalk it up!' she said.

'I am hungry. What is in the fridge, Mum?' Lurleen asked,
but did not bother about an answer.

She went to the fridge, and began to eat a sausage, which
cold and fat had mottled blue.

'I gotta get Mandovani,' she said, and started twiddling the
knob.

'Gee, not Mandovani!' Janis hoped.

She herself felt the necessity to writhe, and was threatened
instead with sticking-plaster.

Lurleen twiddled the knob. Except for a couple of bruises, she was really honey-coloured.

But now somebody was coming in.

'Waddaya know, Fixer?' Mr Hoggett laughed.

He was enjoying it at last. The little one had decided to plaster herself against his ribs. Inside his cotton singlet, his belly was jumping to answer her.

> 'The sun rose over the woolshed,
> The coolabahs stood in a row.
> My mother sat in the cow-paddock,
> And heard the Reverend come. . .'

the abo recited; he no longer felt inclined to sing, and had retreated far from the present room.

'Arr, Mr Jensen,' called the bawd, from the springs of a rusty lounge, where she had extended herself after further revival, 'fix me this abo bloke,' she invited, 'and you are a better man than ever I thought.'

But Fixer Jensen, who was tall, thin, putty-coloured, with his wrinkles pricked out in little black dots, stood and picked his nose as usual. He needed, of course, to get inspired.

He looked at Mrs Godbold. Not that he knew her. But he had not expected exactly to meet a statue in a room.

There one sat.

Fixer said:

'Waddaya got 'ere? A party?'

Then he began to laugh.

'It only needs the constable!' he laughed.

Lurleen pouted.

'The constable has gone home,' she advised, and was stroking herself to the accompaniment of music, and revolving, in her pink slip.

'Business good, eh?' Fixer asked.

'Not since the Heyetalian cow set up,' Mrs Khalil snapped. 'Business got donged on the head.'

Suddenly the abo fell down.

He lay on the harlequin lino.

He was very quiet, and a little gusher of purple blood had spurted from his mouth.

'That man is sick,' said Mrs Khalil, from much farther than the droopy lounge.

'I am not surprised!' laughed Fixer Jensen. 'In such a house!'

'Mr Jensen, *please*!' laughed the owner. 'But he is pretty

282

sick,' she said, serious, because it could happen to herself –
all the things she had read about; she began to push her breasts
around.

The abo lay on the harlequin lino.

Mrs Godbold, who had been growing from just that spot for
the hours of several years, produced a handkerchief which she
had down the front of her dress, and stooped, and wiped the
blood away.

'You should go home,' she said, altering her voice, although
it was some time since she had used it. 'Where do you live?'

'Along the river at the parson's,' he answered. He collected
himself. 'What do you mean? Now?'

'Of course,' she said, gently wiping, speaking for themselves
alone.

'Why, in Barranugli. I got a room with Mrs Noonan, at the
end of Smith Street.'

'Are you comfortable?' she asked. 'At home, I mean.'

As if he was a human being.

He worked his head about on the lino. He could not answer.

The music had stuck its sticky strips over all the other faces,
as if they might break, without it, at any time. Some of them
were sleepy. Some were soothed. Still, a hammer could have
broken any of them.

'What is your name?' Mrs Godbold asked.

He did not seem to hear that.

He was looking, it was difficult to say, whether at or beyond
the gentle woman in the black hat. He held his arm across half
his face, not to protect, rather, to see better.

He said:

'That is how I want it. The faces must be half turned away,
but you still gotta understand what is in the part that is hidden.
Now I think I see. I will get it all in time.'

In a voice so oblivious and convinced that Ruth Joyner was
again sitting in the cathedral of her home town, watching the
scaffolding of music as it was erected, herself taking part in
the exquisitely complicated operation. Nor had she heard a
voice issue with such certainty and authority out of any mouth
since the strange gentleman referred to that same music. Now
it was the abo on Mrs Khalil's floor.

He was saying, she began again to hear:

'When the frosts were over, the Reverend Calderon used to
take us down along the river, and Mrs Pask would bring a
basket. We used to picnic on the banks. But they would soon
be wondering why they had come. I could see that all right.

Mrs Pask would begin to remember daffodils. I could see through anything on those days in early spring. I used to roam around on my own when I got tired of sitting with the whites. I would look into holes in the earth. I would feel the real leaves again. Once I came across a nest of red hornets. Hahhh!' He laughed. 'I soon shot off, like I had found wings myself! And seven red hot needles in me!'

When he had finished laughing, he added:

'Funny I went and remembered that.'

'It was because you was happiest then,' she suggested.

'That is not what you remember clearest,' he insisted with some vehemence. 'It is the other things.'

'I suppose so.'

Because she wished to encourage peace of mind, she accepted what she knew, for herself at least, to be only a half-truth.

'Still,' she offered, tentatively, 'it is the winters I can remember best at home. Because we children were happiest then. We were more dependent on one another. The other seasons we were running in all directions. Seeing and finding things for ourselves. In winter we held hands, and walked together along the hard roads. I can still hear them ringing.' Her eyes shone. 'Or we huddled up together, against the fire, to eat chestnuts, and tell tales. We loved one another most in winter. There was nothing to come between us.'

Such a commotion had broken out in the roomful of music and people. It was something to do with Mrs Khalil's Janis, whom Mr Hoggett wanted badly. He was finally convinced that young flesh must be the only nostrum. But Mrs Khalil herself was of quite an opposite opinion.

'Over my body!' she screamed.

And could have been shaking it to show.

'This ain't no concern of yours,' Mr Hoggett was shouting.

'Whose else, I'd liketa know.'

Fixer Jensen, in his putty-coloured hat with the pulled-down brim, was laughing his head off. He could afford to; nobody had ever known Fixer run a temperature. But the little one was possessed by a far subtler kind of detachment. She suddenly sprang, like a cat, and stuck the point of her tongue in Mr Hoggett's ear. She was almost diabolical in her attitude to love matters. She would jump, and swerve, in her cat's games, and at a certain juncture, leaped on a chair, which collapsed rottenly under her. She became screaming mad then.

Everybody was too well occupied to disturb the abo and the

laundress, who kept to their island, not exactly watching, for they had their thoughts.

'Are you a Christian?' Mrs Godbold asked quickly to get it over.

Even so, she was mortified, knowing that the word did not represent what it was intended to.

'No,' he replied. 'I was educated up to it. But gave it away. Pretty early on, in fact. When I found I could do better. I mean,' he mumbled, 'a man must make use of what he has. There is no point in putting on a pair of boots to walk to town, if you can do it better in your bare feet.'

She smiled at that. It was true, though, and of her own clumsy tongue, as opposed to her skill in passing the iron over the long strips of fresh, fuming, glistening sheets.

'Yes,' she smiled, once more beautiful; her skin was like fresh pudding-crust.

But he coughed.

Then she dabbed again with her handkerchief at the corner of his mouth. This, perhaps, was her work of art, her act of devotion.

All the commotion of life, though, continued tumbling in their ears: the ladies protesting their dignity, the gentlemen calling for their rights. Doors were opening, too. So Mrs Godbold looked at the ball of her handkerchief. Soon, she realized, it would be her turn to bleed.

A woman had come, or marched into the room. Her skin was the greyer for flesh-colour chenille, from which her arms hung down, with veins in them, and a wrist-watch on a brass chain.

'I am shook right out,' she announced. 'I am gunna catch the bus.'

She was no longer distinctive in any way. She could have been a splinter, rather sharp.

'There is Mr Hoggett,' indicated the desperate bawd. 'He has waited all this time.'

But the other was clearing her throat.

'Tell 'im I got a cold. Tell 'im to stuff 'imself,' she said.

She was the lady from Auburn, and was known as Mrs Johnno.

Mrs Khalil near as anything threw a fit. All the blows she was fated to receive in rendering service to mankind.

'Some women are that low,' she complained, 'you can't wonder at the men.'

And looked to Mrs Godbold for support.

Which the latter could no longer give. She had stood up. She did smile, as if to acknowledge guilt in ignoring a request. But must hoard her resources carefully. The room had shrunk. For there was Tom now.

Tom Godbold had followed in Mrs Johnno's tracks, and was offering the bawd a note in payment. His wife would have paid more, and torn off a pretty little brooch besides, if she had felt it might redeem. She would have taken him by the hand, and they would have run up the hill together, through the bush, over the breaking sticks, to reach the lights.

Instead, when the note had been crumpled up and pocketed, Tom Godbold crossed over to his wife, and said:

'You done a lot to show me up, Ruth, in our time, but you just about finished me this go.'

She was standing before him on her sleeping legs, in her clumsy hat, and long, serviceable overcoat. Only a membrane was stretched between her feelings and exposure. He might have kicked her, as in the past, and it would have been a kindness.

'Come on,' he said. 'I got what I wanted. You're the one that's missed out.'

As they left, the whores, it appeared, were finishing their business. The little one had disappeared. The window was blacker than before, whiter where the jasmine held the frame in its tender grip. Whether Mr Hoggett would allow himself to be appeased, might never be known now. He was, at least, accepting refreshment from a bottle which had once contained something else. It made his breath come sharp and quick. While Mrs Khalil continued to deplore the contingencies of life, and Mrs Johnno's toe-nails created havoc in the tunnels of her stockings as her feet entered them.

Godbolds were going out, and away. She followed him as a matter of course. The bush smelled of the leaves they bruised in stumbling. It had rained a little. It was fresh.

When they stood beneath a lamp, in a half-made street, on the edge of Sarsaparilla, she saw that the flesh had quite shrivelled from Tom's skull.

'I was wrong, Tom,' she said. 'I know. I *am* wrong. There!' she said, and made a last attempt to convince him with her hand. 'I will follow you to hell if need be.'

Tom Godbold did not wait to see whether he was strong enough to suffer the full force of his wife's love.

'You won't need to follow me no further,' he said, and began to pick his way between the heaps of blue-metal.

By his deliberate concentration, he appeared, if anything, less his own master. More remorseless than the influence of drink, age seemed also to have mounted on his shoulders, and to hold the reins. So his wife realized, as she watched, there was nothing more she could do for him, and that she herself must accept to be reduced by half.

Several years later, summoned to assume the responsibility of kin, she recovered the token of her lost half. On that occasion they allowed her to sit beside a bed, and observe, beneath a thin blanket, stained by the piss and pus of other dying men, what, they told her, was Tom Godbold. Of the husband she had known before disease and indulgence carried him off, nothing lived without the assistance of memory.

'Not more than half an hour ago,' the kind sister told. 'After a boiled egg. He enjoyed his food up to the last. He spoke about you.'

The wife of the man who had just died did not dare inquire for details of those dying remarks. Besides, the sister was busy. She had looked out between the pleated screens at several giggly girls who were washing the bodies of the living far too lingeringly. The sister frowned, and wondered how she might dispose discreetly of the bereaved. Then did, without further ceremony. She could not endure to watch dereliction of duty.

The widow who remained behind in her little cell of white screens was ever so well controlled. Or it could have been that she had not cared about her husband. In any case, when at last a glossy young probationer peeped in, the person was gone. She had given instructions, however, downstairs.

Mrs Godbold left Tom embedded in the centre of the great, square building, which a recent coat of shiny paint caused to glimmer, appropriately, like a block of ice. She walked a little. The acid of light was poured at nightfall into the city, to eat redundant faces. Yet, she survived. She walked, in the kind of clothes which, early in life, people had grown to expect of her, which no one would ever notice, except in amusement or contempt, and which would only alter when they fitted her out finally.

Mrs Godbold walked by the greenish light of early darkness. A single tram spat violet sparks into the tunnel of brown flannel. Barely clinging to its curve, its metal screeched anachronism. But it was only as she waited at a crossing, watching the stream churn past, that dismay overtook Mrs Godbold, and she began to cry. It seemed as if the group of figures huddled on the bank was ignored not so much by the traffic as by the strong, undeviating flood of time. There they waited, the pale souls, dipping a toe timidly, again retreating, secretly relieved to find their fellows caught in a similar situation, or worse, for here was one who could not conceal her suffering.

The large woman was simply standing and crying, the tears running out at her eyes and down her pudding-coloured face. It was at first fascinating, but became disturbing to the other souls-in-waiting. They seldom enjoyed the luxury of watching the self-exposure of others. Yet, this was a crying in no way convulsed. Soft and steady, it streamed out of the holes of the anonymous woman's eyes. It was, it seemed, the pure abstraction of gentle grief.

The truth of the matter was: Mrs Godbold's self was by now dead, so she could not cry for the part of her which lay in the keeping of the husband she had just left. She cried, rather, for the condition of men, for all those she had loved, burningly, or at a respectful distance, from her father, seated at his bench in his prison of flesh, and her own brood of puzzled little girls, for her former mistress, always clutching at the hem and finding it come away in her hand, for her fellow initiates, the madwoman and the Jew of Sarsaparilla, even for the blackfellow she had met at Mrs Khalil's, and then never again, unless by common agreement in her thoughts and dreams. She cried, finally, for the people beside her in the street, whose doubts she would never dissolve in words, but understood, perhaps, from those she had experienced.

Then, suddenly, the people waiting at the crossing leaped forward in one surge, and Mrs Godbold was carried with them. How the others were hurrying to resume their always importunate lives. But the woman in the black hat drifted when she was not pushed. For the first moment in her life, and no doubt only briefly, she remained above and impervious to the stream of time. So she coasted along for a little after she had reached the opposite side. Although her tears were all run, her eyes still glittered in the distance of their sockets. Fingers of green and crimson neon grappled for possession of her ordinarily suetty face, almost as if it had been a prize, and at moments the strife between light and darkness wrung out a royal purple, which drenched the slow figure in black.

Part Five

10

That summer the structure of Xanadu, which had already entered in a conspiracy with nature, opened still farther. Creatures were admitted that had never been inside before, and what had hitherto appeared to be a curtain, loosely woven of light and leaves, was, in fact, seen to be a wall. That which had been hung for privacy, might in the end, it now seemed, stand solider than the substance of stone and mortar which it had been its duty to conceal.

One Tuesday afternoon, while Mrs Jolley was gone on an errand, of which the end was terribly suspicious, and while Miss Hare herself was walking through the great rooms, for no other purpose than to associate with the many objects and images with which they and her memory were stuffed full, the brindled woman thought she had begun to hear a sound. From where she listened it was faint but sure, although whether it was coming from a great depth, or horizontal distance, it was quite impossible to tell. It was all around and under her: the grey sound that is given out by tunnels, and the mouths of elephants, and sleepers turning in a dream, and earth falling in a veil from a considerable height. As soon as Miss Hare began to suspect, she held her fingers in her ears. As if that might stop it. Though she knew it would not. For she, too, was rocking and trembling. She had always imagined that, when it happened, it would come as a blast of trumpets, or the shudder of a bronze gong, with herself the core of the vibrating metal. But here it was, little more than a sighing of dust, and at the end, the sound of a large, but unmistakable bone which had given way under pressure. (She had always cried and protested when men were breaking the necks of rabbits, as she waited for the final sound of cracking.)

Then it was over. And she had survived. Perhaps Xanadu had not yet fallen.

At once Miss Hare began to run through her house to discover to what extent it had suffered. She was quite demented.

289

Although shadow prevailed in the shuttered rooms, a yellow, rubbery light would belly suddenly out through the glass panels of some of the doors, and her figure flickered fearfully. She was more than ever striped, brown, or red, with patches of a clown's white, as she ran to catch the proud spirit, that had fallen, that could still, she hoped, be falling from the height of the trapeze. She ran helter skelter, and her stumpy, rather grubby fingers were stretched out, tighter than nets. But small.

In the drawing-room she found the first serious evidence of damage – in the drawing-room in which ladies in openwork dresses had accepted tea in Lowestoft cups, and told stories of the voyage out, and dancers had rested between waltzes, on the worn step that leads to matrimony, and her parents had failed to escape each other by hiding behind objects of virtu. It was on the drawing-room side that the foundations of Xanadu were now undeniably, visibly sunk. Where there had been a fissure before, where no more than a branch had been able to finger its way inside, a whole victorious segment of light had replaced the solid plaster and stone. Leaves were plapping and hesitating, advancing and retreating, in whispers and explosions of green. Walls were revealed mottled with chlorosis. The scurf of moss had fallen from an oaken shoulder on to the rags of Italian damask. And dust, dust. There was a newer kind, the colour of familiar biscuit, yet smelling of concealment and age. Now spilled freshly out. It lay on the boards together with the grey domestic dust, a thin bed for some future crumbling of stone.

Miss Hare stood looking. Then she picked up a fragment of her house, just about the size of a fist, and threw it at a malachite urn which had been her parents' pride. The moment of impact, however, was somewhat disappointing. The sound it produced was even dull: almost that of a stone striking on composition, or wood. Yet, the urn had been genuinely mineral – so cold, and dense, and unresponsive – her skin had always assured her as a child, as well as on lonely occasions in after life.

Her mouth, which was working to solve, suddenly subsided on the teeth. All problems had always given way to birds, and here were several, aimed practically at her. Released from the tapestry of light and leaves, the birds whirred and wheeled into life inside the burst drawing-room. What kind, Miss Hare could not have told; names were not of interest. But the plump, shiny, maculated birds, neither black nor grey, but of a common, bird colour, were familiar as her own instinct for air and twigs. And one bird touched her deeply, clinging clumsily to a cornice. Confusion had robbed it of its grace, making it a blunt thing, of ruffled gills. From far below, the woman willed the frightened creature back into its element, where the reunited formation completed a figure to the approving motions of her head. She watched them quiver for an instant in flight, wired, it appeared, for inclusion in the museum of her mind. But they were gone, of course. She was left with the shimmer of brocaded light that hung upon the rent in the wall.

So Miss Hare, too, went at last, nodding her papier-mâché head. She became her most clumsily obscene whenever she ceased to control her own movements, as now, when she was moved, rather, through the wretched house, as much her doom as her property. So she loomed on the stairs, and in unaccountable passages. Pierced by the anxious brooches that barely held the skin together, the folds of her throat were choking her. Her ankles were elephantine in their plodding. She trailed a sad bladder, filled with the heaviest, coldest sand.

Mrs Jolley, when she returned, found her employer occupied with the jigsaw pieces of a bathroom floor.

'This is where you are!' the housekeeper exclaimed, as if it had not been obvious.

She was angry, but intended to be cold and firm. Miss Hare also was trusting to appearance to hide her true state, of despondency and fear. At least she had the advantage of being seated on the floor, beneath her protective wicker hat.

'Why shouldn't I be here?' she answered calmly. 'Or there? Or anywhere?'

'I have never seen this room before,' complained Mrs Jolley, inspecting her surroundings.

Miss Hare produced a key: black, of elegant design.

'There was no reason why you should have. This was my parents' bathroom. I had almost forgotten about it myself. It was considered very lovely. Italian workmen came to make it.'

'Gingerbread!' Mrs Jolley snorted. 'Give me modern plumbing!'

'Oh, plumbing!' said Miss Hare. 'That is a different matter.' She had begun to feel tired. 'Everyone will have plumbing soon. They will be flushed right out.'

'What is that thing?' Mrs Jolley asked, and pointed with her toe at the part of the floor with which her employer had been occupied.

'I would prefer not to say,' Miss Hare replied.

Then Mrs Jolley laughed. Because she knew.

'It is a goat,' she said, perverting the word softly in her mouth. 'What a decoration for a person's bathroom! A black goat! Looking at you!'

'No,' said Miss Hare, with a firm movement of her jaw, 'it would not appeal to you. Goats are perhaps the animals which see the truth most clearly.'

Mrs Jolley could not control her irritation. In fact, where her toe struck the mosaic, there was a rush of loose tesserae across the uneven surface of the floor.

'Oh, I know!' she cried. 'You have to throw up at me, don't you, on account of that old goat of yours. The one that got burnt. That you told me of. And nobody to blame.'

Miss Hare was soothing the scattered tesserae with her freckled hand.

'Have you ever seen an armadillo?' she asked.

'No.' Mrs Jolley was very angry.

'Perhaps you have, though, and don't know it!' Miss Hare laughed.

'What,' asked Mrs Jolley, 'is an armerdiller?'

'It is an animal which, I believe, is practically invulnerable. It *can* be *killed*, of course. Anything can be *killed*. Because I once saw an armadillo that somebody had made into a basket.'

Then she looked up at her companion with such an expression that the latter attempted afterwards to describe it to Mrs Flack.

'I know nothing about any such things,' the housekeeper said rather primly. 'And don't like saucy answers, particularly from those who I have obliged.'

Miss Hare was filling her pockets with the fragments of mosaic.

'Have you engaged a strong boy to carry your box?' she asked.

'Then there is no need to tell you!' said Mrs Jolley.

But was taken aback. And, as a lady of principle, had to defend herself.

'Yes,' she said, 'I have decided to terminate my service. You cannot expect me,' she said, 'to risk my neck in a house that is falling down.'

'You have seen it, then? The drawing-room?'

'I'll say I have!'

'Perhaps even foresaw – to have made your arrangements in advance, on the very afternoon!'

Miss Hare laughed. Momentarily she seemed to have re-

292

covered her balance. The pocketfuls of tesserae rattled jollily when slapped. She had never cared for sweets, but would often suck a smooth pebble.

'I don't propose to become involved in arguments,' Mrs Jolley announced. 'I am giving notice. That is all. Though have never done so in a bathroom. That is,' she stumbled, 'I mean to say, I have never been compelled to discuss matters of importance in any sort of a convenience.'

Miss Hare began to scramble up.

'You will go, I suppose, to Mrs Flack?'

Mrs Jolley blushed.

'For the time being,' she admitted.

'For life, I expect,' Miss Hare murmured.

Mrs Jolley hesitated.

'It is very comfortable,' she said.

But did falter slightly.

'What makes you say,' she asked, 'you speak as if,' she raised her voice, 'as if I was not my own mistress?'

Miss Hare, who had arranged her crumpled skirt, was looking, not at Mrs Jolley.

'There is a point,' she said, 'where we do not, cannot move any farther. There is a point at which there is no point. Who knows, perhaps you have reached it. And your friend is so kind. And her eiderdown, you say, is pale blue.'

'But it may suit me to move,' Mrs Jolley insisted, stretching her neck.

'You will see no more in other parts – I know because they took me as a girl – than you will from Mrs Flack's. And through Mrs Flack's eyes. The two of you will sit in Mrs Flack's *lounge*, watching us behave. Even directing us.'

'Have you met her?'

'No. But I know her.'

'You have seen her at the post office, perhaps?'

'Not to my knowledge,' Miss Hare replied. 'I have seen her in the undergrowth. But you do not go there, of course. Amongst the black sods of rotting leaves. And in the ruins of the little shed in which my poor goat got burnt up. And in my father's eyes. All bad things have a family resemblance, Mrs Jolley, and are easily recognizable. I would recognize Mrs Flack however often she changed her hat. I can smell her when you do not mention her by name.'

Mrs Jolley had begun by now to leave the bathroom. Although she had arranged for her belongings to be fetched, she had till the following day to put in. If only she could think of some temporary occupation of a known and mechanical kind. In her distraction, she was reiterating:

'Mad! Mad!'

To preserve her own sanity.

'A sad, bad word.' Miss Hare sighed.

They were walking down the passages in single file.

'Because it leaves out half,' she added.

They were always walking, with Mrs Jolley at the head, with a careful nonchalance, in case the runners should slip from under them.

'All right, then,' Mrs Jolley gasped. 'You can let me alone, then. We could trot out words till the Judgement, and not get anywhere at all. I am going to my room, thank you.'

But Miss Hare could not tear herself away. She was not so good that she was not fascinated by bad. If they had come across a dead baby lying on that window-sill, she would not have asked herself the reason why, before she had examined the little crimped fingers and limp-violet attitude. She would probably have touched it to see whether it felt of rubber. Only afterwards she would have realized that she, too, had escaped strangling by a miracle.

But now they were walking and walking through the passages of Xanadu, and Mrs Jolley's behind was quaking visibly. It seemed as though her corset could do nothing more for her.

'And so soft at times,' Miss Hare meditated.

And pursued.

'Soft what?' Mrs Jolley's breath was sucked right in.

She would not turn, though.

'Eiderdowns,' Miss Hare clattered. 'Evil, evil eiderdowns!'

Rounding a corner, Mrs Jolley realized she had overshot the flight of stairs which led higher to her room. And here were the passages of Xanadu, endless before her.

Almost at the same moment a pampas wand struck her on the mouth, from a console table, as they passed, and immediately she was turned to stone.

But running, running. Her cold, stone legs must never stop.

'If you must keep on about evil,' she called back, her voice close to brass, or laughter, 'I can remind you of some of the things that go on in this town, to say nothing of house. Or *orchard*!'

She almost screeched, and her skirt too.

While Miss Hare appeared to move on pads of kapok. Or else it was the dust from which the carpets were never free.

'I am not surprised,' Miss Hare gasped at last. 'That you found out. One did expect.'

'And with a dirty Jew!'

Miss Hare was red rage itself. She could not see for the sense of injustice which was rising green out of her. Towering in the perpendicular, it burst into a flower of sparks, like some obscene firework released from the dark of memory.

'My *what* Jew?' The words were choking. 'Dirty? What is true, then? My kind man! My good! Then I am offal, offal! Green, putrefying, out of old, starved sheep. Worse, worse! Though not so bad as some. Offal is cleaner than dishonest women. What is lowest of all? You could tell me! Some women! Lower, even. Some women's shit!'

So her memory spat, and the brown word plastered the accuser's back.

Mrs Jolley, of course, could only stop her ears with the wax of unbelief. When she had opened them again, her white lips pissed back:

'Who did the Jews crucify?'

'The Jew!' Miss Hare panted. 'I know that. Because Peg used to tell me. It was horrible. And blood running out of his hands, and down his poor side. I have never allowed myself to think about it.'

In the absence of what she might have kissed, she crammed her knuckles into her mouth. If all the windows had shattered, and the splinters entered her, she could have borne that.

But just then, Mrs Jolley fell down. There was a little flight of two or three steps leading to a lower level, and from which a rod had worked loose. Mrs Jolley fell.

Crump.

Miss Hare was left standing on an edge. She looked down at her housekeeper, where the latter lay, a bundle of navy, on the carpet. The skirt had rucked up above the knees, the dimples of which looked white and very silly, for Mrs Jolley, apparently, wore her stockings neatly hoist at half-mast.

Miss Hare could have gone on looking at the dimpled knees, but forced herself also to examine the face. The first, dreadful, inky blue began slowly to drain away. It left a blank, though trembly blotting-paper.

Mrs Jolley was gasping now. The tears ran out of her eyes, although she was not crying.

'Oh, dear!' she gasped. 'I could have broken something. And perhaps have.'

'No,' said Miss Hare. 'You are too well protected. And came down all of a piece.'

Mrs Jolley remembered, and her hate returned.

'You will pay a pretty penny if I have!' she announced as hopefully as she was able.

Miss Hare touched with the tip of her toe.

'No,' she said. 'Nothing broken.'

But she was a little bit frightened.

Mrs Jolley moved, and more, she began to heave. She was whimpering windily, but cautiously.

'This is what happens to a mother forced by circumstances to live separated from her family. Oh, dear!'

But although she had fallen smack, she got almost as quickly up. It was her knees that drove her, her blue-and-white, milky knees. She got up, and was wrapping her skirt closer round them, as if there had been a draught blowing.

When she raised her face, it was rather a delicate pink, wasted on Miss Hare.

The two women stood facing each other with nothing but their dead passions lying between, nothing to protect them but the sound of their breathing. They could not endure it for very long, but turned, and walked in opposite directions, touching a curtain, a pampas duster or leaf that had blown in. It was pretty obvious they had decided to pretend nothing had happened – at least, for the time being.

But, in this matter at least, Miss Hare did not succeed in keeping up the deception. Her blood would float the evidence back in sudden, sickening waves. She heard words like stones battering on her memory.

She did not see her housekeeper again, except from a distance. The wages she left on a corner of the kitchen table, under a 2 oz. weight, and presumably the amount was correct, for nobody ever complained.

On the following afternoon the boy came for Mrs Jolley's belongings. There was such a chatter of relief, such a clatter of self-importance, as the owner ran to arrange, lock, direct. The boy had bony wrists, and swollen veins in his muscular arms. He paused for a moment in the hall, to get his breath, and recover from the pressure of embarrassment. The lady had run back up the stairs, to fetch an umberella, she said. He had never set eyes on marble before, only in banks and old washstands. Nor did he dream much, or he might have realized, as he looked about him in the hall, that images and incidents do not depend on probability for life. He was trembling slightly, under the pearls of sweat, particularly after he had touched a square of satin which disintegrated in his hand.

That made him breathe harder, out of his arched chest. And when, from another direction, there appeared, sudden like, the madwoman of Xanadu, and asked him to do her the favour, in strictest confidence, of delivering an urgent message to a friend.

Miss Hare stood on her toes to make the mission more confidential still. Her throat was bursting with its urgency. Her lips fanned the words upward.

The lad gathered she must see the Jew cove from Montebello Avenue, soon, soon, at soonest. He was not, on no account, to tell another soul. For the present, he would have been frightened to.

Then Miss Hare handed her messenger a shilling, as she had seen her parents doing. And disappeared. For Mrs Jolley's voice was clearly announcing, in light-coloured accents, the return of Mrs Jolley.

It was many a day since Miss Hare had run so fast. She ran and climbed to get there in time, almost breaking her knees open, climbing by handfuls of carpet when her toes missed a stair, climbing, and straining, and arriving at last in the little glass dome which had been her father's especial eyrie. Then, venturing out upon a parapet, she peered through a stone balustrade.

Here she was, exalted above her late misery and terror. And there, there was Mrs Jolley, distorted by distance and angle, into a squat, navy figure. How her gay eye-veil gesticulated to the boy who laboured beneath her box, and a case hung from his right arm besides. The mauve veil clapped at a distance, like Mrs Jolley's own tongue extolling the morality of motherhood.

Miss Hare's mouth opened, her throat distended. She spat once, and laughed to see it fall, wide, of course, curving in the wind, glittering in the sun. She could have sung for the deliriousness of height, the clarity of light. All hers.

Until the stanched terrors came seeping back, dressed in the iridescence of slime. Frightful things were threatened, which the Jew, with his experience, might possibly avert. She, in her state of almost complete ignorance, could only undertake to suffer, enough, if necessary, for both of them. So her joy was turned to foreboding. The stone house rocked, and the trees which hid the brick homes of Sarsaparilla. She hung on to the balustrade, sweating at the knees as she tried to reconstruct in physical detail the expression of loving-kindness, to recall its even subtler abstract terms. That alone might save, if it were not obliterated first by conspiracy of evil minds.

So she waited.

Wherever she spent the rest of the afternoon, walking through her house or in the garden – at least there was earth on her shoes, and on her scabby hands, and on her skirt a fringe of burrs – Miss Hare could not have mapped her course with any degree of accuracy.

But the Jew did come.

Late in the afternoon she realized he was walking towards her, through the long, treacly grass, out of the choked garden. As he climbed the slope, it was not his face that he presented, but the top of his head, with its wings of difficult hair, grizzled, but still thick. Some might have described that hair as matted, and they would have been correct. He must, indeed, have set out immediately on arriving home. He was wearing a kind of boiler-suit which he could only have bought at an army disposal store, and which no doubt he wore to his work at the factory. The suit was too big, the stuff too dun, too coarse. It was chafing him, she began to see, around the neck. It was a skinny, scraggy neck. But she remembered this was an elderly man, who had suffered great privations, and who had been worn down still further by the accumulation of knowledge. So Miss Hare reassured herself, not without a tremor, holding up his frail elderliness against what she knew of the brutality of men.

He continued to advance. Once or twice he stumbled, when the grass made loops for him to slip his ankles into, and as he lurched – it was inevitable in such circumstances – his great head tumbled and jerked on his shoulders like that of a human being.

The mistress of Xanadu moistened her lips as she waited. She was so brittle herself, it was doubtful whether such another should be added to the collection. Perhaps that gave her just the extra courage needed to receive him as her mother might have, upon the steps. But her mother had enjoyed full possession of that social and economic faith on which the stone mansions are built, whereas in the daughter's worst dreams those foundations were already sunk; only her faith in light and leaves remained to hold the structure up. Whether the Jew would accept the house as reality or myth, depended not a little on whether a divine intuition, which she hoped, insisted, *knew* him to possess, would inform mere human vision.

Actually the Jew had raised his head. He was looking at her.

She saw his face then, and he had not shaved, as some men did not, of course, preferring to tidy themselves at night. He was old and ravaged under the stubble. He was old, and green, of a pale, a livid soap-colour. He was hideous and old, the Jew. So that her own face crumpled, which she had been careful to spread over a framework of expectation. A gust of wind could have blown her, rattling, across the terrace. But mercifully refrained.

Then she realized that his eyes were expecting something of her. And she immediately remembered. She hurried down the steps, too quickly for anyone who had been restored suddenly to life – she might have taken a tumble – yet not quickly enough for one who recognized that same lovingkindness which might redeem, not only those in whom its lamp stood, but all those who were threatened with darkness.

What was oddest, though, the Jew appeared to rediscover something he had known and respected. His expression was so convinced, she was almost compelled to look behind her, in search of some more tangible reason.

If she had not, it could have been because she had finally descended. She was standing beside him on the level ground, and the situation seemed to demand that exchange of flatnesses, biscuits rather than oxygen, by which people mostly exist.

'Oh,' she gasped, and began to crumble words, 'I am so sorry. Such an inconvenience. Bringing you, I mean. Like this.'

'It is no inconvenience,' he replied, in the strain that had been established. 'It was only fortunate that Bob Tanner caught me so soon after I got off the bus.'

'Bob Tanner?'

'The boy who gave the message.'

'Oh,' she said, thoughtfully, 'I did not know there was anyone called Tanner.'

She sank her chin in. If it had been evening, she might have done something with a fan – if she had had one. But there was only that old flamingo horror of her mother's, so hateful since Mrs Jolley had touched it, and provoked an incident.

He was looking at her. He was waiting.

But she remembered hearing it was vulgar and inept to bring people straight to the point.

So she offered graciously:

'I can see the journey has tired you. I insist that you come in. I shall make you rest for a little. You may like to tell me about your work.'

'It is the same,' he said.

'Oh, no,' she said, after careful consideration. 'Nothing is ever the same.'

'You have not been engaged in boring a hole in a sheet of steel.'

'Why must you do just that?'

It was time, she suspected, to lead him in. Their heels crunched as they turned on what had once been the gravel drive. Her occupation was making her feel kind and adult.

'It is a discipline,' he explained, 'without which my mind might take its own authority for granted. As it did, in fact, in the days when it was allowed freedom. And grew arrogant. And in that arrogance was guilty of omissions.'

Miss Hare shivered, as if he had robbed her of her years.

'I never could bear discipline. Governesses!' she complained. 'It is fortunate I have not got what is called a mind.'

'You have an instinct.'

She smiled. She was quite proud.

'Is that what it is?' she considered. 'I do know a lot. About some things.' They had mounted the terrace. 'That light, for instance. Those two shiny leaves lying together on the twig. That sort of thing I know and understand. But will it do anybody any good? And your sitting and boring the silly old hole?'

'Yes,' he answered. 'Eventually.'

They were standing together on the terrace.

'It is not yet obvious,' he said, 'but will be made clear, how we are to use our knowledge, what link we provide in the chain of events.'

The hour sounded inside the house. The winding of that particular clock had been Mrs Jolley's last attempt to preserve continuity, such as she understood it, at Xanadu. The chiming reminded Miss Hare of her real purpose in sending for the Jew, so she began to wrap her hands in each other.

She said:

'I am alone here now. Which makes it easier to receive, and discuss. My housekeeper left me, you know, this afternoon. Before that, one never could be certain at what point she might burst into one's thoughts. She had no respect for the privacy of other people's minds. But was always opening, or looking out from behind curtains. Not that she *saw*! I do not think Mrs Jolley sees beyond texture-brick and plastic.'

Miss Hare had continued to lead her visitor, so that by now they had crossed the threshold, and were actually standing in the house. Out of the corner of her eye, the throbbing beauty of the hall, with its curved staircase and the fragments of a bird's

300

nest, told her of her great courage in attempting to reveal the truth to a second person, even this Jew, after her experience with someone else.

Of course the Jew had to look; he was also human. His head was turning on his scraggy neck. His nostrils, she saw, were remarkably fine, in spite of the very pronounced nose.

'Extraordinary!' he said.

She heard at least that, but did not feel she would attempt to interpret the accompanying smile.

'Oh, there is a lot,' she said. 'I shall show you in time.'

'But are you not overwhelmed,' he asked, 'by living here?'

'I have always lived here. What is there to overwhelm me?'

Fascinated by what he saw, his answer slipped out from behind his usually careful lips.

'Its desolation.'

The heavy word tolled through marble.

'You, too!' she cried. 'Do you only see what is in front of you?'

He threw back his head, it might have been defensively. His laughter sounded quite metallic.

'God forbid!' he said. 'I could have died of that!'

Then he looked at her very closely, following, as it were, in the lines of her face, the thread of his own argument.

'It is only that I have grown used to living in a small wooden house, Miss Hare. I chose it purposely. Very fragile and ephemeral. I am a Jew, you see.'

She did not see why that condition, whatever it was, might not be shared. She felt the spurt of jealousy. She snorted, and began to suck the hot, rubbery lumps of her exasperated lips.

'Almost a booth,' he continued. 'Which the wind may blow down, when one has closed the door for the last time, and moved on to another part of the desert.'

She hated to contemplate it.

'That,' she protested, 'is morbid.'

He was looking at her intently, and with the greatest amusement.

'It is only realistic to accept what history has proved. And we do not die of it. Even though his limbs may be lopped off from time to time, the Jew cannot die.'

He persisted in looking at her, as if determined to discover something in hiding behind her face.

Could it have been he was sorry for her? When they were sharpening their knives for *him*? When he was the one deserving of pity? Some people, it was true, and more especially those endowed with brilliance, were dazzled by their minds into a state of false security. Unlike animals, for instance. Animals, she well knew, peered out perpetually into what was still to be experienced.

So that again she grew agitated.

'I must tell you,' she almost gasped.

In quite a flurry, she had led him into the little sitting-room to which she had retired with her mother the night of the false suicide. Such was her haste on the present occasion, the door would have banged behind them, if it had not decided many years before that it was never again intended to close. It was too stiff. Like the kind of hard *causeuse* on which she seated herself with her guest, and of which the hospitality had remained strictly theoretical even in the palmy days.

There they were, though.

After she had looked round, Miss Hare managed, painfully:

'I am afraid for you.'

And did the most extraordinary thing.

She took the Jew's hand in her freckled, trembling ones. What she intended to do with it was not apparent to either of them, for they were imprisoned in an attitude. She sat holding the hand as if it had been some thing of value found in the bush: a polished stone, of curious veins, or one of the hooded ground-orchids, or knot of wood, which time, weather, and disease, it was suggested, had related to human disasters. Only, the most exquisite sensation destroyed the detached devotion which Miss Hare would normally have experienced, on being confronted with such rare matter.

'Anybody's life is threatened with a certain amount of hazard,' the Jew answered seriously, after he had recovered with an effort from hilarious surprise, and a thought so obscene, he was humiliated for the capacity of his own mind.

Miss Hare sat making those little noises of protest reminiscent of frogs and leather.

'Clever people,' she was saying, 'are the victims of words.'

She herself could have dwindled into a marvellous silence, her body slipping from her, or elongated into such shapes of love and music as she had only noticed long ago in dancers, swaying and looking, no more governed by precept or reason, but by some other lesson which the flesh might at any moment remember, at the touch of peacock feathers.

Miss Hare had to glance at her companion to see whether he could be aware that her limbs were, in fact, so long and lovely, and her conical white breasts not so cold as they had been taught to behave unless offered the excuse of music.

But the Jew had set himself to observe the strange situation in which his hand had become involved. And at the same time he was saying:

'I agree that intellect can be a serious handicap. There are moments when I like to imagine I have overcome it.' Then, as the wrinkles gathered at the corners of his mouth: 'It is most salutary that you and the drill at which I spend my working life should disillusion me from time to time.'

He accused with a kindliness, even sweetness, which made her almost throw away the hand. Her evanescent beauty was lit with the little mirrors of fury, before it was destroyed.

Which it was, of course. Her condition could not have been less obvious than the sad rags of old cobwebs hanging from a cornice.

'Oh,' she cried, her mouth full of tears and pebbles, 'I am not interested in *you*! Not what you are, think, feel. I am only concerned for your safety. I am responsible for you!' she gasped.

In her anxiety, her tormented skin began to chafe the hand. Whether she had suspected a moment before, probably for the first and only time what it was to be a woman, her passion was more serious, touching, urgent now that she had been reduced to the status of a troubled human being. Although they continued to sit apart on the terribly formal furniture, it was this latest metamorphosis which brought the two closest together.

Himmelfarb stirred inside the aggressive, and in no way personal boiler-suit.

After clearing his throat, he asked:

'Is there any concrete evidence of danger?'

If he played for time, and ignored the last dictates of repulsion which might advise him to withdraw his hand, he could perhaps persuade her into telling him the most secret hiding places.

'Concrete? *You* should know that real danger never begins by being concrete!'

Yes, indeed. He could not deny that.

When she had recovered from the spasm of exasperation which caused her to jerk, almost to twist the unbelievably passive hand, she began a long, dry, but important, because undoubtedly rehearsed, passage of recitative:

'I was going to make a proposal. No. What am I saying? Offer a proposition? It has occurred to me on and off, only there were always too many obstacles. And even now it could sound silly. I mean, it might appear distasteful. But it is what Peg – the old servant – would have called practical. (If only Peg were here, it would be so much easier for all of us.) To cut matters short – because that is necessary since certain things have happened – I want to suggest that you should come here, well, to live.'

Purposely, she did not look at him, because she would not have cared to witness surprise.

'I would hide you,' she continued, with blunt tongue. 'There are so many rooms, there would be no necessity to stay very long in any one. Which would add to the chances of your safety.'

She could feel, through his stillness, that he did accept her motives, while remaining critical of her plan.

'It would be wrong of you to hide me,' he answered, but gently. 'Because I can honestly say I have nothing to hide.'

'They will not ask themselves that,' she said. 'Men usually decide to destroy for very feeble reasons. Oh, I know from experience! It can be the weather, or boredom after lunch. They will torture almost to death someone who has seen into them. Even their own dogs.'

'When the time comes for my destruction,' he replied quite calmly and evenly, 'it will not be decided by men.'

'That makes it more frightening!' she cried.

And burst suddenly into tears.

She was at her ugliest, wet and matted, but any disgust which Himmelfarb might have felt was swallowed up in the conviction that, despite the differences of geography and race, they were, and always had been, engaged on a similar mission. Approaching from opposite directions, it was the same darkness and the same marsh which threatened to engulf their movements, but however lumbering and impeded those movements might be, the precious parcel of secrets carried by each must only be given at the end into certain hands.

Although the Jew blundered on towards the frontier through the mist of experience, he emerged at one point, and found himself on the hard causeuse in the little sitting-room at Xanadu. There he roused himself, and touched his fellow traveller, and said:

'I am going now. I would like to persuade you that the simple acts we have learnt to perform daily are the best protection against evil.'

'They are very consoling,' she admitted.

But sighed.

The lovely, tarnished light of evening lay upon the floors. In that light, with each object most emphatically intact for the last moments of the day, Himmelfarb could have forgotten he had ever been forced to interrupt those simple daily acts which he now advocated as a shield.

Miss Hare followed him across the hall.

'At least I must warn you,' she said, 'when you go from here, that my former housekeeper, Mrs Jolley, suffers from certain delusions. I do not think she is an active agent. But is under the influence of a Mrs Flack, whom I have never met, only suspect. It could be that Mrs Flack also is innocent. But the most devilish ideas will enter the heads of some women as they sit together in a house at dusk and listen to their stomachs rumble. Well, Mrs Jolley is at present staying with Mrs Flack.'

'And where do these ladies live?'

'Oh, in some street. That is unimportant. I think you mentioned, Mr ...' (she was no longer ashamed of her inability to manage a name) '... that we were links in some chain. I am convinced myself that there are two chains. Matched against each other. If Mrs Jolley and Mrs Flack were the only two links in theirs, then, of course, we should have nothing to fear. *But*.'

She was leading him slowly through the house, which the crimson and gold of evening had dyed with a Renaissance splendour. The marble of a torso and crystal shivered for their own beauty.

'Is this the way?' he asked.

'I am taking you out through the back,' she said. 'It is shorter.'

On the kitchen table a knife lay, it, too, a sliver of light.

'I would kill for you, you know,' Miss Hare suddenly said. 'If it would preserve for us what is right.'

'Then it would no longer be right.'

Himmelfarb smiled. He took the knife which she had picked up from the table, and dropped it back into its pool of light.

'Its purpose is to cut bread,' he said. 'An unemotional, though noble one.'

So that she was quenched, and went munching silence on the last stage to the back door.

On the step she stood giving him final directions.

The rather dead, soapy face of the man who had come towards her up the hill, had been touched into life, by last light, or the mysteries of human intercourse.

'You always have to leave me about this time,' she meditated, as she stood looking down on him from her step. 'There is

305

something secret that you do.' she complained, 'in your own house. But I am not jealous.'

'There is nothing secret,' he replied. 'It is the time of evening when I go to say my prayers.'

'Oh, *prayers!*' she mumbled.

Then:

'I have never said any. Except when I was not my own mistress. When I was very young.'

'But you have expressed them in other ways.'

She shook that off rather irritably, and might have been preparing something rude, if another thought had not risen to trouble the surface.

'Oh, dear, what will save us?' she wondered.

Before he could answer, she exclaimed:

'Look!'

And was shading her eyes from the dazzle of gold.

'It was at this time of evening,' her mouth gasped, and worked at words, 'that I would sometimes feel afraid of the consequences. I would fall down in a fit while the wheels were still approaching. It was too much for anyone so weak. And lie sometimes for hours. I think I could not bear to look at it.'

'There is no reason why you should not look now,' Himmelfarb made an effort. 'It is an unusually fine sunset.'

'Yes,' she said.

And laughed somewhat privately.

'And the grey furrows,' she observed, 'where the wheels have sunk in. And the little soft feathers of the wheels.'

Himmelfarb took his leave of the mistress of Xanadu. He was not in a position to dismiss her as a madwoman, as other people did, because of his involvement in the same madness. For now that the tops of the trees had caught fire, the bells of the ambulances were again ringing for him, those of the fire-engines clanging, and he shuddered to realize there could never be an end to the rescue of men from the rubble of their own ideas. So the bodies would continue to be carried out, and hidden under a blanket, while those who were persuaded they were still alive would insist on returning to the wreckage, to search for teeth, watches, and other recognized necessities. Most deceived, however, were the souls, who protested in grey voices that they had already been directed to enter the forms of plants, stones, animals, and in some cases, even human beings. So the souls were crying, and combing their smoked-out hair. They were already exhausted by the bells, prayers, orders, and curses of the many fires at which, in the course of their tormented lives, it had been their misfortune to assist.

Only the Chariot itself rode straight and silent, both now, and on the clouds of recollection.

Himmelfarb plodded up the road which led from Xanadu to Sarsaparilla, comforted by physical weariness and the collaboration of his friend. He yawned once or twice. The white faces of nondescript flowers twitched and glimmered at the touch of darkness. Stones brooded. He, the most stubborn of all souls, might well be told off next to invest a stone. As he went up the hill, the sparks shot out from beneath his boots, from the surface of the road, so far distant that, with all the lovingkindness in the world, his back could not have bent for him to lift them up, so elusive that Hezekiah, David, and Akiba had failed to redeem the lost sparks.

The Jew wandered, and stumbled over stones, and came at last to his frail house, and touched the *Sh'ma* upon the doorpost as he went in.

11

Every work morning Himmelfarb took the bus to Barranugli, where he seated himself at his drill in Rosetree's factory, and made his contribution to Brighta Bicycle Lamps. Under the windows the smooth green river ran, but not so that you could see it, for the windows were placed rather high, and there were days when the Jew, who had been moved in the beginning by the flow of green water, scarcely noticed it even when he knocked off. As he walked alongside it towards the bus-stop, it had become a green squiggle, or symbol of a river.

Once the foreman, Ernie Theobalds, who had just received a flattering bonus, was moved to address the Jew. He asked:

'Howya doin', Mick?'

'Good,' replied the Jew, in the language he had learnt to use.

The foreman, who had already begun to regret things, drove himself still further. He was not unkind.

'Never got yerself a mate?' Ernie Theobalds remarked.

The Jew laughed.

'Anybody is my mate,' he said.

He felt strangely, agreeably relaxed, as though it could have been true.

But it made the foreman suspicious and resentful.

'Yeah, that's all right,' he strained, and sweated. 'I don't say we ain't got a pretty dinkum set-up. But a man stands a better chance of a fair go if he's got a mate. That's all I'm sayin'. See?'

Himmelfarb laughed again – the morning had made him rash – and replied:

'I shall take Providence as my mate.'

Mr Theobalds was horrified. He hated any sort of educated talk. The little beads of moisture were tingling on the tufts of his armpits.

'Okay,' he said. 'Skip it!'

And went away as if he had been treading on eggs.

Immediately Himmelfarb would have run after the foreman, and at least touched him on the shoulder, and looked into his face, for he could not have explained how he had been overcome by a fit of happy foolishness. But already the important figure, bending at the knees as well as at the elbows, was too far distant.

It was true, too, as Ernie Theobalds was conscious, the Jew had not found himself any friend of his own sex, although since his arrival in the country he had made overtures to many men, and for that purpose would take the train, and often walk the streets of the city at night. There were those who had asked him for advice, or money, and according to his ability he had given both. Some had accepted it undemonstratively, as their due, others seemed to regard him as God-sent, with the result that he was forced to retreat, to save them from their presumption, and himself from shame. Others, still, suspected him of being some kind of nark or perv, and cursed him as he lifted them out of their own vomit. Once or twice, outside the synagogues, on the Sabbath, he had spoken to those of his own kind. They were the most suspicious of all. They became so terribly affable. And collected their wives, who were standing stroking their mink as they waited, and got into their cars, and drove towards the brick warrens where they hoped to burrow into safety.

So Himmelfarb remained without a friend.

Or mate, he repeated gingerly.

And at once remembered the blackfellow with whom he had not yet spoken.

For that abo was still around at Rosetree's. A lazy enough bugger, everybody agreed. But somehow or other, it seemed to suit the abo to stick. Sometimes gone on a drunk, he would return, sometimes with a purple eye, or green bruise on yellow. A brute that no decent man would touch, only with a broom.

Yet, with this fellow flotsam, the Jew had formed, he now realized, an extraordinary non-relationship. If that could describe anything so solid, while unratified, so silent, while so eloquent. How he would sense the abo's approach. How he went to meet his silence. How they would lay balm on wounds every time they passed each other.

It was ridiculous. They were both ashamed. And turned their backs. And resumed their waiting. Sometimes the abo would whistle derisively some pop tune he had learnt from the radio. He would blow out his lips to extend an already considerable vulgarity of theme. To destroy, it was suggested. But knew that his friend, old Big Nose, would never be deceived.

They might have left it at that. After all, each in his time had experienced the knife.

Then one day during smoke-o Himmelfarb had gone into the wash-room, of which the scribbled woodwork, sweating concrete, and stained porcelain had grown quite acceptable. There he sat. There he leaned his head. And the introspective accents of a mumbling cistern and a drizzling tap ministered to his throbbing head.

He often sat out smoke-o in the wash-room which would remain deserted until work began. He would sit perfectly still, but, on this particular occasion his hand had touched the book someone hàd left open on the bench. It was only natural for Himmelfarb to read whatever print he set his eyes on. Now he began at once, with surprise flooding over him:

'And I looked and behold, a whirlwind came out of the north, a great cloud, and a fire infolding itself, and a brightness was about it, and out of the midst thereof as the colour of amber, out of the midst of the fire.

'Also out of the midst thereof came the likeness of four living creatures. And this was their appearance: they had the likeness of a man.

'And every one had four faces, and every one had four wings...'

But it was no longer his own voice which the Jew heard above the soft babble of the cistern and the sharper drizzle of the tap. It was the voice of voices – thick, and too throaty, and desolating in its sense of continuity. It could have been the voice of the Cantor Katzmann. Yet the voice no longer attempted to clothe the creatures themselves in allegorical splendour, of Babylonian gold. They were dressed in the flesh of men: the pug of human gargoyles, the rather soapy skin, the pores of which had been enlarged by sweat, the mouth thinned by trial and error, the dead hair of the living human creatures blowing in the wind of circumstance.

The Jew read, or heard:

'. . . two wings of every one were joined one to another, and two covered their bodies . . .'

In spite of which he knew from observing. He could read by heart the veins of the hidden bodies.

Now the lips of the past blew the words a little faster, as if the mouth had adapted itself to the acceleration of time. Time, in fact, was almost up. Belts were tightening. Down in the workshop there was a thwack of leather, metal easing greasily.

But the reader could not interrupt his reading:

'. . . and when the living creatures went, the wheels went by them: and when the living creatures were lifted up from the earth, the wheels were lifted up . . .'

When the machinery in the workshop started up, the whole wash-room revolted, but soon drowned, and floated gently enough. Against the noise from the machines, the voices of the tap and cistern were no longer audible.

But the voice of the Jew continued reading, now utterly his own, and loud, above the natter of the rejuvenated machines:

'. . . And the likeness of the firmament upon the heads of the living creatures was as the colour of the terrible crystal, stretched forth over their heads above. . . .'

When the abo came in. Looking for something he had left.

Immediately on seeing how he was caught, he remained poised, rocking on the balls of his normally flat and squelchy feet. He could not decide what to do.

The Jew was shining.

'It is Ezekiel!' he said, forgetful of that convention by which he and the black fellow refrained from exchanging words. "Somebody is reading Ezekiel I found here. Open on the bench.'

The spit jumped out of his mouth with joy.

The blackfellow stood there, playing with a ball of cotton waste, backwards and forwards, from hand to hand. He was sulking now, though.

'It is your book?' asked the Jew.

Then the blackfellow did something extraordinary. He spoke.

'Yes,' he admitted. 'It's my book.'

'Then you read the Bible. What about the other prophets? Daniel, Ezra, Hosea?' the same unmanageable enthusiasm drove the Jew to ask.

But it did not appear as though the blackfellow would allow himself to be trapped again. His lips were very thick and surly. He said:

'We better go down now.'

And jerked his head in the direction of the workshop.

'Yes,' agreed the Jew.

The abo quickly took the book, and hid it amongst what was apparently a bundle of his private belongings.

Himmelfarb remained spellbound. He was smiling that slow, inward smile, which could exasperate those whom it excluded.

'Interesting,' he had to remark. 'But I shall not ask any questions, as I see you do not wish me to.'

'Where'll it lead?' The abo shrugged. 'I was reared by a parson bloke. That's all. Sometimes I have a read of the Bible, but not for any of *his* reasons. I read it because you can see it all. And it passes the time.'

All of which the abo spoke in a curiously unexpected voice, conjured up from a considerable depth.

After that the two men returned to their work, for the machines were deriding them as they belted hell out of Rosetree's shed.

Now the Jew began to wonder, as he sat at his drill, and stamped the sheet, and stamped the sheet, whether their relationship would be in any way altered by what had happened. But it did not appear to be. It was as though it had set too long in the form it had originally taken. A certain enduring warmth, established in the beginning, had been perhaps intensified. The Jew was conscious of it if ever the blackfellow passed. Something almost tactile took place between them, but scarcely ever again was there any exchange of words. Sometimes the younger man would almost grunt, sometimes the older one would almost nod. Or they would look for each other, even catch each other at it. And once the blackfellow smiled, not for his acquaintance of elaborate standing, but for anyone who cared to receive it. If the Jew did, that was incidental. It was, the latter saw, a demonstration of perfect detachment.

Yet Himmelfarb was heartened by his study of this other living creature, to whom he had become joined, extraordinarily, by silence, and perhaps also, by dedication. On one other occasion, finding they had arrived simultaneously at the outer gate, and there was no avoiding it, they must go out together, he could not resist addressing the black.

'The day we spoke,' the Jew ventured, 'either I did not think, or have the time, to ask your name.'

The abo could have been preparing to sulk. But changed his mind quickly, it appeared, on sensing there was no trap.

'Dubbo,' he answered briskly. 'Alf Dubbo.'

And as briskly went off. He was gay on that day. He picked up a stone, and made it skip, along the surface of the green river. He stood for a moment squinting at the sun, the light from which splintered on his broad teeth. He could have been smiling, but that was more probably the light, concentrated on the planes of his excellent teeth.

Alf Dubbo was reared in a small town on the banks of a river which never wholly dried up, and which, in wet seasons, would overflow its steep banks and flood the houses in the lower town. The river played an important part in the boy's early life, and even after he left his birthplace, his thoughts would frequently return to the dark banks of the brown river, with its curtain of shiny foliage, and the polished stones which he would pick over, always looking for pleasing shapes. Just about dusk the river would become most fascinating for the small boy, and he would hang about at a certain bend where the townspeople had planted a park. The orange knuckles of the big bamboos became accentuated at dusk, and the shiny foliage of the native trees seemed to sweat a deeper green. The boy's dark river would cut right across the evening. Black gins would begin to congregate along the bank, some in clothes which the white women had cast off, others in flash dresses from the stores, which splashed their flowers upon the dark earth, as the gins lay giggling and anticipating. Who would pick them? There were usually white youths hanging around, and older drunks, all with money on them, and a bottle or two. Once he had seen a gin leave her dress in the arms of her lover, and plunge down towards the river, till the black streak that she made was swallowed up in the deepening night. But that was unusual. And in spite of the fact that it was also exciting, he had gone away.

Mrs Pask had been standing at the kitchen door.

'Alf, where ever were you?' she asked.

And her cocky echoed from beneath the shawl:

'Alfwheraryou? AlfwheraryouAlf? Alf.'

Not yet sleeping.

'By the river,' the boy answered.

'That is no place,' she said, 'to loiter about at this time of night. Mr Calderon has been looking for you. He is going to let you conjugate a Latin verb. But first there are several little jobs. Remember, it is the useful boys who are sought after in later life.'

So Alf took the tea-towel. He hung around dozing while she splashed and talked, and hoped the Latin verb would be forgotten.

Actually, Alf Dubbo was not born in that town. He was born not so many miles away, at another bend in the ever-recurring river, on a reserve, to an old gin named Maggie, by which of the whites she had never been able to decide. There he would have remained probably, until work or cunning rescued him. That he was removed earlier, while he was still, in fact, a leggy, awkward little boy, was thanks to the Reverend Timothy Calderon, at that time Anglican rector of Numburra.

Mr Calderon and his widowed sister, Mrs Pask, took the boy to institute what they christened their Great Experiment. For Mr Calderon was a man of high ideals, even though, as his more perceptive parishioners noticed, he failed perpetually to live up to them. If it required the more perceptive to notice, it was because his failures up to date had been for the most part harmless ones. He was, indeed, a harmless man, with the result that he had been moved to Numburra from the larger town of Dumbullen. Such perception on the part of his bishop had caused the rector to shed very bitter tears, but of those, only his sister knew, and together they had prayed that he might receive the strength humbly to endure his martyrdom.

It was the more distressing as the Reverend Timothy Calderon was a cultured man, of birth even, whose ideals had brought him from the Old Country shortly after ordination. Quite apart from the Latin verbs, he was able to unravel the Gospels from the Greek. He knew the dates of battles, and the names of plants, and had inherited a complete edition of the *Encyclopaedia Britannica* as well as a signet-ring. If the souls of Numburra appreciated neither his gentle blood nor his education, that was something further he must bear. That he did bear it was due not only to fervid prayer, but also to the timely conception of his Great Experiment. On little Alf Dubbo, the parson decided, he would lavish all he could: fatherly love, and spiritual guidance, to say nothing of Latin verbs, and the dates of battles.

Alf Dubbo appeared from the beginning to be an exceedingly bright boy. Those who were interested in him were soon convinced that he might grasp almost anything, provided he wanted to. Only, where did his bent lie? That at once became the problem. He was bright, but he was lazy, the most sceptical of the rector's parishioners observed with tigerish satisfaction. Who but the rector would not have expected laziness from the bastard of an old black gin out at the Reserve? It did not occur to the critics, of course, that the boy might have inherited his vice from some Irish ancestor. Propriety alone made them reduce Alf's Irish ancestors to the mythical status of the Great Snake.

The rector himself began to suspect his ward of indolence, when on one occasion the boy asked:

'Mr Calderon, what am I going to do with all these Latin verbs?'

'Well,' said the rector, 'in the first place, they are a discipline. They will help to build character.'

'But I can't see what use they will be,' complained the boy, in his gentle, imitation voice. 'I don't think I can be that kind of character.'

Then he started, regrettably, to sulk. He would sulk, and scribble, and his teacher would have to admit that at such times little more could be done with him.

'Sometimes I wonder whether we are not being terribly unwise,' the rector once confessed to his sister.

'Oh, but in some directions, Timothy, he has made visible progress. In sketching, for instance,' Mrs Pask was vain enough to insist. 'In sketching I cannot show him enough. He has an eye for colour. Alf is an artistic boy.'

'Art, yes. But life.'

The rector sighed, moody for his Latin verbs.

Alf Dubbo did love to draw, and would scribble on the walls of the shed where he milked the rector's horny cow.

'What are you doing, Alf?' they called.

'I was marking up the weeks since she had the bull,' the boy replied.

That stopped them. He had noticed early on that Mrs Pask preferred to avert her eyes from nature. So that once more he was free to scribble on the walls of the shed, the finespun lines of a world he felt to exist but could not yet corroborate.

In the circumstances, he was always undemonstratively happy when Mrs Pask happened to say:

'Dear, oh, dear, I have a head! But we must not neglect your education, must we, Alf? Bring out my watercolour box, and we shall continue where we left off last time. I believe you are beginning to grasp the principles of drawing, and may even have a hidden talent.'

As a young girl, Mrs Pask herself had been compelled to choose between several talents, none of them hidden, it was implied; indeed, they had been far too obvious. What with sketching, and piano, and a light soprano voice, she had led rather a distracted life, until it was revealed to her that she must abandon all personal pretentions for the sake of Our Lord Jesus Christ and the Reverend Arthur Pask. She did, however, retain a reduced interest in sketching and watercolour, and would, on days when the climate allowed, take her easel and dash something off. Her hobby – because, in spite of a technical facility, she would not let herself think of it as more – had proved a particular comfort in the hour of trial. For Mrs Pask was widowed early.

'Never forget, Alf, that art is first and foremost a moral force,' she remarked once to her pupil, while demonstrating the possibilities of white as a livener of unrelieved surfaces. 'Truth,' she added, 'is so beautiful.'

He was, at least, fascinated by her brush.

'See,' she said, dabbing, 'one tiny fleck, and each of these cherries comes to life. One has to admit there is something miraculous in the creative act.'

He could not yet, but became convinced of some potentiality.

'Let,' he said, 'let me, Mrs Pask, now.'

He was so quick. He could do a bowl of cherries – highlights included – or plaster hand which she had in a cupboard, before his teacher had caught on to the thread of narrative she proposed to follow. It exasperated, even humiliated her at first.

'I hope you are not a vain boy,' she would remark.

Which was too silly to answer.

Once she put in front of him a vase of what she said were Crimson Ramblers – only a shadow of what they could be.

For him, they were the substance. He made them stand up stiff and solid. He drew a blue line round each of the crimson roses, so that they were for ever contained.

She laughed. She said:

'You cannot resist colour. There was never anything so red. You must learn in time, though, it is delicacy that counts.'

Mrs Pask loved best of all to talk while her pupil worked. She would lie back in her chair, with her feet on an embroidered stool. Years afterwards, coming across a print in a public library, Dubbo was forced to realize that Mrs Pask, for all her virtue, had been at heart one of the turbaned ladies of another

315

more indolent age, leaning, figuratively in her case, on the shoulder of her little coloured boy.

There in the weatherboard sitting-room at Numburra, under the cracking, corrugated roof, Mrs Pask's voice would join with the drone of blowflies in unbroken antiphon.

'I must tell you, Alf, I gave up all for Mr Pask, even down to face-powder, though of course my skin being of the finest, and my complexion so clear and fresh, that was no very great hardship. And who would not have done the same! He was a lovely man. Of the sweetest disposition. And so slim. But,' she coughed, 'athletic. I can see him jump the net at tennis. Arthur would never think of going round.'

The pupil worked. Or looked up at times, for politeness' sake. Mrs Pask, of former fine complexion, had turned purple by that date. It was blood pressure, and the climate.

Sometimes the boy would sit very still at the drawing-board. Then she would complain:

'Surely you have not finished, Alf, when I have only just set you the subject?'

'No,' he would reply, 'not yet.'

For peace.

And would sit. And would wait.

Then, after he had mixed some fresh colours, he would work. Sometimes she thought his eyes stared too hard. That his chest was too cramped. There was something unhealthy.

She would say:

'We must try to find some companions for you. Rough games once in a while are good for any boy. Not that I approve of brute strength. Only Christian manliness.'

He grunted to appease her. He could not have formed words while under such other pressure. For, he was all the time painting.

And on one occasion the tin box of Mrs Pask's paints had gone clattering.

'Oh!' she cried. 'If the little porcelain containers should get broken! Alf, I should be so upset. The box – I told you, didn't I? – was a gift from Mr Pask.'

Nothing was broken, however.

'But what,' she asked, still breathing hard, 'whatever in the world, Alf, is this?'

Looking at his paper.

It was almost as if she had caught him at something shameful. He sat with his knees together. His innermost being stood erect.

316

'That is a tree,' he said when he was able.

'A most unnatural tree!' She smiled kindly.

He touched it with vermilion, and it bled afresh.

'What are these peculiar objects, or fruit – are they? – hanging on your tree?'

He did not say. The iron roof was cracking.

'They must mean *some*thing,' Mrs Pask insisted.

'Those,' he said, then, 'are dreams.'

He was ashamed, though.

'Dreams! But there is nothing to indicate that they are any such thing. Just a shape. I should have said mis-shapen kidneys!'

So that he was put to worse shame.

'That is because they have not been dreamt yet,' he uttered slowly.

And all the foetuses were palpitating on the porous paper.

'I am afraid it is something unhealthy,' Mrs Pask confided in her brother. 'An untrained mind could not possibly conceive of anything so peculiar unless.'

'But the boy's mind is not totally untrained. Since you have begun to train it,' the parson could not resist.

He still smarted for his Latin verbs, and the obvious hold his sister had over Alf Dubbo, through the medium of paint.

'I have to admit I am a little frightened. I wonder whether I should go on with it,' Mrs Pask meditated.

'You have uncovered his imagination. That is all.' The rector sighed.

Imagination, just a little, was his own misfortune, for it had never been enough to ferment the rest of him, yet too much for failure to support. He was a soggy man, reminiscent of grey bread. If he had been less gentle, more bitter, he might have been admired. He had a handsome nose for a start, which should have cut an offender to the quick. But as it had never occurred to the Reverend Timothy Calderon to use any part of his physical person as a weapon, he was not repaid in fear and respect, not even by his own sister, who only loved him because it would have been shocking not to and because there was no other intimate relationship left to her.

As he conducted the ritual of his parish life: the tepid, but in every way reverential services, the visits to those of his parishioners who were too passive to intimidate him, the annual fête at which the same ladies guessed the weight of a different-coloured cake – the rector was sustained by secrets. Only two, certainly, for his temperament would not have run to more.

But of those two secrets, the one was shocking enough, the other he would never have admitted to, so desperately did he depend upon it for his nourishment.

In that northern diocese of bells and lace, Mr Calderon officiated as befitted one born and reared an Anglican. While the temperature rose, so did the incense, though never enough to offend the nostrils. One was relieved to find that taste and the formalities had not been preserved from Rome to be destroyed by any evangelical fervour. Here original purity prevailed. Even when the lace got torn in scuffles, despite the vigilance of Mrs Pask. Even when the Eucharist lulled in summer, and the best intentions slipped beyond the bounds of concentration. Like Sunday, Mr Calderon came and went. His blameless hand would place the wafer, his unexceptionable voice intone, without disturbing the past, or ladies' minds. Blowflies seconded him, under the window of St George, which the Butter Factory had presented.

It was beneath the Saint, his favourite, the manly, flannel-clad, athletic George, that the rector would most frequently indulge his secret life, while attending to those practical duties of devotional routine which boys regularly forgot. Perhaps the swing of his cassock, not entirely an ascetic garment, suggested to the silent man a somewhat freer choreography for the soul. In any case, as he placed a napkin, or a cruet, or retrieved a battered psalter from underneath a pew, the rector would find himself yearning after some more virile expression of faith which a damp nature and family opinion had never allowed him to profess. In other words, the Reverend Timothy Calderon longed secretly to flame in the demonstration of devotion. But would he really have known how? At least in his imagination, the strong voices of clear-skinned boys, in severest linen surplices, would mount in hymns of praise, carrying his diffident soul towards salvation. He would be saved, not by works, too exhausting in a hot climate, not by words, too banal in any event, but by youth, rather, and ever-straining lung-power.

All that he had never been, all that he had not experienced, was fatally attractive to the humble rector. Under the window of the blond Saint, bursting the Dragon with his lance, his brother-in-law Arthur Pask would appear to Timothy Calderon, and, after jumping the tennis-net, throw his arm around the weaker shoulder. During his brief life, all had been made possible to Arthur: a thrilled, and thrilling faith, the rewards and pains of a missionary fervour, marriage with a lovely girl – nobody had blamed Emily on *seeing* that her reason for de-

318

fection was not altogether evangelical – then martyrdom, more or less, for in spite of his aggressive health, Arthur Pask was carried off, at the early age of twenty-six, by rheumatic fever, on the Birdsville Track. Of those who mourned, perhaps it was not his widow who was cut most deeply. A widow is placated by the drama of it; a woman can sweeten herself on what is bitterest in memory. It was the brother-in-law who suffered. Though nobody knew it.

Not long after Alf Dubbo came to them, the rector had remarked:

'I noticed, Emily, you did not communicate this morning.'

'No,' she said.

Their feet were flogging the dust on the short distance to the rectory.

'I remembered,' she explained, 'it is the anniversary of Arthur's death.'

'You remembered!' He laughed.

It sounded odd, but Emily Pask was of those people who, besides forgetting, failed to divine sensibility in others. If less obtuse, of course, she would have seen that her brother whipped his sorrows to prevent them lagging.

Their life together was full of undercurrents, which sometimes threatened to drag them down. So that the presence of the aboriginal boy did at first relieve, and even promise rescue. If the sister was only partially aware, the brother became fully conscious that his hopes were fastening on Alf Dubbo, and that through him he hoped he might achieve, if not personal salvation, at least a mental cosiness. Until finding he had only added another nail to those he wore.

For the rector had never succeeded in communicating with anyone by words. Nor would the boy, it appeared, attempt to express himself, except by those riddles in paint which his teacher so deplored.

Soon after the morning on which Mrs Pask had found herself faced with her pupil's daemon, Timothy Calderon discovered Alf looking through a book, as though he were not at all sure he should be doing what he was unable to resist.

'Well, Alf,' the kindly man slowly opened, 'have you found something instructive? Or only to your taste?'

He had not meant it that way, but there it was. While the boy continued turning the pages with feverish necessity.

'It is a book I found,' Alf replied, with some obviousness. 'It is interesting,' he added.

He spoke dully, when he was, in fact, consumed.

'Ah,' said the rector, 'I believe that was a present from a school acquaintance of my sister's. Who knew of her interest in the arts.'

The man and boy continued looking together at the book.

Here the world broke into little particles of light. The limbs of the bathers might have remained stone, if light had not informed the observer that this was indeed flesh of flesh; even the water became a vision of original nakedness. Dancers were caught for an instance in the turmoil of their tulle. Laundresses ironed a diagonally divided world of powdered butterflies. Solid lanterns vibrated with thick, joyous bursts of light.

'The French,' remarked Mr Calderon, after he had referred to the title, 'have a different conception of things.'

The boy was throbbing over his discovery.

'They are a different race,' the rector judged, smiling a forgiving smile.

Then the boy stopped at a picture he would always remember, and criticize, and wish to improve on. It was the work, he read, of some French painter, a name to him, then as always. In the picture the chariot rose, behind the wooden horses, along the pathway of the sun. The god's arm – for the text implied it was a god – lit the faces of the four figures, so stiff, in the body of the tinny chariot. The rather ineffectual torch trailed its streamers of material light.

' "Apollo",' read the rector.

He was not prepared to continue, or to comment.

But Alf Dubbo said:

'The arm is not painted good. I could do the arm better. And horses. My horses,' the boy claimed, 'would have the fire flowing from their tails. And dropping sparks. Or stars. Moving. Everything would move in my picture. Because that is the way it ought to be.'

'You are the regular little artist!' the rector accused, and laughed against his painful teeth.

'Fire and light are movement,' the boy persisted.

Then the man could bear his own extinction no longer. He touched the boy's head, but very briefly. He said:

'Come on, Alf, close up the book now. There is something else I want you to think about.'

He brought the Bible, and began to read from the Gospel of St John.

'John,' he explained, 'was the Beloved Disciple.'

The parson told of spiritual love and beauty, how each incident in Our Lord's life had been illuminated with those qualities. Of course the boy had heard it all before, but wondered again how he failed continually to appreciate. It did seem as though he could grasp only what he was able to see. And he had not yet seen Jesus Christ, in spite of his guardian's repeated efforts, and a succession of blurry colour-prints. Now he began to remember a night at the Reserve when his mother had received a quarter-caste called Joe Mullens, who loved her awful bad, and had brought her a bottle of metho to prove it. Soon the boy's memory was lit by the livid jags of the metho love the two had danced together on the squeaky bed. Afterwards his mother had begun to curse, and complain that she was deceived again by love. But for the boy witness, at least, her failure had destroyed the walls. He was alive to the fur of darkness, and a stench of leaves, as he watched the lightning-flicker of receding passion.

'Earthly love is not the faintest reflection of divine compassion,' the rector was explaining. 'But I can tell you are not concentrating, Alf.'

The boy looked down, and saw that his guardian's knees, in their thinning and rather crumpled trousers, were touching his. He sensed that, according to precept, he should have felt compassion for this conscientious man, but all he felt was the pressure of knees. He was fascinated by the network of little creases in the worn serge, and by a smell of what he realized later on in cities was that of hot underclothing, as people struggled together, and clung to the little progress they had made.

'I think we had better stop there,' the rector decided.

But he could not bring himself to alter his position.

It was the boy who shifted, sighing, or grunting, as he looked out into the glare and saw Mrs Pask returning from good works with an empty pudding-basin.

While the rector derived little consolation from his attempts to plant faith in the soul of this aboriginal boy, his sister grew quite skittish with what she liked to think the success of her instruction. Admittedly Mrs Pask had always liked the easy things, and admittedly Alf was learning how to please. Here was a whole sheaf of subjects, tastefully shaded, admirably foreshortened. It seemed that with a few ingratiating strokes the boy might reproduce the whole world as his teacher knew it.

That would have been consummation, indeed. If, from time to time, she had not come across those other fruits of her pupil's talent. Which made her frightened.

And on one occasion the pupil himself rooted out an old,

battered box which she had put so carefully away, even she had forgotten.

'These are more paints,' said Alf.

'Oh,' she began to explain, half-prim, half-casual. 'Yes. Some old paints I gave up using very early. They did not suit the kind of work which interested me.'

Alf squeezed a tube, and there shot out, from beneath the crust of ages, a blue so glistening, so blue, his eyes could not focus on it.

All he could say was:

'Gee, Mrs Pask!'

Even then he had to control his mouth.

Mrs Pask frowned in replying.

'I have tried to explain why we should not, on any account, use such a very horrid expression. I thought you might have remembered.'

'Yes,' he said. 'But can I use the paints?'

After a pause, she decided:

'I think, perhaps, it would not be advisable for you to work in oils.'

'Arrr, Mrs Pask!'

For by now he had coaxed a rosy tongue out of a second tube. And was drowning in a burst of yellow from the bottom of a third.

She said with an effort:

'Oil paints lead to so much that is sensual, so much that is undesirable in art. But of course, you would not understand anything of that, and must take it on trust from those who do.'

All he knew for the moment was his desire to expel the sensation in his stomach, the throbbing of his blood, in surge upon surge of thick, and ever-accumulating colour.

'I could paint good with these,' he maintained.

Mrs Pask looked whimsically sad.

Then Alf Dubbo played an unexpected card. Put into his hand by divine interest, as it were, he had no cause for feeling guilty.

'I could do things with these,' he began, 'that I never ever would have known how to do before.'

He touched the tube of supernatural blue.

'I would paint Jesus Christ,' he ventured, in a voice which he had learnt to be acceptable.

'Oh?'

Mrs Pask sniggered wheezily. The boy had sounded so quaint.

322

'I would not like to paint Jesus, only in oil paints,' he admitted.

Mrs Pask averted her old and rather wobbly face. She remembered her young husband, and the strength and loveliness of his uncovered throat.

'I will show you,' said Alf.

'We shall see,' said Mrs Pask. 'Put away the paints. Now. Please.'

'You don't *know*!'

His voice jumped recklessly.

'Oh, but I do!' she said.

The words were so bleached, she was on the verge of repeating them.

'Well, then?'

'How provoking you can be!' she protested. 'I did not say no *exactly*. Well, on your thirteenth birthday. But I insist you put away the paints now.'

He did. And would wait. Longer if necessary. Nobody else would wait so carefully.

In the meantime he followed around the one who held his life in her hands, and she often took advantage of the situation.

For instance, she might ask:

'If you forget to milk poor Possum when it rains, how can you expect me to remember I have promised to let you use the paints?'

The rector hated his sister at times. Because, of course, she had told him what had taken place, making it sound both touching and ridiculous. It was dreadful to Timothy Calderon that he was so often aware of what he was unable to avert. Cruelty, for example. He was particularly sensitive to the duller, unspectacular kind.

'But you will allow him?' he hoped.

Mrs Pask folded in her lips.

'I shall pray for guidance,' she replied.

Frequently Mr Calderon did, too, without always receiving it.

Once in the dark hall, in the smell of old books and yesterday's mutton, the rector encountered Alf with almost no warning. The boy gave the impression of doing nothing with an air of some significance, and as always at such moments, the man was walled up more completely in his own ineffectuality and lovelessness.

Yet, on this occasion, the suddenness of the encounter, or a rush of self-pity, started him off with:

'I expect you are waiting pretty anxiously for your birthday, Alf?'

The boy's smile acknowledged the superfluousness and slight silliness of the remark.

But the rector blundered on.

'Well, who knows, your gift of painting may have been given to you as a means of expressing your innermost convictions.'

Suddenly the two people involved in the situation began to sweat.

'So that you should have something,' mumbled the rector, and repeated with suppressed emotion: 'At least, something.'

At this point an alarming, but not altogether unexpected incident, the boy realized, began to occur. Mr Calderon fumbled at Alf's head, then pressed it against his stomach. They were standing in awkward conjunction in the semi-darkness and familiar smells.

Although at first doubtful how he ought to behave, Alf decided to submit to the pressure. He could feel buttons and a watch-chain eating ravenously into his cheek, and then, deep down in the rector's stomach, he heard a rather pitiful rumble. The sound that uncoiled itself was both apologetic and old. The boy visualized an old, soft, white worm slowly raising its head, swaying, and lolling, before falling back. He was so fascinated by the image that he had even begun to count the rings with which the ghostly worm was scored.

But Mr Calderon had suddenly decided, it seemed, that he was not sad at all. A kind of jollity which had taken possession of his stomach almost bounced the boy off.

'It is wrong to allow our affections to persuade us we are tragic figures,' the rector announced in an unknown voice.

And, as the boy continued standing, pushed him away.

Mr Calderon then went into his study, where the notes for a sermon were waiting to enmesh him, and in spite of his views on economy, and the early hour, switched on the electric light, with the result that he had never been so exposed before. It was disastrous. The boy crept away, but pursued by the picture of his guardian. For, although the rector's incisive nose was as imposing as ever, right down to the glistening pores at the roots of it, the rest of the face was as white and crumbly as old scones. Or perhaps Mr Calderon had no more than left his teeth out.

The image blazed across the boy's mind and away, because, whatever cropped up *en route*, his thirteenth birthday was only a short distance ahead.

When at last he had arrived at it, he asked above the wrappings of the seemly presents:

'And the paints, Mrs Pask? Can I use the oil paints that you promised?'

There was a dreadful pause.

Then Mrs Pask said:

'You set too much store, Alf, by what is unimportant. But as I promised.'

She seemed to have the wind that morning. It made a little *pffff* against the soft hair on her upper lip.

So he got out the paints. He had found an old tea-chest on a rubbish dump, and had hammered it apart, and extracted the nails, and kept the sides in the feed shed. The ply boards were immaculate. He brought them to the back veranda. After sharing with him such technical points as she could remember, his teacher went away. She would not look. Anything might emerge now.

So Alf Dubbo began to squeeze the tubes. Regardful of some vow, he dedicated the first board with a coat of flat white. He began moodily to dabble in the blue. He moulded the glistening gobs into arbitrary forms, to demolish them almost at once with voluptuous authority. He mixed the blue with white, until it had quite paled. And was moved to lay it at last upon the board in long, smooth tongues, which, he hoped, might convey his still rather nebulous intention. Sometimes he worked with the brushes he had prepared, more often with his trembling fingers. But he could not, in fact, he could not. A white mist continued to creep up and obscure what should have been a vision of blue. So he took the brush with the sharpest end, and with the point he described an unhappy O. From this cipher, the paint was dripping down in stalactites of bluish white. He took the blood-red, and thinned it, and threw it on in drops. It dripped miserably down. He recognized his failure, and turned the board away from him.

He kept on returning, however, to the opaque masses of his paint. He was clogged with it. As he thought about his failure, and wondered how he might penetrate what remained a thick white mist in his mind, he scratched his own face in one of the lower corners of the board. The concave shape, something like that of a banana, was held as if waiting to receive. But he sensed he would never improve on an idea which had come to him in a moment of deceit.

For some time he mooned around, until realizing he had, at least, observed a promise. To a certain extent, he had earned his freedom. He felt better then, and thought how he would put into his next picture all that he had ever known. The brown dust. His mother's tits, black and gravelly, hanging down. The figure of the quarter-caste, Joe Mullens, striking again and again with his thighs as though he meant to kill. And the distance, which was sometimes a blue wire tautened round his own throat, and which at others dissolved into a terrible listlessness. There would be the white people, of course, perpetually naked inside their flash clothes. And the cup of wine held in the air by the Reverend Tim. That was, again, most important. Even through the dented sides you could see the blood tremble in it. And the white worm stirring and fainting in the reverend pants. And love, very sad. He would paint love as a skeleton from which they had picked the flesh – an old goanna – and could not find more, however much they wanted, and hard they looked. Himself with them. He would have liked to discover whether it really existed, how it tasted.

Alf Dubbo was painting at his picture all the morning. Some of it even Mrs Pask and the rector might have understood, but some was so secret, so tender, he could not have borne their getting clumsy with it. Parts of it walked on four legs, but others flowed from his hand in dreams that only he, or some inconceivable stranger, might recognize and interpret.

A little while before it was time to set the pickled onions on the table, Mrs Pask came, and stood behind him.

'Well, I never!' she said. 'That is a funny sort of picture. After all I have taught you! What is it called?'

'That is called *My Life*,' the boy answered.

'And this?' she asked, pointing with her toe.

'That,' he said – he almost could not – 'that is the picture of Jesus. It is no good, though, Mrs Pask. You must not look. I don't understand yet.'

She, too, did not know exactly what to say. She had turned her deepest purple. She was munching on her lips.

She said:

'It all comes of my being so foolish. Things are not like this,' she said. 'It is downright madness. You must not think this way. My brother must speak to you,' she said. 'Oh, dear! It is dirty! When there is so much that is beautiful and holy!'

She went away nearly crying.

And he called after her:

'Mrs Pask! It is beautiful! It is all, really, beautiful. It is only me. I am learning to show it. How it is. In me. I'll show you something that you didn't know. You'll see. And get a surprise.'

But she went away towards the kitchen.

And his lips were spilling over with the bubbles of anguish.

That dinner, which Alf did not share, the rector and his sister had a slap-up row.

'But you have not seen!' she kept on harping, and drumming on the tablecloth.

'I do not wish to see,' he repeated. 'I have confidence in the boy. It is his way of expressing himself.'

'You are weak, Timothy. If you were not, you would take the matter in hand. But you are weak.'

He could not answer that one straight, but said:

'Our Lord recognized that all human beings are weak. And what did He prescribe? Love! That is what you forget, Emily. Or is it that you choose to ignore?'

The window-panes were dancing.

'Oh, love!' she said, real loud.

She began to cry then. For a while the windows rattled, but they did at last subside, and become again flat glass.

After that Alf Dubbo went away, because he was sick from listening. He put his paintings in the shed, behind the bran bin, which had just fallen empty, and which usually stayed that way for some time after it happened.

There was no painting or drawing in the following weeks. Mrs Pask said that he must learn to darn, and sew on buttons, in case he should become a soldier. She gave him many other little jobs, like weeding, and errands, and addressing envelopes for the parish news – it was so good for his hand – while she sat and rested her ankles. Nor did she live aloud any more the incidents of her past life. But thought them instead. Or remembered sick people who needed visiting. She went about much more than before, as if, by staying at home, she might have discovered something she did not want to, just by going into a room.

Mrs Pask went her own way, and the Reverend Timothy Calderon and Alf Dubbo went theirs, all separately. It had always been that way more or less, only now it was as though they had been made to see it. In the case of the rector and his sister, at least they had their purposes, but for Alf Dubbo it was terrible, who walked amongst the furniture, and broken flower-pots, and cow-pats. Once he squelched his hand in a new turd that old Possy had let drop, and his eyes immediately began to water, as the comforting smell shot up, and because at the same time the fresh cow-dung was so lifeless in texture compared with that of the oil paints.

Only twice he looked at the paintings he had hidden in the shed. On the first occasion he could not bear it. On the second it might have been the same, if the rector had not suddenly appeared, looking for something, and said:

'I am the only one, Alf, who has not seen the works of art.'

So Alf Dubbo showed.

Mr Calderon stood holding the boards, one in either hand, looking from one to the other of the pictures. His lips were moving. Then the boy realized his guardian was not looking at the paintings, but somewhere into his own thoughts, at the pictures in his mind. Alf did not blame, because, after all, that was mostly the way people did behave.

'So these are they,' the rector was saying; the veins were old in the backs of his hands. 'Well, well.' Looking, and not, from one to the other. 'I can remember, when I was a boy, before I became aware of my vocation, I had every intention of being an actor. I would learn parts – Shakespeare, you know – just for the fun of it, and even make up characters, the most extraordinary individuals, out of my own rather luxuriant imagination. People told me I had a fine declamatory voice, which, admittedly, I had. I took the part of a Venetian in, I believe it was *The Merchant*. And once,' he giggled, 'I played a lady! I wore a pair of rose stockings. Silk. And on my chest a cameo, which had been lent me by some acquaintance of my aunts.'

The Reverend Timothy Calderon had grown cheerful by now. He stood the painted plywood against the empty bin, and went outside.

'One day, Alf, you must explain your paintings to me,' he said. 'Because I believe, however clearly any artist, or man, for that matter, conveys, there must always remain a hidden half which will need to be explained. And perhaps that is not possible unless implicit trust exists. Between. Between the artist and his audience.'

It was a limpid morning, in which the smoke ascended, and Mrs Pask had discovered a reason for paying a call. As he followed the rector between the rows of bolting lettuces, Alf Dubbo was puzzled to feel that perhaps he was the one who led, for Mr Calderon had turned so very spongy and dependent. The boy walked noticeably well. Upright. He appeared to have grown, too. He was suddenly a young man in whom the scars had healed, of the wounds they had made in his flesh. His nostrils awaited experience.

At one point, at a bend in the path, the rector turned, and seemed in particular need of the youth's attention and understanding.

'One summer, before we came to this country,' he said, 'I made a pilgrimage to Stratford-on-Avon – the Home of the Bard – with my brother-in-law, Arthur Pask. It was very delightful. We had both already decided to take orders, although Arthur had not yet been directed to follow a different path. We slept in a shed, in a tea-garden. We would come in after the plays, and talk,' he said, 'half the night. All that week it was moonlight, I remember. Poor Arthur, you know, was a god. That is, as well as being an extremely saintly man, he was most personable.'

The young blackfellow trod warily, stiffly, through the narrative, and kicked aside the sickly stalks of one or two uprooted cabbages. He was not so much hearing as seeing, and was not altogether convinced by the figure of the second parson, whom moonlight made whiter. He remembered the wooden figure of the god in the chariot, in the French painting. Quite lifeless. Either he could not understand, or gods were perhaps dummies in men's imaginations.

When, somewhat to Alf Dubbo's surprise, Mr Calderon took him by the hand, the better to lead him, it seemed, along paths they already knew, under the clothes-line, with its loops of heavy-hanging, wet linen, and past the ungovernable bushes of lemon-scented geranium. Yet, although the two figures were joined together at the hand, and were crowding through the doorway abreast, bumping at the doorposts with their awkward formation, as if to widen the hole, each could only feel that the other was probably entering a different tunnel.

Mr Calderon had turned a bluish, milky white, and would have liked to appear pitiful, to justify his being led.

'I am leaning on you,' he suggested, 'when you are the one who must need support and guidance. If only on account of your age.' Then he gave a kind of gasp. 'Sometimes I wonder,' he added, 'what will become of me.'

'What, are you sick?' asked the boy, in a tone of brutal indifference.

Because his teeth were almost chattering, he had to aim his words like stones.

'Not exactly,' Mr Calderon replied, and added: 'That is,

there are some to whom I would not admit it. Their efforts to sympathize would be too painful to witness.'

He continued to act rather sick, or old, because by now the boy was learning to guide him along the passages. It was becoming gently agreeable.

But the boy himself was behaving automatically. Guiding under guidance, he was no longer the initiated youth. There were pockets of puppy-fat concealed about his body, and his mind shivered behind the veil which still separated him from life. On normal occasions, delivering a message, or returning a pair of cleaned shoes, he would not have lingered in the rector's room; its personal mystery was too much for him. Now, on arrival at their destination, his movements were ticking painfully.

Halted on the carpet from which the pattern had disappeared, Mr Calderon said formally, and somehow differently:

'Thank you, dear fellow. I am grateful to you in my infirmity.'

In which neither of them believed. But Mr Calderon was pleased to have invented it.

Then, again surprisingly, he opened Alf Dubbo's shirt, and put in his hand.

'It is warmth for which one craves,' he explained, older and more trembly than before.

The boy feared his heart, which was leaping like a river fish, might be scooped up and held by that cold hand.

But he did not resist physically.

At no time in his life was Alf Dubbo able to resist what must happen. He had, at least, to let it begin, for he was hypnotized by the many mysteries which his instinct sensed.

Mr Calderon was mopping his forehead.

'Are you charitable?' he asked. 'Or just another human being?'

Alf did not know, so he only grunted.

As his guardian seemed to ordain it, they were pretty soon divesting themselves of anything that might possibly serve as a refuge for their personalities. The parson's pace became reckless, with the boy following suit, because it would have been worse to have got left behind. They were revolving in the slightly shabby room, their ridiculous shirt-tails flapping like wings. Their shoes were thunderous in coming off. Mr Calderon stubbed his toe on one of the castors of the bedstead, but it was not the moment at which to complain. Time was too short. The past, the future, the appearances of things, his faith, even his

330

desire, could have been escaping from him. Certainly, after the whirlwind of preparation, he was left with his nakedness, always so foolish, and rather bent at the knee. But decided to embrace his intention.

It was a warm-cold morning in autumn. It was a morning devoted to regret rather than fulfilment. They lay together on the honeycomb quilt. Pleasure was brief, fearful, and only grudgingly recognized. Very soon the boy was immersed in the surge of words with which his lover lamented his own downfall.

In between, Mr Calderon revived his trance of touch.

'A kind of dark metal,' he pondered, and would have liked to remember poetry, even to have composed some of his own, to write with his finger. 'But metal does not feel.' So they returned perpetually to where they had left off. 'That is what makes it desirable.'

Metal submitted, however. They lay upon the lumpy bed of words. From under his eyelashes the boy was fascinated for always by a mound of grey stomach.

Mr Calderon resumed quoting from the narrative of his life, and Alf Dubbo snoozed.

When he awoke, his guardian was sneezing, overtaken by catarrh, if not an honest-to-God cold.

'We should put our things on,' he announced irritably, and then: 'I wonder what you will think of me, Alf?'

The boy, who had been dreaming happily, looked contented, all considered. But the man was too obsessed to notice. Groping for his trousers, for his handkerchief, from where he lay, keys, money fell in an ominous cascade.

'How I must appear to you?' he persisted.

The boy began to laugh, showing his broad teeth.

'Well?' asked the man.

Suspicious.

'How you look?'

The boy was practically bound with laughter. Then, with an expression which was rather sheepish, but which might have turned to malice if he had been dealing with an equal, he reached out, and seized a handful of the grey belly, and twisted it round, tight, as if it had been stuff.

'Hhehhyyy?'

Mr Calderon whinged. He did not like the turn affairs had taken. But made himself laugh a little.

'You look to me' – the boy laughed – 'like you was made out of old wichetty grubs.'

And twisted the flesh tighter in support.

It was a situation which Mr Calderon might have handled badly, if the door had not opened and introduced his sister Mrs Pask.

Emily Pask was standing there. On two legs. That was the general impression. In a purple hat.

Everybody was looking. Nobody was in any way assisted. They had, in fact, stuck.

Until Mrs Pask's throat began to thaw. The blood was again moving in her, till it matched her hat. Her eyes were sewn to her face, otherwise they might have fallen, and even so, despite the stitches, almost did.

'You *boy*!' She began to try her tongue. 'You! You devil! What have you done to my brother?'

She began to totter at a chair. And fell upon it without mercy.

'I never allowed myself to suspect,' she rasped. 'But knew. Something. Oh, you devil! Sooner or later.'

The others remained fastened to that bed, the honeycomb pattern eating into their buttocks.

In spite of the shock, Alf Dubbo realized pretty soon that he must dress himself. It took a long time, but was eventually accomplished.

The Reverend Timothy Calderon had resorted to tears, and to calling on his sister's name.

In the blur of white and purple, Alf Dubbo left the room. *AlfwheraryouAlf*, called Mrs Pask's cocky. The boy had thought to knot his shoelaces together, and to hang his shoes round his neck. A practical move, it enabled him to run more easily from the township of Numburra, which he never saw again.

As he wandered through paddocks and along roads, the fugitive did not reflect on the injustice of Mrs Pask's accusation, sensing with her that all which had happened, had to happen, sooner or later. He was only glad to have endured it, and to be able to remember some little spasms of pleasure in a waste of words and bewilderment. Sensual pleasure, certainly, because his arms were strong, and his skin was smooth, and the appeal had been made just then. But he did also recall his protector in many harmless attitudes, and would slow up on his journey, and kick at a stone, or pull a leaf, as he estimated the extent and kind of loss. He felt the wind on him. The absence of his guardian was not unlike that caused by the theft of some old woolly, hitherto undervalued garment snatched from an unsuspecting back on a frosty morning. Less material, more subtly missed, because he would not have admitted, were those equally woolly precepts, of God in cloud and God in man, which the rector had attempted to wind round a mind that found them strange, suffocating, superfluous. Although he had adopted a few of these, in secret, for expediency's sake, and had got into the habit of protecting himself from terrors, by wrapping his thoughts in them, beside some waterhole at night.

What became of the rector, Alf Dubbo often wondered, without ever finding out. Timothy Calderon's end could have been an awful one. Chained to Emily Pask in a hell of common knowledge, they might have lingered for a little, torturing each other with the dreadful secret and the brother's insufficient faith. Actually, what happened was this:

When Mr Calderon had snivelled a while, as he was, on the bed, for even if he had clothed himself it could not have hidden his nakedness, and Mrs Pask had grieved, and brooded, and subsided, the rector, it must be said, did affirm:

'As a Christian of a kind, Emily, and I expect even you will grant there are all kinds, I must protest that poor Alf Dubbo was not to blame.'

Mrs Pask creaked, or the springs of the over-goaded chair.

'To blame?' she asked, dreamily.

'For what has happened,' her brother replied. 'You must understand, in all justice, that I was to blame.' He began to snivel again. 'And will do penance for it ever after.'

'To blame?' repeated Mrs Pask. 'For what has happened?' – dreamier still.

Mr Calderon's mouth opened.

But Mrs Pask got up.

'I do not know, Timothy,' she said, 'what you are referring to.'

And looked right at him, as though he had been clothed in one of his two flannel suits, gun-metal tones, or the blue serge, from Anthony Hordern's.

'I am going to warm up the Cornish pasty,' she announced. 'You must excuse me,' she said, 'if dinner is skimpy. I am feeling off colour. Oh, there will be the bottled plums, of course, for anyone who has the appetite.'

If his sister had not been a good woman, he might have doubted her morality. As it was, he accepted the state of affairs, and counted his money, which had fallen on the floor.

They continued to live together. Mr Calderon was even

humbler than before, lighting a candle, offering a text, holding a chalice at eye level. It might have been pitiful, if anyone had ever noticed, how his faith flickered on its bed of ashes in the painful process of rekindling. There was so much to accomplish in such a short time. He was suffering, his eyes suggested, from something secret and internal, as he placed the wafer, shielded the chalice, and wiped the rim with the linen napkin so beautifully laundered by his sister.

Mrs Pask was leading a seemingly tranquil life.

Only once, she had remarked, over her devilled toast, at tea:

'I often wonder what that boy intended to convey through those horrible, horrible obscenities he painted on his birthday with poor Arthur's oils.'

But quickly mastered her wind, while her brother composed a little mound out of some grains of scattered salt.

Mrs Pask no longer took her easel to dash off a sunset or a gum-tree. She had thrown herself into works, and was respected by almost every member of the Mothers' Union and the Ladies' Guild.

After travelling several weeks, Alf Dubbo reached the town of Mungindribble. Privation and the fear of capture had made him thinner. But he grew confident by degrees. As the weeks passed, time and his last memories of Mr Calderon and Mrs Pask persuaded him that he would be better lost to them. Still, he tended to avoid towns, and to rely on farmers' sentimental wives for crusts. True to his policy, he skirted round Mungindribble. If he had entered it, he might have been shocked to find himself back at Numburra. Except that there were two additional banks. There was more money at Mungindribble.

And its streets were hotter, dustier, its river drier. Wandering along the bank of the river, which on the outskirts of most towns is the life-stream of all outcasts, goats, and aboriginals, Alf could not help feel moved as he remembered the generous waters of Numburra, and the clumps of orange bamboos in which the gins waited at dusk. But at Mungindribble he did come at last to the rubbish dump, filled with objects of use and wonder, including the insides of an old clock, which he thought he might like to keep. He picked about there for a bit. Until he noticed on the edge of the scrub a humpy made of tin, bark, bag, and anything else available, with a woman standing in the doorway, holding up the fringe of a curtain made from a fancier kind of hessian.

The woman appeared to be beckoning.

When he got closer, he called: 'Waddaya want?'

'You!' she answered. 'A woman could blow 'er head off yellin' at some silly-lookin' buggers. Come on over, and 'ave a yarn.'

He went, although his instinct warned him.

'It's only sociable,' she said, when he arrived still in doubt. 'You get lonely shut up in the home. I'm in the empty-bottle business,' she explained. 'I ride around most days in the sulky, all around the town, and pick up bottles, and other things besides, and yarn to people, but the pony's gone and staked 'isself. God knows 'ow long I'm gunna be mucked up.'

The woman must have been white once, but the sun and her pursuits had cured her, until she now presented the colour and texture of mature bacon. She was thin enough, but might have plumped out with teeth. Inside the cotton dress, her breasts suggested small, but active animals. Trying to jump at you, it appeared at times. She had those old, blue eyes which bring back cold, windy days, and not even a crow in the sky. That was not to say she did not see a great deal; she would have identified what was stowed away under the seat of a stranger's sulky, even if the object had been wrapped in several bags.

'Where you from?' she asked Alf.

He named a town of which he had heard, in a far corner of the state.

'You a quarter-caste?' she asked.

'No,' he said. 'Half. I think.'

'You could get into trouble,' she said, almost eagerly.

Then she asked him his age, and about his mum. She showed him that expression which some women put on at mention of a mother. She showed him her rather watery gums.

'You're a big boy,' she said. 'For your age.'

She told him her name was Mrs Spice, but that he might call her Hazel if he liked.

He did not like. At all times during their short association, a kind of fastidiousness prevented him using her first name, though there was much else that he accepted.

An association, he now realized with some horror, was forming on the edge of the rubbish dump between himself and Mrs Spice. Of course he could always run away, but had to be released by some mechanism which circumstance must first set off. The agitation he experienced at such an uncertain prospect transferred itself through his fingers to the old clock he was carrying, which started a gentle tinkling and jingling of shaken metal.

335

'What's that you got?' asked Mrs Spice, only to make conversation like, because of course she saw.

'A clock,' he said. 'Or bits of it.'

'Golly!' She laughed. 'That won't do no one any good. You can't eat the guts of a bloody clock.'

Again he realized that fate was in action. The locked mechanism of his will was allowing Mrs Spice to lead him through the hole of her humpy into a darkness in which she lived. He was at least comforted by the jingling of his little clock.

'A bite to eat is what a growin' boy like you needs before anything else,' the lady said.

And unwrapped something. It was cold, fatty, and tasted rancid. But he ate it, together with some ant-infested bread, because he was hungry, and because it saved him from the possibility of having to do anything else, particularly talk.

Mrs Spice, he soon gathered, was one of those people who do not eat. She rolled herself a cigarette, and poured out a draught into a mug, which made her suck her lips in, right back over the gums, and then blow them out again. The contents of the mug were that strong she was almost sucked into it.

How long Alf Dubbo remained camped with Mrs Spice he often wondered. She fed him as much as she thought necessary. He helped her water the pony, and sort the bottles. But would not join her on her sulky-rides around the town. He was happiest when he could escape and moon around the rubbish-dump, where, it seemed, the inhabitants of Mungindribble had shed their true selves, and he was always making discoveries which corroborated certain suspicions he already had of men. Sometimes he would lie on an old mattress, where its overflow of springs and stuffing allowed, and dream the paintings which circumstances prevented him temporarily from doing. He was painting all the time. Except in paint, of course. In these new pictures which his mind created, the bodies of men were of old springs and rubber, equally, with the hair bursting out of them, and sometimes a rusty rabbit-trap for jaws. He would paint the souls inside the bodies, because Mr Calderon had told him all about the souls. Often he would paint them in the shape of unopened tins – of soup, or asparagus, or some such – but pretty battered, and the contents all fermented, waiting to burst out in answer to a nail. He would snooze and compose. The old, broken-down clock, with the altar lights jingling and tinkling inside it, was very reminiscent of his former guardian. Motion still eluded him, though; he could apprehend it, but knew that he would not have been able to convey it. And sometimes the souls, which were the most interesting and obsessive part of his paintings, should have leapt up in the bodies, like the wind of metho, or the delirious throb and dribble of love.

For, soon after his arrival, Mrs Spice had introduced him to the rest of his duties.

She had uncorked the bottle one night, and said:

'I am running short, Alf' – she always was – 'but will give you a drop to pick you up, and show I am a good sport. You are a big boy now, you know. You are thin. But that don't matter.'

He did not know that he wanted the drink, but took it because it might lead him on to fresh discovery. He made her laugh. Himself, too, eventually. It was like the time, he remembered, when Mrs Pask had tinkered with the switch. It was as if he had drunk down a real electric shock; it just about shot him back against the wall.

He stayed shaky for a little. He felt his skin had gone blue. But Mrs Spice did not seem to notice. She would have mentioned it if, all of a sudden, she had seen him turn blue, because she mentioned almost everything.

'That will grow the hair on yers!' She laughed, that was all, rousing herself so that her tits jumped, and the hurricane lamp.

Then she got serious, and, after pouring them another, reaching over with her leathery, but quite smooth and nice arm, would have liked to talk about things.

'Sometimes I wonder what you think about, Alf,' she said. 'What is inside of you? Everyone has somethink in them, I suppose.'

Then she blinked, because she had made a serious contribution, like as if she was in the habit of reading books.

Alf could not tell her. Because he could not have simply said: Everything is inside of me, waiting for me to understand it. Mrs Spice would not have understood. Any more than he did, altogether, except in flickers. So he had another drink out of the mug. One day he would paint the Fiery Furnace, with the figures walking in it. He could see them quite distinct now.

All the time Mrs Spice was trying to impress. He saw at first faintly, then with cruel bursts of understanding. Her words and gestures were those of some other woman, who already existed in her imagination, and who would at last, with the co-operation of her audience and the bottle, perhaps even exist in fact.

'You gotta realize I was not always like this,' she was saying, holding together her straight and loose hair, with both hands, at the nape of her neck.

Although she succeeded surprisingly in her aim – there she was, a young woman in a cleaner cotton dress, smoother, smelling of laundry above the strong armpits – he knew the act to be dishonest. Had he not on one occasion promised Mrs Pask to paint the picture of Jesus Christ because he wanted something awful bad? And had known himself to be incapable.

At least Mrs Spice was capable of fulfilling promises.

'Nobody never accused me of sittin' on it,' she said. 'Mean is what I am not.'

'You don't wanta be afraid,' she added, when she had crawled over to his side of the shack.

He was not afraid, only surprised at the powers which had been given him.

'And remember,' she shouted, 'I am not some bloody black gin! I am NOT. . . .'

She shut up then, as they became possessed of the same daemon.

During the night she was alternately limp and quarrelsome, until he at last shrank back into the body of a thin and sulky boy.

'Go on!' he called out finally. 'Get to hell!'

He might have rolled himself into a ball, in self-protection, but he was pretty sure she would have picked it open.

So he began to hit the old bag.

'I'll fetch the johns in the mornin'!' she shrieked. 'Layin' into a white woman!'

When she fell asleep. He could hear the breath whistling out of her slack mouth.

Towards dawn, Alf Dubbo crawled out of Mrs Spice's hut. He was wearing his skin, which was all she had left him, but it felt good. It was the pearly hour. Damp blankets fell in folds upon his bare shoulders. He wandered a little way along the bank of the almost dry river. Dim trees disputed with him for possession of the silence, as twig or drop fell, and his hard feet scuffed up the dead leaves. The formlessness of the scene united with the aimlessness of his movements in achieving a kind of negative perfection.

But he could not leave well alone. He had to start mucking around with the smooth bark of one tree and then another, with a nail he had picked up in leaving the camp. The faint line of his longing began to flow out of him and over the white bark of the trees. He drew languorously sometimes, sometimes almost inflicting wounds. And would move on to express some fresh idea. And never finished, and would never, so hopeless and interminable were the circumstances in which, continually, he found himself fixed.

After a bit he began to go back in the direction of the camp. There was nothing else he could do for the moment. Colour was returning to the sky. Out in the open the light was sharpening its edge on tins.

Mrs Spice appeared, giggly and abusive, after rising ladylike and late.

'You're a fair trimmer!' she repeated several times, and tittered. 'But don't think you're goin' to rule the roost,' she hastened to add, 'just because I was good to yers once. Generosity has its limits.'

After which she drew in her chin.

But she could not keep it there for long.

She had acquired a numerous clientele, through her dealings in bottles, as well as by bush telegraph. It was not uncommon for shearers in town on a spree to look up Hazel, or for a drover on the road to hitch his sulky to her tree. Gentlemen would drive out from town, or even walk late at night, arriving with a clink of bottles and a salvo of ribaldry. It must be said she seldom disappointed. Or if she did, it was usually some timid soul who had suddenly thought better of it. And for such there were always the alternatives of conversation and song. Mrs Spice herself was musical, and when squeezed in a certain way, would let out a thin soprano in imitation of an oriental bagpipe. There were nights when the moon reverberated with entertainments at the rubbish dump.

Alf Dubbo preferred to keep out of all that, suspecting how he would be treated – like an idiot, or a black – but sometimes could not avoid being caught, early and innocently asleep, in Mrs Spice's shack.

On one such occasion a shearer from Cowra, particularly leery, and beery, and proud of his easy conquest of a lady, noticed something in the corner, and remarked:

'What-o, Hazel! Takin' a swig at the blackjack on the side?'

But Mrs Spice, when stood up, could demonstrate that coarseness was never the master of delicacy.

'That,' she replied, 'I would have you know, Mr Er, is a young boy apprenticed to the bottle trade.'

In between casual custom and the normal business round, she forgot she had warned the abo not to expect anything further of a lady's generosity, and would become fretfully solicitous. Sometimes he laughed in her face, sometimes he beat her with a little switch, but at others they rode together on the tiger, until that slashed and fiery beast turned into an empty skin.

At last, apathy and some foreboding descended on Alf Dubbo. He would look at himself, puzzled and frightened. He was feeling off, the distance through the doorway glittering with tins and emptiness.

' 'Ere,' she asked, 'what's got inter youse?'

'I feel crook,' he said, and turned.

Then she would swear, and shake the bags on which she slept.

She grew more cantankerous.

'You are not worth your damper,' she said once. 'Layin' around!'

And spat.

A couple of days later she came up to him in the sun. He could see that her thoughts were already spilling out of her. She said:

'You *are* crook! And waddaya done ter me? Eh? A fine present ter give!'

He realized how they hated each other.

'You old rubbish dump!' he cried. 'Who's to know who dropped it on yer? What with drovers, and shearers, and everybody!'

She was cursing, and shaking.

'Those are the last words you say in my place!' she shouted.

'Okay,' he said. 'Okay, Mrs Spice.'

He took his shoes, and went, although it was already four o'clock in the afternoon. He slept under a tree that night, and woke early, to re-examine the mark of his sickness the first moment possible. Then he sat, during the brief space when the sun deceives with gold. And continued sitting as the world stretched before him in its actual colours, of grey-brown.

Alf Dubbo now went bush, figuratively at least, and as far as other human beings were concerned. Never communicative, he retired into the scrub of half-thoughts, amongst the cruel rocks of obsession. Later he learned to prefer the city, that most savage and impenetrable terrain, for the opportunities it gave him of confusing anyone who might attempt to track him down in his personal hinterland. But for the time being, he hung around country towns, and stations, working for a wage, or earning his keep, sometimes even living on a charitable person for a week or two. He never cared to stay anywhere long. There was always the possibility that he might be collected for some crime he began to suspect he had committed, or confined to a reserve, or shut up at a mission, to satisfy the social conscience, or to ensure the salvation of souls that were in the running for it.

He avoided his own people, whatever the degree of colour, because of a certain delicacy with cutlery, acquired from the parson's sister, together with a general niceness or squeamishness of behaviour, which he could sink recklessly enough when forced, as he had throughout the reign of Mrs Spice, but which haunted him in its absence like some indefinable misery.

There was also, of course, his secret gift. Like his disease, he would no more have confessed that to a black than he would have to a white. They were the two poles, the negative and positive of his being: the furtive, destroying sickness, and the almost as furtive, but regenerating, creative act.

As soon as he had saved a few pounds, Dubbo had gone about buying paints through the medium of a store catalogue. They were crude, primary things to amuse children. But they made him tremble. And were quickly used. Then he took to breaking into the tins of paint he discovered in station storerooms, and would slap at any obscure wall until he had exhausted his desire. He would spend Sundays in the shade of an iron water-tank, drawing and tearing off, and drawing, until he had a whole heap of hieroglyphs which perhaps only he could interpret. Not that it would have occurred to him to attempt communication with another. But his forms were crystallizing. While his organism was subjected to the logic of disease, an increased recklessness of mind helped him to take short cuts to solving some of the problems. Many others remained, though as he wandered deeper into himself, or watched the extraordinary behaviour of human beings on the periphery of his own existence, he was often hopeful of arriving eventually at understanding.

Everything he did, any fruit of his own meaningful relationship with life, he would lock up in a tin box, which grew dented and scratched as it travelled with him from job to job, or lay black and secret underneath his bed, while he played the part of factory hand or station rouseabout.

Nobody would have thought of opening that box. Most people respected the moroseness of its owner, and a few were even scared of Dubbo.

He grew up tall, thin, and rather knobbly. He had already matured by the time he developed the courage and curiosity to make for Sydney. Arriving there, he left the tin box in a railways parcels office, and slept in parks at first, until he discovered a house sufficiently dilapidated, a landlady sufficiently low, and hopeful, and predatory, to accept an abo. He settled at last, although two of his fellow lodgers, a couple of prostitutes, objected eloquently to such an arrangement. But only in the beginning. It soon became obvious that the abo was going to disappoint, by his decency, his silence, by his almost non-existence. The landlady, who had been deserted the year previous by a lover, gave up knocking at his door, and shuffled off into the wastes of linoleum, to nurse her grievance and a climacteric.

During those years it was easy to stay in work. However distasteful, Dubbo managed to adapt himself to that monotonous practice for longer stretches by sealing his mind off, and by regarding those dead hours as a period of mental fallow for the cropping of his art. But he longed to close the door of his room, which he had made neat enough to please a parson's sister, and to take from his double-locked box the superior oils he could now afford to buy.

There were also the grey days, and the streaming, patent-leather evenings, which turned his skin a dubious yellow, his mind to a shambles of self-examination and longing. Often he would take refuge by slipping into the Public Library, to look at books. But reading did not come easily; an abstraction of ideas expressed less than the abstraction of forms and the synthesis of colours. There were the art books, of course. Through which he looked with a mixture of disbelief and criticism. On the whole he had little desire to learn from the achievement of other artists, just as he had no wish to profit by or collaborate in the experience of other men. As if his still incomplete vision would complete itself in time, through revelation. But once he came across the painting by a Frenchman of the Apollonian chariot on its trajectory across the sky. And he sat forward, easing his brown raincoat, his yellow fingers steadying themselves on the slippery page. He realized how differently he saw this painting since his first acquaintance with it, and how he would now transcribe the Frenchman's limited composition into his own terms of motion, and forms partly transcendental, partly evolved from his struggle with daily becoming, and experience of suffering.

In the great library, the radiators would be pouring out the consoling soup of warmth. All the readers had found what they had been looking for, the black man noticed with envy. But he was not altogether surprised; words had always been the natural weapons of whites. Only he was defenceless. Only he would be looking around. After reading, and yawning, and skipping, and running his thumb down a handful of pages to hear them rise like a flock of birds, he would arrange the books in an all too solid pile, and stare. On days when he was master of himself, his sense of wonder rewarded him. But in a winter light, if he had not been nourished by his secrets, if he had not enjoyed the actual, physical pleasures of paint, he might have lain down and died, there amongst the varnish and the gratings, instead of resting his head sideways on the table, and falling asleep on the pillow of his hands. Then the sweat would glitter on the one exposed cheekbone, and amongst the stubble at the nape of his neck.

On one such occasion he sat up rather suddenly, yawned, tested a sore throat by swallowing carefully once or twice, and picked up a volume which someone else had abandoned along the table. He was reading again, he found, the sad story of Our Lord Jesus Christ. He could remember many of the incidents, and how he had hoped to love and reverence the individuals involved, at least enough to please his guardians. He read, but the expression of the eyes still eluded him. All was pale, pale, washed in love and charity, but pale. He opened the Gospel of the Beloved Disciple. Then his throat did hurt fearfully. It burned. The bubbles of saliva were choking him.

He got up, and went away, his badly-fitting raincoat, of an ugly and conflicting brown, floating and trailing. He walked a considerable distance that night, with long, sliding steps, and lay down under a sandstone ledge, under some wet lantana bushes, with a woman who told him how she had been done out of a quarter-share in a winning lottery ticket.

The couple proceeded to make love, or rather, they vented on each other their misery and rage. The woman had with her a bag of prawns, of which she was smelling, as well as of something slow and sweet, probably gin. She attempted repeatedly to fasten on him her ambitious sea-anemone of a mouth, and he was as determined to avoid being swallowed down. Consequently, he could have killed that poor, drunken whore. She was a little bit surprised at some of it. As he held her by the thighs, he could have been furiously ramming a wheelbarrow against the darkness. But her misfortunes were alleviated, for the time being, and until she discovered they had been increased. Even after her lover had left her, in the same rage which she had chosen to interpret as passion, she continued to call to him, in between doing up her dress and searching for her prawns.

343

As for Dubbo, he slithered down the slope through the smell of cat which lantana will give out when disturbed after rain. Since his guardians had taught him to entertain a conscience, he would often suffer from guilt with some part of him, particularly on those occasions when his diseased body took control, in spite of the reproaches of his pastor-mind. Now he might have felt better if he had been able to roll his clothes into a ball, and shove them under a bush. But it was no longer possible, of course, to abandon things so easily. And he had to walk on, tormented by the intolerable clothes, and the lingering sensation of the whore's trustful thighs.

In the white hours, he came to the house where he lived, and let himself shivering and groping into the room which was his only certain refuge. When he had switched the light on, the validity of certain forms, which he had begun to work out on a sheet of plywood, made his return a more overwhelming relief, even though his deviation had to appear more terrible. Shambling and fluctuating in the glass, he lay down at last on the bed, and, where other men might have prayed for grace, he proceeded to stare at what could be his only proof of an Absolute, at the same time, in its soaring blues and commentary of blacks, his act of faith.

Dubbo was sufficiently sustained both physically and mentally by his vocation to ignore for the most part what people called life. Only the unhappiness of almost complete isolation from other human beings would flicker up in him at times, and he would hurry away from his job – at that period he was working in a Sydney suburb, in a factory which manufactured cardboard boxes and cartons in oiled paper – he would hurry, hurry, for what, but to roam the streets, and settle down eventually on a straight-backed bench in one of the parks.

There he would indulge in what was commonly called *putting in time*, though it was, in fact, nothing else but *hoping*.

One evening as he was sitting on such a bench in such a park, and the big fig-trees were casting their most substantial shadows on the white grass, a woman came and sat beside him. With no intentions, however. She looked deliberately in her handbag for a cigarette. And lit one. With her own match. Then she blew a trumpet of smoke, and watched the water of the tranquil little bay.

If they had not re-crossed their legs at exactly the same moment, they might never have spoken.

As it was, the woman had to smile. She said :

'Two minds of the same opinion. Eh?'

He did not know what to answer, and looked away. But the attitude of his shoulders must have been a receptive one.

'How do you find it down here?' the woman asked.

Again he was perturbed, but just managed to reply.

'All right.'

Knotting his hands to protect himself.

'I came from up the country,' the woman persisted, and named a north-western town.

'Many of you boys down in the city?' she asked.

She was kind, and polite, but bored by now. She frowned for a shred of tobacco that she could taste as it drifted loose in her mouth.

'No,' he said. Or: 'I dunno.'

He did not like this.

She was looking idly at the colour of his hands.

'What is that you've got?' she asked.

'What?'

'That is an ulcer,' she said. 'On the back of your hand.'

'It is nothing,' he said.

It was a sore which had broken out several weeks before, and which he carried for the most part turned away from strangers, as he waited for it to disappear.

'Are you sick?' she asked.

He did not answer, and was preparing to go away from the seat, from the park, with its dusty grass and little basin of passive water.

'You can tell me,' she said. 'I should know.'

It was very strange. Now he took a look at the strange woman, with her rather full, marshmallowy face, and her lips that she had painted up to shine. She smelled of the powder with which the white women covered their bodies in an effort to soften the impact of their presence.

The woman sighed, and began to tell her life, which he listened to, as though it had been a spoken book.

'You are sick,' she sighed. 'I know. Because I had it. You got a dose of the syph. When I was young and foolish, a handsome young bastard of a Digger put it across me with a hard-luck story. God, I can see 'im! With the strap of his hat hangin' on to 'is lower lip. I can smell the smell the khaki used to have then. Well, that chapter was short, but the consequences was long.'

The woman was a prostitute, it began to emerge, successful, and fairly satisfied in her profession.

She told him that her name was Hannah.

'Of course,' she said, 'I had luck too. I got my own home. An old cove who used to come to me regular left me a couple of semi-detached homes. I let one, live in the other. Oh, I am comfortable!' she said, but aggressively. 'We all laughed when some solicitor wrote about Charlie's will. But it was a *good* joke, as it turned out. No one thought Charlie had the stuff to put away. He was a rag-dealer.'

This story made her audience glad. He loved to listen to the tales in which the action was finished. They had the sad, pale, rather pretty, but unconvincing colours of Mrs Pask's sacred prints.

'Of course,' said Hannah, 'although I am comfortable, I am not all that. That is why I have never retired from business. You never know.'

She threw away her cigarette, and frowned, so that he noticed how the white powder lay in the cracks between her brows.

'Many young fellers would not notice me now,' she said. 'I know that.' Suddenly she screwed up her mouth excruciatingly. 'You would not notice me,' she fired.

He looked down, because he did not know what to answer. He only knew that he would not have noticed Hannah.

'Go on!' She laughed. 'I was not trying you out. Or rather, I was. I have a proposition to make. And did not want you to think I was offering you the job of a ponce. Oh, I am in no need of men. I have my friend, too. No,' she said, sinking her chin. 'Sometimes I will take an interest in a person. And you are sort of down on it. See? Well, I have a small room at the back. Lying idle. What do you say, Jack, to dossing down in my small room? Eh? Of course I won't say you needn't pay me a little something for the privilege.'

He was very, very silent, wondering whether it could be a trap.

'It was only an idea,' she said, looking over a couple of passers-by. 'I never influenced even the cat. Funny, I was to have been a teacher. Can you see me with a mob of kids in a shed beside the road? But do you know what,' she said, turning to him, 'I was frightened at the whole thing. I took up with men instead. Men are stupider.'

The blackfellow laughed.

'I am a man,' he said.

'You are something else as well.' She pondered something she had not yet solved, but could not begin to speak again too quickly. 'I could help you, too.' Pointing at his hand. 'There is a doc I know a little.' She mentioned a certain hospital. 'You are not frightened, are you, Jack?'

Then he knew that he was, and that this floury woman in her dress of lace doilies was leading him poignantly into a dining-room from which the kindness had not yet fled.

'Anyways,' said Hannah, 'if you decide, I would let you have that small room for ten bob.' She had begun suddenly to enunciate very clearly, as some people did for blacks, but dropped her voice a little to give the address at which she lived.

It was getting dark by then. People with tidy lives were setting tables, or leaning bare arms on window-sills. The lights were lit.

'Well,' said Hannah, and began to arrange herself, 'business is business, isn't it? It is a queer thing, but I never liked men one little bit. Only you had to do something, and they told me I was pretty good at it.'

She could not comb too hard.

'Oh,' she said, 'I don't say I don't like a yarn with some man, on a tram, about what he has been doing. I don't mind that. Poor buggers! They are so uninteresting.'

Soon Hannah, who had snapped her handbag on her comb, and dusted off her dandruff, was ready for the streets.

'Then, I might see you,' she said.

But he could tell that something had made her no longer really care. He was the one that did. He had twisted his body right round till his bones were painful on the hard seat.

'At Abercrombie Crescent,' he was saying, in a stupid-sounding, muddy-coloured voice, and repeating other directions she had given.

'Yes,' she called, farther now, throwing the words over her shoulder. 'It is a street, though. No one knows how Abercrombie got stuck with a crescent.' Her voice fell away from her as she went. 'And not before twelve. I'd take the axe to anybody. I am not fit.'

Hannah walked towards the road, inclining somewhat as she went. The night was darkening and purpling across the park, and soon she was sucked up by it.

Alf Dubbo went to live at 27 Abercrombie Crescent, in the small room which Hannah had offered. He did not take long to decide; he was too relieved. He had locked his box, tied a cord round one or two things he had been working on, and gone.

He was happy in the back room, which was stuffed with many objects of doubtful virtue: a spare mattress full of kapok

lumps, a rusted, burnerless kero stove, a dressmaker's dummy,
boxes of feathers, and a scattering of rat pellets. Outside, the
wires of aerials were slackly strung above the slate roofs. He
was fascinated by the wires, and began the first day to paint
them, as they intercepted the sounds of feathers and his own
tentative thanksgiving.

But he kept the door locked.

Some time after the light had gone, Hannah came and rattled
the knob. She announced:

'My friend has come, Alf. I will have to introduce you.'

Dubbo went out to them. Hannah was nervous, but obviously
proud.

'I want you to know Alf Dubbo,' she said. 'Mr Norman
Fussell.'

Doing with her hand as she had seen done.

Normal Fussell had been arranging his waves in front of the
glass.

'Norman,' Hannah explained, 'is a male nurse. He is off duty
for a while, and that is how he is able to be here.'

'Pleased to know you, Alf,' said Mr Norman Fussell.

He was very brisk for one so round and soft. He began
to prepare himself a meal of beans on toast, which was the
kind of thing he liked, and which he ate, holding his head
on one side, half out of delicacy, half because of a difficult
denture.

Hannah was solicitous.

'How is the Sister, Norm?' she asked, but dreaded.

'Bloody,' said Norman Fussell through his beans.

When he had finished, he informed:

'Nurse is feeling better now.'

And sat and smiled, arranging his canary-coloured waves,
and smoking a cigarette which he had taken from a pretty little
box.

Hannah got Alf Dubbo aside.

'They will tell you,' she said, 'that Norman is a pufter. Well,
I am too tired to argue about what anybody is. I am sick of
men acting like they never was. Norm could not impress a
woman even if he tried. And that is what is restful.'

Hannah would attempt not to let business interfere with
Norman Fussell's off-duty, but if it did, he would doss down
with a blanket on the lounge. Though he might also sometimes
go in search of trade. Sunday was religiously kept for Norm,
if he happened to be free. Sunday was bliss, such as is possible.
They would lie in bed overlapping each other, and read the

348

murders and divorces, and consult the stars. Or would slip out to the kitchen to fetch the red tea and snacks they loved: bread spread thickly with condensed milk, or tomato sauce, or squashed banana. Or would snooze and melt together. Dubbo painted them later on, as they appeared to him through the doorway. He painted them in one big egg of flesh, forehead to forehead, knee to knee, compressed into the same dream. It was not his most ambitious painting. But an egg is something; even a sterile one is formally complete.

On going to live at Abercrombie Crescent, Dubbo began to receive treatment as an out-patient at the neighbouring hospital of St Paul's, either from the young doctor known to Hannah, or from one or other of his colleagues. For a long time the patient could hardly tell them apart. Their white coats and aseptic minds made them about as dissimilar as a row of the white urine bottles. As he had anticipated, the blackfellow was frightened at the touch of hands, but realized in time that he was just a case. He even grew bored and irritated by what was being done to him. It was necessary to endure the manufacture of cardboard boxes, but while he waited at the hospital of an evening, he could see the light was failing. He would be straining to prevent it. There were days when he did not take up a brush.

Eventually he was told he had been cured of his venereal condition. He had almost forgotten what it was they were treating him for; it was so much more important to find a way out of other dilemmas. Disease, like his body, was something he had ended by taking for granted. His mind was another matter, because even he could not calculate how it might behave, or what it might become, once it was set free. In the meantime, it would keep jumping and struggling, like a fish left behind in a pool – or two fish, since the white people his guardians had dropped another in.

While he continued painting, and attempting to learn how to think, Dubbo discovered that a war had broken out. So they told him, and he did slowly take it in. Wars do not make all that difference to those who have always been at war, and this one would not greatly have affected the abo's life, if it had not been for the altered behaviour of the people who surrounded him. Certainly, after he had been examined medically, and pronounced unfit, he had been drafted from the stapling of cardboard boxes to the spray-painting of aeroplanes, but that was part of his rather unconvincing, to himself always incredible, communal existence. But there were the people in the house, the people in the street, who now forced their way deeper into his mind. His brush would quiver with their jarring emotions, the forms were disintegrating that he had struggled so painfully and honestly to evolve.

Now he began to dawdle at night in the streets, where there were more people than ever before investigating the lie of the land. Since the men had gone out to kill, a great many of those who had been left were engaged in far more deadly warfare with their own secret beings. Their unprotected, two-headed souls would look out at the abo, who was no longer so very different from themselves, but still different enough not to matter. Mouths, glittering with paint, would open up in the night like self-inflicted wounds. That, of course, was already familiar, and in another light he would have accepted it along with what he sensed to be other tribal customs. Now it was the eyes that disturbed most, of the white people who had always known the answers, until they discovered those were wrong. So they would burst out laughing, or break into little snatches of tinny song. Some of them danced, with open arms, or catching at a stranger. Others fell down, and lay where they were. Or they would lie together on the trampled grass in the attitudes of love. They would try everything sooner or later, but it was obvious they were disappointed to find they had not succeeded in killing the enemy in themselves, and perhaps there would not be time.

Dubbo's workmates were in the habit of allowing him a swig or two, because, when they had got him drunk, he gave them a good laugh. Occasionally he would persuade somebody of an accommodating nature to buy him an illicit bottle. Then he would rediscover the delirious fireworks, as well as the dull hell of disintegration, which he had experienced first in Mrs Spice's shack. Except that by now, an opalescence of contentment would often follow nausea; a heap of his own steaming vomit could yield its treasure. He appeared to succeed, in fact, where the others in the wartime streets failed.

Once, after a bout of drinking, he fell down and lay on the lino inside the front door at Abercrombie Crescent. Hannah, who came in late and unsuccessful, just about broke her neck. After she had switched on the light, and kicked the body again for value, she felt the need to holler:

'Waddaya expect? From a drunken bastard of a useless black?'

But he did not hear that.

Next evening when he got in, she called him, and said:

350

'Look here, love, some john with a sense of his own importance who finds a piebald lurching around, or even *laying* in the street, is going to collect *you*, and plenty more said about it.'

Hannah, without her make-up, was cold, pale, and grave. She was too intent, she let it be understood, on the matter in hand, to bother all that about her lodger's fate. Her naked nails blenched on the little pair of tweezers with which she was pulling the hairs out of her eyebrows.

'Of course,' she said, and pulled, 'it's nothing,' she said, 'to do with me. Every man's business is his *own*. See?'

All the while pulling. She would pull, and squint, and drop the hairs out of the window as if she was doing nothing of the sort.

Alf Dubbo listened, but was more fascinated by what he saw. She had not yet made her bed, and the sheets were the colour of Hannah's natural skin – grey, at least in that light. Hannah herself was the colour of oysters, except for the parting of her breasts, where water could have been dripping, like in an old bath, or kitchen sink.

'By the way,' she mentioned, 'that room of yours is going up to twelve bob. There is a war on now.'

But he remained fascinated by what he saw: Hannah's hand trembling as she worked the tweezers.

'Okay, Hannah,' he agreed, and smiled for other things.

'Don't think I am trying to shake you off, Alf,' she had to explain. 'I need those two bob.'

She was smoothing and peering at her eyebrow, to make it as glossy as it might have been.

'Any tart,' she said, 'even the plush ones, is a fool not to take precautions.'

As she tried rubbing at her eyebrow with spit.

So Hannah, too, he saw, was afraid of what might happen, and most of all in mirrors.

One day when she was running the feather duster over the more obvious surfaces of the lounge-room, she opened one of the compartments of her mind. She left off in the middle of *The Harbour Lights*, to say, or recite, rather:

'Those old women, Alf, the ones with the straight, grey, greasy hair hangin' down to their shoulders, like girls. The old girls. With a couple of yeller teeth, but the rest all watery gums. You can see them with an old blue dog, and sometimes a parcel. Pushin' their bellies ahead of 'em. Gee, that is what frightens me! And the snaky veins crawlin' up their legs!'

But he could not help her, although he saw she was waiting for some sort of easy sign.

He was sitting on the good end of the lounge, the points of his elbows fitted into the shallow grooves of his knee-caps, the slats of his fingers barely open on his cheek-bones. In that position, but for the supporting lounge, he might have been squatted beside a fire.

Fire did protect, of course. Indeed, in deserted places it was not desirable to move at night without it. Alf Dubbo was fortunate in that he had his fire, and would close his eyes, and let it play across his mind in those unearthly colours which he loved to reproduce. But which did not satisfy him yet. Not altogether. His eyes would flash with exasperation. He could not master the innermost, incandescent eye of the feathers of fire.

As he remained seated, and dreaming, and wordless on the lounge, on that occasion when she had been foolish enough to ask for guidance, Hannah was compelled to shout:

'You are no bloody good! Any of yez! That silly sod of a Norm, we know. Not that I don't take 'im for what he is worth. God knows, there is plenty of women without a friend, let alone a human hot-water bottle. But you, Alf, you got something shut up inside of you, and you bloody well won't give another person a look.'

She began laying about her with the duster with such violence that the back fell off a book, which he had never more than noticed, in spite of the fact that it was the only one; it was too old, and black, and dusty, stuck in behind some ornaments which clients had presented to the owner in moments of drink or affluence. He stooped and picked up the brittle strip of leather, which lay in his fingers curled and superfluous as a shred of fallen bark. The rather large gold lettering of a title was still legible, though.

Then he said, quite keen, in that good accent he had learnt somewhere, and would put on at times:

'I would like you to lend me this book, Hannah. Where did it come from?'

'That! Oh, that belonged to Charlie. My old rag-picker that I told you of. My one and only stroke of luck. Yes, you can have a loan of it. I like a good read of some book. But not that!'

The house, squeezed in as it was between two others, had already grown too dark. Dubbo took the book, and went at once to his own room, where light, reduced to its essence, green-white and astonishing, would trickle a little longer, from over the slate roofs, down from the slate-coloured sky, of which they were an extension.

He opened the book beside the window. At that hour even the veiled panes seemed to grow translucent as crystal. So, while the true light remained to him, he continued to read, in such desperate and disorderly haste that he introduced here and there words and phrases, whole images of his own. His secret self was singing at last in great bursts:

'Praise ye Him, sun and moon: praise Him all ye stars of light.
Praise Him, ye heavens of heavens, and ye waters that be above the heavens;
And wires of aerials, and grey, slippery slates, praise, praise the Lord.
Mountains and all hills: fruitful trees, and all cedars: and the grey ghosts of other trees: and soles of the feet on wet leaves: and the dry rivers, praise the name of the Lord. The orange bamboos praise Him with their creaking.
Beasts and all cattle: creeping things and flying fowl, praise, praise. Hands praise the God. . . .'

His own hands were trembling by now, for the light and his eyesight were nearly gone. So he threw himself, face down, on the bed. His upturned heels were quite wooden and lifeless, but in his innermost mind his hands continued to praise, with the colours of which he was capable. They issued like charmed snakes from the tips of his fingers: the crimsons, and the clear yellows, those corrosive greens, and the intolerable purple with which he might dare eventually to clothe the formless form of God.

So he lay and shivered for the audacity of his ambition. Until his body forced him up. Then he switched on the electric light, and did just notice the little dirty trumpet which his mouth must have printed on the pillow. Because it was ugly, he turned it over, so that he should not see the stain.

During the nights which followed Dubbo spent hours reading from the rag-collector's Bible. The voices of the Prophets intoxicated him as he had never been in life, and soon he was laying on the grave splendour of their words with the colours of his mind. At this period, too, he constructed the skeletons of several works which he did not have the strength or knowledge to paint. *The Chariot*, for instance. Ezekiel's vision superimposed upon that of the French painter in the art book, was not yet his own. All the details were assembled in the paper sky, but the light still had to pour in. And suddenly he furled the cartoon, and hid it. To forget about it, at least with the waking part of his mind.

The picture he did paint now was *The Fiery Furnace*, almost the whole of it one Friday – he had gone sick on purpose – then the agony of Saturday, in which he sat, touching the surface of paint once or twice, but not seeing how to solve, or not yet daring. And did at last, in several soft strokes, of such simplicity he was exhausted by them. And sweating. His thighs were as sticky as though he had spilled out over himself.

After that he cleaned his brushes very carefully and solemnly. He was happy.

He went out, past the kitchen. Norm had arrived, and he and Hannah were cutting dainty sandwiches, spreading them with anchovette, or squashed dates. They smiled at him, but guiltily, for the obvious secret they were sharing: there was going to be a party.

'Hi, Alf,' Norm murmured.

That was all.

Dubbo went as far as Oxford Street, where he knew a bar-maid whose friendship did not have principles attached. He could beckon from the street through the bottle door, and sometimes Beat would condescend to see.

Tonight Beat played, and he took his booze down the hill to a dead-end he sometimes frequented, where nobody ever came at night, unless to park a car, or nail a tart against the wall. There he sat on the kerb. He began to drink his neat grog. He went about it at first as though it had been a job he had learnt to do, very conscientious, and holding back some of the finer points of technique for difficult passages ahead. Then spasmodic. Glugging heavily into the bottle. He broke wind once or twice. His digestive tract had caught fire.

He sang a few lines of a song he had made up in similar circumstances:

> 'Hi digger, hi digger,
> My dad is bigger
> Than hiss-sself.
> My uncle is the brother
> Of my mother.
> But the other
> Is a bugger
> No-ho-bodee,
> And not my mother,
> Knows.'

By now the moon had entered even the back alleys, and was rinsing them of rubbish, so the black man stood up, and began to walk precariously along the solid stream. He loved the square-eyed houses, although they were blind to him. He was well-disposed towards the unpredictable traffic eyes. He touched a mudguard or two, and in one instance a flying bonnet. In the big street the dim fruit-shops were all bananas. An open box of dates reminded him that the flies must be collecting at home.

So he began to make for Hannah's place.

During the latter years of the war there was often something doing at Hannah's; the streets were that full, some of it could not help pouring in wherever a door opened. There was the Army, there was the Navy, but better the Navy because of the Yanks, and better than the Yanks, the dollar bills and nylons. Hannah herself was not so far gone she could not occasionally strike a lode deep in the heart of Idaho or Texas: some stoker who would pay real well for an opportunity to tell about his mom. Then Hannah would start swilling the booze around in her glass, and staring deep into it, until the time came to collect.

But there were the other nights at Abercrombie Crescent when Norm's mob came in. When she was in the right mood, Hannah not only did not mind, but encouraged, and took an intelligent interest in the private life of any perv. The whore would nearly pee herself watching a drag act in some of her own clothes. After the monotony and bruises of the flesh show, it could have been that she liked to sink down on the springs, and enjoy the antics of puppets – tricky, ingenious, virulent, lifelike, but strictly papiermâché.

Now as Alf Dubbo wove through the streets back to Hannah's, he guessed it would be queans' night, if only from the special and secret manner she and Norm had worn while spreading the anchovette and dates. The outlook moved him neither way. It was an aspect of life which did not surprise the abo since he had discovered early that almost all human behaviour is surprising; you must begin to worry only for the little that is not. So he went home, as equably as his condition allowed, and prepared for anything.

At Abercrombie Crescent all the inner doors stood open, except that of the room at the back. There were dark whispers in the hall. Somebody was powdering in clouds in front of Hannah's dressing-table, somebody was pulling on stockings. It sounded as though the lavatory cistern would never stop.

Dubbo found Hannah right at the heart of the festivities, seated on the lounge with her friend and colleague Reen, whose hair was waved that tight it would have disappeared altogether if its brillancy had allowed; Reen was one of the golden girls, but thin. In addition to the two whores, there was quite a bunch of queans, who knew, but did not know, Hannah's piebald. There was somebody, besides, whom Dubbo was still too confused to see, but sensed.

Hannah shouted, in what was intended as a social whisper, that Alf had arrived in time for Normie's act. When Norman Fussell did, indeed, make his entrance. He was wearing a bunch of feathers on his head, and a bunch of feathers on his arse, and a kind of diamond G-string wherever else. Otherwise Norm was fairly naked, except that he had painted on a pair of formal nipples, and was prinked and powdered in the right places. The bird began to perform what was intended as a ritual-dance, on Hannah's Wilton with the brown roses. Assisted by gin, and the soul of the original chorus girl, by which he was obviously possessed, Norm extemporized with hands, ruffed up the gorgeous feathers, scratched stiffly at an imaginary earth. Although his bird breathed like a rasp, it did not seem to matter; so do hens when chased around the yard in summer. Just as the chorus girl was smuggled into Norm at birth, her elderly but professional soul had now invaded the body of this pink bird, making it real by the conventions which those present recognized. Indeed, if it ever got around that a bird of paradise had been in conjunction with a brush turkey, Norm Fussell could have provided evidence.

All the queans were shrieking their approval, if it was not their scorn.

Dubbo was laughing loudest and widest. He had squatted down on Hannah's carpet. If there had been space, he, too, would have danced the figures he remembered from some forgotten time. Instead, he clapped his hands. He was so glad, watching Norm strut, and flap his wings of flesh to music, while the stench of bodies caused the small room to shrink still further round the form of the primordial bird.

'You are a proper pufter rorter, Hannah!' Reen had to remark, because she was a cow. 'If it wasn't for you, I wouldn't watch this, not if I was offered a good night's hay. It sends me goosey.'

Hannah, who had let herself be drawn to the mystical core of Norm's act, would have preferred not to interrupt her devotions, but did reply from behind an objective smile:

'What odds! Capon is just another kind of chook.'

At the same time, she realized the person who had come with Norm was present, and rewarded him with a deferential glance.

So that Dubbo also remembered the fellow wearing a good dark suit was seated in a corner, in what was Hannah's best chair. The youngish man could not leave off looking at the abo, not offensively, however, for half his face was shaded by a hand. And in that position he remained, voluntarily obliterated. The extraordinarily long hand, which held and protected the long white face, appeared to sever it from the body, and the richly decorous, dark suit.

After appropriate applause for Norman, and drinks for those to whom respect was due, the party proceeded. Dubbo had cadged a drink or two, and was feeling fine, electrically lit. Soon he would sing his song, and dance his dance. He stood swaying in drink and anticipation.

When Hannah's colleague Reen called:

'What can *you* do, Dubbo? Tear your clothes off, and show your bottom like everybody else?'

She kicked her heels into the carpet and roared. She was shickered, of course, by now, and sour as always.

But Hannah nudged her friend, and looked anxiously at the young fellow who had come with Norm.

Dubbo himself was overtaken by a sudden sadness.

An Eyetalian boy called Fiddle Paganini was finishing singing a number, in the blond wig and black net stockings he had brought for that purpose in a port.

Hannah said in a loud voice:

'Alf can do better than sing and dance. Take it from me. Can't you, Alf?'

She did not look exactly at him, and stuck her tongue into her cheek, because she was just a little bit nervous at what she was about to suggest.

She turned to the young fellow in the corner.

'You don't know what we got here, Humphrey.'

She was addressing the stranger in a voice louder still, in an accent that nobody had ever heard before.

'Alf does oil paintings. Don't you, Alf? How about showing the pictures? That would be a real treat, and one that Mr Mortimer would appreciate and remember.'

Dubbo was struck by lightning right there in the brown lounge.

Everyone was looking. Some of the queers were groaning and yawning.

'Arr, yes, go on, Alf!' Norman Fussell added.

Norm had returned conventionally clothed, and seated himself on his friend's lap, from which he had been dropped almost at once, because he was heavy. This piece of by-play, if of no other significance, forced Humphrey Mortimer's hand to reveal the second half of his face. Which Dubbo saw fully at last.

Now the young man leaned forward, and said:

'Yes, Alf, there is nothing I should like better than to see those paintings. If you would consider showing them.'

He spoke in tones so polite and flat they precluded arrogance, enthusiasm, irony, or any definite emotion. That was the way he had been taught, perhaps. To win confidence, without offending against taste by rousing hopes.

Dubbo stood. Usually he could sense an ambush.

Or was this the one evening when defences might be dropped?

It was vanity that began to persuade him, stroking with the most insidious feathers. All that he was capable of expressing was soon suffocating in his chest, writhing in his belly, tingling in the tips of his fingers. He was looking down almost sardonically into the rather pale, lifeless eyes of Humphrey Mortimer, who was obviously unaware that he might have created an explosive situation.

Until Dubbo was no longer able to endure that such ignorance should be allowed to exist.

'Orright,' he answered, furrily.

He began to walk, or run, along the dark passage to his room, his hands stretched out brittle in front of him, to guard against something. He could not select quickly enough a couple of the paintings, dropped, and recovered them. Started back. At one point his right shoulder struck the wall, which threw him off. But he did arrive in the reeling lounge, where he propped the boards, on the floor, against a chair, in front of the guest of honour.

The whole business was most unorthodox, it was implied by the majority of those present. And the paintings themselves. Some members of the company made it clear they would take no further part in anything so peculiar.

But Humphrey Mortimer sat forward, disclosing through his eyes what he would not have allowed his mouth to attempt; he might have committed himself. Perhaps only Dubbo sensed that an undernourished soul was feeding as though it had never eaten before.

The abo was very straight and aloof.

'Yeeees,' said the connoisseur, because it was time he made a remark, provided it was equivocal.

Dubbo touched the corner of one board with his toe.

'No,' he contradicted. 'These paintings are no good. I was still trying. Half of them is empty. That corner, see how dead it is? I did not know what to fill it with. I'll paint these out later on.'

He was still breathless. But from his vantage point he could afford to be contemptuous, not to say honest.

'Even so,' murmured Humphrey Mortimer.

Possessed by the paintings, whether they were indifferent or not, he had grown completely passive.

Nothing would control Dubbo's passion now. He ran back along the passage. The things in his pockets were flogging him.

He brought paintings and paintings. They lit a bonfire in the mediocre room, the walls of which retreated from the blaze of colour. Although the gramophone continued to piddle manfully, it failed to extinguish even the edges of the fire.

Some of the queers were taking their leave. Some of them had curled up.

'Wonderful, ain't it, what a touch of paint will do?' Hannah said, and yawned.

But in the roomful of dormant or murmurous people, it was the painter and his audience of one that mattered. They were in communication.

Dubbo had just brought an offering of two pictures. Increasing sobriety suggested to him that he ought to withdraw. But he propped the paintings lovingly enough.

The other sat forward. Since he had grasped the idiom, he was more deeply receptive. But, from habit or policy, would continue only lazily to smile his pleasure and acknowledgement.

'Ah,' he began intimately, for the painter alone, 'Shadrach, Meshach, and Abed-nego?'

'Yes!' The abo laughed gently.

It was very like a courtship.

'And the Angel of the Lord,' Dubbo added, in the same caressing voice.

He squatted down, and almost touched with a finger the stiff but effulgent figure. It had emerged completely from the chaos of spirit in which it had been born.

In that it was so very recent, the paint still wet, the creator could not see his work as it must appear and remain. He could at least admire the feathery texture of the angel's wings as a problem overcome, while forgetting that a little boy on a molten morning had held a live cockatoo in his hands, and opened its feathers to look at their roots, and become involved in a mystery of down. Later perhaps, falling asleep, or waking, it might occur to the man how he had understood to render the essence of divinity.

If he could have seen it, the work was already sufficient in itself. All the figures in the furnace were stiff but true. The fire was final. Neither time nor opinion could divert a single tongue of flame into a different shape.

And the two actual men, watching the figures in the fiery furnace, were themselves touched with a heavenly dew which protected them momentarily from other voices and mortal dangers. It seemed that honesty must prevail.

It was the visitor who broke out first. He shivered violently, and shook off the spell. His eyes could have been regretting a surrender.

'You have got something here, Dubbo,' he said, languidly, even cynically.

It was as far as he had ever gone towards committing himself, and it made him nervous.

The abo, too, was nervous, if not angry, as he gathered up what had become an extravagant effusion in paint.

'What is this?' Humphrey Mortimer asked. 'This big cartoon that you brought along last with *The Fiery Furnace*, and didn't explain?'

'That,' said the painter, 'is nothing. It is a drawing I might work from later. I dunno, though.'

Now that he was stone cold, he bitterly regretted having brought out the drawing for *The Chariot*. Bad enough *The Fiery Furnace*. All was exposed and defenceless.

'I like that particularly,' said Mr Mortimer. 'The big cartoon. It is most interesting. Let me look at it a moment.'

'No,' said Dubbo. 'I don't want. It is too late. Another time.' Hurrying his paintings.

'You promise, then?' persisted the other.

'Yes, yes,' said Dubbo.

But his nostrils contradicted.

As the fire that had been kindled in the lounge-room died, Norm's party began to break up. There was a kissing and a hugging. The queans were restoring their habitual atmosphere of crossed lines. While Dubbo carried off the last ember of true passion.

Now he would be able to lock his door and trust the silence.

But footsteps followed in the passage, half-tentative, half-confident.

'Look here, Alf,' Humphrey Mortimer began.

It could not have been anybody else.

'I want to suggest something,' he said.

He had followed the abo as far as his door.

Although it was close in the passage, both men were shivering. Mr Mortimer, whose silhouette seldom fell short of perfect, was standing with his fists clenched in his trouser pockets, and his coat rucked up over a protruding bum. He looked ridiculous.

'I will make you an offer for at least three of the paintings,' he said. 'Which I am very anxious to own.'

He named *The Fiery Furnace* and a couple of others.

'And the drawing of the chariot-thing, when it has fulfilled its purpose. That is to say, when you have finished working from it.'

The young man mentioned a sum, quite the most respectable that had ever been named in Hannah's house of love.

'No. No. Sorry,' said Alf Dubbo.

His voice could not have hacked further words out of his feelings.

'Think it over, at least. It is for your own good, you know.' Humphrey Mortimer pulled that one.

He continued to smile, because life had taught him that his own way was easily bought.

But Dubbo, who had laid himself open at certain moments during the evening, was no longer vulnerable. Since beginning to suspect he had been deceived, he had shrivelled right up, and nobody would coax him out again.

'Paintings which nobody looks at might never have been painted,' the patron argued.

'I will look at them,' Dubbo said. 'Good night,' he said, 'Mr Mortimer.'

And shut the door.

For a week or two the blackfellow experienced no inclination to paint, not even to look at the finished paintings, only to know that they were there. Something seemed to have frightened the daylights out of him. As if, in a moment of exuberant vanity, he had betrayed some mystery, of which he was the humblest and most recent initiate. Now he began to feel sick. He turned the paintings face to the wall, and would lie on his bed for hours, at weekends or at evening, his knees drawn up, protecting his head with his forearms. The palms of his hands had grown clammy.

In that outer and parallel existence, which never altogether convinced him, the war was drawing to a close. The spray-painting of aeroplanes had fizzled out, except on paper. A two-up school was booming in one of the big packing-cases; the hangars were chockful of stuff for anyone who felt inclined to shake it. Many did feel inclined. In fact, all the maggots on all the carcasses began to wriggle, if anything, a bit harder, suspecting that the feast was almost finished. In a few instances, the conscience was felt to stir, as human features returned to the blunt maggot-faces, and it was realized that the true self, whatever metamorphoses it might have undergone, was still horribly present, and hinting at rehabilitation.

Hannah would wake at noon as before, and pluck her eyebrows, and paint her nails, and paddle the big, desperate puff in the shadows of her armpits. But was looking real soggy. Of course, inside the dough of flesh she was still the straight, brown girl, but only she was to know that. And sometimes doubted. Whether she might not have sold herself for a bag of aniseed balls, to some randy kid, under the pepper trees, in break.

Oh, the powder made her cough. She was what they called allergic; that was it. She was that soggy. All steamy, open pores. She was that sick. She was eating the aspros by the handful now. They sat sour. Or returned to burn. But she would also break out sometimes in a lovely sweat, no, a perspiration of relief. Until remembering what you could not exactly have called her sickness. It was like as if she had a sick thought. Her conscience would tick inside her like a cheap alarm clock. If a bell had gone off, she would have screamed out loud.

And the abo would walk along the passage. Quiet. He was quiet all right, except if he got poisoned and fell about the place, and that was the girls in the bars, who had altogether no discretion. Otherwise nobody could complain. It was painting, painting, all the while. That could have been what wore Hannah down: to think there was a man shut up by himself dead quiet in a room at the back, dabbling nonsense on an old board. What some, some of the clever ones, did claim to understand.

Once he came along the passage, quiet as usual, but rather quick. It scared her suddenly to hear him, close by. She broke a nail on the knot of a parcel she had brought back, and was just beginning to untie. If that in itself was not enough to raise the pimples on you. Not that he was any more than only passing. Through the yellower light which poured in, under the blind she had had to adjust, to see what she was doing.

'Gee! You aren't training to bust a safe open?' she was compelled to ask. 'It's those old sandshoes.'

'They're easy on the feet,' he replied.

'Anyways,' she said, 'what's wrong with your job, Alf? You haven't given it away?'

'No,' he said. 'I been feeling crook. I didn't go. Not for two days.'

'What's up?'

'I dunno,' he said. 'Nothing.'

'Ah dear, nothing bad, I hope.' She sighed, but did not care. 'Everybody's sick. It wouldn't be this flamin' war?'

She began again frigging with the parcel, which no longer seemed of much importance. Her mouth was slacker than usual. It shone, because she had had to wet it after she had taken fright.

For a moment there flickered up in him the possibility that he might use, or store, passages of yellow light, or Hannah's broken forms against yellow wood and mirrors.

She only saw that he was looking at her too long.

He went out then, because, he said, he would like to get some air. Although it was doubtful whether he would. That which passed for air would not have squeezed into the lungs, but blocked the tubes like wads of moist blotting paper. A thick, lemony light had been poured into the brick streets and round the roots of the pollarded planes. Somewhere in the distance fire could have been threatening.

When all the frightful accidie and imminence of the last few days bubbled up into Dubbo's mouth, and he spat it out in a brown stream, so that an old woman withdrew into the doorway of her own squalor, away from the hollow blackfellow, who walked casually enough, his hands in his pockets, spitting blood. He did not see, though. He was, to a great extent, released. Now he could have used the impasto of deepening summer, of the thickening, yellow afternoon. He could have wallowed in it. In his own peculiar handwriting, he would have scratched the legend of grey, seamy brick. And against it he would have elongated the already drawn-out face, hollowed still deeper the hollow temples, and conveyed sight through opaque eyelids. For this, he saw, was Humphrey Mortimer's afternoon. Wherever it flowed, it smelled of rotting fruit, of an ether which did not anaesthetize, sweet, but bad.

Again the abo was forced to spit, and this time it was clearer.

This time, besides, he had to notice. Halted by the note of crimson, he stood staring at the grey pavement, remembering his lapse in devotion to a trust. The inexorable crimson stained his wrong deeper still. Then he spat again, and saw that the colour, like all such thoughts, was mercifully fading, though the original cause and weakness must remain. For, had he not revealed to Humphrey Mortimer secret truths which had been given him to keep?

Dubbo sat for a while on a bench, not in a park, but in the street, just where he happened to be passing. From time to time, he spat, to examine the colour, until finding at last that the haemorrhage must have stopped.

Presently a man came and sat beside him, and told him that soon the war would be over, because, said the man, it was written in the Scriptures.

Dubbo made no reply, suspecting it was as the man had said.

And the evil ones, continued the prophet, would be trodden under foot, as would the lesser evil, who betrayed the Lord through pure ignorance and vanity whenever the opportunity occurred. That included the concubines, and sodomites, the black marketeers, and reckless taxi-drivers – all those who in any way betrayed a trust.

The dusk was splitting into little particles. There was nothing, almost nothing left except the movement of disintegration.

Now Dubbo was aching in the chest, now that all goodness was to break. All the solid forms that he could answer for. All the brilliant colours that could lick across the field of vision.

'You'll see,' said the man, in the voice in which it was his habit to prophesy. 'And the price of eggs will fall. And the price of sardines.'

But Alf Dubbo was going. He could scarcely control a longing to look once more at those few paintings in which his innocence remained unimpaired, in which the Lord still permitted a solidity of shapes, a continuity of life, even error.

So he butted the darkness with his head, and the breath rattled behind his ribs, and the streets made way before him.

When he arrived at the house in Abercrombie Crescent he found that Norman Fussell had come. Norm was trying on a white fur in Hannah's glass. His real self had taken over, and the perv sniggered, and snuggled, and considered himself from all angles.

'Hi, Alf!' he called. 'Can you resist my piece of Arctic fox?'

But Hannah had slammed shut with the opening of the front door.

'Lay off it, you silly clown!'

She was in no mood for circuses.

Norm could have been a little drunk. In his desire to continue fooling, he would not allow his stooge to withdraw from their act, as she would, in fact, have preferred. Both were dressed for it, since it was their custom to take off half their clothes in the house, and let their flesh have its slapstick way. Both bulged, if they did not actually sag, and the white fur for which they were now contending seemed to make them softer, nakeder. Norm was certainly the rounder, as his needs had been fulfilled by the touch of fur. His cheeks oozed cheerfulness. Hannah's face, on the contrary, was dry, and curiously flat. It might have been rendered by a couple of strokes of a whitewash brush.

Norm was still arsing about. Obviously he was fairly drunk. He swung, and clung to the tail of the white fox, of which Hannah had recovered the head.

'Shall I tell you, Alf,' he called, 'how us girls got to be financial?'

And jerked the fox.

'I will dong you one,' shouted Hannah, 'before you tear this bloody fur!'

Dubbo laughed, but out of friendship. He could not wait now.

'And financial fanny, anyways!' Hannah had continued to shout.

She told how she had got the fur through the trade, from a Jew who was obliged to her for a favour or two in his reffo days. She spoke that loud and clear, she could have suspected somebody might doubt.

But Dubbo had already passed. And Norm, who had relinquished the fur, was threatening to pee himself. The giggles were glugging. His flesh was flapping. And the handles on the furniture jumped and rattled.

Dubbo had got inside his room at last, in which the blind pictures were standing, and the greeny-black dressmaker's dummy, and all those other irrelevant objects which his life there had made relevant. The room was cracking, it seemed, under the necessity of abandoning its severely finite form. The dummy was inclining forward on its dry-rotten pedestal. Electric wiring whirred. As he began to turn the pictures. And turned. And turned.

And his own life was restored by little twinges and great waves. His hands were no longer bones in gloves of papery

365

skin, as he twitched the pictures over, and gave them the support they needed – against the bed, the rusted kero stove, an angle of the room. Once more the paintings were praising and affirming in accents of which his mouth had never been capable.

Returned into the bosom of conviction, he might not have resisted the impulse to bring out paints there and then, and reproduce the deepening yellow through which he had watched the evening streets, if that yellow had not begun to sicken in him. If he had not dis-covered.

Then the teeth were terrible in his face. He began to fumble and bungle through his own possessions as well as the wretched trash of Hannah's lodger's room. His search toppled the dress-maker's dummy, which went down thumping out its dust. Perhaps he had just failed to see what he was looking for. Often, in moments of passion or withdrawal, he would overlook objects which were there all the time before him. But in the present case, only the hard truth emerged: *The Fiery Furnace* was gone, together with that big drawing. *The Chariot-thing*. What else, he did not stop to consider. Nobody bothers to count the blows when he knows that one of them will prove fatal.

'Hannah!'

A voice had never gone down the passage like that before. He was running on those quiet, spongy feet. And breathing high.

Although he arrived almost at once, she was already advancing to meet him through the doorway of her room. She appeared to have decided she would not do any good by talking. That dry, white look, which her face had only recently acquired, had never been more in evidence than against the controversial fur. She had stretched the fox, straight and teachery, along her otherwise naked shoulders. No swagger any more. There was a sort of chain, with a couple of acorns, holding the furs together above the shabby, yellow parting of her breasts.

'Hannah!' he breathed. 'You done that?'

He couldn't, or not very well, get it past a turn in his throat.

'I will tell you,' Hannah answered, flat, now that the scene was taking place. 'Only don't – there is no need – to do your block before you know.'

And Norm looking over her shoulder. Norman Fussell was very curious to observe how, in the light of what he already knew, the rest of it would turn out.

For the present Dubbo was almost bent up. Breathing and

366

grinning. His ribs would have frightened, if they had been visible.

But Hannah was slow as suet. With a nerve inside of it.

'I will tell you. I will tell you,' she seemed to be saying.

She did not care very much whether she died. She could have exhausted her life by now. It was only the unimaginable act of dying that made her sick nerve tick.

Then Dubbo began to get his hands around her. She went down, quite easy, because she felt that guilty at first, she was offering no resistance. She intended to suffer, if it could not be avoided. She almost wanted to feel his fingers sinking into that soft sickness she had become.

So he got her down against the doorway of her room. The chain which had been fastening the fox burst apart, and she was bundled in her pink slip. Or tearing. Her cheek was grating on the bald carpet when not ploughing the smell of new fur.

The abo was tearing mad, and white beneath his yellow skin.

All his desperate hate breath hopelessness future all of him and more was streaming into his pair of hands.

Then Hannah got her throat free. Perhaps she had expiated enough. She let out:

'Aaaahhhhhhh! Normmm! For Chrissake!'

Norm Fussell just failed to exorcize the ghost of a giggle.

Not that things were getting funny. It had begun to be intolerable for him too, as he was officially a man, and had just been called upon to work a miracle. So now, he who had been hopping around in his normal flesh, after throwing off responsibility with his clothes, began with one arm to apply to the abo a hold which a sailor had once taught him. And which he had never known to work.

But at least they were all three involved. Their breath was knotted together in ropes as solid as their arms.

At one point, Hannah began again:

'Alf, I will tell you. I will tell you.'

Her tongue was rather swollen, though. It would pop out like a parrot's.

In between, she was crying sorry for herself.

'I will tell' – she would manage to get it out. 'That Mort bug Alf *Chrise* MORTIMER honest honest only took a few quid commish *on* Alf.'

That made him fight worse. All the bad that he had to kill might escape him by cunning.

Because all three of the wrestlers understood at last they

were really and truly intended to die at some moment, possibly that one.

Seeing the muck of blood on her arms, on her slip – it could only have been *her* blood – Hannah was whimpering afresh for what she had been made to suffer, ever, and so drawn out, when in the history book they chopped the heads cleanly off.

But at that moment, Norm Fussell, by dint of pressure, or weight, or the sailor's genuinely skilful hold, got the abo off of Hannah.

And Hannah got up. Self-pity did not delay her a second. Her flesh flew. But, of course, she had got thinner. She could not drag out the drawer too quick. Of the dressing-table. Scrabble under handkerchiefs. Fetch out what was flapping more than her own hand.

When the abo came at her afresh, she had the envelope to push against him.

'Honest,' Hannah cried, shaking the paper. 'I wouldn't never bite your ear! Look, Alf! Look, only!'

Dubbo was unable to look, but nature slowed him up.

'See, Alf? There is your name. I wrote. Only took a spot of commission. Bought a fur. What other intention. It was that puf Mortimer would not let me alone. Here, look, Alf, is the rest. I was gunna hand it over, dinkum, when things had settled down.'

Dubbo was all in for the moment.

Seeing the blood on her arms, and her slip reduced to bandages, Hannah began again to cry, for what she had escaped, for all that life had imposed on her. The tufts of her hair, Norman Fussell observed, had turned her into the imitation of a famous clown.

There was a knocking on the door then: some neighbour, some Eyetalian, to see whether they wanted the police. No, said Norman Fussell, it was only a slight difference being settled between friends.

But Hannah cried.

'All the good money!' she blubbed. 'And what is old paintings? We only done it for your own good.'

That, apparently, was something people were unable to resist.

'Yes, Hannah,' Dubbo agreed. 'You are honest. If anybody is.'

He could not get breath for more.

She was relieved to see that the blood she had noticed could not have been her own, but was trickling out of the abo's mouth.

'You knocked a tooth, eh?'

'Yes,' he could just bother.

So now Hannah had to whimper because she was tender-hearted, and blood was sad, like hospitals, and wet nights, and old bags of greasy women, and fallen arches on hot feet, and the faces of people going along beneath the green neon.

'Arr, dear!' she cried, but checked herself enough to call: 'Don't forget your money, Alf. Your money. Arr, well. You know it will be safe with me. You know I never bit anybody's ear.'

For Dubbo had gone along the passage into that room of which the cardboard walls had failed to protect. Perhaps, after all, only a skull was the box for secrets.

But that, too, he knew, and swayed, would not hold for ever; it must burst open from all that would collect inside it. All pouring out, from tadpoles and clumsy lizards, to sheets of lightning and pillars of fire. For there was no containing thoughts, unless you persuaded somebody – only a friend would be willing – to take an axe, and smash up the fatal box for good and all. How it would have scared him, though, to step out from amongst the mess, and face those who would have come in, who would be standing round amongst the furniture, waiting to receive. Then the Reverend Jesus Calderon, for all he raised his pale hand, and exerted the authority of his sad eyes, would not save a piebald soul from the touch of fur and feather, or stem the slither of cold scales.

The weight of night fell heavy at last on the house in Abercrombie Crescent. Norm Fussell, a nervous type, said he was going walk-about. Hannah did not go on the job – she was done up – but took an aspro, or three, and knew she would not drop off. Yet, it was proved, she must have floated on the surface of a sleep.

About five, the whore got up. She was not accustomed to see the grey light sprawling on an empty bed; it gave her the jimmies. She would have liked a yarn, to put the marshmallow back into life by offering right sentiments. There is nothing comforts like worn opinions. But in the absence of opportunity, she looked along the passage, touching her bruises.

There she saw the abo's door was open.

'Alf!' she called once or twice, but low.

She began to go along then, running her hand along the wall.

The room, it appeared, was empty. She had to switch on

369

finally to see, although the electric light was cruel. But Dubbo had gone all right. Had taken his tin box, it seemed, and smoked off.

All around, amongst the junk she had been in the habit of shoving away in that room, was matchwood. He had, she saw, brought the axe from the yard – it was still standing in the room – and split his old pictures up. Nothing else. All those bloody boards of pictures. There they were, laying.

The thin light was screaming down from the bare electric globe.

Well, she realized presently, she could let the stuff lay where it was, and use it up in time as kindling. She was glad then. She had known other men do their blocks, and bust up a whole houseful of valuable furniture.

As she went back slow along the passage, in which the light was beginning to throb, from grey to white, gradually and naturally, it occurred to her the abo had not asked her for his money; it would still be in there under the handkerchiefs. He would come back, of course, and she would surrender up the envelope, because she was an honest woman. But sometimes a person did not come back. Sometimes a person died. Or sometimes what mattered of a person, the will or something, died in advance, and they did not seem to care. She remembered the abo the night before, after he got blown, propping himself in the middle of the carpet, on the bones of legs, all bones and breathlessness. If anyone had knocked on him at that stage, he might have sounded hollow, like a crab. But she did not think he had shown her his eyes, and in her anxiety to reconstruct a situation, she would have liked to remember.

Still, Hannah was throbbing with hopes. In the cool of the morning, she was already on fire. She was back in her room by now. She would move the envelope from the drawer, for safety, since it had been seen. Not that Norm, of course. Norm was honest too.

Dubbo did not return to the house in Abercrombie Crescent. Hannah's place was connected in his mind with some swamp that he remembered without having seen, and from which the white magic of love and charity had failed to exorcize the evil spirits. Certainly he had never expected much, but was sickened afresh each time his attitude was justified. Angels were demons in disguise. Even Mrs Pask had dropped her blue robe, and grown brass nipples and a beak. Such faith as he had, lay in his own hands. Through them he might still redeem what Mr

Calderon would have referred to as the soul, and which remained in his imagining something between a material shape and an infinite desire. So, in those acts of praise which became his paintings, he would try to convey and resolve his condition of mind.

As far as the practical side of his existence was concerned, it was easy enough to find work, and he went from job to job for a while after he had run from Hannah's. He took a room on the outskirts of Barranugli, in the house of a Mrs Noonan, where no questions were asked, and where bare walls, and a stretcher with counterpane of washed-out roses, provided him with a tranquil background for his thoughts. He read a good deal now, both owing to a physical languor caused by his illness, and because of a rage to arrive at understanding. Mostly he read the Bible, or the few art books he had bought, but for preference the Books of the Prophets, and even by now the Gospels. The latter, however, with suspicion and surprise. And he would fail, as he had always failed before, to reconcile those truths with what he had experienced. Where he could accept God because of the spirit that would work in him at times, the duplicity of the white men prevented him considering Christ, except as an ambitious abstraction, or realistically, as a man.

When the white man's war ended, several of the whites bought Dubbo drinks to celebrate the peace, and together they spewed up in the streets, out of stomachs that were, for the occasion, of the same colour. At Rosetree's factory, though, where he began to work shortly after, Dubbo was always the abo. Nor would he have wished it otherwise, for that way he could travel quicker, deeper, into the hunting grounds of his imagination.

The white men had never appeared pursier, hairier, glassier, or so confidently superior as they became at the excuse of peace. As they sat at their benches at Rosetree's, or went up and down between the machines, they threatened to burst right out of their singlets, and assault a far too passive future. Not to say the suspected envoys of another world.

There was a bloke, it was learnt, at one of the drills down the lower end, some kind of bloody foreigner. Whom the abo would watch with interest. But the man seldom raised his eyes. And the abo did not expect.

Until certain signs were exchanged, without gesture or direct glance.

How they began to communicate, the blackfellow could not have explained. But a state of trust became established by subtler than any human means, so that he resented it when the Jew finally addressed him in the wash-room, as if their code of silence might have thus been compromised. Later, he realized, he was comforted to know that the Chariot did exist outside the prophet's vision and his own mind.

Part Six

12

Passover and Easter would fall early that year. The heavy days were still being piled up, and no sign of relief for those who were buried inside. Little wonder that the soul hesitated to prepare itself, whether for deliverance from its perennial Egypt, or redemption through the blood of its Saviour, when the body remained immured in its pyramid of days. Miss Hare burrowed deep, but uselessly, along the tunnels of escape which radiated from Xanadu, and parted the green, her skin palpitating for the moment that did not, would not come. Mrs Godbold, standing in the steam of sheets, awaited the shrill winds of Easter, which sometimes even now would sweep across her memory, out of the fens, rattling the white cherry boughs, and causing the lines of hymns to waver behind shaken panes. But this year, did not blow. For Mrs Flack and Mrs Jolley, mopping themselves amongst the dahlias at *Karma*, it was easier, of course, to invoke an Easter that was their due, as regular communicants, and members of the Ladies' Guild. For Harry Rosetree, however, in his cardboard office at the factory, the season always brought confusion. Which he overcame by over-work, by blasphemy, and by tearing at his groin. There the pants would ruck up regularly, causing him endless discomfort during rush orders and humid weather.

'For Chrissake,' Harry Rosetree bellowed, as he thumped and bumped, and eased that unhappy crotch, in his revolting, tilt-able, chromium-plated chair, 'what for is Easter this year so demmed early? A man cannot fulfil his orders.'

In the outer office Miss Whibley, the plumper of the two ladies who were dashing away at their typewriters, sucked her teeth just enough to censure.

Miss Mudge, on the other hand, sniggered, because it was the boss.

'Can you tell me, please, Miss Whibley?'

Mr Rosetree would insist. He could become intolerable, but paid well for it.

'Because it is a movable feast,' Miss Whibley replied.

She thought perhaps her answer had sounded clever without being altogether rude. Miss Whibley was an adept at remaining the right side of insolence.

'Well, move it, move it, or see that it is moved, Miss Whibley, please,' Mr Rosetree insisted, plodding through the wads of paper, 'next year, well forward, Miss Whibley, please.'

Miss Mudge sniggered, and wiped her arms on her personal towel. The boss would start to get funny, and keep it up during whole afternoons. Miss Mudge approved, guiltily, of jolly men. She lived with a widowed, invalid, pensioned sister, whose excessive misfortune had sapped them both.

'Because I will not rupture myself for any Easter, Miss Whibley, movable or fixed.'

Mr Rosetree had to kill somebody with his wit.

Miss Whibley sucked her teeth harder.

'Dear, dear, Mr Rosetree, it is a good thing neether of us is religious. Miss Mudge is even less than I.'

Miss Mudge blushed, and mumbled something about liking a decent hymn provided nobody expected her to join in.

'I am religious.' Mr Rosetree slapped the papers.

'I am religious! I am religious!' Mr Rosetree sang.

Indeed, he attended the church of St Aloysius at Paradise East, on Sundays, and at all important feasts, and would stuff notes into the hands of nuns, with a lack of discretion which made them lower their eyes, as if they had been a party to some indecent act.

'You gotta be religious, Miss Whibley.' Mr Rosetree laughed. 'Otherwise you will go to hell, and how will you like that?'

Now it was Miss Whibley's turn to blush. Her necklaces of flesh turned their deepest mauve, and she took out a little compact, and began to powder herself, from her forehead down to the yoke of her dress, with the thorough motions of a cat.

'Well, I am not at all religious,' she said, wetting her lips ever so slightly. 'I suppose it is because my friend is a dialectical materialist.'

Mr Rosetree laughed more than ever. He could not resist:

'And what is that?'

He was quite unreasonably happy that afternoon.

'I cannot be expected to explain *every*-thing!' Miss Whibley sulked.

'Ah, you intellectuals!' Mr Rosetree sighed.

Miss Mudge coughed, and shifted her lozenge. She loved to listen to other people, and to watch. In that way, she who had

374

never thought what she might contribute to life, did seem to participate. Now she observed that her colleague was becoming annoyed. Miss Mudge could feel the heartburn rise in sympathy in her own somewhat stringy throat.

'My friend is a Civil Servant,' Miss Whibley was saying. 'In the Taxation Office. He is considered an expert on provisional tax.'

Then she added, rather irrelevantly, only she had been saving it up for some time as a kind of experiment:

'My friend is also a quarter Jewish.'

Mr Rosetree was disengaging the wads of paper, which could only be prised apart, it seemed, at that season. Miss Whibley did not watch, but sensed.

'A quarter Jew? So! A quarter Jew! I am a quarter shoe-fetichist, Miss Whibley, if that is what you wish to know. And five-eighths manic-depressive. That leaves still some small fraction to be accounted for. So we cannot yet work it out what I am.'

Miss Whibley flung her typewriter carriage as far as it would go. Miss Mudge did not understand, but Miss Whibley knew that she should take offence. And she did, with professional efficiency.

'A quarter Jew!' chanted Mr Rosetree.

But Miss Whibley would not hear. She lowered her head to study her shorthand notes, though inwardly she had crossed the line which divides reality from resentment.

Presently it was time for the ladies to leave. They went out most conspicuously on that afternoon. In the workshop the men were knocking off. Some had begun to move towards the bus-stop, others towards the paddockful of ramshackle cars. Whether they marched, carrying prim-looking ports, or gangled leisurely, with sugar-bags slung by cords across the shoulders, no other act performed by the men during the day so clearly proclaimed their independence. Only a boss, it was implied, would presume that their going out was inevitably linked to their coming in.

Although the boss should have left, now that the walls no longer shook, and silence was flowing back into the shed which ostensibly he owned, Harry Rosetree continued to sit. Because he had decided to work on. But did not, in fact. The silence was so impressive he became convinced he was its creator, along with the Brighta Lamps, the Boronia Geometry Sets, the Flannel-Flower Bobby-Pins, and My Own Butterfly Clips. Of course, if he had not been possessed by his irrational joy long before the factory had begun to empty, the illusion might not have endured; he would most probably have been caught out by that same silence which now increased his sense of power and freedom. But his joy, which had made him so distasteful during the afternoon to the ladies he employed, was too rubbery and aggressive to allow itself to be bounced aside. Nor could he have restrained it any more than he could have halted time, which went ticking on through the last week before the Easter closure, and the most formidable silence of all, when the soul is re-born.

Not that Rosetrees were all that observant. But Harry Rosetree was an honest man. If you signed a contract, you had to abide by the clauses. And religion was like any other business. Rosetrees were Christians now; they would do the necessary. Shirl complained, but of course she was a woman. Shirl said she had been brought up to stay at home, to stuff the fish, and knead the dumplings, not to pray along with the men. She did not go much on early mass, but Harry would sometimes persuade, with a bottle of French perfume or pair of stockings. Then Shirl would get herself up in the gold chains which were such a handy investment, and derive quite a lot from the subdued and reverential atmosphere – it was lovely, the elevation of the Host – and the wives of upper-bracket executives in their expensive clothes.

But that Easter they had made their reservations at My Blue Mountain Home. It was all very well to be Christians, Shirl said, but surely to God they were Australians too. So they were going to sing *The Little Brown Jug*, and *Waltzing Matilda*, and *Pack Up Your Troubles*, after tea. Along with a lot of bloody reffos, Harry said. What he understood best, usually he suspected most.

So that it was not altogether the sweet scent of Easter which had flooded Harry Rosetree's soul, as he worked on, or sat in his office, in the brassy light of late afternoon. As he drifted, he was uplifted, but by something faintly anomalous. Until finally he was stunned. It could only be the cinnamon. It was Miss Mudge: my chest, sir, if I do not take precautions in humid weather, hope you do not object to such a penetrating odour. It smelled, all right. Even now that she was gone, it shrieked down the passages of memory, right to the innermost chamber.

They were again seated in the long, but very narrow, dark parlour, raising the mess of brown apple to their lips. The mother had arranged special cushions, on which the father was reclining, or lolling, rather. Such an excess of blood-red plush, with the nap beginning to wear off, filled the chair and made for discomfort. It was the occasion that mattered, and the father throve on occasions. Whatever the state of their fortunes, whatever the temper of the *goyim*, the father would deliver much the same homily: our history is all we have, Haïm, and the peaceful joys of the Sabbath and feast days, the flavour of cinnamon and the scent of spices, the wisdom of Torah and the teaching of the Talmud.

What had been the living words of the father would crackle like parchment whenever Haïm ben Ya'akov allowed himself to remember. Or worse, he would see them, written in columns, on scrolls of human skin.

But now it was the *scent* of words that pervaded. Whatever the occasion – and how many there had been – the father wore the *Yarmulka*. And the wart with the four little black bristles to the side of the right nostril. At *Pessach* the father would explain: this, Haïm, is the apple of remembrance, of the brown clay of Egypt, so you must eat up, eat, the taste of cinnamon is good. Haïm Rosenbaum, the boy, had never cared for the stuff, but long after he had become a man, even after he was supposed, officially, to have stripped the Ark of its Passover trappings, and dressed his hopes in the white robe of Easter, the scent of cinnamon remained connected with the deep joy of *Pessach*.

Now as the molten light was poured into the office where Harry Rosetree sat, the two eyes which were watching him seemed to be set at discrepant angles, which, together with the presentation of the facial planes, suggested that here were two, or even more, distinct faces. Yet, on closer examination, all the versions that evolved, all the lines of vision that could be traced from the discrepant eyes, fell into focus. All those features which had appeared wilfully distorted and unrelated, added up quite naturally to make the one great archetypal face. It was most disturbing, exhilarating, not to say frightening.

Until Mr Rosetree realized the old Jew he had employed for some time, that Himmelfarb, that Mordecai, had approached along the passage without his having heard, and was glancing in through a hatchway. Passing, passing, but hesitating. So the moment fixed in the hatchway suggested. It was one of those instants that will break with the ease of cotton threads.

Mr Rosetree was trembling, whether from anger – he had never been able to stand the face of that old, too humble Jew – or from joy at discovering familiar features transferred from memory to the office hatchway, he would not have been the one to decide.

Although his dry throat was compelled, still tremblingly enough. He was forced to mumble, while his joy and relief, fear and anger, swayed and tittuped in the balance:

'*Shalom! Shalom! Mordecai!*'

The face of the Jew Himmelfarb immediately appeared to brim with light. The windows, of course, were blazing with it at that hour.

'*Shalom, Herr Rosenbaum!*' the Jew Mordecai replied.

But immediately Mr Rosetree cleared his throat of anything that might have threatened his position.

'Why the hell,' he asked, 'don't you knock off along with other peoples?'

He had got up. He was walking about, balanced on the balls of his small feet, rubbery and angry.

'Do you want to make trouble with the union?' Mr Rosetree asked.

'I am late,' Himmelfarb explained, 'because I could not find this case.'

He produced a small, fibre case, of the type carried by school-children and, occasionally, workmen, and laid it as concrete evidence on the hatchway shelf.

Mr Rosetree was furious, but fascinated by the miserable object, which had already begun to assume a kind of monstrous importance.

'How,' he exploded, 'you could not find this case?'

He might have hit, if he would not have loathed so much as to touch it.

'It was mislaid,' the old Jew answered very quietly. 'Perhaps even hidden. As a joke, of course.'

'Which men would play such a wretched joke?'

'Oh,' said Himmelfarb, 'a young man.'

'Which?'

The room was shuddering.

'Oh,' said Himmelfarb, 'I cannot say I know his name. Only that they call him Blue.'

The incident was, of course, ludicrous, but Mr Rosetree had become obsessed by it.

'For Chrissake,' he asked, 'what for do you need this demmed case?'

How repellent he found all miserable reffo Jews. And this one in particular, the owner of the cheap, dented case.

Then the old Jew looked down his cheekbones. He took a key from an inner pocket. The case sprang tinnily, almost indecently open.

'I do not care to leave them at home,' Himmelfarb explained.

Harry Rosetree held his breath. There was no avoiding it; he would have to look inside the case. And did. Briefly. He saw, indeed, what he had feared: the fringes of the *Tallith*, the black thongs of the *Tephillin*, wound round and round the Name.

Mr Rosetree could have been in some agony.

'Put it away, then!' He trembled. 'All this *Quatsch*! Will you Jews never learn that you will be made to suffer for the next time also?'

'If it has to be,' Himmelfarb replied, manipulating the catches of his case.

'A lot of *Quatsch*!' Mr Rosetree repeated.

That intolerable humid weather had the worst effect on him. As his face showed.

The wretched Jew had begun to go.

'Himmelfarb!' Mr Rosetree called, through rubbery, almost unmanageable lips. 'You better take the two days,' he ordered, 'for the *Seder* business. But keep it quiet, the reason why. For all anyone will know,' here he became hatefully congested, 'you could have gone ...' but still choked, with some disgust for phlegm or words.

His veins were protesting, too, to say nothing of his purple skin. '... SICK,' he succeeded finally in shouting.

The employee inclined his head with such discretion, the favour could have been his due. As for the employer, he might have taken further offence, but was a fleshy man, suffering from blood pressure, and already emotionally exhausted.

'Who will decide,' he sighed, 'what forms sickness takes?'

But very soft. And was in no way comforted.

'*Hier! Himmelfarb!*' he bawled, as his inferior was preparing for the second time to leave.

Mr Rosetree had just the strength to remember something, however embarrassing the thought. And was floundering around in his breast pocket. He was flapping a wallet.

'*Für Pessach,*' Mr Rosetree grunted.

The old Jew was rather startled. His employer was dangling what appeared to be a five-pound note.

'*Nehmen Sie! Nehmen Sie!*' Mr Rosetree threatened. '*Himmelfarb! Für Pessach!*'

Harry Rosetree was not so innocent he did not believe a man might pay for his sins. Yet, an abominable innocence seemed to have washed the face of Himmelfarb quite, quite clean of any such suspicion.

He had come back. He said:

'I would ask you, Mr Rosetree, to give it, rather, to somebody in need.'

With that sweetness of innocence which is bitterest to those who taste it.

Then Mr Rosetree grew real angry. He began to curse all demmed Jews. He cursed himself for his foolishness. He dared to curse his own father's loins.

'This is where I will give these few demmed quids!' Harry Rosetree shouted.

As he crumpled up the note. And worried it apart. He did not tear it, exactly, because his fury could not rise to an act of such precision.

'So!'

Revenge made him sound hoarse.

If he had been able to atone in any way for the burst of destruction he had inspired, Himmelfarb would have done so, but for the moment that was impossible. Because, whatever the hatchway suggested, the wall prevented. He could not even have picked up the irregular pieces, which, he saw, had settled round his employer's feet.

So he had to say:

'I am sorry to have caused you such distress.'

Aware that humility can appear, at times, more offensive than arrogance itself, he tried to soften the blow by adding:

'Shalom, Herr Rosenbaum!'

And went.

A passive, but possessive heat ushered in the Season of Freedom. The heads of grass were bowed with summer. Limp wigs of willows, black at the seams, yellowing in hanks, were by now the feeblest disguises. Although carpets had been laid on the afternoon of the *Seder* night, they were of the coarsest, most tarnished yellow that a late-summer light could provide. Mere runners, moreover. But the heavy, felted light did lead, or so it appeared at that hour, over the collapsed grass and tufts of blowsy weed, to the brown house in which the Jew of Sarsaparilla had elected to live.

Neighbours were unaware, of course, that peculiar rites might be expected of the owner of the disgraceful, practically derelict house. Nor had the Jew availed himself for some years of the freedom which the season offered, feeling that his solitary trumpet blast might sound thin and poor in a celebration which called for the jubilance of massed brass. Until, at the present time, some welling of the spirit, need to establish identity of soul, foreboding of impending events, made him long to contribute, if only an isolated note.

So, in the afternoon, Himmelfarb went about setting the *Seder* table, as he had seen done. He layed the tablecloth which his neighbour Mrs Godbold had starched stiff, and ironed flat, and stuck together with its own cleanliness. Moving in a kind of mechanical agitation of recollected gestures, he put the shankbone and the burnt egg. He put the flat *Matsah*, the dish of bitter herbs, and the cup for wine. But was distressed by his own conjuring. The mere recollection of some of the more suggestive wonders would have prevented him performing them. Or the absence of an audience. Or the presence of ghosts: the rows of cousins and aunts, the Cantor Katzmann, the Lady from Czernowitz, the dreadful dyer of his youth – all of them, with the exception of one whom he preferred to leave faceless, expectant of his skill.

At that point he remembered the stranger: how they would stand the door open for anyone who chose to walk in. In imitation, he opened his, and put a stone against it. Though he doubted whether he would have dared lift the cup to any stranger's lips, for fear his own emotion might trouble, or even spill the wine. So that he could no longer bear to look at his property table, with its aching folds of buckram, and the papier-mâché symbols of Pessach. It would not have been illogical if, in the course of the farce he was elaborating, a *Hanswurst* had risen through the floor, and flattened the table with one blow from his bladder. In anticipation, a bird was shrieking out of a bush. Through the open doorway, Himmelfarb saw, the human personality was offered choice of drowning in a grass ocean, or exposure to the great burning-glass of sky.

Then the Jew, who had in his day been given to investigating what is above and what is below, took fright at the prospect of what might be in store for him. He began to walk about his house, with little, short, quick steps. He was quite boxed. All around him, behind the sticks of trees, were the boxes containing other lives, but involved in their own esoteric rites, or mystical union with banality. He would not have presumed to intrude, yet, it was so very necessary to unite.

It was his own open door which finally persuaded that *he* was the stranger whom some doorway must be waiting to receive. He would walk straight in, into the atmosphere of questions, and cinnamon, and songs. He would sit down without being asked, because he had been expected.

It took him seconds to fetch his hat. After first haste, and an episode with the front steps, he settled down quietly enough to the journey. Nor did it disturb him to think he had not locked his house.

In Sarsaparilla, Himmelfarb caught the bus. Buses were always amiable enough. It was the trains that still alarmed at times, because of the passengers substituted for those who had started out. But at Barranugli, where the train was waiting for him, he did not experience distress. His tremendous decision to make the journey had restored to the Jew the gentleness of trust. He smiled at faces he had never seen before. With luck, he calculated, he might arrive in time for *Kiddush*.

So they started again.

It was the kindest hour of evening, strewing the floors with a light of trodden dandelions. Mostly ladies filled the train. As they sat and talked together, of cakes, and illnesses, and relatives – or just talked, they worked the words inside their mouths like the bread of kindness, or sugared lollies. The mauve plastic of their gums shone. Temporarily the slashes in the train upholstery were concealed by corseted behinds, the brown smells of rotten fruit overcome by the scents of blameless but synthetic flowers.

Himmelfarb the Jew sat and smiled at all faces, even those which saw something to resent. He was delivered by his journey as seldom yet by prayer. Journeys implied a promise, as he had been taught, and known, but never dared accept. A promise that he would not dare, yet, envisage. Only an address, which he had heard discussed at smoke-o, of the Home Beautiful, the promised house. In Persimmon Street, Paradise East. So he clung to that promise. He nursed it all the way in the obviously festive train.

Outside, humidity, and conformity remained around ninety-three. Round the homes, the dahlias lolled. Who could have told whose were biggest? Who could have told who was who? Not the plastic ladies, many of whom, as they waited to shove chops in front of men, exchanged statements over fences, or sat drooping over magazines, looking for the answers to the questions.

By such light, Himmelfarb was persuaded he could have answered many of those.

A lady at his side, who, in anticipation of Easter, had pinned kindness to her bosom in letters of glass, told him how she used to bury gramophone needles under hydrangea bushes, when there were gramophone needles, but now there were none.

'And here am I,' she said, 'reared a Congregationalist, but attending the Baptist Church, because it pleases my son-in-law. Are you a Baptist, perhaps?' she asked.

'I am a Jew,' the Jew replied.

'Arrrr!' said the lady.

She had not heard right, only that it sounded something funny. Her skin closed on itself rather fearfully.

All the ladies, it appeared, had paused for a moment in their breathing. They were slavering on their plastic teeth. Before they began to clatter again.

Presently they were carried under the city, and many of the ladies, including Himmelfarb's neighbour, were discharged. The train issued lighter out of the earth, with those whose faith drove them on. As they prepared to cross the water, the Jew sat forward on his seat. The sky opened for them, and the bridge put forth its span, and they passed effortlessly over the glittering water. As it had happened before, so it had been arranged again for that day.

So the Jew had to give thanks as they mounted the other side, through a consecrated landscape, in which the promised homes began to assemble, in pools of evening, and thickets of advanced shrubs.

Where Himmelfarb was at last put down, roses met him, and led him all the way. Had he been blind, he could have walked by holding on to ropes of roses. As it was, the roselight filtering through the nets of leaves intoxicated with its bland liquor. Till the Jew was quite flushed and unsteady from his homecoming. He had grown weak. In fact, on arrival at the gate, he had to get a grip of the post, and ever so slightly bent the metal letter-box, which was in the shape of a little dovecote, empty of doves.

It was Shirl Rosetree who looked out of the apricot brick home, and saw.

She called at once:

'Har-ry! Whaddaya know? It is that old Jew. At this hour. Now what the hell? I can't bear it! Do something quick!'

'What old Jew?' Harry Rosetree asked.

He turned cold. Excitement was bad for him.

'Why, the one from over at the factory, of course.'

'But you never seen him,' her husband protested.

'I know. But just know. It could only be that one.'

Even his diversity did not alter the fact that there was only one Jew. It was her father, and her grandmother in a false moustache, and her cousins, and the cousins of cousins. It was the foetus she had dropped years ago, scrambling into the back of a cart, in darkness, to escape from a Polish village.

Shulamith Rosenbaum struck herself with the flat of her hand just above her breasts. Too hard. It jarred, and made her cough.

'I'm gunna be sick, Harry, if you don't do something about that man.'

Because she had learnt to suffer from various women's ailments, she added:

'I'm not gunna get mixed up in any Jews' arguments. It does things to me. And packing still to finish. I will not be persecuted. First it was the *goy*, now it is the Jew. All I want is peace, and a nice home.'

She would have liked to look frail, but a grievance always made her swell.

'Orright, orright!' Harry Rosetree said. 'For what reasons, Shirl, are you getting hysterical?'

He himself was flickering, for the Jew Mordecai had begun to advance up the gravel drive. If the visitor's pace appeared shambly, his head suggested that he was possessed of a certain strength.

'For what reason?' Mrs Rosetree slashed. 'Because I know me own husband!'

'For Chrissake!' The husband laughed, or flickered.

'And is he *soft*!' Shirl Rosetree shouted. 'Lets himself be bounced by any Jew because it is the *Seder* night. And who will have to bounce the Jew?'

'Orright, Shirl,' her husband said, making it of minor importance. 'We will simply tell him we are packing for our journey.'

'*We!*' Shirl Rosetree laughed. 'Jew or Christian, I am the one that has to tell. Because, Haïm, you do not like to. It is easiest to pour the chicken soup into everyone that comes. *My* chicken soup, *gefüllter Fisch*, *Latkes*, and what have you! You are the big noise, the generous man. Well, I will tell this old bludge there is nothing doing here tonight. We do not know what he even means. We are booked at My Blue Mountain Home for Easter, leaving Good Friday, in our own car, after the Stations of the Cross.'

If she stopped there, it was because she could have shocked herself. They stood looking at each other, but so immersed in the lower depths of the situation, they did not observe that the sweat was streaming from every exposed pore of their skins. They had turned yellow, too.

'We was told at the convent we was never on no account to

lose our tempers,' Rosie Rosetree said, who had come into the hall.

She was growing up a thin child.

'They better learn not to be bold,' her mother said. 'Nobody was losing their tempers.'

'A gentleman has just come,' her father added.

'What gentleman?' Rosie wondered, squinting through the pastel-blue venetians.

She was not interested in people.

'You may well ask!' her mother could not resist.

And laughed, opening a vein of jolly, objective bitterness.

The father was making noises which did not in any way explain.

The child's face had approached close to that of the stranger, the other side of the intervening blind. She squinted up and down through the slats, to look him right over.

'His clothes are awful,' Rose Rosetree announced.

Then she went away, for she had completely lost interest. Charity was an abstraction, or at most a virtue she had not seen reason to adopt. It was something lovely, but superfluous, talked about by nuns.

Yet, her father was a good man.

Now he had opened the door. He sounded funny-loud, but indistinct.

Harry Rosetree said:

'Well, Mr Himmelfarb, it is quite an unexpected visit.'

The machinery of social intercourse was turning again.

Where Himmelfarb had felt there would be no need for explanation, he now saw that eventually he must account for his behaviour. But not now. He was, simply, too tired. He only hoped their common knowledge might be shared as an implicit joy.

'I will sit down. If you don't mind,' said the unexpected guest.

And did so suddenly, on a little rosewood stool that Mrs Rosetree had never intended to be sat on. It caused the owner of the stool to stand forth.

But her husband intervened.

'You better sit there for a bit, and relax. You are pretty well flogged,' Mr Rosetree said, using a word he did not seem to remember ever having used before.

But Mrs Rosetree stood forth. Her house-coat, in one of those colours it was sometimes her good fortune to lose her head over, not only concealed her plumpy forms, it created drama, even tragedy. Earlier that afternoon, she had lacquered her nails. Now she remembered again to stand with her fingers stretched stiff, in an attitude of formal guilt. From the very beginning, the tips of her fingers could have been dripping blood.

'It is a pity my husband did not explain, Mr Himmelfarb,' Mrs Rosetree said.

The fact that nobody had been introduced to anybody did not seem to matter, because by now everybody had grasped the part that each was intended to play.

'Did not explain.' Mrs Rosetree proceeded to. 'That we had planned to go away. For Easter. After tomorrow is already Good Friday, you must know.'

Mrs Rosetree smiled to assist, and the wet-looking lipstick with which she had anointed her otherwise naked skin, glittered like an accident.

'I do not want to appear inhospitable,' she said. 'Not to anybody. But you know what it is, Mr Himmelfarb, to shut up the home. All those little things. And the kids. Not even hardly time to open a tin of baked beans. Because I will not stock up with a lot of fresh food, to leave for rats to gorge on, and ourselves perhaps contract the yellow jaundice.'

Mrs Rosetree's head was all barbed with little pins, at mercilessly regular intervals, to control the waves that were being moulded on her.

Harry Rosetree had to admire his wife for an unfailingly ruthless materialism, such as he himself had been able to cultivate for use in business only. But to Shirl, of course, life was a business.

As he stood looking down upon the crown of the old Jew's head, he said:

'We couldn't run to a pick-me-up, eh, for Himmelfarb, to celebrate an occasion?'

Mrs Rosetree's throat began to debate, or grumble.

'I wouldn't know about occasions. He better sit still first. It isn't right for elderly people to go swilling alcohol after they have been exerting themselves. I wouldn't give it to my own father, for fear it might bring something on.'

Then, with an air of having laid tribute on an altar, Mrs Rosetree went away, to allow matters to take their course.

So that Haïm ben Ya'akov was left with the stranger Mordecai on the *Seder* night.

In the absence of rejoicing, there was nothing he could offer the guest from his full house. Indeed, it was possible that the house no longer belonged to him, that nothing could belong to a Jew beyond his own skin and certain inherited truths.

The stranger did not attempt to deny. He sat with his head bent, in a state of apparent exhaustion, or acceptance. He was too passive to imply, yet did.

So Harry Rosetree, who was, in any case, not a Jew, began to grow impatient, if not actually irritable. Surrounded by veneer, the stranger's shoes were becoming provokingly meek and dusty.

Then Himmelfarb looked up, as if realizing the awkward situation in which he had placed his host.

'It is all right,' he said, and smiled. 'I shall be going soon.'

'Well, Himmelfarb,' Mr Rosetree found it easier to reply, 'it was unexpected, to say the least. And life does not stand still. You must excuse me if I leave you for a little. I gotta water a few shrubs before it is dark.'

Because Mr Rosetree had learnt what was done in the suburb in which he happened to be living for the time being.

'But,' he added, 'you are at liberty to rest here just as long as you feel it is necessary. A man of your age cannot afford to neglect the health.'

Himmelfarb continued sitting in the Rosetrees' hall, which was less a room than a means of protecting the owners from the unwanted; their strength could not be questioned while they remained hidden. At that hour the light was failing. Many of the glassy surfaces were already dulled. But the glint of opulence, together with all the mechanical sounds of success, still issued from the house behind.

Presently a boy appeared. He was already tall, but not yet furnished. In that light the contours of his face shone like yellow wax. He himself could have been holding a taper, if not a scroll.

The boy frowned, who had not bargained for a visitor.

Himmelfarb was grateful even for a presence.

'The *Bar Mitzvah* boy,' he could not help himself.

'Eh?' exclaimed the boy, and frowned deeper.

All of this was part of something he sensed he must resent, but only sensed.

'You are thirteen,' the stranger remarked with certainty.

The boy grunted agreement, but full of hate.

'What is your name?'

'Steve,' answered the boy.

He would get out pretty soon.

'What else?' the man insisted. 'Haven't you a real name?'

The boy's throat was working.

'One of ours?' the stranger persevered.

The boy was full of disgust, not to say horror. He hated the madman in the hall.

And went from there without answering, on his rubber soles.

So that there was nothing with which the stranger might identify himself, and he would have gone if his limbs had allowed him.

But a girl came. She was looking rather feverish. And thin. Her hair was minced up into little, quivering curls.

'Good evening,' he began. 'You are the daughter.'

'Oh, yes,' she admitted, but that was unimportant.'I have been reading the life of the Little Flower,' she said, because she loved to tell about herself. 'It is lovely. It is my favourite book. But any saints are interesting.'

'Have you come across those of Safed and Galicia?'

'Oh,' she said, 'I never heard about *them*. They wouldn't be real, not Catholic saints.'

But even that was unimportant.

She came closer to him to confess.

'Do you know, I am going to have a vocation. I am praying for it, and if you pray hard enough, it comes. I am praying that the wounds will open in my hands.'

In the half-light she was rubbing the thin palms of her hands, and showing.

But the telephone rang, and the mother came. So the daughter hid her hands.

Mrs Rosetree, still wearing her house-coat, of which the colour suddenly illuminated in the old man's mind the whole, exhausting perennial journey, very carefully disentangled the telephone cord, and carried the instrument round the corner. For privacy. Even so, the corner revealed the burning azure of Mrs Rosetree's behind.

'Hello?' answered Mrs Rosetree. 'This is JM 3 ... Marge! Why, Marge!' Mrs Rosetree cried. 'I dunno what's got hold of this line. Come closer into the phone.'

The daughter made a face.

'That is Mumma's friend,' she said. 'And she's a pain.'

'Why, Marge, I would of rung you,' Mrs Rosetree was protesting, 'but went to the hairdresser's ... Yairs, yairs. That one. I gotta leave him, Marge. His wife is having some trouble. Always the same. Every time ...'

The child pressed against the stranger in the dusk. She had to whisper.

'You know about St Tereese and the roses? I think I once saw a rose. A white rose.'

'Arr, nao, nao, Marge! I would of *rung you*,' Mrs Rosetree was saying. 'But then I went to the pictures ... Yairs. Yairs. ... It was a love story ... Yairs. No story much, but it made you feel good. ...'

In the dusk the paper roses twittered round Himmelfarb. The voices of love breathed a synthetic heliotrope.

'Yes, Marge,' Mrs Rosetree laughed. 'I gotta. I gotta have my ration of love.'

'Why do you tell me all this?' Himmelfarb whispered to the little girl. 'The roses, and the wounds?'

'On Good Friday, after. ... Yairs. After the Stations of the Cross ... Yairs,' said Mrs Rosetree with great patience. 'Well, dear, we have our obligations to the Church. Well, you see, Marge, that is something you will never understand if you are not one yourself.'

The daughter was sucking her mouth in, and thinking.

'I like to tell somebody,' she said. 'Once in a while. People I won't ever see again.'

In fact, she had already dismissed her collaborator.

But whirled him back for a moment in a gust of her especial hysteria.

'Besides,' she giggled, 'you are sort of spooky!'

'Nao, Marge,' Mrs Rosetree was insisting. 'There is nobody. ... Sure ... Well, yes, a chap came, but is going. ... Nobody ... Yes, dear, I tell you, he is *go*-ing. ...'

With the result that the stranger got up and went. The door had been standing open ever since he came.

When Mrs Rosetree had finished her conversation, she returned from round the corner with the telephone, and said:

'Don't tell me that man has gone! What can you have done to him?'

Her daughter, who had given up answering her parents, continued to rub her finger round a window that did not open.

'These old Jews,' Mrs Rosetree explained, 'will land on you, and then you have had it.'

'Was he a Jew?' the child asked.

'Was he a Jew!'

Mrs Rosetree spoke and laughed so softly, she could have been referring not to the stranger, but to some part of her own body that was a secret between herself and the doctor – her womb, for instance.

'Like Our Saviour!' exclaimed the little girl.

Who began to cry extravagantly. Because she would never experience a miracle. However long she waited for the hands to touch.

'Arr, now, Rosie,' the mother protested. 'I will fetch the milk of magnesia. Cry, cry! Over nothing.'

'It is the age, perhaps.' The mother sighed.

And went softly, tenderly, into the kitchen, to heat up some chicken soup with *Kneidlach*, and to taste that chopped chicken liver she had bullied the daily into pounding up good.

If her husband did not come – he usually did whenever a smell of food arose – it was because he was still in the bush-house. If he had held no further conversation with the Jew Mordecai before the latter left, it was because the bush-house had prevented him from doing this too. The bush-house – and propagation area – which Mrs Rosetree had wanted so bad until she got it, had fascinated him from the beginning, as well as offering a refuge on occasions, never more needful than that evening, as the familiar stars appeared between the twigs, and the feet of the departing guest were heard on the gravel.

At one end of the balcony above the narrow street in which they used to live, they would weave a few sticks together, into a rough canopy. At that end the dish-clouts hung at normal times, and even during *Succoth* there remained the heavy smell of dish-water. Into which they would drag their mattresses, and lie. The whole family. Their blood almost running together. During the festival of *Succoth* they never seemed to leave their tabernacle, unless the rain came, very unpleasant, causing them to scatter, and the old people to pat one another's clothes to estimate the dangers. But normally they would lie, all through the nights of *Succoth*, under the smell of dish-water, the grandfather groaning, and snoring, and breaking wind, the boy Haïm ben Ya'akov looking at those same stars.

Now Mrs Rosetree called:

'Har-ry? All this good soup will be getting cold. You don't wanta be afraid. He's gone. Tt tt! Har-ry! The night air is gunna play hell with you!'

By the time Himmelfarb returned along the streets of Paradise East, the ropes of roses had disintegrated. The houses, too, had dissolved, although the windows had set into shapes of solid light, thus proving that something does survive. Filled with such certainty, or an evening feed of steak, the bellies of stockbrokers had risen like gasometers. As the stockbrokers stood, pressing their thumbs over the nozzles of hoses, to make the water squirt better, they discussed the rival merits of *thuya orientalis* and *retinospera pisifera plumosa*. All the gardens of Paradise East were planted for posterity. All the homes were architect-planned. From one window, certainly, a voice had begun to scream, strangled, it seemed, by its boa of roses, and so unexpected, the noise could have carried from some more likely suburb.

Himmelfarb reached the station, and caught the little train. Again it appeared to have been waiting for him, as if by arrangement, to run him back into that country which, for the hostage, there is no escaping.

He did not complain actively. It was the train. The train rocked and grumbled, and communicated to his still passive body something of the night of desolation. The plastic ladies, of course, had been too pastel to last, and faded out with afternoon. At night it was the men who prevailed and rumbled in the train. The facts they were exchanging might have sounded brutal if they had not already been worn down by the users: by the thin, copper-coloured blokes, and the bluish, pursy ones, bursting with hair like the slashed upholstery in trains. As they rocked, there was a smell of peanuts, and wet paper bags, and beer, and tunnels.

Here and there, as it lurched, the train threatened to blunder into the private lives of individuals. In the kitchens of many homes, gentlemen in singlets were only now assaulting their plastic sausages, ladies were limply tumbling the spaghetti off the toast on which they had been so careful to put it, daughters daintier than their mums were hurrying to get finished, for ever, but for ever. Over all, the genie of beef dripping still hovered in his blue robe. But magic was lacking. And in narrow rooms, emptied boys, rising from sticky contemplation of some old coloured pin-up, prepared to investigate the dark.

The train burst across the night where it was suspended, miraculously, over water. In the compartments no one but the Jew appeared to notice they were returning to a state of bondage they had never really left. But the Jew now knew he should not have expected anything else.

The train was easing through the city which knives had sliced open to serve up with all the juices running – red, and green, and purple. All the syrups of the sundaes oozing into the streets to sweeten. The neon syrup coloured the pools of vomit and the sailors' piss. By that light, the eyes of the younger, gaberdine men were a blinding, blinder blue, when not actually burnt out. The blue-haired grannies had purpled from the roots of their hair down to the angles of their pants, not from shame, but neon, as their breasts chafed to escape, from shammy-leather back to youth, or else roundly asserted themselves, like chamberpots in concrete. As for the young women, they were necessary. As they swung along, or hung around a corner, or on an arm, they were the embodiment of thoughts and melons. As if the thoughts of the gaberdine men had risen from the ashes behind their fused eyeballs, and put on flesh at last, of purple, and red, and undulating green. There were the kiddies, too. The kiddies would continue to suck at their slabs of neon, until they had learnt to tell the time, until it was time to mouth other sweets.

All along the magnesium lines swayed the drunken train. Because the night itself was drunk, the victims it had seemed to invite were forced to follow suit. Himmelfarb was drunk, not to the extent of brutishness; he had not yet fetched up. Released from the purple embrace, sometimes he tottered. Sometimes hurtled. Watching.

As the darkness spat sparks, and asphalt sinews ran with salt sweat, the fuddled trams would be tunnelling farther into the furry air, over the bottle-tops, through the smell of squashed pennies, and not omitting from time to time to tear an arm out of its screeching socket. But would arrive at last under the frangipani, the breezes sucking with the mouths of sponges. Sodom had not been softer, silkier at night than the sea gardens of Sydney. The streets of Nineveh had not clanged with such metal. The waters of Babylon had not sounded sadder than the sea, ending on a crumpled beach, in a scum of French-letters.

At one point the train in which Himmelfarb huddled on his homeward journey farted extra good. And stopped.

The man opposite paused in stuffing cold potato-chips into his mouth.

'Whoa-err, Matilda!' shouted the rather large man, and brayed.

Through a mash of cold potato.

But the foreign cove did not understand a joke.

Or was listening to the radio which had begun to sing in the stationary night. Some song which the potato-eater did not bother to recognize.

'O city of elastic kisses and retracting dreams! [the psalmist sang];
'O rivers of vomit, O little hills of concupiscence, O immense plains of complacency!
'O great, sprawling body, how will you atone, when your soul is a soft peanut with the weevils in it?
'O city of der-ree....'

But the train choked the voice by starting. And continued. And continued. And after much further travel the old Jew found himself descending the lane – or avenue – in which he lived. He was shaking now, and threatened with falling amongst the swathes of paspalum which tried perpetually to mow him down. He was almost crying for all that he had seen and experienced that night, not because it existed in itself, but because he had made it live in his own heart.

So he reached his door, and felt for the *Mezuzzah* on the doorpost, to touch, to touch the *Sh'ma*, not so much in the hope of being rescued, as to drive the hatred out.

The miracle did, in fact, occur almost at the same moment as he noticed a light approaching, swaying and jumping, as the one who held it negotiated the uneven ground. Distance, shadows, light itself finally made way, and Himmelfarb recognized the figure of Mrs Godbold, carrying an old hurricane-lamp which he had known her take before on missions at night.

'I listened for you, sir, and heard you come, I am sorry,' she apologized, 'if I disturb. But have a reason.'

Even so, she remained embarrassed.

And Himmelfarb could have been happier. The love that he should have returned any living creature was still a shabby, tattered one.

Then he noticed that his neighbour was holding a dish, on it something insignificant and black.

Mrs Godbold looked down. She was made immensely solid by that rudimentary light. Yet, a white transparency of light had transfigured her normally opaque skin.

'This is some lamb, sir,' she explained, at once heavy and tremulous, 'that a lady gives us every year at Easter.'

'Lamb?' Himmelfarb repeated, in some desperation, from a fit of nausea, not for present circumstances, but perhaps a past incident, he could not for the moment remember what.

'Yes,' she said, and repeated: 'For Easter. Have you forgotten? The day after tomorrow – no, tomorrow already is Good Friday. The factory will be closed. You will have to think of how you will be living for quite a number of days.'

'Oh,' he said. 'Yes. It is also Easter.'

Mrs Godbold was again confused. She looked down at the still only partly explained object on her dish.

'The lady gives us the leg,' she said, and blushed by lantern-light. 'But this year the puppy got hold of it. Not all that much. We tidied up the other end for ourselves. And the shank was not touched. I brought it, sir. I thought you might care to make a little celebration.'

'For Easter.'

Now that his voice had stuck, he could not avoid repeating things.

'That is not the point,' Mrs Godbold said, and again she blushed. 'Everybody has got to eat. Whatever the time of year.'

Then he took the dish from her. The long, leaping shadows from the jumping lantern made them both look very awkward.

He began talking, in quick, nervous, little, stabbing phrases, putting his tongue out a good deal.

'You will be glad. Not that it will be, well,' he chose with some care, 'a holiday, exactly. For you. I expect. But for what it signifies.'

'Oh,' she answered, 'I am always glad at Eastertide. Because, then, suffering is over. Or so they tell us. For a little.'

That she should not appear to have offered a variant of her own, she continued rather quickly:

'It was more of Easter at Home, of course. There was the flowers. The scent of flowers. The narcissies. And the white anemones we would pick if we cut across the woods. Oh, and blackthorn!' she remembered; it was, indeed, a joyful find. 'I think I liked the blackthorn best. The flowers were the whitest, on the black sticks. We children would sometimes bring the flowers to decorate our Table. Oh, it would look lovely when they had lit the candles. It would look alive. Then it did seem as though the world was re-born. The mass of blackthorn was like a whole tree flowering on the Table of our church. It was not much of a one, sir, by any great standards. But on Easter Day we would know Our Lord had risen.'

Mrs Godbold's trumpet voluntary sounded solitary, but true.

'But, of course,' she hastened, 'we would have known without all that. All the flowers on earth could wither up, and we would still know.'

Then the Jew hung his head.

But she saw, and at once she touched him with her voice, saying:

'You must forgive me. I must not waste your time. You will not be up for work. The lamb is nothing, but you are welcome to it – only if you would care.'

When she had left, and he had gone inside, and switched the light on, and it had rained down on his almost empty living-room, he realized that he had to face the disaster of his *Seder* table. Still untouched, the past few hours seemed to have made a sculpture of it, not of rejoicing, but of lament. Here, rather, was the tomb of all those, including himself, who had not survived the return journey, and he, risen from the dead, the keeper of it. That he knew, he knew. He touched the clay of Egypt, which time had turned browner. And herbs, never so bitter as facts. That he knew for certainty.

Then the Jew saw that he was still carrying Mrs Godbold's dish, and that the wretched shankbone which his neighbour had brought as an offering was almost the twin of the one he had laid that afternoon on his own *Seder* table.

13

Because the telephone is the darkest, the most sepulchral oracle of all, Mrs Flack would stalk around that instrument for quite a while before she was persuaded to accept the summons. Although a considerable pythoness herself, it might have been that she felt the need for invocation before encounter with superior powers. Or was it, simply, that she feared to hear the voice of doom addressing her personally?

Either way, she would at last be heard:

'Oh? Ah? Yairs. No. No! *Yairs!* Perhaps. Who can tell? I will have to think it over and give you an answer. Well, now! Those who know, need not ask.'

As she parried with a shield of wooden words, it would begin to appear as though she had mislaid her matchless sword, and the armour of disbelief, with which she had been careful to gird herself, had turned audibly to buckram.

Mrs Jolley, who enjoyed the gift of being able to overhear without actually listening, had even known her friend reply:

'You cannot expect me to be wise to everythink. Can you, now?'

It made Mrs Jolley wonder, but she continued to immerse the dishes, which was one of the duties she performed in return for friendship and a very small remuneration.

Mrs Jolley soon learned that, of all the telephone voices, there was perhaps only one to which Mrs Flack could genuinely respond. On such occasions the true glue of prophecy would be poured back, into the funnel of the telephone, on to the missing questions. Mrs Jolley could tell that her friend's rather dry and freckled hands were moulding the warm bakelite into an altogether different shape.

Mrs Jolley would hear:

'If you was so foolish as to leave off your singlet as well, then what can you expect? Oh, dear, dear! I would advise you to rub your chest before retiring, and see as the blanket is pulled right up, and sweat it out with a couple of aspro, and a drop of somethink. It is you who must answer for your own health, whoever else is willin' to.'

On one occasion Mrs Jolley heard:

'I do not expect feelin's where feelin's do not exist. But expect them to be respected where they do. Eh? No, you do not understand. You do not understand. No one understands no more, unless it is put in American.'

When her friend returned to the kitchen, Mrs Jolley could not resist:

'Ah, dear, some people are terrible.'

But Mrs Flack did not appear to hear.

'Some young fellers,' Mrs Jolley ventured further, 'are all for themselves nowadays.'

Mrs Flack had risen to the surface, but her thoughts were floating after her.

'That nephew of yours is giving you a lot of trouble,' said Mrs Jolley, and chipped a plate on the tap.

'There is no trouble,' replied Mrs Flack, 'where a person's life is his own.'

'Oh, no, where a person's life is his own.' Mrs Jolley sighed. She did wonder where.

There was the morning – it was the Thursday of Easter, Mrs Jolley would remember – the telephone had rung that sharp, she broke the little butter-dish with the gum-nuts on it, which she hid behind the dresser to dispose of when convenient.

Mrs Flack answered, as usual, but only after bells had begun to ring at every end of a lady's nerves.

Mrs Jolley heard:

'Waddaya know! I would never ever! Golly, I am pleased, Blue! But watch out now, won't you? I am telling you people will act different. People, when they get a smell of someone else's luck, are very, very different. People, at the best of times, are different underneath their clothes. Eh? You know, Blue, I did not suggest. You will never ever find me descending to anything low – thoughts or talk – never low. Because there is so much that is far from nice. Which reminds me, Blue, someone that we know of was visiting last night, so I am told, by lantern-

396

light, a certain person. Yairs, dear. Forgetting, it would seem, the time of year. It was *them* that crucified Our Saviour. To-morrow. Think of it. Tomorrow! Yet, someone that we know of must *consort* – to put it blunt. Eh? Blue! Blue! I forbid you! Who am I – I would like to know – that you are talking to? Where are you, Blue? I can only think you must be full. In the one across from work? A fat lot of work you'll do this morning, Blue, and what odds!'

Here Mrs Flack laughed like a motor-bike.

'I do not blame you, neither. It is only right that young people in full possession of their health should take their pleasure. And if they come to grief, well, it is the parents will wear the scars. It is not the children on who the sins. Oh, dear, no! Whatever else. Do not think I am bitter, as has sometimes been suggested. I am not. I am realistic, that is all, and must bear the consequences of seeing things as they really are. And suffer every Easter to know the Jews have crucified Our Lord. Again. Blue? Something that the young do not need to under-stand. Not while they have their lovely bodies. Eh? Blue? Enjoy, boy, enjoy, then! Bust your skin open, if that is what you want! It is only a game to let the blood run when there is plenty of it. And so red. Nothing is cruel if you don't see it that way. Besides, it lets the bad out, too, and I would be the last to deny there is plenty of that waiting to turn to pus in anybody's veins.'

'Eh? Blue?' Mrs Flack was calling, it could have been in joy, or desperation.

When she entered the kitchen she was glittering dreadfully.

Mrs Jolley, who had been excited, puzzled, frightened by all that she had overheard, decided to continue looking at the sink.

'Blue,' gasped Mrs Flack, 'and six workmates' – here she sat hard upon an upright chair – 'has gone and won the Lottery. They called the ticket "Lucky Sevens".'

Mrs Jolley was looking at the sink, of which the grey water, suddenly so flat and still, continued to conceal a variety of objects.

'You are not pleased,' Mrs Flack only dreamily accused.

In her entranced state she did not need to glance. Mrs Jolley would be without her shine. She would be wearing the grey look of mornings of dishwater. It was normal for her now to leave her teeth whole days in the tumbler, beneath the handker-chief, beside her bed.

'Some people,' said Mrs Flack, 'do not like to hear the good.'

Mrs Jolley stroked the water.

'I was only thinking,' said Mrs Jolley.

She was not all that grey.

'I was thinking of his poor mother,' she said.

Nor was she reproachful, only sympathetic.

'What was the name,' she asked, 'of your sister, Mrs Flack, that passed on?'

Mrs Flack grew dreamier.

'Eh?' she said. 'My sister. My sister Daisy. Daisy,' she said.

'I was thinking,' said Mrs Jolley, 'it will be lovely for your sister to know as her boy has struck lucky.'

Usually when others expressed suitable sentiments, Mrs Flack would be at a loss how to bridge the gap. If she were unable to prevent the moment occurring, she would find herself, as now, squinting down her front into – nothing.

On that most brilliant of mornings Mrs Jolley had elected for darkness. Her friend suspected she might even be concealing some long-range plan for breaking open safes, and thieving old letters and deeds.

So Mrs Flack arranged her spotless front, and waited.

'I bet your hubby, too, was fond of such a sturdy boy. As much an uncle as you an aunt.'

'Will?' Mrs Flack answered from very far. 'Will died when Blue was still a little kiddy.'

Mrs Jolley sucked her gums.

'It was not my intention,' she said, 'to bring it up. And such a dreadful end.'

But Mrs Flack could not in every way agree; death is so practical.

'I will not deny,' she said, 'that the manner of it was unexpected, Will being so well-thought-of in the trade, so well-remunerated, a first-class tiler. But, it is not the manner of it, Mrs Jolley, that matters – whether a man slips off the roof, or snuffs out in 'is own lounge-room, in an easy chair. The end, why, the *end* is the same.'

Mrs Jolley began to see plainly there might be no escaping from out of that cube of kitchen.

'Well,' she cried, 'are we a pair of crows!'

'It was not me that chose to enter into morbid speculation,' said Mrs Flack, loftier.

Mrs Jolley struck the surface of the water with her hand.

'And on such a day!' she shrieked, looking at the clock. 'I bet that nephew of yours will be full as a piss-ant by eleven!'

'Blue is a good boy,' claimed Mrs Flack.

'No one ever,' conceded Mrs Jolley.

'Blue never got into trouble. Or not much.'

'I do not know what I do not know!' Mrs Jolley laughed.

'Blue never killed a soul,' said Mrs Flack.

'Who killed who?' asked Mrs Jolley, her neck turning on a steel spring.

'It happens every day. A person has only to read the papers.'

'You cannot take the papers for true.'

'Only a person can know the truth, and then not always.'

There the two ladies were caught up in the morning. Their actions were no longer their own because severed from their bodies by thought and light.

Himmelfarb, who had retired late, rose early on that day. Whatever its conditions were to be, he refused, as always, to allow himself to speculate before he had laid the phylacteries on. Only when he was girt with the Word, and the shawl, covering his shoulders, excluded with its fringes those other desires of heart and eyes, had his own day begun, or was again created, sanctified, and praised. As he stood, reciting the *Sh'ma* and Benedictions, from behind closed lids, from the innermost part of him, the face began again to appear in the divine likeness, in the clouds of the little mirror, offering itself for an approval that might always remain withheld.

But the Jew prayed:

'Blessed art thou, O Lord our God, King of the Universe, who hast given to the cock intelligence to distinguish between day and night. . . .'

And the light was poured into the four corners of the room, though silently at Sarsaparilla, for man had known better than God or Levite, and had operated on the cock. But the purest leaf touched the Jew's eyelids; his lids were shaped in gold. His veins were lapis lazuli in a sea of gold, the thongs of the phylacteries were turned to onyx, but the words that fell from his mouth were leaping crystals, each reflecting to infinity the words contained within the words.

The Jew prayed, and the statue which had been broken off the pediment of time, and set down on the edge of the morning, became a man. The rather chapped lips were forming words of their own flesh:

'Let us obtain this day and every day, grace, favour, and mercy in thine eyes, and in the eyes of all who behold us, and bestow lovingkindnesses upon us. Blessed art thou, O Lord. . . .'

And the light which, until now, had been of a mineral order, a matter of crumbling gold, together with the cold slips of elusive feldspar, forming upon the deposits of porphyry and agate with which the solid firmament was streaked, dissolved at last into a sea of moving crimson. The crimson sea lapped at the skin of the man as he stood at prayer, the tips of his ears and the hollows of his temples grew transparent, his cheeks were flushed with crimson, or the intensity of his petition.

The Jew affirmed:

'I believe with perfect faith in the coming of the Messiah, and, though he tarry, I will wait daily for his coming. For thy salvation I hope, O Lord! I hope, O Lord, for thy salvation! O Lord, for thy salvation I hope!'

And the shawl fell back from his shoulders in the moment of complete union, and the breeze from the window twitched at the corner of his old robe, showing him to be, indeed, a man, made to suffer the torments and indignities. The hair lay in thin, grizzled wisps in the hollow between his breasts; the thongs of veins which bound his scraggy legs, from the ankles to the knees, were most arbitrarily, if not viciously entangled.

When he had finished praying, Himmelfarb looked out of the window of his fragile house. Because he had not slept, each act that he observed was of the most innocent, each line the cleanest, each form the simplest. On a ridge the other side of the street, white hens were already picking amongst the black trunks of the wattles. In the street itself, an old man, after unfolding his newspaper, was preparing to read with unconcern of the worst that could have happened. The stream of milk was transfixed between the milkman's measure and the billy-cans. The Jew stood rubbing the stubble on his cheek. Since all was obviously logical, now he could only be prepared.

And went about getting himself ready. He could not prevent his hands fumbling and trembling at times, not only because he was moved by the purity of certain objects which he had to touch, but because these were attached by strings of memory to incidents experienced. He did, however, attempt to eat. He drank part of a cupful of coffee, which on that morning tasted peculiarly bitter in his mouth. From the wreckage of his *Seder* table he tasted a little of the bitter parsley. He pulled splinters from each of the identical shankbones. Only after they had been chewed, moistened in humility and longing, did the splinters begin to suggest meat. Then he had to swallow the fragments in great, hot, sounding lumps.

At the usual hour, he packed the *Tallith* and *Tephillin* into his small fibre case. Although officially excused by Herr Rosenbaum from appearing during *Pessach*, he knew, of course, that his attendance was virtually expected. By others. Even, perhaps, by Rosenbaum. Himmelfarb would not allow himself to remember the threatened expression of his employer's eyes, but walked up the hill, in the shadow of the grey paling fences, to catch the bus for Barranugli.

The morning soon turned grey and resistant, movement rubbery, either slack and disinclined, or taut and desperate. At Rosetree's the machines were already limber. As they ran, they sucked and breathed, but grudgingly. Ladies at their trays were mopping themselves with complaints. One was showing how the night had bruised her. All was as usual. Except everybody knew that this morning would be different.

It was, for one thing, the eve of Good Friday, and who was gunna work when Easter had as good as come? Better to close down was the general opinion, and see to it that the meat was got home, and enough booze to last the holidays. But in the absence of common sense and justice, everybody sat and expected. Or toyed slightly with the metal parts which it was the habit of their second natures to put together. Today the hinges were resentful, spikes inclined to pierce the flesh. Moisture gathered in smears on the brilliant plating.

Then it was realized Blue was absent from the plating-shop, and that several of the boys were not showing up, or only by fits and starts, shoving their dials round the door, and going, and coming, always grinning elastically. It was the Lucky Sevens, of course. One or two of the less lucky had been better informed from the beginning. Mr Theobalds was laughing as he played with the hair of his armpits and awaited developments. He appeared to be a man the softer for experience. Soon it had passed along the lines of grannies and sulkier girls that some of the blokes had pulled off the Lottery. Well, good on 'em! But there were some could have cried. And one lady produced from her pocket a whistle of the postman type, which she had found that morning on her bedside table, and blew it until the veins were ugly at her temples, and her lips had turned pale and cracked in spite of the layers of pillar-box red.

It was humid down on the work-floor. Who was gunna work? Though a few inveterates dabbled. It would be possible very soon to detach from the arms, all-of-a-piece, the films of moisture, or long gloves of greasy skin.

Only the Jew remained dry, and unaffected by the outward

situation. His hands were tingling but prepared as he sat down at his drill, and proceeded to bore the hole, and bore the hole, as would be expected of him, until he was called. In the circumstances, his concentration was distasteful, abominable to many, who could not prevent themselves glancing, however, at the bloody foreign Jew, and especially when he got up, and stamped around his drill, to restore circulation, drive out the pins and needles. When he rubbed his hands together, they sounded sand-papery and dry, unlike the soapy, streaming skins of people. To some it is always unendurable to watch the antithesis of themselves.

But the Jew returned to his stool, and did try to cause as little pain as possible. Though he nodded once at the blackfellow, in spite of their unexpressed agreement not to recognize each other.

The abo did not recognize now.

Although the latter had evidently been sick, and had lost weight to the extent of looking emaciated, he continued to strip to the waist on account of the excessive humidity. If nobody commented on his appearance, not even those who were most disgusted by the presence of sickness, or blacks – antithesis in its extremest forms – it is because he had become by now the abstraction of a man. The eyes of the talkers lingered only absently on the construction of ribs. These had no connexion with the life of brick homes and washing-machines which is led by human beings.

At times the abo would shiver, though. Especially when recognized by the Jew. He did not want that. He did not wish to become involved in a situation which he might not have the strength to endure. But which he must learn ultimately to express.

So he shivered, and at one stage the salient ribs appeared to grow convulsed and separate, in spite of their attachment to one another in his sides.

Round about ten, Mr Rosetree himself came out of his office, after first glancing through the hatchway at the workshop, and deciding that a personal appearance was at least theoretically appropriate. Nobody cared, though. So Mr Rosetree strutted worse than ever on the balls of his rather small feet. And addressed one or two of the absent-minded ladies.

Harry Rosetree was very jolly that day, even when the sweat trickled down his delicatessen skin, at the back of his carefully clipped neck. The sweat trickled under the collar. But Mr Rosetree laughed, ever so jolly, and said what a day it was for the factory, for seven mates to pull the lottery off. And just at Easter. Then he looked at the clock. And laughed again, right back to his gold tooth. The radio was straining all the time from the wall, and one day, if not actually that morning, it would tear itself free at the very moment strangulation was promised.

Just then, one of the Lucky Sevens looked in before returning to the pub across the street. The boys were celebrating, he reported, and his smile produced dimples such as are reserved for mention of beer, Old Ireland, or mothers. There had never been another Easter like it. They were pissed as flies.

Mr Rosetree laughed fit to stagger the machines.

But frowned at the Jew Himmelfarb.

The whole human mechanism of the boss was threatened by events that were developing in his own establishment, and for which he must blame somebody. Of course the mates were out of the question; they were sacrosanct. There remained Harry Rosetree himself, or his conscience Haïm ben Ya'akov, or its goad, Himmelfarb. Blood pressure, heat, noise, all contributed to his distress, and confused his attempts to distinguish a cause.

'What for you come when I told you to lay off over *Pessach*?' Mr Rosetree sputtered.

Himmelfarb replied:

'I have never escaped the consequences by avoiding them.'

'Eh?' shouted Harry Rosetree.

But by now there was too much noise.

Over and above the repeated statement of Himmelfarb's drill, and general emotional jamboree of machinery, something was happening in the street. There were drums, and cornets, and probably one fife. A sharp stench of animals began to mingle with the blander smell of oil.

In the outer office Miss Whibley, who had been powdering herself all the morning, paused and exclaimed:

'Oh, I say, a circus!'

Miss Mudge agreed that it was, and together they flung themselves at the window, with the object, it seemed, of widening the hole, and thus penetrating farther into what they hoped to see.

At the same time, there was such a squealing of stools and thumping of tables in the workshops, as a scaffolding was erected from which to view the spectacle through the rather high-set louvres. Certain gentlemen took advantage of the situation to squeeze close to certain young ladies. Everything so contiguous, the summer blouses grew as unconscious as blancmange. Although the owner of the whistle did not stop blowing.

As the circus returned to the patch of dead grass where some had observed it pitched the night before, fevers that had never been diagnosed sweated their way into the hands and faces of many of the spectators: to see the white bellies of the girls through the fringes of their satins, or to smell the smell of monkeys. A fellow on a skewbald nag could have been anybody's almost-extinguished dream, the way he drew a match along the tight flank of his pants, and almost glanced up, out of his burnt-out eyes.

Most comical was one of the clowns who pretended to enact a public hanging on the platform of a lorry. Nothing but the jolting and his own skill prevented him from adapting his neck to the noose. He would totter, and fall – wide. Yet, it was suggested, as good as strangled by the air. His tongue would loll outside his mouth, before licking up those invisible fragments which restore to life.

'They will kill the silly bugger yet!' screamed one of the grannies of Rosetree's Brighta Bicycle Lamps. 'Look! What did I tell yez? And spoil 'is Easter!'

It did seem as though the clown's act had been played out at last, for a second procession, longer, smoother, less amorphous, had united precipitately with the first. Between the jolting and the screams, flowers were falling, as the second procession was seen to be that of an actual funeral, so well-attended, so black, clothes of such good quality, and faces of such a doubtful cast, it could only have been an alderman that they were putting down quick before the holidays set in.

As the clown spun at the end of his rope, and the little property coffin hesitated on the brink of the lorry, and confusion carried voices, brakes, horses' wind into the upper register, a woman rose in the first funeral car, or stuffed herself, rather, in the window: a large, white woman – could have been the widow – pointing, as if she had recognized at last in the effigy of the clown the depth, and duration, and truth of grief, which she had failed to grasp in connexion with that exacting male her now dead husband. The woman was screeching dry screams. A monumental marble could have been clearing its throat of dust, and would not stop since it had learnt.

It had not been established whether the clown was dead, or again shamming, when the interlocked processions dragged each other round the corner, and out of sight. Those who had longed for a show wondered whether they were appeased, for the clown was surely more or less a puppet, when they had been hoping for a man. On the other hand, the eyes of some of the more thoughtful had receded into their heads as the hand of the controversial clown seemed to jerk at a curtain in their minds.

It occurred to these that their boss had remained stranded with the Jew down at the far end of the shed, and that the soundless attitudes of the two men had nothing and everything to do with events.

Harry Rosetree's hands were trying to part the air, so that he might come closer to the core of it.

He had, in fact, just said:

'I must ask you, I must order you to leave!'

Of course the vibration of the machinery was enough to dash the words out of anybody's mouth.

'It could be for your own good,' Mr Rosetree threatened.

But the Jew smiled sadly. He was not so sure.

'At once. Before.' The boss was booming, and exuding.

The shaped, but silent words bounced like blown egg-shells.

The Jew had replied, in his own vein of sad irony:

'You will not be blamed.'

Sometimes the velvet belting of machinery actually soothed.

'Nobody but myself,' Himmelfarb could have been saying, 'will be held to blame for anything that may happen. You are doubly insured.'

The strangeness of the situation, the employer trying to extract something from the air, and offer it in the shape of a secret message to one of the least skilled of his employees, would have roused curiosity, if it had not disturbed. Those who noticed averted their eyes.

Fortunately there were other things happening. It was just on smoke-o. The machines were easing. Workers were descending from the scaffolding of tables, from which they had been employed enjoying the spectacle of the processions. It was now time to relax.

When the Lucky Sevens returned, from the pub across the street, and the incident of the hanging clown. There was Blue at last, whom many had not seen, let alone congratulated, on the morning of his good fortune. A number of his workmates, noticeably those of the female sex, were rushing to touch, to kiss, to associate, while the shyer waited for him to identify himself in some way, although he had got full enough, to show.

Blue was shickered all right. The beer was running out of his navel.

The partners in chance advanced. All were clothed, conventionally, in singlets and slacks, with the exception of their leader, who wore the gumboots in which he was accustomed to wade through the acid of the plating-shop, and the pair of old shorts stained beyond recognition as a fabric, resembling, rather, something sloughed by nature. Blue had always been primarily a torso, an Antinous of the suburbs, breasts emphatically divided on unfeeling marble, or Roman sandstone. Somebody had battered the head, or else the sculptor had recoiled before giving precise form to a vision of which he was ashamed. Whether damaged, or unfinished, the head was infallibly suggestive. Out of the impervious eyes, which should have conveyed at most the finite beauty of stone, filtered glimpses of an infinite squalor: slops of the saloon, the dissolving cigarette-butts, reflections of the grey monotonies, the greenish lusts. The mouth was a means of devouring. If ever it opened on words – for it was sometimes necessary to communicate – these issued bound with the brass of beer, from between rotting stumps of teeth.

Now Blue called to the surge of his admirers, not with any indication of caring:

'Hayadoin?'

Notwithstanding, the ladies were lapping him up with the same thirst as she who was closest to him by blood. His rudimentary mouth was soon smeared with red.

'Goodonya, mate!' called the heartier of the females, perhaps under the impression that manliness might succeed where feminity had failed.

But he laughed from between his stumps, and pushed the ladies aside, leaving them to trample on one another.

There was no doubt the Lucky Sevens now predominated on the work-floor. Drink had made them gigantic, or so it appeared to Haïm Rosenbaum, in whose past the gestures and faces of the crowd had often assumed alarming proportions. Now he remembered a telephone call he had promised to make weeks ago.

'Take it easy, Blue!' Mr Rosetree called in passing.

As everyone had forgotten the boss, some did pause to wonder at the significance of the remark.

Mr Rosetree continued up the stairs, inadequately protected by the knowledge that he had done his best. If there was an enemy of reason, it was the damned Jew Himmelfarb, who must now accept the consequences.

The latter had just picked up his case, and was about to cross the yard, making for the wash-room, which in the past had provided a certain sanctuary for the spirit.

Haïm ben Ya'akov looked back. Had he graduated, by some miracle, from the rank of actor to that of spectator? Then renewed panic carried him on, and, clearing the remainder of the steps, he reached his office.

Himmelfarb was walking rather slowly. Although aged by circumstances or the weather, he too had increased in stature, to match those figures with whom he was slowly, slowly becoming involved. That much was evident to the abo at least, whose instincts informed his stomach with a sickening certainty.

While standing on the mat floor, Alf Dubbo was stationed as if upon an eminence, watching what he alone was gifted or fated enough to see. Neither the actor, nor the spectator, he was that most miserable of human beings, the artist. All aspects, all possibilities were already splintering, forming in him. His thin belly was in revolt.

Himmelfarb could have touched the nearest of the Lucky Sevens by raising an elbow. But went out. And began to cross the yard. Nobody but the abo had begun yet to attach significance to the Jew of lolling head.

Then Blue, who was hanging his, began to feel lonely, began to feel sad. He could have laid his head on a certain thin bosom, from which the vitriol would spurt in little jets. At the same time he was trying to remember – always a difficult matter where moral problems were concerned. His ear was aching with the effort as it pressed against the telephone of memory. But did at last distinguish the faintest: ... *suffer every Easter to know the Jews have crucified Our Lord*. All the sadness pressing, pressing on a certain nerve. *It was Them, Blue*. All the injustices to which he had ever been subjected grew appreciably sadder. But for all the injustices he had committed, somebody had committed worse. Not to say the worst, so he had been told, the very worst. And must not go unpunished.

'Hey, Mick!' Blue called.

Now several of the Sevens realized what a very scraggy, funny, despicable sight the Jew-cove presented. One who suspected that a joke was being prepared, laughed quite short and high, but another who had the wind, belched, and hated.

The Jew had turned.

'I beg your pardon. Did you speak?' he asked.

Though it was hardly necessary. He did not appear anything but fully informed.

Blue, who always had to rootle around in his mind before he

could find a reason, was not quick enough in finding one now. He knew, though. Reasons which originate in the blood, the belly, or the loins, solicit most persistently. And looking at the Jew, Blue experienced the authentic spasm.

'We gotta have a talk,' he said, 'about something that happened.'

Touching a button on the Jew's shirt, but lightly, even whimsically.

Because Blue the vindicator was also Blue the mate. It was possible to practise all manner of cruelties provided the majority might laugh them off as practical jokes. And there is almost no tragedy which cannot be given a red nose. Blue perhaps sensed this as he lightly touched the shirt-button, or remembered some wowser of a parson who had failed to keep it serious as he droned on against the blowflies.

'I got a bone to pick,' said Blue.

Already some of his confederates were bending their elbows in support of whatever situation their leader might choose to develop.

'So the parson tells me,' Blue pursued. 'Or someone.' He frowned, and faltered. 'Or me auntie,' he added, brighter.

Indeed, that rekindled a fire which might otherwise have died. Now it flickered afresh with a greenish, acid flame.

And Blue began to laugh. He was all gums, and the muscles in his throat.

'You bloody buggers!' Blue laughed. 'You black bastards!'

The Jew's shirt surrendered up, most comically, a long, unprotesting strip.

Dubbo looked into his hands. They were weaponless, and without weapons he felt badly afraid. Officially, of course, he was not a man, but a blackfellow. He could have cried for all his failures, but most of all this one.

Left with the strip of shirt in his hand, Blue had not yet thought what to do with it.

Then the Sevens began to move. It was their simultaneous intention to go into action against the offending Jew, although, for a start, they appeared to be pushing one another around. Their elephant-phalanx rubbed and cannoned. It was in earnest, though. If one or two half-sniggered, it was to clear their mouths of phlegm, or something. They were in earnest all right.

'Christ!' Even if somebody had to laugh, that seemed to hit right home.

It struck Dubbo. Sounds transposed into tones of fear and

horror, both personal and limitless, began to pour out over the yard, on the edge of which the struggle was taking place. If it could be called that. For the Jew did not resist. There was, on one side, the milling of the righteous, even to their own detriment. On the other, the Jew, who did not flinch, except that he was jostled. His expression remained one almost of contentment.

As Dubbo watched, himself a thinking stick, twitched and tossed, the mob surged out across the yard, over the lavings from the plating-shop. Some were giggling and chanting. Of those who hung back or protested, none was willing as yet to forgo a disgraceful spectacle, but would grizzle at their own lack of decision, in bass undertone.

'Go home! Go home!' giggled and chanted the young girls.

'Go home to Germany!' sang the older women.

There was a clapping and a stamping as the men's chorus interpolated:

'Go home! Go home! Go home to hell!'

With a joyful, brassy resonance, because the puppet in their lives had been replaced at last by a man of flesh and blood.

In the yard, Dubbo realized, there was that old jacaranda, which they had lopped back before its season of blue, perhaps for the very purpose of preventing it. But, although deformed and angular in its present state, the painter was made to visualize the divine tree in its intensity of blue, wrapped in shawls of it, standing in pools of it. Towards the present travesty of tree, its mutilated limbs patched with lichens of a dead, stone colour, with nails protruding in places from the trunk, together with a segment of now rusted tin, which somebody had hammered in for reasons unknown, it was agreed by consent of instinct to push the victim. Harder now. Indeed, at one point, the Jew went down. And got trampled for a while. At the risk of spoiling it, some of the rout could not resist trying the resilience of the mushroom that they longed to pick, and one man, braver than the rest, suddenly became aware of the dreadful frailty of the human body as he kicked at the fallen victim's ribs.

Then Blue reached down, and yanked the Jew up. The latter had begun to bleed from above his left eye, which appeared to the mass of the spectators both repulsive and rewarding.

Never more plastic than now, Blue was glittering with sweat. Several of the young girls and married women consigned their souls willingly to the bonfire as they surrendered themselves to his image. Some of the men would have taken a hammer, or plunged a knife, if either weapon had been at hand. Into the Jew, of course.

Nor would the latter have protested. That was what maddened the crowd. His mouth was not even set to endure suffering, but was ever so slightly open, as if to receive any further bitterness.

So they pushed him up against the tree trunk. Ramming. And jamming. His head was heard once.

'Hey, hold hard!' shouted Blue.

He was not exactly protesting, but could not lose sight of the convention which demanded that cruelty, at least amongst mates, must be kept at the level of a joke.

With that perhaps in mind, he broke away briefly, and ran into the plating-shop. And returned with a rope, or coil of lithe cord.

The others were not sure they were going to approve. Some of them felt, in fact, they could have attempted heights of tragedy, they could have made blood run redder and more copiously than ever before. However, the majority were pacified by the prospect of becoming involved in some episode that would degrade them lower than they had known yet; the heights were not for them.

Blue was very active. Fixing and tying. Shouting orders.

Dubbo saw they had begun to hoist the Jew. They would tie him to his tree. Already higher than the crowd, he had been grazed by nail or tin, so that blood, quite a lot of it, did flow. At least one of his hands was pierced. Through the torn shirt, it could be seen that the disgraceful ribs were gashed.

The crowd howled, and pushed.

A lady who had begun to feel sick, saved herself by remembering:

'It is the foreigners that take the homes. It is the Jews. Good old Bluey! Let 'im 'ave it! I'll buy yer one when the job's finished.'

And the lavender curls lolloped on her old head.

Now Dubbo knew that he would never, never act, that he would dream, and suffer, and express some of that suffering in paint – but was, in the end, powerless. In his innocence, he blamed his darker skin.

Somewhere clocks were chiming.

At that hour, descending the stairs at Xanadu, Miss Hare saw the marble shudder, the crack widen a little farther. She waited for the structure to fall. But it did not. And when she

410

had reached the foot of the stairs, she went on out into some unhappiness of trees. Her skin could read the air. She went, touched and fretted, fretting and touching. So she trundled through the misery of that morning, of which she herself was a troubled particle. In fact, as she shuffled over leaves, she followed the narrowing spiral of her dread almost to the cone of it.

At that hour, Mrs Godbold took the sheets which she had washed earlier, and which were dry by now, and smelling of their own freshness. She began to iron the sheets, and soon had them ready in a pile. She would work fast and skilfully, even while remembering painful things: how the women, for instance, had received the body of their Lord. At that time of year Mrs Godbold would experience all that had happened, from bitterest dregs to joyful evidence.

And now was pierced, never more deeply. But accepted it as always.

And would lay the body in her whitest sheets, with the love of which only she was capable.

Mrs Flack, who had just poured them a cup of tea, looked at the surface of it, to see.

'The truth will always out,' she said.

'It depends,' Mrs Jolley dared.

'What depends?' returned Mrs Flack, sucking in her breath.

'It depends on what you believe the truth to be.'

Mrs Flack was awful.

'The truth,' she said, 'is what a decent person knows by instinct. Surely that is so?'

'Yes,' her friend had to agree.

Sometimes now Mrs Jolley took fright, particularly at the leaves of the *monstera deliciosa*, at the holes in their dark surfaces. Suddenly to catch sight of them, looming higher than the window-sill, gave Mrs Jolley a turn, but it would have hurt Mrs Flack to cut them back.

The Jew had been hoisted as high as he was likely to go on the mutilated tree. The rope pulleys had been knotted to a standstill; one of Blue's accomplices had fumblingly, but finally, fastened the ankles. There he was, nobody would have said crucified, because from the beginning it had been a joke, and if some blood had run, it had dried quickly. The hands, the temples, and the side testified to that in dark clots and smears, too poor to attract the flies. If some of the spectators suffered the wounds to remain open, it was due probably to an unhealthy state of conscience, which could have been waiting since childhood to break out. For those few, the drops trembled and lived. How they longed to dip their handkerchiefs, unseen.

Others had to titter for a burlesque, while turning aside their faces in an attempt to disguise what they suspected might be blasphemy.

Blue was laughing, and swallowing his excessive spittle. He stood looking up, with his throat distended on his now rather convulsive torso: a decadence of statuary.

He called up out of the depths:

'Howyadoin up there, eh? 'Ad enough, eh? Bugger me if the cow don't go for it!'

The Jew appeared, in fact, to have been removed from them, while the archtormentor himself might have been asking for respite from torments which he had always suffered, and which, in certain circumstances, were eased, he seemed to remember. So the marble body was contorted into the changing forms of wax at the foot of the tree.

The Jew hung. If he had not been such a contemptible object, he might have excited pity. Hoisted high at the wrists, the weight of the body threatened to cut them through. The arms strained to maintain that uneasy contact between heaven and earth. Through the torn shirt the skin was stretched transparent on the ribs. The head lolled even more heavily than in life. Those who had remained in touch with reality or tradition might have taken him for dead. But the eyes were visionary rather than fixed. The contemplative mouth dwelled on some breathless word spoken by the mind.

Because he was as solitary in the crowd as the man they had crucified, it was again the abo who saw most. All that he had ever suffered, all that he had ever failed to understand, rose to the surface in Dubbo. Instinct and the white man's teaching no longer trampled on each other. As he watched, the colour flowed through the veins of the cold, childhood Christ, at last the nails entered wherever it was acknowledged they should. So he took the cup in his own yellow hands, from those of Mr Calderon, and would have offered it to such celebrants as he was now able to recognize in the crowd. So he understood the concept of the blood, which was sometimes the sick, brown stain on his own pillow, sometimes the clear crimson of redemption. He was blinded now. Choking now. Physically feebler for the revelation that knowledge would never cut the

412

cords which bound the Saviour to the tree. Not that it was asked. Nothing was asked. So he began also to understand acceptance. How he could at last have conveyed it, in its cloak of purple, on the blue tree, the green lips of detached, contemplative suffering.

And love in its many kinds began to trouble him as he looked. He saw the old man, the clergyman, searching the boy's body for the lost image of youth on the bedstead at Numburra, and Mrs Spice whirling to her putrefaction in the never-ending dance of the potato-sacks, and Hannah the prostitute curled together with her white capon, Norman Fussell, in their sterile, yet not imperfect, fleshly egg. Many anonymous faces, too, offered without expecting or frowning. There was the blandest experience of love: the milky light of morning poured out unadulterated over his naked shoulders. And the paints as they swirled, and he swathed them on a bare board, sometimes as tenuously as mist, sometimes moulding them with his fingers like bastions of stone. Perhaps this, his own contribution to love, was least explicable, if most comprehensive, and comprehensible.

Now the Jew stirred on the lump of an ugly tree trunk on which they had stuck him.

The crowd pressed forward to see and hear, jostling the stick of an abo half-caste who did not exist for any member of it.

The Jew had raised his head. He looked out from under those rather heavy, intolerable lids.

From the beginning Himmelfarb had known that he possessed the strength, but did pray for some sign. Through all the cursing, and trampling, and laughter, and hoisting, and aching, and distortion, he had continued to expect. Until now, possibly, it would be given. So, he raised his head. And was conscious of a stillness and clarity, which was the stillness and clarity of pure water, at the centre of which his God was reflected.

The people watched the man they had fastened to the tree. That he did not proceed to speak his thoughts was most unnatural, not to say frustrating. The strain became enormous. If they had seen how to go about it, they would have licked the silence from his lips, as a substitute for words.

Then a young girl of thin mouth and smoothed hair began to run at, and struggle with the backs of the bystanders, who would not let her through. But must. Hysteria would see to it. The scarlet thread of lips was drawn tight on some demon that she would on no account give up. When she reached the foot of the tree, she took an orange she had brought, and flung it with her awkward, girl's throw at the Jew's mouth, but it fell short, of course, and thumped on his hollow chest.

The crowd laughed, or sighed.

Then a young fellow, one of the Sevens, called Rowley Britt, came down, who remembered his mother dying of cancer of the bowel. He had filled his mouth with water, and now attempted to spit it in the mouth of the damn crucified Jew. But it missed. And trickled down the chin.

The young man stood crying at the foot of the tree, swaying a good deal because he was still drunk.

Many of the onlookers, to whom it had begun to occur that they were honest citizens, with kiddies at school, were turning away by this. Who knows, though, how the show might have dragged on, and ended, if authority had not put a stop to it.

The administrative offices were placed in such a way that the three people contained in them had an excellent view, either through the glass hatchway, or the door which led to the workshop, and in spite of their determination to ignore, became involved, whether to positive or negative degree, in the present disgraceful incident.

It had been Mr Rosetree's intention to telephone a business connexion, suddenly remembered, about an order for geometry sets. He sat and sweated, contracting and expanding like a rubber bulb under pressure, while Miss Whibley fiddled at her switchboard.

'For Chrissake, Miss Whibley,' Mr Rosetree shouted, 'I am waiting for this cheppie's number!'

'Bugger it!' blurted Miss Whibley. 'It is the *switch*!'

Most unusual. Miss Whibley never used words.

'It is the switch! The switch!' she attempted.

Her voice could have been nougat.

When Miss Mudge, who had ventured to look through the hatchway, exclaimed too loudly:

'Oh, look! It is that Mr Himmelson. Something terrible is going to happen.'

Mr Rosetree and Miss Whibley had always considered that Miss Mudge, a worthy soul, should not be allowed her freedom. This was not the moment, however, for Mr Rosetree and Miss Whibley to share opinions.

'It is the switch! It is the switch!' the latter repeated, demonstrating too.

Certainly the mechanism seemed most ineffectual.

Mr Rosetree bulged.

'They are doing something to Mr Himmelson!' Miss Mudge harped against the glass.

She was so colourless that any commentary by her sounded the more intolerable.

'They are pulling. On that tree. The jacaranda. Oh, no! They are. Mr Rosetree, they are *crucifying* Mr Himmelson!'

For the first time perhaps the knife was entering Miss Mudge, and the agony was so intense, it frightened her. All else that she had known – her invalid sister, trouble over pensions, the leaking roof – was slit from her, and she stood gulping and shivering.

Mr Rosetree still sat.

Miss Whibley had given the switchboard away. She had begun:

'I will not look. Nobody can compel me.' She took out her compact, to powder, knowing herself to be inundated with the inevitable purple. 'Nobody,' she said. 'To look. I will hand in my resignation, Mr Rosetree, as from the holidays.'

Mr Rosetree had not looked, but knew. Nobody need tell him about any human act: he had experienced them all, before he had succeeded in acquiring adequate protection.

'They are spitting *water*,' Miss Mudge just managed.

If it had been piss, it would not have scalded more.

'On the man,' she protested. 'That good man!'

What degree of goodness Miss Mudge implied, Mr Rosetree did not gather. But it made him feel he would have to look.

Miss Mudge was trembling horribly for the discovery she had made; that she, herself quite blameless, might be responsible for some man, even all men. Now her responsibility was tearing her. Her hitherto immaculate flesh, white and goosey, with the vaccination marks, did not know how to cope.

Mr Rosetree had tiptoed to the door. He was looking and looking.

'I will not look,' announced Miss Whibley, unwisely blowing the powder out of her mirror.

'Do something, please, Mr Rosetree!' Miss Mudge was calling right across the three feet which separated her from the boss. 'They are kill. Do. Do.'

But Mr Rosetree was looking and looking. He might even topple over.

'To Mr Himmelson. They say he is a Jew.'

Mr Rosetree could have burst out laughing. Instead, he started bellowing:

'For Chrissake! Mr Theobalds! Ernie! Do something,

please! What for are you employed in this establishment, if not to keep order? It must be restored at once, please, in the entire premises.'

Then Ernie Theobalds, who was not a bad sort of a cove, not to say as good a mate as a man might expect, strolled out from where he had been standing, exploring the flesh under his singlet, and watching events.

'Okay, Harry!' he called. 'Keep your wool on! It ain't nothun to get worked up over.'

He laughed that rather indolent, but in no way insolent laugh which revealed his comfortable denture. He walked across and kicked the arses of a couple of lads who were standing at one side. Other spectators began at once to turn, the mass to open for the foreman, who might, the waking eyes hoped, accept responsibility.

'What is going on 'ere?' asked Ernie Theobalds, jovial like.

As if he did not know. As if nobody knew.

Nobody did.

Mr Theobalds stood beneath the tree and the shambles of a man. He began, very easy, to negotiate a knot here and there, to loosen the rope pulleys, assisted by a couple of the Sevens who had resumed their own faces. Perce Thompson could not assist enough, but opened his pocket-knife, and sawed through one section of rope, with the result that the figure, in its descent, arrived almost too quickly, and might have fallen in a heap of bones, clothes, and silence, if Mr Theobalds had not caught.

'Hold hard!' he recommended, rather fat and kind, and supported with his arm, big but soft, with orange fur and freckles.

So Himmelfarb was raised too soon from the dead, by the kindness and consideration of those who had never ceased to be his mates. So he must remember not to doubt, or long for a solution that he had never intended to provide.

'Easy does it!' said and laughed the foreman.

Himmelfarb himself was persuaded to attempt a laugh, but the bones rattled, and were hurting besides.

However, he did manage:

'Thank you, Mr Theobalds.'

To which the foreman replied:

'Something you will never learn, Mick, is that I am Ernie to every cove present. That is you included. No man is better than another. It was still early days when Australians found that out. You may say we talk about it a lot, but you can't

416

expect us not to be proud of what we have invented, so to speak. Remember that,' advised Ernie Theobalds, laying the palm of his hand flat against his mate's back.

'Yes,' Himmelfarb said, and nodded.

But was unsteady at the level of reality to which he had been returned.

Purged of the resentment which made them jump and rattle, the machines seemed to be running smoother in their oil. The muted dies might have been cutting into felt instead of metal.

'Remember,' Ernie Theobalds continued, 'we have a sense of humour, and when the boys start to horse around, it is that that is gettin' the better of 'em. They can't resist a joke. Even when a man is full of beer, you will find the old sense of humour hard at work underneath. It has to play a joke. See? No offence can be taken where a joke is intended.'

So the foreman spoke, and everyone believed. If Blue had gone into the plating-shop, and was holding his semblance of a head, it was because he felt real crook. It was the beer. It was the beer. It was the fount of blue and crimson sparks. It was the blood that had not touched his lips, in driest memory, or now. But would, in fact, have turned him up. So that, between longing and revulsion, not to mention the hiccups, he went into a corner, and vomited.

When Ernie Theobalds had delivered his kind and reasonable speech, he squeezed the elbow of the one to whom it had been addressed.

'You oughta get along now,' he said. 'I will mention it to the boss that you have gone off sick.'

Himmelfarb agreed that he was feeling far from well. But the pulses of his body expressed gratitude for the resolved situation in which he found himself so simply and so naturally placed.

And his property returned.

For, Alf Dubbo the blackfellow had brought the shawl and the phylacteries which had burst from the small fibre case during the hilarious scrimmage, and got somewhat trampled on. The leather cylinder of one phylactery was crushed, there was blood, besides, on the fringes of the shawl.

Which the blackfellow handed back. The latter did not speak, though. He would not speak, now, or ever. His mouth could never offer passage to all that he knew to be inside him.

'There we are!' the foreman shouted above the noise of the machinery. 'There is your old gadgets!'

417

But did frown slightly, and would not have cared to touch. Only when the dubious objects were safely inside the case, Ernie Theobalds fastened the surviving catch, as the Jew seemed unable to.

The machinery was working and working.

The blackfellow would have done something, but was not told what.

The Jew was going, he saw, with the gentle, uncertain motion of an eggshell tossed by flowing water.

The blackfellow would have run after him to tell what he had seen and understood. But could not. Unless it burst from his fingertips. Never from his mouth.

Very quietly Himmelfarb left the factory in which it had not been accorded to him to expiate the sins of the world.

Although nobody watched, everybody saw.

14

When Mrs Flack returned to the back garden, her friend Mrs Jolley was still watching the glow from the fire. It was the hour of green, when the acid light that summer has distilled from foliage eats the copper plate of evening. Mrs Jolley, standing with her arms beneath her apron, had given herself a pregnant look. But Mrs Flack was never impressed by the pregnancies of others.

'I do like a fire,' Mrs Jolley remarked, out of her girl's face, for the rather peculiar light had swilled away the dross of wrinkles. 'I mean,' she said, 'a *good* fire. That is not, I mean to say, that I do not sympathize with those concerned. I *do*. But do like a fire.'

'If you are in need of it,' Mrs Flack pronounced, 'then it is beneficial.'

'Eh?' Mrs Jolley asked.

Mrs Flack did not reply, nor did Mrs Jolley bother, for she was able to stand and watch the fire, and knew, besides, that answers would not cure her permanent uneasiness, her only really chronic illness.

The greenish light of evening had formed a cool cup in which the orange potion would sometimes seethe up into a head of blond sparks. The fire was not so far away, but far enough, for anyone who needed it.

'Some people, though,' Mrs Flack murmured, and not necessarily for her friend, 'some people need to be given a taste of what is coming to them, but will not burn, most likely, not even then.'

At which point she looked behind her.

'Not,' she said, 'if they was born of fire.'

Mrs Jolley would have liked to descend from the heights of prophecy, but as she did not dare, she continued staring at the conflagration. This she did with such intensity, her head began to wobble gently. So Mrs Flack noticed. Often she could have pushed her friend, and risked damage to the mechanism.

Mrs Jolley, in her innocence, ventured finally to remark:

'I would give anything to know whose fire that is.'

Mrs Flack cleared her throat.

'But surely I told you?' she said, so flat. 'I told, and always tell.'

Mrs Jolley did not answer.

Mrs Flack drew hard on the surrounding air, the better to expel a reply.

'It is *his* fire,' she said. 'That man's. It is the Jew, so they tell me, in Montebello Avenue.'

'Not *that* man!' Mrs Jolley cried, now quite light and girlish; she held one corner of her apron between a thumb and a finger, and crooked her little finger.

'It is the insurance, no doubt,' Mrs Jolley cried, and tittered.

She could have danced, twitching her apron like a girl.

'I doubt,' said Mrs Flack, 'in fact, I know the insurance does not enter into it.'

She looked around, at the darkness which was clotting under the few tailored shrubs.

'Mrs Jolley,' she said, 'this is nothing,' she said, 'if not strickly between ourselves.'

'Oh, yes!' said Mrs Jolley.

Mrs Flack tore off an evergreen leaf which a bird had spattered.

'It is a bunch of young fellers,' she said, 'whose sense of decency was outraged by a certain person. So I am told, mind you. Who come up. Only to give warning, they say. They was flicking little balls of paper, soaked in somethink, into the Jew's place, to put the wind up him like. When matters got out of hand. In a weatherboard home.'

Mrs Flack sucked her teeth to appease convention.

In the last light Mrs Jolley glowed with fire.

'It is terrible,' Mrs Jolley said.

'It is terrible all right,' Mrs Flack agreed, 'but it is not for us to decide who will burn for it.'

Which was strange, Mrs Jolley found – that Mrs Flack should feel unable to decide.

From Xanadu, Miss Hare caught sight of the light of fire. It was too jubilant to ignore, blaring out, trumpet-shaped, from amongst the deciduous exotics and shabbier native trees. The complexion of the firelight might have conveyed a ruddy, boisterous, country beauty in other less personal circumstances, although all fire is personal to all animals, as they watch, listen, sniff, from their lair of bushes; fire is the last warning. Of course, Miss Hare, in her equal relationship with air and earth, and responding as she did to the motion of leaves, had known about the fire some little time before she saw it, just as, when placed right at the core of her great house, she would sense mist climbing up out of the gullies – she would feel it behind her knees – or she would usually learn of the approach of strangers, partly by collaboration of the elements, partly by a contraction of her own confidence.

On that evening of fire, she had known. Rootling after what she could not remember, in a drawer somewhere in the inner gloom, amongst old letters, hanks of yellow string, bent nails, and pumpkin seeds, her head had suddenly gone up. Very slowly at first she had begun to negotiate the cells and corridors of Xanadu, together with the spiral of her own skull, gathering impetus as the gusts of fear and hatred played upon her out of the remaining shreds of curtains. So that she was soon compelled to run, and by the time she tumbled out on the terrace, her skin was tingling with all the implications of fire, the little hairs were standing up along the line of her jaw-bone, almost preparing to be singed.

There, above the normal spectacle of trees, was the brassy thing, clapping and vibrating as she had expected. Even at a distance the smoke confused her.

Miss Hare began to mumble. She ran this way and that. The air was furry with indecision.

And all the time the fire-thing, singing in the exhausted evening, dared her to reject her complete association with that place, or to forget that her spirit might be called upon to take part in some painful, last rite.

Then her foot crunched the little bone. It was the thigh-bone, she saw, of a rabbit. Lying on the terrace, amongst dandelion and grit, the bone had been weathered to a whiteness that disturbed the memory as orange fire seared the present. In search of a clue to her distress, Miss Hare's toe stirred the bone. She even picked the sharp white reminder up.

Because, of course, she remembered at once: the attitude in which he had been standing, and how she had led him in, and held his hands, as if it had been some curious object she had found, bone, or leaf, of which she had to learn the shape and history.

It was the Jew who was concerned, she now knew for certain, the Jew for whom the fire had been lit. And at once the air was palpitating with dangers past and present. Faced with the illogic of fire, birds had fallen silent. For the moment it was quite still, except that a solitary church-bell had begun to call believers into the Gothic thicket of prayer.

Miss Hare did not waste time – she who always wore a hat did not have to put one on – but set out along the most direct of several tracks that she and animals had flattened through the long grass. Always she knew where to squeeze most easily, or crawl. All around, her kingdom was quivering in agreement. Her skin was not submitted to pricking, rather, to a confirmation of existence. Leaves, which would have whipped at other intruders, made dashing love-play. The waters of a little creek consoled her ankles. The structure of her world might have risen vaster, soaring with her breath out of the merely incidental cage of ribs, if it had not been reduced finally by anguish. In the circumstances, the spirit returned, wounded and doubtful, into the dumb, trundling body of the beast.

At one point Miss Hare put her foot in a rabbit burrow, and fell. She was terrified by a blue breathlessness. Which passed. She continued. Moaning from time to time. Not for her present situation, but because she was trying to remember the name of an old servant – Meg? – whose strength had become desirable. The old Meg – Peg, was it? Peg! Peg! – appeared to see the truth quite clearly from behind steel-rimmed spectacles. Of course, truth took many forms, Miss Hare suspected. Or was crouched in the formlessness that she herself best knew: of wind and rain, the falling of a leaf, the whirling of the white sky. Whereas Peg's truth was a perfect statue. Miss Hare would have liked to touch her servant's skirt, as she had in girlhood, to be comforted. She would have liked to take the Jew's hand, and shut it up in her withered bosom, together with all those images which could only be preserved in love, as Peg the immemorial had bottled plums. There Miss Hare almost fell again, remembering her lack of skill in the methods of love, and that her own experience had taught her disintegration was the only permanent, perhaps the only desirable state. In the end, if not always, truth was a stillness and a light. So she continued, lumbering, scurrying wherever an absence of obstacles allowed, licking her gelatinous lips, more from habit, than in hopes of restoring shape, chafing through the immensity of the kingdom which separated her from the fire.

When this being burst at last out of the scrub, she found a fairly respectable blaze in Montebello Avenue. It was, as she had known, the brown house in which her friend lived, which she had seen, but never entered.

But must now. That was clear. In order to love and honour the more, she had invested the Jew with a goodness so pure as to render the possessor practically powerless against the consummate forms of evil. Already she saw the dead-seeming face lying upon its pillow of fire, upturned in its indifference to the canopy of golden stalactites.

A number of persons had come down to watch, or trail hoses for which taps had never been provided. The fire brigade, they assured themselves, must have either failed, or gone away for the holidays. Even so, some of the spectators kept watch, over a shoulder, while continuing to enjoy the progress of the fire.

'But if there is a man inside!' Miss Hare protested.

Although that was not known for certain, there were those who would have dearly loved to know.

Only Miss Hare was shaggy love itself.

She was walking at the fiery house with her hands outstretched to trap its rather dangerous spiders. She had never experienced fear of insects, and only momentarily of fire, because, after all, the elemental must come to terms with the elements.

So that those who were watching saw the most inhuman behaviour develop in one they had taken to be human until now.

'Miss Hare!' they called. 'Are you mad?'

Almost as though they had always thought her to be sane.

And now were overwhelmed by ugliness and terror, as the woman in her great, wicker hat walked into the burning house.

By this time the framework had become quite a little temple of fire, with lovely dionysiac frieze writhing on its pediment.

Similarly, all its golden columns danced. But Miss Hare, who was involved in the inner tragedy, did not notice any of that.

The fire came at her first to push her out, but returned as quickly to suck her in. And she was drawn, drawn, stumblingly, inside. The agony might have been more intense if she herself had not been molten. The molten stream of her passion ran down the skin of her cheeks and her outstretched hands, the tears ran out of her eyes to burn fire.

So she stood in the everlasting moment. A revelation should have been made to one possessed of her especial powers, and indeed, a more rational curtain of flame was almost twitched back for her to see. She did almost, from under her by now transparent eyelids. The sparks were halted. She almost saw the body of her friend, a rather frail old man, or at most, inflammable prophet, his ribs burning like the joists of a house. But it was not possible, she moaned, to go to him as she would have chosen. Or not yet. She was, after all, crinkling up. Under threat of burning, the sticks of her arms were becoming distorted. Her singed trunk was presented to the shimmering, rushing, revolving teeth of fire.

Then, mercifully, she was returned to her animal self. She began to scream. The smell of burning fur or feathers had always terrified her.

Nobody who saw would ever forget how Miss Hare had emerged from the burning house. She was a blackened thing, yet awful. Her wicker hat was turned to a fizzy Catherine wheel, wings of flame were sprouting from the shoulders of her cardigan, her worsted heels were spurred with fire. Most alarming was the swollen throat from which the terror, or more probable, the spectators felt, the orders and the accusations would not immediately pour. Moving forward, she halted those who might have come to meet her. Then one or two more responsible men did get possession of themselves, ran towards her, and began to beat at the avenging angel with their coats. Until she was at least materially extinguished.

All the time this monster of truth was struggling to give vent to her feelings, and did finally bring out:

'You have killed him!'

'Who?' they asked.

'There is no reason to suppose there is anyone,' they said, 'inside.'

And continued to belt at her, now with their dislike and their consciences, in addition to their coats.

423

Miss Hare was crying and choking. She hated those who were saving her.

'You have burnt my dearest friend!' she bellowed. 'I am going to report to the police.'

Parrying the blows of hateful coats.

'I will take the matter, if necessary, to court. By raising funds. By some means. My cousin in Jersey.'

Just then two ladies, who had come down in second-best hats to enjoy the spectacle, happened to reach the brink of the fire. They realized at once how things stood, though too late, alas, to choose a better moment.

Miss Hare saw, too, and advanced.

'You,' she cried, 'are the devils!'

More she could not.

Mrs Jolley retreated a few paces, and might have escaped altogether if she had not been chained to her protector. The latter stood, pointing a toe at their accuser. She was thinner, yellow perhaps, but retained considerable faith in her oblique powers.

Mrs Flack said:

'For your own sake, I would not care to hear you repeat that, madam. Accusations are very often confessions.'

The crowd grew murmurous in appreciation.

But Miss Hare, perhaps because of her powerlessness, did dare once again.

'The devils!' she repeated, certainly aiming more at random, through the bubbles and the blisters.

Then she began to walk away, trailing ribbons of smoke, and, of course, crying mad.

Longer than any other witness would Constable McFaggott remember that night, and the object which presented itself in the station doorway.

'You have done nothing,' it cried, 'to protect my friend from persecution and arson.'

'Himmelfarb,' Miss Hare at last succeeded in wrenching out the name, 'Himmelfarb has been burnt to death.'

McFaggott, a personable man, of pretty teeth, strong legs, and white eyeballs, was somewhat in dishabille, considering the importance of the evening. Now he touched the holy medal which he wore in the hair of his chest, and which had accompanied him in the past through the most unlikely circumstances.

'I will hold you responsible!' the mad thing was shouting.

'Steady on!' called the constable, in the high, soft tenor that they liked. 'There is such a thing as libel, my lady!'

424

'There is such a thing as truth,' replied Miss Hare. 'Until it gets into the mouth of the Law. Where it seems to fork.'

It was fortunate for McFaggott that, on the evening of the fire, a difference of opinion with his wife had delayed his going on duty as usual at Mrs Khalil's. Thanks to his wife's contemptuous behaviour, he was available to investigate facts, not to mention face the press. Now he was tired, but amiable. He even touched the crazy creature as she stood in front of him, touched her with gentle, though manly authority, in the way that made normal ladies thrill inside their blouses.

McFaggott said:

'It is all fate, you know, Miss Hare.'

With promotion approaching, he would not have been so injudicious to have called it anything else.

'It was fate, you might say, that caused the mechanical defect in the fire-engine, which did not arrive – or, by crikey, there it is!'

Indeed, it could be heard clanging, its tyres groaning roundly on the stones of Montebello Avenue.

'Which did not arrive in time, you might say, to prevent the gutting of this Jewish gentleman's residence.'

Miss Hare was marooned in her own emotions and the constable's sea of words.

'It was fate, too, which removed this same gentleman from his home before the conflagration had broken out.'

'Removed?' Miss Hare moaned.

The constable reaped the harvest of his power and knowledge. He laughed, or showed his excellent teeth – real, as everybody knew.

'That is what I said,' said the constable. 'By Mrs Godbold, and Bob Tanner, the young feller who is going with her eldest girl.'

'Then where is Mr Himmelfarb?' Miss Hare demanded.

'In the temporary dwelling in which Mrs Godbold lives,' the constable informed.

'Oh,' Miss Hare said. 'Yes,' she said. 'I might have known. Mrs Godbold would never allow anything to happen. I mean, anything that might be averted.'

The constable had to laugh again.

'Mrs Godbold is only a woman,' he said.

Constable McFaggott would wrinkle up his face to laugh, because he knew how crisp the skin would appear at the corners of his eyes. Now he could not laugh too much.

'One day, Miss Hare,' he said and laughed, never so silkily, 'we'll have to get your opinion of we men.'

But the phone was again calling him from distant places.

'Oh, the men,' she protested. 'I do not know.' Sputtering and muttering. 'Not the men. A cock is for treading hens.'

When she got outside, the sparks were settling down again into stars. The moist, blackberry darkness nuzzled against her drawn skin. She could no longer run, only stump, and flounder, past what she knew to be there. The framework of her friend's house was hissing by now beneath the play of water, but she did not really care whether the fire was extinguished or not.

On arrival at Mrs Godbold's shed, she forgot to knock, but went in, quite as though she were expected, which, indeed, she was.

'Ah, there you are,' the owner said.

Mrs Godbold stood smiling in the depths of her one room, her solid form fluctuating inside its glistening apron of light. Children were distributed on all sides, watching, or taking for granted. More than this Miss Hare did not attempt to notice. Without wasting any time, she surged forward on the last gust of her physical strength. But her instincts, it seemed, had only to open their reserves of power, as she knelt to lay her scorched face, against the cotton quilt, at the foot of the huge, iron bed.

Himmelfarb had returned to his house round about noon. By then his physical distress was considerably increased, not so much from the bruises, cuts, and possibly one or two broken ribs inflicted on him at the factory, but a deeper, numbing pain, above which his mind would burn and flicker with the obsessive blue clarity of an acetylene flame.

In the circumstances, the emptiness and silence of his wooden house offered him perfect consolation. How the carvings on the walnut surfaces would have oppressed, the plush fingers desolated, even at their most tenderly solicitous. Instead he lay down on the narrow bed in his bare room. His face was sculptured most economically in dead, but convincing, yellow wax, from which he issued, between spasms, to contend with the figure of Moshe his father, who flickered longingly within the acetylene nebula. Always separate during the illusory life of men, now they touched, it seemed, at the point of failure.

How long Mordecai lay there, loved and tormented by his

father, he could not have calculated, but when he opened his eyes, things were still preserved in their apparent shapes, and he was relieved to explore from a distance that of his single chair, down to the last crack and familiar abrasion.

At the same time he realized he was not alone. That somebody was touching his forehead and his wrists. That a presence of unwavering strength had begun to envelop his momentarily distracted being.

It was, he saw, his neighbour, Mrs Godbold.

'I have no intention of disturbing you,' she said, speaking in tones both practical and absent, 'but wonder what to do for the best.'

In her state of doubt, she only half-addressed him, standing by the bed with her face averted, her attention concentrated on a distant and still confused idea. Her statue had been set down, it appeared, on the edge of a great, open space, whether lake or plain he did not bother to investigate, only it was vast, he knew, from the expression of the face, and the unobstructed waves of afternoon.

'Yes,' she decided at last, though still hesitant. 'I shall fetch you down to my place, sir, if you do not mind, as it is close, and where I can give you every attention.'

Watching the heavy knot of hair in the nape of the thick, but appropriate neck, he did not protest.

'I will go now,' she said quietly, still addressing someone else; 'I will go, but come soon with the others.'

He did not answer, but waited for that and anything more to be done.

He could see now the rightness and inevitability of all that his wife Reha had been allowed in her simplicity to understand, and which she had attempted to convey, not so much by words, for which she had no gift, but by the light of her conviction. It seemed to him as though the mystery of failure might be pierced only by those of extreme simplicity of soul, or else by one who was about to doff the outgrown garment of the body. He was weak enough, certainly, by now, to make the attempt which demands the ultimate in strength.

In the meantime, as he prepared, or rid himself of minor objections, he had agreed unreservedly that Reha should become his voice and hands. They had seldom enjoyed such intimacy of spirit as when, in the course of the afternoon, a wind got up from the sea, and hollowed the shell of the house until its walls were thinner still. Willows whipped deliriously, and the rushing of air could have engulfed, if it had not been

427

for his spasms of pain, and the rows of beansticks dividing the immense colourlessness at regular intervals.

At one such point she put her hand on his shoulder, and he opened his eyes, and saw that Mrs Godbold had returned.

The woman who was bending over him straightened at once, for modesty's sake, it seemed.

She said:

'We are here, sir, as I promised. Else, you know, and this is Bob Tanner, a friend.'

Else was blushing, and looking into corners, not for what she might discover, but so that she might not be forced to see. She was reddening most prettily, with a blush of hedge-roses along her milky skin. Bob Tanner, in whom Himmelfarb recognized the lad sent on a former occasion to summon him to Xanadu, was all boots and muscles. He was ashamed of the noises that he made by moving on the bare floors, or, simply, in the act of breathing.

'Now,' explained Mrs Godbold, 'we are going to move you on to this contraption.'

They had made a kind of stretcher out of two saplings and several chaff-bags, on to which they began, awkwardly, to ease the Jew. Bob Tanner, who could carry full sacks on his back, would have undertaken it alone after his fashion, but the women had to have their part.

Mrs Godbold bit her lips till the blood almost ran.

Else could have cried for her lover's clumsy strength.

'Silly thing! Stupid thing!' Else would hiss, and hook an elbow into Bob Tanner's ribs.

She could not be too critical. She could not be too close. She loved the veins that were bursting in his strong, but clumsy arms.

So they moved the man out of the house in which he had never expected to live for more than a short interval.

They brought Himmelfarb down on the stretcher to Mrs Godbold's place. His head lolled. There was a rushing of willows, and a whispering of grass. As he passed, the spearheads of the dead grass pricked his wrists, but without malice now. Whatever the length of the journey, it was consecrated for the sick man by the love and participation of his people. So, whole deserts were crossed. He opened his eyes, and already they had left the most grievous of them far behind. From the fringes of Kadesch, a blue haze promised Nebo over on the right. How they jolted and swayed. Endlessly. But the back of the young man, the bearer at his feet, was a pillar of solid flesh, and the woman who bent above his head supported him less with the strength of her arms, than with a pervasive warmth of spirit.

'There, sir,' she grunted sturdily. 'Not much farther now.'

Sometimes she stumbled, but would not fall.

Mrs Godbold was quite exalted by the burden it had been given her to bear. Her large breasts were proud inside the washed-out cotton dress, as the procession of faithful staggered at last to a standstill underneath her roof.

Two little solemn girls, whom Himmelfarb connected with pushing and singing, had prepared a bed, as ordered, and were standing by. Mottled green by bruised grass, their arms were glowing golden against the white of sheets. Gold of light and green of vines were tangled together in the window, to make a curtain, of which a reflection hung, shimmering and insubstantial, on the wall above the great bed. Gently and rationally somebody was undressing him. After which, inside the tingling, sun-baked sheets, he might have surrendered completely to the pleasures of unconsciouness, if only the vice of pain had offered him release.

At one point he was almost crushed by it, and opened his eyes, wondering, with the result that several of the watchers recoiled, and two of Mrs Godbold's younger girls, who had dared to peer into depths for which they were not prepared, began to cry.

The mother shushed and shoved.

Then she addressed the patient, saying:

'I will send one of them to fetch Dr Herborn.'

But the sick man's face rejected her suggestion, so that she decided to humour him, for the moment at least.

Doing as she knew how, she warmed a brick, and put it inside the bed, against his feet. At which he smiled. Or, again, when his lips, dried and cracked by suffering, opened on some request she was unable to interpret, she brought a watery soup made that same day out of a scrag-end of mutton, and tried to tempt him with a little of it. But his expression of nausea restrained her, and immediately she was ashamed for the poorness of her soup, indeed, for her whole house, unworthy even of lesser guests.

Perhaps realizing, he opened his eyes at her, and spoke rather odd.

'I am content, thank you,' he said.

Then Mrs Godbold was overwhelmed by that compassion which all suffering roused in her. The sudden pangs forced

429

her to go and put down the cup, which had begun to clatter in its saucer.

During the afternoon, Himmelfarb drifted into a doze. He was swallowed up by the whiteness. He was received, as seldom. Of course there had been other occasions when he might have allowed himself: the hills of Zion, spreading their brown pillows in the evening light, had almost opened; the silence of his last and humblest house had promised frequent ladders of escape; as he knelt on the stones, in his blindness, the flames of Friedensdorf had offered certain release. But the rope-end of dedication had always driven him on. Even now it was torturing his side, although the goat-mask and hair shawl had slipped, leaving him hanging abandoned on a tree. Again, he was the Man Kadmon, descending from the Tree of Light to take the Bride. Trembling with white, holding the cup in her chapped hands, she advanced to stand beneath the *Chuppah*. So they were brought together in the smell of all primordial velvets. This, explained the cousins and aunts, is at last the *Shecchinah*, whom you have carried all these years under your left breast. As he received her, she bent and kissed the wound in his hand. Then they were truly one. They did not break the cup, as the wedding guests expected, but took and drank, again and again.

Afterwards Else Godbold straightened his pillows. Else could only improvise little acts to cover up her inexperience. And the sick man was grateful for the touch of balsam, for the almost imperceptible dew brushing the craggy surfaces of pain.

But Else withdrew quickly from what she sensed she, too, must eventually suffer. The iron shed which contained them all had begun to stifle, not to say menace. How she longed to slip outside, and hang about the lane, and feel the moonlight slide along her arms and throat, and return the touch of moonlight, until it became impossible to distinguish intention from intention.

Then Bob Tanner, who had gone out earlier, returned, and told them of the fire which had started at the Jew's – the continued heaping of orange light confirmed – and she saw that for her lover something was happening which would leave him changed. She saw that his rather clumsy, lad's honesty, which she had loved and derided from the start, was setting in a shape that even she would not alter. He realized that his girl was the uglier for pity, and would alter many times yet. Each was choking with discovery. But the lovers were grateful to

430

know they could still recognize each other, and did not doubt they must continue to, whatever the disguise.

Then Else Godbold tore herself out of what was becoming an unbearable embrace of thoughts. She leaned towards the sick man, and said:

'Mr Himmelfarb, I wish you would tell me of anything you want, of anything I could do, or bring.'

She sounded as though she were threatening him, because, she realized bitterly, she was still too young.

'If I brought cold water,' Else suggested desperately, 'to sponge your face with? Eh?'

But Himmelfarb had no requests.

When he was not dozing, when he was not removed from the compartment of his body into a freedom of time and space, his expression would appear composed, observant, peering out through the vizor of his face, from out of what had by now become the protective armature of pain. Once or twice he glanced towards the window, at the scarcely extra-ordinary orange light, to follow an event that was taking place, at a distance, but of no concern. In the same way, from under his eyelids, he experienced the apparition of Miss Hare. He was not surprised. Nor did the weight of his faithful disciple weigh heavy on his dead feet.

Miss Hare came in, and even the older children were afraid, who had known this mad woman ever since they could re-member, and looked for her at windows, or in and out the bush, always to be found, like owls in certain trees, or some old possum-inmate of particular shed or chimney. Now this amiable and familiar beast lay whimpering and grunting across the foot of their mother's bed. She smelled still of burning, but fire could have been the least cause of her distress.

The mother, of course, handled this like any other situation. Coming forward, she said:

'I am glad you have come, Miss. I thought you would. There is perhaps something that only you can do for him.'

And touched the scorched shoulder.

But Miss Hare would not answer at first, or would only moan, which could yet have been a manner of communication with some other soul present.

The sick man, however, gave no sign of acknowledgement, but lay with his eyes closed.

'Will you take off your jacket, perhaps?' Mrs Godbold asked of her most recent guest.

But Miss Hare would only moan, not from pain, it seemed, but because she had again succeeded in closing the circle of her happiness. Yet she must have been suffering, for those of the children who had advanced closest saw that the red down was singed close along her chops, and the skin shiny from the basting it had got.

Horrid though her appearance was, all those around her remained rooted in respect. Although the great wicker hat had gone askew, its spokes burnt black, not even Mrs Godbold dared suggest the wearer should remove it. Miss Hare had never been seen without, unless by Mrs Godbold herself, who had nursed her years before in sickness. Nobody else cared to speculate on what might be hidden underneath.

Then Miss Hare sat up, as straight as her fubsy body would allow.

'His feet,' she said, 'are cold.'

For she had stuck her hand under the blanket.

'So very, very cold.' Miss Hare's slow words followed her fingers, ending in a shiver.

'Yes.' Mrs Godbold could not evade it. 'But you shall warm them.'

Miss Hare cheered up then, as everybody saw. She sat and chafed her spirits back. Or gradually lolled lower, until her face rested on the forms of feet, printing them on her cheek.

All this time the man's face was breathing gently on the pillow, but the air could have been rarefied.

'Gracie will go for Dr Herborn,' Mrs Godbold had at last decided.

But Himmelfarb opened his eyes. He said:

'No. No. Not now. Thank you. For the moment I have not the strength to submit to any doctor.'

And smiled with the least possible irony, to absolve who-ever it had been for conceiving a superfluous idea.

He was as content by now as he would ever have allowed himself to be in life. Children and chairs conversed with him intimately. Thanks to the texture of their skin, the language of animals was no longer a mystery, as, of course, the Baal Shem had always insisted.

So he breathed more gently, and resumed his journey.

So Miss Hare was translated. Her animal body became the least part of her, as breathing thoughts turned to being.

The night rose and fell, to which the dying fire gave its last touch of purple through the frame of vines and window.

Maudie Godbold did think for a moment that she saw a

face, but by that hour all the watchers were sleepy, some of them even sleeping.

After leaving the factory on the eve of the holidays for which they had all been longing and waiting, Dubbo went straight to the house where he lodged, on the outskirts of Barranugli. In other years he might have stopped at shops to lay in food against Easter, but now, because something had happened, his sandshoes hurried. Something had happened of extreme importance, but which he would attempt to dismiss. He washed his hands first. He sat for a little on the edge of the bed. He ate some bread, with cold sausage, which tasted of sawdust. He spat it out. But gathered it up at once from the floor. Something he had done contradicted what he had been taught. He sat. In the dusk he washed his hands again. It was so important. He was clean at least by education. He sat in the dusk, and would have liked to look at his few recent paintings, all turned to the wall, but knew he would find them receded into their frames. The disappearing room abandoned him to hopelessness. Shadows would flutter at that hour like insubstantial bats. He remembered his mother had once told him how the spirit of his grandfather was a guardian on whom he might rely, but during one of the many phases of flight, he and his protector had, he suspected, parted company. In any case, for quite some time he had sensed himself to be alone.

Now he began to tremble. The frame of the stretcher creaked, creaked. He was ill, of course. Run down, Mrs Pask would have said, and prescribed a tonic. He coughed for a while, too long, and with such force that the joints of that rickety room were heard to protest wheezily. Again he washed his hands, Mrs Pask breathing approval over his shoulder.

Then he began to cry as he stood propped against the basin, a sick, hollow crying above the basinful of water. There were days when the blood would not stop.

The blood ran down the hands, along the bones of the fingers. The pain was opening again in his side.

In his agony, on his knees, Dubbo saw that he was remembering his Lord Jesus. His own guilt was breaking him. He began to crack his finger-joints, of the fingers that had failed to unknot the ropes, which had tied the body to the tree.

He had not borne witness. But did not love the less. It came pouring out of him, like blood, or paint. In time, when he could muster the strength for such an undertaking, he would touch the tree to life with blue. Nobody knew the secret of the blue that he would use; no one would have suspected such a jewellery of wounds, who had not watched their own blood glitter and dry slowly under sunlight.

Dubbo got up now. He began to move purposefully. He had to put an end to darkness. He switched the light on, and there at least his room was, quite neat, square, and wooden. He changed his singlet, put on best pants, smoothed his rather crinkly hair with water, and went out in the sandshoes which he always wore.

In the steamy, bluish night, he caught the bus for Sarsaparilla. It was an hour when nobody else thought to travel, and the abo had to cling, like a beetle in a lurching tin. Everybody else was already there. All along the road women and girls were entering the brick churches for preliminary Easter services. Without altogether believing they had consented to a murder, the sand-coloured faces saw it would not harm them to be cleared in public. They had dressed themselves nicely for the hearing, all in blameless, pale colours, hats, and so forth. Some of them were wearing jewels of glass.

Dubbo knew these parts by heart, both from looking, and from dreaming. He had drawn the houses of Sarsaparilla, with the mushrooms brooding inside. He had drawn the thick, serge-hidden thighs of numerous gentlemen, many from Government departments, some with the ink still wet on them. He had drawn Mrs Khalil's two juicy girls, their mouths burst open like pomegranates, their teeth like the bitter pomegranate seeds. And as the serge gentlemen continued to pulp the luminous flesh, all was disappointment and coronary occlusion. So Dubbo had seen to draw.

Sometimes in his wanderings through Sarsaparilla, the painter had pushed deep into his own true nature, which men had failed to contaminate, and there where the houses stopped, he had found his thoughts snapping again like sticks in silence. But subordinate to silence. For silence is everything. Then he had come back and drawn the arabesques of thinking leaves. He had drawn the fox-coloured woman looking out of a bush, her nose twitching as the wind altered.

He would have liked to draw the touch of air. Once, though, he had attempted, and failed miserably to convey the skin of silence nailed to a tree.

Now, remembering the real purpose of his visit to Sarsaparilla in the night, Dubbo's hands grew slithery on the chromium rail of the empty bus. Ostensibly he was steadying himself. The bus was such a void, the conductor came along at

434

last, and after clearing his throat, condescended to enter into conversation with a black.

The conductor said, extra loud, there had been a fire at Sarsaparilla – some Jew's place.

'Yes?' Dubbo replied.

And smiled.

'Oh, yes!' he repeated, almost eagerly.

'You know about it?' the conductor asked. 'Know the bloke perhaps? Worked at Rosetree's.'

'No,' Dubbo said. 'No. I don't. I don't know.'

Because, he saw, with widening horror, it was his nature to betray.

So he smiled.

'Anyway,' said the conductor, 'these bloody foreigners, the country's lousy with them.'

Dubbo smiled. But the cage of his chest was crushing him.

'What happened to the bloke?' he asked.

His voice was pitched rather too high.

'Arr,' said the conductor. 'I dunno.' And yawned. 'I didn't hear.'

He was tired, and began to clean his ears with a key.

Dubbo continued to smile away his love and faith. Early on they had told him it was his nature to betray, and often since, they had proved it to him. He had even betrayed his secret gift, but only once, and with that, he knew almost for certain, he would make amends eventually. That would bear witness to his faith, in the man they had crucified, as well as in the risen Lord.

When the bus reached Sarsaparilla, the abo got down at the post-office corner, and descended the hill to where he knew the Jew had lived. There, sure enough, was the skeleton of what had been a house. The little, mild blue beads of fire ran and dropped from what remained. Contorted sheets of iron glowed fainter now, and hissed. The sparks, however, were still very beautiful if in any way encouraged.

A few women were standing around, hoping something of a personal sort might explode in the ashes to revive their interest, and a couple of volunteers were examining a limp-looking length of hose. To these men the abo called.

'Where,' he began to ask from a distance.

Everybody turned and stared. The voice the strange black-fellow used was slewing round in the slight wind.

The firemen were too tired to bother, but their flat faces waited for a little.

'Where would,' the abo began again; and: 'Can you tell us.' His question fell, broken.

For he had begun to cough, and went stumbling humiliated away. He could only cough, and stagger over ground that might have been designed for his downfall. And after a brief passage through some blackberry bushes, came up abruptly against a shed.

There was a light in it. He steadied himself. His hands were holding a window-sill.

Then Dubbo looked inside, and saw as well as remembered that this was the shed in which lived Mrs Godbold, whom he had first encountered at Mrs Khalil's, and who had bent down and wiped his mouth as nobody had ever done. Consequently, as she had already testified her love, it did not surprise him now to find the same woman caring for the Jew. There in the bosom of her light the latter lay, amongst the heaps of sleeping children, and the drowsy ones, who still clung to whatever was upright, watching what had never happened before. And the fox-coloured woman from Xanadu lay across the Jew's feet, warming them by methods which her instincts taught her.

As Dubbo watched, his picture nagged at him, increasing in miraculous detail, as he had always hoped, and known it must. In fact, the Jew was protesting at something – it could have been the weight of the bedclothes – and the women were preparing to raise him up. The solid, white woman had supported him against her breasts. and the young girl her daughter, of such a delicate, greenish white, had bent to take part, with the result that some of her hair was paddling in the Jew's cheek, and the young fellow, his back moulded by the strain, was raising the body of the sick man, almost by his own strength, from out of the sheets, higher on the stacked pillows.

The act itself was insignificant, but became, as the watcher saw it, the supreme act of love.

So, in his mind, he loaded with panegyric blue the tree from which the women, and the young man His disciple, were lowering their Lord. And the flowers of the tree lay at its roots in pools of deepening blue. And the blue was reflected in the skins of the women and the young girl. As they lowered their Lord with that almost breathless love, the first Mary received him with her whitest linen, and the second Mary, who had appointed herself the guardian of his feet, kissed the bones which were showing through the cold, yellow skin.

Dubbo, taking part at the window, did not think he could survive this Deposition, which, finally, he had conceived. There

436

he stood, sweating, and at last threatened with coughing. So he went away as he had come. He would have been discovered if he had stayed, and could not have explained his vision, any more than declared his secret love.

As soon as the women had settled their charge, his head lay marvellously still.

Mrs Godbold, who had arranged the sheet neatly underneath the yellow chin, touched him with the tips of her fingers. She could not feel life, but knew from having carried the body of her brother, and closed the eyes of several babies, that life was there yet.

Indeed, nothing would now divert Mordecai ben Moshe from his intention of following to its source that narrower, but still reliable stream. So he would ignore the many hands which tweaked at his cap, or became involved in the flowing folds of his white gown, to distract, to supplicate. As he strode, the particles of petitions fluttered in his face in tinkling scraps, to melt against his hot skin. Pressure of time would not allow him to stop, to piece together, to communicate, although he was expected, he was expected to know.

And did, of course, now.

He knew all the possible permutations and combinations. Whereas, at Bienenstadt, his green and supple soul had been forced to struggle for release, the scarred and leathery object which it had become would now stand forth with very little effort. So, too, he had only to touch tongues, including his own, and they would speak.

As the purple stream – for it was evening now – wound through the rather stony hills, there came to him thousands asking him to tell them of the immediate past, so that they might be prepared against the future, since many of them feared they might soon be expected to return. The strange part was: he knew, he knew. The cliffs of rock were his scroll. He had only to open the flesh of their leaves to identify himself with the souls of plants. So the thousands waited for him along the banks of the interminable river. Sometimes the faces were those of Jews, sometimes they were gentile faces, but no matter; the change could be effected from one to the other simply by twitching a little shutter. Only, he who had drilled holes, could not stop now for souls, whatever the will, whatever the love. His own soul was carrying him forward. The mountains of darkness must be crossed.

Such was his anxiety and haste, Himmelfarb shifted his feet

beneath the bedclothes: little more than a fluttering of bones, but not so faint that Miss Hare did not feel it against her cheek. For a moment Mrs Godbold was afraid the old creature might be going off into one of her attacks; there was such a convulsion of the body, such a plunging of the blackened hat. But Miss Hare only settled deeper into a state where her friend was too discreet to follow. As she turned to occupy herself with other things, Mrs Godbold saw on the blistered mouth evidence of gentlest joy.

Miss Hare had, in fact, entered that state of complete union which her nature had never yet achieved. The softest matter her memory could muster – the fallen breast-feathers, tufts of fur torn in courtship, the downy, brown crooks of bracken – was what she now willed upon the spirit of her love. Their most private union she hid in sheets of silence, such as she had learnt from the approach of early light, or from holding her ear to stone, or walking on thicknesses of rotted leaves. So she wrapped and cherished the heavenly spirit which had entered her, quite simply and painlessly, as Peg had suggested that it might. And all the dancing demons fled out, in peacock feathers, with a tinkling of the fitful little mirrors set in the stuff of their cunning thighs. And the stones of Xanadu could crumble, and she would touch its kinder dust. She herself would embrace the dust, the spirit of which she was able to understand at last.

Himmelfarb's face had sunk very deep into the pillow, it seemed to Else Godbold as she watched. He was stretched straight, terrible straight.

But warmer now. For it was at this point that he glanced back at the last blaze of earthly fire. It rose up, through the cracks in the now colourless earth, not to consume, but to illuminate the departing spirit. His ankles were wreathed with little anklets of joyous fire. He had passed, he noticed, the two date-palms of smoking plumes. By that light, even the most pitiable or monstrous incidents experienced by human understanding were justified, it seemed, as their statuary stood grouped together on the plain he was about to leave.

So he turned, and went on, arranging the white *Kittel*, in which, he realized, he was dressed, and which he had thought abandoned many years ago in the house on the Holzgraben, at Holunderthal.

Then Miss Hare uttered a great cry, which reverberated through the iron shed like the last earthly torment, and began to beat the quilt with the flat of her hands.

'Himmelfarb,' she cried, 'Himmelfarb,' the name was choking her. 'Himmelfarb is dead! Oh! *Ohhhhhh!*'

It died away, but she continued to blubber, and feel the quilt for something she hoped might be left.

All the little girls had woken, but not one could find the courage to cry.

And now Mrs Godbold herself had come, and when she had touched, and listened, and her intuition had confirmed, she saw fit to pronounce:

'He will not suffer any more, the poor soul. We should give thanks, Miss Hare, that he went so peaceful, after all.'

Just then the alarm-clock, with which one of the children must have been tinkering during the day, went off before its usual hour, with a jubilance of whirring tin to stir the deepest sleeper, and Mrs Godbold turned towards the mantel.

When she was satisfied, she said:

'Mr Himmelfarb, too, has died on the Friday.'

Although her remark was so thoughtfully spoken, its inference was not conveyed to anybody else. Nor had she intended exactly to share what was too precious a conviction.

Then the woman and her eldest daughter quietly went about doing the several simple things which had to be done for the man that had died, while Maudie Godbold pulled on her stiff shoes, and trailed up the hill to fetch the previously rejected Dr Herborn.

It was very still now, almost cold for the time of year. The lilies of moonlight dropped their cold, slow pearls. The blackberry bushes were glittering. At that hour, before the first cock, if such a bird survived at Sarsaparilla, the only movement was one of dew and moonlight, the only sound that of a goat scattering her pellets.

At that hour, Miss Hare came out of the Godbolds' shed, since there was no longer cause for her remaining. She had witnessed everything but the doctor's signature. In the friable white light, she too was crumbling, it seemed, shambling as always, but no longer held in check by the many purposes which direct animal or human life. She might have reasoned that she had fulfilled her purpose, if she had not always mistrusted reason. Her instinct suggested, rather, that she was being dispersed, but that, in so experiencing, she was entering the final ecstasy. Walking and walking through the unresistant thorns and twigs. Ploughing through the soft, opalescent remnants of night. Never actually arriving, but that was to be expected, since she had become all-pervasive: scent, sound, the steely dew, the blue glare of white light off rocks. She was all but identified.

So Miss Hare stumbled through the night. If she did not choose the obvious direction, it was because direction had at last chosen her.

15

Rosetrees did not go away at Easter. Harry Rosetree said he could not face it.

'But we got the reservations,' his wife protested frequently.

'We shall lose the deposit, Harry,' Mrs Rosetree pointed out. 'You know what those Hungarians are.'

Harry Rosetree said that he was feeling sick. Deposit or no deposit, he just could not go away. But went into the lounge-room, and pulled the blinds down.

'You are *sick*?' Mrs Rosetree cried at last. 'You are neurotic! I am the one that will get sick, living with a neurotic man.'

Soon afterwards, she began to cry. She did not dress for several days, but went around in the azure housecoat she had been wearing the evening of that old Jew's visit. It blazed less, perhaps, on Mrs Rosetree now, and the seams were going at the armpits.

Nor did Harry Rosetree dress, but sat in pyjamas, over his underwear, and smoked. Or he would just sit, a hand on either thigh. He was tired, really; that was it. He would have preferred to be a turnip.

Mrs Rosetree would come in and sit around.

'Neurotic,' she repeated rather often, which was the worst she could say of anybody after: 'What can you expect of Jews?'

Then she would peer out through the slats of the venetians. From a certain angle, Shirl Rosetree still appeared to wear the varnish, but there was another side, where her husband's sudden denial of life had crushed and matted the perm, giving her the look of a crippled bird, or, for Haïm ben Ya'akov at least, his wife's grandmother, that black old woman whose innocent and almost only joy had been to welcome in the Bride with cup and candle. So that in the room at Paradise East, which normally was just right – oyster satin, rosewood, and the net *Vorhänge* – Harry Rosetree would be shading his eyes, from some distressing effect of light, or flapping of a great, rusty bird.

There were moments when the intensity of his experience was such that his wife, who never stopped moving around, or feeling her side, or suspecting her breath, or re-arranging the furniture, or again, crying on account of everything, would sit down, and lay her head, the side of crumpled hair, on a little rosewood table, and watch through the slats of her fingers the husband whom she despised, but needed still. Of course Shulamith could not see by the light of reason and the shadowy room what was devouring Haïm, although the surge of her blood would suddenly almost suggest. But she would not accept. She would jump up, and return to the venetian blinds.

Mrs Rosetree would have liked very much to know whether the house in Persimmon Street conveyed an impression of abnormality from the outside. Needless to say, it did not. Since normality alone was recognized in Paradise East, tragedy, vice, retribution would remain incredible until the Angel of the Lord stepped down and split the homes open with his sword, or the Bomb crumbled their ant-hill texture, violating the period suites. For the present, it seemed, from the outside, reality was as square as it was built. The mornings droned on. There was Stevie Rosetree, kicking his heels amongst the standard roses, picking his nose behind the variegated pittosporum, as on any other holiday. There was Rosie Rosetree trotting off to mass, again – was it? – or again? – holding the book from which the markers had a habit of scattering, and paper rose-petals of grace.

Rosie Rosetree attended all the masses; it was no trouble at all to one trembling on that delicious verge where the self becomes beatified. Even the return to superfluous questions could not destroy bliss at Easter.

'Did Father Pelletier wonder why we was not there?' Mrs Rosetree asked.

'He asked whether Mumma was sick.'

'And what did you say, Rosie?'

'I said that Dadda was undergoing a mental crisis,' Rosie Rosetree answered.

And withdrew into that part of her where, she had recently discovered, her parents were unable to follow.

Mrs Rosetree was practical enough to respect a certain coldness in her children, because she had, so to speak, paid for it. But she had to resent *some* thing. So now she returned to the usually deserted lounge-room which her husband had hoped might be his refuge. She leaned her forearms on the rosewood table, so that her bottom stuck out behind her. She was both formal and dramatic, in azure satin. She said, with some force:

'You gotta tell me, Harry, or I'm gunna go plain loopy. Did something happen to that old Jew?'

Harry Rosetree was fanning the smoke away from his eyes, although nobody was smoking. She realized, with some horror, she might always have hated his small, cushiony hand.

'Eh?' Mrs Rosetree persisted, and the table on which she was leaning tottered.

But her husband said:

'You let me alone, Shirl.'

She was frightened then. All that she had ever experienced in darkness and wailing seemed to surge through her bowels. And she went out, out of the house, and was walking up and down in her housecoat, moaning just enough to be heard – fearfully, deafeningly, it sounded to the children on whom she had conferred immunity – as she trod the unconscious, foreign, Torrens-titled soil, beside the barbecue.

That way Rosetrees spent their Easter, while for other, less disordered families, Jesus Christ was taken down, and put away, and resurrected, with customary efficiency and varying taste. Outside the churches everyone was smiling to find they had finished with it; they had done their duty, and might continue on their unimpeded way.

While Harry Rosetree sat.

On the Wednesday Mrs Rosetree, who had begun once more to dress, came and said, neither too casual, nor too loud:

'Mr Theobalds is on the phone.'

Harry had to take the call; there was no way out.

His wife was unable to follow, though. The conversation was all on Mr Theobalds' end, and Harry, if he answered, that froggy.

Afterwards Harry rang a Mr Schildkraut. There was to be *Minyan* for Mordecai Himmelfarb.

And however much she was afraid to be, Shirl Rosetree knew that she was glad. She had survived the dangers of the flesh, but did not think she could have endured an interrogation of the spirit. Sometimes she thought she was happiest with her own furniture. So now she began to run the shammy leather over the rosewood and maple veneer, until wood was exalted to a state of almost pure reflection. She got the hiccups in the end.

Shortly after he had shaved himself, Harry Rosetree went out without telling his wife, who knew about it, nevertheless. Through the sealed window in the hall, she watched him get inside the car. He was fumbling a good deal, she could tell; he made the lights wink, over and over, in the car's glass buttocks, as if it had been night. Before he drove away with a jerk.

Mr Rosetree drove out towards Sarsaparilla along the main highway, where morning had conspired with the Tudor-style, luxury homes to wrap them in cellophane, thus increasing their market value. But soon he was taking lesser roads, which led him by degrees through the remnants of a countryside: grey sheds, and barbed wire, a repetition of shabby hills – at which he did not care to look. Rural scenes made him nervous, unless some sunlit forest, remembered or illusory he had never decided, through which he loitered, gathering wild strawberries at the foot of a convent's mottled wall. Unequivocal forms, whether topographical or human, depressed this small, soft man, who saw that he might come to grief. So he would turn aside, on principle, from axe-faced women and muscular men. He liked to eat *Gänsebraten* and *Torte*. His lips were rather red, and full, with a division in the lower one. But, confronted with the bones of a situation, as in the last few days, the juices had run out of him. He was appalled.

Harry Rosetree continued to drive – the long, glass car was almost too biddable – towards a duty which he had accepted, less from compulsion than from sentiment, he was trying to believe. But as he drove in his incredible car, Haïm ben Ya'akov found himself abandoning the controls of reason, not to say the whole impressive, steel-and-plastic structure of the present, for the stuffy rooms of memory. His father, who was never far distant, entered almost at once, in *Yarmulka* and rather frowzy curls. He took the boy by the hand, and they stood before the Ark, which the beadle had uncovered as a favour, so that they might read the inscription on the wrapper. See, Haïm, the father was explaining, your own wrapper covering the Scroll. Read, he insisted, since I have paid for you to learn the letters. Read, he said, and let me hear. So the boy read, fearfully: *The Commandment of the Lord is clear.* Then the beadle pulled the cord, and the wonders and terrors were again veiled by the little curtain. Wonders and terrors alternated. Why, you are trembling, Haïm. Once more it was the father, as they stood outside the privy in the unmistakable smell of urine-saturated wood. But there is no reason, the father attempted to persuade, and went so far as to squeeze an elbow as they continued standing in the yard. His eyeballs shone greenish in the last of the pale light which trickled in between the cramped houses. I will let you into a secret, he apparently decided there and then, to give you courage, though perhaps it is too soon to understand more than a little of what is promised. Such light as there was, converged on those glittering eyeballs. I have just come, the father confided, from a conversation with two *Rabbanim*, in which we discussed the One who is Expected. Here the eyeballs threatened, and the urine smelled most terribly. The One who, in our time, we are convinced, must come, to lead and save, as it was not, it seems, David, or Hezekiah, and not, most certainly, Sabbatai Zvi, though *all that* is something you will not have heard about. Listen, Haïm, because this is what concerns you. You will be amongst the first to receive our Saviour. I have prayed for it, and prayed, and know. That you. YOU. It was written on the whitest scrap of sky. Then they called to the father from the shop, to attend to business. Soon there was the sound of hardware, and the shattered boy was left saddled with the greatest wonder, the greatest terror of all.

Now Harry Rosetree, whose swirling car had brought him to the outskirts of Sarsaparilla, realized that his tongue was sticking to the roof of his mouth, his throat might have swallowed a handful of dust, his nails were brittle unto breaking. They told him at the post office that the woman Mrs Godbold lived just down there. In the shed. Other side of the blackberry bushes. He left the car, and began to walk, tottering over the uneven ground, the archway of his legs only groggily dependent on their unhappy union.

In a kind of lean-to adjoining the shed there was a woman he took to be Mrs Godbold, bending down to stoke a copper, from which she rose redder over pale. For a moment he hoped such a very simple person might not understand his manner of speech, as regularly there were some who did not. Then he could apologize, and go away. But the situation continued to develop. And now the woman had turned to face him, while remaining withdrawn, hair harassed, arms wet, for it so happened she was occupied with laundry matters.

'My name is Mr Rosetree,' her visitor began, but did not add, as was his habit: 'Of Brighta Bicycle Lamps at Barranugli.'

'Ah, yes,' said Mrs Godbold, in a voice that was clear, and light, and could have been unlike her own, a voice, moreover, which might not reveal, and certainly would not ask.

'I own a business down here,' Mr Rosetree mumbled, and

waved his arm in any direction. 'And have come in connexion with a disagreeable incident, involving an *Individuum* of my employment.'

Mrs Godbold was re-arranging her sodden wash. In the blue water, in the zinc tubs, she pushed the heavy forms around. Once or twice she plunged her arms, and on drawing them out, the skeins of suds fell back. She was so intent, Mr Rosetree doubted he would ever reach her.

'An *Individuum* who died,' he added rather hopelessly.

At this point Mrs Godbold was at last persuaded to assist.

'On Good Friday. Early. Mr Himmelfarb,' she said.

It was so conclusive, there seemed no reason for looking at her visitor.

Then, although he did not wish to, Mr Rosetree had to inquire:

'Where, please, is the corpse of this Himmelfarb?'

Nothing had ever appeared so brutal as the surfaces of the zinc washtubs.

'That is to say,' he said, 'I wish to know with which funeral establishment you have placed the body. There are friends who will take charge of it.'

Mrs Godbold was examining a beam of light, in which invisible things were perhaps disclosed.

'But he is buried,' she said, at last. 'Like any Christian.'

Mr Rosetree opened the mouth which he hoped most desperately to use.

'But this Himmelfarb was,' he said, 'a Jew.'

Mrs Godbold's throat had contracted inside its thick, porous skin. The intruder was prickling all over. The woman, too, he saw, had broken out in an ugly gooseflesh.

'It is the same,' she said, and when she had cleared her voice of hoarseness, continued as though she were compelled by much previous consideration: 'Men are the same before they are born. They are the same at birth, perhaps you will agree. It is only the coat they are told to put on that makes them all that different. There are some, of course, who feel they are not suited. They think they will change their coat. But remain the same, in themselves. Only at the end, when everything is taken from them, it seems there was never any need. There are the poor souls, at rest, and all naked again, as they were in the beginning. That is how it strikes me, sir. Perhaps you will remember, on thinking it over, that is how Our Lord Himself wished us to see it.'

Mr Rosetree was confused.

'But Himmelfarb was a Jew,' something forced him to repeat. Mrs Godbold touched the edge of zinc.

'So, they say, was Our Lord and Saviour who we have buried too.'

Mr Rosetree was no longer able to connect the facts he wanted to communicate. In between, his mouth would form disconcerting bursts of bubbles.

'Schildkraut who is waiting. And other nine men. To hold *Minyan*.'

'I did not know as Mr Himmelfarb had any particular friends. He was too well disposed to all,' Mrs Godbold thought aloud, then added in unequivocal words: 'Tell his friends it was a lovely morning, the morning that we buried him. It was yesterday, it seems. Early, so as Mr Pargeter – that is the minister – and the undertakers, could fit it in. Of course I would have been capable of doing everything myself, and did do many little things that professional undertakers will not recognize. But he was buried official by Thomas & Thomas, a credited firm, of Boundary Street, Barranugli.'

Her visitor sensed while looking at the floor that Mrs Godbold had become inspired.

'I walked to the ground – it is not far – with a couple of my more sensible girls. And was there to receive him. It was that clear. It was that still. You could hear the magpies from all around. The rabbits would not bother themselves to move. There was a heavy dew lying from the night, on grass and bushes. No one would have cried, sir, not at such a peaceful burial, as on yesterday morning when we stood, and afterwards, we was glad to dawdle, and feel the sun lovely on our backs.'

So they buried Himmelfarb again.

Mrs Godbold stirred those same sheets which lay soaking in the blue water.

'He was, you might say, overlooked,' she ventured to judge. 'But some of us will remember and love him.'

Then her visitor began to move. He felt himself to be super-fluous. While all the time Mrs Godbold's stream flowed, warmer, stronger, all-healing. Only, Haïm ben Ya'akov regretted, certain wounds will not close.

'Ah!' she cried suddenly.

Life was too insistent.

'I was forgetting!' she panted.

And pushed inside the main shed, with such force that she shook it.

'It is the bread,' she said.

When she had flung the oven open, there, indeed, was the bread. The loaves had risen golden. The scent was rushing out of them.

'Will I make you a quick cup?' she asked. 'With a slice of fresh bread to it? There is quince jam,' she coaxed.

'No,' Mr Rosetree replied. 'I have business. Other business.'

She came out again, almost too close to him; he could smell the agonizing smell of bread.

'You have not taken offence?' she asked. 'At what I did? To bury the gentleman on Christian ground?'

'What for should I go crook?' Rosetree protested, stiff now. 'It is this Schildkraut. I am no Jew.'

'No,' said Mrs Godbold.

As he could feel she had begun to pity, he went away very quickly, stumbling over the rough ground.

Even so, he heard her voice:

'Dr Herborn certified it was the heart.'

Harry Rosetree drove home so smoothly nobody would have guessed. So much chromium. Such a vision of pink paint. He had turned the radio on as a matter of course, and the car was flying streamers, of pretty music, in addition to those it stripped from the wind. It was only inside, amongst the beige upholstery, and faced with the controls, that the music broke up into little tinkly bits of foil, and nervous glass splinters, and ugly, torn sheets of zinc.

He drove faster in order to arrive, and did, although it was only at his own house.

Shirl said:

'Well, Harry, you look as though you seen an accident, or something. You wanta take a good stiff Scotch and a couple of aspro. Though I know it is wrong to offer advice.'

She would have been interested to examine him closely, but he was walking through their house. He was grunting sort of funny. He sat on the edge of an already overflowing chair, grunting, or belching – grey.

'Gee,' she said, who had followed him, 'you are not going to put the wind up me, are you?'

When he began to cry, she was at first too shocked to continue. Mrs Rosetree had a secret longing for hard, blond men, in sweatshirts that revealed their torsos. Not this soft sister, whom she had loved, however, by contract, and even, she could swear, by impulse.

Harry was blubbering, and rubbing his knee-caps.

'It is the same!' he was saying, she thought.

She stared.

'It is the same!' he kept on blubbering.

Then she did get angry.

'It is the same? It is the same?' she shouted back. 'I am the same dill that always stuck around!'

She began to punch the cushions.

'But have had enough for now! At least,' she said, 'I am gunna ring Marge Pendlebury, and go to some nice picture. To forget. Oh,' she called, 'I have my sense of duty, too. I will not forget that.'

Harry Rosetree continued sitting on the over-upholstered, grey chair until his wife had left the house. She had looked in once, but they were still far too naked to address each other. When she had gone, he went into the bathroom, where she had been powdering her body, and gargling. There was steam on the mirror, in which he began to write, or print, in big letters.

MORD . . . , he put.

But rubbed it out.

But began again to cry.

And stopped.

Quite suddenly he bared his teeth at the glass, and the least vein in his terrible eyeballs was fully revealed to him.

When Mrs Rosetree got home, the strings of the parcels were eating into her plump gloves. She was trailing the fox cape as if the bull had been too much for her.

'Hoo-oo!' she called. 'Hiya?'

That was for Colonel Livermore, who made careful noises back. His wife would avert her eyes from the Rosetrees' side, but the colonel, a mild man, and just, had in the beginning offered cuttings of Pussy Willow, and imparted several Latin names.

'Home again!' replied the colonel with his usual exactitude.

But Mrs Rosetree seldom listened to the words her neighbour spoke. She was content to bathe in the desirable if rather colourless distinction the colonel's dried-up person still managed to exude.

Now Mrs Rosetree chose to remark, with a special kind of tenderness, from her side of the photinias:

'That, I always think, is such a pretty little thing.'

Although she was in no mood for any bally plant.

'That,' replied the colonel, 'is oxalis.'

And pulled it smartly up.

Mrs Rosetree could not care.

'Well,' she said, 'I am quite fagged out.'

She had learnt it from Colonel Livermore himself.

'I am going to lay – lie down, I don't mind telling you, Colonel,' she said, 'and rest my poor, exhausted feet before the kids come in.'

At that hour the shapes of the garden, in which she had never really felt at home, were beginning to dissolve, the bricks of the house were crumbling. If the interior resisted, it was because her instincts kept the rooms stretched tight, at least the essential part of them, or comforting primeval form, and she could have wandered endlessly at dusk through her version of the stuffy, felted tents, touching, when her spirit craved for reassurance, the material advantages with which she had filled a too heroic prototype.

So she trailed now. But frowning for her husband. She had no intention of announcing her return. But would let him come to her, out of the shadows, and kiss her on a dimple, or the nape of her neck.

But she could not stop frowning. It was for Marge now, who had kept on not exactly looking at her. Somehow sideways. Sort of peculiar. All through that lousy picture.

So Mrs Rosetree frowned her way into the bathroom. She had very little confidence, not even in her own breath, but would gargle every so often.

The bathroom was lighter, of course, than the other rooms, because it was full of glass, as well as the translucence of pastel plastic. But brittler, too. And constricted. With the window shut, the airlessness would sometimes make a person choke.

All of a sudden Mrs Rosetree could have felt a cord tighten round her throat. She began to scream, right down, it seemed, to the source of breath. She was ballooning with it.

'*Aacccchhhh!*' she screamed.

Then held back what remained. To force out the words when she had mustered them.

She did moan a little, in between.

'*Oÿ-yoÿ-yoÿ-yoÿ!*'

For the forgotten tendernesses. But her shame hung too heavy. Its bulk bumped against her.

Du! DU!' she was shouting at the tiles. '*Du verweister Mamser!*'

Mrs Rosetree was running through the house, forgetful of the furniture she knew. One particularly brutal chair struck

449

her in a private place. She kicked free once, hobbled by the soft shadows, or a fox cape.

And reached the garden, a place of malice, which she had always hated, she realized, for its twigs messing her hair, spiders tossed down her front, and the voices of the *goyim* laughing for no reason, at a distance, through redundant trees.

'*Hilfe! Hilfe! Hören Sie!*' Mrs Rosetree was imploring quite hysterically by the time she reached the photinia hedge. '*Mein verrückter Mann hat sich....*'

Colonel Livermore's emaciated face was shocked by such lack of control.

Mrs Rosetree remembered as quickly as she had forgotten.

'Colonel,' she said, 'I am terribly distressed. You will forgive, Colonel Livermore. But my husband. If you will do me the favour, please, to come. My hubby has hung hisself. In the bathroom. With the robe cord.'

'Great Scott!' cried Colonel Livermore, and started to climb through the photinias. 'In the *bathroom*!'

Fleetingly, Mrs Rosetree feared it might have been a lapse of taste.

'My husband was nervous, Colonel Livermore. He was sick. *Yoÿ-Yoÿ!* Nobody is to blame. It was never ever anybody's fault when the mind was sick. Eh?'

Unless the fault of that old Jew who came. Shulamith remembered. Before darkness slapped her in the face with a bunch of damp leaves.

'*Nein!*' she moaned, right from the depths, and continued protesting from some region her companion had never suspected, let alone entered. 'There is also the power of evil, that they tell us about in the beginning – oh, long! long! – and we forget, because we are leading this modern life – until we are reminded.'

Colonel Livermore was relieved that his wife had gone for the day to cousins at Vaucluse, thus avoiding such a distasteful experience. He, who hated to be touched, could feel the rings of the hysterical Jewess eating into his dry skin. So he was borne along, detached, a splinter stuck in the scented flesh of darkness.

The night was whirling with insects and implications. His wooden soul might have practised indefinite acceptance, if the brick steps had not jarred him from the toes upward, back into his human form. The woman, too, was jolted back to reason. This return made them both, it seemed, top-heavy, and as they mounted the steps, they were jostling each other with their shoulders and elbows, almost knocking each other down.

'Excuse me, Colonel!' Mrs Rosetree laughed, but coughed it away.

Rejuvenated by some power unidentified, she was becoming obsessed by a need for tidiness.

'So many little details arise out of a sudden death in the family,' she had to explain. 'I must ring Mr Theobalds. Must come over. Put me in the picture. It is only right. Only practical. With two young kids. To show where I stand.'

So the details accumulated, and the blood was distending their fingers, but finally there was no reason for delaying their entry into the house of the man who had hanged himself.

16

From where he was lying the window contained nothing but sky, and he was content with that. Around the frame the bare walls, white once, and still presentable in spite of flies, did not detract from the abstraction which the faulty glass perpetuated. Details were added in certain lights: a burst of little colourless bubbles would emerge, to imprint their chain of craters on the landscape of hitherto unblemished blue, which was swelling, moreover, with rosy hillocks, and invested with depressions of mauve. Sometimes he was forced to set to work on what he saw someone else had failed to finish. His Adam's-apple would move with unconscious arrogance as he surveyed the composition, and added from memory flat masses of the red earth, or a faint wash of the salad-coloured foliage that belonged along the river banks of Numburra. He passed his days in this way, and might have felt happy, if it had not been for his physical inertia, and the knowledge that he still had to commit himself. Then he would begin to torture the quilt. Mrs Noonan's quilt was turned to lint anywhere within reach of his fingers.

Dubbo had not returned to Rosetree's factory after the Easter closure. If it had not been for other, catastrophic events, someone might have come in search of him, but in the circumstances, he was left alone, forgotten. Which accorded well enough with his intentions. Often in the past he had left a job in order to work. To have discovered the reason would have made them laugh their heads off. If only for a moment or two. As soon as they had spat the phlegm out, they would have turned, of course, and continued tending the machinery of labour. But his cult of secrecy had always protected him from ridicule. And now, more than ever, even the walls of silence were suspect.

Already on the second day after he had taken to his bed – in preparation for the plunge, he persuaded himself, to avoid dwelling on his helplessness – there had been a knocking at the door, and he had scrambled up resentfully to open.

It was Mrs Noonan, the landlady herself. Which had never happened before.

He scowled at her through the crack.

'Ah,' she said, and smiled; she was one of the sandy things, and shy.

'I got it inter me head like, yer might be feelin' bad. I got a potta tea goin',' she explained. 'If yer would care for a cuppa tea, it has not stood all that long.'

Her scaly eyelids were flickering, he saw, like those of sandy hens.

'No,' he answered, brutally.

'Ah, well,' said Mrs Noonan.

Flickering and smiling.

When she was once more received into the darkness of the hall, he ran to the edge of the landing, and called out over the banisters:

'I gave my job away. I've got other business now. For several days. I've gotta be left private.'

'Ah,' her voice floated up. 'Business.'

And he knew from the sound that her mouth would be wavering on the sandy smile.

'Thank you,' he called, rather woody, as an afterthought.

But she must have gone away already.

That probability desolated the man stranded on the landing, and he soon went back into his room. He sat on the stretcher. He did not at once lie down, and for several days there recurred to his inward eye the shape of Mrs Noonan's floating smile.

On the morning of the fifth day, his melancholy was so intense, his guts so shrivelled, his situation so unresolved, he got up with determination, and went out into the streets. He drank a pint of milk at the Sicilian's, bought two pounds of tomatoes, and a packet of bacon. A bland, almost autumnal light had simplified the architecture of Barranugli to the extent that its purposes could no longer be avoided. All the faces in the streets were expectant down to the last pore.

So Dubbo saw, and knew that he had reached the point of compulsion. On returning to Mrs Noonan's, his spirit was running ahead of him, while his cold hand slowly advanced over certain welts on the handrail, which had come to mark the stages in his progress up the stairs.

When he arrived, the empty room was full of the yellowest light. The tawny plane tree in the yard below tossed up bursts of green with the flat of its leaves. The wind-screen of a lorry flashed. So that his eyes became pacified by the assistance he was all at once receiving. He began to arrange things with the precision that was peculiar to him. He cleaned the already clean brushes. He ate into a tomato, and some of the golden juice trickled down as far as his chin. He ate a couple of the pink rashers, chewing with teeth that had remained strong and good, and swallowing the laces of rind.

Only then he brought out the first of the two canvases which he had bought months before, in anticipation. Of more commanding surface than the boards of ply or masonite which he normally used, the black canvas no longer frightened him.

He took his time preparing the surface, soothed by the scent of shellac with which he was anointing the colourless waste, preoccupied by the proportions of the picture he intended to paint. These suddenly appeared so convincing, so unshakeably right, they might have existed many years in his mind. Behind the superficial doubts, and more recent physical listlessness, the structure had been growing. Now his fingers were reaching out, steely and surprising. Not to himself, of course. He was no longer in any way surprised. But knew. He had always known.

Dubbo was unaware how many days he had been at work. The act itself destroyed the artificial divisions created both by time and habit. All the emotional whirlpools were waiting to swallow him down, in whorls of blue and crimson, through the long funnel of his most corrosive green, but he clung tenaciously to the structure of his picture, and in that way was saved from disaster. Once on emerging from behind the barricade of planes, the curtain of textures, he ventured to retouch the wounds of the dead Christ with the love that he had never dared express in life, and at once the blood was gushing from his own mouth, the wounds in the canvas were shining and palpitating with his own conviction.

After that he rested for a bit. He could have allowed himself to be carried off on any one of the waves of exhaustion. But his prickly eyelids refused him such a suave release.

Towards the end of that day, he rose, dipped his face in the basin, and when he had shaken the water out of his eyes, was driven again to give expression to the love he had witnessed, and which, inwardly, he had always known must exist. He touched the cheek of the First Mary quite as she had wiped his mouth with the ball of her handkerchief as he lay on the lino the night at Mollie Khalil's. Her arms, which conveyed the strength of stone, together with that slight and necessary roughness, wore the green badges of all bruised flesh. As he painted, his pinched nostrils were determined to reject the smell of milk that stole gently over him, for the breasts of the immemorial woman were running with a milk that had never, in fact, dried. If he had known opulence, he might have been able to reconcile it with compassion. As it was, such riches of the flesh were distasteful to him, and he began to slash. He hacked at the paint to humble it. He tried to recall the seams of her coat, the hem of her dress, the dust on her blunt shoes, the exact bulge below the armpit as she leaned forward from her chair to wipe his mouth. Perhaps he succeeded at one point, for he smiled at his vision of the Mother of God waiting to clothe the dead Christ in white, and almost at once went into another part of the room, where he stood trembling and sweating. He thought he might not be able to continue.

On and off he was bedevilled by that fear. He would go out into the streets. He bought food, and ate it, sometimes standing at a street corner, tearing at the carcass of one of the synthetic, delicatessen chickens, or picking distractedly at little grains of pink popcorn. While all the time men and women were lumbering past, pursuing their own, heavy lives.

Almost always he would leave his room when the light had gone. At night the streets of the model town were practically deserted, all its vices put away; only an emptiness remained, and a sputtering of neon. As he hurried along in his sandshoes, beneath the tubes of ectoplasm, the solitary blackfellow might have been escaping from some crime, the frenzy of which was still reflected in his eyeballs and the plate glass. It drove him past the courts of light, where the judges were about to take their places on the blazing furniture, and past the darkened caves, in which plastic fern lay wilting on grey, marble slabs. So he would arrive at outer darkness, crunching the last few hundred yards along a strip of clinker, which could have been the residue of all those night thoughts that had ever tortured dark minds.

After such a night, and a delayed dawn, he got up to wrestle with the figure of the second woman, whose skeleton huddled, or curled, rather, at the foot of the tree. Once he might have attempted to portray a human desperation in the hands preparing to steady the feet of their dead Lord. But since he had ruffled the coat of darkness, his mind was shooting with little, illuminating sparks. Now he began to paint the madwoman of Xanadu, not as he had seen her in her covert of leaves beside the road, but as he knew her from their brief communion, when he had entered that brindled soul subtly and suddenly as light. So he painted her hands like the curled, hairy crooks of ferns. He painted the Second Mary curled, like a ring-tail possum, in a dreamtime womb of transparent skin, or at centre of a whorl of faintly perceptible wind. As he worked, his memory re-enacted the trustful attitudes of many oblivious animals: drinking, scratching, or biting at their own fur, abandoning themselves to grass and sun. But he painted the rather strange smile on the mouth of the fox-coloured woman from remembering a flower that had opened under his eyes with a rush, when he had not been expecting it. His vanity was flattered by his version of this Second Servant of their Lord. The risk of spoiling did not prevent him touching and touching, as he wrapped the bristled creature closer in the almost too skilful paint, or visual rendering of wind. There she was, harsh to the eye, but for all her snouted substance, illuminated by the light of instinct inside the transparent weft of whirling, procreative wind.

Dubbo added many other details to his painting, both for his own pleasure, and from the exigencies of composition. He painted flowers, a fierce regiment, the spears and words of flowers, together with those cooler kinds which were good to lay against the burning skin. He painted the Godbold children, as he sensed them, some upright with horror for the nightmare into which they had been introducd, others heaped, and dreaming of a different state. There were the workers, too, armed with their rights, together with doubts and oranges. There was the trampled blue of fallen jacaranda. There was the blue showing between the branches of the living tree, and on those same branches, a bird or two, of silent commentary.

The Christ, of course, was the tattered Jew from Sarsaparilla and Rosetree's factory. Who had, it was seen, experienced other lives, together with those diseases of body and mind to

455

which men are subject. If Dubbo portrayed the Christ darker than convention would have approved, it was because he could not resist the impulse. Much was omitted, which, in its absence, conveyed. It could have been that the observer himself contributed the hieroglyphs of his own fears to the flat, almost skimped figure, with elliptical mouth, and divided, canvas face, of the Jew-Christ.

Although the painter could not feel that he would ever add the last stroke, a moment came when he threw his brush into a corner of the room. He groped his way towards the bed, and got beneath the blanket as he was. There he remained, shut in a solid slab of sleep, except when he emerged for a little to walk along the river bank, beside the Reverend Timothy Calderon. But drew away from the rector, who continued mumbling of eels, and sins too slippery to hold. So that, in the end, the figures were waving at each other from a distance. They continued waving, to and back, separated, it seemed, by the great, transparent sinlessness of morning. Joyful parrots celebrated, and only that *Alfwheraryou* could not have borne their playful beaks, would have entered, and sat picking, inside his cage of ribs.

He woke then, with mixed fears and smiles. It was night, and he could not feel the grass, but worked his body deeper in the bed, to widen the hole if possible, for protection. Comfort did not come, and he lay there shivering and whinging, frightened to discover he had remained practically unchanged since boyhood. Only his visions had increased in size, and he had overcome a number of the technical problems connected with them.

The painting of his Deposition left Dubbo as flat as bore water. Water might have been trickling through his veins, if a brief haemorrhage experienced at this stage had not reminded him of the truth. He had very little desire for food, but continued to make himself eat, to be prepared for possible events. In the meantime, he would lie and suck his finger-joints. Or hold his elbows, tight. His strength was reduced by now, except when his imagination rose to meet some conjunction of light and colour in the window, in that always changing, but unfinished, abstraction of sky.

Then, on a yellow morning of returning summer, when the black lines between the floor-boards were pointing towards him, and the window-panes were temporarily unable to contain the blaze, he found himself again regretting that large drawing they had stolen while he was at Hannah's. Because he had grown physically incapable of hating, his capacity for wonder led him to embrace objects he had refused to contemplate until now. So he would examine the face of Humphrey Mortimer, for instance, with the same interest that he might have brought to bear on a flock of pastured maggots, or block of virgin lard. Everything, finally, was a source of wonder, not to say love. Most wonderful was the Jew's voice heard again above the sound of the cistern and the wash-room tap:

'... And I looked and behold, a whirlwind came out of the north, a great cloud, and a fire infolding itself, and a brightness was about it, and out of the midst thereof as the colour of amber, out of the midst of the fire....'

The blackfellow rolled over on the bed, biting the back of his hand. The window was blinding him, with its four living creatures in the likeness of a man.

As he remembered the voice, so Dubbo was still able to see the drawing of *The Chariot-thing*. He would have known how to draw it, detail by detail, inch by inch, for he never forgot those places where he had been. There was simply the question of physical strength. Whether he could still paint, he doubted.

All that night he was haunted by the wings of the Four Living Creatures. The tips of their wings stroked his eyelids. He would reach up and touch the feathers, to become acquainted with their texture. But he woke horribly from one sleep, in which he had found himself lying stretched under the skin of a dead man. There it had been, sagging slightly above the bed, to shelter, it would have seemed, only for the cold drip, drip, drip.

He lay awake through the false dawn. Then, at sunrise, he got up, and stood at the window, and some of that rekindled fire was distributed through his dead veins. His fingers were liberated, and he began to trace on the glass the lines, not of his lost drawing, but the actual vision as it was revealed.

About seven o'clock Dubbo made himself a pannikin of tea. He ate some stale bread, with butter that could have been rancid. But the food comforted him. He felt quite brisk, though brittle. And began at once to restate his conception of the Chariot. The drawing was perhaps too quickly done, but came away so easily, almost as a print, from his memory. There it was in front of him. He knew then that, whatever his condition, he would paint his picture of the Chariot as he had originally intended.

The next two days his movements took control of his body,

although his mind hovered above, as it were – rather stern, beaky, ready to refuse collaboration in dishonesty. So the firmament was again created. First the foundations were laid in solid blue, very deep, on which he began to build the gold. The road ran obliquely, and cruel enough to deter any but sure-footed horses. The latter could have been rough brumbies, of a speckled grey, rather too coarse, *earthbound* might have been a legitimate comment, if their manes and tails had not streamed beyond possibility, and the skeins of cloud shed by their flanks appeared at any point to catch on the rocks of heavenly gold.

One curious fact emerged. From certain angles the canvas presented a reversal of the relationship between permanence and motion, as though the banks of a river were to begin to flow alongside its stationary waters. The effect pleased the painter, who had achieved more or less by accident what he had discovered years before while lying in the gutter. So he encouraged an illusion which was also a truth, and from which the timid might retreat simply by changing their position.

The days grew kind in which Dubbo painted his picture. They were of a fixed, yellow stillness. The creaking of cicadas was not so much a noise, as a thick, unbroken, yellow curtain, hung to protect his exposed senses. All other sound seemed to have been wound into a ball at the centre of the town, as he stood and transferred the effulgence of his spirit on to canvas, or, when overcome by weakness, sat on the edge of a scraping chair, leaning forward so as not to miss anything taking place in the world of his creation.

Where he cheated a little was over the form of the Chariot itself. Just as he had not dared completely realize the body of the Christ, here the Chariot was shyly offered. But its tentative nature became, if anything, its glory, causing it to blaze across the sky, or into the soul of the beholder.

The Four Living Creatures were a different proposition, of course. He could not shirk those. So, set to work painfully to carve their semblance out of the solid paint. One figure might have been done in marble, massive, white, inviolable. A second was conceived in wire, with a star inside the cage, and a crown of barbed wire. The wind was ruffling the harsh, fox-coloured coat of the third, flattening the pig's-snout, while the human eye reflected all that was ever likely to happen. The fourth was constructed of bleeding twigs and spattered leaves, but the head could have been a whirling spectrum. As they sat facing one another in the chariot-sociable, the souls of his four living creatures were illuminating their bodies, in various colours. Their hands, which he painted open, had surrendered their sufferings, but not yet received beatitude. So they were carried on, along the oblique trajectory, towards the top left corner. And the painter signed his name, in the bottom right, in neat red, as Mrs Pask had taught him:

A. DUBBO

With a line underneath.

It was again evening when he had finished. The light was pouring into his room, and might have blinded, if the will to see had continued in him. He sat down stiffly on the bed. The sharp pain poured in crimson tones into the limited space of room, and overflowed. It poured and overflowed his hands. These were gilded, he was forced to observe, with his own gold.

Mrs Noonan was a stranger in her own house, which had belonged, in fact, to her mother-in-law, which caused her to go softly in her rag hat, and coast along the walls in anticipation of strictures, smiling. She had no friends, but two acquaintances, a carrier and his wife, whom she could seldom bear to disturb. But drank a great deal of tea on her own. And loved her hens. And set store by the presence of a lodger, a decent sort of man, whom she did not see.

And was puzzled at last, on running a duster along the landing wainscot, to detect an unorthodox smell coming from under the door of the room that she let. It was so peculiar, not to say nasty, she did at last venture to call:

'Eh, Mis-ter?'

And to knock once or twice.

To rattle the knob of the locked door, though diffidently, because she could never bring herself to consider the rented room any longer part of Mother's house, let alone her own.

'Mister! Mister!' She rattled, and smiled, cocking an ear. 'Anything wrong? It is me – Mrs Noonan.'

'It is Mrs Noonan,' she repeated, but fainter.

Perhaps that was to reassure herself, but she was not really convinced by the sound of her own name, and went away wondering whether she dare disturb her acquaintances, the carrier and his wife. On deciding not, she put on a better hat, and some shoes, and went to a house several blocks away, where she had noticed from a brass plate that a doctor had set up.

The young doctor, who was reading a detective story, and scratching himself through his flies, was bored on being disturbed, but also relieved to be asked for advice, since an unpleasantness at the butcher's over credit.

'What sort of smell?' the doctor asked.

Mrs Noonan flickered her eyelids.

'I dunno, Doctor,' she said, and smiled. 'A sort of peculiar smell like.'

She breathed more freely when he fetched his bag, and felt important as they walked along the street, not quite abreast, but near enough to signify that they were temporarily connected. It was still hot, and they trod with difficulty through the pavement of heavy yellow sunlight, which had assisted Dubbo in the painting of his picture.

'Had he been depressed?' the doctor asked.

'Ah, no,' she answered. 'Not that you could say. Quiet, though. He was always quiet.'

'Sick?'

'Well,' she hesitated. Then, when she had considered, she burst out in amazement: 'Yes! Sick! I reckon that dark feller was real sick. And that is what it could be. He could of died!'

Her own voice abandoned her to a terrible loneliness in the middle of the street, because the doctor was above a human being. They went on, and she tried to think of her hens, now that that decent blackfellow was gone.

When they reached the room door, the doctor asked for a key, but as there was no duplicate, he did not suggest anything else; he burst the papery thing open.

They went in on the draught, rather too quickly, and at once were pushed back by the stench.

The doctor made a noise, and opened the window.

'How long since you saw him?'

'Could be three days,' Mrs Noonan answered from behind her handkerchief, and smiled.

Dubbo was lying on the bed. He was twisted round, but natural-looking, more like some animal, some bird that had experienced the necessity of dying. There was a good deal of blood, though, on the pillow, on his hands, although it had dried by then, with the result that he could have been lying in the midst of a papiermâché joke.

The doctor was carrying out a distasteful examination.

'Is he dead?' Mrs Noonan was asking. 'Eh, Doctor? Is he dead?'

'He is dead,' she replied, for herself.

'Probably a tubercular haemorrhage,' mumbled the doctor. He breathed harder to indicate his disapproval.

'Ah,' said Mrs Noonan.

Then she caught sight of the oil paintings, and was flabbergasted.

'What do you make of these, Doctor?' she asked, and laughed, or choked behind her handkerchief.

The doctor glanced over his shoulder, but only to frown formally. He certainly had no intention of looking.

When he had finished, and given all necessary instructions to that inconsiderable object the landlady, and banged the street door shut, Mrs Noonan prepared to go in search of her acquaintances, the carrier and his wife.

But she did look once more at the body of the dead man, and the house was less than ever hers.

The body of Alf Dubbo was quickly and easily disposed of. He had left money enough – it was found in a condensed-milk tin – so that the funeral expenses were settled, the landlady was paid, and everybody satisfied. The dead man's spirit was more of a problem: the oil paintings became a source of embarrassment to Mrs Noonan. Finally, the helpful carrier advised her to put them in an auction, and for a remuneration carried them there, where they fetched a few shillings, and caused a certain ribaldry. Mrs Noonan was relieved when it was done, but sometimes wondered what became of the paintings.

Not even the auctioneers could have told her that, for their books were lost soon after in a fire. Anyway, the paintings disappeared, and, if not destroyed when they ceased to give the buyers a laugh, have still to be discovered.

Part Seven

17

They had started to demolish Xanadu. A very short time after the wreckers went in, it seemed as though most of the secret life of the house had been exposed, and the stage set for a play of divine retribution; only the doors into the jagged rooms continued closed, the actors failed to make their entrance. Of course, the reason might have been that vengeance was fully inflicted, and the play finished, where wallpaper now twittered, and starlings plastered the cornices. Even so, people came down hopefully from Sarsaparilla to watch, to brace themselves against the impending scream of tragedy, to stroll amongst the grass while keeping a lookout for souvenirs, a jade bead perhaps, or coral claw, or the photographs that are washed up out of the yellow past.

It was no more than a gleaning, because the furniture had been removed immediately it was decided to demolish and subdivide. Solicitors had presided. A young man turned up, in black, and a rustier, elderly individual. They had supervised the inventories, and were present at the arrival of the vans, on the authority of the legatee and relative, a Mr Cleugh, of the island of Jersey, U.K. All was arranged by correspondence, as the fortunate gentleman was too old to undertake the voyage – besides, he had done it once – and could have been interested only in the theory of wealth by now. So the malachite urns were removed at last from Xanadu, and the limping cedar, and the buhl table of brass hackles. Some of the inhabitants of Sarsaparilla claimed to have been informed that it all fetched a pretty penny, though there were others who heard that it went for a song.

The strange part was that the old woman had thought to consult solicitors. She had, it appeared, called them in soon after the death of her mother, when some transparency of memory prompted her to dictate a will in favour of her cousin, Eustace. Not even those who invariably failed to understand motives could have interpreted the inheritance as a simple

463

reversion, for Mary Hare was closer by blood to several Urquhart-Smiths.

So, it seemed, Miss Hare had chosen. She who had lurked in the scrub, and frequently scuttled from the eyes of strangers, who had stood at a window holding the rag of a curtain over half her face, or drifted directionless through the corridors and rooms of her nominal home at Xanadu, she who was at most an animal, at least a leaf, had always chosen, people came to think, and had chosen for the last time, the night the Jew's house got burnt, to go away from Sarsaparilla, where she was never seen again.

There had been a hue and cry, and speculation in the press, and two bodies offered, one from a river in the south of New South Wales, the second from the sea, off the Queensland coast. Neither corpse was recognizable. But it was decided by reasoning too devious to disentangle that Miss Hare was she who had stepped into the cold waters of the southern river, where trout had nibbled at her till the state of anonymity was reached. So it was published officially. But there were those who knew that that was not Miss Hare. Mrs Godbold knew. Several of the latter's daughters knew. Though the matter was never, never discussed amongst them, they knew that Miss Hare was somewhere closer, and would not leave those parts, perhaps in poor, crumpled, disintegrated flesh, but never more than temporarily in spirit. So the Godbolds would push the hair out of their eyes, and squint at the sun, and keep quiet, if ever the subject of Miss Hare's end crept into the conversation of the inhabitants of Sarsaparilla.

It remained something of a mystery, while Xanadu itself was the broken comb from which the honey of mystery had soon all run. People listened for the next crump, from a distance, or approached close enough to enjoy the spectacle of the complicated copper bath-heater, although from that level they could not have caught sight of the tessellated Italian floor, from which time and Mrs Jolley had already half-scattered the medallion depicting a black goat.

Sometimes, in the absence of actors, the workmen would appear on one of the several planes of the deserted stage, and perform against the dead colours for the pleasure of the thin but enthusiastic audience. The spectators would enter right into the play, because all those workmen were regular blokes with whom they could have exchanged sentiments as well as words. Which made the act of desecration more violent and personal, adding to it, as it were, the destructive animus of banality.

464

So the few ladies from Sarsaparilla, and handful of kiddies, and three or four stubbly pensioners, roared their heads off the morning the young chap – the wag of the bunch – stood on the landing at Xanadu with a bit of an old fan he had found, and there, amongst the lazy sunlight which the trees allowed to filter on to the brown wallpaper and dustmarks, improvised a dance which celebrated the history of that place. How the young labourer became inspired enough to describe those great sweeping arcs with his moulted fan, nobody understood, nor did the artist himself realize that, for all its elasticity of grimace and swivelling impudence of bum, his creation was a creaking death dance. But the young man danced. For the audience, his lithe thighs introduced an obscenity of life into the dead house. The candid morning did not close down on his most outrageous pantomime. The people hooted, but in approval. Until at the end, suddenly, the tattered fan seemed to fly apart in the dancer's hand, the tufts of feathers blew upward in puffs of greyish-pink smoke, and the young man was left looking at a few sticks of tortoiseshell.

At once he began to feel embarrassed, and went off stage, careful to close the door upon his exit. The audience dispersed shyly.

Xanadu continued to crumble, when it did not crash. In the evenings when the wreckers had gone, and the long gold of evening had succumbed to cold blue, other figures would appear. They were the couples of lovers, avoiding one another, which was easy eventually, since there was enough silence for everyone, and the grass meeting in arches above the extended bodies made a world that might have been China or Peru.·

Else Godbold walked there with her lover Bob Tanner. They, who had experienced life, frowned on recognizing ignorance, skirted obstructions in the rather difficult terrain, stalking stiffly. Locked together precariously by the little finger, they swung hands, but gravely, and made plans for the future. As if they had actually tamed it.

But once Else bent down, and picked up a scrap of paper, some old page, from some old book, only of handwriting, of a funny, educated kind, which they took the trouble to decipher, some of it at least, under a rampant elder bush.

'July 20. . . .' Else Godbold began to mumble syllables, and Bob Tanner chose that moment to approach his head.

'. . . heat *oppressive* as we left Florence for Fiesole, and the villa of Signora Grandi, the acquaintance of Lucy Urquhart-Smith's. I hope life may become more tolerable, though Signora G. has made it clear that it will remain *exorbitant*! Bathed face, and put on my reseda Liberty. *Feeling much improved!*

'Norbert *indefatigable*. Italy his *spiritual home*. Only a few nights ago he embarked on a long poem on the theme of *Fra Angelico*. Doubtful, however, whether his physical condition will allow him to bring it to an altogether satisfactory conclusion. Poor fellow, the oil is a constant upset to his stomach! Now that we are in a villa of our own, hope to discover some respectable woman who will know how to prepare him his mutton chop.

'My little girl is unhappy. She is a puzzle. Says she *wishes she were a stick*! Often wonder how M. will adapt herself. She is so *plain*! And will not learn to converse. Her statements stop a person short. Will not deny that M.'s remarks usually contain the truth. But the world, I fear, will not tolerate the truth, at least in concentrated form. A man who drinks his whisky neat quickly becomes unsociable. *As we know from personal experience.*

'July 21. Norbert insisted on returning to Florence for the day. Did San Marco, Santa Maria del Carmine, Santa Maria Novella, Santo Spirito, etc., etc. Exhausted. Bilious.

'July 26. Have not written since Thursday. Too distressed. On Thursday night Norbert took too much. Threatened to open his veins. Decided against, because, he claimed, it was what Urquhart-Smiths expected.

'Yesterday evening, as though the other were not enough, our poor M. had a kind of little "fit". Quickly over, but *dreadful*. Sat up and said she had never been so far before, that she had found *lovingkindness* to exist at the roots of trees and plants, not to mention *hair*, provided it was not *of human variety*.

'Most distressing. Must consider how I may show her that *affection*, of which I *know* I am capable. Remember in future to pray particularly.

'Oh dear, to see the future! Time must solve problems which prove too great a tangle at close quarters. Had always dreamt of an old age made comfortable by a daughter with cool, lovely hands. No question of a tranquil husband. Sometimes am forced to conclude only the air soothes. But where? Not at Florence. . . .'

'Waddayaknow!' It was too much for Else Godbold.

But Bob Tanner had taken a blade of grass, and was inserting it strategically into the opening of his girl's ear.

'Ah, *Bob*!' Else cried.

She laughed, but down her nose, because she was interrupted in contemplation of higher things.

Then he put his face almost into the angle of her neck, until there remained only a thin band of burning air to separate them. Outside, the cold air spilled down, almost to the roots of the elder bush, where it was repelled. They were warm there, nesting in the grass.

Else could have cried. She crumpled up the yellow paper from which she had been reading.

Then Bob took the lobe of her ear between his teeth, and could not hold his breath, but snorted hot into her ear.

'Ah, Bob,' she had to protest, 'didn't you listen to what I was readin' out?'

'All that old stuff?'

She had never seen him angry.

'Ah,' she cried, 'I would give anything to see what will become of us!'

'I could tell you,' Bob said.

But did not attempt.

The flesh, she saw, was slipping from his face, so that, with nothing to intervene, she was brought all that closer to him.

They were very close now. Their mouths were melting, flowing into one.

Until Else came up for breath.

'I am afraid, Bob.'

'What of?' he asked.

'I dunno,' Else said, because she could not have conveyed the world of darkness.

Owls were flapping through the rooms of Xanadu. Somewhere a branch cracked, and fell.

'I used to think,' Else said, 'you could make the future what you wanted.'

Then Bob Tanner, who was determined to resist the future, when the present was so very palpable, blazed up:

'What odds the future! I know enough. Can't you see me, Else? Look at me, Else. Eh? Else!'

Then she did.

'That's all right,' he said. 'Eh? That's all right.'

The present welcomed them with open arms. As they rocked together, underneath the elder bush, it did not seem likely that anything would ever withstand Bob Tanner's blunt conviction.

'I will show you! I will hold you! I will give you the future!'

'Ah, Bob! Bob!' Else cried.

As if she had not always known that all certainty was here, and goodness must return, like grass.

One morning, Mrs Jolley put on her hat, and went down to Xanadu, to have a look. Without her friend, though, who suffered from the gallstones, and the varicose veins, to say nothing of a heart. It was too far for Mrs Flack. So Mrs Jolley went on the quiet, and might have developed palpitations herself, such was her anxiety to arrive, and determine to what extent her resentments had been appeased.

The house had been mashed pretty well down by then, the surroundings trampled hard, much of the stone carted away, leaving a desert of blond dust. Veins and arteries still quivered from the severing. Elbows of ironwork lay around amongst the shattered slates, and in a shrubbery which she had never entered before, due to a distaste for nature, the revenant came across an old, battered, black umbrella. It gave her quite a turn; at first she thought it was a person.

Now, where she had intended to stroll, and give the impression of ownership, she scuttled, rather, as if to avoid getting crushed, and the slight trembling of her head, which her friend had already begun to notice, blurred her perception. All should have been clear, yet objects loomed, and disappointments, out of the haze of Mrs Jolley's thoughts. She barked her shin on a piece of scrapped balcony, and whimpered for the blows she had sustained at various times.

The truth was: this victim's resentments had not been exorcized by the demolition of Xanadu; they had merely taken different shapes. There were the three daughters, in their bubble nylon, walking just far enough ahead; she could never reduce the distance. There were the thoughtless kiddies, pulling at catapults, thrashing the paths with their skipping-ropes, regardless of their nan. There was that tight knot, the sons-in-law, who did not appreciate relationship, but discussed among themselves dahlias, pensions, and Australian rules. In the circumstances, could she afford to reject even a friend whose friendship she already questioned?

Mrs Jolley almost tripped over a length of rusty flue, from which there rose a cloud of soot, one would have said, deliberately. Her friend!

Then, stranger, but true, at a turn in the path, where they had dumped the Diana of the broken wrist, the actual Mrs Flack was conjured up.

'Oh!' cried Mrs Jolley.

She had to hold her left side.

'Ha!' cried Mrs Flack.

Or hiccupped.

'It is you!'

'It is me!'

Their complexions also were in agreement.

468

'I would not of suggested,' said Mrs Jolley, 'in your state of health.'

'No, dear,' Mrs Flack replied, 'but the morning was that lovely, I decided to surprise myself. And here I am.'

They began slowly, though at once, to walk towards some objective, which neither, perhaps, could have specified. Mrs Flack had taken Mrs Jolley's arm. Mrs Jolley did not refuse it. So they walked, and came, Mrs Jolley discovered, to the house in Mildred Street, which they might never have left, and before the lid closed again, of the brick box, the prisoner did have time to wonder what her intention had been that morning in visiting the ruins of Xanadu.

The two women continued with their lives. At night, from under her eiderdown, each would listen to the other, clearing her throat, at a great distance, from deep down, perfectly dry.

There were the days, though, when Mrs Jolley got the upper hand. There were the evenings in particular, when she would glance through the daily paper, when she would feel brighter for reading of the deaths, the storms, and any acts of God.

There was the evening Mrs Jolley shook out the newspaper, and laughed.

'Young people are the devil,' she remarked.

And her milky dimple had returned.

'What does it say?' Mrs Flack asked, but hoarse.

Her eyes were shifting, from point to point, to avoid some eventuality.

'Nothing.' Mrs Jolley sighed. 'I was thinking only.'

And the restless paper was turned to sheets of thinnest metal.

'I was thinking,' she said, 'they would murder you for tuppence.'

'There is always someone must get murdered,' Mrs Flack replied, 'and always someone to do it, independent, you might say, of age.'

Mrs Flack had impressed many.

But Mrs Jolley laughed, and sighed.

'That young nephew of yours,' she began again, after a decent time had elapsed, 'that *Blue* is a caution, never looking in, never giving another thought to his auntie. Who was that good. Always buying the best fillet.'

'Blue?' Mrs Flack cried, and paused.

Something could have been eating her friend: so Mrs Jolley recognized. From experience, she would almost have diagnosed a growth.

Then Mrs Flack resumed, purely conversational:

'Blue is not here. He has gone away. Blue is travellin' inter-state.'

'For some firm?' Mrs Jolley asked.

'No,' said Mrs Flack. 'That is – no. Not for any particular firm.'

'Ah.' Mrs Jolley sighed, but laughed. 'A lone wolf, sort of.'

If Mrs Flack did not test the edge of her knife, it was because, temporarily, she had lost possession of it.

There were mornings when Mrs Jolley sang. Then her rather girlish voice would run off the sparkling dishes, and fall in little pearly drops.

There was the morning a gentleman came. Mrs Jolley flung off the water. Her milky dimple was recurring.

'No,' she said. 'Mrs Flack is at the Cash-and-Carry. If there is anything,' she said, 'I am her friend.'

He was a gentleman on the stout side, but she liked the big manly men.

He did wonder whether. But his original intention finally opened him up.

'I am Mr Theobalds,' he said, 'from where Blue was, previous.'

Mrs Jolley had grown even more infatuated. Her face made it clear she would lend every assistance.

'I am the foreman, like,' Mr Theobalds explained. 'And me and Blue was always good mates. See? Now he drops a line to say everything is O.K. Got a job with a firm in Queensland. Sent me a snap, too. Blue is fat. They turn into ripe bananas up there, from layin' in the sun.'

'Oh,' cried Mrs Jolley, with such candour, the visitor was compelled to look right into that decent woman's face, 'his auntie will be *glad*!'

Mr Theobalds had to laugh. It sounded rather loose. Some of the big men, the pursy ones, could not control their flesh or laughter.

'I wouldn't of thought 'is auntie would of turned a hair,' Mr Theobalds replied. 'Though they do say it continues to grow on 'em after the lid is screwed down.'

'The *lid*?' Mrs Jolley was surprised. ' 'Is auntie?'

'His Aunt Daise died of something, I forget what.'

Mr Theobalds could afford to look jovial for that which had happened long ago, and did not concern him.

'But was his poor mother,' Mrs Jolley insisted.

'*She* is his mum.' Mr Theobalds looked out through his eye-lashes, which made a gingery fringe.

Mrs Jolley was confounded.

'I thought everybody knew as Ada Flack was Bluey's mum,' Mr Theobalds said, 'but perhaps you have forgot.'

'*She* is his mother!' Mrs Jolley repeated.

She could never forgive.

'I am not that foolish, Mr Theobalds,' she protested quickly, 'to forget what I was never told. Ever. I am obliged to you, incidentally, for important information.'

Mr Theobalds did not care for what he had started. Although the outcome would be no concern of his.

'And the father?' Mrs Jolley could not resist.

'No official father. Only opinions.'

Mrs Jolley rattled.

'One thing is sure,' Mr Theobalds said, 'it was never Will Flack.'

'Who slipped off the roof.'

Mrs Jolley was following the progress of the doomed sand-shoe on the fatal tile. Her face had turned a chalky blue.

Mr Theobalds laughed again.

'Will never slipped.'

'Jumped?'

Her informant did not answer at first.

'Mr Flack was *pushed*, then?' Mrs Jolley almost screeched. It startled the visitor.

'I would not care to say,' Mr Theobalds said, 'not in any court. Not pushed. Not with hands, anyhow. Will Flack was a weak sort of coot, but good. He could not face an ugly situation. That is the way I see it.'

'She as good as pushed her own husband off the roof! That is what it amounts to!'

'I did not say it,' Mr Theobalds said.

He had gone rather soft, and his size made him look all the softer.

Mrs Jolley realized she was still standing on the step. She asked:

'Would you care to take somethink, Mr – Er?'

But her visitor did not. He was having trouble with the carby. He would probably have to take it down.

Then Mrs Jolley remembered that she was partial to big men. Even the softish ones.

She said:

'You mechanical men! I could look inside of an engine, and not know the first thing about it.'

She would continue looking, though, if it would help.

But her visitor had been caught once, so he went away.

'I am glad that your nephew is so well and happy,' Mrs Jolley kept repeating to her friend. 'And that he should have thought to write, even if it was only to Mr Theobalds, though he seems a nice sort of man.'

Mrs Flack's lips had never looked paler.

'Oh, Ernie Theobalds,' she said. 'He was always mates with everyone.'

If she had not been continually ailing, she might have complained of not feeling well, but in the circumstances, she had to think of something else. So she kept on parting the little rosettes of hair, matted above her forehead, and which were of a strangely listless brown.

All things considered, Mrs Jolley would no longer have been surprised if Mrs Flack wore a wig.

'Some men are to be trusted only so far,' Mrs Flack remarked.

And dabbed at the steely perspiration which glittered on her yellow forehead.

'You are telling me!' Mrs Jolley laughed. 'Not that some women,' she added, 'don't wear the same pants.'

Mrs Flack was in some distress.

'Pardon me!' she said. 'It is the herrings. I have not been myself since we opened that tin. I should never ever touch a herring in tomato sauce.'

'No, dear,' Mrs Jolley agreed, 'and you with a sour stomach; it is asking for resurrections.'

Nobody could have said that Mrs Jolley was not solicitous for her friend. She would bring her cups of red tea. She would change the water in the vases, because by now, Mrs Flack had forgotten. When Mrs Jolley poured the opaque stream of flower-water, the smell of which becomes ubiquitous, Mrs Flack would begin to walk about her brick home, and examine the ornaments, to avoid what was unthinkable. She herself had the look of pressed flowers, not exactly dead, and rustling slightly.

Winter evenings were cosiest at Mildred Street, even when it rained on a slant. Then the two ladies, in winter dressing-gowns, would sip the steamy cups of tea. Mrs Jolley would hold her cup as though she must not lose a drop: it was so good, so absolving, such a crime not to show appreciation. But Mrs Flack, teacup in hand, might have been supporting air.

One evening Mrs Jolley put down her cup, and when she had rearranged her chenille, looked up, and speculated:

'I wonder what that Mr Theobalds does of an evening. There is a real man's man.'

Mrs Flack wet her lips, which tea had already wetted.

'I would not give a thought to Ernie Theobalds,' she said. 'I would not.'

Looking right through her friend.

'I would not,' she said.

She was looking that yellow, and somewhere in the side of her neck, a pulse.

'All right! All right!' Mrs Jolley said. 'I was making conversation like.'

She smiled so soft. She had that blue eye. She had a mother's skin.

'I would not believe the tales,' Mrs Flack ejaculated, 'of any Ernie Theobalds.'

Mrs Jolley must have done some very quick thinking, for her eyes shifted in such a way. Then she sat forward in her soft, blue chenille.

'But I do believe,' she said. 'Because I am a mother.'

It was most extraordinary, but Mrs Flack's tongue began sticking straight out of her mouth, the tip of it curled slightly up. She dropped her teacup. She was making noises of an uncommon kind.

Mrs Jolley rose, and went and slapped her friend's wrists.

'There!' she said. 'There is no need, you know, to create. I am one that understands. Look,' she said, and stooped. 'The cup! It is not broken. Isn't that just luck!'

But Mrs Flack was looking right through the wall.

'It is what takes hold of you,' she said. 'A person is not responsible for all that happens.'

It could have been the presence of Mrs Jolley which made her add, slower:

'That is – not everybody is responsible for everythink.'

Mrs Jolley did not like to play the role of conscience, but since it had been thrust upon her, she did her best. From beneath the pale blue eiderdown she would hear that poor, guilty soul, her friend, get up several times a night, almost as if her bladder – though that was one part of her which Mrs Flack herself had forgotten to accuse.

At all events, the condemned woman would wander through her temporary abode, touching objects, trailing her dressing-gown of beige. For Mrs Flack was all of a beige colour now. Worst of all, as she drifted in the dark, she would know that her conscience was stretched beneath a pale blue eiderdown, waiting to tangle with her thoughts. Left alone, she might have found refreshment by dwelling at times on the pleasures of sin, for remorse need not be all dry, even in a shrivelled sinner. And Mrs Flack was that. Indeed, her breasts would not have existed if it had not been for coming to an agreement with her vest. Which night would cancel. The knife of time descended again, and all the fumbling, bungling, exquisite agonies of fullness might only have been illusion.

'If I was you,' Mrs Jolley once advised at breakfast, 'I would consider asking the chemist to recommend a reliable pill.'

'I will not drug myself,' Mrs Flack replied. 'You will never persuade me it is right. It is not. It is not ethical.'

'Oh, I will not try to *persuade*! It was only for your own good,' Mrs Jolley protested. 'I cannot bear to watch a human being suffer.'

And averted her eyes. Or watched, instead, her victim's toast.

'Sometimes I wonder whether I am all that good for you,' she murmured, thoughtful.

Without looking up, but watching.

'Not good?' Mrs Flack stirred, dry as toast.

'Whether our two personalities do not click, like,' Mrs Jolley explained. 'I would go away if I could convince myself it was the case. Never ever did I think of going away, not even when you was unkind, dear, but would consider it now, if I thought it would be in any way beneficial to another.'

Mrs Jolley did not look. She listened to hear the silence expostulate in pain.

Then Mrs Flack moved, her chair was bumping on the lino, her slippers had discovered grit. For a moment Mrs Jolley suspected her friend might have revived.

'I have often wondered,' said Mrs Flack, 'why you did not think to go, and your good home, let at a nominal rent, to a friend. And your three daughters so affectionate. And all the grand-kiddies. All the advantages. All sacrificed for poor me.'

So that Mrs Jolley no longer suspected, she knew that Mrs Flack was escaping, was stronger than her fate.

So Mrs Jolley blew her nose.

'It is not the advantages,' she said, 'it is the memories.'

It was the tune, she had remembered, on some old banjo, that made Mrs Jolley water.

Mrs Flack cut the crust off her toast, and freed her fingers of the crumbs.

'If you was to go, of course I would suffer,' she admitted.

Mrs Jolley hung her head, in gratitude, or satisfaction. She might, perhaps, have been mistaken.

'I would suffer, wondering,' said Mrs Flack, 'how you was makin' out, down there, in that nice home, with all that family, and memories of your hubby who has passed on.'

Then Mrs Jolley actually cried.

Remembering the hurdy-gurdy tunes of life made her more assiduous. Frequently she would jump up and scrub the scullery out at night. She wrote letters, and tore them up. She would walk to the post office, and back. Or to the chemist's.

'If someone told me you had gone away,' Mrs Flack remarked, 'I would believe it.'

'It is the weather,' said Mrs Jolley. 'It unsettles you.'

'Bad news, perhaps. There is nothing so unsettling as a letter,' suggested Mrs Flack.

Mrs Jolley did not answer, and Mrs Flack watched the little soft white down that moved very slightly on her friend's cheeks, with emotion, or a draught. The two women would listen to each other intolerably, but could not refrain from such a pleasure.

One day, when Mrs Jolley had gone to the chemist's, Mrs Flack entered her friend's room – only, of course, it was Mrs Flack's – and began to act as though she were drowning, but might just be saved. Her hands were, in fact, frenzied, but found, for her salvation, under the handkerchief sachet which some kiddy had embroidered, a letter, perhaps *the* letter.

Mrs Flack was foolish with achievement. She held the page so close, closer than she need have. How she drank it down, in gulps of visible words:

Dear Mum [Mrs Flack read, or regurgitated],

I received your letter last week. You will wonder why I have not answered quicker, but was giving the matter consideration – Dot and Elma as much as me. Fred also had to be told, as you will understand, it concerns him so very closely. He is sitting here in the lounge-room with me as I write, listening to some Light Music.

Well, Mum, to put it plain, none of us think it is a good idea. You know what people's nerves are when living on top of one another. Elma is particularly cramped for space, Dot and Arch are always paying something off, if not several articles at once – I wonder they ever keep track of the dockets. Well, that is how the others are placed.

As for Fred, he said he would have no part of any plan to bring you to live under the same roof. He just would not, you know how stubborn Fred can be. Well, Mum, it all sounds pretty hard. I will admit that, and perhaps it is. I will admit you are our mother. We are the ungrateful daughters, anyone would say, of the mother who made the sacrifices. Yes, Mum, and I think perhaps the biggest sacrifice you ever made was Dad. Not that any blood was let. It was all done clean and quiet. Nobody read about it in the papers. But I will never forget his face the night he died of married love, which is sometimes also called coronary occlusion.

There, I have said it – with my own hubby sitting in the room, waiting to read what I have wrote. I am not afraid. Because we expect the least, we have found something in each other to respect. I know Fred would not tread on yours truly, even if he discovered I was just a slug. That is the great temptation, Mum, that you was never able to resist, you and other human beings.

There you have it, then. The kids are good. I am sorry if your friend is so very awful, but perhaps she will bear further looking into. Every mirror has its double.

With remembrances from
Your daughter
Merle

PS. Who was driven to it, Mum.

Mrs Flack had only once witnessed an indecent act. This could have been the second. On which the drawer stuck. She had shot it back crooked, but straightened it at last.

When Mrs Jolley returned she noticed that her friend appeared to have solved one of the many riddles, and was not altogether pleased with the answer. But she herself could not care. She volunteered:

'I am going to lay down for a while. It is those sinuses.'

'Yes, dear,' answered Mrs Flack. 'I will bring you a cup of tea.'

'No!' Mrs Jolley discouraged. 'I will lie and sniff something up, that Mr Broad has given me.'

They did, in fact, from then on, bring each other endless cups of tea, for which each showed herself to be grateful. It did not, however, prevent Mrs Jolley more than once emptying hers down the lavatory, or Mrs Flack from pouring hers, on several occasions, into the *monstera deliciosa*, after giving the matter thought.

Thought was a knife they no longer hesitated to try upon themselves, whereas in the past it had almost invariably been used upon another.

'That handkerchief sachet which I have, with the pansies on it, and which you must have seen, dear,' Mrs Jolley once remarked.

Mrs Flack coughed dry.

'Yes, dear, I seem to have noticed.'

476

'That,' said Mrs Jolley, 'was embroidered for me by little Deedree, Elma's eldest.'

'I never ever owned a handkerchief sachet,' Mrs Flack considered, 'but for many years retained a small bottle full of first teeth.'

'Oh!' cried Mrs Jolley, almost in pain; she would have so loved to see. 'And what became of that bottle?'

'I threw it out,' said Mrs Flack, 'at last. But sometimes wonder whether I ought to have done.'

Night thoughts were cruellest, and often the two women, in their long, soft, trailing growns, would bump against each other in the passages, or fingers encounter fingers, and they would lead each other gently back to the origins of darkness. They were desperately necessary to each other in threading the labyrinth. Without proper guidance, a soul in hell might lose itself.

Just before the house was completely razed, the bulldozers went into the scrub at Xanadu. The steel caterpillars mounted the rise, to say nothing of any sapling, or shrubby growth that stood in their way, and down went resistance. The wirier clumps might rise again, tremblingly, on their nerves, as it were, but would be fixed for ever on a later run. Gashes appeared upon what had been the lawns. Gaps were grinning in the shrubberies. Most savage was the carnage in the rose garden, where the clay, which Norbert Hare had had carted from somewhere else, opened up in red wounds, and the screeching of metal as it ploughed and wheeled competed with the agony of old rose-wood, torn off at the roots, and dragged briefly in rough faggots. A mobile saw was introduced to deal with those of the larger trees which offered commercial possibilities. The sound of its teeth eating into timber made the silence spin, and they were sober individuals indeed, who were able to inhale the smell of destruction without experiencing a secret drunkenness. Many of those present were forced to steady themselves. Because most of the inhabitants of Sarsaparilla came down to watch the garden being cleared, just as they had felt the need to assist at the demolition of the house. In time even the indifferent, the timid, the indolent, the unaware, and the invalid had taken part.

Only Mrs Godbold appeared untouched by these historic local events, but remained more or less unnoticed, as a person of little substance and no importance. Only dimly was a woman seen to emerge from a shed, and hang out the washing. The

477

thick arms were reaching repeatedly up, and there were the loops of limp, transparent linen, hanging at first so heavy, then twitching at a corner, lifting at last, blowing, in glad, white flags.

Mrs Godbold, when she was noticed at all, seemed to live for irrelevance. In the course of her life, she had developed a love and respect for common objects and trivial acts. Did they, perhaps, conceal a core, reveal a sequence? Whatever the explanation, she would go about planting a row of beans, not as though she were covering seed, rather as if she were learning a secret of immense importance, over and over. She would go amongst her pots of ferns, freeing the young crooks from the bonds of spiders. In her later years at least, she might sit for sometimes half an hour beside her ironing table, in the shed where it seemed by then she was ordained to live. Obviously, the scored surface of the yellow board, together with the various vessels and utensils of her office, could not have been housed anywhere else with due sacral dignity. So she and they remained enshrined. There she would sit, at the mercy of the sun, squinting, or it could have been smiling for such glimmers of truth as she had been allowed to glimpse.

But then, Mrs Godbold was such a very simple person. Always there. Nobody could remember having seen her except in some such cotton dress, a cardigan in winter, or the perennial, flared overcoat. Her massive form had never altered, except to grow more massive in its pregnancies.

If she indulged herself at all in her almost vegetable existence, it was to walk a little way down the hill, before the children returned, after the breeze had got up in the south, to walk and look, it seemed incuriously, at the ground, pursued by a galloping cat.

Then she might turn, and call.

'Tib! Tib! Tib!' she would call, and: 'Poor Tibby! Nobody was going to leave you!'

And gather up her many-angled cat, into her bosom, and laugh for the joy of giving shelter, holding up her throat to the sun; it was as though a trumpet were being raised.

If she had been worthy of notice, Mrs Godbold's simplicity might have become proverbial.

The farthest tables were always the most coveted. There one was in a position to view the room from the slight eminence of a platform, and never be outstared. One of those desirable tables had been reserved for the three ladies advancing down the ash-infested carpet, clinging to the chromium handrail to prevent their heels pitching them head-first at their goal. But the handrail, to say nothing of their appearance, lent them a certain crazy dignity. All the cutlery on all the tables seemed to applaud their arrival. If there had been an orchestra, it would have played them down the stairs, but there was never any music at lunch, beyond the sustained pizzicato of conversation; words might ping their way without deflexion into the unprotected eardrum.

These were obviously three ladies of importance who had reached the safey of the floor after the dangers of the street stairs. They stood around, agreeably helpless, while waiters flew like homing swallows. From the tables, early patrons craned outrageously, which might have been disquieting to the objects of their interest if it had not been desired. For the three ladies were wearing rather amusing hats. The first, and perhaps least confident of the three, had chosen an enormous satin bon-bon, of screeching pink, swathed so excessively on one side that the head conveyed an impression of disproportion, of deformity, of bulbous growth. But the uncertain lady was palpitating with her own daring, and glanced at the closer of her two companions, fishing for a scrap of praise. Her friend would not concede it, however. For the second lady was secure in her own seasoned carapace, and would not have recognized her acquaintance except by compulsion. The second lady was wearing on her head a lacquered crab-shell. She was quite oblivious of it, of course. But there it sat, one real claw offering a diamond starfish, the other dangling a miniature conch in polished crystal. The unconscious wearer had divested herself conventionally of her gloves, and was restoring suppleness to her hands. As she tried her nails on the air, it was seen that those, by some chance, were exactly the same shade of audacious crab.

How the waiters adored the three insolent ladies, but it was at the third and obviously eldest that their most Italianate smiles were directed.

The third, or by now the first, lady affected the most amusing hat of all. On her blue curls she had perched an innocent little conical felt, of a drab, an earth colour, so simple and unassuming that the owner might have been mistaken for some old, displaced clown, until it was noticed that fashion had tweaked the felt almost imperceptibly, and that smoke – yes, actual smoke – was issuing out of the ingenious cone. There she stood at the centre of the smart restaurant in her volcanic hat, her mouth crimped with pleasure, for she had reached an age of social innocence where she was again dependent on success. So she smiled, in the abstract, for the blinding bulbs of two photographers, and because she was trying to ignore the arthritis in her knees.

Soon the ladies were as comfortably arranged as their clothes and their ailments would allow. All three had accepted advice to order lobster Thermidor, in spite of an heretical *gaucherie* on the part of the Satin Bon-bon, who had to remark on the popularity of shellfish.

'Dare we?' she had sniggered. 'Is it tactful?'

Too pleased for her provincial joke.

The Crab-shell saw that the Bon-bon had a natural gap between her centre, upper teeth, which gave her an expression both vulgar and predatory.

But the Volcano no longer had to notice more than she wanted, or needed to.

She leaned forward, and said with an irrelevance not without its kind of tired charm:

'You are two people I have been longing to bring together, because I feel that you can become an influence for good on the Committees.'

The Crab-shell was incredulous, but polite. Even the speaker did not appear to believe entirely in what she had said, for she added vaguely:

'What I mean to say is that friendship – the personal touch – is better able to achieve charitable objectives. And I do want the Harlequin Ball to be a great success.'

'Jinny is a darling. But an idealist. Isn't that pure idealism, Mrs Wolfson?' the Crab-shell asked, turning to the Bon-bon, not because she wanted to, but because it was part of a technique.

Nor did she allow an answer, but went off into a studied neighing, which produced in her that infusion of redness peculiar to most hard women. The whole operation proved, moreover, that her neck was far too muscular.

The Volcano put her old, soft, white hand on the Crab-shell's stronger, brownish one.

'Mrs Colquhoun and I have been friends so long, I doubt we could misunderstand each other,' the Volcano said, addressing Mrs Wolfson.

Trying to bring the latter in, though only succeeding in keeping her out.

'Idealism again!' neighed Mrs Colquhoun, as if she would

480

never rid her system of its mirth. She had been several years without a husband.

'I am an idealist,' said Mrs Wolfson carefully, 'like Mrs Chalmers-Robinson. That is why I think it is so important to help these little spastic children. Mr Wolfson – who is an idealist too – has promised us a nice fat cheque over and above the takings at the Ball.'

'Splendid!' cried Mrs Chalmers-Robinson, paying for charity with charity.

'Oh, it is most important to do good,' asserted Mrs Wolfson, slowly negotiating the fillets of her lobster Thermidor.

It was most laudable, but the more carefully Mrs Wolfson rounded out her words, the more Mrs Colquhoun was convinced she could detect the accents of that Dorothy Drury, from whom she, too, had taken a course in the beginning, and almost forgotten. Mrs Colquhoun felt less than ever prepared to endure her neighbour Mrs Wolfson.

'Take the Church,' the latter continued, 'Mr Wolfson – Louis,' she corrected, catching sight of Mrs Colquhoun, 'my husband is all for assisting the Church. At St Mark's Church of England, which we attend regularly, he has given the fluorescent lighting, and although a very busy man, he is about to organize a barbecue.'

Mrs Chalmers-Robinson had fixed her still handsome eyes on something distant and intangible.

'Lovely old church!' she intoned in traditional key.

She loved star-sapphires, and powder-blue. The remnants of her beauty seemed to demand tranquillity.

'Then you will know Canon Ironside.' Mrs Colquhoun dared Mrs Wolfson not to.

Under her inquisitor's wintry eye, the latter was glad of the protection of mutation mink, and settled deeper into it.

'Before my time.' She coughed.

It was a gift to Mrs Colquhoun.

'But I am pretty certain,' she calculated, 'the Canon did not leave for Home, above, I should say, six, certainly not more than seven, months ago.'

Mrs Wolfson contemplated her plateful of forbidden sauce. Food had made her melancholy.

'Yes, yes.' The Bon-bon bobbed. 'We did not attend prior to that.'

At the wretched little, impersonal table, her two friends were waiting for something of a painful, but illuminating nature to occur.

'I was married in St Mark's Church of England,' Mrs Wolfson ventured, and showed that gap which Mrs Colquhoun so deplored, between her upper, centre teeth.

'And you were not done by Canon Ironside?' Mrs Colquhoun persisted.

'Sheila only recently married Louis Wolfson,' Mrs Chalmers-Robinson explained. 'He is her second.'

'Yes,' sighed Mrs Wolfson, trying chords on the cutlery that remained to her. 'Haïm – Harry passed on.'

But Mrs Colquhoun might have been unhappier than Mrs Wolfson.

In all that restaurant the hour seemed to have hushed the patrons. The eyes, glancing about through their slits, began to accuse the mask of being but a dry disguise. It was too early to repair a mouth that must be destroyed afresh. So the women sat. Even Mrs Chalmers-Robinson, of certain inner resources, it had been implied, though of a fragile nature, had ceased to vibrate. For the moment she mistrusted memory, because she might have remembered men. All the women in the room could have been visited by the same thought: that the men went first, that the intolerable, but necessary virtuosi died of their virtuosity, whereas the instruments they had played upon, and left, continued from habit to twang and murmur. Momentarily the instruments were still. Although they must begin again, since silence is the death of music.

So Mrs Chalmers-Robinson listened, and heard herself distantly vibrate. She had fastened on her face the fixed, blue, misty expression, which of all the disguises in her possession had won her most acclaim, and which she would have labelled Radiance.

She said:

'I was confirmed at St Mark's. I can remember the veins on the backs of the Bishop's hands. I knelt on the wrong step. I was so nervous, so intense. I think I expected some kind of miracle.'

'I am told they can happen!' Mrs Colquhoun laughed, and looked over her shoulder at the emptying room.

'My little girl was interested in miracles when she was younger,' Mrs Wolfson remarked.

Her companions waited for the worst.

'She had a nervous breakdown,' the mother informed. '*Ach*, yes, beginning and ending is difficult for women! But my Rosie is working for a florist now. Not because she has to, of course. (There is her own father's business, which the boy is managing

very competently. And Louis – the soul of generosity.) But a
florist is so clean. And Mr Wolfson – Louis – thought it might
have some therapeutic value.'

All three ladies had ordered ice-cream, with fruit salad, and
marshmallow sauce. They were pleased they were agreed on that.

'Then, you know St Mark's.' Mrs Wolfson harked back, and
smiled.

It was comforting to return to a subject. She would have
liked to feel at home.

'I have not been for years. Except, of course, to weddings.
You see, I became interested in Science,' Mrs Chalmers-
Robinson said.

'In Science!'

Now Mrs Wolfson could not believe.

'*Christian* Science, Jinny means,' Mrs Colquhoun explained.

Everyone listened to the word drop. Mrs Wolfson might by
this time have called out: All right, all right, it dogs you like
your shadow, but you get used to it at last, and a shadow cannot harm.

Instead she said:

'You don't say!'

And noted down Science in her mind, to investigate at a
future date.

'You should try it,' suggested Mrs Colquhoun, and laughed,
but it became a yawn, and she had to turn her head.

'I do not believe Science ever really took on with Europeans,'
Mrs Chalmers-Robinson earnestly remarked.

'I *adore* Europeans,' said Mrs Colquhoun, looking at the
almost empty room.

She did, too. She collected consuls, excepting those who were
really black.

It bewildered Mrs Wolfson. First she had learnt not to be,
and now she must learn what she had forgot. But she would
remember. Life, for her too, had been a series of disguises,
which she had whisked on, and off, whether Sheila Wolfson, or
Shirl Rosetree, or Shulamith Rosenbaum, as circumstances
demanded.

So the black, matted girl settled herself inside the perm, behind the powdered cleavage, under the mutation mink. She was
reassured.

'Speaking of miracles,' Mrs Chalmers-Robinson said, 'Mrs
Colquhoun lived for some years at Sarsaparilla.'

The informant advanced her face over the table to the point
at which confidences are afterwards exchanged.

'Sarsaparilla!' exclaimed Mrs Colquhoun with some disgust. 'One could not continue living at Sarsaparilla. Nobody lives at Sarsaparilla now.'

'But the miracle?' Mrs Wolfson dared, in spite of her foreboding.

'There was no miracle.' Mrs Colquhoun frowned.

She was most annoyed. Her mouth, her chin had almost disappeared.

'I understood,' Mrs Chalmers-Robinson murmured, her smile conveying disbelief, 'something of a supernatural kind.'

She was too old, too charming, to allow that indiscretion on her part was indiscretion.

'No question of any miracle,' Mrs Colquhoun was repeating.

A stream of melted ice-cream threatened to spill from one corner of what had been her mouth.

'Certainly,' she admitted, 'there was an unpleasant incident, I am told, at Barranugli. Certain drunken thugs, and ignorant, not to say hysterical, women were involved. Both there, and later at Sarsaparilla. Only, there was no miracle. Definitely no miracle!'

Mrs Colquhoun was almost shouting.

'It is much too unpleasant to discuss.'

'But the Jew they crucified,' Mrs Chalmers-Robinson insisted in a voice she had divested deliberately of all charm; she might have been taking off her rings at night.

'*Oÿ-yoÿ-yoÿ!*' cried Mrs Wolfson.

The latter was frowning, or wrinkling up black, through all that beige powder. She was played upon again. She was rocked by those discords on bleeding catgut, which she did, did wish, and not wish, to hear.

'You know about it?' Mrs Chalmers-Robinson asked.

But Mrs Wolfson was racked and rocked. The cello in her groaned audibly.

'Oh, no!' she moaned. 'That is,' she said, 'I did hear somethink. Oh, yes! There was somethink!'

Did she know! In herself, it seemed, she knew everything. Each of her several lives carried its burden of similar knowledge.

'I warned you!' shouted Mrs Colquhoun.

Although it was never established which, fortunately one of the three upset a cup of coffee into the powder-blue lap of Mrs Chalmers-Robinson. For the moment everyone was mopping and talking.

'Darling, darling Jinny! How absolutely *ghastly!*'

'*Waj geschrien!* The good dress! All quite spoiled! No, it is too much, Mrs Chalmers-Robinson!'

Mrs Wolfson decided to absolve herself of any possible guilt by sending some fine present, something that would last, some little trinket of a semi-precious nature. She had found that such gestures paid.

But a young Italian waiter had got down on his knees, and was sponging the lap of Mrs Chalmers-Robinson with fascinating hands. As she watched the movements of the hands, she knew the damage was as good as repaired. Only she could not reconcile the indestructible shape of the young waiter's perfect head with the life that was slipping from her in daily, almost hourly driblets.

'Thank you,' she said at last, when he stood before her, and she was looking up into his face, with that radiance of which she had once been completely mistress, but which was growing flickery.

'So much for miracles!' She laughed.

'I told you!' said Mrs Colquhoun.

Even though Mrs Wolfson was still being tossed on her ugly wave, it was fast receding. All three began to feel guiltless, though empty.

The women no longer made any effort. They were sitting with their legs apart at their table in the darkened restaurant – for the waiters were turning out the lights, between lunch and dinner, and rolling the used napkins into balls.

'I used to have a maid, who married some man, and went, I believe, to live at Sarsaparilla,' Mrs Chalmers-Robinson recollected.

The ingenious smoke-making contrivance concealed in the crown of the little hat produced a last, desperate feather.

'Not actually a maid!' Mrs Colquhoun had begun again to mutter and hate.

'An excellent girl, although she would breathe down the guest's neck while handing the vegetables at luncheon. I forget her name, but have often wondered what became of such a person. She was – how shall I put it?' Mrs Chalmers-Robinson asked herself, or more, she appeared to be reaching out through the dark plain in which they were sitting. 'Yes,' she said, at last convinced. 'You will laugh, Esmé, I know. She was a kind of saint.'

'A saint? My poor Jinny! A saint in the pantry! How perfectly *ghastly* for you!'

Mrs Colquhoun had gone off into uncontrollable giggles, not

to say hysterics, to which the lolling claw of the crab-shell on her head beat a hollow time.

'How interesting my little girl would have found this conversation. Before the nervous breakdown,' Mrs Wolfson said. 'In what way, Mrs Robinson, did this maid of yours show she was a saint?'

Mrs Chalmers-Robinson was groping in the darkness. Her face had developed a tic, but she was determined to reach a conclusion.

'It is difficult to explain – exactly,' she began. 'By *being*, I suppose. She was so stupid, so trusting. But her trustfulness could have been her strength,' the visionary pursued drunkenly. 'She was a rock to which we clung.'

Then she added, without any shame at all, perhaps sensing that ultimately she would come no closer to understanding:

'She was the rock of love.'

'On which we have all foundered!' cried Mrs Colquhoun, biting on her lipstick.

'Oh, I do wish I could see her,' Mrs Chalmers-Robinson murmured, craning in hopes that saving grace might just become visible in the depths of the obscure purgatory in which they sat. 'If only I could find that good woman, who knows, who knew even then, I am sure, what we may expect!'

The old thing had exhausted herself, Mrs Wolfson saw. At her age, it was unwise.

Indeed, Mrs Chalmers-Robinson's crater was by now extinct. She continued to sit for a little, however, together with her companions, while each of the three tried to remember where she should go next.

When Xanadu had been shaved right down to a bald, red, rudimentary hill, they began to erect the fibro homes. Two or three days, or so it seemed, and there were the combs of homes clinging to the bare earth. The rotary clothes-lines had risen, together with the Iceland poppies, and after them the glads. The privies were never so private that it was not possible to listen to the drone of someone else's blowflies. The wafer-walls of the new homes would rub together at night, and sleepers might have been encouraged to enter into one another's dreams, if these had not been similar. Sometimes the rats of anxiety could be heard gnawing already at bakelite, or plastic, or recalcitrant maidenhead. So that, in the circumstances, it was not unusual for people to run outside and jump into their cars. All of Sunday they would visit, or be visited, though sometimes they would cross one another, midway, while remaining unaware of it. Then, on finding nothing at the end, they would drive around, or around. They would drive and look for something to look at. Until motion became an expression of truth, the only true permanence – certainly more convincing than the sugar-cubes of homes. If the latter were not melted down by the action of time or weather, then they could only be reserved for some more terrifying catalysis, by hate, or even love. So the owners of the homes drove. They drove around.

Mrs Godbold could not have counted how many years it was since the razing of Xanadu, when the fancy suddenly took her to put on her hat and go down. It was a Tuesday in June, the sky watering with cold, but fair. Mrs Godbold had not changed, not in appearance anyway, for life had dealt her an early blow, then forgotten her for other victims. All around her, change was creeping, though that side of the hill where she lived was still choked with blackberry bushes, still strewn with jagged bottles and rusty springs. It was, in fact, a crying shame, but people had stopped crying about it, since the ulterior motives of a speculator seemed in accord with some more obscure, possibly divine, plan. So, there Mrs Godbold continued to live, and had worn several tracks, to suit her habits and her needs, amongst the enamelled blackberry bushes.

Now she chose the appropriate track into Montebello Avenue, and was followed, as usual, a little of the way, by that same, or perhaps another, cat.

'Shoo!' she cried. 'Silly thing! It is too far. For once!' She laughed. 'This will be a proper journey!'

So that her cat was persuaded to turn, and wove its way back, velvety amongst the thorns.

The cold rushed at Mrs Godbold, but her vision remained clear. She broke off a twig, and sucked it for company.

'Who are you?' she asked at one of the gates along the road. 'Eh?' she asked. 'Who are you?'

It was a joke, of course. It was her grandchild. Even better than her voice, he knew the drowsy smell of soap, and was now made silent, or reverent, by recollections of intimacy.

She touched the little boy's cheek once. He submitted, but without raising his eyes.

'And who is this?' Mrs Godbold asked of a second little boy, who came down the path munching, his face full of crumbs.

'Bob Tanner,' the elder little boy answered straight.

She could have eaten him.

487

'And you are Ruth Joyner,' he shouted.

'Ah,' she laughed, 'you are the same cheeky boy who never gets smacked by his mother!'

The little boy kicked the ground. His younger brother pushed him, and showed the liveliest approval of the joke.

'Well,' said the grandmother, her lips trembling, such was her own approval of all her children, 'give my regards to your mum, then.'

'Arr, nan!' cried the elder boy. 'Come on in! There's corn-flour cakes!'

'Not today,' said the grandmother. 'I am going on a journey.' And almost laughed again, but coughed.

'Take me with you,' begged the boy.

'It is too far,' she answered.

'Arr, no!' he cried. 'I can walk good!'

But she was already slowly on her way, making the little noises of deprecation and love, which disappointment would prevent the boy from interpreting at once.

Mrs Godbold continued along a road which progress had left rather neglected.

Two of her girls had been given by now, and two others were promised, and the youngest pair practically in shoes. The six Godbold girls would sometimes forgather still on the trodden ground outside the shed, together with the little, strange, toy children of the eldest sisters. The girls would weave garlands in the green light – any old common flowers, morning-glory, say, and sarsaparilla, and the crumpled wild freesias. They would wear their flowers, and clown amongst themselves, and sing as one:

> 'I will slap
> Any chap
> Who's bold enough
> To cheek me.
> The one that matters
> Never flatters,
> But hangs around
> When he's found.
> He's the one
> I'll kiss,
> And kiss, and kiss, and kiss!'

Although Poppy Godbold would exclaim:

'I am not gunna kiss any feller! Never, never, never!'

Then she might modify her vow, and swoop, and cry:

'Without I kiss young Bob Tanner!'

And the little boy would shout, and protect himself from the onslaught by his silly, youngest, clumsy aunt, who was burning red above him.

So Mrs Godbold had her children. She had her girls. But for how long?. With two already gone. Sometimes she would continue to sit in front of the shed after all those straight girls had slipped from her into the evening, leaving in her lap their necklaces of wilted flowers. Then it would seem as though she had shot her last arrow, and was used and empty. She would feel the touch of darkness. She would sit, and attempt to rub the rheumatism out of her knuckles. Often she would recall the night her friend the Jew died, in the shed behind her. Even the youngest children, who had been sleeping at the time, remembered that night, for sleep did not seem to have prevented them participating in the event. So their eyes saw farther than those of other girls. Tempered on that night, their metal was tougher. Finally the woman sitting alone in front of the deserted shed would sense how she had shot her six arrows at the face of darkness, and halted it. And wherever her arrows struck, she saw other arrows breed. And out of those arrows, others still would split off, from the straight white shafts.

So her arrows would continue to be aimed at the forms of darkness, and she herself was, in fact, the infinite quiver.

'Multiplication!' Mrs Godbold loudly declared, and blushed, for the nonsense it must have sounded, there on the road to Xanadu.

She looked back once more, however, at the two little boys, who were swinging the gate enough to break it.

Mrs Godbold meandered along past the raggedy wattles. She remembered the winter Miss Hare had been laid up, how she had gone down to nurse the poor thing, and how they had been together in the silent house, and spoken of the Chariot. Well, everybody saw things different. There was Miss Hare, who, they said, was mad. For that reason. Miss Hare had seen the chariot of fire. Mrs Godbold, who would never have contradicted her superior in any of her opinions, especially when the latter was sick, knew different too. She had her own vision of the Chariot. Even now, at the thought of it, her very centre was touched by the wings of love and charity. So that she closed her eyes for a moment as she walked, and put her arms around her own body, tight, for fear that the melting marrow might spill out of it.

When she opened her eyes again, there, already, was the new settlement of Xanadu, which they had built on the land Mr

Cleugh, the relative, had sold. Mrs Godbold could not help admiring the houses for their signs of life: for the children coming home from school, for a row of young cauliflowers, for a convalescent woman, who had stepped outside in her dressing-gown to gather a late rose.

'It is too cold, though! Too cold!' Mrs Godbold called, wrapping up her own throat, to illustrate.

'Eh?' mumbled the woman, as she stood tearing at the stalk of the resistant rose.

'You will catch *cold*!' Mrs Godbold insisted.

She could have offered more love than was acceptable.

The woman in the dressing-gown stood, apparently not wishing to hear, and went inside presently, after she had succeeded in twisting off the rose.

Children stared at the stranger in passing, and decided she was probably a loop.

'You will be glad to be home at last,' she said.

'Nah,' the boys answered.

Some of the girls snickered.

But Mrs Godbold was satisfied simply to stand and observe Xanadu. On subsequent occasions people got to know her, and would look for her again, not only those whom she had healed of some anxiety, but those who suspected her of possessing an enviable secret; they would watch for the unchanging woman in her black prototype of a hat.

There in particular, on the spot where she had sat with her sick friend in the old, disintegrating house, there where the new homes rocked and shouted with life, the edifice of memory would also rise in all its structural diversity, its whirling, involuted detail, and perhaps most moving, the unfinished archways, opening on to distances and mist. Mrs Godbold would build. Or restore. She would lay the stones methodically, in years, almost in days that she had lived. But sometimes the columns of trees would intervene. The black trunks of oak and elm, and ghostlier gums which Mr Norbert Hare had overlooked, would rise again out of the suburban lots, and obscure the present, as they struggled to meet at last in nave or chancel. Light would have its part, and music. The grey light from off the fens in winter would search the paving in shafts from opening doors, branches of the whitest light flower upon the Easter Table, smouldering jewels of evening pour through the tracery of twigs and stone. With such riches of the spirit, she could not resist the secular touch, but had to drag in the green, slippery urns, of reflective, worshipful magnificence, of which she had been shy at first, in the hall at Xanadu. There was some peculiar gentleman, too, who had talked to her about the music, she could not remember clearly, but recalled him as a truthful presence. The music itself she would remember frequently, and again allow its scaffolding to shine, as it climbed always higher inside the accommodating spire. Sometimes, though, the grey pipes blew blasts that made her shudder. And there was that intolerable, hovering note, which rounded out her brother's head, crushed by the wheel, and blood still in the sockets of the eyes.

Mrs Godbold grew cold at times for the Gothic profusion of her vision. The stone figures she had laid upon their tombs would struggle inside the armour of eternity. Then she would try to free, at least for a moment, as many of them as she could remember: Miss Hare in a fever of words, the earth still caking her freckled hands; that abo fellow, with whom she had celebrated a mystery the night she went to fetch Tom from Mrs Khalil's.

Time had broken into a mosaic much that had seemed complete, obsessive, actual, painful. Now she could approach her work of living, as an artist, after an interval, will approach and judge his work of art. So, at last, the figure of her Lord and Saviour would stand before her in the chancel, looking down at her from beneath the yellow eyelids, along the strong, but gentle beak of a nose. She was content to leave then, since all converged finally upon the Risen Christ, and her own eyes had confirmed that the wounds were healed.

On that first occasion of her revisiting the altered Xanadu, Mrs Godbold did not think she could bear to go there again, in spite of her pleasure in many present, lively matters. But did, of course. On that first occasion of her venturesome walk and momentous achievement, she was so jostled and shaken by the past she tore off a little sapling to lean on. She was holding her handkerchief to her mouth as she returned towards her home at Sarsaparilla. Even at the height of her experience, it was true there had been much that she had only darkly sensed. Even though it was her habit to tread straight, she would remain a plodding simpleton. From behind, her great beam, under the stretchy cardigan, might have appeared something of a joke, except to the few who happened to perceive that she also wore the crown.

That evening, as she walked along the road, it was the hour at which the other gold sank its furrows in the softer sky. The lids of her eyes, flickering beneath its glow, were gilded with an identical splendour. But for all its weight, it lay lightly, lifted her, in fact, to where she remained an instant in the company of the Living Creatures she had known, and many others she had not. All was ratified again by hands.

If, on further visits to Xanadu, she experienced nothing comparable, it was probably because Mrs Godbold's feet were still planted firmly on the earth. She would lower her eyes to avoid the dazzle, and walk on, breathing heavily, for it was a stiff pull up the hill, to the shed in which she continued to live.

READ MORE IN PENGUIN

In every corner of the world, on every subject under the sun, Penguin represents quality and variety – the very best in publishing today.

For complete information about books available from Penguin – including Puffins, Penguin Classics and Arkana – and how to order them, write to us at the appropriate address below. Please note that for copyright reasons the selection of books varies from country to country.

In the United Kingdom: Please write to *Dept. JC, Penguin Books Ltd, FREEPOST, West Drayton, Middlesex UB7 OBR*

If you have any difficulty in obtaining a title, please send your order with the correct money, plus ten per cent for postage and packaging, to *PO Box No. 11, West Drayton, Middlesex UB7 OBR*

In the United States: Please write to *Penguin USA Inc., 375 Hudson Street, New York, NY 10014*

In Canada: Please write to *Penguin Books Canada Ltd, 10 Alcorn Avenue, Suite 300, Toronto, Ontario M4V 3B2*

In Australia: Please write to *Penguin Books Australia Ltd, 487 Maroondah Highway, Ringwood, Victoria 3134*

In New Zealand: Please write to *Penguin Books (NZ) Ltd, 182–190 Wairau Road, Private Bag, Takapuna, Auckland 9*

In India: Please write to *Penguin Books India Pvt Ltd, 706 Eros Apartments, 56 Nehru Place, New Delhi 110 019*

In the Netherlands: Please write to *Penguin Books Netherlands B.V., Keizersgracht 231 NL–1016 DV Amsterdam*

In Germany: Please write to *Penguin Books Deutschland GmbH, Friedrichstrasse 10–12, W–6000 Frankfurt/Main 1*

In Spain: Please write to *Penguin Books S. A., C. San Bernardo 117–6 E–28015 Madrid*

In Italy: Please write to *Penguin Italia s.r.l., Via Felice Casati 20, I–20124 Milano*

In France: Please write to *Penguin France S. A., 17 rue Lejeune, F–31000 Toulouse*

In Japan: Please write to *Penguin Books Japan, Ishikiribashi Building, 2–5–4, Suido, Tokyo 112*

In Greece: Please write to *Penguin Hellas Ltd, Dimocritou 3, GR–106 71 Athens*

In South Africa: Please write to *Longman Penguin Southern Africa (Pty) Ltd, Private Bag X08, Bertsham 2013*

BY THE SAME AUTHOR

Voss

The plot of this novel is of epic simplicity: in 1845 Voss sets out with a small band to cross the Australian continent for the first time. The tragic story of their terrible journey and its inevitable end is told with imaginative understanding.

The figure of Voss takes on superhuman proportions, until he appears to those around him as both deliverer and destroyer. His relationship with Laura Trevelyan is the central personal theme of the story.

The true record of Ludwig Leichhardt, who died in the Australian desert in 1848, suggested Voss to the author.

'. . . by far the most impressive new novel I have read this year' – Walter Allen in the *New Statesman*

The Twyborn Affair

Eddie Twyborn is bisexual and beautiful, the son of a Judge and a drunken mother. With his androgynous hero – Eudoxia/Eddie/Eadith Twyborn – and through his search for identity, for self-affirmation and love in its many forms, Patrick White takes us on a journey into the ambiguous landscapes, sexual, psychological and spiritual, of the human condition.

'It challenges comparison with some of the world's most bizarre masterpieces' – Isobel Murray in the *Financial Times*

A Fringe of Leaves

Returning home to England from Van Diemen's Land, the *Bristol Rose* is shipwrecked on the Queensland Coast and Mrs Roxburgh is taken prisoner by a tribe of Aborigines, along with the rest of the passengers and crew. In the course of her escape, she is torn by conflicting loyalties – to her dead husband, to her rescuer, to her own and to her adoptive class.

'A complete success. He uses cruelty and savagery to write of tenderness and beauty; this is one of his best novels' – Paul Theroux in *The Times*

BY THE SAME AUTHOR

Memoirs of Many in One

Elegant and outrageous, Alex Gray has as many 'lives' as a cat – from Cassiani, the nun with unexpected blue eyes, to Dolly Formosa, 'star turn' of Alex Gray's Theatrical Tour of Outback Australia.

Inhabiting a fantastic world of adventures, daydreams and recollections, Alex has finally settled in Sydney to finish her memoirs. She asks an old friend, Patrick White, to act as the literary executor and editor of her extraordinary diary. In this amusing, sparkling document she records among other things her exotic journeys overseas, her flamboyant religious escapades, her dramatic successes in experimental theatre and her present 'real-life' role as a suburban shoplifter.

'An irreverent and moving literary *trompe l'oeil* . . . bizarre and witty' – David Leavitt, author of *Lost Language of Cranes*

'To read Patrick White . . . is to touch a source of power, to move through areas made new and fresh, to see men and women with a sharpened gaze' – *Daily Telegraph*

Also published:

The Aunt's Story
The Burnt Ones
The Cockatoos
The Eye of the Storm
The Living and the Dead
The Solid Mandala
Three Uneasy Pieces
Travels in the Drifting Dawn
The Tree of Man
The Vivisector

and his autobiography

Flaws in the Glass